the Golden Specific

MAPMAKERS

BOOK TWO

S. E. Grove

PUFFIN BOOKS

PUFFIN BOOKS
An imprint of Penguin Random House LLC
375 Hudson Street
New York, New York 10014

First published in the United States of America by Viking,
an imprint of Penguin Group (USA) LLC, 2015
Published by Puffin Books, an imprint of Penguin Random House LLC, 2016

THE LIBRARY OF CONGRESS HAS CATALOGED THE VIKING EDITION AS FOLLOWS:
Grove, S. E.
The golden specific / S. E. Grove ; maps by Dave A. Stevenson.
pages cm.—(Mapmakers ; book 2)
Summary: Thirteen-year-old Sophia Tims, with her friend Theo,
continues to search for her parents, explorers who have vanished as the
borders shift within a world transformed by the Great Disruption of 1799.
ISBN 978-0-670-78503-2 (hardcover)
[1. Fantasy. 2. Maps—Fiction. 3. Missing persons—Fiction.]
I. Stevenson, Dave A., illustrator.
II. Title.
PZ7.G9273Gol 2015
[Fic]—dc23
2014034892

Puffin Books ISBN 9780142423677

Printed in the United States of America

1 3 5 7 9 10 8 6 4 2

Designed by Eileen Savage

Praise for
The Glass Sentence

"Refreshing . . . refulgent with nervy invention . . . I am in no doubt about the energy of S. E. Grove as a full-fledged, pathfinding fantasist."
—Gregory Maguire, *The New York Times Book Review*

★ "Wholly original and marvelous beyond compare."
—*Kirkus Reviews*, starred review

★ "A thrilling, time-bending debut . . . It's a cracking adventure."
—*Publishers Weekly*, starred review

★ "Mind-blowing . . . will attract Harry Potter fans."
—Shelf Awareness, starred review

★ "Stellar . . . richly layered and emotionally engaging."
—*BCCB*, starred review

"[A] page-turner . . . thoughtful, intelligent." —*The Wall Street Journal*

"Densely imaginative . . . Grove's protagonists are compelling, and she enriches her story by introducing fascinating secondary characters."
—*The Boston Globe*

"The narrative . . . is action-packed; the world that Grove has created is rich and interesting; and the characters are complex and endearing. It's hard to say which part is more compelling." —*BookPage*

"Absolutely marvelous [and] completely original. I love this book."
—Nancy Farmer, National Book Award–winning author
of *The House of the Scorpion*

"Exuberantly imagined [and] exquisite."
—Elizabeth Wein, *New York Times* bestselling author of *Code Name Verity*

A National Indie Bestseller
A Summer/Fall 2014 Indies Introduce New Voices Selection
A Kids' Indie Next Top Ten Book
A *Publishers Weekly* Flying Start
A *Washington Post* Summer Book Club Pick
A Junior Library Guild Selection
One of *Publishers Weekly*'s Best Summer Reads
An Amazon Editors' Pick, Summer 2014

BOOKS BY S. E. GROVE

MAPMAKERS
The Glass Sentence
The Golden Specific
The Crimson Skew

For Alton

It is difficult for us to grasp the peculiar glamour and significance the yellow metal held for the conquistadores. We respond instantly to the cool irony of a Hernán Cortés explaining to a Mexican chief that Spaniards suffer from a disease of the heart, for which gold is the only specific; but in that coolness and irony, as in almost everything else, Cortés is atypical.

—Inga Clendinnen,
Ambivalent Conquests: Maya and Spaniard in Yucatan, 1517–1570

CONTENTS

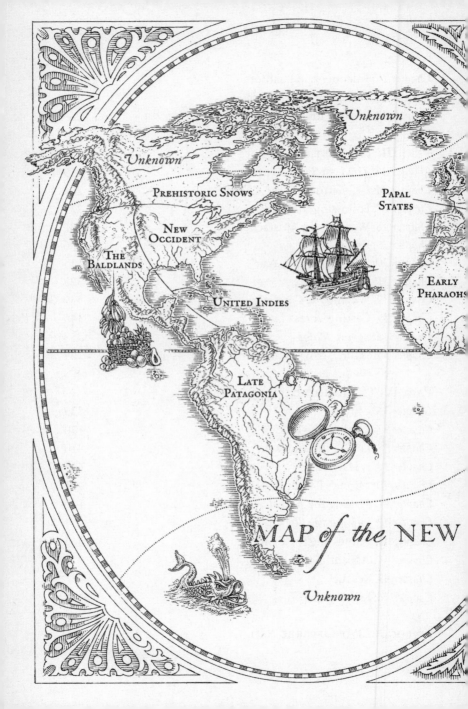

Unknown

Unknown

Prehistoric Snows

Papal States

New Occident

The Baldlands

Early Pharaohs

United Indies

Late Patagonia

MAP *of the* NEW

Unknown

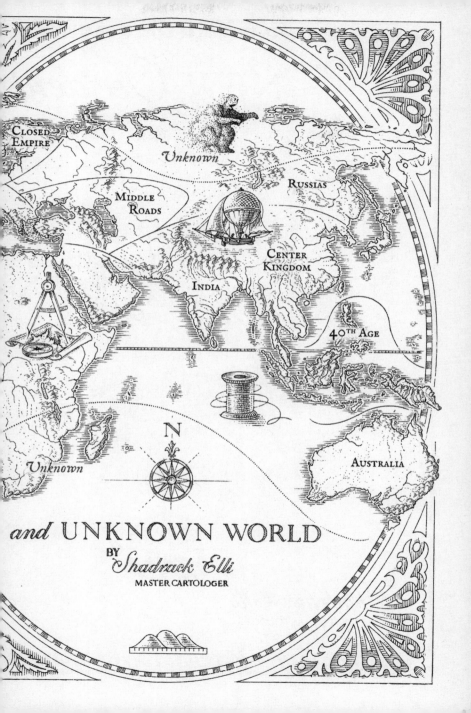

CLOSED
EMPIRE

Unknown

RUSSIAS

MIDDLE
ROADS

CENTER
KINGDOM

INDIA

40TH AGE

N

Unknown

AUSTRALIA

and UNKNOWN WORLD

BY *Shadrack Elli*

MASTER CARTOLOGER

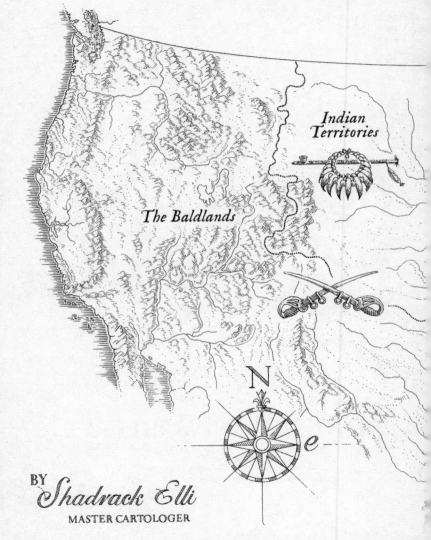

NEW *Occident*

Indian
Territories

The Baldlands

N

e

BY *Shadrack Elli*
MASTER CARTOLOGER

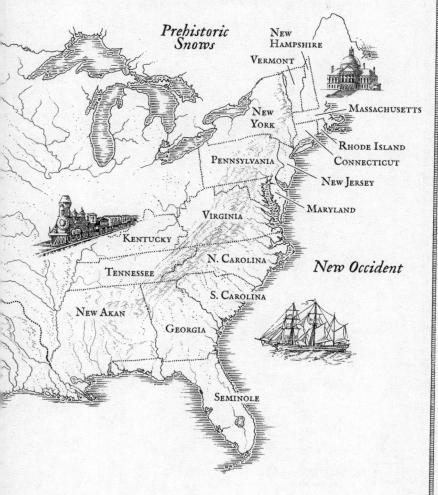

and ITS
ADJOINING AGES

Prehistoric Snows

NEW HAMPSHIRE

VERMONT

NEW YORK

MASSACHUSETTS

RHODE ISLAND
CONNECTICUT

PENNSYLVANIA

NEW JERSEY

MARYLAND

VIRGINIA

KENTUCKY

N. CAROLINA

New Occident

TENNESSEE

S. CAROLINA

NEW AKAN

GEORGIA

SEMINOLE

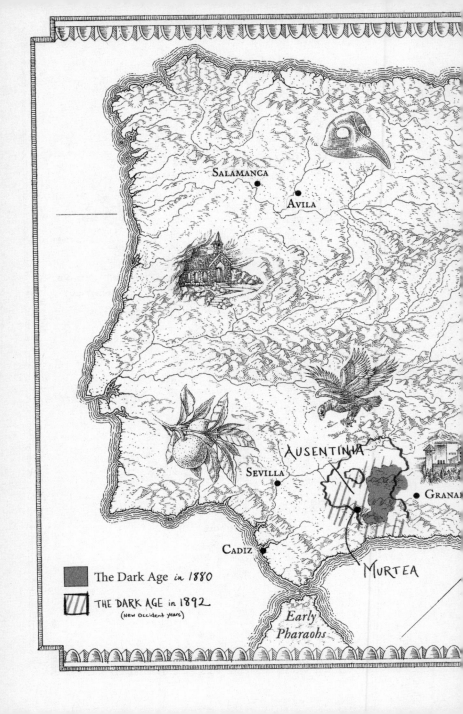

SALAMANCA

AVILA

AUSENTINIA

SEVILLA

GRANA

CADIZ

MURTEA

The Dark Age *in 1880*

THE DARK AGE *in 1892*
(New Occident years)

Early
Pharaohs

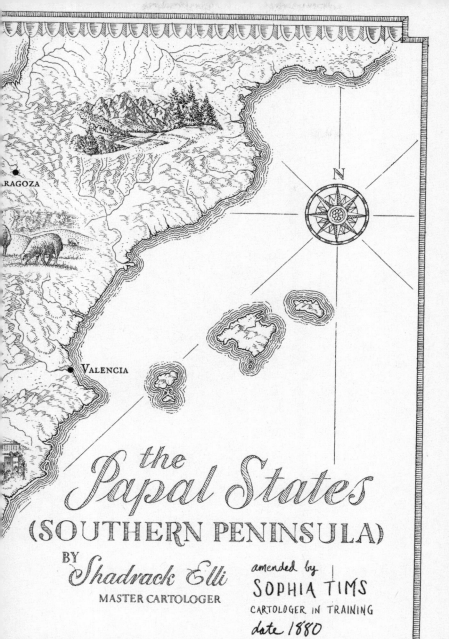

RAGOZA

VALENCIA

N

the
Papal States
(SOUTHERN PENINSULA)

BY *Shadrack Elli*
MASTER CARTOLOGER

amended by
SOPHIA TIMS
CARTOLOGER IN TRAINING
date 1880

In Boston it was still 1799, but elsewhere the Ages had gone their different ways. To the north lay prehistoric snows. Across the ocean lay medieval ports. To the south lay a land of many intermingled futures and pasts. And beyond that—who could say? The world had been remade. Scholars and scientists studied the problem and found no solution. Too much was unknown. Too much of the new world was inexplicable. Consider that we do not even know for certain whether the Great Disruption was caused by mankind and, if so, which Age of mankind caused it.

—From Shadrack Elli's *History of the New World*

PROLOGUE

September 4, 1891

Dear Shadrack,

You ask me for news of the Eerie, and I can tell you that there is no recent news of them in the Indian Territories. For more than five years they have not been seen here.

But the rumors are true—I traveled in search of them three years ago, when I had need of a healer. It began with a boy trapped in one of the mines. For days his cries had echoed up through the shaft, terrifying any who came near it. His laments were so painful that all who heard them felt themselves sinking into paralyzed despair, and every attempt to rescue him failed. Finally, they came to me. Four of us hardened our hearts and went into the mines, seeking the lost child. We found him in the deep, deep dark, clawing uselessly at the walls. He came with us quietly, whimpering along the way. Only when we emerged from the mine did we realize that the boy had no face.

The creatures, called "Wailings" here and "Lachrima" in the Baldlands, appear rarely in the Territories. Until I saw him myself, I had only half believed in their existence. Now I had no doubts. I had been moved by the duties of my office to rescue a trapped child; now that I saw his condition, I was moved by pity to seek a remedy. I left Salt Lick in the hands of my deputies and took the Wailing boy north, toward the Eerie Sea, in search of the Eerie and their legendary healers.

The journey became much longer than intended, and the presence of the boy, much as I pitied him, left me despondent—almost fatally so. It was only by chance that, at the edge of the Sea, we came across an Eerie who was traveling east. She understood my errand at once. "How far has he traveled since becoming faceless?" she asked me. I could not tell her. She examined his hands, as if to answer her own question. "We will try," she concluded. Without more discussion she agreed to lead us to the nearest Weatherer— their name for those Eerie who are most gifted as healers.

We traveled for ten days to a place I have tried to find since and cannot. A strange corner among the pine trees, where the winds from the glacial sea make sounds like the voices of murmuring mourners. The Weatherer lived in an earth-sheltered house made of pine, with a roof of sod. It was dusk as we approached, and I saw deer and birds, squirrels and rabbits hurrying into the woods, avoiding our arrival. They scurried over the pine needles and fluttered into the branches, and they left the place in total stillness.

The Weatherer was hardly more than a boy himself, and I never learned his name. He stood waiting for us; he had anticipated our arrival. Without even glancing at me, he led the Wailing boy by the hand to a smoothed tree stump. He placed his hands over the Wailing's face, as if protecting it from the cold. Then the Weatherer closed his own eyes, and I could sense all of his thoughts and intentions moving through him into the boy. The Wailing leaned forward into his hands, as if accepting a blessing.

I felt the change before I saw it. The forest around us seemed to pause, as if every tree and rock and cloud had taken notice and stopped to watch. The light shifted from the gray murkiness of dusk to a clear and pure silver. I could see dust motes in the air, unmoving as a constellation of stars. The pine needles nearest me seemed to shine like blades. The tree trunks became elaborate labyrinths of curved bark and pierced holes. Everything around me had become more vivid, crystalline, sharp. I felt the sense of despondency that I had grown accustomed to lift and dissipate. Suddenly, the clean forest air seemed to reach through my lungs into every corner of my body, surging through me with a kind of fierce, possessive joy. I have never felt more alive.

I had not closed my eyes, but my attention had drifted to the world made new around me. When I looked again at the Weatherer, he had stepped back from the Wailing. A boy stood before him, whole and intact, an expression of wonder on his realized face.

Since then, I have often contemplated what occurred in those woods, and I have determined that the clarity granted to me in that moment was not unlike that which transformed the Wailing boy. We are all, to some degree, dulled in our senses and our experience of the world. We are all, to some degree, suppressed by layers of accumulated grief. My unmarred features belie the gradual dulling of all those faculties that should animate a human being. We are all, to some degree, faceless.

So, you ask me if I know the Eerie. Hardly. We left the pine woods, the boy and I, having exchanged fewer than twenty words with our guide and fewer still with the Weatherer.

You ask if I could find them again. I cannot. As I said, I have searched again for that forest, and somehow it seems to have vanished.

You ask if the healing powers of the Eerie are true. Without doubt. One who can heal the Lachrima can surely heal those other maladies for which we find only imperfect cures.

Yours,
Adler Fox
Sheriff, Salt Lick City, Indian Territories

PART I
The Leads

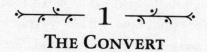

1

THE CONVERT

—*1892, May 31: 9-Hour 07*—

In New Occident, the majority of the people cleave to the Fates, all-powerful deities who are believed to weave the future and past of every living being into their great tapestry of time. Some smaller number follow the True Cross, which has more followers in the Baldlands. The remainder adhere to more obscure sects, Nihilismianism being the most dominant among them.

—From Shadrack Elli's History of New Occident

ON THE MORNING of May 31, Sophia Tims stood on Beacon Street, staring through a gap in the iron fence at the monolith before her. Junipers, tall and immobile, lined the winding lane that rose to the mansion's entrance. The building itself, from a distance, seemed cold and forbidding, all stone walls and curtained windows. Sophia took a deep breath and glanced up again at the sign beside the gated entryway. It read:

The Nihilismian Archive
Boston Depository

For the hundredth time that morning, Sophia wondered if she was making a mistake. Reaching into her skirt pocket, she took hold of the two tokens that always traveled with her: a pocket watch and a spool of silver thread. She clasped them tightly, willing them to send her some sign of assurance.

The note leading her to the Nihilismian Archive had arrived three days earlier. Returning from yet another fruitless excursion to the Boston Public Library, she had found an envelope waiting for her on the kitchen table where Mrs. Clay, the housekeeper, had left it. There was no return address and she did not recognize the handwriting; she opened it at once. Inside was a pamphlet. On the front, an illustration of a gargoyle wearing a blindfold squatted below the title:

THE NIHILISMIAN ARCHIVE: BOSTON DEPOSITORY

On the inside, two long columns of text explained the archive's purpose. It began:

THE WORLD YOU SEE AROUND YOU IS A false world. The true world, the Age of Verity, vanished in 1799, at the time of the Great Disruption. At the Nihilismian Archive, archivists and preservationists have dedicated their lives to finding and collecting the documents of the true world that we have lost—documents from the Age of Verity. With extensive collections pertaining to the lost Age of Verity as well as this Apocryphal Age that we inhabit, the Archive strives to ascertain how far we have strayed from the true path.

The pamphlet boasted of the archive's forty-eight rooms of documents pertaining to every corner of the known world: newspapers, personal correspondence, manuscripts, rare books, and all other manner of printed text. It ended with one short but important sentence:

Only Nihilismians are permitted to consult the Archive.

On the back, in the same hand that had addressed the envelope, was written,

Sophia—if you are still looking for your mother, you will find her here.

Had the pamphlet arrived some months earlier, Sophia might have thrown it out with a shudder the moment she saw what it contained. She knew Nihilismians; she knew the ferocity of their convictions, and she knew that those convictions made them dangerous. Sometimes she still awoke from nightmares in which she tried to run along the roof of a speeding train, her feet heavy as lead, while a Nihilismian behind her threw a shining grappling hook straight toward her heart.

But the last year had changed things.

SOPHIA COULD REMEMBER clearly the moment in December when she ran down the stairs to the hidden map room at 34 East Ending Street, clutching the clue to her long-lost parents' disappearance. Her uncle Shadrack Elli sat at the leather-topped table beside his close friend, the famous explorer Miles Countryman, and Theodore Constantine Thackary, the boy from the Baldlands who had become one of their small family. The three were silent as Sophia, her voice choked with emotion, read the letter from her father.

He had written it eight years before, telling Sophia that their journey had taken an unexpected turn: they were planning to follow the lost signs toward Ausentinia.

Miles whooped for joy at the discovery, pounding a laughing Theo on the back, and begun making plans for their immediate departure. Shadrack listened with elation, which turned to bewilderment as he reread the message once, twice, three times. "I have never heard of Ausentinia or the lost signs," Shadrack declared, perplexed. "But no matter! *Someone* will have heard of them."

And yet, it became blindingly clear as the days turned to weeks, no one had. Shadrack Elli, the greatest cartologer of New Occident, the man who could create and read nearly every sort of map in the known world, wrote to every explorer and every cartologer and every librarian he had ever known, along with many he had never met. No one had so much as heard or read the words.

Still, Sophia had held out hope. She had faith that while she continued to learn cartology, the Fates, in their wisdom, were planning how to lead her onward with a promising thread of discovery. Their guidance had steered her true before, and surely it would again.

Every so often, a possible lead would emerge, and Shadrack would send Miles or some other explorer friend to hunt it down. Each lead dwindled into a dead end. And as the months went by, and the list of failed attempts grew, Sophia remained convinced that surely another, better lead—perhaps the one that would finally point to Minna and Bronson—would appear.

Then in late winter, with the election of a new prime minister, Shadrack was offered a government position as the Minister of Relations with Foreign Ages. Prime Minister Bligh was a trusted friend, and Shadrack could not refuse the offer to replace another friend, Carlton Hopish, who still languished in the Boston City Hospital. Left horribly injured and deprived of his senses by a violent attack, Carlton showed no sign of even the slightest recovery.

As he left at dawn and returned after dinner, Shadrack's days at the ministry grew longer and longer. Sophia still waited at home for him each evening, eager to discuss her day's findings, but Shadrack seemingly wearied more each day. His eyes were tired, his gaze, abstracted. One evening at dinner, Sophia left to get her notebook, and when she returned, she found Shadrack slumped over the kitchen table, fast asleep. Little by little, Shadrack's searching stopped. The lessons in cartology, which Sophia had waited desperately for each evening, stopped as well.

The winter stretched on, and Sophia sank into a long gloom. Shadrack had no time. Miles departed in pursuit of a slim lead, taking Theo with him. Sophia struggled against the feeling that she was alone. She tried, fruitlessly for the most part, to continue the cartology lessons on her own. After school, she haunted the Boston Public Library, poring over every relevant book she could find, and at home she plumbed the depths of the map room, finding more riddles than solutions in Shadrack's obscure collection. By the time spring arrived, she felt her hope wearing thin. She had difficulty sleeping, and this made her feel forgetful, unsteady, and unsure. There were times, as she drew in her notebook recounting the day, when tears spilled over onto the page. The careful lines of text became great gray clouds; the drawings blurred and puckered; and she could not point to the reason.

And then, finally, the Fates sent her a sign. It first appeared at dusk. Sophia had been watching for Shadrack from her bedroom window when she saw a pale figure lingering by the front gate. It stood indecisively, taking a step toward the street and then a step back toward the house. The cobblestones shone from a recent rain shower, and a low fog had settled in around the streetlamps.

The woman seemed familiar. She had to be a neighbor, but which one? The woman placed her hand on her heart and then lifted her palm toward Sophia's window: a gentle gesture of affection.

It struck Sophia like a blow. For a moment she stared,

unmoving. Then she bolted from her room, throwing herself down the stairs, through the kitchen, and out into the street. The woman was still there, pale and uncertain, by the gate. Sophia stepped haltingly toward her, hardly daring to breathe. "Mother?" she whispered. Then the figure vanished.

The following evening, she appeared again. Sophia had partly persuaded herself over the course of the long day that her mind was playing tricks on her and that the figure she had seen was conjured by exhaustion and misplaced hope. Still, she waited by the window. When she saw Minna by the gate, silent and hesitant, Sophia rose shakily and rushed out of the house.

This time, Minna waited. She took a step backward onto the sidewalk and another onto the street. Sophia opened the gate and stepped after her. Minna moved silently over the cobblestones. "Wait, please," Sophia pleaded.

Minna stopped. As Sophia approached, her footsteps loud in the silence, she could see her mother's face: pallid and insubstantial, but still discernible in the dusk light. There was something odd about her that Sophia could not place until she had closed the distance between them: the figure appeared to be made of paper. She seemed a perfect rendering of Minna Tims brought to life. She reached her hand out plaintively as Sophia neared, and then she spoke: *"Missing but not lost, absent but not gone, unseen but not unheard. Find us while we still draw breath."* The last words seemed to prove the substance of the riddle, for they sounded after Minna had, once again, disappeared.

But Sophia did not care. She felt as if she had just taken air into her lungs for the first time in months, as if she had been drowning and the words spoken at dusk by Minna's semblance had pulled her from the deep. She was still in those dark waters, but now, at least, she could breathe. The paralyzing sadness that had gripped her all winter was something she could look at: she could see how vast it was; she could see how far she had to swim.

The next day, the second sign appeared: the Nihilismian pamphlet. Sophia told herself, as she read the handwritten note over and over, that the Fates could not have spoken more clearly.

She had not mentioned seeing Minna or receiving the pamphlet to Shadrack.

There are some things that only keep their enchantment, their full promise, when they remain unspoken. Sophia knew the pale figure she had seen at dusk was improbable, and when she imagined speaking of it, she felt the power of Minna's presence dissipate like fog. The wonder of it, the potency of the whispered words, were uncommunicable. Indeed, even in her own mind she could not approach the thought of what she had seen and heard too closely, for the moment she did a flurry of troubling questions rushed forward: *What is she? Is she real? What does it mean that I can see and hear her?* Sophia turned away from these questions resolutely, and she did not contemplate the vision too closely. She accepted a simpler and, to her, undeniable pair of truths: her mother was asking for her help, and the Fates were sending her a sign.

Shadrack did not believe in the Fates. Even if she could somehow convey the sense of desperation in Minna's message, the sense of clarity from the pamphlet, Shadrack would not see their guiding hand at work. He would see something else, and Sophia wanted to see what she saw now: an unmistakable urgency, a clear way forward. Instead of telling him, she thought about it for two days. And then she made a decision.

STANDING NOW BEFORE the soaring iron gates, Sophia took a deep breath. She pushed, and they swung soundlessly inward. Her boots crunched on the gravel path as she walked slowly uphill, bringing the great house into closer view. Here and there the curtains hung open. A groundskeeper near the mansion's entrance was carefully raking the gravel, making a perfect set of concentric circles. Other than the sound of the rake combing the fine stones, the air was still.

The groundskeeper ignored Sophia as she walked toward the granite steps. On the roof above the open doorway, the blindfolded gargoyle depicted on the pamphlet perched comfortably, its stone tongue impossibly long.

A crimson runner beyond the open doors led across the marble floor to a tall wooden desk. Sophia held her head high and walked steadily toward it. The man behind the desk looked up as she approached and put down the book he was holding. He nodded. "Good morning."

"Good morning," Sophia said. She forced herself to look the

attendant in the eye. He was bald, with blue eyes so pale they seemed almost colorless. Sophia swallowed. "I am here to consult the archive."

The bald man nodded again without taking his eyes from her. "Patrons wishing to consult the archive may apply for an investigator's card, which will allow them unlimited access to the depository. However," he paused, "access is only permitted to Nihilismians."

"Yes, I understand," she replied. "I am Nihilismian."

2

THE NIHILISMIAN APOCRYPHA

—1892, May 31: 9-Hour 09—

The Nihilismians began sending missions to other Ages in the 1850s. The missions are intended to encourage past Ages to unfold as they did in New Occident's past. The practical and philosophical obstacles are myriad. Imagine, for example, the folly of ensuring that explorers from the Papal States sail east to "discover" the Western Hemisphere. Nonetheless, the missions continue, and Boston alone sends dozens of missionaries to the Papal States, the Closed Empire, and the Early Pharaohs every year.

—From Shadrack Elli's History of New Occident

AT FIRST, SOPHIA thought the Nihilismian pamphlet might have been sent by someone at the Boston Public Library who had been helping with her search for so many months. Perhaps one of them was secretly Nihilismian.

Then it occurred to her that it might have come from a friend of Shadrack's who believed, quite rightly, that he would balk at the idea of consulting a Nihilismian archive himself. Shadrack was not closed-minded, but the events of the previous summer had set him decidedly against Nihilismians. He had always believed their ideas misconceived; now, he also believed them to be dangerous.

Then Sophia considered that the anonymous sender might be someone who actually worked at the archive: someone who knew for certain that the collection contained something of value for her search. Unlikely as it seemed that a strange Nihilismian would want to help her, the idea that some real clue existed and had already been spotted made her tremble with anticipation.

Perhaps, she thought, as she stared at the attendant on the other side of the desk, this very man was the ally who had sent her the message. Though his persistently unblinking stare made it seem unlikely. Sophia reached to clasp the pendant that hung around her neck, clearing her throat quietly. The Nihilismian's attention obligingly drifted to the circular amulet. Then he turned slowly and opened a drawer in his desk. He drew out a piece of paper and handed it across to Sophia with a pen. "Here is the application for an investigator's card."

"Thank you."

"I am required to emphasize," he said quietly, indicating the signature line, "that this application functions as a legal contract. If you sign the form and anything written there is discovered to be untrue, it will be considered fraud."

"I understand." Sophia paused, but went on despite herself. "What happens when it is considered fraud?"

The bald man gazed at her without expression. "It depends on whether the archive pursues the matter in court. The archive pursued three such fraud cases last year and won them all." He cocked his head slightly to one side, as if considering an unspoken question. "The only thing these 'investigators' will be reading for some time is the mail they receive in prison."

Sophia nodded briskly. "I see. Thank you." She took the pen and the form to one of the ample burgundy armchairs that made up the sitting area in the foyer. Her hands were trembling. She sat quietly for a moment, collecting herself; then she reached into her pocket and clasped the spool of silver thread for encouragement.

She took her notebook from her satchel and placed it under the form, filling out each portion as quickly as possible.

Name? *Every Tims.* Date of birth? *January 28, 1878.* Address? *34 East Ending Street, Boston.* Was she a citizen of New Occident? *Yes.* Did she hereby swear that she was of the Nihilismian faith? Sophia hesitated for the barest instant. *Yes.* Had she been Nihilismian from birth or was she a convert? *A convert.* If the latter, what was the name and address of the Nihilismian who had officiated at her conversion? *Seeking Montfort, 290 Commonwealth Avenue, Boston.*

Sophia signed at the bottom, slipped her notebook back into the satchel, and rose to hand the form back to the attendant.

"We will be in touch with Seeking Montfort to confirm," he said quietly, without looking up.

"Of course."

"'Every,'" he said thoughtfully. "March twenty-fifth. '*Every vision around you is false, every object an illusion, every sentiment as false as a dream. You live in the Age of the apocryphal.*'" He looked up at Sophia, waiting.

"Truth of Amitto," she murmured, pressing the amulet around her neck. Since Nihilismians adopted new names from the Book of Amitto when they converted, Sophia had chosen the name that seemed least objectionable, avoiding ones like "Purity," "Lament," and "Beneath."

The attendant cocked his head to the side again. "Please have a seat. I will call one of the archivists. Your card will be ready to pick up when you leave the archive today."

"Thank you." Sophia began to turn away.

"Every," the attendant remarked. "Your amulet is very unusual." Sophia raised her eyebrows. "Did you make it yourself?"

"Yes, I did." She held his gaze while she clasped the circular pillow of midnight blue embroidered in silver thread with a small hand, open-palmed, fingers outstretched.

"We see that in many cases where families don't approve. The faithful find a way." He nodded his own approval.

Sophia watched as he left the foyer, his heels echoing on the marble floor. Then she took a deep breath and sank back into the burgundy armchair.

SEEKING MONTFORT WAS, in fact, a genuine Nihilismian. But he had not officiated at any ceremony for Sophia's conversion, and he no longer resided at 290 Commonwealth Avenue. He had passed away the previous year, leaving only his widow and an aging pair of lapdogs. Sophia calculated that she had at least three days and perhaps as many as six before the Nihilismians of the Boston Depository discovered the truth. It all depended on the zealousness of their inquiry and the cooperation of Mrs. Montfort.

A letter sent today would arrive tomorrow. Montfort's widow would take at least a day to reply. Sophia had visited her, in the cramped rooms made pungent by the spoiled lapdogs, with a question about a made-up relative who had converted to Nihilismianism and left on a mission to the Closed Empire. She had seen the formidable wooden cabinet where Seeking Montfort's records resided, and she had watched as Mrs. Montfort searched rather carelessly for the imaginary document. After a few minutes, the woman had given up; she was much more interested in her yapping dogs than the history of her husband's legal practice. If the Fates smiled upon her, Sophia figured that Mrs. Montfort might take several days to search fruitlessly through the cabinet and reply.

Or, on the other hand, she might reply immediately.

Sophia rose from the chair as the attendant returned, now accompanied by a tall man with a gray mustache. The man made a slight bow toward her. "Whether Moreau," he said, extending his hand.

"Every Tims," Sophia replied, taking it.

"It is a pleasure to welcome you to the Boston Depository."

"Thank you."

"Please follow me." Walking toward the archive's main corridor, Whether Moreau left Sophia to hurry after him. Despite the warm spring weather, the building was silent and uncommonly cold. Crimson carpeting muffled their footsteps. Sophia caught a glimpse of several rooms as they passed: high ceilings, oak bookshelves, dark wallpaper, and spherical flame lamps. Dark curtains over the windows prevented sunlight from reaching the documents.

They arrived at a marble staircase. As they climbed, Sophia determined, glancing at him sideways, that Whether was no secret ally. He stared ahead, eyes withdrawn, almost as if he had already forgotten Sophia's presence beside him. The dark suit he wore was pressed with a precision that bordered on ferocious, and its darkness was reflected in his well-polished shoes.

On the second floor, they followed another corridor, finally stopping at one of its many open doorways. Sophia peered past him into a room much like the ones she had seen below.

"Are you familiar with the structure of the Nihilismian Archive?" Whether asked, looking over her head at a point on the wall.

"I know only what is explained in the informational pamphlet."

"Let me explain our organizational system before I ask about your line of inquiry." He paused. "The archive contains forty-eight rooms," Whether said, gesturing down the hallway. "Rooms one through thirteen are dedicated to the Age of Verity—*Veritas*, as we call it here. Meaning 'truth,' of course. These are where chronicles of time before the Great Disruption, as well as texts produced during that time, are stored. The Apocrypha rooms contain the chronicles of the Age of Delusion—the time elapsed since the Great Disruption—and, as you may note from the number of rooms, fourteen through forty-eight, that collection is larger. This would seem counterintuitive," he continued, "as less time has elapsed since the Disruption than before it. But you will discover that documents and texts from before the Disruption are exceedingly rare. Each room has its own curator. I am the curator of room forty-five." He indicated the open doorway.

"So the archive is organized chronologically?"

Whether nodded. "That is correct. We arrange all the chronicles and texts sequentially, since this method lies at the heart of the archive's mission: to demonstrate the great abyss that separates our world from that world we lost more than ninety years ago." He led Sophia into room 45. "We pursue this mission by contrasting and comparing the recorded differences between occurrences in the Age of Verity and the Age of Delusion."

Whether took Sophia to a mahogany reading table. "Please have a seat. I'll demonstrate more clearly what I mean."

As Whether headed toward the back of the room, Sophia studied the space around her. Room 45 had high windows that overlooked the gardens at the rear of the building, but the curtains were again drawn, and flame lamps illuminated every corner. Bookshelves filled the walls from floor to ceiling, separated halfway up by an iron balcony that connected to a spiral staircase. Along the carpeted floor near the reading table, freestanding shelves bore the weight of row after row of precisely labeled volumes and document boxes. A young woman wearing unusual clothes—loose pants and a man's dress shirt—was putting books from a cart onto one of the shelves. She glanced at Sophia and paused for a moment.

Perhaps this is my secret ally, Sophia thought. She gave a slight nod. The young woman did not acknowledge her, but turned back to her task.

Sophia swallowed. She sat up straighter in her chair, determined not to be undone by the chilliness of the Nihilismian archivists.

A moment later, Whether returned with a large box. He spread its contents out across the table, placing side by side before Sophia two items: a folded newspaper that looked quite new and a torn single page of newspaper that looked quite old. He tapped the first with long, white fingers. "This paper, as you can see, was printed earlier this month." The copy of *The New-York Times* was dated May 1, 1892. Sophia leaned forward to glance at the headlines, which included a story about the deportation of a major financier who had been discovered to be an unnaturalized native of the Baldlands, a short report about pirate raids near Seminole, and a long article about the ongoing dispute with the Indian Territories. "This, however," Whether said, framing the older fragment of newspaper with his thumb and forefinger, "was also printed on May 1, 1892." He leaned back and waited.

At first glance, the paper looked identical. It was labeled *New-York Times* in the familiar font, and the date said "New-York, Sunday, May 1, 1892." But then, as she examined the headlines, Sophia realized that the stories were very different. "Is Sherman's Eye Upon It," the page said near the middle. "The Ohio Senator declines to answer a hypothetical question," declared the subtitle. "A Return to Barbarism," read another headline at the far right, and below it, "Europe trembles before the Anarchist bombs. Paris and Brussels fear May Day—Foreign ignorance of the Chicago Bomb Throwing." "Minnesota Still Wants Blaine," said a smaller headline farther down.

"It's a different paper," Sophia said, intrigued. "I don't recognize most of these people and places."

"They belong to the Age of Verity," Whether assented. "This is the 1892 that we *should* be living, that we lost—the 1892 that would have been without the Great Disruption."

"So this document survived the Disruption?"

"Precisely. It was found in an old cabinet in the western Baldlands. Someone had used the newspaper to line a drawer. The cabinet was sold to a collector of curiosities, and the paper was recognized only then as something of value. The collector passed it on to a rare-book dealer, who in turn brought it to our attention. It is immensely illuminating—an invaluable find."

"Is there any overlap between the two papers?"

"You have asked the very question that the archive strives to answer. How much does our Age of Delusion coincide, if at all, with the Age of Verity? How much of this false world can we consider true? This is what we labor continually to find, study, and prove. In this case," he said grimly, "it seems that we have strayed very far from our intended route. Indeed, New Occident as a whole has deviated terribly. Between these two papers, there are no two stories that are alike. The Age of Verity paper mentions—as you rightly pointed out—many places and people that seem not even to exist in our world."

Sophia considered the room around her. "The pamphlet said your collection covers other places beyond New Occident. Is that true of every room?"

"Indeed. Every piece of pertinent text that we can find is collected here, or in one of our affiliated archives. There are some areas for which we have more documentation than others, but this is only to be expected. In addition," he went on, picking up a leather-bound volume, "the Apocrypha are cross-listed in indexes that use our own method of time-keeping." He opened the volume at random and showed Sophia that it read, at the top, "A.D. 43."

"To us, in New Occident, today is the thirty-first of May, 1892. For inhabitants of the Closed Empire, today is May thirty-first, 1131. Yet we are living in the same moment," Whether continued, "and our indexes take this into account." He slid the book toward Sophia. The top left of the page read:

> 1642—Accounts ledger by Tomas Batiste.
> Location: United Indies Depository.
>
> 1642—Convent log kept by Sister Maria Therese.
> Location: United Indies Depository.
>
> 1642—Broadsheets, collected, published in Havana.
> Location: United Indies Depository.

Sophia looked up. "There is another depository in the Indies?"

"There are depositories all over the world. Sixteen, to be exact. Twice a year, they send us updates of their collections so that we may enter the information in our indexes. If you look ahead a few pages," Whether said, doing so, "you'll see that other ages are included as well."

Still looking under the heading "A.D. 43," Sophia scanned a list of documents from New Occident, dated 1842:

1842—Newspapers, collected, published in New York.
Location: Boston Depository.

1842—Private diary of Maxwell Osmond.
Location: Boston Depository.

1842—Collected letters of Peter Simmons.
Location: Boston Depository.

"I understand," Sophia said slowly. "These all were written at the same time, but in different Ages."

Whether nodded slightly. "These were all written—or dated, for the purposes of the archive—in A.D. 43: After the Disruption, Year 43; or, as we call it, Age of Delusion, Year 43. If you wish to review all the Apocrypha produced in a given year, you can simply consult the index. It is," he concluded seriously, "a vivid indication of just how scattered and disrupted our apocryphal world has become."

"It certainly is," she agreed. She turned back to the index, realizing with growing dread the size of the task ahead. She had no idea what she was looking for, much less the year in which it was originally written. Working in the Nihilismian Archive would present a formidable challenge in drudgery, not unlike searching for a needle in a carefully arranged haystack.

How will I find anything useful in three days? Sophia asked herself, gazing at the entries with a feeling of dismay bordering on panic.

"What is it you wish to consult at the archive?" Whether queried.

Sophia took out her notebook and withdrew a letter. "I received this in December, long after it was written. There has been no word of its author all these years, and I was hoping the archive might contain information about the place mentioned in it."

Whether read the letter silently. Then he placed it on the table and looked at Sophia as if seeing her for the first time. "Bronson Tims," he said. His expression was unreadable. "Are you related to Shadrack Elli, the cartologer?"

"Yes. He is my uncle."

"You are a recent convert. Your family are not Nihilismian." They were statements, not questions.

"No, they are not. And yes, I am a recent convert." There was a long pause. Whether continued to gaze at her, his face unnervingly somber. Sophia realized that the assistant who had been shelving books had stopped shelving. She stood with her hand on the cart, making no effort to conceal her stare.

"And yet you seek two people in this world—this apocryphal world."

"You misunderstand my search," Sophia said composedly. "I am Nihilismian, yes, but like my uncle I am still a cartologer. Just as your objective is to reveal the diverging histories between our world and the Age of Verity, so it is my objective to map the differences between them. I wish to confirm the location of this Ausentinia, for I have found no mention of it elsewhere."

Whether gazed at her pensively for a moment. "I see," he finally said. He rose from his chair and carefully returned the two newspapers to the document box. "I will ask Remorse to assist you, since I tend to work with more experienced patrons," he said, making no effort to conceal his condescension. "Remorse?" he asked, over his shoulder.

"Thank you, Mr. Moreau," Sophia said, rising from her seat. "I appreciate the introduction to the archive."

"Not at all," Whether said, turning away, box in hand.

Remorse sat down across from Sophia. "May I see the letter?" she asked without preamble. She took a pair of amber-tinted spectacles from her shirt pocket.

Sophia studied the young woman as she read. She could not have been more than twenty years old. Her small hands, delicate and slightly tapered, still looked like the hands of a child. The buttoned work shirt she wore was frayed but carefully ironed, as were her unexpected pants. Short black hair and dark eyebrows framed her face; behind the spectacles, her eyes, as she read, were resolutely inexpressive. *Probably not my ally either,* Sophia concluded.

Remorse handed the letter back and crossed her arms. "'March fifteen, 1881,'" she said, her voice flat. "'Dearest Sophia. Your mother and I have thought of you every moment of every day during this journey. Now, as we near what may be the end of it, the thought of you is foremost in our minds. This letter will take ages to reach you, and if we are fortunate, we will reach you before my written words ever do. But if this letter reaches you and we do not, you should know that we are following the lost signs into Ausentinia. Do not think of pursuing us, dearest; Shadrack will know what to do. It is a road of great peril. We had no wish to travel into Ausentinia. It traveled to us. All my love. Your father, Bronson.'"

Sophia stared at her. It was disconcerting to hear her father's affectionate words voiced so entirely without emotion by a stranger. But it was more perplexing that the stranger knew the words at all. "How did you do that?" Sophia asked.

"I can remember anything after seeing it once," Remorse said impassively.

"That is an enviable skill."

Remorse looked away. "It depends upon what you see. There are things you want to remember. And things you don't."

Sophia blinked. "Yes. There certainly are."

"So you are looking for Ausentinia." Remorse said.

"Yes. Have you ever heard of it?" She realized suddenly that Remorse might be the best shortcut through the archive. "If you remember everything you've seen, perhaps you have seen the name somewhere?"

"I haven't," Remorse said. She looked back at Sophia. Then she rose abruptly from her seat. "I think you should look at the index for the year the letter was written. A.D. 82. I'll go get it." Without waiting for Sophia's reply, she left the table and disappeared among the bookcases.

A few minutes later, she returned pushing a library cart.

"I've brought you the first thirty." She began heaving the heavy volumes onto the reading table.

Sophia frowned at the cart. "The first thirty what?"

"The first thirty volumes of the index for A.D. 82." Remorse paused, and for the first time her face shifted from studied blankness to mirth. "You didn't think the index for each year was just one book? A.D. 82 contains more than three hundred volumes."

Three hundred volumes! Sophia thought, appalled. *How will I ever read three hundred volumes in three days?*

3
THE *Kestrel*

February 20, 1881

I awoke on our tenth and final night aboard the *Kestrel* to a terrible howling. As I turned to wake Bronson, a sudden jolt threw him against me. We disentangled ourselves hurriedly and dressed. From the violent rocking of the ship and the cries of the crew, barely audible over the howling, we knew we were in the midst of a ferocious storm. Utter blackness, cut through by brilliant silver when lightning struck, filled the world beyond our porthole. I understood in that moment, with unequivocal clarity, that the night would not end well. I had missed Sophia from the moment we left Boston. Now the thought of her in her small bed, sleeping peacefully, pierced me like a blade. She was there and we were here—in a perilous storm on a vast ocean. What had we done?

There was nothing to do but confront the disaster that awaited. Through the roar of the storm and the crashing of the waves, we heard the shouts become screams, and Bronson took my hand.

"My love," he said, "whatever we find outside that door, we stay together."

"Yes." I squeezed his hand. He squeezed back.

Then he took a length of rope that we had used to keep our trunks in place against the floorboards and rapidly tied it around his waist; the other end he tied around mine. "We'll need our hands. If we have to swim, we swim together."

"Yes, Bronson," I said again. "I love you, dearest."

He placed his hand against my cheek. "And I you, Minna." In a flash of lightning, I saw him smile. Then his face was thrown into darkness once more, and I felt him turn to open the door.

Water fell upon us as if dropped from a great height. I lost my balance immediately and tipped backward. The pull of the rope gave me enough time to steady myself. I stepped tentatively onto the deck, seeing nothing but feeling a tug at my waist as Bronson emerged from the cabin.

We moved hand over hand toward the main deck. A terrible scream pierced the air, and the howling of the wind rose and fell unabated. Suddenly the ship ceased to pitch. I peered into the darkness, seeking some guidance for my slipping feet and some clue as to what had stilled us. As if to grant my wish, another flash of lightning cut across the sky, illuminating the mottled clouds.

At first I could not understand what I saw. The stern of the ship was embedded in a rocky mass covered with kelp, as if some gigantic stone jaw had taken the *Kestrel* in its teeth. I heard Captain Gibbons shout, over the howling, "Abandon ship!" Then, in the next flash, I saw the scurrying of dark shapes. They emerged from the rocky mass that held the *Kestrel*, and I realized then, as the howling changed, that it was not made by the wind. It was more like the howling of animate creatures: dogs, or perhaps beasts.

The shape nearest to us advanced toward the captain with the unmistakable movements of a man. Amid the thick kelp that hung like hair about his head I saw a face: white and fierce, with bared teeth, grassy beard, and glassy eyes. In the next flash, I saw the creature fling out his arms, making the sound that I had mistaken for the wind; the massive weeds that formed his lower body surged, pushing him upward; the white arms—faintly green and luminescent, as if lit from within—cast a kelp-made net that caught the sailor closest to him in its slippery mesh, throwing him flat onto the deck.

"Minna, to the bow!" Bronson shouted, as the world plunged once more into darkness. He steered me away, and I knew he aimed for the front of the ship so that we could leap into the waves, putting ourselves at the mercy of the sea.

The captain and his crew were of the same mind. We could hear them as we walked unsteadily toward the bow. The scene that met us there was chaos. Shapes hurled themselves into the water; others were caught and dragged by the weed nets; and still others, locked in vicious embrace, struggled against each other. There were shouts and howls, but there was no semblance of command, and as I discerned Captain Gibbons only a few steps away, fiercely wielding his blade against the creature that was attempting to seize him, I realized what would happen next.

A net cast from behind fell upon the captain, and he was flung to the ground. "*Captain!*" Bronson shouted, leaping forward. I stumbled after him, almost sending us both crashing against the hapless Gibbons, who was struggling mightily. But the captain had dropped his knife. Bronson took it up before the water could carry it away, and he hacked at the net as urgently as he dared without cutting Gibbons. I fell to my knees beside him and pulled uselessly at the slick kelp; it was like trying to rend the water itself—hopeless.

I knew that we had only a few moments before we were captured. Suddenly, the captain, roaring like a boar, was whisked away, and then, before we could stand, the net I had awaited fell upon us.

Bronson sliced into it with a cry of frustration. I had to scream in his ear so that he would hear me. "*No, Bronson, don't. Don't cut—pull!*"

For a moment he did not comprehend me, but then he realized, as I had, that our feet were still upon the wooden deck, and that with our combined weight we could pull against the creature that held the net. "*Now,*" I cried.

We hurled ourselves against the nearby rail. Caught by surprise, the kelp creature let go. We pitched into the air, a tangled mass, leaving the ship behind.

For a few seconds, all sound seemed to have been sucked away. Then I plunged into the water and felt the cold pressure of its weight all around me. The net of kelp had been yanked away. I was too shocked to struggle. I seemed to lose sight of where I was, and the thought passed through my mind—gently, like a curiosity—that I might be losing consciousness.

It happened to me then: the tendency I have struggled to rein in from childhood; the habit I have almost banished, but that returns at times, unpredictable and unstoppable, throwing me off balance. I lost track of time.

I drifted. The water was dark with patches of orange light, as beautiful as some marine phantom. Instead of seeking the surface, I found myself contemplating a vision—no, a memory—from the previous night. Bronson and I sat at Captain Gibbons's table, sharing dinner with him as we had throughout the journey. I took a mouthful of stew, which tasted of squash and butter. The room was quiet and peaceful and the food wonderfully filling. Still, there was a source of unquiet within me, and I decided to voice it.

"We cannot help but notice," I said, glancing at Bronson, who nodded, "that the crew grows increasingly uneasy as we sail east."

Gibbons paused, staring at his bowl of stew. He took a long drink of water from his crystal glass. "It's nothing," he assured us, picking up his spoon. "You have sailed east before—you know mariners maintain all manner of superstition about the open seas."

Bronson shot me a look. "Yes, we have sailed east, though not by this route," he said.

"Is there a particular 'superstition,' as you put it, we should know of?" I asked.

Gibbons shook his head. "My men are very level-headed on land, but there is always a point halfway across the Atlantic that seems to transform them into frightened children, cowering under their covers at the prospect of nightmares." He smoothed his hands over the tablecloth, calming the wrinkles of the white linen.

"Gibbons," Bronson said amiably. "Come, tell us what it is they fear. Minna and I are not prone to panic at the telling of mariners' tales."

"Of course; I apologize." Gibbons looked up at us with a smile. "I did not wish to alarm you, but you are quite right. You are both far too reasonable to be alarmed without cause." He shrugged. "The men believe that crossing the Atlantic carries us across a barrier—an invisible barrier, that is— separating the old world of the Papal States, the Closed Empire, the Middle Roads, and the Early Pharaohs from our Western Hemisphere."

"If it is invisible," I asked, "then what does it consist of?"

"Ah." He smiled. "That is where the tales differ. Mariners believe that some mysterious power guards this barrier, but they do not agree on its form. You'll hear my men talk of the Fellweeds, creatures with the Mark of the Vine who guard the old world." He laughed and scraped the bottom of his bowl, the silver spoon clinking against the fine china. "Fellweeds," he scoffed. "I think the real danger in the Atlantic crossing is boredom! Too many men with too much idle time, letting their minds wander every which way. Absurd." He pushed aside his bowl, as if to push aside all thought of his men's superstitions. "My cook has made us lemon pudding for dessert," he announced happily.

The memory faded, as if all the light had gone out of it. I moved listlessly with the water. Suddenly I felt a faint tug at my waist. The thought of Bronson jolted through me. My arms flailed and seized the rope; I scrambled along it hand over hand until I realized my fear—there was nothing at the other end. Only then did I fight for the surface, clawing desperately.

When I reached it, a rush of sound filled my ears. I could not see. I heard the storm and the great howls of the Fellweeds, but where I was, and where Bronson was, I could not tell. Sinking once again below the surface, I was submerged in terror; if I did not move, I would drown. My arms fought the waves; my legs kicked frantically. When my head struck something solid I reached for it, blindly, and found myself clutching a large piece of wood.

I took in air and opened my eyes. A piece of the ship's mast had saved me, but the *Kestrel* itself was beyond salvation. In the near distance I saw the fragments of the mighty ship fall and disappear, like the bits of a broken toy, beneath the waves.

4
TRUTH TELLING

—*1892, May 31: 17-Hour #*—

"Indian Country" at the time of the Great Disruption was an unofficial designation for the region to the west of the eastern seaboard of the former United States. Treaties from before the Disruption had guaranteed Indian tribes particular parcels of land, but the treaties were often violated. After the Disruption, in 1805, New Occident formalized its relationship with the Indian Territories, setting firm boundaries in a series of treaties and granting it special status as an organized incorporated territory. Unfortunately, but unsurprisingly, the settlers in the states continued to ignore the new boundaries.

—From Shadrack Elli's History of New Occident

PART OF WHAT had made the winter and spring so difficult was the broken clock. The city of Boston had clocks on every corner, and every citizen of New Occident carried a lifewatch. Moreover, every citizen carried an inner clock, reliably marking the hours of the twenty-hour day, in his or her mind—every citizen other than Sophia. Her inner clock was broken. It had caused her endless inconvenience and considerable shame to lose track of time so easily, but the previous summer she had made her peace with it. She had realized that a wayward inner clock could be useful. If she concentrated on a single thought, poring over its every detail, a whole hour could feel like a second. And if she concentrated on the passing moment, imagining its hidden depths, a second could feel like an hour.

But the sadness that had crept in with the cold of winter, first in a trickle and then in an engulfing wave, had made it impossible to concentrate. She could no longer expand and contract the time around her, bending it to her will. Once again, she found herself at the mercy of those boundless hours and seconds, helpless in their limitlessness.

Now she felt her powers of concentration returning. They filled her with a contented thrum, a sense of steady and accomplished intention. Her first day at the Nihilismian Archive, Sophia had scanned as many of the indexes as she could until Remorse shooed her from room 45 so the archive could close. Sophia collected her membership card from the front desk and rushed home to be back by dusk.

Minna did not appear.

Buoyed by her new sense of purpose, Sophia was not deterred. She had decided to tell Shadrack about the Nihilismian Archive. Settling into the chair at her desk, where she had a clear view of East Ending Street, she waited.

To make the time pass quickly, she concentrated on her last sighting of Minna, bringing forth all its detail as if immersing herself in a memory map: the dimming light, the scent of lilacs that tumbled over the gate, the distant rumble of the trolleys. And she imagined Minna herself, dark hair braided and coiled around her head, clad in a colorless traveling dress that reached the ground. A long row of buttons trailed down the front and along each sleeve. Her voice was gentle and muted, as if she spoke from behind a curtain: "*Missing but not lost, absent but not gone, unseen but not unheard. Find us while we still draw breath.*" When she reached out toward Sophia, her face bore a mixture of tenderness and regret. Her dress hung on her loosely, as if she had grown thin, and the hem was stained with water and mud.

Sophia frowned. Her thoughts had taken an unexpected turn. She shook her head, trying to recall the elation that had coursed through her at the sight of her mother, but it was gone.

Sophia opened her eyes, hearing a rapid step on the cobblestones. As she watched her uncle walk up to the side door, she felt a sudden wave of sadness. She floundered. Was it seeing Shadrack, or was it the marred memory of Minna that had overturned the smooth vessel in which she had sailed through the day? She took a deep breath to steady herself, considering the sadness critically so that she would not be engulfed by it.

It was not sadness about one particular thing, but about many things all at once. She regretted that Shadrack was arriving so late from the ministry and that he would probably have to work more at home. It saddened her to see him tired all the time. And it saddened her that there would be no time, once again, to study cartology. The thought of all the untouched maps in the underground map room filled her with frustration. She felt bad for begrudging Shadrack his time, since everything he did for the ministry was so important. Most of all, she felt wretched about how things seemed so different between them. She could not tell if it was Shadrack's exhaustion or her own resentment that had brought about the sense of distance, but it was there. In the past, Sophia thought unhappily, she would have run down the steps to meet him. Now, she rose slowly from her chair, dreading his weary look and his rapid departure to the study.

Sophia walked down the steps to the kitchen, where she found Shadrack unpacking a canvas shopping bag at the kitchen table. "You're home," she said, putting her arms around him.

"I'm finally home, Soph," he replied, embracing her wearily in return. "You needn't have waited for me. You must be hungry."

"Oh, I don't mind waiting." Sophia took up unpacking the food while Shadrack sat down exhaustedly. She heard in her own voice the resentment, the opposite meaning, pleading to be heard: *I do mind. I mind waiting. Every night.* It surprised her. She could hear it now, in the same way that she could see the great expanse of sadness. Could Shadrack hear it?

"Well, *I'm* hungry," Shadrack said, throwing himself back in his chair. "So hungry that I just took things off the shelves at Morton's without really thinking. I'm glad Mrs. Clay has the chance to escape us on her night off, but our stomachs always suffer when she does."

He could not hear it.

Sophia turned to the bag and stared at it, overcome by the realization. Slowly and steadily, she pushed the discovery aside. She forced herself to look at the contents of the bag. "Pickles, cold pork, cheddar cheese, a loaf of rye bread, and four toma-toes," she said woodenly. "I'll get plates." It was suddenly apparent to her that this happened every night: she said things she did not mean because she wanted them to be true.

"Another impossible day," Shadrack sighed. He rested his elbows on the table and put his head in his hands. "Raiders in the Indian Territories, as usual. Or 'settlers,' as they call them-selves. They simply won't see sense. To them, any piece of land without a fence around it is land for the taking. Most of them are simply scoundrels, but some of them are Nihilismian, and they insist on pushing west, because that's what happened in the 'Age of Verity.'" He rolled his eyes. "They seem incapable of understanding that we inhabit this world around us, not a different one."

Sophia looked at him. *Now is the moment to tell him about the archive,* she thought. *He will be upset. Then I'll explain, and he'll understand.* She opened her mouth to speak, but the words would not come.

Shadrack shook his head and moved on. "But enough about the ministry—I have more immediate news. Good news and bad news."

Sophia sank down into her chair. "What is it?"

"I received a letter from Miles today. The man they had gone to find near the Eerie Sea who supposedly knew about Aus-entinia is, very recently it seems, deceased." He stared down at his plate before looking up to meet her gaze. "I'm sorry, Soph."

She had hoped for better news. "They didn't learn anything?"

"Miles only said that the man was dead. Most of his letter

was about an attack they witnessed. Well, they witnessed the aftermath. Settlers from Connecticut on an Indian town near the border." Shadrack ran a hand through his hair. "Prime Minister Bligh and I spent three hours today finding absolutely *nothing* by way of solution."

Ever since the previous summer, when parliament had adopted an uncompromising posture toward foreigners, closing the borders and deporting people of foreign birth, New Occident had changed. To Sophia it was most apparent in the empty storefronts, the neighbors from the Indies who had moved away, the trolley drivers she no longer saw, and the undefinable sense of *sameness* of Boston's inhabitants. There were no more vendors from the Baldlands selling turquoise or palm readers from the Indies offering to tell one's fortune. Even people from the Indian Territories and the state of New Akan, who had every right to be in Boston, had gradually drifted away.

To them, the border closure was pointless. The Territories and New Akan were next door to the Baldlands; their families and friends lived there. People came and went all the time. The *real* foreigners, they argued, were settlers from places like Connecticut, who ignored existing treaties and tried to seize land in the Indian Territories. Tensions between settlers and existing residents had grown strained. Prime Minister Cyril Bligh, who wished to overturn the border closure and who sought a peaceable solution to the disagreements, had been appointed, it seemed, too late. By the time he was appointed in January, so many altercations had erupted that even his well-known skill at negotiation was ineffectual. Sophia took a deep breath. "And what's the good news?"

"The good news is that Miles said they are returning. It sounds to me as if they are making their way back to us now, even as we speak." Shadrack attempted a smile. "So they will be home soon."

Finally, Sophia thought. "When do you think they'll be here?"

"It could be any day now. I know you'll be glad to have Theo back."

"Yes." It was true, she would be glad. The search for Minna and Bronson—and things in general—had become so much more difficult in his absence.

Theo had not been particularly helpful with the search. When they went to the Boston Public Library to look for leads, Sophia spent hours reading, while Theo, after reading for a few minutes, inevitably drifted from his desk to chat with the other library patrons. Moreover, he made a joke out of everything, even things that were very serious. When a promising lead turned into a dead end, his ridiculous comments went on and on until Sophia had to laugh. Perhaps this was why things were worse without him. Dead ends were not funny, but Theo could make them seem like the funniest thing in the world.

Sophia and Shadrack sat in silence, staring down at their untouched food. The kitchen clock over their heads ticked loudly. *This is when I should say something*, Sophia told herself. *I must tell him about the archive.* "I went to a new archive today," she said, before she could reason her way out of talking.

There was a pause. "Did you?" Shadrack asked. His voice

was falsely bright. Sophia could see in his eyes that he hated himself for that falseness, and it filled her with sympathy. *I feel the same way,* she thought. *I hate the falseness, too.* She wanted to say something that would make it all right—something that would explain that she missed the lessons in cartology and desperately wanted his help, but that she understood, and that even though she was disappointed, he was still her beloved uncle Shadrack.

Somehow, talking about the search for Minna and Bronson had become something that made them both feel guilty: Shadrack, because he was not doing enough to help; and Sophia, because it felt like she was accusing Shadrack of not doing enough to help. Suddenly, she did not want to tell him about the Nihilismian Archive at all. "I did." She gave her own false smile back. "Nothing useful yet. I'll let you know if I find something."

"That sounds like an excellent proposal. Come," he said. "We should eat. We've both had long days. And I'm afraid I'll have to hole up in the study to do more work after dinner."

Sophia nodded, burying the sense of disappointment. "Let's eat, then."

—1892, June 1: 7-Hour 59—

SHE WAS WAITING at the Nihilismian Archive when the doors opened the next day. As the bald attendant appeared in the doorway, Sophia scanned his face quickly for some sign: outrage, suspicion, alarm. None of it was there. He nodded expressionlessly when she showed him her card and ushered her in. *Safe for today, then.* She nodded in return and made her way up to room 45.

Remorse had offered to leave the A.D. 82 indexes on one of the mahogany tables so that Sophia could return to her work without interruption. As she began, she found that the volumes had been moved. *A.D. 82: v. 1* through *A.D. 82: v. 5*, which she had read already, were still neatly placed to the left of her work space. But instead of *A.D. 82: v. 6*, which she had left out to work on next, Sophia found *A.D. 82: v. 27* in front of her. She returned the volume to the cart, where it belonged, and withdrew *A.D. 82: v. 6*.

She began working her way through the volumes as quickly as possible, scanning each line and moving on to the next. Every once in a while, as her eye moved over the index entries, she heard the echo of that unforgettable voice, urging her onward: *Find us while we still draw breath.*

I'm trying, she replied silently. *I am trying.*

Remorse worked steadily nearby, dusting bookshelves and reorganizing volumes. At one point, when Whether had left the room, she wandered up to the table and set down her duster. "How goes the reading?" she asked expressionlessly.

"It goes," Sophia replied. She turned back to the index. A moment later, she realized that Remorse was still standing there. She looked up, disconcerted. "How goes your work?"

"It goes as well." Remorse sat down abruptly. "I won't be here many more days. I've accepted a Nihilismian mission."

Sophia blinked. "Where are you going?"

"The Papal States." Remorse paused. Then she asked, "What do you think about the missions?"

Sophia frowned. "I am not sure," she said truthfully.

Remorse nodded. "Some Niles think it is the most devout work in the world, going to other Ages to keep them on the right path. Last year, I heard, the mission to the Papal States prevented a disaster that would have resulted in the early death of Christopher Columbus."

Remorse's voice was neutral, but Sophia replied carefully. "That does seem important. Though surely Columbus's voyages cannot happen now the way they did in our own past."

Remorse cocked her head. "That is what Whether says. He says that the missions are pointless because we live in an apocryphal Age, so why should what happens in it matter? This is not a real world, anyway."

Sophia hesitated. Clearly Remorse did not believe this, or she would not be undertaking a mission. "I think both explanations make sense."

"If this is not a real world," Remorse continued, as if Sophia had not spoken, "then why do we feel sad and angry and happy in it? We should feel nothing if this is all not real."

Sophia had learned enough about Nihilismians to know why they behaved as they did. They were attempting to demonstrate that they felt nothing: that they felt no sadness or happiness, because there was no reason for emotions in a false world. But she had never considered that Nihilismians might genuinely struggle to conceal what they felt. More—that they struggled *not* to feel. She felt a twinge of unexpected pity. "That is difficult to answer," she said slowly. "I don't know."

"Nor do I," Remorse replied. She looked down at the table.

"Can you say more about what your mission will be?"

Remorse rose from her seat as abruptly as she'd taken it. "No. But I am leaving soon." She tucked the duster under her arm. "It is not always most productive to read the volumes in order," she said, changing the subject.

"It is easiest to keep track of what I've done this way."

Remorse looked at her a moment longer. "Very well." She turned away and resumed her work.

Sophia regarded the Nihilismian, wondering about her comment. She considered that Remorse had been the one to suggest the 1881 index. Was she offering something more than general advice? Sophia looked for some flickering sign, some further indication of her meaning. But the Nihilismian dusted with perfect discipline, and she betrayed nothing.

5

NEWS FROM THE EERIE SEA

—1892, June 2: 15-Hour 22—

Once called "great lakes," the bodies of water in the northwest corner of New Occident transformed with the Great Disruption. They are now glacial expanses trafficked by few. The name "Eerie Sea" has multiple meanings. One of the lakes was known as Lake Erie before the Disruption, named for the Indian tribes that lived near it. Now the sea is home to these tribes as well as the Eerie, a people who migrated east from the Pacific Coast. And lastly, there can be no doubt that the sea is, indeed, eerie. Glacial palaces with great caverns and frozen pools, the icy chambers of the sea have befuddled explorers with strange lights, sudden fogs, and mysterious sounds.

—From Shadrack Elli's History of New Occident

SOPHIA HAD SPENT three days reading the indexes for A.D. 82. In those three days she had read through nineteen volumes. Remorse encouraged her by commenting impassively that she read very fast. But Sophia knew otherwise: it was not fast enough. The three days she had known would be safe were over, and she would now need to gamble every morning as she arrived at the archive with the likelihood that she would be discovered and accused of fraud.

Find us while we still draw breath, she heard in her head, as she walked back to East Ending Street from the trolley stop. *I don't know how to,* she thought. *I don't know what else to do.* There was no guarantee that A.D. 82 was even the right year. What if the clue she was looking for lay three shelves away on A.D. 83?

So it was an especially disheartened Sophia who walked up the steps to 34 East Ending Street. She opened the side door, dropped her satchel on the bench, and suddenly froze.

The sound of laughter reached her from somewhere inside the house. Three voices—no, four. Her pulse quickened. She listened a moment longer as a slow smile crept across her face. Then she raced down the hall, into Shadrack's study, and down through the open doorway to the underground map room. "There she is!" she heard Shadrack say merrily as she clambered down the stairs.

Sophia burst into the room, dimly aware that Shadrack was seated at the table and that Mrs. Clay and Miles Countryman were in the armchairs near him. Standing at the foot of the stairs, with his arms crossed over his chest and his brown eyes looking up at her expectantly, was Theo. Sophia pulled herself up short just one step shy of where he stood. Pausing for a few moments—which felt to Sophia like no time at all—she registered the astonishing sense of happiness and relief that flooded through her at the sight of him: worn-looking, taller than she remembered, but essentially the same.

He uncrossed his arms and held out his scarred hand, a surprising tremor running through it. "Are you going to make me wait another hour for a hug, or what?" he demanded gruffly.

Sophia pitched herself forward with a delighted laugh and wrapped her arms around him. "Where have you *been*?" she cried. "You've been gone forever!"

"Still having trouble keeping time, I see," he said laughingly, but the pleased smile on his face as Sophia pulled back left her no doubt that Theo had missed her, too.

She turned away with effort to greet Miles, who embraced her happily, and whose mane of white hair, looking even more unkempt than usual, threatened her with imminent suffocation. "My dear Sophia," Miles exclaimed, finally releasing her, "we have fought our way back to you tooth and nail, and here we are at last, back where we belong." He grinned conspiratorially. "Although if you ask me, it is the perfect moment for another journey." Shadrack and Mrs. Clay groaned. "It is!" Miles protested. "Sophia is finally done with her classes, the forecast in the *Farmer's Almanac* is very auspicious, and I love the smell of foreign breezes in June!"

Shadrack shook his head with mock exasperation. "At least take a few minutes to tell us about the Indian Territories before you leave in search of savory foreign breezes, Miles."

"Well, if we all leave together, Theo and I can report along the way!"

Sophia and Mrs. Clay laughed.

"Miles," Shadrack remonstrated, "I am forced to conclude that you expressly intend to torment me. Knowing full well that the Ministry confines me to Boston like a rabbit in a pen, or a chicken in a coop, or—more accurately—a helpless prisoner in jail . . ."

"Very well, very well," scoffed Miles. "I can see that the Ministry has given you license to put on airs, and that now there are too many other issues of importance competing for your time, so that even the merest little sea voyage—a slight skip and a jump—is an interruption to Great Matters of State."

Sophia and Theo exchanged grins.

"By all means, Miles," Shadrack burst out, "let me resign my post at once and nominate you. I would do anything to rid myself of the unfathomable Matters of State and the inevitable headaches that accompany them." He sighed and said in a more serious tone, "In truth, I would not wish the Ministry position on my greatest enemy."

"Not even the magnificent, handsome, and brilliant Gordon Broadgirdle?" Miles's voice was heavy with sarcasm. "Surely you could spare the esteemed member of parliament a headache or two, if only to remind him of how it feels to be mortal."

"Well." Shadrack smiled, as if determined to see the problem humorously. "Perhaps Broadgirdle." He stood up with sudden energy. "But on such a night we should be celebrating, not inviting thoughts of our least favorite MP into our midst! If you'll join me upstairs, you'll see that I'm not entirely unprepared for a small celebration. I have ginger beer and two meat pies from the Stamp and Whistle, and Mrs. Clay bought the largest maple-sugar cake she could find at Oliver Hamilton's.

Miles and Theo, if you would kindly bring the maps to show us every mile of your progress, we will have everything we need."

Miles bounded for the stairs. "Theo will have to do the talking; my mouth will be full."

Mrs. Clay followed him, muslin skirts bunched in her hands to avoid tripping on the stairs, with Shadrack close on her heels. "Hurry, Mrs. Clay, for Fates' sake," Shadrack urged her. "The man will leave us nothing to eat, and we'll be forced to make a meal of the crumbs on the floor."

"What a good thing the maple cake is upstairs in my apartment, then," Mrs. Clay replied.

"Oh, he'll find it," Shadrack cried. "Nothing is safe from that man's stomach, not even the kitchen table."

Sophia and Theo laughingly followed. "Hey," Theo said, grasping Sophia's hand as they climbed the stairs. "How have you been?"

Sophia smiled, the sudden shyness she had felt at first seeing him momentarily returning. "Fine." She squeezed his hand. "I'm glad you're back."

"Me, too. Shadrack says you've been spending all your time at the library."

Sophia looked down at her feet. "Yes. Just trying to decipher the letter. I've made no progress. Right now I'm trying to read through three hundred volumes that might possibly have some clue."

"Well, now it's summer. Maybe," he went on, his voice light, "it's time to take a little break from that letter."

Sophia looked up at him with surprise. They had reached the top of the stairs. "Take a break from the letter?" she asked, astonished, as if he had suggested burning it in the fireplace.

"Sure. You know, sometimes things look different after a break. Rest your head a bit. Do something other than read for a while."

Sophia pulled her hand away. "I'm not taking a break."

"I don't mean forget about the letter—I'm not saying that. Just a break. We could persuade Shadrack to let us sail for a month with Calixta and Burr. Maybe you'll have some new ideas."

"I don't want to take a break. I want to find my parents."

"All right, all right," Theo said at once, his tone conciliatory. "I just got back. I don't want you mad at me already." He grinned. "I can come along. We'll go read those three hundred volumes together, and it will go twice as fast. What do you say?" He reached for her hand again.

Sophia looked up at him, her expression softening. "I have to read them myself. But thanks. I'm glad you're back."

"Sophia, Theo," Shadrack called. He appeared in the doorway of the study. "Are you going to help us fight Miles for the food or not? He has already plunged a fork into one of the pies, and I'm not sure we can hold him off much longer."

"The scoundrel!" Theo exclaimed, pulling Sophia after him. The meat pies and bottles of ginger beer had pride of place on the kitchen table; as Mrs. Clay laid out the plates, napkins, and utensils, she swatted Miles's hands away from the main course.

When they were all seated, Shadrack divided up the first pie, poured ginger beer out for all, and raised his glass in a toast. "Welcome home, Theo and Miles. Here's to a safe voyage concluded."

"And many more to come," Miles added, raising his own glass. "Starting tomorrow."

They all laughed and dove into the pies, which were every bit as good as Shadrack had promised. When they had finished, leaving only crumbs and empty glasses, Mrs. Clay brought dessert down from upstairs and served generous portions of the soft yellow cake slathered in maple sugar frosting alongside cups of Charleston tea.

Miles sat back with a satisfied sigh after his third piece. Then he began his account of the journey, describing the long route west through New York and the northwest corner of Pennsylvania that led to the Indian Territories. At times flaring into argument with Theo where his recollection of certain circumstances differed, Miles admitted that their travels west had been fairly uneventful, even up to their arrival at the Eerie Sea. "The only difficulty we encountered was a decidedly prejudicial view toward Bostonians," Miles said sourly. "The border closure has not improved our popularity. An old man in Salt Lick actually spat at me when I told him where we came from."

Theo chuckled at the memory. "Miles spat back, of course."

"Well, I had to!" Miles protested. "I had to explain why I loathe the border closure more than he does."

"Apart from that lively event, the only obstacle was finding

Cabeza de Cabra. We took as many days doing that, once we reached the Eerie Sea, as we did getting there from Boston."

"That's true," Miles assented.

"No one could agree on where he lived," Theo explained to the others, "and the lead we were following was so vague to begin with."

Miles and Theo had departed in late winter in pursuit of a rumor. Word had reached Boston of a hermit living near the glacial Eerie Sea, a man from the Papal States named Cabeza de Cabra who, for three hundred and sixty-four days of the year, shunned all human contact. Then, on the three hundred and sixty-fifth—the day of the winter solstice—he emerged from his solitude to rant about the end of the world, the next Great Disruption, and the mysteries of Ausentinia. He spoke a curious amalgam of Erie, Castilian, and English, and the unsolicited sermons were dismissed by the villagers as the wanderings of a madman.

But the distant echoes of his annual ravings had traveled all the way to Boston, along with the name "Ausentinia," which had been mentioned nowhere else except Bronson's letter. The March snows were still falling when Miles and Theo journeyed west.

"By the time we found the tree house where Cabeza de Cabra had been living," Miles continued, "it was late April, and his body had been lying unattended so long the crows had taken it to pieces."

"Ugh," Mrs. Clay said, shuddering.

Shadrack sighed with disappointment. "And did you find anything there, in his home, to indicate how he might know of Ausentinia?"

"Cabeza de Cabra lived like an animal," Miles said, frowning. "He dressed in skins and slept on a filthy piece of hide. There were no pots and pans, shoes or books or tools. I have no idea how he fed himself. We were about to leave the place, after finding it so barren, when Theo noticed something that I, frankly, would have missed."

"And *I* only noticed it thanks to the mapmakers back home who were on my mind now and then," Theo added, with a slight smile at Sophia. "It was a curtain. Or more like a screen. A square of dark fabric, nailed over the small window to block the sun. I was surprised how clean it was. Everything else was filthy. We pried out the nails and took it down. Sure enough, when I let it flutter in the breeze—"

"It was a map!" exclaimed Sophia.

"Yes," Miles said. "Although I will eat my warmest winter hat if you or Shadrack is able to make any sense of it."

"Well, bring it out!" Shadrack demanded. "And get your hat, because it's going right onto that empty cake plate."

"All right, all right. We'll see how far your threats go once you've seen it."

Theo disappeared into Shadrack's study, where he and Miles had left their packs, and returned with a bulky white bundle the length of his forearm. Shadrack and Mrs. Clay cleared the table, and Theo unrolled the fabric gently, revealing inside it a square piece of forest-green linen.

At first, the fabric seemed unremarkable. Its edges were worn and frayed, but the surface remained clean, unbroken, and smooth. Theo carefully turned it over, and Sophia and Shadrack both gasped. The other side of the linen square was densely covered with tiny beads—even smaller than peppercorns—that had been carefully stitched onto the fabric. "Yes," Theo said, in response to their gasps. "The moment we pulled it down we saw the beadwork, but it took me a little while to figure out what it was, since the beads don't make any pattern or picture."

"Metal, clay, and glass," Sophia breathed.

"Exquisite," Shadrack exclaimed, bending over the table to examine the map more closely. "I have never seen this technique, but what a simple and beautiful method—incorporating the other layers of mapping *into* the weather map. Brilliant."

"This is nothing like the maps I recall from the academy in Nochtland," Mrs. Clay observed, looking at it with a baffled expression.

"I have not the benefit of experience in any cartologic academy," Miles said. "And Shadrack has never bothered to explain to me the mysterious techniques acquired there."

"Never *bothered*?" Shadrack protested. "Every time I attempt to explain these maps, you tell me they are no substitute for exploration, and then you turn a deaf ear."

Theo laughed. "He did the same to me."

"It is not my fault that you make them sound so very

scholarly," Miles said with distaste. "Are they *useful*? That is what I wish to know."

"Incredibly useful," Sophia explained eagerly. "They can tell you everything that happened in a particular place and time. Usually a cloth map shows the weather, and if you layer it with other kinds of memory maps—a clay map to show the earth, a metal map to show everything man-made, and a glass map to show human life—you have a complete impression of what was happening."

Shadrack looked up with an expression of delight. "But this map has omitted the need for the others by creating a single layer of clay, metal, and glass beads. It is a significant innovation. And I have never seen a metal map made of gold—too costly—but these beads are almost certainly gold." He paused. "Do you see any glass beads here, Soph? My impression is that they are mostly clay, with about a quarter gold and—"

"Five glass," Theo put in. "It took me a while to find them." One by one, he pointed out the five clear glass beads hidden in an irregular pattern among the others.

"Five people?" Mrs. Clay asked.

"More than five," Shadrack said. "But perhaps not many more."

"There isn't much human life on this map," Sophia said thoughtfully.

"There isn't much of anything!" Miles complained. "Go ahead, take a look at it."

Theo lifted it up and released a puff of air, making the cloth flutter. Then he placed it back on the table with the beads facing down. A fine network of white lines spread across the linen surface.

"Now that the map has woken," Shadrack said in anticipation, "we can specify the time." He indicated a nested set of concentric circles at one corner. The outermost circle was numbered to sixty, as was the second; the third was numbered to eight, the fourth to thirty, and the innermost to twelve. "Seconds, minutes, hours, days, and months," he murmured, "and the hours are not New Occident hours. No year. Sophia . . . ?"

She had already gone to the cupboard. "What about barley? Or rice?"

"I think rice." After a brief search, she returned with a small handful of rice, which she poured onto the table. "You choose," Shadrack said, looking up at her with a smile.

Sophia felt a flood of happiness as she placed a grain of rice within each circle. It felt almost like old times; here they were, reading maps together, just as they used to. "To make it easy to remember," she said, smiling back at him. "The fourth of April at four-hour, four-minute, four-second."

They each set a fingertip on one of the white lines fanning out across the square of fabric. Immediately, Sophia's mind was filled with a vivid memory of a place and time she had never seen. A vast, dry landscape surrounded her in every direction. The ground was flat and dotted here and there with dark green scrub. In the distance, a few hills rose dustily into the blue sky; it was a blue so brilliant that it almost blinded her. The sun bore down heavily, and the dry heat left her breathless. The air was perfectly still. For a few moments more, Sophia surveyed in her memory the arid plain around her, and then she lifted her finger.

"Hm," Shadrack said. He had sat back in his chair, his arms crossed over his chest.

"I'll say," Miles commented. "It's all like that. Hot and dry and empty. Quite useless."

"But it can't *all* be like that," Theo countered, "Because there are those metal beads and the few glass ones. Somewhere in this map there must be some people and lots of things made by them—a city or a town or roads, or something. We just haven't had time to look through it all yet. I mean, the map covers a whole year, so you actually need to spend a whole year in every place pictured here, and it looks like it covers at least a hundred square miles."

Miles shook his head. "You could spend a lifetime combing through that map. No, thank you. I'll leave the maps to you. I'd rather go there in person."

"It's in the Papal States, I think," Shadrack said pensively.

Miles nodded. "I agree. The landscape is undoubtedly Papal States—I would guess the southern portion of the peninsula."

"Yes. And supposedly Cabeza de Cabra was *from* the Papal States," said Shadrack.

"So these could be his memories?" Sophia wondered.

"Or someone else's, but the map likely came with him from the Papal States," Shadrack concluded. "Unless . . . It could be that it was made in the Indian Territories using Cabeza de Cabra's memories."

"We came to the same conclusion," Miles said. "But, as I said before, remarkable as the map may be as an artifact, I can see no value in it for our search. I'm afraid that Cabeza de Cabra, if he knew anything about Ausentinia, took his secrets with him to the grave."

Sophia gazed at the white lines webbed across the linen square, her mind turning over each piece of information. Cabeza de Cabra had spoken of Ausentinia. He came from the Papal States, and his map showed a year's worth of time lived there. Despite this clear connection, they had learned nothing certain. Cabeza de Cabra might not have been speaking about Ausentinia; a word so unfamiliar could easily have been distorted as it traveled so many miles by word of mouth. Nevertheless, she thought, her eyes narrowing, the map might contain some useful secret. There was no telling yet.

Her thoughts, as well as the conversation that had been going on without her, were interrupted by a sudden knock at the front door. Then another knock sounded, rapid and light. No one ever used the front door at 34 East Ending Street. They all fell silent, and after a moment's pause the knock was repeated. Mrs. Clay rose nervously to her feet. "Who could it be?"

Shadrack frowned. "It is probably someone from the ministry."

Mrs. Clay left the kitchen, her heels clicking on the wooden floorboards.

They waited, listening, as she opened the door, and a male voice announced itself. Moments later, Mrs. Clay reappeared, followed by a slight man in a pale gray suit.

"Bligh!" Shadrack exclaimed, getting to his feet. "What has happened?"

"I'm very sorry to interrupt your celebration," Prime Minister Bligh said, taking in the half-eaten cake and the gathering at a glance, "but the matter is urgent. Broadgirdle is making his way here at this very moment. He will be attempting to persuade you to take steps to dissolve the treaties with the Indian Territories. He has some leverage to force your hand, but I do not know what it is. He does not know that I know, and he cannot know that I am here. But I had to warn you."

Shadrack stared at him, aghast. "Dissolve the treaties? That's as good as declaring war."

Bligh shook his head. "Ignore that for the moment. What leverage might he have? What does he know about you that could hurt you? And what can we do to make it ineffective?"

"I don't know. I—" Shadrack ran a hand through his hair. "Nothing. Or any number of things. It depends on how dirty he is willing to get."

"I believe very dirty." Bligh set his mouth in a firm line.

There was another knock at the front door, this one loud and steady. They all stood frozen. "You must answer it," Bligh said tersely. "It will seems suspicious otherwise."

Shadrack took a deep breath. "Miles, take Bligh to the map room and do not leave until I come down to find you. Sophia, Theo—upstairs. Mrs. Clay, I will wait for Broadgirdle in the study." He quickly rolled up the map on the table.

"Very well, Mr. Elli," Mrs. Clay said, her voice unsteady. She left the kitchen. Bligh followed Miles out of the room in the opposite direction.

Sophia stood rooted to the ground. "Come on," Theo said, pulling at her hand.

"It will be fine," Shadrack said. He squeezed her shoulder. "Go on up. I'll call you when this is over."

6

WREN'S ROOST

February 20, 1881

I clung to the piece of the *Kestrel*'s mast as the sea heaved around me, laden with the ship's wreckage. While the sky remained dark and inscrutable, the howling of the Fellweeds had subsided, and I heard a distant call over the continuing crash of the waves: *"Minna! Minna!"* It was my husband. My throat rasped and raw with salt water, I shouted back as loudly as I could. Finally, he heard me. *"Stay where you are and call my name!"* he cried. *"I'll swim to you."*

I called his name until my voice was shredded, until I saw a piece of debris moving toward me through the settling waters. Kneeling on a large, jagged piece of the deck, Bronson was using a broken plank as an oar. He pulled me up onto the makeshift raft carefully, and then we collapsed, exhausted, into each other's arms.

The relief was short-lived. Soon, the terror of being so lost on such a great expanse of water overtook us. I would have cried, but that my body and mind were too spent, and for a time I slept, or lost consciousness, or simply drifted in that vast emptiness made by the ocean at night.

When I returned to the world, Bronson and I were still tightly wrapped around one another. The waters were as calm as I had ever seen them on the open sea, and the sky had begun to lighten. I realized that I had been roused by the sound of shouting voices, and I shook Bronson awake.

We turned as one to look at the ship that sailed toward us: similar in size to the *Kestrel*, its figurehead was a mermaid with a small bird in her cupped, outstretched hands. The *Roost*, as the ship declared itself to be in fine, white letters, moved gently toward us, and a pair of deckhands tossed down a rope ladder. I thought for several seconds that I was imagining it. I could not believe our luck.

From the ship's name, its familiar aspect and equipment, and the loud cries in English of the sailors, we took it to be from New Occident. Indeed, Captain Wren, who met us on deck, confirmed that he had sailed from a remote port neither of us had heard of in Upper Massachusetts. Incredibly tall—as, indeed, was his entire crew—he had a keen blue gaze that spoke powerfully of both his competence as a captain and his curiosity as to our circumstances.

The captain ushered us immediately into his cabin, where he provided us with clean clothes and tumblers of fresh water. He left us to bathe and compose ourselves. "I am anxious to be informed of your misadventure as soon as you are well enough to speak of it," he said with a kind of formality, even stiffness, that I have not often observed in sea captains. "But I know you must be completely exhausted. Please rest, and then find me on deck when you are able." We thanked him warmly for his kindness and set about following his generous instructions.

Bronson has often claimed that I was as taken in as he was, and that neither of us observed anything unusual about Captain Wren and his crew. He argues with me that we were half ruined by the destruction of the *Kestrel* and the long night on the open sea, and that we could not have been alert, observant, and circumspect. But I maintain that my memory is correct, and that even from that first moment in Captain Wren's cabin—indeed, from the very moment he welcomed us aboard the *Roost*—I suspected that he was not who he claimed to be.

The clothes he had provided were too well made. It will sound absurd, but this made me uneasy from the start. They were finer and more compact than ours. I have mentioned that Wren and his crew were all tall men; they also had extraordinarily white and even teeth. They seemed too healthy, too well kept to be mariners. The items in Wren's cabin, too, seemed unlike the objects in Captain Gibbons's. I cannot explain how they seemed wrong to me, other than to say that while half of them seemed peculiarly new, as if they had never been used, the other half seemed entirely too old, as if unearthed in a curiosity shop. Some of the nautical charts, for example, which I glimpsed on his desk as I was drying myself, were printed on a paper so white that I had never seen the like. At the same time, the magnifying glass—identical to one owned by Gibbons, and made by a manufacturer in Boston—seemed to carry centuries of use. The wooden handle was cracked and blackened as if from a thousand Atlantic crossings. I can observe these things now, with hindsight, more clearly. At the time, I knew only that the sum total of Captain Wren's cabin, however familiar in its form and composition, made me ill at ease; something was not quite right. I said as much to Bronson before we made our way up to the deck. "What do you make of him?" I asked.

"Seems a good man," Bronson said. He reached out to cup my chin. "Don't worry, my love. We're safe now."

"Yes. Yes, we're safe." I paused. "Does it not strike you that there is something different about him and his crew? He's not like any man from Upper Mass I've ever known."

Bronson laughed. "True. Probably not from Upper Mass, though. He said that he had sailed from a port there, not that he was *from* there." He put his arm around me. "Don't worry yourself. If he had wanted to do us harm, he had only to leave us in the ocean."

I could not deny such sound logic, and my sense of unease was shortly put to rest by the captain's friendly reception, even while many aspects of his bearing and the ship itself continued to strike me as unusual. He wanted to hear every detail of our misadventure.

Bronson began by showing him the letter from Bruno Casavetti that had precipitated our voyage:

December 2, 1880

Minna and Bronson, my dear friends—

I write to you in great need, with the most desperate of pleas.

As you know, I departed from Boston six months ago to map the border between the Middle Roads and the Papal States. I cannot at this moment recount the details of how this objective changed along the way, so that I lost all possibility of fulfilling my purpose. My friends, something terrible has happened. In this place I thought I knew so well, I have discovered a new Age. I cannot explain how it came to be here, but it brings with it fear, intolerance, and persecution.

I write to you now—on smuggled paper—thanks to the kindness of a child, whom I saved from a fate that I, sadly, was unable to escape. They believed this child to be a witch, and they believe me to be some similar agent of devilry. A terrible plague that they call lapena has wreaked havoc on the region, and the people see witchery in everything and everyone. I was able to prove them wrong in the case of the girl, Rosemary, but the case against me is stronger, and I have not the advantage of being a winsome, likable child native to their Age.

At present I am imprisoned in the town of Murtea (I have also seen it Murcia or Mursiya in some of Shadrack's volumes—do not trust my spelling), and the judges slowly gather evidence against me. Loath as I am to call you here, I feel that you are my only hope. The child Rosemary will deliver my letter to a distant town so that through the royal mail it may

reach the port and, from there, I hope, some traveler head-
ing to Boston. I enclose a map and directions for locating her
when you arrive. Protect her if you can—she is not to blame
for this.

I am sorry, my friends, to bring this misfortune into your
path. My life is in your hands.

Bruno Casavetti

"Very serious indeed," Wren agreed, handing the letter
back. "And you decided to respond in person to his call for
aid?"

We described the voyage aboard the *Kestrel* and the terrible encounter with the Fellweeds. Captain Wren's eyes lit
up with something near excitement when we described the
creatures that had destroyed our ship. "I have never seen a
Fellweed," he said, in a low, awed voice, "though I have heard
them described."

"Frankly," Bronson admitted, "we both thought it a mere
fancy. I would never have believed the things existed if I had
not seen them with my own eyes."

"I would have said the same before this morning," Captain Wren agreed. "Although some part of me always wanted
them to be real."

"Why should you wish such a thing?" I asked him, astonished. "The Fellweeds were merciless."

"Well, yes," Wren replied, somewhat embarrassed. He

wore an amber-tinted monocle on a golden chain, and whenever he was at ease he would twirl the monocle idly. Now the monocle came to an abrupt halt. "An idle curiosity, I suppose. In any case," he went on, changing the subject, "it will be no difficulty to take you to Seville, if that was your destination."

"It was. Are you certain this does not make you deviate from your intended route?" Bronson asked.

"Not in the least," Captain Wren replied, without actually telling us what his intended route was. "We have ten days of sailing ahead of us, and I will look forward to your company during that time." Wren's tanned face and white, even teeth seemed to shine at the prospect. And he did, indeed, appear to savor our conversation. Over the next few days, we told him about our past journeys, and our dear Sophia, and how we had planned to take her with us on this voyage, but the dangers Bruno had written of prevented it. He had a thousand questions for us about Boston, which he justified by saying that he was from a remote and isolated part of Seminole, and that he had never visited our capital. I would have believed this explanation but for his unwillingness to talk about the area he claimed to call home and—more strikingly—what emerged as his surprising ignorance regarding New Occident in general.

This ignorance was hard to place, as he certainly seemed to know a great deal about some aspects of life in New Occident. Yet at other moments he would ask a question or use a phrase that baffled us. Finally, on the third night aboard the *Roost*, my discomfort prompted me to confront him more directly. We had been telling him about our journey, some years prior, into the Indian Territories. Bronson, with his skillful pen, drew quick sketches of the people and places we had seen along the way. Captain Wren leaned in over the wooden table, quite literally on the edge of his seat. His bronzed hands clasped each other; his blue eyes were wide with interest at our description of riding through upper New York toward Six Nations City. "I have never been to Six Nations City. What is it like?" he asked eagerly.

"A great trading city," Bronson said, "much like Charleston or New York. People from all over the territories and New Occident live and trade there—more or less peaceably."

"An Eerie woman once told me that Six Nations City should more rightly be called 'Sixty Nations City,' given the variety of languages and peoples one finds there," Wren remarked.

Bronson and I glanced at one another. "That's true," Bronson finally said.

"You've met the Eerie, then?" I asked. "Few people in New Occident ever have."

Captain Wren sat back. He looked flustered. "Yes, I had trade with some of the Eerie not long ago."

Now it was our turn to ask wondering questions. "There are many stories about them in New Occident," Bronson said, "but little is known for certain. We hear that they are great healers who traveled all the way from the Pacific after the Great Disruption. Is that true?"

"I couldn't say," Wren demurred. "Yes," he added after a moment, "I believe so."

"Their territory is very difficult to reach," I pressed him.

"Is it?" the captain asked, with a cautious air. "We reached the Great Lakes from the north, not through New Occident, so perhaps I took an easier route."

Bronson and I glanced at one another again, this time with greater meaning. "The Great Lakes?" I queried. "Do you mean the Eerie Sea? No one in New Occident calls them 'lakes,' as far as I know."

Wren flushed. "Of course, I mean the Eerie Sea. It's a local phrase—a seaman's term. We have difficulty conceiving of those frozen expanses as a 'sea.' You can imagine."

By now, even Bronson had observed the patchy pattern of Wren's knowledge. We had discussed it at length in private and reached no conclusion, other than to agree that whatever Wren was concealing could not be ill-intention toward us. He seemed to genuinely care for our well-being. Sensing this prompted me further to seek the cause of his sudden confusion. I fully expected that the explanation would be illuminating, not incriminating. "You seem to be very familiar with some aspects of New Occident, Captain Wren," I said gently, "and very unfamiliar with others. How is that?"

He sat silently for a moment, taken aback by my direct question. Then he smiled, and his white teeth gleamed. "I set sail for the first time when I was only a boy. I've spent most of my life at sea, and I've never had any formal schooling. You must excuse my ignorance. I am sure most of my secondhand knowledge is very ill-informed."

Bronson and I listened silently to this explanation, which I, at least, found entirely inadequate. My husband seemed more inclined to indulge Wren, not because he believed him, but because he trusted Wren's motives. Politeness prevented me from pushing further, and so that evening we learned nothing more. I was ignoring my better instincts; I knew, then, that Captain Wren had no personal knowledge of New Occident at all. But I could not imagine what interest he had in pretending so arduously otherwise. So I remained silent, and the deception continued.

7

GORDON BROADGIRDLE, MP

—1892, June 2: 18-Hour 11—

Few explorers have encountered the Eerie, and yet rumors about them abound. The last documented contact took place in 1871, when an injured explorer from New York took refuge with an Eerie during a winter storm. He had slipped on the ice and injured his leg, and the Eerie came upon him some hours later. The explorer recounted spending the two-day storm in a refuge built high in the pines, south of the Eerie Sea; he claimed to wake to find his leg mended and his frostbite healed. One can only imagine how the exposure to cold must have clouded his mind.

—From Shadrack Elli's History of New Occident

SOPHIA LEFT THE kitchen reluctantly, following Theo through the corridor and up to the second floor. They had reached the landing when they heard a booming voice: heavy and commanding, in a tone long practiced at the podium, it crashed through the house like a wave.

"My dear Shadrack! So sorry to surprise you like this, but I simply could not wait until tomorrow."

Theo froze on the landing, his hand still clasping Sophia's. His fingers gripped hers with a sudden intensity. "Ow!" Sophia exclaimed, trying to pull away as she looked at him in surprise. "What was *that* for?"

His face was blank with panic. Sophia had seen that look once before, but she could not remember when or where. Fear was so unusual in Theo that it sent a flash of sharp unease through her. "What is it?" she whispered. "What's wrong?"

Theo's eyes fastened abruptly on hers. "We have to go back down," he whispered back. "Now."

She stared at him. "Why?"

"Just come."

Sophia hesitated, more troubled by the moment. "Shadrack told us to go upstairs."

"They won't see us."

Theo tugged at her hand, and Sophia gave in. She thought for a moment that he was leading her back to the kitchen, but instead he opened the short door to the closet tucked beneath the stairs. He edged silently past a broom, a dustpan, and a precarious pile of hatboxes to kneel on the wooden floorboards. Then he turned to Sophia, a finger raised in warning to his lips. She stepped in after him and crouched down.

"Take a look," Theo whispered. He pointed to a crack in the wall.

Sophia peered through and realized she was looking into the study—the closet was situated behind a set of floor-to-ceiling bookshelves. She pulled back. "This wasn't here before!" she exclaimed as indignantly as whispering would allow.

"*Shhh!*" Theo glared at her. "I cut the wallpaper in the study.

It's behind the shelf. Not even noticeable." He turned back toward the wall. "What do you see?"

Sophia shook her head, dumbfounded. "I can't believe you cut the wallpaper. What for? There's nothing to see in there."

"Well, I think right now there probably *is*, if you would only bother to *look*."

Sophia took a deep breath, shelving her outrage for the moment. She leaned in toward the crack in the wall. She saw the tops of several books. Inching herself down, she saw the back of Shadrack's chair, his shoulders, and the back of his head. Beyond him, in front of the curtained windows, sat a huge black-haired man whom she had only seen depicted in the Boston papers: MP Gordon Broadgirdle. He wore black and gray, with a charcoal felt hat that he held loosely in his lap. She realized then that the room was silent. Shadrack was staring at an open book.

She drew back. "Shadrack is reading something. Broadgirdle is just sitting there."

"What does he look like?"

"Shadrack?"

"*No*—Broadgirdle."

She leaned back toward the wall. "Relaxed. Arrogant." She hesitated. "Scary. I can't say why."

"But what does he *look* like?"

"Oh. Very tall. Broad-shouldered. He has black hair and a full beard and a wrinkly sort of mustache. I don't like his eyes."

"What about his teeth?"

"His *teeth*?" She turned to Theo in astonishment.

"Yes, his teeth," he whispered nervously.

Then Sophia remembered when and where she had seen that look of panic on Theo's face: Veracruz, almost one year ago, when a raider with sharp metal teeth had chased them through the market. "You recognize him," she said, eyes wide.

"I recognized his voice," Theo replied. "I've never heard another like it. But I might be wrong. It could be a coincidence. Can you see his teeth?"

Sophia tried again. "I can't," she said soberly. "His mouth is closed. But I think someone would have mentioned it if Broadgirdle had metal teeth. No one in New Occident has them." She paused. "Why don't you look?"

Theo took a deep breath and wiped his palms on his pants. "Okay. Okay, I'll look at him." He dove forward and peered through the crack. After several seconds, he pulled back.

Just as he did, Shadrack spoke; his voice, wary and more than a little defensive, reached them clearly in the closet. "I didn't write this."

Sophia leaned in to watch. Broadgirdle was smiling, revealing a row of very large, very white teeth. "Not yet, perhaps."

"No. Not ever. I have not written this and never will. This is not me."

"Shadrack," Broadgirdle said earnestly, bending forward so that his massive shoulders crowded the space between them, "there is a larger purpose here. We are behind. Terribly behind. Those maps prove it."

"I don't see it that way. You know I have a very clearly defined view on policy for the Indian Territories. It is not our land."

Broadgirdle suddenly rose from his seat and placed his hat carefully on his head. "I want you to think carefully about your next move, Shadrack. You have a choice, and it could be the right choice or the wrong one. I would be so disappointed if you made the wrong one. So let me say that I *will* be very glad to hear it is the right one." He was still smiling, the thin mustache, wiry and mobile, contorting with the effort. But his words had no warmth to them. "Good evening. I will see you at the ministry tomorrow. I'll let myself out." He nodded. "Keep the book."

Shadrack sat motionless in his chair as Broadgirdle left the room. "I don't understand," Sophia whispered anxiously to Theo, still watching. "What choice? What is he talking about?"

Theo didn't answer. She turned and saw him slumped against the closet wall with a lost, pained look on his face. "Theo," she said, reaching out to clasp his scarred hand. "Is it him? The man you know?"

His words were almost inaudible. "It's him."

"But he had white teeth. They were normal."

"He must have covered them somehow. Ivory caps or something."

"Who is he? Is he another raider?"

Theo shook his head. "I don't want to talk about it."

Sophia frowned. She was about to remonstrate him when she heard Shadrack finally rising from his chair. Through the peephole, she watched him open the hidden door to the map room. "Miles, Bligh. He's gone," Shadrack called down. Then he dropped back into his seat.

A moment later, the two men emerged from the map room. Sophia could not see the prime minister, but Miles went to Shadrack immediately. "What did he say?" he demanded.

Shadrack simply handed Miles the book. "He gave me this."

Bligh joined Miles, looking over his shoulder as the explorer first frowned at the cover, and then began furiously turning the pages. "What does he mean by giving you this dreck?"

Shadrack did not answer.

"I believe I understand," Bligh said slowly, a sad expression in his gray eyes. "He wants you to feel as though you are already committed to this path. That this future is inevitable."

"Because of *this*?" Miles protested. "But that's absurd!"

"Of course it is." Shadrack's voice was weary. "But Cyril is right. That is what he wants. Naturally, I did not accede to his demands."

"And what will be the consequence?"

"He did not say," Shadrack replied. "We are to speak tomorrow."

"We are pressed on both sides," Bligh said quietly. At Shadrack's inquiring look, he added, "I was just telling Miles what Lorange informed me today. While Broadgirdle is bent on dissolving treaties with the Indian Territories, the United Indies are threatening an embargo if we do not reopen the borders."

Shadrack let out a breath. "An embargo would ruin us. Half our trade is to the Indies. Boston would starve."

"Of course it would. We must stop it at any cost." He put

his hand on Shadrack's shoulder. "But you have been burdened with enough for one evening. Get your rest, and we will speak of it tomorrow."

Shadrack rose to his feet. "Thank you, Cyril. Though I'm afraid it will be a sleepless night. And we have one more matter to discuss," he added. "The Eerie."

Miles shook his head. "I told him when we were downstairs. I could find no trace of where they are this season."

The prime minister sighed. "Poor Goldenrod. I'm afraid she's going to die on our hands, my friends."

"I am sorry to let you down," Miles said, his voice heavy with regret. "I was certain I would find them. I was somewhat constrained by Theo's presence, but in any case I needed to return. My best contact told me that the Eerie had departed for the Prehistoric Snows, which will require a different manner of expedition."

"You plan to head north?" asked Shadrack.

"At the end of the week. I'll take a route directly into the snows."

"Very well," the prime minister said as he left the study, his footsteps falling lightly on the floorboards. "Though I worry that Goldenrod may not make it through the summer."

"Believe me," Shadrack said quietly, "we are well aware of it."

As Shadrack and Miles followed Bligh out, Sophia sat back, her brow furrowed. She turned to ask Theo what he knew about the Eerie and Goldenrod but found, to her surprise, that he was gone.

IN THE FALL and early winter, before Theo had departed with Miles for the Eerie Sea, Sophia and Theo would sometimes stay awake talking until the early hours. Theo's room—a fourth bedroom on the second floor that had previously been tenanted by roughly five thousand disordered maps—was across the hall from Sophia's, and it shared a wall with the house next door. Almost every night, the neighbors would play music on their Edison phonograph—a wondrous invention as yet owned by no one else in the neighborhood. Sophia and Theo would listen to the music, or talk and listen, or just talk. Many late nights were spent laughing so hard they had to cover their faces with pillows to avoid waking Shadrack. Many nights were spent remembering the previous summer: their trip by train to New Orleans, the pirates, their journey into Nochtland, and their confrontation with Blanca and the Sandmen.

Sophia had not realized how important those evenings with the Edison phonograph had been until Theo and Miles had gone. And she had not realized, until she found Theo vanished from the closet, that she had been expecting to end this evening talking conspiratorially with her best friend, listening to the muted music next door. When Miles and Shadrack returned to the study and then descended to the map room, clearly intent on further discussion of Broadgirdle's visit, Sophia crept out of the closet and up the stairs.

Theo's door was closed. When Sophia knocked quietly,

there was no answer. "Theo?" Sophia said, knocking again. "Are you all right?" She waited, her ear to the door. After several seconds she began to worry. "Theo. Are you there?"

There was a quiet scuffle as Theo walked across the room toward the door. "I'm here," came the muffled reply.

"May I come in?"

There was a long pause. "I'm sorry. I can't talk right now."

Sophia stood at the door, astonished. "All right," she finally said.

In her own room, she took out her notebook, struggling with what she knew was an unreasonable sense of injury. Theo had been frightened by something, and she understood the impulse to shut himself away. But she did wish he could have taken comfort in her company.

For a time she wrote and drew, filling a page with the news of the evening: an account of the beaded map; a drawing of Bligh; and Broadgirdle, hulking and full of menace. When she heard Shadrack's footstep on the stairs, she looked at her watch and found that it was already two-hour.

"You are still awake?" Shadrack asked, standing in her doorway.

"I was waiting for you," she replied.

He stayed in the doorway. "Sorry to keep you up so long."

"What happened?"

Sophia watched Shadrack's tired face contract slightly. "Broadgirdle had some ludicrous proposal about dissolving the treaties, just as Cyril said." He looked at the notebook before her. "Writing your thoughts for the day?"

"But what did the prime minister mean by 'leverage'?" Sophia asked, ignoring his question.

Shadrack ran a hand through his hair. "Broadgirdle has a nasty habit of using information about people to threaten them. If he found out I wasn't really a cartologer, but that all my maps were drawn by you and Mrs. Clay, I would do anything he asked for him to keep my secret."

Sophia didn't smile at the feeble joke. "Did he threaten you?"

"No, no. He didn't threaten me. He's an unsavory character, and I have no wish to lock horns with him. But he was on good behavior tonight." He smiled. "Truly. I would tell you if there were reason to worry."

"Would you?"

"Of course." Shadrack smiled reassuringly, but there was nothing reassuring about the emptiness of his smile, or the worry in his eyes.

—*1892, June 3: 5-Hour 32*—

The Papal States emerged from the Great Disruption in what historians of the past would have termed the fifteenth century. And yet not entirely: within the Papal States, pockets of other Ages were gradually identified. Some were unpopulated and hardly noticeable; others were so small as to be insignificant; still others, no doubt, have yet to be found. But one was impossible to ignore: an Age from a past so remote, its landscape was unrecognizable. Occupying a hundred square miles west of Seville and east of Granada, it is known as the Dark Age.

—From *Shadrack Elli's* Atlas of the New World

A SLIGHT SOUND woke Sophia the next morning. She opened her eyes a crack. All the familiar occupants of her bedroom rested quietly in the gray light of early dawn: the neatly ordered desk, the painting of Salem above it, the rows of books, the wooden desk chair piled with pillows, and the folded clothes over the back of the chair. But there was one unexpected occupant—a figure standing by the window.

"Shadrack?" she mumbled. The figure turned. Sophia opened her eyes and saw a familiar shape in a long traveling dress. Her voice, low in timbre and just above a whisper, seemed to fill the room: *"Take the offered sail."* Then her face came into focus. It was Minna.

Sophia sat up abruptly. "What?" she whispered.

Minna smiled slightly. In the dawn light, the peculiar texture of her dress and skin were more clearly visible: she seemed made of crumpled paper, translucent but tangible. Sophia could just see the contours of the desk behind her. *"Take the offered sail."*

"What do you mean, the offered sail?" Sophia rose, ready to take a step closer—

The figure was gone.

Sophia stood staring, eyes wide and heart pounding, at the place where her mother had been. Then she sat back down slowly. As before, the sight of Minna made her overjoyed and anxious at the same time. What did it mean? What sail? Sophia felt a flash of frustration at the riddle, and then she reminded herself that whether or not she understood the words, Minna's appearance was a sign—a sign from the Fates.

I have to find what I'm looking for at the Nihilismian Archive, she said to herself. *Today.* She hurriedly pulled on the clothes from her chair—a cotton skirt with side pockets, a linen shirt with horn buttons, gray socks, and her worn brown boots—and thrust her lifewatch and the spool of silver thread into her skirt pocket.

As she brushed and then braided her hair, glancing at herself in the small oval mirror hanging inside her wardrobe, a door opened and closed downstairs: Shadrack was already leaving for the ministry. Sophia quickly packed her satchel and descended to the kitchen, casting a glance at Theo's closed door on the way. She ate breakfast alone in the silent house.

The beaded map lay on the kitchen table where Shadrack had left it the night before. She unrolled the square of linen and eyed it thoughtfully, remembering the sense of delight she had felt when they all began reading it together. It had been short-lived.

The unexpected sound of a door opening on the second floor interrupted her thoughts. A moment later, Theo padded down the stairs and joined her at the table, reaching comfortably across it for the bread and butter. She studied him. The fear she had seen in his face the day before had vanished. He was once again the unflappable Theo she knew so well.

He smiled. "Morning."

Sophia stared. "That's *it*?" she asked indignantly.

He gave her a look of wide-eyed innocence. "What?"

"You wouldn't even open your door last night. Are you going to tell me why?"

Theo shrugged, buttering his bread liberally.

"Is he a raider?"

"Yeah," he replied, noncommittally.

"I guess what you said before about not lying to me isn't true anymore," she murmured.

Theo put the bread down. "I'm sorry." His voice was sober and serious. "I just can't talk about it. I have to figure some things out first."

Sophia leaned back in her chair. She reminded herself that the previous summer, she had so often doubted Theo; she had pressed him for answers, and he had kept his silence for good reason. For a moment the sight of his scarred hand, cut again by the guard of Nochtland, flashed before her. "All right. I won't ask more. But just the same," she added, "when you're ready to talk about who he is, I'd like to know."

He grinned, giving her a snap of the fingers that ended in a gesture like a pointed gun. "You'll be the first to hear." He nodded at the map, changing the subject. "Made any progress?"

"No—I haven't started reading it yet."

"We can do it today, if you want. Head over to see Miles and read it there."

Sophia looked down at the table. "I have to go to the archive."

Theo chewed thoughtfully. "Okay. When are you getting back?"

"Not until the end of the day."

"I guess I'll head over to see Miles on my own, then," Theo said, reaching for another piece of bread.

"To ask him about the Eerie?" At his obvious confusion, she added, "You must have left before he started talking about it." She recounted the overheard conversation and the worried comments about someone named Goldenrod who might not make it through the summer. "Did you know Miles was looking for the Eerie?"

"He didn't say a thing about it. Deceitful old codger. Keeping things from me." Theo didn't seem particularly bothered.

Sophia took the spool of silver thread from her pocket and

worried the top of it, running her thumb over the wood. "You're not the only one. Shadrack didn't mention it to me, either. Maybe that was the whole reason for the trip— nothing to do with my parents or Ausentinia. Just to look for the Eerie."

"I'm sure Shadrack had good reasons for not telling you."

"And do you think he had good reason for pretending the conversation with Broadgirdle went well? Because he did."

Theo finished buttering his second piece of bread. "I'm not totally surprised."

Sophia frowned. "What does that mean?"

He chewed, avoiding Sophia's eyes. "Let's just say that peephole has been very informative."

Sophia's frown deepened. "It's wrong to spy on Shadrack. We shouldn't have done it." Then she realized more fully what Theo meant. "You mean he lies to us about other things?"

Theo looked uncomfortable. "I didn't say that. But you know he has an important job, with complicated things happening all the time. He probably *can't* tell you everything."

Sophia rose from the kitchen table. "I have to go."

"I didn't mean to upset you."

She felt a wave of frustration. "Maybe not, but you did. And since we were spying, I can't just ask him outright about what I heard."

"Well, I can ask Miles. I'll tell him I overheard it all and I'll get what I can out of him."

Sophia shook her head. "That just means more lying."

"Let me handle it," Theo said earnestly. "I'll figure it out—

you'll see." He stood up as Sophia left, but she did not turn back. "I'll let you know what I find out," he called after her.

As Sophia walked to the trolley stop, she reflected on the hypocrisy of her comment to Theo—she had concealed the truth from Shadrack about the Nihilismian Archive, and she had outright lied at the archive about who she was. She felt a disconcerting sense of wrongness in her stomach and did not know what to do about it. *And now,* she thought, feeling even worse, *I'll find out if my lies have been discovered.*

Insensible to the bright morning sun, the chattering of swallows, and the blooming lilacs, Sophia gazed blankly at the cobblestones until the trolley arrived. Then she paid her fare and boarded. She sat perfectly still, staring at her boots, until the trolley reached her stop.

Before she entered the Nihilismian Archive, Sophia paused for a moment at the base of the hill. The archive almost certainly held a vital clue: a way to find her parents, an answer to Minna's pleas, a route forward. But it might also be the end of a route. She had planned her way in carefully, but she had not planned a way out. If the attendant accused her of fraud, she had no recourse other than to run.

She opened the gates and slowly made her way up the drive. It was too early for the gardener, and almost all of the curtains were drawn. The great mansion seemed even quieter and more forbidding than usual. She checked her lifewatch and found that it was still twenty-seven minutes to the hour. As Sophia stood in the circular gravel drive, attempting to quell her nervousness, she saw Remorse open the gates. The Nihilismian walked steadily up the path and joined Sophia. "You are here early," she said.

"I just want to make the most of the day," Sophia said.

"As do I." Remorse took a key from her pocket. "This is my last day at the archive."

Sophia looked at her in surprise. "I didn't realize you were going so soon."

Remorse nodded, fitting the key in the lock. "My mission leaves tomorrow for the Papal States. I have a few things to conclude here before then."

Sophia followed her into the cool foyer, realizing that by arriving early she had avoided the encounter with the bald attendant. *But he could receive the reply any time today,* she reminded herself. *And then I won't even be near the door so I can run.* She pushed these thoughts aside as they ascended to the second floor.

"I'm glad you're here early," Remorse said, opening the door to room 45 and gesturing for Sophia to enter. "There's something I wanted to tell you about your search. Give me just a moment."

Sophia stood by the doorway of the dark room while the young woman opened the drapes on the north side of the room and one by one lit all of the flame lamps, bringing the dark wooden shelves and polished worktables, the leather chairs and deep carpets gradually into view. Sophia went to her customary table, where the volumes of A.D. 82 were piled, and waited.

Brisk footsteps echoed in the hallway. Sophia looked with apprehension at the open doorway, fearing the attendant, but it was Whether Moreau, who said a brief good morning and settled himself at his desk without another word.

Remorse looked over at Sophia and shook her head.

As Remorse began pulling books from a shelf at the back of the room, Sophia sat down and tried to make sense of what had just occurred. Remorse wanted to tell her something, but not in front of Whether Moreau. What could it be? She thought back and realized that this morning had been one of only two occasions when Whether had not been there. And on the other occasion, an archive patron had been working nearby.

Suddenly the obvious struck her: Remorse was her ally at the archive. She had sent the Nihilismian pamphlet, and she knew what and who Sophia was looking for. How Remorse knew and why she wished to help were inexplicable, but it didn't seem to matter. She knew.

Sophia felt her pulse quicken. Her mind flew back over their brief conversations. They had talked about Nihilismian missions and Columbus and the falsity of feelings. What else? Remorse had commented on her reading: *It is not always most productive to read the volumes in order,* she had said.

That's it! Sophia realized. *She brought this index for me to read, but she told me not to read it in order.* Which volume had been waiting for her on the second morning? She pushed her chair back and ran her finger over the books, trying to remember. Seventeen? No, she had already looked at seventeen. *Twenty-seven!*

As she opened it, she glanced up and saw Remorse at

another table nearby. She had begun mending the books she had pulled from the shelf. Working with a curved needle and heavy thread, she punctured the folded sheets of paper in practiced loops, pulling and puncturing, pulling and puncturing. She flipped through the pages of the newly sewn bundles, making sure they were even and tight. Each finished set of pages went into a pile.

Sophia watched her for a minute before taking up volume 27. Instead of reading, she propped the book upright, on its spine. The pages ruffled across her thumb, and then they stopped of their own accord at a point halfway through. As the pages opened, she found that they had yielded to a purple ribbon of the finest velvet that lay coiled like a sleeping snake near the fold. She reached for it, her eyes wide. This was her mother's way of marking pages. Sometimes Sophia still found lengths of ribbon in the books at East Ending Street.

As she pulled the ribbon from between the pages, her gaze was caught on a line of text: a cluster of words that jumped out at her clearly. For a moment, she could not believe what she saw. She blinked, hard. But it was no illusion; the line of text was there, looking no different from all the other lines above and below and beside it.

Sophia forgot to breathe. The curved shape of the letters swam before her eyes. She pushed back her chair so quickly it almost tipped backward.

Whether cleared his throat and frowned from across the room. Remorse, putting down a bundle of pages, looked at her levelly.

"Remorse, could I ask you a question?" Sophia said, her voice cracking on the last word.

Remorse rose to join her. "How can I help you?" she replied.

"Can I show you what I found?" At the Nihilismian's nod, Sophia pointed to the page.

"'Diary of Wilhelmina Tims, Granada Depository,'" Remorse read aloud. "This is very good news," she murmured.

Sophia's mind whirled. Her mother had written a diary! She had written a diary after leaving Boston, and the diary was in a place called the Granada Depository. She held up the sliver of purple velvet. "This was coiled up on the page and then I saw it—my mother's name."

"Remarkable," Remorse said, her face impassive.

Sophia felt overwhelmed by a sudden wave of gratitude that she knew she could not voice. "Where is the Granada Depository? Can I go there? Or can the diary be sent here?"

Remorse took the velvet ribbon and slowly curled it around her finger. "The depository is in the Papal States. In Granada, which lies beyond the Dark Age. And our archives do not lend their materials."

"So I would have to go in person?"

Remorse inclined her head. "Precisely. And, as is the case here, only Nihilismians are granted entry. Your investigator's card from Boston would not give you access, but you could apply again for a card in Granada."

Sophia took a moment to absorb this information, her understanding of what lay before her quickly reshaping itself to accommodate the circumstances. *I'll have to go in person.*

Shadrack and I can go. But . . . Shadrack may not have time. Even if he wanted to go halfway across the world to visit a Nihilismian archive, he might not be able to. But I could go with Burr and Calixta. They wouldn't mind sailing to the Papal States, would they? Maybe I could persuade them. The question is, can I persuade Shadrack to let me go all the way to the Papal States without him? And how am I going to get an investigator's card in Granada? I don't even speak Castilian. . . .

She saw the diary disappearing from view, like a boat sinking into the horizon.

"Thank you. I have to go," she heard herself saying. "I have to . . . make some plans." Quickly, she copied the entry into her notebook. Remorse watched silently as she closed volume 27, put it back on the cart, and packed her satchel. "Thank you for all your help," Sophia said.

"Every—" Remorse said, getting to her feet. She glanced up at Whether and stopped. "I'm very glad you have found what you were looking for."

"Thank you, Remorse. You've been very kind."

She hurried out of room 45. Shadrack would be at the ministry. *I just have to persuade him,* she said to herself. *I just have to tell him the truth, and he'll understand.*

"Every." Remorse had followed her into the corridor. "Wait just a moment. I wanted to tell you something. About the Papal States."

Sophia looked up at her. "Yes?"

Remorse drew close and lowered her voice. "My mission is to the Papal States, you may recall."

"I remember."

"As I mentioned this morning, my ship departs tomorrow." She glanced at the open doorway of room 45 and lowered her voice even more. "If you like, I could ask the captain if there is room for you and your uncle."

Sophia's eyes widened. "For me and Shadrack?"

"You have Nihilismian credentials," she said with a meaningful look, "and though your uncle does not, exceptions have been made in the past for relatives and paying passengers. I believe Captain Ponder could be persuaded." She paused. "If you travel with me, I could easily gain access to the Granada archive. After you read the diary, you can return to Boston with your uncle."

The Papal States. Tomorrow. Sophia could barely conceive of it. And yet, she realized the opportunity Remorse had placed before her would never occur again. Was it rash to accept? Or was she simply following the signs sent to her by the Fates? Suddenly the words Minna had spoken that morning found her, winding their way into the dark corridor of the Nihilismian Archive: *Take the offered sail.*

Sophia felt a surge of elation. "Yes," she said. "Yes, we'll go."

Remorse reached out impulsively and squeezed Sophia's hand. "I'm glad. We leave at fifteen-hour, and you can board any time after midday. The ship is called the *Verity*. Speak to Captain Ponder when you arrive."

"I will. I just have to tell Shadrack. But I promise—I'll be there."

THE LEAGUE OF ENCEPHALON AGES

February 24, 1881

Finally, on our fifth night aboard the *Roost*, we made a discovery that exposed the breadth of Captain Wren's deceit.

Some part of me had been expecting it, of course, but neither Bronson nor I anticipated the form it took. We were waiting for the captain in his cabin. He had invited us to dine with him, as he always did, but on this occasion he immediately excused himself, saying he had to attend to something on the ship. He urged us to make ourselves comfortable until he returned.

Bronson and I sat in silence. The last two days had been tense between us. While I felt increasingly ill at ease aboard the *Roost*, certain as I was that something was not right, Bronson was increasingly enthralled by Captain Wren and his crew, certain that they were the kindest, canniest fellows in the world. The night before, we had almost argued about it. I insisted that we should reveal nothing more about ourselves, and Bronson fairly laughed at my insistence. I called him a fool for being so easily won over, and Bronson called me a fool for being so easily suspicious.

So we sat in silence in Wren's cabin, until I got up, somewhat impatiently, and went to the back of the cabin, where I began to peruse the shelves that held the captain's library and nautical instruments. Shelves full of books always put me in mind of my brother Shadrack and make me feel at home. I ran my finger idly along the spines, none of which had titles I recognized. Imagine my surprise when I saw the very name that had just come to mind: *Shadrack Elli*. I exclaimed in delight.

"What is it?" Bronson asked, condescending to speak to me.

"Wren has a book by Shadrack!" As I said these words, however, I found myself suddenly confused. The author was, indeed, Shadrack Elli. But I knew my brother's books quite well, and this was one I had never seen—*Maps of California, the Mexican Border, and the Mexican-American War*. I stared at the cover. "Could it be he published a book without telling me? There couldn't possibly be another author with the same name. It doesn't make any sense."

Bronson came up behind me and read the title over my shoulder. "That's not one of Shadrack's books."

"I know," I said quietly. "And what is California?"

"Check the printer's information," he suggested.

I turned to the front of the book, and what I saw there gave me sudden pause: *Roberts Bros., Boston, 1899*. "How is this possible?" I whispered to Bronson, aghast. "When it is now 1881?"

Bronson was frowning at the book, equally baffled, when the door opened.

Captain Wren saw at once that something had happened. With a nervous air, he pocketed the amber monocle. Instead of speaking or asking what the matter was, he simply stared at us. I was surprised and even more confused to see fear pinching at the edges of his eyes.

"Captain Wren," I asked, holding up my discovery, "how is it that you have a book here written by my brother and published *eighteen years from now*?"

Wren held up his hands as if to appease us, the apprehension in his eyes giving way to an equally disturbing look of resigned sorrow. "Please," he said. "Please, do not be alarmed."

"I *am* alarmed," I said, somewhat more loudly than I intended. I could feel Bronson's arm slip around my waist, steadying me. "I don't understand what this means."

"I will explain—I will explain it to you," he assured us. "Please, sit down. Allow me to call for dinner as I had planned, and I will explain everything to you."

If Wren had wanted to harm us, some part of me reasoned, he would have had many opportunities. And besides, I *wanted* an explanation.

Bronson and I took our seats. Wren rang the handbell, calling for dinner, and, as he always did, poured us glasses of wine. I noticed that the wine, which he usually took from a glass cabinet, came from a drawer in his desk and had a very unusual, pristine label, unlike any I had ever seen. For some seconds, he seemed lost in thought. Bronson took my hand—the discovery had erased the tension between us—and squeezed it.

"It will seem to you," Wren began with a sigh, "that I am a liar of the worst sort. And there is no doubt that I have lied to you. But I would beg you to keep in mind, as you learn of my deceit, that the deceit is not only perpetuated for a very good reason, it is required of me—by my government, by the League of Encephalon Ages, and by my own sense of honor."

Bronson and I shared an astonished look. A knock on the door announced the arrival of our dinner.

Wren served us roasted chicken, broiled potatoes, and carrots with minted butter. We'd had no cause to complain of the meals aboard the *Roost*. They were always exceptional, if mysterious—I had never been able to get a straight answer about where all the fresh vegetables came from. But though Wren encouraged us to eat, we could not. Our food sat there, getting cold, as he began his account.

"I am not from New Occident at all," Wren began, looking each of us straight in the eye in turn. "I am from Australia. My entire crew is from Australia. We are carefully—meticulously, even—outfitted to resemble a ship and crew from New Occident. Each of us has been trained in the history, customs, and speech of your Age. But, as you have discovered, Minna, our training is not perfect. In point of fact, we are not permitted to have contact with anyone from your Age without approval, so there are few occasions to test the adequacy of our training."

"Then why the deceit?" I asked, utterly perplexed. "Why go to so much effort if you do not even speak to us?"

"There are circumstances," Wren continued, "in which communication is permitted. One is the circumstance that allowed me to take you on board: when a person's life is at risk. The second, more common circumstance, relates to our mission aboard the *Roost*: to infiltrate and gather information about your Age."

We digested this. "Information?" Bronson said.

And I said, at the same time, "Then you are spies?"

"Yes," Wren sighed. "I expected you to see it that way. Yes, we are spies. But let me explain further; I promise you that our intentions—at least the intentions of those aboard this ship—are entirely benign. A moment earlier, I mentioned to you the League of Encephalon Ages. Our Age, Australia, belongs to it, as do the other Ages that lie temporally beyond New Occident."

"What does that mean?" asked Bronson.

"Your cartologers and historians have begun to map the 'new world,' as you call it, is that right?" We nodded. "If the new world were to be ordered by place in linear time according to the pre-Disruption world, some places would lie behind New Occident and others would lie before it. So the Prehistoric Snows are in the distant past, and New Occident in the nineteenth century." We nodded once again in agreement.

"The Ages that lie beyond your Age, beginning with ours, Australia—which experienced the Disruption in the twentieth century—form an alliance: the League of Encephalon Ages."

Wren paused, as if he had reached a difficult point in his narration. He looked down at his food and, apparently seeking a distraction, took two or three mouthfuls of chicken and potatoes. "Have you never wondered," Wren asked, putting down his fork and reluctantly continuing, "why you have not received envoys from what you consider 'future' Ages?"

This left us momentarily dumbstruck. "Of course we have. The challenges of travel are forbidding," I suggested.

Wren shook his head. "Not for everyone. In certain Ages, travel is less of a challenge. Australia would be easily able to send hundreds, thousands of people to your shores—every week."

"Future Ages would have no interest in dwelling on the past," Bronson argued. "For the same reason that we do not pack up and move to the Papal States, where they are on the verge of burning our friend thanks to superstitious backwardness, you would not want to travel to New Occident."

Wren shook his head. "Bronson, you know better than anyone the curiosity of an explorer. You are, yourselves, journeying as explorers to the Papal States. Does it not seem odd that no explorers from Australia have ever turned up in Boston?"

"I suppose you are right," I conceded.

"The League of Encephalon Ages," Wren explained, after another mouthful of food, "was formed shortly after what you know as the Great Disruption. Your Age, New Occident, lies at the cusp of the divide. All the Ages after it belong to the league, and we agreed not to venture into your Age, or any earlier one."

"There are future Ages in the Baldlands, and we venture back and forth all the time."

"But those Ages are mere fragments," Wren explained, "that lost their encephalon qualities soon after the Disruption. They do not qualify for the league."

"But what is the *purpose* of the league?" Bronson demanded.

"The purpose," Wren said, sitting back, his face suddenly weary, "is to protect all of you from us." For a moment, he sat and looked off into the middle distance. Wren was so consistently a cheerful man, always radiating such good humor, that the sudden gravity of his expression seemed to alter him completely. He appeared ten years older. The lines of his tanned face seemed grooves of worry rather than laughter. He passed his large hand over his forehead, momentarily covering his eyes. "To tell you why such protection is necessary would defeat the very purpose. All our Ages are agreed that yours should not know of"—he paused, taking a deep breath—"the misfortune in ours. We are protecting you from knowledge. And we aboard the *Roost* are only a few among the thousands who make it our task to sustain this protection and enforce the terms of the league. In most cases, we are communicating with agents of our own; we need only be persuasive enough to pass muster from a distance."

"Agents?" Bronson echoed.

"Yes," Wren replied with an apologetic look. "There are among you—in all the pre-cephalon Ages—people from our league, pretending to be of your Age." I opened my mouth to speak, but he continued: "I know how it must seem, but understand that we are there primarily to police ourselves: to track down and capture people of our Ages who have no permission to travel, who have broken the terms of the league treaties, who would corrupt your Ages with knowledge from ours. We were, in fact, returning from a failed mission to apprehend one of these wrongdoers when we found you. Since your lives were in danger, the terms of the league did not prevent me from hauling you from the water. But the crew and I are not accustomed to such constant and percep- tive attention." He smiled. "I feared that it was only a matter of time before we gave ourselves away."

Bronson and I still could not eat; we needed to absorb the captain's words. Staggering as the information seemed, there was such an air of truth to it, and such an earnestness to Wren's demeanor, that we did not for a moment doubt his explanation.

I reviewed the last five days in light of this new knowl- edge. All the things I had considered suspicious—the subtle but noticeable difference in the health and stature of the men, the odd mixture of old and new aboard the ship, the misinformation scattered throughout Wren's conversation—now made sense to me. It also made sense that, as I had keenly felt, Wren meant us no ill will. The curiosity I might have felt about the Encephalon Ages, their league, and their mysterious secret was superseded by my sudden, sharp appreciation of all that Wren had done for us. He had not only saved us from the sea; he had, touchingly, done his best to fit his world to ours, thereby honoring his own allegiances. I could not, perhaps, understand the secret of the Encephalon Ages, but I could certainly understand the effort it cost Wren to adhere to his principles.

"Thank you, Captain Wren," I finally said, "not only for your explanation but for your kindness to us. I can see, given all you have told us, that many in your position would have left us to our fate in the ocean."

Bronson, who had, after all, formed a greater attachment to Wren and thereby felt the deception more acutely, was somewhat slower to come around. "Yes," he said, his face slightly flushed. "We certainly thank you for your continued hospitality aboard the ship—however strange to us its origins."

Wren looked vastly relieved. "It's very good of you to say so. I wouldn't blame you in the least for throwing such duplicitous hospitality in my face."

"And then?" Bronson asked. He has too forgiving a heart to stay angry long with anyone, and Wren was no exception.

"It would be highly impractical now to jump into the sea because we did not like your hospitality! We may not like it," he declared, making clear he meant just the opposite, "but we will simply have to put up with your fine wine and delicious meals and excellent company a little bit longer."

Wren laughed. "Very well, very well. You are most welcome to it."

"What I still do not understand," I put in, placing my hand on the volume beside me on the table, "is this book by my brother."

"Ah," Wren said, reaching for it. "Yes, of course. Well, it would be more accurate to say that it was written by someone with the same name as your brother. They are not the same person. In my Age, about a century ago, a man with the name Shadrack Elli who lived in Boston wrote this wonderful book. I bought it, kept it, and unwisely brought it with me. It does not, strictly speaking, meet protocol. But you can imagine the challenges of creating an entire ship that does. Your Age is not identical to the nineteenth century that existed one hundred years ago in mine. Keeping the environment accurate is very difficult."

"I see," I said slowly, when Wren had finished. "Then . . ." I paused. "Does this mean there was also a woman in your Age by the name of Wilhelmina Tims? And a man named Bronson Tims? And a little girl named Sophia?"

Wren gave me a keen glance and smiled. "Truthfully, I do not know. It is possible, given that you have found a book by someone with your brother's name. But many things happened differently in that past, Minna," he added gently. "It is more different from your Age than similar to it."

"Of course," I agreed. "I asked merely out of curiosity."

"Now that we know all of this," Bronson said, "will you and the crew drop the pretense? Will we have a chance to see what Australians are really like?"

"I'm afraid not, my friend," Wren replied ruefully. "Well, of course we will drop the pretense in the sense that we will none of us claim to be from your Age. And perhaps we can introduce a few of the comforts familiar to us that we usually keep hidden." He tapped the wine bottle and grinned. "But we cannot entirely yank off the veil, lest we imperil the integrity of our regulations. The more unfortunate circumstance," he said, "is that we will be unable to travel with you into Seville. We are already deviating from our set course, but I considered it essential that we take you safely to port."

"We certainly understand," I said. "We are very grateful to you for adjusting your route."

"Of course. And the other thing we can do is travel at our accustomed speed. The crew will be relieved, I'm sure. Doing so, we'll arrive in Seville tomorrow, instead of five days from now." Bronson and I both exclaimed in surprise. "Yes. I'm happy to bend the rules on that score. Though, sadly, it means we will be saying good-bye rather soon. Once we arrive in Seville tomorrow, you will be on your own."

—*1892, June 3: 9-Hour 10*—

The New States Party, founded in 1861, has long advocated peaceful integration with other Ages, rather than conquest. It has, in years past, advocated an accelerated path to statehood for the Indian Territories, and even a treaty with the western Baldlands. Its popularity tends to ebb and flow with the perceived danger posed by other Ages.

—From Shadrack Elli's History of New Occident

WHEN HE HAD finished his breakfast, Theo headed to Miles's house on Beacon Hill, a rambling and profoundly untidy brick edifice crammed from basement to attic with relics from countless journeys. However untidy, the mansion still cut an impressive figure. Miles was one of the wealthiest men in Boston. He was certainly the wealthiest explorer; but he was not one of those residents of Beacon Hill whose family had always enjoyed a fortune.

Miles's grandparents had been slaves at the time of the Disruption, and they had joined the rebellion that formed New

Akan. In those early years after the rebellion, when the eastern seaboard looked upon the state populated by former slaves with distrust, Miles's grandfather had built his fortune selling sugar, cotton, and rice from New Akan in the eastern states. Being a former slave himself, he was one of the few who would buy from the men and women who now ran their own farms, and who would hire former slaves in his textile mills. John Countryman acquired the mansion on Beacon Hill when he was building his fortune, as a signal to Boston of what trade with the powerful state of New Akan might accomplish. Now his grandson, Miles, occupied the palatial home with little thought of trade but with a similar ardor for exploration, the pursuit that had become his life's passion.

Even if Theo had not overheard the previous night's conversation, he would probably have gone to see Miles anyway, dropped happily into an armchair, and discussed the high points of their expedition all day. As it was, he had a more particular purpose. He spent more than an hour leading Miles in a roundabout way closer and closer to the topic, until he finally was able to ask casually, "Why was Bligh so worried about Broadgirdle? He sounded friendly enough."

Miles snorted and threw up his hands, almost dropping the pottery he was holding. The only tidy spots in the house were the great glass cabinets in which he displayed the treasures acquired on his expeditions. He was reorganizing one now to accommodate the pieces they had just brought back. "Oh, believe me, he has good reason to be worried. Broadgirdle is the most inveterate blackmailer in New Occident. Any stain, however small—that man will find it and make it spread until his poor victim is good and dirty all the way through. How do you think he rose to become leader of his party so quickly?"

"Where did he come from?"

"Who knows. He bought his seat in parliament only five years ago. Apparently he made a fortune in the soap industry." Miles gently dusted the ears of a sculpted bear.

Theo gave a wry smile. "How perfect."

"Meaning?"

"He's washed away all traces of his past, hasn't he?"

"I would say it's not very good soap." Miles scowled. He closed the cabinet and sat down in the leather chair next to Theo. "Despite the clean, sweet-smelling appearance that the people of Boston seem to believe in, the man is still the dirtiest politician in town."

"Does anyone know more about him?"

Miles looked at Theo keenly, as if suddenly hearing a different question. He leaned forward in his leather chair, his strong, wrinkled hands clasping his knees. "Why are you so interested?"

Theo shrugged. He had planned to play his next card later on, but he did not want Miles to consider his persistence too closely. "I *might* have overheard him threatening Shadrack."

Miles groaned. "You are incorrigible. How much did you hear?"

"Not much. Just something about the right choice and the wrong choice. I was trying to figure him out. Should we be worried?"

"I can't be sure," Miles said. He shook his mane of white hair. "Broadgirdle is so cunning that everything I have ever heard is pure rumor. No one has actual proof of what he does. If the rumors are true, then I suppose yes—we should worry." He narrowed his eyes. "Did you hear the rest? About the Eerie?"

Theo gave a broad smile. "It *is* a shame you didn't find the Eerie, isn't it?"

Miles grimaced. "I'm sorry for deceiving you. The prime minister himself had given me the charge and forbidden me to disclose it." He shook his head. "Believe me, it would have made everything much easier for me if I could have told you."

"You might be more than four times my age, old man," Theo said affectionately, "but you still haven't learned to break the rules when you need to. You *should* have told me." At Miles's rueful look, he went on: "Well, will you tell me now? What's this all about?"

"The thing is . . ." Miles began. "There are aspects of this that would be better for you not to know—for your own good." Theo rolled his eyes. "No, truly; I am serious. Until we identify where—*who*—the threat comes from, it would be irresponsible to expose you to their unwanted attention." He sighed. "On the other hand, I have never believed safety lies in ignorance."

"This gets more and more interesting. Spill it."

Miles stood up and considered his disordered study. Beside the glass cabinet, a collection of terrifying masks covered one wall, and framed maps covered the rest. The floor was a tapestry of strewn newspapers and books. On the desk, which Miles almost never used, lay a jumble of magnifying glasses, compasses, coffee cups, pencils, and crumpled papers. "Let's go to the conservatory," Miles said.

Theo looked at him in surprise. "What? It's going to be blazing hot there."

"Yes," Miles said distractedly, getting up to leave. Theo hurried to catch up.

The conservatory lay at the rear of the house. Though the weather was mild, the summer sun had warmed the glass-paned room, and the plants were luxuriating in the humidity. Immediately, the heat began to overwhelm them. Miles closed the door. He wiped his forehead with a white handkerchief and folded it carefully, tucking it into his striped cotton shirt. Theo patiently waited for an explanation.

"What I can tell you is brief," Miles said in a low voice, "but even my staff should not hear it." By "staff," he meant the elderly couple, Mr. and Mrs. Biddle, who respectively maintained the house and cooked his meals. Theo did not believe Mr. Biddle's hearing was robust enough for eavesdropping, and he was certain Mrs. Biddle did not care in the least about the personal matters of her eccentric employer, but he nodded sagely and did not contradict. "I was attempting to find the Eerie," Miles said, "because of their well-known healing powers. Someone is in great need of them." He frowned with his bushy white eyebrows.

Theo waited. "That's it?" he asked after a moment. "That's all you're going to tell me?"

"I am about to explain!" At Theo's impatient look, Miles settled himself in one of the wrought-iron chairs, gesturing to the one opposite. Then he leaned in. "The Eerie are legendary healers. No one knows how many of them there are altogether. Some call them not the Eerie but the Numinous. They live near the Eerie Sea—exactly where, we do not know—but occasionally a few travel beyond their realm, and where they travel they leave a trail of marvels. They might simply be a compassionate people, but Shadrack believes they are bound by a code that obliges them to heal anyone who crosses their path. Only this, he says, can explain such profound secrecy combined with such undisguised curative miracles.

"The most gifted among them are called 'Weatherers,' and they are gifted indeed, if the stories are true. A blind woman gaining sight; a drowned man gaining breath; there is even a story, which I find hard to fathom, of a grievously injured child regrowing a limb that had been torn off by a bear."

Theo raised his eyebrows.

"Yes," Miles agreed. "It beggars belief. But let me tell you something more. Shadrack had sent word to the Eerie Sea last August, asking for the aid of a Weatherer. You know what happened to his dear friend Carlton Hopish—so horribly injured by Blanca and the Sandmen that he has never regained consciousness. Shadrack, in his desperation, turned to the Eerie for help. There was no reply, and this did not entirely surprise him, for they are so impossible to reach. Then, to his astonishment, in January he received a letter from an Eerie woman named Goldenrod. She begged him for news of three Weatherers who had left for Boston in response to his call for aid. They had never returned to the Eerie Sea."

Theo whistled. "So they came to help Shadrack after all."

"Apparently they did. Or they tried. No one had seen them in or even near Boston. By then, Bligh had been elected, and Shadrack showed him Goldenrod's letter. Bligh took matters into his own hands, sending trusted delegates to search high and low for the Weatherers. He found nothing.

"Then, in February—you remember, when the snows were at their heaviest—a most inexplicable thing happened. At a farm on the outskirts of Boston, there was a pounding on the door in the dead of night. The farmer opened his door to find a man with an unconscious woman in his arms, the snowstorm raging behind them. The woman was grievously wounded. The man wept, and he gave no explanation but this: 'I tried to kill her, and still she healed me.' He repeated this time and again— 'and still she healed me.' The farmer and his wife tended to the injured woman as best they could, and they sent the strange man, so overcome with remorse, for a doctor.

"In the morning, the doctor arrived. But what he discovered confounded him. The farmer's wife had settled the injured woman in bed, and she was still there, still unconscious—and surrounded by yellow flowers."

"Flowers?" Theo looked past Miles at the greenery surrounding them.

"Indeed. Flowers that grew from her clothes, and her skin, and even from the bedsheets! I cannot conceive it myself. The doctor examined her, unable to make any sense of her condition, but he did find something vital: letters in her pocket sent by Prime Minister Bligh. The woman was the Eerie named

Goldenrod." Miles studied his worn boots and shook his head. "Bligh has consulted the best doctors in Boston, but nothing has changed. Though her body appears to have healed, her mind is still closed. She has been unconscious ever since she was brought to the farm." His expression was vexed. "Bligh has cared for her as best he can, but she is fading."

"And what about the man who brought her?"

"Ah!" Miles said with a shrewd smile. "That is the deepest mystery. He vanished. After leaving to get the doctor, he was never seen again. Bligh naturally asked the doctor and the couple to describe him as best they could, but there was nothing of substance—tall, narrow of shoulder, long of face—with the exception of one detail. The weapon he carried. It was a grappling hook, attached to a long rope."

Theo gasped. "A Sandman."

"A Sandman," Miles nodded.

"But I thought the Sandmen—"

"Had vanished? Well, they must have gone somewhere. Shadrack and I thought that without Blanca to lead them they would disband, each drifting his own way. But it seems we were wrong. Someone sent this Sandman to attack Goldenrod. And Goldenrod, instead of defending herself, healed him." Miles sat back with a frown and wiped his forehead again. "That is what we know. As you can imagine, we want nothing more than to help her. But every attempt to reach the Eerie has failed. This is why I searched for them when we traveled west."

Theo mulled all this over in silence. He gazed at the ferns

and the hibiscus, trying to picture them growing from clothes and skin. Where were the roots? How did they draw water? It was unimaginable. "You could have told me," he said once more.

Miles shook his head. "It would have made no difference. The Eerie refuse to be found." He sighed. "I head off again in a few days to make another attempt."

"What if Sophia and I go with you?"

"I'm afraid that won't be possible. This will be a different kind of expedition."

"What does that mean?"

"I will be posing as someone I am not."

"I do that better than you, old man!"

"Undeniable. But it does not alter the fact that I must go alone."

—12-Hour 11—

THE TRIP INTO the city center from the Nihilismian Archive felt interminable. Sophia tried concentrating on her discovery to make the time pass quickly, but it had the opposite effect. Every block drifted by too slowly; every corner brought a lingering pause. A man swept the sidewalk before a shop selling rubber boots. The store beside it advertised oysters in bright, white letters. Workers lingered during their break outside a dye shop; an engraving shop announced a summer sale; and a young servant cleaned the windows of a boardinghouse two doors down. Near the State House, a cemetery with crooked stones offered a quiet corner of shade in the busy city. After what seemed like hours, the trolley finally stopped near Boston Common. Sophia ran as fast as she could and at twelve-hour wound her way up the stairs to the ministry offices in the State House.

The serious-looking young man at the front desk in Shadrack's office had met Sophia once or twice before, but he either didn't remember her or pretended not to. "Is my uncle, Shadrack Elli, here?" she asked breathlessly.

He gave her a severe look, as though breathing audibly in the august offices of the ministry was a serious discourtesy. "He is very busy at the moment."

"Please just tell him that Sophia is here and that Minna wrote a diary. He'll know what it means."

The young man did not deign to answer, but he rose from his chair and left by the corridor at the rear of the room, returning only a moment later with Shadrack close on his heels.

"Sophia?"

"Shadrack! I found a lead—a real one, this time. She wrote a diary!"

Shadrack looked at her with astonishment. "Come," he said, reaching out a hand. "Let's talk in my office."

She hurried after him, not even sparing a glance for the disapproving clerk. As soon as Shadrack had closed his office door, Sophia related her discovery in one long, excited burst. "Remember how I told you about the new archive I visited? It was the Nihilismian Archive on Beacon Street." Shadrack's eyebrows rose, but he did not interrupt. "I was looking through an index of things written in 1881. The year they left. I thought it would lead to nothing, but it was Remorse's idea. She works there—she's Nihilismian but she's very kind, not at all like the ones we know; she's really been helping me, Shadrack. And today I was reading the index and it said 'Diary of Wilhelmina Tims'—I couldn't believe it. Her diary! It's at the Granada Depository. But the depository doesn't send materials or give access to anyone other than Nihilismians, so Remorse said that we could go with her. She's going on a mission to the Papal States and she's leaving tomorrow, and she said she would ask the captain for permission for you and me to come, too, and she'll get us into the archive. And then we can come back. Maybe the pirates will bring us back—do you think we could ask them? But we have to go with her tomorrow."

Shadrack seemed to have been rendered speechless.

Sophia watched him anxiously, searching his face for some sign of the same elation she was feeling. "It's too wonderful to pass up, don't you think?"

"I think," her uncle said slowly, "that this is certainly a wonderful lead. And though I am curious how you gained access to the Nihilismian Archive, I am very glad to know that the diary exists. But I don't think leaving tomorrow on a Nihilismian vessel is the best way to acquire it."

Sophia felt something slow and unpleasant uncoiling in her stomach.

"The diary isn't going anywhere," he continued. "I can send someone to get it—someone who is familiar with the Papal States."

"But we need a Nihilismian to get us access to the archive!"

Shadrack gave her a pointed look. "Yes, but Sophia—how did you get into the archive in Boston?"

Sophia felt herself blushing. "I said I was Nihilismian."

Shadrack shook his head. "You took a grave risk. But having done so, you realize the possibilities. If you could lie to get into the Boston archive, why couldn't someone else do the same in Granada? This Nihilismian friend of yours is helpful, perhaps, but not essential."

Something began to shift inside of Sophia, as if an hourglass that had been lying on its side had been tipped and its inner sand was now, grain by grain, accumulating into a pile. She realized that what she felt was anger. "So *I* shouldn't lie, but it's acceptable for someone else to lie for the same purpose?"

Shadrack looked apologetic in the way a person does when he expects to be forgiven: rueful, but without remorse. He could not see her anger, just as he could not see what that look of halfhearted apology had cost her for so many months. "I am simply pointing out that this particular access into the Granada Depository is not the only one. It is long and arduous and wholly unnecessary. As it happens, Soph, we will not need to lie at all. I have a contact in the Papal States who has connections with all its archives and libraries, and he can requisition a copy even if he cannot gain personal access to the Granada Depository. There is no need for us to go."

Sophia simply looked at him.

She could not explain why she felt so betrayed, when she was the one who had concealed the truth. As she opened her mouth to speak, she knew her words would be hurtful ones, but she did not know how to express what she was feeling otherwise. "Last summer you started teaching me to read maps," she said, her voice quiet but shaking.

Shadrack looked down at the floor. "I know."

"You were teaching me to read maps so that we could go out into the world and find Minna and Bronson. Now it seems we no longer have need for maps. We no longer plan to go anywhere. Why?"

Shadrack considered this in silence. Sophia waited, urging him to understand what she was asking. *I want you to care about this as much as I do. Forget about the ministry. Think about your sister. Think about me. I want you back.*

But when Shadrack spoke, his air of weary regret was unchanged. "The circumstances are different now. Bligh hopes to overturn the border closure. And, as you know, I have obligations here that prevent me from traveling. I am sorry, Sophia."

She looked at him without speaking.

"This clue you have found is very worthwhile," Shadrack said, his tone placating, "and I will send for a copy of the diary at once. But it does not require us to sail across the Atlantic."

The sand slipping down inside her reached its peak and stopped, leaving some upper part of her empty. "I understand," she said. She had an odd thought, as she turned to leave, about the Nihilismians and their desire to feel nothing in a world that was untrue. Their intentions made sense to her now. She felt nothing at all.

"Sophia," Shadrack said, putting out his hand to stop her.

"It's a wonderful find—the diary. Congratulations."

"Yes. It is." She left his office and walked quietly through the narrow corridor into the waiting room, then out into the main hallway. Then she left the State House and worked her way home.

—*13-Hour 09*—

THEO FOUND HER in her room, holding the spool of silver thread. Her face was wet with tears. He edged in and sat down on the floor, then gave her a friendly smile. "Want to tell me about it?"

Sophia held up the spool. "The Fates gave me a sign."

Theo waited.

"I was at the Nihilismian Archive. I found out that there's a diary written by Mother in a depository in Granada. And my friend Remorse at the archive says she can take us there—tomorrow. She can get us into the archive. But when I told Shadrack, he said no, that someone else would get a copy of it and send it."

Theo pondered this. "You wanted to go to Granada."

Sophia sighed. "This is the best clue we've found! And they *need* me. Mother needs me. Don't ask me how I know. I *know*. I thought—I thought that he and I would go, and then the diary would tell us where she is, and then we would go from there, maybe. You were right—I want to *do* something. And I thought Shadrack would, too. But he has the ministry, and he says things are different now."

"This friend of yours, Remorse—she's a Nihilismian?"

"Yes."

"And you trust her?"

"I do. She's different. I like her."

"She said you could go with her tomorrow? What, by sail?"

Sophia nodded.

Theo looked out the window and then at Sophia. He gave a slow smile that ended in a grin.

"What?"

"Let's go with her."

The spool of thread in Sophia's hand caught the sunlight and glimmered faintly. She felt her breath expanding in her lungs. "Go with her?" she echoed.

"You and me. We pack, we plan—or, *you* plan, more like—and we go. We did it before, didn't we? We can do it again."

Sophia felt the tears welling up in her eyes, and she realized it was due to a surprising gain and a surprising loss. They had come about gradually, but now, in a single hour, she saw they were both decisive. That ease she had felt with her beloved uncle, the sense of always being encompassed and known, had drifted away. In its place was the certainty of finding comprehension and sympathy and humor somewhere else. Shadrack no longer understood her; Theo did.

"I guess we could," she whispered.

11
ALONE AMONG THE MAPS

—1892, June 4: 10-Hour 20—

BOSTON: *The Atlas Book Shop. Founded in 1868, the Atlas has a reputation for procuring rarities. Its proximity to the Boston State House makes it a popular source for official expeditions to remote Ages.*

—From Neville Chipping's Map Vendors in Every (Known) Age

THE ATLAS BOOK SHOP, as the hanging sign with Atlas shouldering the globe suggested, specialized in travel books, historical geography, and maps. As the bell above the door rang and Sophia crossed the worn threshold, she heard a cheery "Hullo!" from the back. "Mr. Crawford, it's Sophia," she called.

"Sophia!" The top of Cornelius Crawford's mostly bald head, his blue eyes, and a red nose emerged from behind a precarious stack of books. "Good to see you. I'm buried back here with new inventory. Let me know if you need anything."

"Thanks, I will." Sophia gave him a brief wave and began searching the tight, crammed aisles for the section on the Papal States.

She and Theo had packed their bags that morning, but Sophia could not bring herself to take any of Shadrack's books and maps to help them. It seemed like theft to her, paired with the deception.

Theo insisted, unconvincingly, that the two of them had not lied. Shadrack had come home late the previous evening, his face furrowed by some unvoiced concern: Over a silent dinner, it became clear to Sophia that he had either forgotten about the diary or become so preoccupied with matters at the ministry that the diary seemed unimportant by comparison. She felt a sharp stab of sadness, and her resolve hardened. When she heard him leaving the house in the morning, she sat up in bed and hugged her knees, wishing everything were different. Then she got out of bed and began packing for the journey.

Now she was at the Atlas, buying the books and maps they would need, before meeting Theo at the *Verity*. She had to admit that despite the difficulty of leaving Shadrack under such circumstances, a slow pulse of excitement had begun to move through her.

The shop was filled with the comforting smell of worn paper and leather bindings, and the sun filtered in through the half-closed blinds, as if through the branches of a tree onto the disordered floor of a paper forest. Stepping carefully over little piles of books that seemed to sprout like mushrooms from the floorboards, Sophia found the Papal States section, sat gingerly down on a pile of large volumes, and was soon lost in the pages of a history written by Fulgencio Esparragosa. Its dozens of maps and long chapters were organized around the pilgrimage routes to the religious shrines that dotted the vast peninsula. The routes had been crippled, Esparragosa explained, by the spread of the plague known in the Papal States as *lapena*, a dreadful illness that had paralyzed trade, dried up commerce along the pilgrimage routes, and decimated entire villages.

No other customers entered the Atlas while she read. From time to time Cornelius, hidden at the back, spoke querulously to himself, protesting how much he had paid for the *Encyclopedia of the Russias* or wondering where he had put the maps of the Middle Roads.

When Sophia looked at her pocket watch again, it was almost eleven-hour. She got to her feet and made her way to the front of the shop. "Mr. Crawford," she called out when she reached the cashier's box, "can I buy this book on the Papal States?"

"Of course you can, dear," came the muffled reply. "Just a minute."

While Sophia waited, she flipped through the booklet displayed on a stand nearby: *Map Vendors in Every (Known) Age*. It was a surprisingly useful little book, containing the addresses of prominent map sellers in New Occident, the Baldlands, the Papal States, and the Russias; there were even some entries for the Closed Empire. Sophia placed it atop the Esparragosa, and as she did so Cornelius finally emerged, huffing and puffing as though he had hauled himself out from the bottom of a volcano.

He made a cursory attempt to straighten the wisps of hair that sprang like antennae from his head. "All right," he said, heaving a tremendous sigh; he reached into his vest pocket for a gold monocle with an amber-tinted lens and peered through it at the books. "Fulgencio Esparragosa and *Map Vendors in Every (Known) Age*," he said, writing down the titles and their prices in a little notebook. As he wrapped the books in brown paper and string, he glanced at her pack and asked, winking, "Planning a trip somewhere?"

Sophia smiled, her excitement getting the better of her. "Perhaps."

"Very exciting," Cornelius declared. He always told his customers, with faint regret, that he had never traveled out of Boston; the bookstore kept him too busy. "Well, let me know if you need anything else before you go."

"Don't I need to pay you?"

"Shadrack has an account with me, dear. He's in here so often he just settles the bill at the end of each month."

Sophia handed him a pair of notes. "I want to buy these myself," she said.

"Very well," he agreed, counting out the change.

"Thank you." Sophia placed the books in her satchel, beside her notebook and the beaded map. *Now we have everything we need,* she thought with satisfaction.

As Sophia closed the door behind her and the bell ceased its ringing, Cornelius Crawford ambled slowly into the Atlas's back room. His office made the store look tidy. A wooden chair with a worn cushion stood like a lone small tree in a city of books: towers so high they blocked the window, sagging shelves overpopulated by bound books, leaning stacks that threatened to collapse if nudged the wrong way. Cornelius sat down in the chair with a deep sigh and looked at his visitor, who was perched quietly on one of the more stable book piles.

"Well, that was unexpected," Cornelius said.

The visitor, a slight young woman who wore a man's buttoned shirt and trousers, tucked her black hair behind her ears and nervously fingered the pendant of her necklace. "She didn't hear me?"

"You were very quiet."

"Why was she here, Sam?"

Cornelius shrugged. "To buy books on the Papal States. Very natural, I'd say."

"Yes, but I mean why? It is too coincidental. Ten minutes after I got here?" She shook her head. "I don't like it."

Sophia would not have recognized her calm, expressionless friend from the Nihilismian Archive. Though Remorse had not changed her appearance, an unrestrained vitality now animated her every word and gesture.

She plunged her hands into her hair and held her head. "You know what this means."

"It doesn't mean anything, Cassia," Cornelius said soothingly.

"I hate when this happens."

"Some coincidences are just coincidences."

"Sam!" Remorse sprang to her feet and crossed the room, toppling a low stack of books in the process. "You know better. A coincidence is never a coincidence. Coincidence is how pre-cephalon Ages explain what they don't understand."

"I'm pretty sure I've seen some real ones," Cornelius ventured. "Last week, I was looking for a book on dinosaurs, and I found one on parliament politicians from the 1820s."

"That's not a coincidence, Sam, that's a joke," Remorse said dismissively. "And really kind of a bad one."

Cornelius sighed. "Okay. What are you going to do?"

Remorse tapped her front teeth with her forefinger. "Nothing. We have to stick with the plan. We've already moved the container, and I have to get it to Seville. There's no other way." She took a deep breath and put her hands on her hips. "We shouldn't have meddled this much. I'm afraid we've gone too far."

—11-Hour 55—

THEO HAD HAPPILY distracted Mrs. Clay in the kitchen while Sophia came downstairs and left by the front door, carrying her bulky travel gear. He had spent the rest of the morning and early afternoon in half-pretended idleness, throwing himself repeatedly in the way of Mrs. Clay's housekeeping until she announced, exasperated, that she was off to do the shopping. "I am happy to have you back, Theodore," she said, "but you have such a talent for inconvenience." Theo smiled to himself as he watched her leaving with her basket.

He tossed the last few things into his pack, pulled the drawstring tight, and fastened the flap. Shouldering the pack, he bounded down the stairs to the first floor. He was congratulating himself on how smoothly his and Sophia's plan had gone so far when he heard, to his surprise, Miles and Shadrack arguing at the side door. He pulled off the pack and thrust it under the kitchen table just as Shadrack came in.

"I have already tried," Shadrack said, scowling.

"He must be somewhere," Miles insisted.

"Miles." Shadrack turned to face him. "I beg you to say something useful. Telling me that 'he must be somewhere' helps me not at all."

Theo raised his eyebrows. Miles was prone to frequent displays of temper, but Shadrack was rarely as angry as he was now. It was disconcerting to see the old explorer relatively calm while Shadrack seethed. "Who is somewhere?" Theo asked.

Shadrack glanced at him and began to pace. "The prime minister. I have had no word of him since yesterday morning. No one, in fact, has seen him."

Theo shrugged. "Maybe he needed a holiday?"

"Bligh is not on holiday," Shadrack snapped. "And he is not at home and he is not at the State House, and I begin to worry that something very serious has happened to him. He would never vanish in the middle—" Shadrack turned on his heel and headed for the library.

"This has something to do with your conversation with Broadgirdle yesterday morning," Miles accused him.

Theo followed them, both his plans and his pack beneath the kitchen table temporarily forgotten.

"Why is the door to the map room open?" Shadrack asked, pausing at the bookshelf. "Is Sophia here?" he asked Theo.

"She's out."

"It is really very offensive," Miles said, beginning to look perturbed. "I take it that you told Bligh, but you will not tell me. What happened? Did Broadgirdle threaten you?"

Shadrack held up his hand. "I am sorry, Miles, but I have told you I will not discuss it."

"Listen to me, Shadrack. It is not like you to be this obstinate, and while I am the first to admit that I often too readily take to argument, in this case you must see that the provocation is extreme. I demand," he continued, raising his voice as he followed Shadrack down the stairs, "as probably your closest and certainly your oldest friend, I demand that you tell me *this instant* what happened during that conversation." All of Miles's huffing indignation was suddenly deflated as he reached the bottom of the stairs and collided directly with the back of his closest and oldest friend. Theo, a few steps above him, gave a small, involuntary gasp.

They all stared at the horror that confronted them: Prime Minister Cyril Bligh sat in one of the chairs, his face frozen in surprise. His jacket was neatly hung on another chair. The black waistcoat he wore shone unnaturally, and the white shirt beneath it was stained dark with blood.

Shadrack leaped forward, insensible of how the congealed blood on the carpet was staining his shoes and the blood on Bligh's body was staining his hands. "Bligh," he cried. "For Fates' sake, Bligh, answer me!" He put his hands to the man's neck for a pulse.

Miles flew after him, seizing the prime minister's wrist. "He is cold," he said. "Completely cold."

Theo's eyes darted around the room, taking it all in. On the table beside the prime minister lay a short knife. The blade was encrusted with blood. The mother-of-pearl handle was perfectly clean. Beside the knife were a blood-spattered heavy cotton robe and a pair of gloves. There were no footprints anywhere. The carpet on the stairs was clean.

A deafening crash sounded above.

Abruptly, Miles and Shadrack stopped their futile efforts to revive the prime minister. "Sophia!" Shadrack shouted, rushing toward the stairs, as the sound of pounding footsteps filled the house. Theo grabbed the bloody instruments from the table and made for the familiar wardrobe at the back of the room. In a matter of seconds, he was closeted within it.

A phalanx of police officers rushed down the stairs, meeting Shadrack halfway with their pistols drawn. "Shadrack Elli and Miles Countryman," the leading officer shouted, far louder than was necessary. "Put your hands over your heads. You are under arrest for conspiracy and treason, and for the murder of Prime Minister Cyril Bligh."

12
ADRIFT

—1892, June 4: 13-Hour 00—

Scholars who have examined the Book of Amitto, the sacred text of the Nihilismians, have raised interesting questions about its authenticity. It is undeniable that the tone of the prose throughout is consistent and likely composed by a single author. But that author may not be, as Nihilismians maintain, from New Occident. Vocabulary and usage suggest other possible backgrounds. Therefore scholars very rightly ask: why would Amitto pretend to be from New Occident?

—From Shadrack Elli's History of New Occident

BOSTON HARBOR WAS hectic with the cries of gulls and the shouts of mariners. Its distinctive smells—molasses and sugar, coffee and rum, ocean air and seaweed—drifted by like restless travelers disembarking from their long voyages. Sophia wove her way through the crowd to the harbormaster's office, where she posted a letter to Calixta and Burr asking them to meet her and Theo in Seville in one month. She showed her papers to one of the officers who patrolled the harbor, ensuring that no foreigners entered and that any traveling citizens had the proper paperwork. Then, her pulse quickening, she searched for the *Verity*.

She found the name in white paint on a ship with tall masts and a smooth hull. The figurehead, a woman in blue wearing a white blindfold, echoed the blindfolded gargoyle at the entrance of the Nihilismian Archive. The tightly furled sails seemed ready to spring open, anticipating an imminent journey.

As she stood gazing at the ship, a middle-aged man in a trim blue uniform approached her. He carried a Nihilismian amulet around his neck and a notebook and pencil in his hands. "Are you sailing with the mission to the Papal States?" he asked.

"Yes," she replied with a shaky exhalation.

"Your name?"

"Every Tims."

He scanned the pages of his notebook. "Here you are. I remember now. Remorse arranged for your passage. And you are traveling with someone else? It says 'Every Tims and her guest, Shadrack Elli.'"

"The name Remorse gave you is incorrect. And he isn't here yet."

"You may board and I will direct him when he arrives. What is the correct name?"

"Theodore Constantine Thackary."

"Very well." He gave a brief nod. "Welcome aboard the *Verity*, Miss Tims. Your cabin is number seven."

"Thank you."

Sophia climbed the gangplank. The moment she reached the top, she felt the waters of the harbor gently rocking the *Verity*, and the seasickness she had come to know so well the previous summer struck her with full force. She took a deep breath and steadied herself, then slowly followed the signs to the cabins. As she passed the open doors, she saw more than one Nihilismian unpacking: other missionaries, like Remorse, preparing for the long Atlantic crossing. With deliberate movements, they placed folded clothes in drawers, books onto shelves, bedding onto the mattresses. Sophia opened the door to cabin 7 and surveyed the tiny room. A bunk bed with netted curtains filled half the space. A wooden chair and a desk stood under the round window, its frame painted blue.

Sophia put her pack on the floor and her satchel on the desk. She sat down and inhaled deeply, trying to calm her stomach. She reached into her pocket and clasped the spool of silver thread. *I'm here,* she said to herself. *I'm here and this is going to be fine. Theo and I faced worse together last year. This will be easy.* Through the open door, she could hear the seagulls and the waves splashing against the ship. There was no other sound. She watched the curtains on the bed ruffle gently in the breeze in smooth, unpredictable patterns.

The seasickness troubled her less when she closed her eyes; she had been told that ordinary seasickness improved by fixing the eye upon a steady horizon, but she knew the malady that arose from being adrift in the timelessness of the ocean manifested differently. Closing her eyes, Sophia focused on a single point in time: the morning before, when Minna had appeared to her and spoken those simple words: *Take the offered sail.* She saw the figure's hazy contours and heard the voice; she pictured the rest of her room in the dawn light;

slowly, she began to feel herself settle and the seasickness abate. It was such a relief to feel well again that she kept herself in the moment for as long as she could.

The sound of the waves beyond the open doorway changed. Sophia opened her eyes and realized at once that the light had shifted and yellowed. She scrambled for her watch but could not believe what it said: fifteen-hour, seven.

With panicked steps, she flung herself from her cabin and out into the corridor, running until she reached the rail. The city of Boston was rapidly shrinking. The *Verity* had set sail. And as far as she knew, neither Theo nor Remorse was aboard.

PART II
The Hunt

13

THE MALADY

February 25, 1881

The *Roost* arrived in Seville the following day, as Captain Wren had predicted. The parting from Wren and his crew left us rather wistful, for the final twenty hours were the most enjoyable we spent aboard. Released from their self-imposed subterfuge, the Australians were able to behave as they really were—that is, loud, inquisitive, and riotously good-humored.

Much of the afternoon was spent in eager interrogation of our history and habits; they were infinitely curious about the world of New Occident and the Baldlands, which most had never seen. We found them less forthcoming about their Age, and we quickly learned that if we were to keep them cheerful, we were not to ask questions. But the evening was enjoyable as well, and we went to bed far too late and woke to find we had nearly docked. For the last portion of our journey, Captain Wren slowed the ship to a less astonishing speed, so as not to draw attention.

As we disembarked in Seville, Captain Wren made us a gift of a watch on a heavy chain. While at first glance it seemed ordinary, a watch that might be found in any Boston shop, on closer inspection it proved to have twelve hours on its face, rather than twenty. It was Australian in more ways than this, according to Captain Wren. "I'm really not supposed to give you anything," he said, "but as I've bent the rules so far already, I figured I may as well bend them a little more." He turned the watch over. "If you press here, you'll see that the back flips open." We watched as he revealed a compartment with three bronze buttons the size of pinheads. "Think of this watch as a kind of magnet," Wren explained, to our surprise, "that draws me to you should you ever need assistance. The top button will activate the magnet, and I will be alerted. Should you be in serious danger, do not hesitate to press it. I'll find a way to reach you."

"What do the others do?" Bronson asked.

"You won't need them; they won't be useful while you're in the Papal States—or New Occident, for that matter."

"Thank you, Captain Wren, for all your kindness," I said, pressing his hand. "I hope we never have an emergency that requires calling you, but this watch will serve as a wonderful reminder of you and the days we spent aboard the *Roost*."

After we said our good-byes, Wren sailed almost immediately, without so much as restocking his ship. He had explained that there were more than enough provisions in the hold, and that they needed to make up for lost time. We were left, rather forlornly, by ourselves on the streets of Seville.

The city is probably quite beautiful, though I am sure we did not enjoy it as we might have. The mood of the populace was withdrawn and uneasy. On the way to the city center, we were nearly robbed twice, and it is only thanks to Bronson's long sword and my passable Castilian that we arrived safely in the Jewish quarter, where we knew of a map store and an inn friendly to foreign travelers. Our information proved correct, and the elderly innkeeper demonstrated himself to be the kindest man we met in all the Papal States. Hearing we had nearly been robbed, Gilberto Jerez shook his head of white hair with exaggerated grief and thanked the heavens for our safe delivery. He showed us to our small but very clean room and fed us excessively with a stew of chicken and chickpeas and a dessert of figs and almonds.

Though Seville was, on the whole, as backward and primitive as is to be expected of such an early Age, I would have stayed in Gilberto's little inn quite happily for an entire month.

If only the Fates had allowed us some foresight, so that we might have done so.

Instead, we explained the urgency of our mission to the kindly Gilberto, who insisted the following day on accompanying us personally to the home of his nephew, a reliable if taciturn man of roughly my years by the name of Ildefonso. Gilberto had suggested that Ildefonso, who was a merchant and often traveled the route east, might accompany us to Murtea. Ildefonso admitted that he had no plans to travel for another few weeks in that direction, but we were able to persuade him to serve as our guide by offering fair payment in gold. Shadrack had told us, and he was right, that the Papal States value gold above all else. It is well known that in the Spains and their empire—that is to say, in the place that existed in our Age, hundreds of years earlier—gold was also valued highly. But, as with so many things, the world was not the same after the Great Disruption; the Papal States are not the Spains. In the Papal States, gold is valued above all else for a different reason.

The dreaded Dark Age, which sits on the road between Seville and Granada, is thought to be the source of a plague known as *lapena*. Bruno had warned us of it in his letter, and his warning proved correct: even in Seville, where the other dangers of the Dark Age are proximate, the plague is the most feared.

The illness begins with a marked wave of exhaustion and lethargy. The victim's spirits become very downcast, such that all the world seems dark and oppressive. It has been described by survivors as a gradual loss of vision, so that the victim's world seems to shrink from the edges outward. As the days pass, the victim languishes more and more, turning away all food and drink, feeling nothing for loved ones, and, finally, caring nothing for his or her own life. I have seen people afflicted with *lapena,* and I can confirm that it is terrible to witness. Usually, the victim dies slowly of thirst or starvation, making the grief of the victim's family all the more terrible. It seems a choice, though clearly it is not; it is a disease that the sufferer has no power to resist. And there is one other thing which I should have mentioned at the start: *lapena* is contagious. Terribly so.

There is no proven cure, but for reasons that physicians do not fully understand, there is one substance that on occasion has been observed to have an ameliorating or preventative effect: gold. More often than not, it has no effect at all. But rumor has it that the precious metal has more than once prevented the disease from taking root or even kept a sufferer from death. Gilberto himself told us that he had seen a distant relative cured after she was forced to look at her face in a mirror of beaten gold. But people have attempted far more radical cures: wearing a golden breastplate like a shield; drinking water mixed with gold flakes; even piercing the body with gold needles. For this reason, gold is in high demand in the Papal States, and every ounce of it is gathered for the purpose of warding off *lapena*.

In any case, we arrived well equipped. We had spent a small fortune in Boston changing currency for gold in preparation for the journey, and we considered the gold we gave Ildefonso well spent if it would carry us to our destination safely. Shadrack had also equipped us with the best possible maps: his own of the Papal States, a glass map from a friend who had journeyed to Toledo a decade earlier, and a tea map to find lodging.

I will say little of our journey east to Murtea, because thanks to Ildefonso it was mostly uneventful. We had thought that our gold was buying only his services as a guide, but perhaps due to Gilberto's urging, or perhaps due to a surprising generosity, he brought along two cousins for additional protection. Ostensibly, they were to defend us from the *cuatro-ala* or "fourwing," a fearsome beast, with, as the name would suggest, four wings; it resides in the Dark Age and ventures from that black forest to pillage and scavenge for food. We did not encounter any fourwings, but the presence of the two cousins, whom we only knew by their nicknames—"Rubio" and "El Sapo"—effectively dissuaded any highway robber who might have been tempted to make our journey difficult. Rubio, a tall, thin man with curly blond locks, carried a long sword and a dagger and made a great show of cleaning his teeth with the short blade whenever we stopped for a meal. El Sapo, who was nearly as wide as he was tall, had lost most of his teeth in previous brawls, and his callused fists were like clubs. Thanks to them and Ildefonso's vaguely menacing silence, everyone left us to ourselves.

The country outside of Seville was dry, even in February, and though Ildefonso considered it hilly, the landscape was in reality quite flat. We traveled on horseback, fed the horses at the roadside inns, and saw very little of the villages along the way. The farther east we traveled, the closer we came to the Dark Age, and we saw empty villages everywhere. The people in those villages still populated kept to themselves and were wary of strangers. We appreciated all the more that our guide was well-known on the route as a merchant. Instead of viewing us with suspicion, innkeepers almost universally accepted us without comment. It was evident, nonetheless, that the epidemic had done more than isolate the villages. It had also, to my eye, made the population generally sullen, unwelcoming, and hostile. As we continued along, encountering the hard faces of innkeepers and other travelers, I realized how exceptional Gilberto's lively and generous outpouring of kindness had been.

Our traveling companions had been very quiet on the last day of our journey; though, to be fair, they were rarely talkative. Rubio occasionally had moments of effervescent sociability, but for the most part they were a serious—that is to say, dull—trio of bodyguards. I was beginning to feel nervous about the encounter that lay before us. Either we would find Bruno dead, or we would be faced with an unpleasant confrontation with the village authorities. Riding into Murtea around midday, we asked directions from the sentry, and he pointed us to the sheriff's office.

Murtea was ringed by a stone wall, and once we had passed through its gate we found ourselves in a labyrinth of narrow streets, some of them cobbled, some of them dirt. It took several tries to reach the fountain at the village center and then locate beside it the sheriff's office. Bronson and I rode in front, and our supposed guides, riding more and more slowly, followed. Here and there we passed villagers on the street, and they glanced at us warily and made no sign of welcome. When we finally found the sheriff's office, we were greeted at the doorway—if such a scowl can be considered greeting—by a thin man wearing a long sword tipped with gold and a tattered black cape.

We had agreed some days earlier that, while my Castilian was adequate, Ildefonso would be the one to ask the Murtean sheriff what had happened to Bruno. However, as we dismounted, I found that our three bodyguards were no longer beside us. Their horses stood with ours, seemingly as perplexed as Bronson and I; they shook their loose reins with surprised gratification. Looking quickly around the plaza, I realized that Ildefonso, Rubio, and El Sapo were sitting at some distance from each other, near the fountain. My first thought was that they were exhausted by the heat. But then, with dawning horror, I saw El Sapo fall to his side listlessly as if in a faint. He lay there, insensible to the dust and punishing sun. I knew then, without any doubt, what afflicted him. Bronson and I looked at each other, sharing the same, panicked thought: *What are we to do?*

The decision was made for us. A woman we had not seen, who was standing in the shade of a building not far from the fountain, let out a piercing scream. *"Lapena, lapena!"* she cried, her voice rising to a shriek as she repeated the dread word over and over again, running from the plaza. Our three companions did not so much as move. Bronson and I turned as one to the sheriff, but he had already disappeared. For one deluded moment, we imagined we would go free. I think, to my shame, I actually contemplated riding off and leaving Ildefonso, Rubio, and El Sapo.

Then four figures emerged from the sheriff's office. They wore full suits of armor under white capes with hoods, and upon their faces were long-beaked masks of pounded gold. The white fabric of the capes glinted in the bright sunlight, and I realized that golden thread had been woven into the cloth. With their beaks and armor and white garments, the men seemed like strange, silent raptors. I recognized the sheriff only by the gold-tipped sword with which he held us at bay. While his three assistants strode purposefully toward the fountain, the sheriff curtly ordered us to raise our hands.

In a rapid, unnerving procession, we were guided back out through the labyrinth of narrow streets. I heard some disturbance behind us, and I turned to see that the sheriff's deputies had thrown Ildefonso, Rubio, and El Sapo face-down over their saddles and were leading them along behind us. Once again, I felt a wave of unfounded hope that they would simply turn us out of the village. It was not to be. After passing one shuttered window after another, we reached the now unmanned sentry post and stepped past the city walls onto the dry, featureless plain. We walked south, branching off the road we had arrived on, and I saw our destination on the slope of a hill: a low, long building of stone with grating on the open windows. It was the village jail, doubling as a station for quarantine, set at a safe distance from the village walls. The sheriff opened the door and motioned for us to enter. His deputies tied up the five horses and carried our inert guides into the dark jail.

"Please, sir," I begged him in Castilian. "Let me explain why we are here. We can leave at once if you will only tell us the whereabouts of our friend—a man who was imprisoned here some months ago . . ." It was impossible to read the sheriff's expression under the sinister golden beak, but his actions were clear enough. Forcing us into the jail at sword's point, he threw the door closed behind us and locked it. Bronson and I were left there together in the darkness, along with three men who were already, inexorably, succumbing to *lapena*.

14
KEEPING SECRETS

—*1892, June 4: 13-Hour 27*—

Prior to the Disruption, law enforcement in Boston relied upon sher-
iffs, constables, and watchmen. In some parts of New Occident, this system
is still in place. But beginning in the 1840s, many of the larger cities—
namely Boston, New York, Charleston, and New Orleans—established
police forces aimed at preventing and detecting crime. Since then, the police
force has become a pillar of the criminal justice system in New Occident.

—From Shadrack Elli's History of New Occident

CLUTCHING THE KNIFE and the blood-stained bundle of clothing, Theo sat perfectly still in the darkness, his back against the
wardrobe wall. He breathed as quietly as he could and used the
trick he always did when he needed to calm himself: he imagined himself watching from overhead. Beyond the wardrobe
lay the map room, and beyond the map room stood the rest of
house; East Ending Street spread out in either direction, and the
streets he knew so well branched out from it until they filled
the city and reached the bay. From that vantage point, he could
see all the routes connecting him, in the wardrobe at 34 East

Ending Street, to the innumerable places in the larger world. He wasn't trapped—he was hiding. Watching from overhead reminded him that no matter what the circumstances, he could find a way out. There was always a way out.

The police had taken Shadrack and Miles—the former calling for Sophia, the latter raging furiously—and left two officers guarding Bligh's body. Theo heard them grumbling when they were assigned to stay behind.

"When's Grey coming, then?" one of the police officers asked the other, after more than half an hour had passed.

"He's on his way. Having his dinner at home, I heard, and wouldn't be interrupted."

The two men shared a low chuckle. "And I heard he didn't have a choice about it."

They laughed again. "You don't have a daughter," the officer with the older voice said more soberly. "They boss you something shocking."

"And you don't have a Nettie Grey," the younger man replied. "I met her last year when Grey got the medal. She asked me why we hadn't arrested Juniper in the Park Street burglary."

"Fates above. How did she know about that?"

"Grey tells her everything, the old fool. He's all stone to us and all honey to her. Worships the ground she walks on. Makes her think she owns the whole of Boston."

"Terrifying."

"I'll say. If it were me I wouldn't interrupt dinner, either."

There was a noise overhead, and the officers fell silent. Theo heard slow, even steps descending the stairs. "Ives, Johnson," said a level voice. "Good evening."

"Evening, Inspector Grey," the older voice replied. "Not a good one though."

"So I see. Nothing has been moved?"

"The two suspects made a bit of a mess before we could pin them."

"Which I suppose accounts for the carpet."

"Most likely, sir."

"Thank you. I'll take a few minutes."

Silence ensued. Theo heard only quiet movements for almost half an hour, and he had to force himself to wait for their voices or their footsteps on the stairs. *They are still here,* he said to himself. *Wait for them. Wait.*

Finally, Inspector Grey's voice interrupted the silence. "Thank you. You may take the body. Is anyone else at home?"

"The housekeeper is outside, sir. She arrived while we were here, and we've kept her waiting so as not to interfere."

"I'll speak with her upstairs."

Theo heard first the even footsteps of Grey climbing the steps and then the messier sounds of the two officers moving and wrapping Bligh's body. With sounds of effort they, too, left the map room.

Theo stretched his legs with a sigh of relief. He would have to wait a while longer, but at least now he could move. The darkness made it impossible to check his watch. He sensed that it was nearing fifteen-hour. Sophia was surely waiting for him at the harbor, and he would not be there. He shook his head, telling himself that once she came home, she would understand.

The footsteps above and the occasional high-pitched lament told him that Mrs. Clay was speaking with Grey. Their interview lasted some forty minutes, and then Theo waited roughly half that time again to be certain that the footsteps he heard overhead belonged to Mrs. Clay alone.

Bundle and knife in hand, he climbed quietly out of the wardrobe, sidestepping the gruesome carpet and the overturned chair. He took the stairs silently and peered into the study. There was no one there. The house had grown ominously quiet. "Mrs. Clay?" he called.

"*Theo!* Is that you?" A chair in the kitchen scraped against the floor, and Mrs. Clay rushed to meet him. She let out a shriek. "Fates above!"

"This isn't my blood—it's Bligh's." She stared at him, uncomprehending. "These things are Shadrack's; I had to take them."

Her eyes grew round with horror. "What have you done, Theo?"

"I was with them when we found Bligh. I saw the knife, these gloves, and the robe—they're Shadrack's. So I took them and hid in the wardrobe."

"You've been in the wardrobe this whole time?"

"Yes." They stared at one another in silence. Theo was remembering the previous summer and considering the odd coincidence of being forced to take refuge twice in the basement wardrobe of 34 East Ending Street.

Mrs. Clay was attempting to understand what had happened, and as yet she could not. "So the police did not see you?"

"They didn't see me."

"But what about those—*things* you're holding? The police will want them."

Theo held the knife up meaningly, as if to remind her what it was. "Shadrack didn't kill Bligh. But anyone who finds this will think he did. I had to take them."

"I need to sit down," Mrs. Clay said. She walked back to the kitchen, and Theo followed her. "Put those horrible things in the sink."

"Is Sophia back?"

"That is the other tragedy." Mrs. Clay shook her head and took a piece of notepaper from her skirt pocket. "What on earth does this mean?"

Theo could see it was in Sophia's hand, and his stomach sank. "What does it say?"

"'Shadrack, I am sorry, but I had to go. You said to me last summer that I needed something to do. What was true then is true now. I will be in good company. And I've asked Calixta and Burr to meet me in Seville. Love, Sophia.' She can't really mean *Seville*?"

"What time is it now?" Theo asked, ignoring the question. He wrapped the knife and gloves in the robe with the clean part on the outside and began washing his hands vigorously in the sink.

"Fifteen-hour, fifteen. Your shirt has blood on it."

She'll be back any moment now, Theo reassured himself. *When I don't show up, she'll be upset, but she'll just come home.* He pulled off his shirt, dried his hands, and then joined Mrs. Clay at the kitchen table. "I think Sophia can explain it herself. She should be back soon. That letter . . . She and Shadrack had a little argument, that's all."

"The Fates have turned against us," Mrs. Clay said, her voice catching. "I can think of no other explanation. I have always warned Mr. Elli that his irreverence toward them would have consequences, but he would not listen." She sniffled.

"The Fates had nothing to do with it." Theo took stock of the housekeeper's disordered hair, her tears, and her ashen face. "Mrs. Clay," he said more gently, reaching across the table to take her hand. "This wasn't the Fates. It was Gordon Broadgirdle."

She blinked at him. "What do you mean?"

"I have no doubt—it was him. He was here the other day threatening Shadrack, and this is just the kind of thing he would do. Commit some terrible crime and frame someone else for it."

"But he's a member of parliament."

Theo gave a dry laugh. "He is now, sure, but he hasn't always been. He's a scoundrel, through and through."

"You speak as if you know him."

"I do." Theo dropped her hand and leaned back in his chair, crossing his arms over his chest. He could see how the next month would unfold, as clearly as he could see his escape route from Boston. Sophia would come back to the house, and she would be devastated to find her uncle in prison. The evidence would all, neatly and precisely, confirm Shadrack's guilt. A plodding procession of criminal justice officials would convict Shadrack and Miles of murder. Broadgirdle, the unseen architect of the entire grotesque edifice, would chuckle in the background, enjoying the spectacle.

Theo saw his escape route crumbling as if it had been built of sand. The motto that had served him well for many years, "Every man for himself," was of no help here. *What will happen to Sophia?* Theo thought. *She can't fix this by herself, nor can Mrs. Clay.* He could not imagine abandoning Shadrack and Miles now, not while he had a chance to prevent what would happen. Indeed, he was perhaps the only person who *could* prevent it, since he knew with certainty who was responsible.

The thought of confronting Broadgirdle made him quail. *But that won't happen,* Theo thought firmly. *I don't have to talk to him or even see him. I just have to prove he's guilty.*

He realized that Mrs. Clay was waiting for him to speak. "I know him from before," he said. "Before I met all of you. When I lived in the Baldlands."

"Do you mean to say that he is not from New Occident?"

"That's right."

"But no one knows this. He pretends to be from Boston." Mrs. Clay twisted her handkerchief. "He has no right to be in parliament!"

"You got it. He's just like us—forged papers and everything, I'll bet."

"You must tell someone! Now—at once. Someone in parliament."

"That's not a good idea."

"Why not? It's an obligation, Theo! You must."

Theo wanted to tell Mrs. Clay the truth, and in fact he had planned to, so that she would see the rightness of what he intended. But now the words he had meant to say lodged somewhere in his chest, and other words—easier words that felt so much more palatable and that were not, in fact, entirely untrue—took their place. "Here's the thing. Remember the other night, when Bligh asked Shadrack about leverage?" She nodded. "You know what Broadgirdle does with leverage? He blackmails people."

Mrs. Clay stared at him. "But Shadrack has not done anything wrong."

"We don't know what kind of leverage Broadgirdle has. It could be something we don't know about—something from his past." He felt a twinge as he said it; the words cut unexpectedly close. "If we just go to parliament and burst out with it—'Broadgirdle is not from New Occident!'—he might do the same with what he has on Shadrack."

"I see what you mean," she said slowly. "But who *is* he? You still haven't told me."

Theo opened his mouth to speak, not knowing what he would say until the words were out. "He was a banker on the Baldlands side of the border. He made a fortune off of railroad speculators—took their money and then found some dirty secret they were keeping and made it impossible for that money to ever leave. I saw it happen to more than a dozen people." It sounded plausible. And it fit the circumstances of their present dilemma perfectly.

"How did you find out?" Mrs. Clay asked, more horrified than doubtful.

"Friend of mine who worked at the bank," he said matter-of-factly.

"That's simply appalling!"

"Yes," Theo agreed. "Appalling." *And not half as bad as the truth,* he thought.

15
VERITY REVEALED

—1892, June 4: 15-Hour 15—

Before the plague began to take its terrible toll, pilgrims from Ages near and far would travel to the Papal States to visit the shrines decorating the peninsula like so many precious jewels: monuments to the wondrous miracles that have taken place in this once-blessèd land. Now the shrines are less trafficked, and some have, tragically, fallen into decay. But the miracles they preserve within their crumbling walls are no less marvelous today than they were then.

—From Fulgencio Esparragosa's
Complete and Authoritative History of the Papal States

SOPHIA RACED BACK toward her cabin, trying to ignore the returning nausea that she had overcome at such a high cost. *They must have put Theo in a different cabin,* she told herself. *He got caught up talking to someone. Or he's exploring the ship.* She felt a flash of frustration. *Of course he would forget to come find me.* It struck her as strange that Remorse had not visited her, either, but perhaps she had obligations to do with the mission.

She worked her way down the covered passageway, noticing that all of the cabin doors were open and the rooms were empty. *Why is there no one here?* she wondered uneasily. She went up the first flight of stairs that she encountered and found a passageway identical to the one below—also empty. The fantastical, unreasonable thought flashed through her mind that she was the only passenger aboard. She could not help but remember Grandmother Pearl's story aboard the *Swan*, about a Lachrima who had been set adrift on a ship it would not abandon. Sophia took a deep breath to steady her nerves and her stomach. *I'm not thinking clearly,* she told herself firmly. *There is an explanation for this.*

A moment later, she discovered it. From a large room at the end of the passageway came the smell of roasted chicken; it turned her stomach, even as it reminded her that she was very hungry. Some thirty Nihilismians were sitting at three long dining tables, eating and conversing quietly. Sophia tumbled through the doorway. She could not see Remorse or Theo, but then again there were so many people and she was having difficulty taking them all in.

As she hesitated, a tall man with a gray mustache rose from his seat and approached her. "Miss Tims," he greeted her with a slight bow. "I am Captain Ponder. Are you feeling better?"

Sophia looked at him, baffled. "I am still seasick," she said. "I am looking for my travel companions—Theodore and Remorse."

The captain paused a moment. Then he turned and beckoned to the middle-aged man who had ushered her aboard ship. Wiping his mouth quickly with his napkin, he joined them. "Yes, Captain?"

"Miss Tims is asking after her guest, Theodore Constantine Thackary."

The man gave her an apologetic look. "I am afraid he did not arrive, Miss Tims. I was standing where you saw me the entire afternoon, welcoming passengers until fifteen-hour."

"There was no note, or anything?" she asked weakly.

"I am sorry. No."

Sophia swallowed hard. "I see. What about Remorse?"

"Thank you, Veering," the captain said, dismissing the man. "Remorse suspected that you would be unwell and chose not to disturb you," he told Sophia, "asking that we do the same. She left this for you." He took an envelope from his jacket and withdrew an envelope.

Sophia took it numbly. "Do you mean she isn't here?"

The captain cleared his throat. "Did you expect her to be? Perhaps there has been some misunderstanding. Remorse is not aboard the *Verity*."

"But she is sailing to the Papal States for her mission."

The captain met her with silence. Then he spoke carefully. "This is not the case. Remorse booked a ticket for you, Every Tims, and your guest some weeks ago, but never for herself. You are Every Tims?"

Sophia stared at him, stunned. "Yes," she said, her voice just above a whisper.

"I cannot say how this misunderstanding arose, but perhaps the letter holds some explanation." Taking Sophia by the elbow, he led her to an armchair at the side of the dining room.

"If you are feeling well enough afterward, please join us for the evening meal."

Sophia watched in silence as Captain Ponder returned to his seat. Then, with shaking hands, she opened the envelope.

Sophia—

I apologize for what will seem a terrible deception. It is a deception, but a necessary one. Maintain that you are traveling to the Papal States as Every Tims, and the captain will look after you well. He has sailed this route many times, and you are certain to have an uneventful journey. Ponder is more open-minded than other Nihilismians, and you will find him not discourteous to your uncle.

You and Shadrack will be met in Seville by my associate, who will mention me by name. I expect he will also explain the need for this elaborate ruse more fully. There is something else: I have left cargo in the hold marked with your name. Give the cargo to my associate when you disembark, and he will get you access to the diary.

Sophia, I am sorry that I could not travel with you, and I am sorry for my deceit. There are reasons why I must remain in Boston. However my actions may appear, please believe in my good intentions. This was a good decision, truly. You will not regret it.

Your friend,
Cassia (Remorse)

The letter fell from her hands. Sophia did not notice. Looking up at the dining room, she realized fully what had occurred. She was traveling alone across the Atlantic, under a false identity, on a ship full of strangers, to meet another stranger. She understood, then, that this had not been a good decision at all: it was the most thoughtless, dangerous, misguided thing she had ever done.

16
LOSING BLIGH

—*1892, June 4: 17-Hour 17*—

Members of parliament pay for their seats and, based upon their views, fall in with one party or another. Every six years, voters in New Occident select which of these parties will designate the prime minister, who must already be an MP. Almost invariably, the prime minister chosen by the elected party is already a popular party leader.

—From Shadrack Elli's History of New Occident

GORDON BROADGIRDLE STOOD in front of the full-length mirror in his office, surveying his ensemble. He understood, in a way many of his colleagues in parliament did not, that a man's appearance could make the difference between success and failure. Those who admired MP Broadgirdle, which was to say most of parliament and the larger part of Boston, called him "handsome"; those who feared him, which was to say everyone who knew him, called him "imposing"; and those who feared but did not admire him called him nothing at all.

The very few brave enough to admit that something about the handsome, imposing member of parliament made them uneasy had difficulty explaining why. Perhaps it had to do with how he parted his thick black hair right down the center of his sizable head, making a severe white line down his skull. Or perhaps it had to do with how his piercing black eyes seemed to say one thing from beneath his dark brows, while his words said another. Or perhaps it had to do with the thin mustache that clung to his upper lip like a centipede, spindly above the imposing black beard that covered much of his face. The centipede seemed to have a mind of its own. When Broadgirdle smiled, it squirmed unpleasantly.

He caressed one end of the centipede now with a large hand, white-powdered and finely manicured; his other hand rested on his broad chest. It was a great matter of pride that his name matched his girth, and he relished the intimidating effect of his presence. It was enough to walk into a room and advance purposefully toward a slim or average-sized man, then stare down at him from a great height, like a mountain contemplating a rickety cart at its base. People who laughed at Broadgirdle's name before meeting him were invariably reduced to silence when presented with the massive chest, the formidable black beard, and the piercing stare.

Broadgirdle used this to his advantage. He relied on his appearance as the primary instrument of blunt force, and he reserved his words for when they were most needed. This had the effect of making those words, when he used them, seem all the more potent.

He turned away from the mirror and examined the speech he had prepared for this occasion. It filled three white pages, and he looked it over once more, mouthing the words as he would deliver them to the Boston public, which was anxiously waiting to hear whether the rumors regarding the prime minister's murder were just that—rumors—or whether they were based on fact.

A light knock at the door indicated that the time had arrived. Notes in powdered hand, he strode to the door. Accompanied by his assistant, he proceeded to the long colonnade that looked out onto the steps of the State House. The crowd below, which poured out across the steps and onto Boston Common, buzzed like a hive. Its palpable anxiety was tinged with an edge of morbid excitement.

Alone, Broadgirdle walked to the center of the colonnade and stepped up to the dais so that he was clearly visible to all below. As he came into sight the crowd hushed in a wave that fanned outward until it reached the very edges of the common. Broadgirdle waited, calm and confident.

The task of announcing Bligh's murder should have fallen to the parliament's majority leader. But Broadgirdle, the minority leader, had asked to do it, and everyone was too afraid of him to refuse. Ostensibly, they had chosen Broadgirdle because of his voice—and it was true that along with his size and his stare, his voice was powerful. Rich and stentorian, it rang like the deep pealing of bells when he spoke before an audience. In private, he moderated it to a restrained but forceful current. He waited now, gazing down, until everyone in the crowd was silent. Then he spoke.

"People of Boston, friends. My colleagues in parliament

have asked me to make this urgent announcement because of the extraordinary turn of events that has taken place today." He paused, and let his words hang over the crowd. No one stirred. It seemed the entire city was listening.

"As you know, Prime Minister Cyril Bligh and I have had our differences these last few months. We have had different visions for New Occident. I wished to see a nation that was mighty in its dominance. Cyril wished to see a nation that was mighty in its compassion. These are fundamentally different ways of viewing the nation, and the world." He paused again, and it almost seemed that his audience had grown even quieter. "It made me terribly happy," he said, and the centipede curled awkwardly as Broadgirdle smiled, "when only three days ago our visions became radically more compatible. Cyril expressed to me his change of heart, and his desire to follow the plan I have advanced to him since the winter—the plan to unify our Western Age by force, where necessary; by expansion, where advantageous; and indeed by compassion, where possible."

There was wave of murmuring below: whispers of disbelief and confusion. Broadgirdle waited only a moment before moving on. "Unfortunately, by so doing, by agreeing to my plan for asserting the dominance of New Occident, Cyril made my enemies his enemies. Shadrack Elli and Miles Countryman, two of Cyril's closest supporters, suddenly became his fiercest foes. And the foreigner who had been living secretly with Cyril these many months, an Eerie woman by the name of Goldenrod, no doubt resented his change of heart." Broadgirdle unrolled the last sentence with a faint sneer and heavy innuendo, and the crowd obligingly gasped.

"I am sadly accustomed to the malicious retribution of my opponents and their underhanded methods. I am thereby prepared to deal with them. Cyril, as a man championing compassion even in the face of certain aggression, was not so accustomed or so prepared.

"I regret very much to tell you that today, this afternoon, Prime Minister Cyril Bligh was found murdered.

"The prime minister is dead. May he rest in peace."

Broadgirdle had intentionally planned his speech so that the announcement of Bligh's death would be his final words. He knew that once the words were out the public would erupt, and he was right. A roar rose from the crowd that was part wail of lament, part howl of outrage, part cry of incomprehension. The hive had been attacked, and it swarmed now, fierce and angry and confused.

Broadgirdle turned his massive back on the confusion and left the dais. The members of parliament who stood by the colonnade waited to shake his hand as he passed. Even the members of his own party were a little taken aback by how he had managed to insult the prime minister while seeming to eulogize him and how he had used the opportunity of Bligh's death to make a political gambit. But they were accustomed to Broadgirdle's bold moves, and those who had been bold enough in turn to confront him had, without exception, lived to regret it. So, one by one, his colleagues congratulated him as he walked by—some sincerely, some more ambiva-lently; all of them fearfully.

Once back in his office, Broadgirdle put the speech aside to be filed and called to his assistant, a thin wisp of a man by the name of Bertram Peel. Duly scurrying to his side, Peel prepared the wooden writing desk he carried everywhere: he smoothed the paper, lifted the pencil, and looked up expectantly as he always did, at the ready.

Bertie Peel was Broadgirdle's greatest admirer, which was just as well, because they spent most of every day together. There is a certain kind of person who, from many years of being bullied, becomes convinced that bullies run the world, and that if they run the world they must have a right to run the world, and that if they have a right to run the world they must be running it as it is supposed to be run.

Peel was such a person, and from this conviction he derived a great admiration for the greatest bully of them all, Gordon Broadgirdle. To Peel, Broadgirdle was a figure to be carefully observed and emulated, for even if he could never hold sway as Broadgirdle did, it fell upon him—Peel—to do his very best to try. So, in imitation of his supervisor's habits, Peel made a vigorous center part down the middle of his head, kept well-powdered hands, and cultivated a wilted centipede of a mustache. He looked like a younger, emaciated version of Broadgirdle, which made the supposedly handsome and imposing MP appear all the more so.

"I would like you to take a letter to our accused minister, Shadrack Elli."

"Certainly, sir." Peel waited expectantly.

"Dear Minister Elli, comma. I was aggrieved and shocked to hear of your wrongful arrest in connection with our prime minister's death, full stop. I would like nothing more than to see you restored to freedom, full stop. In the meantime, comma, please do not hesitate to contact me if I can be of any assistance, full stop. Yours sincerely, et cetera. And deliver the letter by hand, Peel. Wait for a reply. He will say 'yes' or 'no.' We have already agreed on terms. If they do not allow correspondence put through at the jail, you will let me know, and I will speak to the warden."

"Very well, sir."

"And on your way back from police headquarters, stop by my house and tell my housekeeper to bring dinner to the State House. We have a long night of work ahead of us, Peel."

"Yes, we do, sir. Thank you, sir." Peel scribbled a final note to himself so he would not forget about the dinner, and then he turned on his heel, trembling but also slightly exhilarated, as he always was when Gordon Broadgirdle, MP, showed the world what he was made of.

—17-Hour 57—

THEO SAW THE dispersing crowd as he made his way back to East Ending Street from Boston Harbor. When he arrived, he found Inspector Grey sitting at the kitchen table with Mrs. Clay, the one writing notes tirelessly in his notebook while the other sat rigidly, eyes damp from recent tears.

"Inspector Grey is here to speak with you and Sophia," Mrs.

Clay said. "I told him I was worried, since you took off again so soon after coming home." She gave him a significant look.

Grey stood up and offered Theo his hand. "If you have a moment, I have some questions for you, young man."

Theo disliked anyone who called him "young man," but he had a feeling Inspector Grey used the words more out of thoughtlessness than condescension. He seemed like the type who followed rules without ever pausing to consider what use they served. "Of course," Theo said, attempting to strike a balance between helpful and aggrieved. "Anything I can do."

"Is Sophia Tims not with you?"

"I'm afraid not," Theo answered gravely, avoiding Mrs. Clay's eyes. "It seems she has sailed to the Papal States."

"*What?*" Mrs. Clay exclaimed.

Grey looked from her to Theo. "This was unexpected?"

"She had spoken of her plans to me and to Shadrack. But she came to a decision very recently."

Mrs. Clay burst into tears. "I can't believe it," she said, burying her face in her handkerchief.

"Why is she sailing to the Papal States?"

"Sophia's parents disappeared when she was very young. They were explorers. She recently learned of a clue to their whereabouts in Granada."

Grey eyed him in silence. "I see," he finally said. He bent over his notebook and wrote quietly. "And where were you this morning and afternoon?"

"I was here in the morning," Theo said truthfully. "Then I went to meet Sophia at the public library. She never showed up." He felt an unexpected pang of guilt at his words. They made him imagine how Sophia must have waited and waited at the harbor, finally accepting that he would not arrive. Had she suspected that something had detained him? Or had she assumed that he had simply failed her? "I came home and Mrs. Clay told me what had happened and that Sophia wasn't here. I realized she might have left for the Papal States. So I went to the harbor. Her name is on a manifest for a ship called the *Verity*. It sailed at fifteen-hour."

Mrs. Clay sobbed into her handkerchief.

"Fifteen-hour," Grey repeated. "Several hours after Bligh was found. Had you seen Sophia at home earlier in the day?"

Theo couldn't believe Grey would consider a fourteen-year-old girl a likely murder suspect, but apparently the possibility did not strike the detective as too far-fetched. He was a rule follower, no doubt about it. "She left in the early morning. This was always the day she had in mind for leaving," he said pointedly. "I just didn't think she would go."

"These circumstances will need to be examined further," Grey said, his expression grim. "When will Miss Tims return?"

"Friends of ours are meeting her in Seville at the end of the month," Theo said.

Mrs. Clay looked up hopefully. "Are they?"

"She should come back with them in July."

Grey shook his head. "That is much too late for my purposes." He made a brief note. "I will need to see your identity papers."

Theo rose from his chair. "They're just upstairs."

Grey eyed him placidly. "You should know better, young man. I was saying the same to Mrs. Clay. As foreigners, you would be well-advised to carry your papers with you always."

Theo gave him an easy grin. "What a good idea. It never occurred to me." He left the kitchen and returned a minute later with his papers.

Grey looked them over. Then he took Theo's identity papers and Mrs. Clay's, which lay on the table, and tucked them into his jacket. "I will keep these for the time being."

"That will make it tough to carry them around with me," Theo said with a wry smile.

"Not at all," Grey replied calmly. "You and Mrs. Clay will be confined to 34 East Ending Street for the duration of this investigation."

"What?" she exclaimed. "But we've done nothing wrong!"

"Perhaps not," conceded Grey. "And yet this is a very serious crime, and it took place in this house. No one is above suspicion. Especially foreigners."

There was a long silence.

"We aren't foreigners," Theo said quietly. "We live here now."

Grey rose from his chair, ignoring the comment. "There will be officers at the side door and front door at all times."

Mrs. Clay put her face in her handkerchief and filled it with quiet sobs. Theo fixed Grey with a cold stare. "It will be difficult to eat if we can't leave the house for groceries."

"An officer will accompany you for essential errands. Naturally, if you are found alone beyond the confines of the house, it will be difficult to interpret it as anything other than willful uncooperativeness. And it will be necessary to arrest you."

"This isn't right," Mrs. Clay said feebly.

"What isn't right, madam, is the murder of a prime minister. Bear that in mind as you consider what is right and what is wrong."

17
Verity's Helm

—*1892, June*—

None know whence the Dark Age emerged. It offers a window onto a distant past too terrible to contemplate. Like a fatal leech on the fair skin of the States, it clings tenaciously to the peninsula. Only the labors of the Orders, particularly the Order of the Golden Cross, keep the dangers of the Dark Age at bay.

—From Fulgencio Esparragosa's
Complete and Authoritative History of the Papal States

SOPHIA AGONIZED OVER whether she should demand that the *Verity* return her to Boston Harbor. She had no notion of how difficult it would be nor how kindly the captain would respond. And then there was Theo's absence. Why had he not appeared? What could have stopped him? She felt injured by his betrayal one moment and worried on his behalf the next. Various possibilities occurred to her, none of them satisfying: Miles had asked for his company north into the snows, and Theo had decided to go; Shadrack had found her note and extracted an explanation; some terrible accident had befallen him on the way to the harbor. They all seemed possible and impossible, and her mind would not settle. One day she felt certain he had let her down; the next she felt just as certain he never willingly would have.

Nor could she fathom Remorse's deception. For several days, as she learned the rhythm of the *Verity* and its passengers, she contemplated her conversations with the archivist, aghast at her own inadequate sense of judgment. *How could I have trusted her so easily? What was I thinking? This is what comes of lying to Shadrack. And lying at the archive.* She went over and over the decisions she had made. *I should never have gone to the archive alone. I should have told Shadrack about the pamphlet. I should have waited for Theo at the harbor. I should have wondered why Remorse wasn't aboard. I should have wondered why she was helping me.* Sophia could see now, in hindsight, that her eagerness to find the diary and her willingness to trust the signs given by the Fates had made her rash and impulsive, qualities she sometimes admired in others but could not live with in herself.

With time, her storm of vexation subsided. She was able to look past the humiliation, and she gradually reconciled herself to the circumstances. However foolish the route she had taken to reach it, the diary was still worth searching for. More—it was worth any number of humiliations. *I would do it all again if it meant getting the diary,* Sophia said to herself resolutely. And so she focused on what lay ahead. Though she had no conception of why or how, someone who could lead her to Minna's diary was going to meet her in Seville. She reminded herself of this as she clutched her spool of silver thread and hoped, fiercely, that even this misstep was part of the plan. *And if I'm being fooled again,* she thought, *at least I know I can count on Burr and Calixta to meet me there in July.*

Captain Ponder, just as Remorse had promised, was a very able captain. Smooth sailing left Sophia to worry about her own journey, rather than the *Verity's*. The Nihilismians politely ignored her. It became clear that they considered her a recent convert, one who had not yet learned to fully school her demeanor and was thereby prone to unseemly displays of emotion. They gave her a wide berth.

Sophia had no difficulty politely ignoring them back. For the first few days, she was too busy battling the seasickness and her dismay. When she grew tired of rebuking herself and decided to follow the path set before her, she turned her attention to the beaded map, which had remained untouched in her pack.

With a sigh, Sophia unrolled the beaded map and set it on the little desk of her cabin. Placing her fingers on the linen sent her into the dry, changeless, and stationary landscape of the Papal States. To her surprise, the seasickness vanished. From then on, she took refuge in the barren land for long hours of the day, and sometimes when she emerged from it, the sense of solidity stayed with her long enough to keep the nausea at bay a short while.

Sophia slipped into a routine. She fell asleep at night in the landscape of the beaded map, where the dark night sky, heavy with stars, was wonderfully still. She awoke with a lurching stomach at dawn. She retreated into the map again for an hour to calm herself before joining the Nihilismians at breakfast. In the morning, she read Esparragosa. After lunch, she wrote in her notebook and sat on the deck if the weather was fair. After dinner, she withdrew into the beaded map again, letting the brilliant sunsets remind her that somewhere, beyond the turbulent waters, lay a land where she would find firm footing.

The map was limitless. She could spend years drifting through its landscapes. But Esparragosa was finite, and she found herself rereading him by the end of the first week. Captain Ponder surprised her on the eighth day of the journey by arriving in her cabin with a pile of books. "I cannot take credit for noticing," he said quietly, "but another passenger observed that you were wanting in reading material. You will find my cabin well stocked, and you should feel welcome to borrow from it when you are finished with these."

He had brought her other histories of the Papal States. One recounted the history of the plague. Another described the Order of the Golden Cross. A third, entirely on the Dark Age, was written by none other than Fulgencio Esparragosa. Sophia dove into them with pleasure, deeply grateful to the Nihilismians for their consideration—however careful they might be to conceal it.

She had heard of the Dark Age, but even among Shadrack's wide circle of explorers, none had traveled to it. "To the inhabitants of the Papal States," Esparragosa's volume began, "the Dark Age is both familiar and strange."

It is familiar because we all live in its shadow, and strange because however proximate it is, we do not know it well. Soon after the Disruption, the Papacy forbade travel into the Dark Age. Its borders are patrolled by the Order of the Golden Cross. And yet the Order cannot watch the entire perimeter at every moment, and people continually pass in—to their great peril. The Spines or Espinas, with their iridescent black trunks and branches, bear thorns like teeth on every limb. Their bite, occasioned by even a slight breeze, is fatal. The Fourwing is the avian sister to the Spine: its iridescent black feathers catch and reflect the sun. Its sharp talons and beak, a more muted black, are as ferocious as its yellow eye. Fully as tall as a man, the Fourwing will devour a flock of sheep, chase away the horses, and drive an entire family from its home to lay eggs. They are now rarer, having been hunted indefatigably by the Orders in the early decades. And yet none of these horrors is so deadly as the Plague, lapena, which has already taken so many lives.

The volume you have in your hands recounts the history of the Dark Age as it is known to cartologers today, though you must recognize, dear reader, that this knowledge is riddled with holes and embellished with fictions. Only a cartological expedition into the Dark Age, sent for the purposes of exploration, will result in a true history.

Sophia smiled wistfully to herself, recognizing in Esparragosa's writing the same spirit of exploration that motivated

Shadrack. And so, even on a ship full of strangers, she felt rather more at home.

ON THE SECOND week of the journey, Sophia saw Minna again. Her absence had been disheartening, but not surprising. Without understanding what the specter was or how it appeared, Sophia had assumed it remained earthbound. She was wrong.

It happened at dusk, when Sophia emerged from reading the beaded map and found that she felt well enough to go out on deck. She walked along it slowly, taking deep breaths and feeling grateful for her settled stomach. The moon, heavy and yellow, hung low in the cloudless sky.

She saw a shape several paces away. At first, she thought it was one of the Nihilismians, taking the night air as she was. Then she realized the figure was faintly luminous, as if touched by the moonlight. She stopped. The figure turned and approached, though its face was still indecipherable. Then it spoke, and Sophia felt a jolt of recognition as the voice reached her. *"Do not regret those you leave behind."* Sophia started and took a step backward. *"Do not regret those you leave behind."*

"How are you here?" Sophia asked, her voice shaking.

"Do not regret those you leave behind."

"Why not?" she whispered.

"Miss Tims?" A stern voice called her to attention, and she turned to find Captain Ponder standing in a nearby doorway. "Is everything well?"

Sophia looked back at Minna, but she was gone. She shook her head, dazed. "I thought I saw something. Someone."

Captain Ponder observed her for a moment. "I have been to Seville every year for the last decade, and word has reached me of a new peril emerging from the Dark Age."

"What is it?" Sophia asked, her throat tight.

"Wraiths that appear from among the spines. They lure the living away, into the dark forest, never to be seen again."

Sophia said nothing.

"The Papal States are not as they should be, as they were in the Age of Verity." He paused. "Dangerous illusions abound. You know this better than most: *'Every vision around you is false, every object an illusion, every sentiment as false as a dream.'*"

"Truth of Amitto," Sophia said reflexively. But her thoughts rebelled. She could not believe that the beloved figure that had guided her this far was a terrible wraith from the Dark Age. It was impossible. "Good night, Captain Ponder." She turned her back on the captain and slowly made her way back to cabin 7.

18

THE ROAD TO AUSENTINIA

March 15, 1881

Rubio died on the sixth day, and Ildefonso and El Sapo died on the seventh. Whatever food and water Bronson and I did not consume remained untouched, and our jailers observed these signs without comment. For several days the fear that we, too, would fall ill paralyzed us. I think at times the fear itself was enough to make me lose my appetite. Watching three grown men kill themselves slowly, passing out of the world as if they had never belonged to it, was horrifying.

As the days wore on, Bronson and I realized that we remained, somehow, unaffected. I was frightened and disheartened, but I still wanted to live. Every morning when I awoke I searched Bronson's face with apprehension, terrified that I would find there the weary indifference that marked the first signs of the plague. But every morning he bore an anxious concern that mirrored mine. The desperate wish to escape, to flee that plagued continent, to return to our dearest Sophia, shone brightly in his eyes.

We had pressed the button on Wren's watch on the first day and every day since, but nothing came of it. I still held out hope that he might arrive—with a ship like the *Roost*, anything was possible. But perhaps my hope was naive.

Even more naive was our hope that resisting the plague would be our deliverance. Surely they could not keep us quarantined if we were not ill? But on the eighth day, after the sheriff's men in golden masks had carried away the corpses and burned them on the plain beside the jail, we discovered our error.

We were visited by the sheriff and two other men: a scribe in black robes with a portable desk who wrote down every word of our long exchange, and a small, plump man in red and white robes. Like the sheriff's men, he wore a beaked mask made out of pounded gold and a magnificent golden cross on a gold chain across his chest. From the sheriff's explanation, I understood the second man to be Murtea's priest. Communicating through the barred window, the priest asked us a series of questions, all the while clasping his pudgy, rather dirty hands reverently over his belly.

"State your names and place of origin."

"Minna and Bronson Tims of Boston in New Occident."

"Why does your husband not answer?" the priest asked. I could not make out his expression behind the golden mask, but the tone of disapproval was unmistakable.

"He does not speak Castilian."

There was a short pause. "Very well," the priest said, making clear that it was not. "Why have you traveled to the Papal States?"

"We came here to find news of our friend, Bruno Casavetti, who contacted us some months ago. I believe he was here, in Murtea. Was he here? Can you tell us where he is now?"

This caused some consternation. The three men consulted with each other, and though they spoke too rapidly and quietly for me to follow their entire conversation, I heard the name "Rosemary" and the word *brujo*—meaning "witch"—repeatedly.

When the priest turned back to us, it seemed that they had already formed some conclusion, for his line of questioning changed. "By what spells or dark arts do you repel the plague?"

I was so stunned that I could not reply. "What did he say?" Bronson asked.

"He asked what spells we use to protect ourselves from the plague," I said, aghast.

"Fates above," he murmured. "This bodes ill."

I turned back to the cleric. "We are astonished by your question. We do not believe in spells or dark arts. We have no more idea than you do why we did not catch the disease carried by our companions. Truly, it is entirely a mystery to us."

"You do not believe in the dark arts?" the priest said, his voice hard. "You deny the existence of such dangerous evil?"

"Please," I said quickly, realizing my mistake, "we do not know what to believe. This illness and the means of treating it are entirely unknown to us. What I meant to say is that we have no knowledge of any spells or dark arts."

The priest and sheriff conferred once more, while the scribe diligently took notes. This time I understood nothing of their conversation, and when the priest faced me again, an air of dismissal evident in his every movement, I felt a terrible sense of foreboding. "Your sentence will be determined by midday tomorrow and communicated to you by the sheriff." Without another word, he began to walk away, followed by the other two men.

"Please!" I called after him. "Please let us go on our way and we promise never to return. We are not ill! We will cause you no harm."

They made no sign of having heard me, but continued without pause toward the walled village of Murtea, kicking up a cloud of dust in their wake.

The relief we had felt at escaping the plague gave way to a contained panic. Bronson spent the long afternoon trying to weaken the mortar holding the bars on the rear window, and I began writing this account with the notepaper in my pack. My thoughts turned somber. I began to feel that escape would be impossible, and that whatever dread fate had befallen Bruno would befall us, too. I did not regret that we had responded to his call for aid, but I regretted with all my heart that we had arrived so precipitously and thereby placed ourselves in peril. We might have stayed longer with Gilberto Jerez. We might have sent someone on ahead of us to inquire what had happened. We might have called upon the authority of the bishop in Seville. All the alternatives seemed, from the vantage point of the Murtea jail, wiser than the one we had chosen.

As the afternoon darkened into dusk, Bronson abandoned

his hopeless task at the window and I put down my pen. I lost track of time as I wandered down the dark pathways of what might have been, before Bronson finally recalled me to the present. We sat in the growing darkness, our hands entwined, not speaking. But our thoughts traveled together over the past, lingering on Sophia and the world we had left behind in Boston. The sun set, and our spirits sank with it.

Then, as the hours dragged, we were surprised to hear a light footstep approaching the jail. Had the sheriff arrived with our sentence? We rose and went to the barred window. But it was not the sheriff. We saw a girl—no more than twelve or thirteen years of age—approaching us.

She wore a long dress and a shawl that covered her head. When she reached the window of the jail, she lowered the shawl so that we could see her face in the faltering light. "You are friends of Bruno?" she asked in slightly accented English.

"Yes," I answered, surprised. My mind leaped to the letter he had sent us. "Are you Rosemary?"

She nodded.

"Thank the Fates," Bronson exclaimed. "We have found you. Or you have found us. We received the letter you sent for Bruno. Is he here? Is he well?"

Rosemary bit her lip. Her eyes were filled with sorrow. "He is not here. He was sentenced in December, only a week after I sent the letter."

Bronson and I were dumbstruck. Our worst fears had come true. "What was his sentence?" I asked hoarsely.

"He was banished to the hills north of here to follow

the *señas perdidas*. The lost signs—the paths that once led to Ausentinia."

"Banished?" I echoed. "But then he is alive? We could find him by also following these—lost signs?"

"I fear not. I will explain it to you. I have come here partly for this purpose, to explain to you what happened to Bruno, because I fear," she paused, "it is the same as what will happen to you." She fell silent. "It is difficult to tell."

"We understand, Rosemary." I was suddenly conscious of the risk she must have taken to visit us. "We appreciate your generosity in bringing us this news. Yours is the only kind word we have had since arriving here."

Rosemary looked pained, but she nodded. "I will tell you what happened to Bruno." She paused. "It all happened because of Ausentinia."

"Ausentinia?" I echoed.

"Yes." She sighed. "Ausentinia. For as long as we in Murtea can remember, there has been another Age in the hills to the north—the hills of Ausentinia. My mother told me of it from the time I was very little, before I ever visited myself.

"From the moment you cross the stone bridge into the hills, you leave our Age behind. The paths through the hills are a labyrinth—mysterious and changing paths, that shift every time you turn your head. Yet every traveler knew how to find the way. At each juncture in the road, there is a path to the left, a path in the middle, and a path to the right. However much they might change, by always choosing the middle path, you would arrive after an hour's travel in a beautiful valley where the city of Ausentinia shone like a piece of polished copper in the sun.

"Pilgrims from every corner of the Papal States traveled to it, always taking the stone bridge, always following the middle path, and always finding their way to the hidden city. This is why your friend Bruno came—to visit Ausentinia." Rosemary paused.

"But why?" asked Bronson.

"We call it Ausentinia here, but elsewhere it is known as *La Casa de San Antonio*—'The House of Saint Antony,' after Saint Antony of Padua, the patron saint of lost things. Ausentinia offered every person who visited something marvelous: the miracle of way-finding."

"What do you mean?" I asked.

"Imagine you had lost something very precious: the key to a trunk full of treasures; a brother who had left home, never to return; a secret whispered in your ear and then forgotten. Then imagine that someone with knowledge of all things that could and would happen drew you a map: a map that told exactly where to go and what to do when, so that you would find the key, or the brother, or the whispered secret. Wouldn't you travel any distance for such a map?"

It sounded like something out of a dream. "Of course I would."

"Let me tell you of my own visit so that you may understand," Rosemary said. "When I was little, I lived with my mother on a farm outside Murtea, some half hour's walk from the walls. I had never known my father, and my mother was the world to me. We were very happy.

"My mother loved to sing, and she had a beautiful voice. Wishing to be just like her, I sang, too—she called me her little warbler. The sound of our voices, filling the house and the field behind it, day and night, made me glad.

"Then, three years ago, when I was ten, she fell ill. You know the signs now, as I did: she lost her appetite; in the mornings, she had no desire to rise from her bed. We both knew it was *lapena*. Before it could get worse, she did something both cruel and merciful. She left me. The note I found in her place explained that she wished to spare me not only the illness but also the sight of her losing care for everything she loved, including me.

"I searched, day after day, in all the places where I thought she might go, but I could not find her. After two weeks had passed, I knew. She was gone. She had met her death somewhere out on the dry plains, alone. Worse still, her remains would never be buried on consecrated ground, and her soul would wander forever in purgatory. All this she had done just to spare me.

"That was a terrible time. I cried until my eyes were swollen shut. Why had the plague not taken me, too? I wished for it and it would not come.

"When I emerged from my grief, alive despite myself, I found that I had lost my voice. Not only my singing voice—I had entirely lost the power of speech. At first, I did not care. I had lost my mother, and any loss compared to that great loss was as nothing.

"But as the weeks passed, something changed. The silence that settled upon the house was killing me—and I no longer wished to die. Singing would have reminded me of her and brought the memory of her into the house. I needed my voice to return.

"So, for the first time, I crossed the stone bridge, taking the middle path at each juncture, following the dusty footpaths until, after an hour's walking, I reached the city of Ausentinia. I remember that I arrived at midday, when the sun was high. In Murtea, the heat would be unbearable, and everyone would be indoors. But here it was cool. The city was ringed with pine and cypress trees, and their aroma filled the air. Lovely stone houses, with their shining copper roofs, basked in the sun. The market was full of vendors, and every man, woman, and child seemed to radiate contentment. I realized, as I walked along, seeking a map vendor, the cause of their happiness: nothing was ever lost for long in Ausentinia. Anything lost would soon be found. And the departure of those things that left the world forever—my mother among them—caused them less agony, I thought, for they understood the loss as final and necessary.

"Almost half the shops on the streets sold maps. I chose one simply because I liked the sign hanging above the doorway; there was a bird on it that reminded me of a warbler. Inside, there were low counters on three sides, and behind the counters the walls were entirely covered with tiny drawers, each one the size and round shape of a Seville orange. Standing at the till was a man with a long beard and bright eyes who smiled at me as I entered.

"I had not realized until that moment that I would not be able to explain what I needed. How could I request a map to find my voice if I had no voice? But the man simply smiled again, seeing my expression of consternation, and said, in Castilian, 'Have no fear, Rosemary.' He leaned forward, his elbows on the counter. 'You have lost your voice, and you seek to find it. But I believe you seek something else as well, do you not?' I looked at him in bafflement. 'Your mother's resting place,' he said gently. I felt my eyes filling with tears. I nodded. 'Well, child,' he said kindly, 'there is a map here for you, waiting only to be read.'

"He walked along a drawer-lined wall, running his fingertips along the labels, until he found the one he wanted. Opening the drawer, he pulled out a sheet of paper that was curled into a tube and tied with a piece of white string. I weighed it in my hand—this was a famed map of Ausentinia? 'Doesn't look like much, does it?' he remarked with a smile. 'Don't worry. It will contain what you need.' I reached into my purse to pay him, but he stopped me. 'No, no. We don't accept that kind of payment. Instead, you must guide someone else, like yourself, who is out in the world, seeking just as you are seeking. Here,' he said, handing me a second roll of paper, this one tied with a blue string, 'is your payment. Your map will explain for whom it is intended.'

"Giving him thanks—although I did not wholly understand him—I left the shop, and once I was out in the street I quickly unrolled the scroll with the white ribbon. There was a map drawn upon it. Below, it said, *A map for the little warbler.* My tears overflowed, and the page became a blur. When I had composed myself and was able to clear my eyes, I saw something that made little sense. It bore the appearance of a map—but where did it lead?

"In the corner, a compass pointed an arrow toward 'The Future.' There were 'Mountains of Solitude,' a 'Forest of Regret,' and other strangely labeled regions. But a clear path stretched across it—or, rather, one clear path with many branches. The path began at Ausentinia. And on the back of the map were several paragraphs written in a fine hand. The opening read:

> *Soundless, we scream in the heart; silent, we wait in the shadows; speechless, we speak of the past. Find us at either end of eleven years.*
>
> *Taking the Trail of Uncertainty, accept the guide who arrives under the full moon. Travel with him into the Meadow of Friendship, and when the cart breaks, go to the Goat's Head. Your traveling companion is falsely accused. Speak then, and speak the truth, for both truth and falsehood lead to the Steep Ravine of Loss.*

"The map went on, explaining how I might navigate the branching paths and strange landscapes to find, at the end, my mother's remains. Despite the many incomprehensible markings on the map and equally incomprehensible directions, I understood the beginning, and I understood the end. Tucking the scroll in my pocket, I opened the second one. It was very much like my own, but written in a language I could not read.

"And so, with the maps I had sought, I returned home to wait.

"At the next full moon, as the map had promised, I heard someone making his way along the path to my house. Sound carries easily on the dry plain, and while he was still at some distance, I heard not only his footsteps, but also his voice. He was singing. His voice was low and gentle, and he sang something in a foreign tongue that sounded merry and full of laughter.

"I went to the door and opened it, watching the moon shine down upon him. When he arrived, he looked upon me with a broad smile. His sweet-sounding song was still in my ears. Of middle years, with a dark beard and a round belly, he was, I fancied, like the father I had never had, arriving at last in my hour of need. 'My name is Bruno Casavetti,' he said in Castilian, giving a slight bow, 'and the monks in Granada suggested I might find lodging here. I can pay in gold, or in melodies,' he added, with a wink. 'Or both. Any chance you might spare a bed for an aging traveler with a heavy pack?'"

19

WINNING NETTIE

—*1892, June 5: 9-Hour 38*—

The New States Party was founded mid-century by parliament members who wished to offer a progressive approach to foreign and domestic policy. They first made their mark with the Hospital Reforms of 1864, whereby high standards were set for the care of patients in New Occident hospitals and houses of charity.

—From Shadrack Elli's History of New Occident

INSPECTOR ROSCOE GREY lived not far from East Ending Street, in a neighborhood called "the Little Nickel" after a counterfeiting scandal that had taken place decades earlier. The inspector kept a small but orderly household: a pair of servants, Mr. and Mrs. Culcutty, who ran things so smoothly that it was almost imperceptible when one of Grey's long cases kept him on the street for days at a time; and the inspector's daughter, Nettie, who was sixteen. The three adult members of the household doted on Nettie, in part because she had lost her mother when she was only an infant, and in part because she was such a sweet and charming young person.

The inspector, who by some accounts had become a severe

man after the death of his wife, considered Nettie his sun, moon, and stars. When he returned at the end of a long day, his spirits were lifted by the sound of his daughter at the piano, and his angular face, with its sad eyes, narrow nose, and close-trimmed brown beard, seemed to lift along with them. Mr. and Mrs. Culcutty, the gentlest and most amiable couple in the Little Nickel, worshipped the very ground she walked upon. The pair had their few disagreements over matters involving Nettie, principally when one of them was thoughtless enough to disappoint her and the other was compelled to righteously champion her cause.

There had been one such disagreement the night before, when the inspector was out very late attending to his new case, the terrible murder of Prime Minister Bligh. Nettie had wished to seek some companionship and comfort at her friend Anna's, and Mrs. Culcutty had felt obliged to point out that it was nearly nineteen-hour and her father would not want her to leave the house, and Nettie had consequently cried, and Mr. Culcutty had indignantly told his wife that he would accompany Nettie to Anna's house or to the end of the earth, be it nineteen-hour or not.

There were some in the neighborhood who found Nettie Grey perhaps a little too sweet. The dressmaker two doors down, Agnes Dubois, had been known to roll her eyes when Nettie walked down the cobbled street, carrying a basket laced with ribbons and singing a sweet little tune. And the dressmaker's friend, a music teacher named Edgar Blunt who instructed Nettie at the piano every Friday, had difficulty understanding why everyone thought he should consider it such a privilege to teach a student who was, to his ear, quite mediocre and a trifle too earnest. And the dressmaker's neighbor, a librarian named Maud Everly, could not bring herself to admire a girl who spent so much time on her appearance and so little time on reading. But apart from these exceptional cases, the neighborhood and the Greys' circle of acquaintances were generally inclined to think very highly of Nettie, with her broad smile and her bright blue eyes and her cascade of brown curls and her sweet, high voice.

Theo's first impression was rather different. From the moment he saw her through the window, dutifully practicing her scales with a look of contented self-satisfaction, he thought, *What a princess.* He smiled to himself.

Theo had made his plan as soon as Inspector Grey left 34 East Ending Street the previous evening. It was simple: He would keep track of the inspector's investigation by befriending Nettie Grey. He would prove Broadgirdle had planned Bligh's murder. Once he had evidence that Broadgirdle was guilty, he would make sure Grey got hold of it. Shadrack and Miles would go free. Everything would return to the way it had been, and he would never have to hear another word about Gordon Broadgirdle.

It had required patience but no ingenuity to avoid the officers at East Ending Street. The library window had provided the means, and the boredom of the police officers had offered the opportunity. Theo waited for them to drift toward one another, as they inevitably would, so that they could converse idly on the corner. They each had their respective doorways in sight, but from the corner they could see nothing happening at the rear of the house. Theo swung out into the narrow garden bed, hopped two fences into the yard of a house on East Wrinkle Street, and emerged well out of sight. It took him an hour to discover Grey's address in the Little Nickel.

He watched the house for another hour to make certain the inspector was not home. Then, after Nettie had been practicing scales for some twenty minutes, he knocked on the window. Nettie stopped her playing at once and turned. She blushed and gave a tentative smile.

Theo returned the smile with a friendly wave. Finally, after several seconds of pink-cheeked hesitation, Nettie made her way to the tall casement window and opened it.

"Hi," Theo said, widening his smile.

"Hi," Nettie replied. She brushed a brown curl out of her eyes.

"I heard you playing," he continued, "and I couldn't help myself; I had to see where such beautiful music was coming from."

Nettie batted her eyelashes. "Oh, I was just playing scales. It's nothing."

"Really? Just scales? Can you play anything else?"

Nettie nodded happily. "Of course." She returned to the piano bench and settled in, riffling nervously through a stack of music sheets until she found the one she wanted. With a quick smile back at the opened window, she set her choice on the stand and began to play. It was a Chopin waltz, and a rather long one. The piece clearly strained the limits of Nettie's technical abilities and affective range, but she blazed through it bravely, leaving the misplayed notes behind her like a trail of debris.

As she played, Theo quietly climbed up through the casement window and seated himself on the upholstered chair beside it. He did his best to ignore the destruction of the Chopin waltz and studied the room. It was clearly decorated to suit Nettie: poppies on the upholstery, lace on the curtains, and porcelain figurines on the delicate side tables. In one corner was a worn leather chair and a footstool piled with books: Inspector Grey's outpost. Grey did not keep his work here, Theo surmised, but hopefully it was all neatly stored in Nettie's silly head.

Nettie finished the piece and turned to Theo with a look of triumph. She seemed a little startled to find him sitting in the chair rather than leaning in through the window, but she recovered as Theo applauded loudly.

"That was just amazing!" he cried. "Wow! You must give concerts, don't you?"

Nettie smiled happily. "I'm glad you liked it. I would love to give a concert someday," she confided. "Although," she added, her brow wrinkling slightly, "Mr. Blunt says I do not have the soul for it, whatever that means."

Theo shook his head. "Ridiculous. You must give a concert, even if the first is only a small one for your friends. Once they hear you, the word will spread."

"That's a very good idea," Nettie said, her eyes opening wide.

"I'd be happy to help you organize it," he offered, extending his scarred hand. "I'm Charles, by the way."

"Nettie."

As they shook hands, the distant sound of the front door opening reached them. "I'm home, Nettie," a woman's voice called out. "And I brought you a maple cake."

Nettie's face flickered with momentary aversion.

"Must you stop practicing now?" Theo asked with some concern.

"No," Nettie said, shaking her dark curls and frowning. "That's just Mrs. Culcutty."

"How kind of her to bring you a maple cake."

"It is not especially kind of her," Nettie said airily, "because she is making life very difficult for me at the moment, and the maple cake does not help one bit to make it easier." In the end, Mrs. Culcutty's concerns the previous evening had overridden Mr. Culcutty's indignant chivalry, and Inspector Grey had even thanked the housekeeper for not letting Nettie out so late. Now, Mrs. Culcutty was attempting to make it up to Nettie for being strict and being right.

Theo was the very picture of sympathetic concern. "And how is she making life difficult?"

"She wouldn't let me go see my friend Anna last night, even though it was a terrible night and I needed desperately to speak with her."

Theo shook his head with a sigh. "I completely understand. It *was* certainly a terrible night. Learning of the prime minister's murder. Discovering that he'd been living with a foreigner, of all things. It is shocking." He blinked, as if struck by a sudden realization. "Forgive me—perhaps you had a terrible night in some other way."

Nettie seemed touched by Theo's thoughtfulness. "I did mean about the prime minister." Her expression shifted from gratified to appalled. "Isn't it simply ghastly how he was found?"

"Horrifying."

"Did you happen to hear any of Broadgirdle's speech?" Nettie asked in a low voice, leaning in.

"I did not. But supposedly he made rather clear that Minister Elli, Miles Countryman, and the foreign woman were responsible for the murder."

Nettie gave a little sigh, no doubt overcome by the wickedness of the world.

"I also heard," Theo continued, "that the best police inspector in Boston had taken the case. I'm sure he'll discover the truth of it."

Nettie gave him a sly smile. "Did you hear that?"

Theo paused deliberately. "Someone named . . . Grey, I believe."

Nettie's smiled widened, her eyes bright. "As it happens," she said confidingly, "Inspector Roscoe Grey is my father."

"No!"

"Yes! He was called away in the afternoon, and he was gone for hours, and then when he finally returned he said it would be better to tell me the details, because they were so gruesome that I would probably faint if I read them in the paper."

"That would certainly be worse," Theo agreed. "And did he tell you?"

"Certainly. I did not faint," Nettie said with some dignity. "Even at the most disturbing aspects of the case."

"What were those?" Theo asked, his eyes wide.

Nettie leaned in and spoke in a stage whisper. "He said the prime minister was absolutely *coated* with blood."

"Monsters," Theo replied, widening his eyes as far as they would go. "I hope they confess."

"They are not likely to, since there was no murder weapon found on the scene."

Theo urged his face into an expression of amazed stupidity. "What does that mean?"

"It means that someone took the weapon. Someone else helped Elli and Countryman commit the murder."

"The Eerie woman!" Theo exclaimed.

"Precisely." Nettie sat back with a complacent air. "The Eerie woman. Who mysteriously vanished the day Bligh was found dead."

Theo shook his head and eyed Nettie with frank admiration. "Astounding. Well, he certainly knows what he's doing. I have no doubt your father will find her in no time."

—*10-Hour 31*—

THEO LEFT THE home of Inspector Grey in high spirits. He had learned little new about the murder, other than the fact that Goldenrod had disappeared, but he had learned everything he had hoped to about the detective's progress. He felt certain that any new development would be passed along to him by Nettie with alacrity. Grey was certainly on the wrong track. Perhaps with a little time and a few discreetly planted ideas, the investigation might find itself on the right one.

Theo was grinning as he passed a street corner where a boy was selling the midday paper. His grin froze and then evaporated when he read the top headline.

MP BROADGIRDLE VOWS TO CLEAR
MINISTER ELLI'S NAME

He snatched the paper.

"Hey, you have to pay for that," the boy protested.

Theo ignored him and read quickly, his eyes flying over the page.

I N A SURPRISE move, the minority leader, MP Gordon Broadgirdle, has recanted and declared himself the incarcerated minister's champion. Before a silent and rather nonplused parliament, Broadgirdle made a seven-minute speech on the morning of June 5, insisting that he was now convinced Minister of Relations with Foreign Ages Shadrack Elli and the explorer Miles Countryman had been wrongly accused of murder. He vowed to find the foreigner mentioned in his speech, an Eerie woman by the name of Goldenrod, whom he accused of being the true perpetrator of the crime.

Broadgirdle's speech astonished many in his own Western Party, who consider Minister Elli more of an adversary than a candidate for support and sympathy. Having been appointed by the murdered Prime Minister Bligh of the opposing New States Party, Elli frequently pursued policies directly against the Western Party's stated principles. Yet MP Broadgirdle contends that such partisan concerns cannot influence the pursuit of justice. "I know Minister Elli to be an honest, reliable, and patriotic man," he said near the end of his speech. "He would never commit such an atrocity and we owe it to both him and Bligh to find the real criminal." Broadgirdle's actions were immediately lauded by all and sundry as magnanimous and worthy of a great political leader.

"Pay for it or give it back," the boy growled at Theo.

Wordlessly, Theo returned it. He continued on his way, but his euphoric mood had been obliterated. What might have looked like good news at first glance was undoubtedly bad news. Theo knew what Broadgirdle's sudden and spirited defense really meant. It meant that he had used his leverage, and Shadrack had ceded. He had agreed to Broadgirdle's terms.

20
STALKING GRAVES

—1892, June 5: 12-Hour 39—

The Western Party was founded in 1870, with an acquisitive eye on the northern Baldlands. Always considered an unrealistic pursuit by the New States Party, expansion into the northern Baldlands was first proposed as a means of reining in the excesses of raiders, slavers, and ranchers who flourished in that region as lords in their improvised fiefdoms.

—From Shadrack Elli's History of New Occident

IT HAD TAKEN Theo more than two hours to climb the six blocks up Beacon Hill. The thought of setting eyes on the man known in Boston as Gordon Broadgirdle made him want to run and run until he could run no farther. Realizing he would see Broadgirdle—and that Broadgirdle would see *him*—turned his legs to stone. He stopped, wheeled his stolen Goodyear around, and walked slowly back down the hill. Then the thought of Shadrack and Miles in prison brought him to a halt once more. He considered that they had no way to discover the truth while they sat behind bars. He reminded himself of Grey's misguided investigation. Punching his leg, furious at his own unforgivable weakness, he turned and climbed two blocks uphill. He stopped again, overcome.

And so it went, for more than two hours, until he arrived at the corner, already exhausted, his palms sweating. But he arrived determined. *I'm here to prove he's guilty,* Theo told himself firmly. *I know he is, and I know there's evidence. I just have to find it. And once I find it, Shadrack and Miles will be let free.*

Broadgirdle owned one of the largest homes on Beacon Hill: a brick mansion on a corner lot. Most of the others crowded the curb, but his flaunted a long front yard protected from the street by a low, black fence of wrought iron. The curtains were open in every room, as if to declare that the occupant had nothing to hide from anyone.

Theo stood on the opposite corner, watching the mansion with a bitter smile. He could remember when the man known as Gordon Broadgirdle would not have been fit to appear on the sidewalk in Beacon Hill, much less inhabit one of its mansions. In those days, he went by "Wilkie Graves," and every piece of his tattered clothing was hung with silver bells. His teeth were long, jagged slivers of iron. He even wore gloves with iron claws, the better to make his point when someone disagreed with him—which was often.

It was quite a transformation, Theo admitted, as he watched Broadgirdle alighting from his coach and striding up his front drive. His hair and teeth and beard were new; even his walk was new—he carried himself with a kind of easy imperious- ness that suggested a long life of privilege. Theo remembered a more urgent, aggressive posture to his old adversary. But the eyes and the voice had not changed. Those were the same: terrifying.

Watching Broadgirdle in his fine suit, Theo thought involuntarily about the day he had met Wilkie Graves. The memory was one he had long ago tried to bury, along with everything else that touched upon Graves in the slightest. But it returned now, unbidden, fiercely vivid despite the years it had spent hidden away.

It had happened in a town very mistakenly named Paradise, a town as dry and dusty as any Theo had ever seen. He'd been on his own for two weeks, and food had been scarce.

The wagon was tied outside a tavern, and it was not the usual kind of wagon. Most travelers in the Baldlands used cotton canvas that would let the light through but block the worst of the heat and cold. This one was closed, made entirely of wood, with a door at the back. The door was chained and locked. Theo calculated that the wagon had to be full of valuables. Gold bars? Paper currency? *Food.* He began to imagine the links of sausages hung on hooks, the bags of grain, the barrels full of apples and potatoes. He was so hungry he would have eaten an onion raw and found it delicious. So alluring was the vision that he was drawn inexorably to the wagon, even though there were many easier marks in Paradise.

In retrospect, he always chided himself for not paying attention to the condition of the horses. If he hadn't been so hungry, he would have thought for a moment about their mistreated hooves and the lines of dried blood on their haunches. But the vision of what lay inside the wagon drew him onward, and he slipped his tools from his pouch and began working at the lock, the imagined feast becoming more fantastic by the moment.

That was how Graves found him: with his pick still in the lock and a stupid look of dreamy anticipation on his face. Graves had grinned, showing all his jagged teeth. He was holding a black guard dog on a leash, and the dog looked as hungry as Theo felt. "Take him, Sally," Graves said, in that booming voice Theo came to know so well. The dog leaped at him, and Theo put out his hand with the iron bones, knowing it would not be enough to stop the dog but hoping it would be enough to save his life.

Theo flinched at the memory. His heart was pounding. He raised the open newspaper he was holding as Broadgirdle paused in his doorway and turned to survey the street. Truly, he was almost unrecognizable. Only the voice really gave him away, for there were many men with cruel eyes. He said a brief word to his butler before passing into the foyer. The butler waved to the driver, who headed for the coach house.

But Wilkie Graves wasn't the only one who had transformed over the years; Theo had, too. He hadn't changed his name, but he was many years older and many years wiser. He'd last seen Graves when he was a boy of eleven: a lot shorter, a lot dirtier, and a lot sorrier. *He wouldn't recognize me if I stood right in front of him in full sunlight,* Theo told himself resolutely.

This thought, wrested out of the barest sliver of confidence, gave him the boost he needed. Wheeling his Goodyear away from the corner, he circled Broadgirdle's property. The mansion and its surrounding property took up a large portion of the block; its back garden bordered the street, instead of another yard. At either side of the house was a high brick wall covered with ivy; a door in the wall was firmly shut. But there was a decorative pattern—the silhouette of an owl—cut into the door, and it allowed a clear view into the garden.

Theo crouched down and peered through. He saw a shovel stuck into the ground beside a recently turned flower bed. Theo shifted to the right. Now he saw two pairs of men's legs. They stood on either side of the door to Broadgirdle's garden shed. Theo stood back up. *What are you up to, Graves?* he thought. *Why do you have men guarding your garden shed? Is this one of your old tricks, or something new?* Stepping up on one of the pedals of his Goodyear, he peered in through the owl cutaway higher up on the door.

With a muffled exclamation, Theo abruptly dropped down. He gave a low exhalation, long and slow. *Well, Graves,* he thought, *this is new. This is definitely new.* He swung his leg over the seat of the Goodyear and pedaled away as fast as he was able. Soon the steep descents of Beacon Hill had carried him far from Broadgirdle's house, but Theo's heart was still racing. He had seen the two men guarding the shed quite clearly. They were dressed in nondescript suits, they wore grappling hooks on their belts, and they had unmistakable scars along their cheeks: long lines that stretched from the corners of their mouths to their ears; scars that had been made by wires pulled tight against the skin.

21
QUARANTINE

—*1892, June 28: 6-Hour 00*—

The Order of the Golden Cross is among the most militant. It has built its wealth by collecting property abandoned by victims of the plague. Some have criticized the Order for benefitting from misfortune, but the Order argues that it functions as custodian for the plague, clearing the land of contagion and overseeing the houses of quarantine.

—From Fulgencio Esparragosa's
Complete and Authoritative History of the Papal States

SOPHIA FOLLOWED CAPTAIN Ponder through the ship and down into the hold. Dark and low-ceilinged, it was filled with crates stamped CANNED COD and JARRED MOLASSES and PRESERVES. The captain led her along a circuitous route through the piles of crates until they reached the very back of the hold. He held his lamp aloft. There, a tall box on wheels stood waiting. It was difficult to make out much beyond its shape. It was made of wood, and the lid, which presumably opened on hinges, had evenly spaced holes for aeration. She stood on tiptoe and tried to peer in, but the holes were too small and the hold too dark. A flutter of something green and brown was all she could see. The lid was held in place with a formidable padlock. Experimentally, she pushed her weight against one end of the box, and it rolled easily across the wooden floorboards.

Sophia was taken aback. She had been imagining something smaller: a letter or some precious packet. The planter looked less valuable and more cumbersome than she had expected. "Remorse left me a planter?"

"This is it."

Sophia considered her alternatives. They had arrived in Seville safely and in good time. In fact, they had arrived a few days early. The person sent by Remorse would not be expecting her yet, and Burr and Calixta would not arrive until July. She could not remain on the *Verity*; it would sail on for several months before returning to Boston. *If this is what I have to do to get the diary,* she said to herself, *then this is what I will do.* "I guess I will take it," she said reluctantly.

"I expect it will be difficult to move single-handedly," Captain Ponder said. "But I will ask the crew to roll it up while the plague cleric questions you."

"Thank you." As Sophia followed him back through the hold, she asked: "Do they take long? The plague clerics?"

"It will depend on whether there has been a recent outbreak. At times they are excessively meticulous, considering that we come from a foreign port. The threat is from within, not without, but the plague clerics are not ones to overly rely on logic." He stopped on the stairs and turned to her. "You don't have the cold that has afflicted some of the others, do you?"

"No—I'm fine."

"Just as well. A cold is a cold, but, as I said—the clerics are not renowned for their sound logic."

Sophia considered this. "Have you ever known someone who suffered from the plague?"

"Once I almost stopped in a port farther north, where the plague had struck years earlier. As far as I could tell there was no one left alive. Even from a distance, I could see the bones of the inhabitants littering the dock."

—9-Hour 42—

THE ENTRY TO Seville was by the Rio de Guadalquivir, which divided the city into one greater and one lesser portion. The long harbor along the riverbank was almost deserted. One ship near the *Verity* was casually guarded by a sleeping mariner and a brown dog. Three more ships lay abandoned, their masts sagging wearily toward the murky water. Dusty orange trees lined a road to a great stone archway, beyond which a slow traffic of people and horses made its way along the cobblestones. The buildings near the river, with chipped white walls and red tiles, had a faded aspect, as if they had been exhausted by the sun.

Sophia had been waiting on the dock for more than an hour. The pealing of bells from the cathedral sounded, echoed by bells from smaller chapels throughout the city. For a moment Seville seemed a lively place, filled with cheerful cacophony. Then the chiming faded, and the silence seemed all the more mournful and ominous.

Sophia wanted only to get out of the sun. She was last in

line to be questioned by the plague cleric. One by one, the Nihilismian missionaries had been allowed to pass into the city, carrying their few belongings. The two remaining Nihilismians, Whence and Partial, middle-aged women who were singular only by virtue of their occasional displays of kindness to one another, stood quietly, studiously ignoring her.

The punishing sun reminded Sophia of the Baldlands. She tried to take what relief she could by crouching behind the planter, but even in the rectangle of shade, the heat was overwhelming. The cleric conferred with his scribe as he approached Whence and Partial. He was an older man, with only a few strands of hair, a pair of bushy eyebrows, and no chin to speak of. His teeth were yellowed and crooked. The robes he wore, in white, black, and red, seemed entirely unsuited to the fierce Seville sun, but he appeared not to notice the heat.

The cleric stopped before Partial, examined her in silence, and then spoke rapidly in Castilian to his scribe, who made a series of slow, deliberate annotations. He held his hands clasped before him and peered at Partial with milky blue eyes. "You arrive today from New Occident?" the cleric asked, in accented English.

Partial nodded.

"Why do you arrive?"

"I am Nihilismian. I am here on a mission."

"What is this mission?"

She sighed. "To set the Papal States on the true path."

"And what is the true path?"

Partial did not respond. She seemed to be melting where

she stood. Coughing suddenly, she let her head drop onto Whence's shoulder. "Whence can tell you about the true path," she murmured.

The cleric glanced at his scribe, and the scribe nodded. "Are you feeling unwell?"

"She is unwell," Whence said, "but it is only a common cold. She is tired from the journey and the heat." She put her arm around Partial.

"How long has she been unwell?"

"Some four days. She needs water and rest, that is all."

The cleric eyed Whence dispassionately and turned once more to Partial. Eyes closed, breathing deeply, she appeared to have fallen asleep on Whence's shoulder. There were beads of sweat on her upper lip and forehead. The cleric's bushy eyebrows drew together in a frown. He spoke quietly in Castilian and the scribe nodded. Walking quickly along the dock, the scribe disappeared into the stone archway that led to the city.

"Where is he going?" Whence asked irritably. "We have been here for an hour already. Are we almost done?"

"Almost," the cleric said with composure. He clasped his hands before him again, and waited.

Sophia felt the time pass slowly, but it was only a few minutes later that a pair of horsemen emerged, accompanied by the scribe. A flash of cold traveled down her spine, and she rose to her feet with a sense of foreboding. The two horsemen wore white, hooded robes that glittered in the sunlight. Their faces were obscured by golden masks: long, hooked beaks and narrow slits for eyes made them into ominous, brilliant birds.

Sophia found herself thinking of the Nochtland guard; somehow, these golden horsemen appeared even more forbidding.

They dismounted when they reached the dock and walked unhurriedly beside the scribe. As they approached, Sophia saw that their long robes shimmered from golden thread that had been woven into the white cloth. Each wore a heavy belt and a long sword in a scabbard. One of the men tossed back his hood as he approached, revealing a mass of golden curls. They did not remove their masks. With a brief nod, the plague cleric spoke to the horsemen and gestured to Partial. The golden beaks nodded in reply. Then, without so much as a word, they stepped forward and took Partial by the arms.

"What are you doing?" Whence exclaimed. She reached out, clinging to her friend's listless hand.

Partial awoke enough to object and push feebly at the hands that held her. The horsemen took no notice. Half guiding, half carrying her toward the horses, they led her away. "Where are you taking me?" Partial protested. She batted ineffectually at the masked men.

"What is happening?" Whence asked the cleric at the same time.

"Your companion has *lapena*," the cleric said calmly.

"*What?* No—no, she doesn't. It's just a cold and she is exhausted by the heat."

"We shall see."

"But where are they taking her?"

"To quarantine."

"You can't take her to quarantine. There will be others with the plague there!"

The cleric nodded. "All those with plague must be isolated."

"But she doesn't *have* the plague!" Whence's voice had grown shrill.

The cleric examined her for a moment in silence. "How can you be certain? She has all the signs. She is tired and does not care for life. She can hardly be roused."

"*Does not care for life? She is tired, that's all!*"

"Her signs are advanced," the cleric said with an air of finality. The men with the golden beaks were leaving the dock, one of them leading the horses and the other leading Partial. "You are her travel companion, are you not? What remains is to see if you, also, have any signs of these plagues."

Whence fell suddenly silent. She stared at the cleric with horror. Then she straightened her skirts and stood at her full height. "Very well. Ask me your questions. You will see that I am not in the least unwell."

The cleric squinted at her thoughtfully. "You arrive today from New Occident?" he asked, commencing his litany of questions once more.

As Whence answered, Sophia watched, wide-eyed. She could hardly believe it had happened so fast. The Nihilismian was gone. She would be placed in quarantine, and if there was anyone there with the plague, she would surely fall ill. Sophia's heart pounded, and her attention drifted. She felt a mixture of relief, shame, and fear: relief that she was not being led away by the men with golden masks; shame at her sense of relief; and fear that the same fate would befall her. It could not. It would not.

The plague cleric nodded at Whence, concluding his questioning. "It is well; you may enter Seville."

Whence nodded in return. "Thank you." Sophia could see that the Nihilismian was deeply shaken. She picked up her satchel and Partial's without a word and walked slowly toward the city.

The plague cleric turned to Sophia and the scribe looked up, expectantly, prepared to take down her replies.

"You arrive today from New Occident?" the cleric asked.

"Yes," Sophia replied, a false smile stretching across her face.

"Why do you arrive?"

"I am here to look for my parents. They came this way many years ago, and I hope to find them."

The man considered this in silence. Then he echoed, "You hope to find them."

"Yes. I am on my way to Granada, to the Nihilismian depository, to find a document written by my mother."

The cleric took this in. Then he nodded slightly in the direction of the planter. "And what is this?"

"This is a container with plants." Sophia realized, as she gave her reply, that the heavy lock might cause some suspicion. But she could not pretend it was hers. If the cleric asked to see inside the box, she would be unable to open it.

"And why do you bring it?"

"I am transporting it for a friend. It is a gift for someone in Seville."

"Do you have the name and address of this person?"

Sophia opened her satchel and took out *Map Vendors in Every (Known) Age*. She had seen an entry for Seville, and she turned the pages as calmly as she could. "Gilberto Jerez," she said to the cleric, finding the entry in her book. "Calle Abades."

The cleric looked at her in silence for a moment. He spoke rapidly in Castilian to the scribe, who had been making careful note of Sophia's replies, and the scribe responded. Then the cleric asked her, in a practiced way, "Have you recently been visited by visions or apparitions of any kind?"

Sophia paused, feeling her heart lurch. "No, I haven't."

"Do you assert that you love the life granted to you by God?"

"Yes."

"Do you wish this life to end?"

"No."

"Do you suffer from any declining spirits or do you know anyone," he paused, "anyone in addition to the traveler called"—he turned to the scribe, who made a brief reply from his notes— "called Par-shal, who suffers from such declining spirits?"

"No, I don't."

"If you should fall into a decline of spirits, do you accept that you must leave the city, isolating yourself, so that you may die without contaminating those who love life?"

Sophia hesitated at the sudden prospect of such a terrible fate. The cleric watched her closely. "Yes, I do accept," Sophia said.

"State your name and place of origin."

"Every Tims, Boston, New Occident."

"It is well. You may enter Seville," the cleric said. The scribe finished his notes.

"Thank you," Sophia said.

"You will find," the cleric added, as he prepared to leave, "that you will not be able to make the delivery of this plant. Gilberto Jerez died last year of the plague."

22
FALCONER AND PHANTOM

—June 29: 10-Hour 13—

*It was soon discovered by those who hunted them that the Fourwings'
golden eyes remained bright and luminous, even after the creatures died.
Longer lasting than beeswax or tallow, the eyes could be used in place of
candles or oil lamps. For a time they were used in the streetlamps of Seville
and Granada, until it became clear that the residents would steal every last
one of the precious orbs. Now they are only used in private homes.*

—From Fulgencio Esparragosa's
Complete and Authoritative History of the Papal States

THE PLANTER WAS far heavier than Sophia had imagined. She
was able to pull it along the wooden dock without too much
difficulty, but once she reached the cobblestone streets her
progress slowed. The stones were rounded and uneven, and
the planter pitched and jammed at every step. Sophia's pack,
riding on the lower shelf of the planter, shifted back and forth,
sliding off more than once.

The dusty orange trees were motionless in the brilliant sun.
With significant effort, Sophia reached the main plaza, where
the half-built cathedral of Seville stretched upward into the

blue sky, all vaulted towers and pointed spires. Sophia had read in Esparragosa's history that construction had begun centuries before the Great Disruption. Now, with the stagnation brought about by the plague, the unfinished cathedral seemed like an abandoned fantasy.

Her progress drew some attention. A woman wearing a long veil walked by holding two little girls by the hands. The girls, dressed in long white dresses that trailed over the paving stones, stared at Sophia with undisguised fascination. Three old men who sat near the cathedral talking, their faces withered as dried apricots, chuckled silently with their toothless mouths, pointing at the planter. At the corner where she turned off the plaza, an old woman knelt on a folded woolen blanket, her hands outstretched in supplication.

Sophia had nothing to give her. With a desperate yank, she left the plaza and trudged on, pulling the planter into the shade. She had as her goal the bookstore listed in *Map Vendors in Every (Known) Age*. Even if Gilberto Jerez had died, perhaps the store was still open. And she had to find food. Though she had brought New Occident money, she had no gold or currency of any kind accepted in the Papal States.

She had consulted her map of Seville while still at the harbor, and she followed it now in her mind, stubbornly hauling the planter over the cobblestones, even though her legs trembled and the sweat ran down her forehead. Sophia began to question her choice. Perhaps leaving the planter on the *Verity* would have been better. Surely she could negotiate help from

Remorse's associate without it. If he appeared, that would mean he wanted to help her and would be disposed to overlook the missing planter—wouldn't he? Sophia felt her thoughts grow muddled in the heat.

Suddenly, the planter seemed to glide forward of its own accord, and Sophia stumbled forward. Hurriedly stepping aside, she turned to see what had happened. A tall man wearing a hooded cape had pushed the planter with the palm of his hand; now he stopped. "Looked like you could use a hand," he said dryly in English. His voice was deep and accented. Sophia had heard the accent before from explorers who visited Shadrack; he was from the Closed Empire. Beneath the hood she saw a stubbled chin, dark blond hair the color and length of her own, and a Roman nose. His eyes were obscured by the hood's shadow. Sophia squinted dubiously, taking in his worn boots, the long sword visible under his cape, and the bow and quiver slung over his shoulder. His hand was still resting against the planter. "Go on," he said, as if he were a mule driver. "I'll push."

Too tired to argue, Sophia took up the handle at the front of the planter. They made quick progress, and Sophia strained to keep the map straight in her mind. They passed a street packed with butcher shops, where the meat hung in the shade and the flies described slow circles at every entryway. Then they turned on a narrow passage where two young women sat in a doorway, carding wool. A chapel tucked back from the road filled the air with the heavy scent of incense. Sophia glanced into an open shop where dried lavender hung in bunches from the ceiling. White candles of all sizes were neatly stacked on the store's wooden shelves. After several minutes of walking through the quiet streets, they reached the address in the Jewish quarter. Sophia stopped and wiped her brow. "This is it," she said. She turned to the gray-hooded man. "Thank you."

"You are welcome," he said shortly, and headed back the way they'd come.

Sophia watched him go, astonished. *Even the friendly people in Seville are unfriendly,* she thought. As the hooded man walked away, he raised his left wrist, and with an almost silent flutter of wings, a gray-brown bird of prey settled on his leather-bound forearm. The bird turned to stare back at Sophia, its black eyes disconcertingly bright.

There was a tiny patch of shade where the rooftops blocked the sun, and she stood there, catching her breath. The narrow street could have been beautiful, with its flower boxes and painted doorways and colorfully shuttered windows. The cobblestones, wretched as they were for hauling the planter, reminded her of East Ending Street. But the very air seemed to carry suspicion and neglect. Several of the houses were visibly abandoned, with littered doorways and broken windows. The plague had taken a heavy toll.

She knocked on the door of the map store with a sense of apprehension. Its sign hung lopsided on a single nail, and the shuttered windows did not appear to invite customers. No one answered, and Sophia knocked again with a sinking heart. After knocking a third time and receiving no reply, she slumped down in the doorway. Finding the map store had been her only inspiration.

Sophia let her head fall back against the door of the map store and tried to prevent herself from panicking. Reaching into her pocket, she clutched the spool of silver thread for reassurance. She longed to be safely home in Boston. When she thought about home—Shadrack, Theo's homecoming, Mrs. Clay's maple cake—she felt tears welling up in her eyes. She wished powerfully for Theo, who not only would have known what to do in such a situation but would have made light of it. She smiled at the thought, but it did not stop the tears from falling. They were so salty they hurt. *I need water,* Sophia realized. *That's why I'm so weak and confused.* The thought made her feel even more overwhelmed and helpless. Somewhere down the street, a door opened and closed. Sophia opened her eyes and peered in both directions, shielding her face with her hand. *I am not helpless,* she told herself. *I will knock on every one of these doors—someone must be kind enough to give me some food and water.*

Dragging herself to her feet, Sophia shouldered her satchel, crossed the narrow street, and knocked on the low blue door directly in front of her. No one answered. She knocked again. A sound came from within, and though the door did not open a small window within it, covered with iron grating, did. Sophia looked hopefully at the window, which was just at eye level. An old woman peered out at her. "Please," Sophia said in English. "Can you spare some food or water?" She bunched her fingers together and lifted them to her mouth, then pretended to hold a glass and tipped it back. "Please?" The woman stared at her for a moment longer, and then, without a word, the little window was slammed shut.

It felt to Sophia like a physical blow, but the first rejection stung the most. Next door, no one answered, and in the third house she had a string of incomprehensible words hurled at her and another window slammed in her face. The fourth and fifth houses looked abandoned, but she knocked anyway. No one answered. The sixth had flowers in its flowerpots, and the shutters were open. The door, to match the shutters, was painted bright yellow. Unlike the others, it had no little window. Sophia knocked as firmly as she dared.

After only a few seconds, the door opened slightly, and a young woman looked out. "Could you please spare any food or water?" Sophia asked, miming again. The woman paused, as if undecided. Her hair was tied back with a handkerchief, and she wore a full apron over her blue dress. The apron was covered with flour. Suddenly, there was a tussle of movement at her skirts and a small boy, no more than three years old, appeared at the woman's knee. He pushed the door wider to get a better view and gaped up at Sophia. His cheeks were dusted with flour. Sophia smiled at him, her dry lips cracking. "Hi," she said to him with a small wave.

"Ay," he said back, mimicking her wave.

The woman had watched in silence, and then she bent forward and said something to the little boy, who disappeared abruptly as if pulled away by a string. She turned back to Sophia and, saying something in Castilian, pointed down the street. Her tone seemed encouraging, but Sophia had no idea what she meant.

"I don't understand," Sophia said.

"*Agua*," the woman said. "*Agua*," she repeated for emphasis. She made a motion with her hands, placing one over the other as if, Sophia thought, she were climbing a rope. No, she realized—drawing water from a well!

"Oh! Thank you."

The woman held up her finger, signalling for Sophia to wait. A moment later the little boy reappeared, and he held up to his mother a brown loaf dotted with raisins. The woman smiled, kissed the boy on the top of the head, and whispered something. Obediently, he turned and offered the loaf to Sophia.

Clearly, the exhaustion was making her weepy. She felt tears in her eyes for the second time that hour as she reached out to take the loaf. "Thank you so much," she said. "I will never forget your kindness. Thank you."

The boy gave her a shy smile and folded his hands together over his stomach. The woman smiled as well, pointing again down the street.

With another effusive expression of thanks, Sophia waved and turned away. She bit into the loaf of bread as she walked, and even though her mouth was dry and she had difficulty swallowing, it tasted delicious. The loaf was sweetened with honey, and the raisins seemed to explode on her tongue. As the narrow street curved, she found herself entering a tiny plaza. At the very middle of the deserted plaza was a stone well. Sophia hurried toward it with a gratified cry of victory. Placing the precious, unfinished loaf in her satchel, she hooked the bucket onto the clasp and lowered it into the well. The sound of the bucket hitting the water was more exquisite than she could have imagined. She drew it up, hauling hand over hand, and seized it as soon as it was within view. The water was wonderful. Drinking her fill, she placed the bucket on the stone lip of the well and sank down with a sigh. She felt immeasurably better. Her circumstances no longer seemed quite so dire; after all, she had food and water, and wasn't that the most important thing?

Sophia got up to retrieve the planter and her pack, and as she did so she suddenly thought about the plants. If she was parched from the heat and sun, how must they be? Sophia hauled up a full bucket of water from the well and carried it out of the tiny plaza and along the narrow street. Pouring the water in through the perforated lid required a little creative climbing, but once she had a foothold on the window ledge of the abandoned map shop, she was able to empty the bucket. She peered down into the small, round holes and thought she could make out some green stems here and there.

After returning the bucket to the well, Sophia again began to feel exhausted. She had no idea what she would do next, but having secured food and water felt like sufficient accomplishment. Finding as much shade as she could behind the planter in the doorway of the abandoned shop, Sophia curled up against her pack. Within minutes, she was fast asleep.

—6-Hour 42—

SOPHIA AWOKE TO an unpleasant prodding sensation, and she opened her eyes to a street that was already gray with dusk. Standing in front of her and speaking urgently in Castilian was an old man. He jabbed her shoulder with a long pole. "Ow," Sophia said, seizing the end of the cane. "Don't do that. I'm awake."

The man responded angrily in Castilian, and Sophia got to her feet. "I don't understand you." She frowned, and the combined effect of her frown and her words seemed to temporarily silence him.

"*La-pe-na?*" he asked very slowly and distinctly.

"No," Sophia replied emphatically, shaking her head. "No, I'm not sick. I'm just tired." She tucked her hands beside her head to mime sleeping, and then for good measure she threw in the gestures for food and water. Perhaps if the old man was concerned, he would want to help.

Instead, these gestures seemed to make him immediately lose interest. Placing the end of his pole firmly on the cobblestones and glaring at her with the full weight of his bushy eyebrows, he said something dismissive and turned away. Sophia watched him limp slowly down the street and sighed. She wondered if the young woman who had given her bread was the only kind person in all of Seville. The old man walked a few more paces, then raised his pole to the nearest streetlamp. With an expert movement he passed a tiny flame into the lamp, lighting the candle within. He lowered the pole and moved on.

Sinking down again in the doorway, Sophia rubbed her eyes. Even with the lamplight the narrow street was getting dark. It had not yet grown cold, but the declining sun had left the air cool and dry, and Sophia had no wish to spend the night out of doors. Nor did she want to ask for help again from the kind young woman. Rising to her feet, she looked both ways and tried to gauge her chances of finding shelter in one of the empty homes. She squinted. It was really getting dark, she realized.

Suddenly, a shape at the end of the street near the plaza caught her eye. Was someone standing in one of the doorways? It looked like a woman—Sophia could see the shape of her skirts. For a moment Sophia thought it might be the woman who had helped her, but then she realized that it was a different door. The figure began to move, gliding along the cobblestones in Sophia's direction. Sophia stepped out into the street, a little flicker of hope lighting within her. Perhaps someone had seen her sleeping and would take pity on her. "Hello?"

The figure moved closer, but it remained in the shadows. Sophia squinted. "Hello?" she repeated. Then the figure made a gesture, and Sophia recognized her.

"Is it you?" Sophia whispered. The pale figure took another step. "You followed me here?" Her voice shook. She paused, and the word slipped out like a secret breathed into the ear of the Fates. "Mother?"

Sophia drew closer. Though she could discern Minna's pale outline, the details of her face and dress were obscured. Her face lifted slightly, and more by this than by any expression she appeared to smile. *"The falconer and the hand that blooms will go with you,"* Minna whispered.

"What?" Sophia replied.

"The falconer and the hand that blooms will go with you." Minna raised her hand, stretching it outward.

Sophia took another step forward, her arm raised in response.

Without warning, a sound like a whistling reed hissed past her ear. At the same moment, a whir of movement disturbed the air. The object that had hurtled past her collided directly with the pale figure, embedding itself deeply and soundlessly, like a knife plunged into a pillow. The apparition collapsed and disintegrated.

"No!" Sophia cried, rushing forward. She ran to where the figure had fallen, but all that remained was a long stem of a pale green wood with a blunt point: a rude arrow cut fresh from a branch. It was unmarked, intact, as if it had hit nothing at all. Sophia looked down the street and saw the man with the gray hood, his hood now pushed back, walking toward her with his bow in his hand. "What have you done?" she cried.

"Nothing of consequence," he said brusquely.

"Where is she? She might still be here." Sophia looked wildly up and down the street.

The bowman took her firmly by the arm. "Stop," he said. "She's not here."

"Let go of me! I have to find her." She tried to shake him off.

"I said stop," the bowman repeated evenly. "Listen to me. That specter in the shadows is not what you think it is or who you think it is. It is an illusion."

"How do you know?" Sophia realized she was weeping. "How do you know? You know nothing about her. I have to find her." She tried to pull away against the bowman's grip.

"I can tell you for sure." He took her shoulders in his hands so that his face was directly in front of hers. "I promise you on my life," he said slowly, "that the thing you saw a moment ago was an illusion. It was sent for one purpose: to draw you away and into oblivion."

Sophia cried and shook her head.

"I can prove it to you," he said softly. "Would you like me to prove it to you?"

She shook her head again.

"Look over my shoulder." He knelt on the cobblestones so that Sophia could easily see the street behind him.

She gasped and started, but the bowman held her fast. "Look carefully," he insisted. There was a pale figure in the shadows several houses away. Tall, broad-shouldered, and with a slightly drooping head, it stood languidly by the wall.

"Who is it?" Sophia whispered.

"It is no one. Watch." Without rising, he swiveled on his knees. He took the freshly cut branch that lay at Sophia's feet, drew his bow, and loosed the arrow. It struck home, plunging soundlessly into the pale figure, which disintegrated as if it had never been. The arrow clattered onto the cobblestones. "Did you see that?" the archer asked.

"Yes."

"And do you know how I know that specter is no one I have ever loved or wished with all my heart to find?" he asked, his voice hard.

"How?"

"Because I have sent my arrow into its heart every night for the last two years."

23

DOUBTING THE CHAMPION

—1892, June 6: 9-Hour 00—

During the first half of the century, most members of parliament lived on Beacon Hill. Its proximity to the State House makes it convenient, and its views are not unpleasant. After 1850, MPs began acquiring homes on Commonwealth Avenue, near the public garden. The promenade, the flatter walkways, and the greater space for erecting palatial residences have drawn wealthier residents of Boston—MPs and ordinary citizens alike.

—From Shadrack Elli's History of New Occident

THEO APPROACHED NETTIE Grey's house with high hopes. He had spent the night pondering the case, and while he could not quite see the connections yet, he knew they were there.

The Eerie whom Miles had told him about, Goldenrod, had been attacked by a Sandman. The Sandmen were working for Broadgirdle. Goldenrod had been convalescing at Bligh's house. And now Bligh was dead and Goldenrod was gone. The connections lay somewhere in the questions he still could not answer. How had Broadgirdle come to work with the Sandmen? Why would he want to attack an Eerie woman? Where had Goldenrod vanished to? What did she have to do with Bligh's death? Theo shook his head. He wished, for the hundredth time, that

Sophia were there to help him think it through. She always saw the connections before anyone else did.

But he hoped, as he approached the window of the Grey residence, that Inspector Grey had discovered something in the last twenty hours that would make all the connections clear.

Nettie was practicing scales again. Theo watched her with a bemused smile. She played a scale, stopped, stared out over the piano, twirled her hair around one of her fingers, stared some more, and played another scale. Theo tapped on the glass.

He was rewarded with a look of wide-eyed excitement; she had been expecting him. She gave a little wave. "Good morning!" she said happily, as she opened the window. "Is it already nine?"

Theo smiled broadly. "Good morning, Nettie. It is. I wanted to arrive earlier, but we said nine and I waited until nine. I was ready to see you hours earlier."

Nettie gave a pleased little smile in response and opened the window more widely. Then her face collapsed into an expression of dismay. "I'm so glad you're here, because I have the most shocking thing to tell you. I've been going over it and over it in my mind, and the weight of it is almost unbearable."

Climbing deftly over the sill and guiding her over to the poppy-patterned sofa, Theo said with concern, "Of course, Nettie. You can tell me anything. What is it?"

Nettie fanned her face, as if the unbearable thoughts were breaking out like blisters on her cheeks. "Charles, I am so worried. I knew when my father began this investigation that it would relate to Matters of State, but I had no idea how much.

Now I'm afraid Matters of State have come crashing down upon us like a tidal wave, and it has fallen to my poor father to somehow turn the tide."

Theo shook his head sympathetically. "Your poor father," he echoed.

"Oh, Charles, you have no idea." She dropped her voice. "New Occident is on the brink of disaster, and my father is the only one who can prevent it."

Theo's face obligingly took on an expression of awe, admiration, and anxiety. "What in Fates' name do you mean?"

"Here is the thing," she said, pausing for a moment in order to draw out the suspense. "Father spoke yesterday to the prisoners who were arrested for murdering Prime Minister Bligh."

"Yes?" Theo asked encouragingly.

"At first one of the prisoners resisted and would not speak to him at all."

He pursed his lips. "How rude."

"But finally Father won them over, and persuaded them to tell him everything."

"They confessed?"

"No." Nettie shook her head, and her curls bounced. "But he learned that Prime Minister Bligh was trying to prevent the New Occident parliament from declaring an embargo on the United Indies."

"You mean the Indies embargo on New Occident," Theo corrected her automatically. "How shocking."

Nettie stood up and crossed her arms. She looked down at him with narrowed eyes, her expression entirely altered. "Yes, shocking." Her voice had lost its high-pitched lilt. "I am shocked that you already knew that the embargo would be an Indies embargo. I am shocked that you've pretended not to know anything about any of this, when you clearly know a great deal." She gave him a shrewd smile. "Who are you? And why are you so interested in the investigation into Bligh's murder?"

Theo looked up at her, thunderstruck. He hardly recognized the girl who stood before him. She had the same elaborately ribboned shoes and the same frilly dress with the same smattering of pearls, but her pretty face was twisted into a fierce scowl. "I . . ." He was momentarily lost for words.

"You thought I was a brainless brat who would spill information to a stranger. You thought it was an easy way to get to Inspector Grey. I can see that. It's quite obvious, Charles. What I can't see is why. Are you working for the murderer? Are *you* the murderer?"

"No!" Theo exclaimed, aghast. He jumped to his feet. "No, I'm not the murderer. I knew Bligh; I liked him. I . . ." He ran a hand through his hair. "Look, I'll be straight with you."

"Please," Nettie replied.

"I work for Shadrack Elli. He's my employer—and a friend. And he is innocent. I know he is. I'm just trying to do everything I can to prove it. He and Miles didn't commit this murder, but someone else did, and that person has to be found."

"Why not leave that to the police?"

"I'm sure the police will conduct a good investigation. But what if the person who murdered Bligh is smart enough to make it seem like Shadrack and Miles really did commit the crime? The police don't know them like I do. It's their job to suspect anyone and everyone. Just by doing their jobs, they might accuse the wrong people."

Nettie listened to him pensively, and when he was done she tapped her fingers on her arm as if playing rapid notes. Then she sighed. "As it happens, I agree with you."

"You do?"

"Yes. I don't think Elli and Countryman are guilty. The evidence is both neat and partial in a suspicious way. And they really have no motive. I don't believe the hogwash about Bligh changing his entire political outlook. He wasn't the type. His political philosophy was formed over decades, matured deeply through personal experience. He would not throw it over for expedience or ambition or greed."

Theo stared at her with genuine astonishment.

Nettie laughed. "I wish you could see your face."

"I just . . ." He shook his head. "The act is very convincing," he said with admiration. "You're a real pro."

"Thank you," she said, smiling slightly. "I appreciate the compliment. This one is sincere, apparently."

"It is." Theo grinned.

Nettie gave a little pout, seeming for a brief second like her old self. "I know my piano playing is monstrous." She sat on the couch. "But it helps me think."

Theo joined her. "So if you don't think Miles and Shadrack are guilty, do you think your father will figure it out?"

Nettie waved her hand dismissively. "My dear father! He is

a sweetheart, but he is the most literal-minded man in New Occident. He has no imagination. He thinks of evidence as little building blocks, to be stacked up into a rigid tower, when they are really pieces of a story."

"But then how is he so successful?"

Nettie looked at him with raised eyebrows. "Really? Still haven't figured that out?"

Theo was newly shocked. "*You?*"

"There's a reason he's done so well in the last three years."

"How do you do it?"

She sighed. "I can't injure his pride, poor man. So I break into his study. I read all his notes on a case. And I see what's there—what's *really* there. Then I make little suggestions. Oh, believe me, it is tricky," she continued, fully engaged. "Most of the time he only gives me an overall sense of the case, and it taxes my ingenuity something awful to think of ways to point him in the right direction without letting on that I know as much as I do."

Theo whistled. "Wow." He sat up straighter. "Why are you telling me all this?"

Nettie sat back and twirled a curl around her finger. "Because I could use some help. Someone on the ground. I don't have the mobility you have." The fierce scowl was back. "On the night of Bligh's murder I tried to go out and investigate, and look what happened. Mrs. Culcutty worked herself up into a frenzy." She shook her head with frustration. "This is going to be the most important crime of the decade, and I want to solve it."

Theo considered her, impressed. He had no doubt that Nettie Grey would make a formidable ally or a formidable foe. It was far better to have her on his side. "Well, *I* am mobile."

Nettie grinned. "Excellent. We have a deal. You tell me what you find and I'll tell you what I find."

"Done." As he spoke, Theo realized he would not be able to tell Nettie about the knife and the bloodied clothes, because he could not tell her who he really was and why he had been present at the discovery of Bligh's body. And he was reluctant to talk about Broadgirdle, since his reasons for suspecting the man were ones he would never discuss. *But I can tell her some things without telling her how I know them,* he decided. "You first."

"No, *you* first," Nettie replied, "as a show of good faith."

Theo grinned. "Fair enough. The woman everyone thinks murdered Bligh—Goldenrod? I know who she is, and I know how she ended up at Bligh's." He repeated what Miles had told him, omitting nothing but the explanation of how he had tangled with Sandmen the previous summer. "I've tracked down one or two men in Boston who use grappling hooks," he finished. "That's the lead I'm following now."

"Fascinating." Nettie had listened attentively and without interruption, more than once pulling on a brown curl and giving it a pensive chew. "Especially given what I have to tell you. About the examiner's report of the body."

"Which is?"

"The injuries were not made by a knife. In fact, the examiner could not say what instrument made them. He said there were fourteen entry wounds, and the instrument had barbed points."

"Grappling hooks have barbed points," Theo said.

"They do." Nettie twirled her hair thoughtfully. "So whoever attacked Goldenrod may have killed Bligh. There's a story here we're not seeing. Perhaps Goldenrod knows something about what's happening in the Indian Territories—something she reported to Bligh, something that someone wants concealed."

"Like what?"

"Like a railroad being built illegally or something like that."

"Maybe," Theo said, unconvinced.

"Or it could have to do with these Weatherers—the missing Eerie who never made it to Boston. Perhaps something happened to them, and Goldenrod was prevented from discovering it."

"That would make sense."

"Well, we need more, Charles," Nettie concluded. "We need more pieces of the story." She raised her eyebrows. "What is your next step?"

"I'm going to keep an eye on these men with grappling hooks. See if I can learn more about what they're doing."

"That sounds good. And I'm going to see what I can find in Bligh's papers. Father brought several boxes of them home." She gave a sly smile. "And he never looks at the sheet music I keep on the piano stand. You know how my teacher *insists* on my practicing scales."

BEACON HILL WAS picturesque even in darkness. The streetlamps cast yellow light into the humid summer air, and the brick buildings seemed to lean away from them, their windows tightly shuttered. Theo walked silently across the cobblestones. He had left his stolen Goodyear at the foot of the hill, tied to a lamppost. As he approached Broadgirdle's mansion, he slowed his pace. When he reached the brick wall, he peered through the hole in the garden door. Ordinarily, it would have been difficult to see anything in the darkness, but the back of the house was illuminated by a pair of flame lamps. Sure enough, two Sandmen were stationed before the garden shed.

Theo waited. As twenty-hour approached, he heard the footsteps that he was expecting: four police officers hurriedly made their way up Broadgirdle's front walk. They passed through the gate, and one of the officers pounded on the door. A light went on in a second-story window. Theo smiled to himself in the darkness, but the smile was as much to encourage himself as it was to celebrate the success of this first step. He was deeply nervous.

More lights appeared, and finally, some minutes later, Theo heard the front door open. Broadgirdle's booming voice cut through the still night. "Well, officers? What are you doing here at this hour?"

"Mr. Broadgirdle, we received an anonymous tip that your life was in danger."

"In danger? From what?"

"The note said that you were entertaining guests this evening and that one of them meant to assassinate you."

There was a pause. "Does it look to you like I am entertaining guests?"

"Well, no, Mr. Broadgirdle, but we would nonetheless like to be certain. Especially after the tip that warned us of the prime minister's murder at Minister Elli's house. That one was correct, after all."

"Very well. Come in."

The officers entered, closing the door behind them. More lights were illumined on the ground floor. And then the rear door of the house opened.

"Mortify, Until!" Broadgirdle bellowed into the darkness.

Theo heard the scuffle of boots and then the rear door closing. He hurried to where the wrought-iron fence met the brick wall. Scrabbling up the fence, he peered into the garden. It looked deserted. He swung up onto the top of the wall, then dropped down. As his feet landed, the tension in his stomach crested, setting all of his nerves off like alarm bells. He did not have much time. Broadgirdle would allow the policemen to search the house, but his patience would soon wear thin.

Theo padded quickly and quietly toward the shed. A light was on inside; it shone dully through the dirty windows. The door was padlocked. *Of course it is,* Theo thought grimly. He could hear Broadgirdle protesting from somewhere inside the house. Rounding the shed, Theo found two windows—firmly latched—and one small casement window, facing the brick wall, that was propped open. *Gotcha, Graves!* he thought. The space between the garden shed and the brick wall was tight—perhaps a foot and a half. Climbing into the shed was out of the question. But perhaps the window would open wide enough to let him see inside.

Theo shimmied up the wall, propping one foot on the bricks and the other on the shed until he was just below the window. Then he pulled it open as far as the wall behind him would allow and peered in.

A single gas lamp sat on a worn wooden worktable in the center of the room. Pruning shears, a watering can, and a roll of twine sat beside the lamp. Rakes and brooms, shovels, and a few broken beams filled one corner; empty wooden planters were stacked in another. Along the walls were more work-tables covered with gardening supplies: pots, spades, burlap sacks of dirt. A chair stood by the worktable.

There was nothing unusual in the room. It looked just like an ordinary potting shed. Theo squinted, willing the room to come into focus, waiting for the secret guarded by the Sandmen to reveal itself. Nothing happened.

Broadgirdle's voice reached him clearly from an open window on the second floor. "Are you satisfied now? I would like to get back to sleep."

Theo shook his head in frustration. He had only a moment before the Sandmen returned. Suddenly the lamp flickered, and the pruning shears, left carelessly open, took on a different aspect. Was that rust on the cutting edge of the shears, or blood?

Unbidden, a memory of driving Graves's wagon broke over him. It was the first time Theo had been tasked with driving it, and Graves assigned it to him only because the wagon was empty. The air was deadly dry. The horses were slow and, as always, they were injured. Their smell wafted up behind them, and Theo felt like he was just one more pile of waste, sitting on the wagon bench downwind from the horses. He was driving alone from Refugio to Castle, where he would meet Graves. At the time, he had only been aware of how he hated the wagon and hated Graves and hated himself for driving one to the other. He hated himself most for not running away, now that he was left alone and in command of two horses—albeit two very worn and rather useless horses.

In later years, when he allowed himself to think about it, he understood that Graves had given him the task precisely with this objective in mind. He didn't care about getting to Castle sooner on his own fast horse. He only wanted Theo to feel gutted by a lack of courage; he wanted him to feel fully, during every one of those fifty-six miles, that he was *incapable* of running away. Graves was good at that. He knew what the slow cultivation of fear could do to someone, especially a child. It made you totally powerless, so that even when you seemed to have your freedom, you did not.

Theo had seen enough. He let himself drop down into the narrow space between the wall and the shed. As he hit the ground, the casement window that had been propped open suddenly slammed shut, and the sound reverberated through the quiet garden. He froze.

There was silence from inside the house. Then several pairs of feet hurried out into the yard. "The rest of you stay inside," one of the officers commanded. "Secure the front door and the ground-floor windows. Did that sound come from your shed?" he asked the MP.

"I cannot say," Broadgirdle responded gruffly. "My guess is that it is one of the neighborhood cats. I very much doubt you will find an assassin hiding in my shed."

His voice was terribly near. Theo felt himself shrink against the wall, wishing he could disappear into the ivy.

"Nevertheless, sir, we'd like to check."

"Very well." There was a brief pause as Broadgirdle fussed with his keys, and then the shed was unlocked. Theo crouched down. "As you see, I have nothing here but gardening supplies."

Theo realized that this was his only moment to escape unnoticed, unless he wanted to spend the entire night crouching in the damp darkness. While they were searching the shed, he would have to circle around it and flee through the garden. Theo knew he had to, but he could not bring himself to do it. Graves's presence, so close and hidden by only the thin wall of a garden shed, muddled his thoughts. He felt like he was nine years old again, and shifting even a foot from where he had hidden himself seemed impossible. *You can't stay here,* a voice in Theo's head shouted at him. *Move. Move now!*

With a burst of effort, he stepped as quietly as he could

along the wall, away from the main house and into the darkness. Once he was clear of the shed he took a deep breath. The garden spread out before him; it seemed a mile long. *I can't do it,* he thought. *Someone is going to see me.* Before he could doubt what he was doing, he turned to the garden wall and hauled himself up it, struggling with the creepers that tore, tore again, and finally held him. He rolled himself over the top and landed blindly in the neighbor's garden. Crouching against the wall, he fought to steady his breathing.

Theo could hear the men on the other side hurrying out of the shed. "A cat, you said?" the officer asked tersely. "I believe your garden has been invaded by something rather larger. I will leave two officers here—"

"That really is not necessary."

"I insist. And we will wake the neighbors to see what manner of 'cat' has visited them."

Theo closed his eyes and pictured himself from overhead. He was sitting against the wall, and beyond it was the street, and beyond the street lay all of Beacon Hill, twinkling with lamps on every corner. His Goodyear was only a few blocks away. There were any number of escape routes. He just had to take one of them.

Rising quietly from the damp ground, he walked to the rear of the much smaller garden. Broadgirdle's neighbor, he realized with relief, was a reasonable human being who didn't hide bloody shears in his shed. There was a simple back gate with a latch and no lock. Theo opened it and stepped out onto the sidewalk. He closed the gate soundlessly behind him and took a deep breath. Walking slowly, steadily, as if he had decided to take a turn around the neighborhood to get some fresh air, he crossed to the other side of the street. He thrust his hands into his pockets. They were shaking.

As he walked downhill toward the Goodyear, he began to feel better. He had learned something and he had not been caught. The euphoria started to make him giddy, and all that had seemed so frightening minutes before seemed suddenly laughable. *I'm on to you, Graves,* he thought, grinning fiercely in the darkness. *You're guilty as sin, and I'm going to prove it. This time, you won't get off so easy.*

—1892, June 29: 17-Hour 15—

It was thought at first that the plague befell only those who ventured into the Dark Age, but it soon became clear that it was not so discriminating. What has been observed in the decades since is that travelers from other Ages, particularly later Ages, carry a greater resistance. This has caused the papacy to suspect, logically, that some devilry practiced in future Ages protects their inhabitants unnaturally from the plague.

—From Fulgencio Esparragosa's History of the Dark Age

ERROL FORSYTH, THE phantom hunter, sat at the table, mending his cape by the faint light of the fire. Seneca, the falcon, stood at the far end of the table, preening his feathers. They both glanced occasionally at the girl, Sophia, who, some half an hour after sighting the phantom, was still visibly upset. She had not protested when Errol began dragging the heavy wooden crate on wheels, but instead followed him dumbly, half weeping into her cupped hands. Now the planter stood outside in the courtyard of the abandoned house where he had been taking shelter for the past week, and the chickpea stew he had made earlier was bubbling over the fire.

The girl reminded him powerfully of his younger sister Catherine, whom he had not seen for so many years. She had the same unyieldingly serious face, pensive when she was glad, brooding and sorry when she was upset. Errol smiled to himself, thinking of the time he had banished that sorry look by teaching Cat to make the thrushes eat seeds from her palm. Observing the girl, he thought to himself grimly that it would take more than a few thrushes to expunge the memory of the phantom. *Poor child,* he thought. He finished the seam, tied a knot, and snapped off the thread with his teeth. Then he got up and ladled the stew into two ceramic bowls painted white and blue. He placed the bowls on the table, placed a pair of spoons beside them, and turned to Sophia.

"Come eat," he said.

Sophia got up wordlessly. Before sitting down, she opened her battered satchel and took out an equally battered half-eaten loaf of bread. She gazed at it a little mournfully. "It tastes better than it looks."

"Thank you," Errol said gravely.

"Thank *you,*" murmured Sophia. "For taking me in." She looked up and met his gaze. "And for before, in the street. Though I don't understand what happened."

"I will explain all of that to you soon enough. For now, let's eat."

Sophia found, to her surprise, that the chickpeas were delicious. She was so eager to eat them that she burned her tongue. Without saying a word, Errol ladled more into her bowl and sat back to eat his own. After the second bowl, a hunk of the bread, and a glass of water, Sophia began to feel somewhat better. She looked around the room.

They were in a house that had once been comfortable. The shelves were carefully built into the wall and stacked with the blue-and-white dishes. The mullioned windows had fine lace curtains, and copper pots hung above the open fire. The table and chairs were worn but well cared for, and above the table hung an iron candelabrum that at one point had fully illuminated the room. Now there were only two candles, burned down to pale stumps.

The phantom hunter looked entirely out of place among the pretty crockery and dainty curtains. Even without his gray hood, he seemed like a creature more fit for the wild outdoors than a candlelit kitchen. Tall and angular, he had broad, callused hands with blunt fingers. His dark blue eyes met Sophia's and held them, making her more uncomfortable by the second. She could read nothing in those eyes about the man behind them, but she felt that her every thought, every moment of her past, was visible to him.

"Does your bird eat bread?" Sophia asked, scattering crumbs on the table. It examined them coldly.

"Seneca is a falcon. He eats meat, and he hunts it himself."

"Oh. So you are both hunters."

"I suppose you could say that. Seneca hunts mice; I hunt phantoms. You can see which one of us is wiser." Errol lifted his finger and Seneca clacked closer to him, then pushed his head against it. "I found him near Córdoba when he was only a ball of white feathers. Could not hunt at all, then." Seneca bit his finger gently in protest. "Even now he is a lazy hunter. You are more philosopher than predator, are you not, Seneca?" The falcon turned away from Errol and walked back to his corner of the table, then contemplated the fire with a beady eye.

Sophia gazed solemnly at the falcon and then turned back to Errol.

He put his spoon down. "You want me to explain what the apparitions are," he said flatly.

"Yes."

"People here believe they emerge from the Dark Age. That they are sent to lure us into those dark pathways so we will be eaten to pieces by the spines." He stood up, stretched, and put another log on the fire. Though the day had been blisteringly hot, the warmth had vanished with the sun, and now the night was sharp and cool. Errol sat back down. Despite his height, he moved smoothly, almost gracefully, as though every motion had a foreseen and intended conclusion. "Perhaps they are right. I do not know for certain what they are. I can only tell you how I have come to know them."

"All right," she agreed.

"I come from the Closed Empire. You may have noticed it from my speech." Sophia nodded. "I serve a lord there, my family does, near York. I was the falconer before I left three years ago. My twin brother worked with milord's horses." He looked up at Sophia, as if expecting some response. She looked back at him expectantly. "My twin brother is named Oswin," he went on. "It was three years and seventeen days ago that I saw Oswin drawn away by a specter."

Sophia caught her breath. "Drawn away?"

Errol gave a small nod. "He saw an apparition—unclear, insubstantial, but still recognizable—and was transfixed by it. I saw it all happen, for I was not far away. We stood in the field at dusk. I was returning from the stables, and he waited for me, as he often did, so that we might walk together and talk before sitting down to supper. But before I reached him, the phantom appeared."

"Who was it?"

"It was not a person. It was the phantom of a thing—an animal. A horse that ran away when we were children. I recognized it by the toss of its head, and so did Oswin. I heard Oswin call to it by name. I followed, thinking as my brother did that some strange spirit of the horse, or the horse itself, had returned to us." He shook his head. "But it was not the horse or its spirit. It was a fell thing that drew him across one field and then another. I pursued him, caring nothing for the horse but gravely distressed by how my brother seemed not to heed or even hear me. The night deepened, and we passed into the forest." Errol turned to the fire. Sophia waited. "I lost him there," he said, in a hard voice. "In the darkness. Though I could still pursue his trail. In the town beyond the forest they had seen him, and in the town farther south they had, also." He passed a hand quickly over his eyes. "I will not tire you by telling you of every sign I sought and found, but suffice to say that I pursued Oswin for a year, farther and farther south, until we were at the very edge of the Papal States, and I began to doubt my own sanity.

"But here," he said slowly, "I found that others had seen phantoms. It was not so uncommon as it had seemed to me in York. I saw them for myself—other specters. As dusk fell, they emerged, each with its intended destination. The people in the cities and towns north of here live in mortal fear of the phantoms, believing if they are bewitched by them, they will be drawn into the Dark Age.

"Then I had a chance discovery. I ran out of arrows." Errol paused and smiled briefly to himself. "The mistake of a novice. So I cut new ones from an orange tree—crude things with too much bend and hardly a point. And when I launched them at the apparitions, they vanished. Now I cut fresh arrows each day. The green wood is, as yet, the only method I have found for banishing the shadows—at least for a single night. They always reappear."

Sophia felt a rapid pulse of relief. *She'll be back again tomorrow,* she thought. *She's not gone.*

Errol picked up his spoon, then put it down again. "By then, I had reached the road from Seville to the border of the Dark Age. And there I lost the trail. No one had seen Oswin, though plenty had seen him farther north. He was easy to mark—a pale, blond youth from the Closed Empire, identical in appearance to me. Many before had seen him. But then all sign of him vanished. That was two years ago."

He was silent for so long Sophia thought his story had

ended. Seneca walked across the table once, examined Errol's plate, then retreated to his corner and turned his back on them. Sophia felt her caution of the phantom hunter fading. He was just like her, this Errol Forsyth: seeking lost family, across great distances and with impossible prospects. *Here,* she thought, reaching into the pocket for the spool of thread, *is someone who will understand what I am doing. The Fates have been kind to place him in my way.*

Suddenly Errol spoke again. "Then I began to see Oswin's likeness. It always arrives at dusk—that was what you saw. A sad, pathetic thing. With a strange face that seemed made of some page from a monk's book. I do not know what it means." He frowned, and his eyes, reflecting the fire, seemed filled with flames. "I refuse to believe that he is dead. I have seen the phantoms of the dead, and this is not one of them. True phantoms are heavy, toxic with grief. These are light, as if illuminated by a searching flame. He is alive," he said fiercely. "I am sure of it."

"Does he speak to you, too?"

"Yes. Always some nonsense."

"He says the same thing each time?"

"No. Different things. I have long since stopped listening. The words have no meaning. It is not Oswin, that specter." He took a breath and his face relaxed, growing pensive. "For the last two years, I have traveled all throughout the towns and cities here, but I have had no further sign of him. I have circled the perimeter of the Dark Age twice, but I will not venture into it."

Sophia considered him. "Because it is not allowed by the Orders, or because it is too dangerous?"

"I care nothing for what the Orders allow or do not allow. But the Dark Age is not to be trifled with. It may belong to some distant past, but it is still here. It is the dark heart of the Papal States. We all have one," he said, his eyes narrowing, "a dark point at our center, where it is wise not to enter or look too closely. My Dark Age is as dark as any other." He flexed his hands. "I refuse to believe he is there. Not Oswin." He took his eyes from the fire to look at her. "And you must have lost your mother, or she would not have appeared to you as a phantom."

Sophia nodded. The piercing blue gaze seemed kinder now, though the expression on Errol's face was unchanged. "She and my father disappeared when I was small. They were explorers. I'm here because I think there may be word of them in Granada. My mother left a diary there. I was to travel with another woman from Boston. Remorse. But she never boarded the ship. She . . . I don't know. She made arrangements for me to meet someone in Seville at the port. They weren't there. I am not sure if they ever will be. So who knows if I will ever get to Granada." Errol gazed at her a moment longer after she had stopped speaking, then nodded.

"I will go with you," he said without looking at her, standing up to throw another log on the fire.

She hesitated, surprised by the offer. "Thank you. But I can't keep you from your search."

"You are not keeping me from it. And it is a long road to

Granada. It circles north all the way around the border of the Dark Age. Besides, this is what I do: wander futilely, hunting my brother's ghost while my brother himself continues to elude me." He spoke without bitterness, but with a heavy sadness that sounded to Sophia very like defeat.

"I should wait here, in Seville," she said with a sigh. Then she looked up and was surprised to see the phantom hunter smiling.

It was the first time she had seen him smile, and it made him look suddenly younger. He let out a brief laugh. "You do not trust me!" he exclaimed.

"That's not true," Sophia replied earnestly. "I am grateful for your offer to help—very grateful. But I did sent word to friends in the United Indies before leaving Boston. I think perhaps I should wait for them here. They can be trusted—they are not Nihilismian like the others."

"Ah. Nihilismians." He paused. "And this woman who left you alone on the ship and made arrangements for you that did not come through—she was Nihilismian?"

"Yes."

Errol raised his eyebrows. His face was serious once more as he turned to look at the fire. "In truth you would be wise," he said, "to be cautious of strangers. I am surprised you found a Nihilismian trustworthy. And you do not know me—cannot know what I am or am not." He shook his head. "You have nothing to fear from me, but you should bolt the door of my room, to make sure. A cautious young lady would not easily stay the night in an empty house with a hooded stranger. We will bolt the outside door as well."

Sophia felt embarrassed by the reprimand. No doubt he was right. She trusted too readily. "All right. Thank you."

—19-Hour 42—

THE BED IN the little room overlooking the courtyard was softer and more comfortable than Sophia had imagined. But she could not sleep. Restless thoughts and persistent uncertainties kept her mind turning. The pretty room, which had clearly belonged to a girl her own age or younger, filled her with morbid thoughts about the deaths that had likely occurred in her place of refuge. *Perhaps,* she comforted herself, *the family moved away to avoid* lapena. *But then, why would they leave all their belongings?*

Sophia sighed and turned over restlessly. She could not decide what to do. Was it wiser to stay in Seville and wait for Remorse's ally? Or would it be better to travel east to the Granada Archive at once? Sitting up, she leaned forward and opened the shutters to the window overlooking the courtyard. Moonlight poured into the room. She looked out at the roofs of Seville and imagined the plague creeping through the city on shadowy feet. Despite her exhaustion, she realized, she would not be sleeping.

Sophia took her notebook from her satchel. She filled the pages, drawing and writing by the light of the moon. The plague cleric, Whence and Partial, the boy and his mother who had given her bread, the lamplighter, Errol Forsyth, and the specter of Minna Tims. She could hardly believe it had all happened in one day. As she drew, the tolling of bells marked the night hours: the second vigil, the third vigil, the fourth vigil, and matins.

It was close to dawn, though the sky was still dark, when Sophia suddenly heard a strange sound: a stretching and creaking, like the wall of a house resisting the wind. Then a sharp cracking and splintering cut through the air: the sound of wood being smashed to pieces. For a moment, she thought of the front door, but no—the sound came from the courtyard. A clattering explosion, followed by the report of wood on stone, drove her to the window.

She looked down and saw the planter in pieces. The plants that had been growing inside the wooden container were now bursting from it; the soil lay scattered, the fully blossomed flowers partly trampled, as if someone had walked through them.

Sophia pulled away from the window with a gasp. "Errol!" she shouted. She unbolted her door and rushed out into the corridor. She could hear him in the room across the narrow hall, stumbling across the floorboards.

He pounded on the door of his room. "Open the door. Sophia. *Sophia!* Unbar the door!"

But Sophia stood motionless in the corridor. She stared up at the figure that stood not five paces away, blocking her path. Tall and strangely illuminated, emitting a golden light like the flame of a candle, the woman held her hand out toward Sophia, commanding her stillness. "Do not move," she said, her voice sinuous as a velvet ribbon, winding its way around Sophia so that she felt rooted to the floor. Then the woman turned her palm upward, and a cluster of golden blossoms sprang from her hand. "Be gone," the woman whispered. With a slight movement, she tossed the blossoms toward Sophia. They burst into a dense fog of petals and pollen, heavy and thick as a storm cloud. Sophia could see nothing but a yellow mist, and her breath seemed to lodge in her throat. She could hardly breathe.

PART III
The Test

25

THE LOST SIGNS ARE LOST

March 15, 1881

It was no surprise to us that Bruno had not only been kind to Rosemary but had become her teacher and friend. She told us how, during the year he stayed at the farm, Bruno had related stories of all his adventures, sung often, and laughed more. He tried to coax her out of silence with his poor Castilian, and when this did not work, he switched to his native English. Neither drew Rosemary into speech, but she slowly learned the unfamiliar language, even as she communicated with him mostly by signs. Bruno read out loud to her from his many books in English, sharing the world of New Occident through their pages. Bruno was never impatient or vexed at her muteness, which he treated with a delicacy that, at times, almost allowed her to forget its existence.

These qualities were the same ones that had endeared Bruno Casavetti to us when we first met him in Boston years earlier, and they were the qualities that had made him such a beloved companion on more than one expedition. They were the reasons why we had gone into such a remote Age to find him, leaving little Sophia behind. We listened with great emotion to Rosemary's stories of Bruno's kindness—

and, finally, with dread to her account of his final months in Murtea.

"Bruno became captivated by Ausentinia," she told us, "as I knew he would. He had originally traveled to the Papal States with the intention of mapping the perimeter of the Dark Age, but Ausentinia had distracted him. Rumor of the House of Saint Antony drew him to Murtea, and once he discovered the rumors were true, its marvels kept him close by. Bruno wanted to understand how such a wondrous Age had come to be. He crossed the stone bridge to Ausentinia every day, returning only at dusk. He visited each map store asking every manner of question and receiving friendly but uninformative replies. None of them had a map for Bruno. He became convinced that the entire origin and existence of Ausentinia was something the inhabitants concealed: the one lost answer for which no map would be drawn.

"And then, one day in November, he returned to the farm with a stricken look that filled me with fear. He would hardly meet my gaze. I pressed his arm and signed to ask him what had happened. He looked up at me then, his expression filled with grief. 'It is gone,' he said quietly. 'Ausentinia is gone. The Dark Age has taken it.'

"I was shocked, naturally, and my face said as much. Bruno explained as best he could. 'As I took the path to the stone bridge, I came across Pantaleón, the priest's nephew. He was heading into Ausentinia as well. We walked together, talking, toward the stone bridge. But then when we crested the hill we saw'—he swallowed—'we saw that the paths to Ausentinia were gone. Not even the hills were there. Black moss met the stone bridge on the other side. I saw the spines—they were young ones, with their thorny trunks and long limbs. I have seen the Dark Age before, as I stood at a safe distance, and there is no doubt in my mind. Somehow, inconceivably, it has arrived, taking the hills of Ausentinia with it.

"'It was Pantaleón who saw the yellow hills in the distance. He pointed, and I could see that he was right. Pieces of Ausentinia had yet survived, like amber islands in a sea of black. As we looked, something even more unbelievable occurred. The shape of the Age before us changed. An Ausentinian hill in the near distance expanded, replacing a portion of the dark forest. Then, more shocking still, the earth on the far side of the stone bridge transformed as well—the familiar tall, yellowed grass appeared. Pantaleón and I stared, dumbfounded. I did not understand what I was seeing. But Pantaleón, with his typical impulsiveness, ran to look more closely. I called him back, but he ignored me.'

"Bruno wiped his brow. 'If only I had stopped him!

"'Pantaleón crossed the bridge and rushed across the grass to the very edge of the black moss, and as he did I heard a rush of wind like the sound of an approaching storm. Pantaleón reached to touch the moss, an expression of wonder on his face. I saw behind him what appeared to be a gust of wind, moving through the spines. Pantaleón rose, but he was too late. When I uncovered my eyes, everything beyond the bridge was black once more, as if darkness had extinguished a frail yellow flame. I could not see Pantaleón.' Bruno looked up at me then, his face filled with horror. 'But I could hear him screaming, running through the spines. And then... nothing.'

"Bruno and I sat in silence; both of us struck dumb now. After a time, he sighed. 'I do not understand what I saw.' He got to his feet. 'But I must tell the priest what has happened to his nephew. Perhaps some brave soul will go in search of him and see if he is still alive.' I nodded, understanding that the errand was necessary, but I felt a curious sense of unease and then dread, which grew in my stomach after he had gone. The story had unsettled me, of course, but I felt a fear of something much nearer: some impending danger that I could not fathom. Finally, unsure what else to do, I hurried to the village to find Bruno at the priest's house.

"As I neared Murtea's walls, I saw the peddler who travels between Granada and Murtea. He is an old man, hunched and dried as the hills, but he still walks the route every other week. He was arguing with a man from the village, and I heard their voices grow shrill. Suddenly, the enraged customer raised his sword, and with vicious strokes he began to hack the old man's cart to pieces. For a moment, I felt a strange relief that he was attacking the cart and not the old man. And then my mind understood what my eyes were seeing. A broken cart. *A broken cart.* The words from the map came back to me. *When the cart breaks, go to the goat's head.* I lost no time; I did as the map instructed me."

"But what is the goat's head?" I asked Rosemary.

"Our sheriff," she said. "Alvar Cabeza de Cabra. His name means 'head of goat,'" she explained for Bronson's benefit. "I ran to the village plaza, where I knew the sheriff would be, and there I found my dear Bruno already bound, looking at the sheriff and the priest with an expression of complete bewilderment. I ran up to him and clawed at his bonds. 'Seize her,' the priest said. 'No doubt this little witch assisted him.' I was no match for the sheriff, who held my hands behind my back before I could even turn to face him. 'Did you teach the *brujo* a trick or two?' the priest asked me cruelly. 'Did you tell him to bring the Dark Age upon us? To send my nephew into its depths?'

"Then, as if it had never been gone, my voice returned. '*No!*' I screamed. 'He is no witch. He wanted to help Pantaleón. You must believe him!'

"The priest regarded me with disgust. 'No doubt it was his witchcraft,' he hissed, 'that gave you back your voice as well. Was it a pact of some kind? An exchange of his soul for your wretched voice? I will see that you both pay for this.'"

Rosemary broke off. "I cannot bear to tell you the rest of it," she said quietly.

"Please," I said, though my eyes were already damp with tears. "I am sorry for the pain it causes you, but I beg you to tell us what became of him."

"They placed us both in this same jail," Rosemary went on, with effort, "and in time the villagers discovered that what Bruno had said was indeed true. The Dark Age had overtaken Ausentinia. It had reached the very edge of the stone bridge. None dared enter in search of Pantaleón. Bruno began to lose hope that they would ever listen to reason. Certainly the priest did not.

"Without telling me, he decided to confess to the charges. He could not explain how the Dark Age had arrived, but he pretended that he had made a pact with the Devil, sending Pantaleón into the Dark Age in exchange for my voice. He told them that I was innocent.

"It was then they let me go, and I sent the letter that brought you here. The following week they sentenced him. His sentence was cruel. He was condemned to cross the stone bridge, so that he would suffer the same fate Pantaleón suffered."

Bronson and I gasped.

Rosemary covered her eyes with her hand, aggrieved. "That was before they truly understood the consequences of passing into the Dark Age."

"What consequences do you mean?" I asked her—

My account is interrupted. I have no more time. I must write my final thoughts, and I hope that someone—perhaps the sheriff, who has been kinder than I expected—will see that these pages are safeguarded. I will be able to write nothing more in them.

We have been condemned for witchcraft—for resisting the plague by means of dark arts. At noon we will be taken to the stone bridge. If we are able to avoid the Dark Age, we will follow the lost signs to the city of Ausentinia. It is our only chance of finding safety. Perhaps they are still there, beneath the dreaded darkness.

I wish I could say otherwise, but I confess that as the hour draws near, I am afraid. I see my husband sitting across from me, as handsome as the day I met him. His skin is powdered with dust from the dry air; his gentle eyes are filled with sadness. He tries to smile at me. . . .

What will become of us? Will we survive, and what does survival through such a trial mean? I wonder what our Sophia is doing at this moment. Drawing at her little desk, perhaps. Walking with Shadrack by the river. Sleeping with that look of surprised calm that overtakes her.

I promise you, dear heart, that we will find our way to you again.

Minna Tims
March 17, 1881
Murtea, Papal States

26

GOLDENROD'S CURE

—1892, June 30: 4-Hour 11—

And yet the people of the Papal States are far more divided as to the plague's cause and its treatment. Some believe it is a curse sent northward from the Early Pharaohs. Others, particularly those sympathetic to Nihilismian explanations, believe it is essentially a fatal melancholy brought on by the grief of inhabiting the world of the Great Disruption.

—From Fulgencio Esparragosa's
Complete and Authoritative History of the Papal States

SOPHIA REELED AND fell backward. She felt as though all the air had been wrenched from her lungs in one solid mass. From a great distance, she heard an insistent pounding and a loud voice calling her name: Errol. She realized that she was not on the floor but was being held—cradled. The strange woman had caught her. "What—" she said thickly, trying to raise her head.

"It will take a few moments," the woman said, in her low voice. "I have called it away and it has obeyed me, but you will need a moment to recover."

"Sophia!" Errol shouted. "Sophia, answer me!"

"Called what away?" Sophia asked weakly.

"The wanderer that was beginning to make a home inside you."

Sophia shook her head. She was feeling better, but the woman's words confused her. "Wanderer?" she repeated.

"What people here call a sickness—the plague."

Horrified, Sophia sat up suddenly, still dizzy and dazed. "I had the *plague*?"

"A wanderer crept into your head a few hours ago, and it was thinking about staying a while." The woman smiled. "I called it away." She looked around her with a sense of observation. "This house is full of them."

"Sophia!" Errol pounded on the door.

Sophia scrambled to her feet. "My friend—Errol—might be sick, too. Please, can you help him?"

The woman rose to her feet and without a word threw back the bolt and stepped aside. The door flew open. Errol leaped forward, his sword held high. Seneca beat the air over his head and whirled, screaming, into the dark hallway. "No!" Sophia cried. The woman's back was already to the wall, the point of Errol's sword at her neck. She eyed him coldly.

Sophia rushed between them. "She didn't hurt me! She didn't hurt me, Errol."

Errol had not taken his eyes off of the woman. Slowly, he lowered his sword, but only by a little. He pulled Sophia toward him and held her protectively. "Who are you?" he growled at the woman. "And where did you come from?"

A slight smile pulled at the edge of her mouth. "Goldenrod," she said quietly. "I come from the Eerie Sea."

"How did you get here?" Errol demanded.

Goldenrod motioned with her chin. "I came across the ocean in a wooden coffin."

Sophia gasped. "You were in the planter!"

"I was fading—I had been for months. You, Sophia, gave me sun and water, and they revived me." She gave a slight bow. "I owe you my life."

Sophia blinked. "Sun and water?"

"People of New Occident know little about us," Goldenrod said, "and I suspect you cured me by chance."

"You are one of the Eerie?"

"That is your name for us, yes."

"I thought the planter held . . . plants."

Goldenrod smiled. "You were not entirely wrong." She held out her hands. It was difficult to see in the dawn light that seeped into the corridor, but Sophia thought that Goldenrod's hands looked faintly green.

Errol had relaxed his grip, though he still had one hand on Sophia's shoulder and the other on his sword. "What manner of creature lives on sun and water?"

Goldenrod reflected. "The wanderer has been with you longer. In a few hours, you will begin to feel its presence."

Sophia whirled and looked up at Errol's scowling face with concern. "He has it? He's sick?" She turned back to Goldenrod. "Please help him."

"What do you mean?" Errol retorted, raising his sword again.

"She means the plague." Sophia wrapped her hands around

his arm, lowering the sword. "Let her help you, Errol. She can make it go away. The whole house is contaminated."

"I have withstood the plague for two years," he scoffed, "and it seems unlikely I would fall to it now."

"Sophia, step aside," Goldenrod said calmly.

"Stop!" Errol commanded, raising his sword.

Sophia pulled away, and in the same moment Goldenrod raised a cluster of blossoms in her open palm. Errol's eyes opened wide. With her slight toss, the petals expanded, enveloping Errol in a pale cloud that clung to the air around him. "Be gone," Goldenrod said quietly. "Find another place to wander."

Errol sneezed violently and staggered backward, dropping the sword. Sophia jumped forward and tried to catch him, but his weight was such that they both collapsed. Seneca, from where he perched in a windowsill, gave a brief squawk of disapproval. Errol sneezed again. "Good God," he said. He put his hand to his head.

Sophia waited, partly crushed by the weight of Errol's head and shoulders, which she had at least prevented from hitting the floor.

Errol shook his head once or twice and opened his eyes. He struggled to push himself upright, fumbling for his sword. "You'll not bury me in your foul powders again," he said, eyeing Goldenrod threateningly. "My sword will find that hand before you can use it."

"We should leave this place," Goldenrod said, ignoring him to peer into the rooms on either side of the corridor. "There are wanderers in every room, and they are restless."

"All right," Sophia said, looking around worriedly. "Are you feeling better, Errol?"

Errol reached out his hand, still sitting propped up against the wall, and seized Sophia's arm. "What did I tell you about trusting too readily? You have only just met her."

"From what I heard as I awoke in the streets of Seville," Goldenrod said calmly, "Sophia has only just met you, as well."

Errol clambered to his feet and glared at the Eerie. Sophia watched them with apprehension. He seemed as tightly wound as a spring; his fists were clenched, and his eyes were narrowed to slits. Goldenrod stood with her arms at her sides, but her still face shone with a quiet intensity. The air between them in the narrow corridor seemed to grow heavier; the silence deepened.

As Sophia considered how best to disturb it, an urgent pounding on the front door reverberated through the house. Errol scowled, not taking his eyes from Goldenrod. The pounding continued. At the sound of a shout, Errol turned his head, his expression altered. "It is the Golden Cross," he said quietly. "Wait here." He took a few steps toward the stairway, but the barked commands, clearly audible if not intelligible to the other two, stopped him in his tracks. He turned back and stared at Sophia. "They are looking for a girl—a foreigner, who was seen lying in the street last night speaking with a lamplighter. An informer has accused her of carrying *lapena*."

Sophia gasped. "How did they know I was here?"

"The informers are paid in gold for their intelligence. They will go to great lengths for it." He walked brusquely in his bare feet to the bedroom. "Get your things. We have less than a minute before they break down the door."

Sophia rushed to her bedroom and collected her things. Without bothering to change out of her nightgown, she stuffed her strewn clothes into her pack and pulled on her boots. She hurried into the hallway to find Errol already dressed, wearing his cape and carrying his bow and quiver. He pointed down the corridor. "There is a back stairway in the last room on the right. It leads down to the courtyard, and from there we exit onto a narrow alley behind the house."

The pounding on the door and the shouted commands stopped. A sudden crash of wood against wood broke the dawn air.

"We are out of time," Errol said. He rushed down the corridor, entering the room on the right and racing down the narrow stairway in the corner. Sophia plunged after him with Goldenrod in her wake. They emerged in the stone patio, where the broken planter lay as if exploded. From the shouts behind them, Sophia could tell that the Order had made their way inside. She heard them crashing through the rooms as Errol opened the door to the alley and ushered them through, closing it carefully behind them.

"Now we do not run," he said. "We walk calmly. Hood up," he said to Goldenrod, giving her a sharp look. "And conceal your arms, for God's sake." Goldenrod pulled her brown hood over her head and withdrew a pair of long brown gloves from her cape, which she pulled on swiftly. "Take Sophia's hand. We are a family of travelers heading east."

"But anyone can see that we do not belong here," Sophia whispered frantically.

"That is why we are leaving the city," Errol said, pulling up his own hood. "We head east, toward Granada, on the road that circles north of the Dark Age."

—5-Hour 32—

ERROL FORSYTH HAD always heard about the Faierie from his mother and father when he was a child, and more especially from his grandfather, who maintained that the soul of a childhood friend had been stolen by one when they were both in the forest, climbing a tree. But he had never seen one. Nonetheless, Errol believed in their existence just as he believed in the existence of people from the Russias: though he did not know any personally, he accepted that they were real.

As the dawn light met them on the streets of Seville, Errol took the opportunity to study the woman who called herself an Eerie. She wore long, green robes and a hooded cape of dark brown. Her hazel eyes had a disconcerting stillness to them that mirrored the calm of her face: a slight nose, a wide and firm mouth, and prominent bones. Her face was pale, as were her neck and shoulders—pale and white. But at the edges of her forehead, where her brown hair began, the skin was brown, and her long hair seemed to shift and spin unlike any hair he had ever seen. Before she had donned the gloves, he had seen her hands: where her arms tapered at the wrists her skin became green, so that her fingers were as bright as new maple leaves. She claimed to be human, Errol reflected, but clearly was not.

"How did you come to find yourself in a wooden coffin?" he asked, as they walked steadily through the winding streets.

Her expression was aloof. "I do not know. I presume someone familiar with our ways placed me in it, because I was buried in soil. It would have been the only way for me to survive a voyage of such length."

Sophia, despite her pounding heart and her worries about the Golden Cross, looked up at her in surprise. "Remorse did that?"

"Who is Remorse?" Goldenrod asked.

"The woman who put us on that ship."

"I do not know her. I remember nothing after the attack in Boston."

Sophia's eyes opened wide. "What attack?"

"At the outskirts of Boston, I was attacked in the darkness. A single attacker, but with more strength than I expected. I resisted for some time. Eventually I was too injured and fell into unconsciousness. Then came a long sleep from which I awoke in Seville."

"And why were you traveling to Boston?" Errol asked. "You said you came from the Eerie Sea."

For the first time, Goldenrod looked troubled. "I thought I would find what I had been seeking for months. Three of our people have disappeared, and we are in search of them. I had received word that they were in Boston. Now that so much time has passed, I am certain others have gone there in my place. I only hope they fared better. I am sure they have," she murmured, reassuring herself.

After a brief pause, Errol made a noise of assent. "I see."

He could not deny, with a wry smile inside his hood, that there was something fitting in the predicament of three travelers, all of them from distant Ages, all seeking people dear to them. But Goldenrod's explanation of her circumstances struck him as entirely improbable. There was something more to the story, he felt certain. Perhaps a Faierie with no weapons could in fact have resisted a surprise attack in the darkness, but why had she been placed under lock and key in a wooden coffin? Was she so dangerous that she had to be not only locked up but shipped across the ocean? Or could it be that the very sight of those green hands had frightened the Bostonians into taking unnecessary measures?

"Why are we going to Granada?" Goldenrod asked.

"Sophia has an urgent mission there, and we cannot stay in Seville. You need not go with us." Sophia gave him a look of admonishment. "In fact, now that we are clear of the house and immediate danger, you are welcome to leave at any time."

Goldenrod, untroubled, did not flinch. "We are not out of danger."

"We will be out of the city in fifteen minutes. As long as we do not encounter any others from the Order, we will have no difficulties."

"I believe you will need my help."

Errol snorted. "I don't see why." He looked up briefly and

then held out his arm. Seneca, who had taken flight once they reached the patio, descended smoothly onto his leather-bound forearm.

"You may think you know this land better than I do," Goldenrod replied calmly. "But believe me—I know it in ways you do not."

Errol paused in his thoughts. That could be true, he realized. If she was Faierie, there were probably many things about her he did not yet know. "I suppose it would do no harm to have a Faierie on our side."

"I am not a Faierie, any more than you"—she paused, glancing at Seneca—"are a falcon." She fixed her brown eyes on Errol's. "But I understand how to you it must seem a likely explanation."

"You may travel with us. But you must wear your hood and your gloves at all times. Your appearance will draw the suspicions of the clerics."

Goldenrod did not reply.

They were reaching the city limits. The bells of the cathedral and all the churches tolled laudes, and already they sounded distant. Errol felt the first rush of heat as the sun began to warm Seville in earnest. "This will be a difficult first day," he said, pausing where the last few houses gave way to scrubby grass and dusty olive trees. "We must walk at least as far as the first inn, and in less than an hour the sun will be scorching." He held out a leather water sack to Sophia. "Drink. There are wells along the way."

Sophia obligingly took a long drink of water and then

passed the sack to Goldenrod. She lifted it, turned her face upward, and with her mouth open poured water over her face and head. Errol watched her, eyebrows raised. "Faierie ways," he murmured, shaking his head. He took the water sack back and tied it to his belt. "If we are approached by travelers on the road, let me speak to them. And if we see the Order approaching from either direction, get off the road and take what cover you can. They will meet a steel-tipped arrow of mine before they can come near us." He stepped forward onto the dry road.

"Falcon ways," Goldenrod said quietly.

—*June 7: 12-Hour 31*—

The Remember England Party is the oldest, having been founded in 1800 on the first anniversary of the Great Disruption. Its founders, poignantly, could themselves remember the England of 1799 and earlier, having traveled there or even, in some cases, being of English birth.

—From Shadrack Elli's History of New Occident

MRS. CULCUTTY ENTERED the parlor, carrying a tray loaded with tea things and a fair-sized cake. "Good afternoon, Charles," she said with a smile. Though Mrs. Culcutty tended to be rather overprotective of Nettie, Charles had struck her from the first as a very amiable, polite young man. Most young men who visited Nettie were either wolfish fellows who took too many liberties or sheepish fellows who brought too many flowers. Charles was neither: while scrupulously proper in his behavior, he seemed pleased but not overawed in her company. When they visited together she could always hear them talking seriously, and that was a good thing. Dear Nettie had precious few moments of seriousness in her life.

"Good afternoon, Mrs. Culcutty!" Theo replied, taking the heavy tray and placing it on the table. "How are you?"

"I am well, thank you, but my cousin across town is suffering from a summer cold, so I will be leaving shortly to see her." She poured Nettie and Theo each a cup of Charleston tea.

"Oh, poor Agatha!" Nettie exclaimed. "You will take her your molasses remedy, won't you?"

"I certainly will. Mr. Culcutty is in the back mending the fence if you should need anything. I'll be back for supper."

"Thank you, Mrs. Culcutty." Nettie gave a sweet smile. She waited for the door to close. "Now," she said, leaning forward, "tell me the rest."

Theo shrugged. "There isn't much more to tell. There was nothing there. After a few minutes, they came outside, so I hopped the fence into the neighbor's yard."

Nettie closed her eyes and chewed on a lock of hair. "Describe everything you remember from inside the shed. Everything."

"A worktable with a lamp, a ball of twine, a watering can, and the pruning shears. Some tools in the corner."

"Which tools?"

"A shovel. A couple rakes. Hand spade. Things like that."

Nettie opened her eyes, scowling. "Charles, I said *everything*."

"Well, I couldn't very well take notes, could I?"

She huffed with frustration. "What else?"

"Lots of empty pots, some of them broken."

"What did the ball of twine look like?"

"What do you mean, what did it look like? A ball of twine."

"Was it rolled tight, or was it loose, as if the twine had been used?"

Theo considered. "Loose. It had been used."

"What was in the watering can?"

"I couldn't see."

Nettie sat back with a sigh. "If you are right, and those shears had blood on them, then someone was hurt in that shed."

"I don't doubt it. Problem is who."

"It could be one of the missing Eerie—one of the Weatherers or Goldenrod."

"Or it could be the man who brought her to the farm," Theo put in. "Don't forget about him. If he was supposed to kill Goldenrod and he didn't, Broadgirdle wouldn't have been happy."

"I haven't forgotten about him," Nettie said pensively. "But I have another piece of evidence that you haven't seen yet." She pulled a crumpled sheet of note paper from between the music books beside her. "Read this," she said, handing it to Theo.

February 4, 1892

Goldenrod—

I have found the Weatherers. I have even seen them. Their situation is dire, and it requires either great force or great ingenuity. I am devising alternatives. Part of the obstacle lies in how visible the Mark is upon them: if I expose their captivity publicly, their appearance will invite suspicion in Boston. I fear the outcome would be disastrous, given the prejudice toward foreigners. The *solution must be stealthy, and I would welcome Eerie assistance. Further, I regret to say, they will be in need of your curative powers once they are freed.*

They send you the enclosed rule. It seemed pressing.

—B

Theo had seen enough governmental paperwork in Shadrack's study to recognize the late prime minister's writing. "Where was this?" he asked.

"In one of the boxes of Bligh's papers," Nettie said. She grimaced. "I was up all night reading."

"What about the rule at the end?"

She shook her head. "This was mixed in with a lot of other documents. It's clearly the letter that brought Goldenrod to Boston. My guess is that she had it with her at the farm, and Bligh saved it once she was in his care. Who knows what she did with the rule."

"I'm not even sure what kind of rule he means. A written rule?"

Nettie's eyes widened with sudden awareness and she gave a little gasp. "Of course!" she exclaimed. "Not rules but rule. How could I not have realized?"

Theo looked at her, perplexed. "Yes, that's what it says."

Nettie jumped up from her chair. "We have a little time before Mrs. Culcutty returns. Hurry!"

Theo followed her out of the piano room and into the elegant hallway at the rear of the house. It was the first time he had seen it. Patterned wallpaper and a set of pastoral landscapes in oval frames covered the wall. Nettie stopped before a heavy oak door on the right-hand side and quickly pulled a key from her skirt pocket. "I had a copy made ages ago," she whispered. "Easier than using a hairpin every time."

Inspector Grey's office was what Theo had expected. Heavy wooden cabinets and the mahogany desk darkened the room. A navy carpet from the Indies and two worn armchairs formed a tidy sitting area where more than a dozen boxes stood in neat piles. "I should have realized the minute I read it," Nettie muttered. She opened the top box and rifled through it, then moved on to the next. "No one says 'rule' unless they mean . . . *this*!" She held up a folded wooden ruler, worn from years of use. "I thought it was just an object from his desk, but it must be what Bligh mentioned in the letter."

Theo took it up skeptically. "Really? It looks like an ordinary ruler."

"Except for the date," Nettie said triumphantly.

"The date?" Theo examined the ruler more closely, and on the unruled side he saw, faintly scrawled in red: *Feb 2 1892*. "I see what you mean. The date would fit with the date on the letter."

"The Weatherers gave this to Bligh, and he sent it to Goldenrod."

"But what is it?" Theo asked, baffled. He handed it back to her.

Nettie dropped into one of the worn armchairs. "I don't know." She seemed to think with her entire face. "No other markings in red. It must be some kind of cipher. Or perhaps it belongs to one of the Weatherers, and sending it is proof of something. Or the ruler might remind Goldenrod of a particular event that they all were part of." She wound a curl around her index finger and tugged. "Too many alternatives. I just don't know." She got up again and began arranging the boxes into their original tidy stack. "Do you think Elli knows about the Weatherers as well? Could you go and ask him?"

"They still aren't allowed visitors." In truth, the prison did allow visitors, and Theo's investigation would have benefited from a long conversation with Shadrack and Miles. But it was rather difficult to visit them when he was not supposed to leave East Ending Street. Nettie Grey might be fooled by a false name, but he didn't wish to test his luck at the New Jail. "Has your father seen the letter?" he asked in the hallway as Nettie locked the study door.

"I'm not sure. But he wouldn't necessarily think it's important. He doesn't know what we know." Nettie wound her way back to the piano room and sat down among the poppies.

"But you're going to give it to him, right?" Theo asked. "It practically proves it."

"Proves what, exactly?" Nettie asked, more to herself than to him. She twirled her hair thoughtfully. "We can speculate that Gordon Broadgirdle kidnapped the Weatherers, and Bligh discovered it. He sent a note to Goldenrod asking her for help, and she came. She was attacked by one of the grappling-hook brutes, but survived. Bligh found her and tried to take care of her. Bligh confronted Broadgirdle on his own about the captive Weatherers, and it got him killed."

"That's it," Theo said in earnest agreement. "It makes perfect sense."

"It does," Nettie agreed, "but it's not enough. There's no proof. And there are too many questions. Where has Goldenrod vanished to? What about the man who attacked her? And this is the most important: Why would Broadgirdle kidnap the Weatherers?" She tapped her chin. "We need more."

Theo ran a hand through his hair. "We need to find the Weatherers."

"You need to get closer to Broadgirdle."

He stood and walked over to the window. He looked out into the side garden, where the neighbor's roses hung heavy with faded petals. "Maybe there's a different way to do it."

"Perhaps, but this is the fastest. What other way do you have in mind?"

Theo pressed his forehead against the glass and tried to think. *Sophia would come up with some other way,* he thought. *But I can't see one.* He turned back to face Nettie. "Let me think about it."

—13-Hour 15—

HAVING RETURNED TO East Ending Street and fended off Mrs. Clay's anxious questions about where he had been, Theo went to his room to ponder his dilemma. There was some part of him that wanted to forget about the problem altogether. *I could still leave Boston,* he thought. *There's no one forcing me to stay here.* But he knew this was untrue, even as the escape route unfurled in his mind. He could leave Boston, but he could not leave Shadrack and Miles and Mrs. Clay; he could not leave Sophia.

It felt strange every time he thought about it, but every time he reached the same conclusion: even facing Broadgirdle would not be as bad as losing the people who now knew him best.

What is the solution Sophia would suggest that I can't see? He smiled as he realized the solution Sophia would propose almost certainly resided in a book. But there was no book to tell him what Broadgirdle had done with the Weatherers. He slapped his forehead in frustration. *The Weatherers. They're in the dead center of this, and I have to figure out where they are. I have to figure out who they are.*

Bligh's letter had referred to "the Mark." Given what Miles had said about Goldenrod and the bed of flowers, it was almost certainly the Mark of the Vine. Suddenly, Theo remembered one of the books Veressa Metl had given Sophia the previous summer. He hurried into her room and scanned the bookshelf until he found it: *Origins and Manifestations of the Mark of the Vine,* by Veressa Metl. Theo began paging through it, skimming as quickly as he could for some mention of the Eerie or Weatherers. Neither was in the index.

Much of the first half of the book was theoretical, for no one could point with certainty to where or when the Mark had emerged. The second half contained observations on how the Mark of the Vine appeared in different people, and these were organized into chapters titled "Physiological Characteristics," "Aptitudes," "Care and Healing," and "Behavioral Tendencies." Those with the Mark most often manifested it on their limbs, though in one case a man's chest was encased in bark, and in others leaves sprouted from the back like wings. Many with the Mark were gifted at working with plants, and in some cases they could grow new plants from their own bodies, without the use of seeds or shoots. Veressa posited that the Mark was not something one did or did not have; rather, it was a spectrum. Some people had very little of the Vine, and some people had a great deal. Perhaps one person might have a single thorn growing from a knuckle, while another might have the Mark on every part of the body.

Theo only put the book aside for dinner, and it was late in the evening when he reached the penultimate chapter, "Care and Healing." There, following a disturbing section on tree diseases, was one called "Winter Sleep." Theo skimmed it without really taking it in. Then a light flared in his mind, and he read it again:

> *Just as bulbs sleep in the earth during winter, so do some with the fullest manifestation of the Mark. Well packed in nourishing soil, such a person might comfortably rest for weeks or even months, as long as this does not extend beyond a single season. In cases where disease or injury has taxed the body to extremes, such winter sleep can even be a necessary remedy.*

Theo pictured the contents of the shed: a worktable with a few objects; a wall of tools; and three empty planters stacked beside it. They were long and wide—like coffins. *I was looking at the wrong thing,* he realized. *Not the pruning shears, but the planters. The Weatherers were there. He kept them in winter sleep, and then he took them out. The question is, where are they now?*

He slowly closed the book, replaced it on Sophia's shelf, and returned to his own room. There, he curled up on his bed and considered the objects around him. What were they, really? A bed, a chair, a desk, a collection of souvenirs from the pirates, and a bundle of clothes. They were, in reality, worthless. He could have easily stolen their value ten times over. And yet, at the same time, they were priceless. This room, in this house, with the people who lived in it, were worth more than anything. If need be, they were worth his life.

There was really no choice, Theo realized. He didn't want to, but he had to. Nettie was right—he had to get closer to Broadgirdle.

—*June 8: 12-Hour 20*—

While the hospital reform initiated by the New States Party did improve conditions for patients, it did not alter the rules for admittance, which continued to prove problematic—particularly at hospitals and houses of charity ministering to patients suffering from madness. Many are assumed to suffer from madness when, in fact, their symptoms disguise other conditions—at times more dangerous, at times entirely innocuous.

—From Shadrack Elli's History of New Occident

THEO LEARNED OF the job because he was lingering by the State House, trying to find a way of approaching it that would not be too obvious. He kept his distance from the crowd of younger and more ragged boys that loitered just across the street, waiting for a message or a package to carry. The guards always made sure that these boys didn't make it onto the steps, but Theo looked older and tidier, and when he approached the steps with a doubtful expression a guard immediately pointed to his right. "You're looking for job postings? Rear door by the servants' entrance."

"Thank you," Theo said amiably. He had been looking for nothing of the kind, but this would be an easier and less visible way of gaining entry. When he reached the servants' entrance, he found a wooden board covered with paper advertisements, and while he waited to get a sense of how much foot traffic there was, and what was required to get in, he looked over the postings. One in the center sprang out:

> JUNE 6: Bertram Peel, in the office of MP Gordon Broadgirdle, seeks a responsible and diligent assistant of good character to work full-time, beginning immediately. Inquire within.

Theo reread the advertisement and the date three times, unable to believe what it said. Then he turned on his heel and went home.

He did not return for two days. Theo told himself that he needed the time to work on his knowledge of parliament, but in reality it took those two days to work up his nerve.

It was true that his knowledge of parliament was negligible. He had heard a great deal about the Ministry of Relations with Foreign Ages from Shadrack, but he had no interest in the workings of the legislature. If he was going to do this, he would have to learn. Plunging into a pile of newspapers at Miles's house, he read everything he could about recent happenings. He was aware that a temporary prime minister had been appointed in place of Bligh and that a proper election would be held at the end of the month. He also knew, as did all of Boston, that Broadgirdle would be the candidate for the Western Party.

Theo suspected that the position he was applying for was due to an increased workload resulting from Broadgirdle's campaign. But he had not known or suspected much beyond this, and over the course of two days he did his best to memorize as many names of MPs and as many details about the histories of each party as his brain could hold.

He arrived at the State House on June 10, dressed in a way that was meant to both flatter and disguise. The thin mustache and severely parted hair were there for Broadgirdle's vanity; he knew that Graves, as ever, thought himself a handsome man, and he would be pleased to think that he had imitators. The kidskin gloves and the pressed suit were there for concealment: in proper clothes, with his scarred hand hidden, Theo felt confident that he would be unrecognizable.

Or, at least, he felt confident at the State House entrance. By the time he arrived at Broadgirdle's offices on the top floor, he was having difficulty breathing. He stood in the corridor for a moment and took deep lungfuls of air. There was sweat on his brow, and he wiped it away quickly.

Then he walked to the door of Broadgirdle's offices and knocked. A thin, reedy voice called, "Come in."

Theo found himself facing a gaunt and unbecoming personage with a hairstyle and mustache identical to his. He felt a bubble of mirth rising through his nervousness. "Mr. Bertram Peel?"

"Yes?"

"I am here to inquire about the office assistant position."

The man looked him over in silence for several seconds. Then he glanced at his watch. "You are fortunate to have arrived at a good time," he said. "If you will have a seat, I would like to ask you a few preliminary questions."

"Certainly," Theo said, taking the seat by the desk.

Peel made a great show of procuring a clean pad of paper and testing his pen. "Your name?"

"Archibald Slade."

"How did you learn of the position? Were you referred by anyone?"

"No, I saw it posted near the servants' entrance. I had been hoping—waiting, really—to see a position in MP Broadgirdle's office for such a long time."

Peel pressed his lips together with approval or skepticism—it was hard to tell. "You are a supporter of MP Broadgirdle?"

"Oh, absolutely," Theo replied. "I think his vision for New Occident is exactly what we need."

Peel let his pen pause over the paper. "How, exactly?"

Theo took a deep breath. Broadgirdle had made numerous campaign speeches, and his agenda was simple, at least as he presented it to the public: *Look west and conquer.* The self-righteous bombast with which he spoke of conquering the west managed to conceal its messiness, impracticality, and, in some cases, downright impossibility. There were not enough people in New Occident to "conquer" much of anything. The standing army was minuscule. Only people on the border with the Indian Territories had any desire to edge westward, and they were already doing it. Broadgirdle's campaign could have easily been brought to a halt with one question: "Who?" That is, "Who will look west and conquer?"

Theo did not say any of this. Instead, he said what Peel wanted to hear: "'Look west and conquer!' It is such an inspiring message. This is what people really need—a strong leader with a bold plan."

Peel allowed his face to relax slightly. "The other parties also have leaders with plans. Why not support those?"

Bligh's party, the New States Party, had chosen Gamaliel Shore, a rope maker from Plymouth, as its candidate. Like Bligh, Shore wanted to overturn the border closure because it isolated New Occident and made it a poor trade partner. This was true, but it did not sound as daring as Broadgirdle's argument. Shore also wanted to grant the Indian Territories statehood, which would have benefitted the nation as a whole but did not have quite the same ring to it as "Look west and conquer." Those who bothered to listen carefully realized that Shore's policies, as a continuation of Bligh's, were prudent and wise, while his competitor's were brash and delusional. But not many people listened carefully.

The third party, the vigorous but small Remember England Party, had chosen Pliny Grimes. Their campaign rested on a simple premise expressed aptly by its name. Dedicated to preserving the memory of that vanished colonial power—which, of course, had ceased to rule the states well before the Great Disruption—the Remember England Party made its decisions based entirely on the speculation of how England would have wanted it. This was a frequent refrain in their debates and discussions. "England would have wanted us to stop the pirates at all cost." Or, "England would have warned us about the dangers of paper currency." Or, "England would have said, 'No land, no vote!'" In reality, the party strained its imagination and credibility at every turn, attempting to envision what an England that had not existed for more than ninety years would have done in crises trivial or extreme, none of which was conceivable in 1799. And, in any case, it was unclear who or what they meant by "England." Surely all of England did not think the same way? As critics were keen to point out, England had itself been a hotbed of highly contradictory politics at the moment of the Great Disruption, before it was plunged into medieval obscurity.

"I believe the entire foundation of the Remember England Party is questionable," Theo said truthfully. "And though I have tried, I cannot understand how their plan for New Occident is even feasible. MP Gamaliel Shore," he continued, less truthfully, "seems to me weak-willed in a situation that requires force. New Occident must take a commanding role with its neighbors."

Peel, who had stopped taking notes, sat back in his chair. "Very good, Mr. Slade." He considered for a moment. "Let me see if the MP is available. I would like him to meet you briefly, if he is."

Theo knew that this meant he had done well, and yet his mouth had suddenly gone dry. He forced the words out. "Thank you."

While he waited for Peel to return, he looked around the office. A second desk—bare apart from a lamp—had been added for the new assistant. The walls were lined with tall wooden cabinets labeled carefully in what Theo already recognized as Peel's hand. A door at the rear of the room led to a narrow corridor and an inner office. It was from this corridor that Peel now reemerged, pressing his mustache with satisfaction. "The MP has a moment to see you. Follow me." He tucked his small wooden writing desk under one arm.

Theo watched Peel's retreating back, unsure that he would be able to move forward. His legs felt as though they were filled with water. He closed his eyes and imagined his escape route: back through the door of the office, down the corridor, down the stairs, out through the colonnade, and across the common. Then he opened his eyes and stepped forward, following Peel's gaunt figure into the narrow corridor.

Peel turned into an office on the right. Graves—*Broadgirdle*, Theo told himself firmly—was there. He sat behind a massive desk, his back to the doorway, contemplating the view from the window. "Here is Mr. Archibald Slade, sir," Peel said.

Broadgirdle turned in his chair. Theo's first impression, seeing him at close range, was that he had not changed so much after all. The clothes and teeth and beard were new, but it was still the same face, the same expression, the same penetrating eyes. "Mr. Slade," Broadgirdle said smoothly, putting out his hand. Though he had long arms, he barely leaned forward, forcing Theo to step up to the desk and stretch across it.

"It's an honor, sir." Theo noticed, as they shook hands, that

Broadgirdle glanced at the kidskin gloves. "Please excuse the gloves," he added apologetically. "I have a skin condition."

"Nothing contagious, I hope?" Broadgirdle asked, smiling faintly.

"Oh, no, sir. Nothing contagious." He smiled back, feeling suddenly a little sick. "Just unsightly."

"Well, as long as it doesn't get in the way of your writing and filing."

"No, certainly not."

Broadgirdle gave a lavish smile, showing all his white teeth. "Peel tells me you believe in forceful leadership."

"I do, sir. I think New Occident needs a forceful leader. Now more than ever." Theo knew he was saying the right words, but he felt that if required to think or elaborate upon them, he would be unable to. Broadgirdle's grin was dizzying. The too-familiar way he tapped his hand upon the desk—pattering against the surface with his third and fourth fingers, as if sending a message to the underworld—made Theo want to turn and run.

"The opinion speaks well of you. Let me ask you the question I asked Peel when I hired him, which I like to ask of anyone who works in this office."

"Certainly, sir."

"Pretend that you are already employed here. You are walking down the corridor, and you overhear an MP from one of the opposition parties discussing a measure that would surprise and undermine our plans. The MP sees you. He demands your word that you will not mention what you have overheard to anyone. What do you do?"

Theo knew that there were only one or two right answers, and he felt with relief that in this instance, his past knowledge of Graves—Broadgirdle—worked to his advantage. Some might think that he wanted an ethical reply. But Theo knew that Graves valued shrewdness greatly and ethics not at all. He took a deep breath. "If the MP is demanding my word, I would give it. Then I would report to you what I overheard. Finally, if the MP protested later on, I would say that he had spoken carelessly to let his words be overheard, and that he had not given me a choice in promising to stay silent."

Broadgirdle raised his heavy eyebrows and gave a slight smile. He sat without speaking. "Well said," he finally replied. Theo felt gratification at the compliment and then a flood of nausea for being gratified. He sensed Peel relax slightly. "Working in the State House raises all manner of ethical dilemmas. It is important to know where one's loyalties lie and to not be overly nice with one's virtues."

"I understand, sir," Theo said. "Thank you for the explanation."

Broadgirdle gave him one last, appraising look and then turned to Peel. He nodded slightly.

"We'll return to the front office now, Mr. Slade," Peel said.

"Thank you for the interview, sir."

Broadgirdle acknowledged him and turned to the window once again.

"Mr. Slade, I will contact you soon about the position," Peel said when they reached his desk. He glanced at the sheet of paper on his writing desk. "Care of the South End Post office?"

"Correct."

"Thank you for coming in."

"Thank you." Theo felt too shaky to say anything else. His legs carried him along his escape route: down the corridor, down the steps, and out through the colonnade to the main entrance. When he reached the common he tried to remove his gloves, but he found that the sweat had glued them to his palms. He shook his hands furiously, suddenly desperate to take them off. Finally, pulling them inside out, he was able to yank them from his fingers. He walked unsteadily across the common, feeling great relief and some surprise that he had survived.

—June 12: 13-Hour 45—

THE LETTER FROM Broadgirdle's office arrived on the eleventh, announcing that he had been offered the position and asking him to present himself for work on the twelfth. Theo tried to visit Nettie's house to tell her, but the inspector was home. He left her a note addressed *To Nettie from your friend Charles* in the mailbox. He spent the rest of the day preparing himself, and on the next he did what he once would have considered impossible: he worked his first day in the offices of MP Gordon Broadgirdle.

He realized, as morning gave way to afternoon, that his contact with Broadgirdle would be limited. For one thing, Peel was fiercely jealous of his time with Broadgirdle, and he tried to be the sole point of contact with the powerful MP. Theo did not protest. Moreover, Broadgirdle spent very little time in his office; he spent most of it moving stealthily through the halls of the State House, meeting with various members of parliament and no doubt applying his leverage in as many places as he could.

Theo tensed every time someone turned the doorknob, but by the end of the day his tension had begun to lessen. The avalanche of busywork deposited on his desk by Peel helped, too. When a young woman in a pinstripe shirt and sharply creased trousers came in, Theo welcomed the interruption with relief. "Can I help you?" he asked, getting to his feet. Peel had scrambled out of the office with his writing desk some time earlier in response to a summons from Broadgirdle.

"I just wanted to introduce myself," the young woman said, putting out her hand. "Cassandra Pierce. I work down the hall in MP Gamaliel Shore's office."

"Archibald Slade. Very nice to meet you."

She gave a firm handshake. "How are you settling in?"

"Fine, thank you." Theo gestured at the pile of paperwork on his desk. "I have plenty to do already."

Cassandra smiled, tilting her head slightly. "It seems I was spared."

"How do you mean?"

"I applied for your position, but was not chosen."

"Ah. Very sorry."

"Not at all." She tucked her short black hair behind her ears.

"It can be overwhelming here. All the little snubs and things that go unspoken. Let me know if I can help."

"Thank you. That's very kind."

Cassandra paused and looked around the office. "Well, it's nice to meet you. The assistants all have lunch together on Fridays, if you'd like to join us."

"Maybe I will—I appreciate it."

She gave him a brief wave as she left. Theo looked down at his desk and realized it was almost fourteen-hour. He tidied the papers on his desk, took his jacket from the coat stand, and left the State House.

He felt exhausted, but the day had been a tremendous accomplishment. Though he had learned nothing new, he had successfully implanted himself in Broadgirdle's office. He felt suddenly, exultantly certain that this would work. Broadgirdle had no idea who he was. In a day or two, he would start searching in earnest, and he would find something that explained the presence of the Sandmen, or pointed to the location of the Weatherers, or proved Broadgirdle's involvement in Bligh's murder. It had to be there. With luck, he would have what he needed by the end of the week.

Distracted by these thoughts, Theo did not notice that he was being followed.

The boy was easy to overlook. He was barefoot, because the soles of his boots had given out that winter and the way they slapped the pavement made it difficult to walk around unnoticed. *Untidy* did not begin to describe his hair, which looked more like a pile of crushed straw than a covering for his scalp;

dirty did not begin to describe his skin, which was so covered with dust it was impossible to determine its color; and *torn* did not begin to describe his clothes, which seemed in danger of disintegrating entirely. His pants were held up with twine. His shirt had only one sleeve. At the very top of this bedraggled arrangement perched a very fine and well-made cap, which he had acquired the day before and was sure to keep for only a day or two longer. The best pieces were always bound to be stolen.

The boy padded silently on his bare feet, receiving only the occasional look of pity or disgust from passing pedestrians, and he followed Theo all the way through the Little Nickel to the South End and onto East Wrinkle Street. The boy observed how Theo tousled his hair with a rather desperate movement and accelerated his pace. Running up behind Theo, he scurried around so that he was standing in front of him and stood in his way, arms crossed.

"Uh . . . hello," Theo said, eyeing the diminutive figure in his path. The boy had large ears and freckles, which made it difficult for him to appear menacing, however piercing his glare.

"Hello, Archibald. Or should I say Charles. Or should I say Theodore."

Theo squinted and eyed the boy thoughtfully. He looked familiar—not familiar in the sense that Theo knew this particular boy, but familiar in the sense that Theo himself had once been very like this boy. It was like seeing a younger version of himself. "Scram," he said, not unkindly. He moved to walk past him.

"You don't want to do that."

"What? Go home?"

The boy scowled. "Ignore me. It's a bad idea."

Theo smiled. It was true, he reflected. Ignoring himself when he was this age would have been a bad idea. "Okay. I'm not ignoring you. You figured out that I have three names."

The boy seemed momentarily disconcerted. "I did," he asserted, attempting to keep his tone confrontational.

Theo shrugged and looked away. "Probably someone told you. And now you want to pretend you figured it out all by yourself."

"No one told me! I did figure it out all by myself."

Theo gave him a skeptical look. "Prove it. How did you know?"

"Easy. Saw you leaving the State House. Followed you here. Saw you sneak in. Saw you sneak out again the next day. Saw you leaving love letters over in the Little Nickel. I've got eyes and ears, and I'm just about invisible. It's a good way to figure things out."

"All right," Theo conceded. "But you don't know what I'm actually doing or why I'm doing it."

"No, I don't," the boy replied stoutly, "but it seems to me that whatever you're doing, you ought to calculate me into your expenses if you plan on staying undercover."

Theo laughed. "Not likely. Nice try, though." He tried to walk away, but the boy stuck out a dirty hand to stop him.

"I know what he has on Shadrack." He looked up at Theo, his eyes sharp.

"What?"

"Broadsy made an agreement with Shadrack. I know what it is."

Theo made an effort to appear mildly impressed rather than desperately curious. "What is it, then?"

"Ha," he replied dryly. "No chance. You and I agree to terms. Then I'll tell you what I've got. If you don't like it, the terms are only good for one week. If you do, the terms are good indefinitely."

Theo tapped his chin, speculating. "All right. Let's talk. What's your name?"

The boy looked suddenly greatly relieved. The tough talk had proved something of a strain for him. "Winston. Winston Pendle. Go by Winnie."

"And you're one of the boys who work near the State House, right?"

"Right."

"How many people know about this?"

"No one, just me," Winnie said with a touch of pride.

"All right. First part of the terms. That's how it has to stay."

"Obviously. Second part. I want a nickel a day."

Theo's eyes narrowed. "Are you blackmailing me like 'Broadsy' does?"

"No!" Winnie said heatedly. "I want a nickel a day for my work. I can take messages, I can hear things no one else does, and I can follow people. Like I said. I'm invisible."

"Okay. But we keep it at a nickel, even if things get a bit rough—which they might. No haggling."

Winnie looked down at the cobblestones in an attempt to conceal his glee. A nickel a day would mean three meals and maybe a pair of shoes, if he saved up. "I can handle rough work. But it can be expensive."

"I said no haggling."

"Fine."

"It's a great deal and you know it," Theo said.

"Yeah. Yeah, I guess it is," Winnie agreed.

"All right. Let's hear what you've got. I'll go in this way, and you go around and knock on the side door of 34 East Ending Street in five minutes. I'm going to introduce you to Mrs. Clay. First test for you. Mrs. Clay has no idea what I'm doing at the State House, see?"

Winnie nodded.

"It's for her own good. She's a worrier. She thinks I've been spending all my time hanging out like you do on the common. We're going to keep it that way, all right?"

—*15-Hour 34*—

MRS. CLAY WAS more than a little shocked by the state of Winnie's attire, and for several minutes, while Theo explained who he was and how they had met lingering near the State House, she could do little more than stare at him. She had seen such children on the street before, of course, but she had the vague sense that their state was always temporary, and she had never had the chance to speak to one of them to ascertain whether this was true. Nodding absently as Theo finished his introductions, Mrs. Clay frowned. "And where do you sleep at night, Winnie?" she asked.

"You know, here and there."

Her frown deepened. "Where are your parents?"

Theo rolled his eyes; this line of questioning was all too familiar, and he knew it would lead nowhere. Winnie squirmed. "No idea about my father. My mother's upstate."

"What do you mean, 'upstate'?"

"At the 'stitution."

"The what?"

"The 'stitution." Winnie looked decidedly uncomfortable. He examined his bare feet.

Theo pushed him into one of the kitchen chairs and sat down next to him. "I have always thought, when they put you in an institution," he said, enunciating clearly for Mrs. Clay's benefit, "it usually means that you are too talkative in the wrong company or quiet in the wrong company or smart in the wrong company or persistent in the wrong company. Basically, it means you have been yourself but in the wrong company. Isn't that the way of it?"

"That's right," Winnie said, crossing his arms with an expression of indignant disdain that did not entirely conceal the gratitude shining in his eyes like tiny flames.

Mrs. Clay sat down slowly, her face pale. "I see. Well, Winnie. You are always welcome to a meal here." She had the sense that this was woefully inadequate, but the complications of doing more struck her forcibly, and she realized that she would have to think long and hard about this problem. Opening the breadbox that sat on the counter, she removed a loaf of currant bread, cut a few slices, and placed the butter beside it while the conversation continued.

"Winnie wants to help us," Theo went on, "and he's going to start by telling us what he found out about the agreement between Shadrack and Broadgirdle."

Drawn away from thoughts of the institution by the currant bread and Theo's prompt, Winnie straightened up in his chair. "Broadgirdle has a book. He was going to give it to Shadrack."

"Yes, he gave it to him. But we don't know what it is."

"It's a book written by another Shadrack."

Theo squinted. "What do you mean?"

"A book written by another Shadrack Elli. Published in 1899. It's about maps for places that don't exist, and a war."

Theo's face eased with understanding. "Ah—it's dreck."

"What's dreck?" Winnie asked. He took the opportunity to seize a piece of currant bread.

"A word from another Age. It means trash. But really it means things from another Age that don't belong in ours. Like that book."

"Well, Broadsy used the book to explain to Shadrack what he wanted. He calls it 'westwood spansion.'"

Theo and Mrs. Clay exchanged a glance. "He wants to take the Indian Territories and the Baldlands," Theo said slowly, thinking aloud. "Westward expansion."

"And," Winnie added with his mouth full, "he wants

Shadrack to help him. He's even agreed to get Shadrack out of jail so he can do it."

"But why would Mr. Elli agree to that?" Mrs. Clay protested.

"Because of you," Winnie said, swallowing. "Both of you."

Theo and Mrs. Clay stared at him, uncomprehending. "You're from the Baldlands, aren't you? And your papers are forged? Well, Broadsy knows. And he's making Shadrack pay for it."

—1892, June 30: 7-Hour 00—

The silkworm that feeds from the grapevine rather than the mulberry tree was introduced by merchants from the Middle Roads. From these merchants, too, was learned the unique properties of its silk. As long as she is the exclusive wearer, the owner of such silk will impart to it a sense of her character. Even when she has left this world, one may sense her presence in the fabric made by these extraordinary creatures. It has become common practice to wear a silk, or "silkshell," to bequeath to loved ones upon one's death.

—From Fulgencio Esparragosa's
Complete and Authoritative History of the Papal States

ERROL AND GOLDENROD had each traveled hundreds of miles on foot in the last year, and for each this was a point of pride. Goldenrod could not conceive of any people but hers moving smoothly and quickly over long distances; Errol, who now knew every inch of road between Seville and Granada, could not imagine anyone navigating the route more competently than he did. He glanced skeptically at Goldenrod's dark hood more than once, thinking to himself that she was probably roasting. Likewise, Goldenrod observed his heavy boots and weaponry with a knowing smile, thinking to herself that they must weigh a good thirty pounds altogether.

So the two traveled quickly, without speaking, but each intently aware of the other. Indeed, Errol was so focused on Goldenrod's quick steps and Goldenrod so focused on the sound of Errol's boots that neither noticed the difficulty Sophia had keeping up with them.

Leaving Seville, they passed more than one traveler headed in the same direction, and after a quarter of a mile Sophia saw a great number of people clustered around a tiny stone chapel. "What is that place?" she asked, trying not to pant.

"It is a shrine for Saint Leonora, whose silkshell lies within," Errol replied. "The pilgrims come daily to visit."

"What is a silkshell?" She hoped faintly that the explanation might slow him down.

Goldenrod stopped, dismayed. "Sophia, you are winded."

"Your legs are longer," she said ruefully.

"I am very sorry. We must keep a more reasonable pace, no matter the danger," Goldenrod said, giving Errol a stern look.

From then on, the falconer and the Eerie walked more slowly, and while Sophia felt that her lungs were filling with dust, she no longer had difficulty keeping pace. They passed another shrine that stood in the shade of a towering oak tree; two young women wearing veils murmured to one another in the shrine's entrance. Errol nodded to them as he passed.

"Do you follow the religion of the cross?" Goldenrod asked.

"I do," Errol said with a sharp glance in her direction. "Many of the shrines along this route are worth visiting."

"I suppose they mark the sites of miracles."

"They do indeed," Errol said, his tone defensive. "The clerics of the Papal States do not inspire my faith in the least, but some of the miracles that have taken place here would inspire wonder in the heart of the most hardened heathen." He spoke the last word meaningly.

Goldenrod smiled. "Such as?"

"At the site of that shrine we passed, a blind woman took shelter from a storm beneath the old oak tree. She not only stayed dry—when the storm passed, her vision had been restored."

"Truly miraculous," Sophia agreed.

"What a kindhearted tree," observed Goldenrod.

Errol looked at her, scandalized. "Perhaps I was wrong. Some heathens are too hardened, after all."

"Not in the least—I am really quite touched to hear of such generosity," Goldenrod said matter-of-factly. She looked off at the horizon, where something had caught her eye. In the short time they had spent walking, Sophia had realized that the Eerie walked with her attention elsewhere, as if she were listening to a conversation in the air around her. Her impression was confirmed when Goldenrod stopped on the dusty road, her eyes alert and focused. "Four riders," she said. "From the direction of Seville."

Errol looked down the road and saw nothing. "How do you know?"

"I know," she told him. "We have a little time. There is an abandoned house some minutes up the road—we should take shelter there."

"I know the house. How could you possibly know of it?"

"Does it matter?" Goldenrod asked, walking on.

The abandoned building was a stone farmhouse with broken shutters. They crouched inside, against the stone walls, which were still cool from the cold night. Minutes later, four riders of the Golden Cross thundered past on horseback, their masks shining like torches in the sun. They left a cloud of dust behind them that swirled and subsided, unsettling the air.

"We should wait here until dusk," Goldenrod said, when the road was quiet once more.

"It will be safest," Errol agreed. "I will travel up the road to get water."

"I will go," Goldenrod said, rising. "It will be safest."

Errol shook his head impatiently. "It will not. And you do not know where the water is."

"Yes, I do." Her voice was calm. "And you are better equipped to protect Sophia, should anything occur in my absence."

Sophia watched them, suspecting that Goldenrod knew quite well nothing would occur in her absence and knew, too, that she had made the one argument Errol would be incapable of denying. "Very well," he finally said.

Goldenrod took his water sack and two jugs from the farmhouse and headed off toward the east, her hooded cape wrapped around her. Sophia watched anxiously through the window until the Eerie reappeared, a wavering, shimmering figure in the morning heat. Goldenrod gave the first jug to Sophia and placed the other in a cool corner. She handed Errol his water sack. Under her hood, her hair and clothes were still wet from the water she had poured over herself at the well. She took off the cape with some relief and hung it on a peg, as if the little farmhouse were hers and she had just arrived from an outing. "I realize the sun is taxing to you," she said, pulling off her gloves and placing them on the table, "but I have need of it. I will be on the other side of the house, away from the road. If there is any disturbance approaching, I will let you know."

Errol frowned and said nothing. "Thank you," Sophia said. She took a long drink from the jug. Then she went to the back of the farmhouse and changed from her nightgown to her traveling clothes. After a moment's hesitation, she left the Nihilismian amulet in her pack. Through the window, she saw Goldenrod lying on her back on the earth, her hair fanning out in every direction, absorbing the sunlight.

Sophia smiled to herself. She had no doubt that Goldenrod bore the Mark of the Vine, as people in Nochtland called it. But Goldenrod did not describe it as such, and she seemed different, somehow, from Veressa and Martin, Sophia's friends there. Perhaps she seemed different because among the Eerie the mark was common, rather than a sign of prestige. Moreover, what person in Nochtland could summon yellow blossoms on their palms? She was no doubt at the "far end of the spectrum," as Veressa had described it.

Errol sat with his eyes closed, though his forearms rested on his bent knees and his expression indicated that he was awake.

Sophia sat down against the wall and took the beaded map from her satchel. Blowing gently on the fabric, she watched as the white lines took shape and then placed it on her lap. Sophia glanced at her watch to make sure she didn't drift too long—it was eight-hour, thirty-two—and then she placed her fingers on the map, marking the time on the clock with one hand and viewing its contents with the other.

It was early April. The parched landscape around her looked indistinguishable from the one she had just been traveling, and she felt an odd sense of recognition. She stood upon a yellow plain that stretched almost to the horizon. The land grew mustard-colored and then faintly green—almost blue—as it gave way to hills. Sophia moved along the road. She knew that her finger upon the map was allowing her to move, but she felt entirely immersed in the memory, as if she had physically traveled into it. The road ran straight, then reached a crossroads with signs that had been bleached empty by sun and wind. She chose one of the paths east, but the landscape did not change. Standing again near the crossroads, she altered the time with the fingers of her left hand, moving up an hour, then two, then an entire day. The weary hours progressed; the sun rose and set overhead. But the crossroads were empty and quiet.

Sophia traveled farther east, following the long ribbon of road. She retraced her steps for one day, and then another, covering the middle of the map over and over again, until she was certain that while the crossroads marked the center of the map, there was nothing to be seen there.

Suddenly Sophia remembered where she was, and that she

had covered weeks of travel along the memory map's dusty road. Lifting her finger from the map abruptly, she fumbled for her watch. Eight-hour, thirty-three—only a minute had passed? Was it a whole day later? But Errol was sitting as she had last seen him: eyes closed, head resting against the stones. No, it was true. Only a minute had passed.

How could this be? It had not happened in all the time she had spent aboard the *Verity* dwelling in the beaded map. She had just now spent many days on the changeless road, yet only a short amount of time had passed in the farmhouse. *Could it be*—Sophia wondered, with dawning awareness—*could it be something I did by losing track of time? Am I letting the time expand in one place in the map, while almost no time passes here?*

Eager to test her theory, Sophia placed her fingers upon the map once again. She set the time to its earliest point and returned to the crossroads, traveling quickly east until she thought she could go no farther. Then, as she flew along the dusty road, she saw something on the horizon. Hills, yes, but hills of a different sort. She stopped abruptly. The landscape had changed.

She was facing directly east. To the south, she could see the walls of a town or village. To the north, the blue hills loomed within striking distance. In all her time within the map aboard the *Verity*, she had never seen the village or the blue hills.

Sophia hurried to the village. Her finger dropped off the edge of the map, pulling her from the landscape; she reimmersed herself. A high stone wall bordered the village, and though she could see the entrance gate, she could not approach it. Taking the road northward, she saw a farmhouse with a sod roof and stone walls. She neared it and heard a young woman's voice, slow and sweet, singing. Her heart pounded. Here was the first glass bead: the first person she had encountered in the map's memories. She did not know how, for the song was surely in Castilian, but Sophia understood the words: they told the story of a lovely gray dove, struck down by an arrow, never to fly again. The song was tender and unspeakably sad. She felt pained by the sound of the girl's voice, and she knew that the person whose memories were inscribed upon the map had known this girl and felt compassion for her. But although she could hear the song and see sections of the farmhouse, she could not see the singer. Sophia lifted her finger in frustration.

She understand now how the map worked. Cabeza de Cabra's map was unlike the memory maps in Shadrack's library, because those had been the careful compilation of many memories. This map contained only his experiences— no one else's. Sophia frowned. Truly, she was looking for a few drops of water in an ocean; a few glass beads among hundreds; a few minutes in a whole year. She sighed and looked at her watch: eight-hour, thirty-five. *At least I have plenty of time to search,* she thought.

Sophia returned to the farmhouse and decided to piece together a chronology. January, February, March—she traveled northward along a dusty road that led to the hills. A stone bridge crossed a dry gully and the hills fanned out, dry and yellow but unexpectedly green and verdant farther on. Sophia's fingers held her in early April. She inched forward to the middle of the month. Suddenly, on the twentieth, as she stood on the stone bridge facing east, she saw a figure coming toward her out of the hills: an old man, walking slowly with the support of a staff. He stopped and looked up at her. He seemed to scrutinize her—or, rather, scrutinize the person whose memories she inhabited, and finally asked, "Good morning, sheriff. First time, I take it?"

"Yes," Sophia found herself saying. She felt a spasm of tension in her chest. "First and last, I hope."

The old man smiled. "There is nothing to fear. Simply follow the middle path at each juncture. This is my third visit."

"And did you find what you were looking for?"

"Always." The stranger produced a scroll of paper from inside his tattered shirt.

"I confess to harboring some skepticism."

"Young man," he replied with a shake of his head, "the maps require some interpretation, and not a little patience. But they are the truest, canniest pieces of wisdom and prophecy I have ever known. It's no wonder the papacy fears this place. If someone had lost Heaven and came to ask for a map back, they would get it. Believe me. No matter what you have lost, Ausentinia will help you find it."

—1892, June 30: 8-Hour 37—
and —1880: April 20—

Many parts of the Papal States remain barren and unexplored. And wherever lands remain unexplored, of course, rumors about them abound. Most are undoubtedly spurious: tales of an Age in the northern mountains inhabited by people made entirely of lead; or a cave on the coast leading to an Age of mermen; or a region in the south where the pathways worn by travelers appear and disappear at whim.

—From Fulgencio Esparragosa's
Complete and Authoritative History of the Papal States

SOPHIA GASPED, THE part of her that sat in the farmhouse with Errol and Goldenrod tensing with excitement while the part of her that traveled through the map continued to converse with the traveler on the bridge.

The old man smiled. "Are you from Murtea, sheriff?"

"I am."

"Tell me your name so that I might find you the next time I am there. I will come to see what guidance your map from Ausentinia has given you."

"Alvar. Alvar Cabeza de Cabra."

The old man offered his dry, withered hand. "Juan Pedrosa, of Granada. I will look for you, Alvar, and I hope your map will be auspicious."

"Thank you. Safe travels." Cabeza de Cabra walked on, pausing once to turn and watch the retreating figure of the old man, who walked slowly with his staff. Then he proceeded along the path before him. It ran straight over a hill. On the other side it split three ways; Cabeza de Cabra took the middle path. He walked along until it split again, taking the middle path once more. As he walked, the way grew less dusty, and the grass on either side grew greener and taller. At the next juncture, the middle path took him through a small grove that obscured the hills, and then it began to ascend in earnest. The trees grew more densely and filled the air with a quiet rustle. Fig, lemon, orange, and olive orchards covered the hillsides, while maples and a few elms shaded the trail. As he climbed, the woods became piney, the air sharp with the scent of sap. Always taking the middle way, Cabeza de Cabra walked tirelessly, until almost an hour had passed. Then he crested a hill and paused to look out over the valley.

The city of Ausentinia lay at its heart, the copper roofs winking in the bright sun. The steep hillsides were ribboned with narrow trails. Hurrying along the descent, Cabeza de Cabra soon arrived at the low stone wall of the entrance.

The people he passed on the streets nodded politely. Cabeza de Cabra touched his forehead in return, taking in the buildings made of a tidy red brick and shingled with black wood or hammered copper. The houses had window boxes filled with flowers, and Cabeza de Cabra heard the deep, rolling sound of some stringed instrument from one open window and the splash of running water from another. He reached a street lined with stores, most with copper globes hung above the signs: map stores.

The one nearest him had a broad, many-paned window, and a middle-aged woman was cleaning it pane by square pane with a look of concentration. Seeing him, the woman stopped what she was doing, studied him, and then indicated that he should enter. Cabeza de Cabra opened the door, setting off a tiny bell. A round silver table in the center of the room held a standing globe. The innumerable little drawers that lined the walls had glass fronts, so that the rolled papers in each were visible.

"Good morning, Alvar," the woman said. She wore a brightly colored apron, and her plump face was slightly pink.

"Good morning," Cabeza de Cabra replied with some surprise. "How do you know my name?"

"It is one of the things we know, those of us with maps to give," she said with a little wave of the hand. "You might say that my map shows you visiting me this fine morning in April."

"I see."

"But you are here not about my map. You are here to find your own."

"Yes, I—I have lost something. Something very dear to me." Cabeza de Cabra cleared his throat. "Something I cannot live without."

"I understand," the woman said gently. "It was the plague cleric who made you lose your faith, was it not?"

Cabeza de Cabra was again surprised. He took a deep breath and regarded the floor for a long while. "Yes," he finally said.

"I have the map that you require." She walked along the wall of drawers, standing on tiptoe to peek into one, bending slightly to peer at another. "Ah, here it is." She opened one halfway down and drew out a scroll of paper tied with white string and what looked like a rolled-up piece of fabric tied with blue string. "This," she said, handing him the paper, "is your map. It may be a long and difficult path, but it will guide you."

"Thank you," Cabeza de Cabra said.

"And you may have heard that we do not accept coin or currency?" At his nod, she gave him the roll of cloth. "This is the payment you will make some time in the future, as your own map describes."

"What is it?"

"I believe it is a map that is yet to be written." She smiled. "You will write it someday."

Cabeza de Cabra shook his head. "Very well, though all of this is beyond my comprehension. If I still believed in the teachings of the clerics, I would call it witchcraft."

"What a good thing you don't, then—at the moment."

"I suppose so." He touched his forehead. "Thank you." He turned to leave the shop, pausing a moment on the street to watch the woman return to her task at the window. Then he walked on, passing the way he had come, until he found himself once again at the stone wall bordering the city. Reaching into his shirt, he withdrew the scroll of paper and opened it. On one side, a map labeled "A Map for the Faithless" showed a long route through strange lands—the Broad Plains of Privation, the Glaciers of Discontent, the Eerie Sea. Drawn in a faint, unsteady hand with black ink, the peculiar landscapes bloomed across the heavy paper like haphazard stains. On the reverse were written the following directions:

Beaten on the edge of a threat; broken by the sound of loathing; destroyed by the dearth of mercy. I am no more than a whisper at the edge of the world, and you may never find me.

You will travel for almost a year through the Desert of Bitter Disillusion, finding no relief in the pious waters offered you. When you see the three faces, your more arduous journey begins. Two of the faces will be empty. The third face, which binds the other two, will have twelve hours. Follow the three faces wherever they lead you, across the many Ages, for your search lies with them. You will traverse the Broad Plains of Privation and find passage across the Glaciers of Discontent. As the glaciers give way to the Mountains of Dawning Hope, you will find yourself entering the fifth Age of your journey. There, you will pass into the Limitless Plains of Learning, and find meaning where there was none before. When you see the first snowfall on the Eerie Sea, you will be ready.

Let the three faces go on alone. Put down roots in the Forest of Belief, and make the map as the Eerie teach you. Let the gold you have saved serve a new purpose. Let the story it tells restore you. Let the map it makes shield you *from the summer sun. A wanderer you have long eluded will join you, and bring you death. There, in that place, and after these travels, you may find what you seek.*

—1892, June 30: 8-Hour 37—

AS THE SHERIFF contemplated the Ausentinian map, Sophia drew herself partially out of the memories to study it more slowly. *Three faces? Twelve hours?* The face with twelve hours could be a watch or a clock, but she had no idea about the two others. Perhaps three clocks, but only one with a face? The portion of the directions that stood out to her clearly involved the Eerie Sea. She did not understand the prophetic riddles any more than she understood the man whose memories she shared, but it was clear from what she knew about his future that this map had somehow led him all the way to another Age—to the Indian Territories, and then to the Eerie Sea. Surely the map that he was meant to make with the Eerie was the very one she now was reading.

It was marvelous, and beyond comprehension, but the map from Ausentinia had drawn a tidy circle: sending Cabeza de Cabra from Ausentinia to the Indian Territories, prompting him to write a map, and guiding Sophia through that map back to Ausentinia itself. "Incredible," she whispered.

She lifted her finger from the cloth, dimly aware of movement in the room. Goldenrod stood in the doorway of the farmhouse, her expression troubled. "Errol," she said.

The falconer opened his eyes. "What is it?"

"There are four more riders coming this way." She paused. "But these are not pursuing us. They bring captives."

Errol rose to his feet. He did not ask how she knew. "Plague victims. They take them to a site of quarantine along this road."

"We must help them," she said simply.

After a moment he replied. "Very well."

Sophia rolled the beaded map and stowed it hastily into her satchel. "What can I do?" she asked.

"You can stay in that corner," Errol said, "until this is over."

"If you would," Goldenrod told him, "wait to loose your arrows until the horsemen flee."

"Flee what?" Errol asked, readying his quiver at the window.

"The dust from the road."

He gave her a look. "I think it more likely they will run from their captives than the dusty road."

"If you loose arrows from the farmhouse, they will come toward it."

"Lamentably, I cannot loose arrows from anywhere else while I am in the farmhouse." He stood by the window holding his bow.

A faint crease of exasperation furrowed Goldenrod's brow. Then she went to the other window that looked out over the road and stood still, waiting. She watched Errol rather than the road.

Sophia crouched in the corner, hugging her knees. How she wished that Theo was with them! He would be making her laugh, making it seem that the approaching danger was a thing he had planned because he thought it would be funny. But without him there, nothing funny came to mind.

When she heard the slow shuffling of horses and people, she leaned to peer out through Goldenrod's window. Four horsemen with gleaming masks and white cloaks rode past, just as the Eerie had said. They wore heavy golden crosses strung on chains. Behind them were ten, twelve, perhaps more people of various ages tied together at their waists and strung, as if on a leash, to one of the horse's halters. The people stared at nothing, listlessly, vacantly. One of them suddenly sat down, and around her the rest followed suit. The rider whose horse held the leash yanked. He rode onward, dragging the prisoners.

"Good God," Errol muttered.

"Wait," Goldenrod whispered urgently.

Errol loosed an arrow, striking the horseman's shoulder. The other three riders turned, momentarily confused, and in a moment looked as one to the farmhouse. Errol loosed another arrow, striking a second rider, and as his horse veered, dust began to rise behind them. The cluster of captives was lost in a yellow cloud. As the last two riders advanced toward the farmhouse, the cloud became a funnel. Sophia's eyes opened wide. It was a weirwind, narrow and tall as the spire of a church. The rider closest to it turned in his saddle. His horse skidded as the rider faced the weirwind. The next moment it swallowed them, and they disappeared into the edifice of wind and dust as if entering another world. The other rider turned to look behind him, and when he saw the weirwind he whirled, digging in his heels. *Brujos!* he shouted.

He galloped toward the farmhouse, sword raised. Errol ran to meet him. Sophia crouched in the corner and listened as metal met metal. "So eager to meet death," Goldenrod commented. She watched for some minutes. The sound of clanging metal stopped.

Sophia dared to look through the window and saw Errol standing with his sword drawn. The man lay strewn before him, immobile. The weirwind was gone.

Errol turned back toward the farmhouse, sheathing his sword. "How did you do that? Where did that windstorm come from?" he demanded as he entered.

Goldenrod ignored his questions. "We must see to the captives," she said, edging past him through the doorway.

Errol shook his head, but he followed without protest. Pack and satchel in hand, Sophia hurried after them.

The string of prisoners sat, heedless of the heat and dust, by the side of the road. Some were sprawled, however their bonds allowed, flat upon the ground. "You mean to douse them with Faierie powder?" Errol asked, coming up beside Goldenrod.

"Will you cut their bonds, Errol? They will panic if they return to their senses and find themselves bound."

Errol went among the prisoners, cutting the ropes that held them to each other. Most were women. Two were aging, white-haired men. Three were children, and one of these was only just old enough to walk alone. Errol carefully cut the ropes around their waists until all were free, and then he stepped back. "Wait a moment, now," he said to Goldenrod. "I have no need of another dose."

"These wanderers are cannier than the ones I know," Goldenrod said, more to herself than to them. "I wonder where they come from." She raised her bare hands in front of her, palms up, and they filled with yellow blooms. Errol and Sophia watched as she tossed them before her, the petals expanding like a cloud that then sank, slowly, onto the oblivious sufferers. Several of them coughed. Some began to speak, as if waking from a long slumber, and one of the children started crying. "They will be fine now."

"Where will they go?" Sophia asked worriedly.

Errol was looking to the west. "They will go back to Seville. We must go on without them. And quickly."

"The other rider?" Goldenrod asked.

"Yes. Who called us witches. It will not be long before he returns with reinforcements. We will have to leave, despite the sun and the risk. Come along, miting," he said to Sophia. "Do not worry about them," he added, indicating the recovering, disoriented plague victims. "We have greater worries."

Goldenrod looked at him attentively. "Is this Order of the Golden Cross so powerful? Can we not simply avoid them?"

Errol laughed. "They cannot be avoided. They have informers everywhere, and more clerics than you can imagine. Now they suspect Sophia of carrying the plague and us of practicing witchcraft." He frowned. "You do not like it when I accuse you of being a Faierie. Well, then. I wonder how you will like it when they accuse you of being a witch."

—1892, June 30: 17-Hour 20—

It is not known whether the Eerie come from a far future Age or a far past Age. What is known is that they first appeared on the Pacific coast. They traveled west into the Indian Territories in pursuit of the Erie, whom they thought might be their kin. It is unknown to Erie and Eerie alike whether they share a bloodline, but the Eerie settled near their possible relations.

—From Shadrack Elli's History of New Occident

"WHAT IS A miting?" Sophia asked Errol as they rode east. She sat behind Goldenrod, her arms wrapped around the Eerie's waist. Errol had captured the horses of the two fallen riders, and Goldenrod had been able to calm them. They moved twice as fast toward Granada now, the horses kicking up dust as they went.

"It is a little mite," Errol said, smiling from under his gray hood.

"What is a mite?"

"It is like a tick. A little insect that bites you and gets under your skin and is impossible to pull out."

Sophia was momentarily too indignant to reply. "You think I am like a bloodsucking insect."

Errol laughed, a soft, low sound. "I say it with admiration. You hold on—a tough little thing with a tough little shell."

"Oh," she said, somewhat appeased. "I'm not that little."

"No, you are not. But you are the smallest of our company and possibly the sturdiest, so I reserve the right to call you 'miting.'"

"But I am not the sturdiest either."

Errol considered. "It is not that you are the sturdiest altogether, but you are resilient in your kindheartedness. I have seen it more than once now. You worry for others when the peril is to yourself." He smiled at her. "It is as foolish as it is honorable."

Sophia did not know what to say to this. "At your age," Errol continued, "I would not have worried so for the plight of others. And you, Faierie?" His voice changed. There was a note of respect that had not been there before. "Were you so driven to rescue the helpless when you were younger?"

Sophia could not see Goldenrod's face, but she imagined the Eerie looking calmly ahead, untroubled. "It is our custom to offer aid to anyone we encounter, if we are able to provide it. We are all this way—it is not my particular quality."

SOPHIA EXPLAINED TO Goldenrod, as she had to Errol, why she had come to the Papal States, what had happened aboard the *Verity*, and what waited for her at the Nihilismian depository in

Granada. Goldenrod did not say that the journey seemed long for a diary, and she did not question the wisdom of leaving the port of Seville when aid was forthcoming.

For most of the long day, Errol and Goldenrod listened for the signs they anticipated of the Golden Cross. But the hours passed quietly. By dusk, Sophia had fallen asleep against the Eerie's back. She woke to the sound of Errol's bow twanging in the stillness. Before her on the horse, Goldenrod sat more alertly. "What were those?"

"Phantoms," Errol replied quietly.

Sophia shifted to look, but she saw only Errol, retrieving his two arrows, and a sign. LA PALOMA GRIS, the sign read, over a cracked painting of a pigeon. She felt a pang of sharp regret that she had missed seeing Minna.

"What do you mean, 'phantoms'?" Goldenrod asked.

"Just that."

"But they spoke."

"Nothing of substance," Errol replied tersely. "They will return again tomorrow at dusk if you wish to exchange words with them, though I doubt you will find it a useful conversation." He lifted Sophia down from the horse. "I know the innkeeper here at the Gray Pigeon. She will hide us if the Order arrives."

The innkeeper greeted Errol with a toothless smile and a warm embrace. There were no other travelers, and after bringing them a jug of water, a pot of stew, a plate of almonds and olives, and a wide loaf of bread, she hung up her apron and retreated to her own rooms.

They rested in a common room hung with hammocks—

evidence of days long gone in which the Papal States still traded with the United Indies. As Errol and Goldenrod settled in, Sophia took the beaded map from her satchel. "Goldenrod?" Sophia peeked through the weave of her hammock to see if the Eerie was awake.

"Yes?"

"How did you do it? The flowers in your hands. Can all the Eerie heal that way?"

Goldenrod's brown hair was spread out across the hammock, and her green skirts spilled over its edges. She had removed her white headscarf and dropped it to the floor. Her soft-soled leather shoes, with long laces like her gloves, lay beside it, and her small green feet were propped on the hammock's webbing. She shifted so that she was sitting upright and looked across at Sophia. Errol, his arms crossed over his chest where he hung in his own hammock, was listening attentively as well.

"We call ourselves not Eerie," she began, "but the Elodea—Elodeans. I believe we are called 'Eerie' by people in New Occident because we live near the Eerie Sea. They confuse us with the Erielhonan, the true Erie, who were long ago dispersed by war. It is a habit I have observed in New Occident—the misnaming of people and places based on fragmentary knowledge. We are from the far west, from the ocean. In a better world, our knowledge would not be secret. But we have learned from long experience that many people use this knowledge for ill.

"People of the Baldlands and New Occident believe we are healers," she said. She contemplated her palms. "But we are not healers so much as interpreters. You see how Errol can speak both the language of his people in the Closed Empire and the language of people here, in the Papal States?"

"Yes," Sophia said.

"What I do is the same, only I speak not the languages of different people but the languages of different beings."

Errol and Sophia considered this, each imagining it to mean different things. Errol's mind drifted to all the strange creatures—goblins, pixies, elves—of his grandfather's stories, while Sophia thought about badgers and bears. "Do you mean beings like animals?" she asked.

"Partly. I spoke to the horses earlier, and they told me a good deal about this Order of the Golden Cross. And Seneca, while of a reserved nature, has shared some interesting stories about Errol." She glanced smilingly at Errol, who looked distinctly uncomfortable. "But I mean other beings, as well. In our Age— and in our history before the Great Disruption—Elodeans have always had the gift of many languages. To us, it seemed ordinary; the way of the world. It was only through contact with the people of the Baldlands and the Indian Territories— and later, people of eastern New Occident—that we realized you do not communicate as we do. This results in many conflicts, some of which you perceive and some of which you do not. The world is filled with beings with which you hold no communication."

"You mean the Fey world," Errol said.

"No, not what you believe is the Fey world, although perhaps some of those beings are the ones I mean. Consider what people call the plague here—*lapena*. Yes, it is an illness, much like a fever brought on by typhus or some other disease. But *lapena* is actually a fever of the heart. Just as with typhus, it is caused by creatures imperceptible to the eye. The tiny wanderers who cause the plague are, themselves, displaced beings; I have not understood yet from where. But they are troubled, discontented, and rootless. They take company with people in a misguided effort to make space for themselves. I speak to them, and the goldenrod blossoms give them something to cling to—like a rope thrown into the sea. They hear me, and take hold of the rope, and climb out. Yet people in the Papal States do not perceive these beings at all; they think of *lapena* as a kind of corruption, or a curse. The being itself goes unnoticed. So it is with other beings, too."

Sophia and Errol digested this. "That does not explain how you knew what was happening farther up the road," he objected. "Or what you did with the dust."

Goldenrod looked up at the ceiling, her hands in her lap. "I am afraid I can say no more. I have already said too much."

"Can you tell us why—why you can't say more?" Sophia tried again.

"I can tell you this much: for some, our abilities seem a thing of power, so that beings of all kinds might be made to jump and dance and do their bidding." Her voice was somber.

Sophia was shocked. "The Elodea do that?"

"No, we do not—none of us would do so willingly. But others, who have seen what we do, have tried to use us for those ends."

"How terrible. You mean . . ." Sophia thought through the

consequences of what Goldenrod had explained. "You mean someone could tell the plague where to go, whom to make sick?"

"Yes. And you must take my word for it that this would be as nothing, compared to the havoc that can be wrought." Goldenrod sounded weary. She swung her legs over the side of the hammock and stepped onto the dirt floor. "I will take some night air, now that the innkeeper has gone to rest."

WHILE GOLDENROD WALKED outside and Errol rested in his hammock, Sophia unrolled Cabeza de Cabra's map. With some effort, she drew her thoughts away from the inn and rejoined the sheriff of Murtea where she had left him: the memory of reading the map that would guide him to the Eerie Sea.

Cabeza de Cabra returned to the stone bridge, taking the middle path at each juncture, and walked back to Murtea without encountering anyone. He entered the walled village and was lost from sight.

Sophia was beginning to understand why there were so few glass beads on the map. The city of Ausentinia accounted for many of the metal ones, but the people Cabeza de Cabra remembered were few and far between. She let the time in the map expand while she waited by the village wall; months passed. No doubt many people had come and gone, but Cabeza de Cabra had remained within, policing Murtea, overseeing his deputies, going about his day within the village's narrow confines.

Then, in November, there was a brief memory that appeared suddenly before her: Cabeza de Cabra led two people out of Murtea. It was clear they were prisoners. One was a man with a shaggy head of brown hair and a beard; his hands were tied. The other, accompanied by a deputy, was a girl of about Sophia's age, who kicked and screamed so viciously the deputy lost patience and threw her over his shoulder. "Calm yourself, Rosemary, please," the other prisoner said in English, with the unmistakable accent of New Occident.

Sophia felt her pulse quicken. *Bruno,* she thought. *This is Bruno Casavetti and the girl Rosemary who helped him. Cabeza de Cabra is the sheriff of Murtea.*

"No! No! No!" Rosemary cried. "He is not guilty! He is not a witch!"

The deputy took a sharp step, jolting Rosemary on his armored shoulder.

Sophia felt pity flooding through her—Cabeza de Cabra had compassion for this girl. "Be gentle," he said gruffly to his deputy. "She is only a child."

"I beg you, Rosemary," Bruno said, "they will only hurt you if you protest. And think of how sad that will make me."

Rosemary quieted, and the group moved on. Suddenly, they were gone; their path had taken them past the map's limit.

With some frustration, Sophia kept her finger on the map's edge. A few minutes later, Cabeza de Cabra and his deputy reappeared. They walked back to Murtea in silence.

In the weeks that followed, the sheriff made frequent journeys along the short stretch of road that connected the village to what Sophia presumed was the jail. Sometimes he went alone, sometimes he went with a deputy, and a few times he walked alongside a short, round man who wore a heavy golden cross. The Order of the Golden Cross had a cleric in Murtea, she realized.

Then, in December, the sheriff visited the jail and returned with Rosemary, who, though visibly upset, did not fight him. In silence, they walked the road north, but instead of entering the village they continued to the farmhouse where Sophia had heard the song of the gray dove. She knew, then, that Rosemary had been the one singing.

When they reached the doorway, Cabeza de Cabra paused. "I wish I could, but I can do nothing for him," he said.

Rosemary nodded without looking at him. "He asked me to send a letter to his friends. I do not know how to send something to New Occident. Will you help me?"

"I will, but let it be soon, because now that Casavetti has confessed, the priest will be seeking a quick sentence."

"I know. I will visit him in the jail tonight so that he may write it, and then I will bring it to you."

"Very well." He sighed. "Be careful, Rosemary."

She nodded and turned to enter the farmhouse. Cabeza de Cabra walked back to Murtea, and his footsteps felt heavy and slow.

Only a few days later, he left the village walls once more, this time accompanied by a small crowd. The deputies and the priest were there, but so were others: grown men, old women, even a few children. They returned from the jail with Bruno in tow. He was thin and his clothes were terribly dirty.

The procession reached the farmhouse, where Rosemary stood waiting like a sentinel, and she joined them as they walked farther north, to the stone bridge. The landscape beyond it had changed. Black trees with sharp thorns grew amid hillocks of dark purple moss. Here and there, the familiar dry grass still clung to the earth in patches.

Sophia could not understand the fierce pounding of the sheriff's heart, or the anxiety that he felt as he untied the prisoner's hands. Why? What were they doing to him? Bruno turned and spoke to the crowd in English: "Fear not. I know these hills and they know me. Ausentinia will protect me. I will follow the lost signs to the city. Though I may not return here, you may trust that I will find my way to safety." Sophia heard Rosemary weeping quietly nearby.

Bruno crossed the bridge, stepping onto a patch of yellow grass. Then, head tucked down, he ran into the hills as if his life depended on it. There was a sudden roar of wind, and a gust moved through the black trees, pulling their limbs like desperate arms. The small crowd of people stood watching. Minutes passed. It was impossible to say if the windstorm had died down or if it had merely retreated farther into the dark hills. There was no sign of Bruno.

"Justice has been served," the priest declared, putting his hand upon the golden cross that hung from his neck.

The crowd, with seeming reluctance, turned to go. There

was some grumbling, as if for most of the spectators disappointment, rather than justice, had been served. Rosemary remained where she was, and Cabeza de Cabra approached her. "Come. There is nothing to see."

"He will return," she said quietly, still watching the hills.

"It is not likely."

"He said he would find Ausentinia. He may not be hurt."

"And what if his soul is taken by the Dark Age? If his face is stolen, as the sentence intends? What then, Rosemary?"

The words emerged, as if from her own mouth, and Sophia felt a sudden fracturing within herself.

The part of her in the Gray Pigeon knew that Cabeza de Cabra was speaking of the Lachrima, and the realization set off a sudden avalanche in her mind, a torrent of fragments that made a comprehensible whole: the letter sent to her parents; their disappearance; the vanished existence of Ausentinia and the lost signs. She understood everything that had happened as surely as if she had seen it.

At the same time, the shock of understanding left her numb. She lost awareness of herself lying in the cool room of the roadside inn. She was no longer Sophia; she was only something that moved and thought as Cabeza de Cabra. It was as if she were truly living in the map, and nothing else existed.

Rosemary stared fiercely at the bridge. "If he returns, I will take care of him."

Cabeza de Cabra rested his hand on her shoulder. "I will come back for you at sunset and take you home."

After that, he went to the farmhouse at least once a week

to see that she was well. Later in the month, he approached the farmhouse and heard her singing a song of a gray dove, pierced by an arrow and felled. His heart was heavy, and not only because of the mourning girl. There were worse things.

After Bruno's sentence had been carried out, the priest condemned others to walk the stone bridge. The crowds that came to watch grew larger. The second prisoner, a young woman, was dispatched more to the priest's satisfaction. She stepped into the tall grass near the bridge and stood, trembling. The roar of wind gathered, and the ground beneath her feet changed, transforming into black moss. Everyone could hear her terrible screams, and when she stumbled back onto the bridge, Cabeza de Cabra recoiled. Her face was gone. She had smooth skin where her face had once been. And yet from that absent mouth came terrible cries—wails that shredded their ears.

Two other prisoners were sentenced to the same fate in February.

And then, in March, five strangers were taken to the jail: a man and woman, explorers from New Occident, and their plague-stricken guides. Cabeza de Cabra felt curiosity and sorrow in equal measure at their arrival: they had brought *lapena* and, with it, a bundle of troubles. At their sentencing, he felt a stab of sympathy. The woman was fierce and determined; when the priest pronounced their sentence at the stone bridge, she looked at him as if studying a viper. Her husband was patient, with not an ounce of malice or resentment even as Cabeza de Cabra cut his bonds and explained the priest's words.

"You are condemned to enter the Dark Age where it has

overtaken the roads that lead to Ausentinia," he said. "Should you manage to escape, you are never to return to Murtea. You may speak your final words."

The priest and much of the town stood watching. The woman reached into her skirts and took out a bundle of papers and a watch on a long chain. She handed the papers to Cabeza de Cabra. "Will you please preserve these?" she asked quietly.

"I will."

She handed the watch to her husband. "Shall we try Wren one last time, Bronson?"

He smiled. "I suppose it can't hurt." He opened the timepiece and pressed his finger against something inside, then closed it. They stood looking at one another.

"Tell them their time is up," the priest said harshly.

Cabeza de Cabra was silent.

"Shadrack will take care of her, Minna," Bronson said.

"Yes. I know he will. He loves her as much as we do, doesn't he?" She gave a small laugh that caught in her throat. There were tears in her eyes.

"He does," Bronson agreed quietly. "Now we do here as we did on the *Kestrel*." He took the long chain of the watch and circled it around his wife's wrist, and then his own. "Wherever we go, we go together. Whatever else we may lose in those hills, we will not lose each other."

"Yes, Bronson," Minna said. Their wrists bound by the watch's chain, they held hands and walked over the stone bridge. They stood for a moment at its far edge and then stepped forward, deliberately and with certainty, as if they knew exactly where they were going. The wind lifted up and howled and stormed in pursuit. Just as Bruno had vanished, so did Minna and Bronson, and after several minutes the crowd began to lose interest and drift away in disappointment.

"I think we can be confident that the sentence was carried out," the priest said to Cabeza de Cabra. When the sheriff did not respond, he added, "Do you not return to the village?"

"I will remain here until they emerge," he replied, still looking at the stone bridge.

"Suit yourself." The priest shrugged and walked away, and Cabeza de Cabra was alone.

"Two of the faces will be empty," he said softly to himself. *"The third face, which binds the other two, will have twelve hours. Follow the three faces wherever they lead you, across the many Ages, for your search lies with them."*

32
WAGING THE CAMPAIGN

—1892, June 22: 14-Hour 00—

Well into the nineteenth century, the Remember England Party continued to frame a national policy around the memory of that lost imperial power, Britain. The party gradually but decisively lost what little credibility it had ever claimed. All but the most nostalgic residents of New Occident recognize that closer relations with that part of the world now called the Closed Empire would be a costly, dangerous, and no doubt depressing enterprise.

—From Shadrack Elli's History of New Occident

KNOWING BROADGIRDLE HAD forced Shadrack into an agreement, and knowing that agreement was partly to protect him, Theo felt a kind of reckless fury that rose and fell in the MP's presence. It seemed that everyone in Boston was lying, and they were lying because of Broadgirdle. Shadrack had concealed Broadgirdle's coercion. Bligh had concealed Broadgirdle's crime. And of course Theo himself was lying to find the explanations for the greater lies with which Broadgirdle had concealed his coercion and his crimes.

Worse still, he realized now that his ability to lie, that comfortable talent which he had cherished as a skill, was no ability at all. It was a malignancy planted there long ago by Graves himself. Graves's lies were a contagion. A lie from Graves engendered fear, and the fear engendered another lie, and soon the way of telling truth was entirely lost. Theo had never considered the point in his life when his own deceitfulness had begun, but now he saw clearly that it began with Graves.

As the days passed, he plunged into the labyrinth of memories that made up those two years of his life, trying to find the first instance. He could not be sure. He recalled a moment when a concerned woman at a horse ranch accused him of being underfed. Theo had lied without considering the alternative and without considering what it signified to defend Graves. *By then I was already sick with it,* he thought. *By then I already lied without a thought.*

He hated the lies now, including his own. He hated that he had lied to Nettie about who he really was. He hated that he had lied to Mrs. Clay about his job at the State House, and he hated that he had lied to obtain the job in the first place. He hated that Shadrack, who told the truth by instinct, had been made to tell lies as well. When Broadgirdle was absent, he raged at the injustice of it, telling himself over and over that Graves would pay—for Shadrack, for Bligh, for all of it.

When Broadgirdle was near, looming over Peel's desk or writing speeches in his office, the rage seemed to grow cold and still, like an ember trapped in ice. Then Broadgirdle would swagger out of the office and the rage would return, slow and silent and tormented by its powerlessness. The reckless fury made Theo more audacious in his search. He examined files when Peel left the office; he asked questions whenever they could be construed as even tangentially work-related; he observed every detail he could for its possible relevance, knowing Winnie was also watching beyond the State House.

But, to his frustration, he had learned nothing new. A week had come and gone, and he was no closer to leaving with proof than he had been on the day of his interview. He could find nothing pointing to the location of the Weatherers; he could find no explanation for why Broadgirdle was working with the Sandmen; and he found nothing directly tying the MP to Bligh's murder. Moreover, the revelation of how Shadrack had been pressured only made things more confusing: if Broadgirdle wanted Shadrack's help, why would he frame him for Bligh's murder?

Theo felt like he was banging his head against a wall. The answer was there, on the other side, but it was impossible to get at. He was learning more than he had ever wanted about Broadgirdle's plans for the future of New Occident, but he was learning nothing about the man's secrets.

Finally, on the twenty-second, Theo unexpectedly discovered a vital piece of the puzzle. Broadgirdle was once again preparing a speech; with the campaign now in full swing, he gave speeches two or three times a day. Later in the evening, he would explain to the Boston Merchants' Guild how his policy for keeping the eastern borders closed and expanding west would, presumably, bring them great trade opportunities and wealth. With disgust, Theo heard him practicing in his office: cutting off legal trade with the Baldlands and the United Indies would help the merchants how, exactly? He shook his head and returned to the filing left to him by Bertie Peel, who was being an enthusiastic audience to Broadgirdle's speech.

The papers were rather dull reports on parliament minutes purchased during May, but as he was neatening the pile, something fell out onto the carpet. Theo stooped to pick it up, and his heart began to race. It was a little pamphlet whose cover said:

Theo opened it and read the contents.

Do you find yourself wondering about
the purpose of life?
Do you ask yourself unanswerable questions about
why the world is the way it is?
NIHILISMIANS HAVE THE ANSWER.

Long ago, during the Great Disruption,
the prophet Amitto wrote a book of reckoning and prophecy.
The *Chronicles of the Great Disruption* account for how
the world changed, proving that the true world
disappeared with the Great Disruption.

We live in a world of illusion.
Nothing in this world is as it should be.
Nihilismianism can explain why.
Nihilismianism is the way of truth.
Find the answers you are seeking.
"Remorse will overcome those who
follow the false path and
do not seek the Age of Verity."
—*Chronicles of the Great Disruption*

Theo read with growing excitement. The pamphlet had been there, in the middle of the accounting papers. It gave him an excuse to ask Broadgirdle or Peel directly about why it was in the office. Perhaps now he would finally discover the nature of the connection between Broadgirdle and the Sandmen.

As the fourth iteration of the speech to the Merchants' Guild came to a close, Theo tucked the pamphlet in his shirt pocket and made a decision. The door to the inner office opened and shut; there were sharp, mincing steps in the hallway announcing Peel's return; then Peel himself walked into the front office. "Mr. Slade," Peel said.

"Yes, Mr. Peel?"

"I need to step out to collect the printed materials our MP will be distributing tonight at the guild meeting. Please continue your filing until I return."

"Certainly, Mr. Peel."

Peel left the office with a jubilant spring to his step—the campaign was making him downright giddy—and after a minute or two had passed, Theo quietly made his way to the inner office. He knocked.

"Come in," came the booming reply.

Broadgirdle was standing by the window, speech in hand, surveying the common with a critical eye, as if considering what he would do with it once the common, and Boston, and New Occident were his. "Yes?" he asked, without turning.

"Sir," Theo said, in his meekest voice, "I wanted to ask you something very particular."

Broadgirdle turned from the window. "What is it, Slade?"

"I found this paper among the materials I was filing, sir, and I was wondering—could it be—? Is it—? Are you . . . ?" Deliberately trailing off, Theo handed Broadgirdle the pamphlet and waited, doing his best to look cowed and hopeful at the same time.

"Ah, yes," Broadgirdle said, dropping the pamphlet on his desk. He ran his carefully manicured fingers over the thick black beard and eyed Theo keenly. "Are you Nihilismian? I had not seen you wearing a talisman."

Theo hesitated. Broadgirdle's reply had told him nothing about his own beliefs. "No," he admitted. "But I'm interested. I was hoping to learn more about it."

The MP nodded approvingly. "It is well worth learning about. The Nihilismians are excellent allies in the plan for westward expansion. According to their beliefs, we should by this point be a much larger nation, stretching from this eastern shore to the western shore of the Baldlands."

Theo was appalled. "Really?" he said with awe.

"Yes, and I wish the entire population of New Occident looked west with as much zeal as they do. They consider it our right, as a nation, since this is the course we took in the Age of Verity." He tapped his fingers thoughtfully.

"How fascinating."

"Fascinating and helpful. I plan to work closely with the Nihilismians once I am elected. They have the right vision for what this nation should be doing: looking west, expanding, bringing gain and profit along the way."

"So you are not Nihilismian yourself, sir?" Broadgirdle frowned, and Theo worried that his question had been too direct. "I was hoping to talk to someone who—" He shrugged with an air of embarrassment. "I guess I need a bit of guidance."

Broadgirdle's frown eased. "I was Nihilismian," he said, his voice more subdued than usual, "once. It was through Nihilismianism that I discovered my mission. I learned of the Age of Verity, and the westward expansion that should have occurred long ago." He considered the clean surface of his desk. "Nevertheless, a successful politician needs to be flexible in his beliefs." He looked at Theo and smiled with the air of easy charm that won him so many adherents. "And Nihilismians are not flexible. But I maintain a . . . sympathy for their views. For their predicament." He extended his open hand in a gesture of offering. "If you like, I could put you in touch with the Nihilismian outreach in Boston."

"Thank you, sir."

With a nod, Broadgirdle returned to his contemplation of Boston Common.

33
CASTING VOTES

—*1892, June 30*—

In part, New Occident embraced the notion of purchased parliament seats so readily because it had seen enough voter fraud to last a century. A wealthy candidate could quite easily buy votes or buy muscle to compel votes. Why not, many argued, simply buy the seat outright?

—From Shadrack Elli's History of New Occident

ELECTIONS WERE ALWAYS tense affairs in Boston, as they were in almost every city and town of New Occident. As the sole opportunity to exercise voting rights at the national level, the election of the ruling party became a serious and somber duty. At the same time, because of the difficulties involved in keeping each vote fair and legal, Election Day inevitably became something of a circus. Some people didn't mind—they liked the bedlam, the sense that anything could happen and everything was up for grabs.

Winnie was not among them. He had been curled up in an alley near the State House since dawn, his eyes still half closed with sleep, watching the growing buzz of activity. He was uneasy. Winnie sometimes had presentiments—curious and inexplicable feelings about the future that seemed to be based on nothing at all and nonetheless often ended up being true. Winnie's mother had been prone to similar presentiments, which, given her present circumstances, made them seem to him more dangerous than useful. Only people who had earned his absolute trust ever heard about them. He called these peculiar sensations "tweakies," and he was having one now, on June thirtieth, Election Day.

Even though people were moving calmly enough past the State House, Winnie had the sense that something truly explosive was going to happen, and he could not put his finger on why. The air felt still; the morning fog muffled the comforting clank and clang of the trolleys, then unveiled the cars suddenly when they turned the corner, as a magician would. The other boys who hung about the State House began to materialize from out of the fog, hungry or full, depending on their luck. At eight-hour, the polls opened, and a steady stream of voters began filing in with their printed tickets.

All three parties—the New States Party, the Remember England Party, and the Western Party—had printed plentiful tickets with the party name and had each set up booths all over the city so that voters could pick up their tickets of choice and carry them to the State House. It was not uncommon to see some sort of chicanery around the booths, as one party stole the tickets of another or a voter was waylaid. But near where Winnie stood, Boston city police officers lined the steps of the State House, and there was no chicanery of any kind: only people climbing the steps to cast their votes.

Despite the orderly start to the day, Winnie had a definite tweaky sense about things going awry. He would have reported this tweakiness to Theo, who could be trusted absolutely, but Theo was already closeted away in Broadgirdle's offices, helping the MP prepare his final speech, and though Winnie had free rein of the city, trying to enter the State House would make him stick out like a fly in a bowl of pudding.

Broadgirdle practiced his final speech only twice on the morning of June 30, so confident was he of its persuasiveness. Peel, after preparing a clean copy, fidgeted at his desk in trembling anticipation of the great event.

At long last, Broadgirdle emerged from the inner office and stood between the desks of the first assistant and second assistant, the very picture of Political Dignity. His black hair was lacquered and combed so that it shone like a brilliant helmet. The black beard made a lustrous complement. The senior centipede appeared calm and primed, ready for anything. The carefully manicured hands were tucked away in white cotton gloves, and the imposing trunk of the MP's person was appropriately clad in a sober-looking brown suit. Broadgirdle checked his watch and tucked it into his vest pocket. "Let us proceed, gentlemen," he said, his voice echoing portentously through the outer office.

Gamaliel Shore and Pliny Grimes had already given their speeches; Broadgirdle had, naturally, engineered it so that his would be last. The other candidates were safely back in their offices, and the fair-sized crowd of people outside the State House stood ready to hear the third. Ostensibly, the speeches gave undecided voters an opportunity to hear the parties' arguments for the last time. In reality, Theo saw, as he looked out over the crowd, most of the voters had already made up their minds and had arrived to boo or cheer.

Broadgirdle stood at the podium and looked out over the crowd. He noted that it was much smaller than the one he had addressed earlier that month, on the occasion of the prime minister's death. Then he lifted his proud head and began:

"People of Boston. It is my belief that a good politician uses both words and actions only as necessary, and the sparing use of both is generally advisable. I will therefore keep my comments brief. The sad loss of our beloved Prime Minister Bligh has necessitated this emergency election, and I am here to tell you why our party, the Western Party, offers not only the best plan, but the plan Bligh would have liked best. He understood, tragically too late, that this great Age of ours holds great promise. We have too long played the passive part—like a sponge, we have sat upon the eastern seaboard, soaking up the waves of foreigners who arrive from the Baldlands and the United Indies and farther, allowing them the full benefits of membership and yet gaining little in exchange. I ask you: Is this what we are? Are we a sponge? Is that how we wish to be thought of by the other Ages? The Sponge Age?"

Broadgirdle's voice rose with indignation, and there were cries of "Nay!" and "No sponges!" from the crowd.

"I say to you," he continued, "that we should not be the sponge.

We must be the wave! We are a mighty Age, and we should act as is fitting for a mighty Age. We must keep our borders closed to the east, and we must surge west into the Indian Territories and into the Northern Baldlands, lifting those lands to prominence just as a powerful wave carries a vessel on its crest."

Broadgirdle paused for a cheer, but the reply that cut into the silence was unexpected.

"Protect our homelands!" came a shrill shout. "Leave the Indian Territories to Indians!" Theo, standing close to the railing, looked down and saw a small group of people holding a printed banner with the words PRESERVE THE TREATIES, PROTECT OUR HOMES. They were from the Indian Territories— men and women, young and old, and the woman who had cried out in protest had a determined look. "New Occident has taken enough. The very place you stand on used to be Indian lands. And now look at it. Preserve the treaties, protect our homes!" Those with her repeated her refrain, lifting the sign high. "Preserve the treaties, protect our homes!"

The crowd around the protesters was momentarily dumbstruck. Some of them looked up at Broadgirdle, waiting to see his reaction. Theo could see his fury building, and there was a long, tense pause.

Theo held his breath. There was nothing Graves hated so much as public embarrassment. Most affronts struck him as amusing opportunities for repayment with interest, but insults that shamed him before a crowd enraged him, for he could not insult the entire crowd.

Theo remembered watching, horrified, when a tavern

keeper in New Orleans with less flexible morals than most of his kind had refused to serve Graves. It had not even occurred to Theo to feel pleasure at Graves's humiliation; he knew too well the cost. Graves had grinned at the tavern keeper, showing every one of his sharp metal teeth. The tavern was silent. The patrons who knew his reputation stared in dread. "If you refused food and drink to every man with questionable dealings, you'd soon lose your business." There was an edge of menace to his voice.

"No matter," the tavern keeper said firmly. He was a sandy-haired man with a reddish beard and a broad chest of his own. He crossed his arms over it. "I'd rather lose my business than give it to men such as you."

In response, Graves let out a low laugh. "So be it, then," he said, but with the tone of a man who has accepted his enemy's surrender.

Theo had breathed a sigh of relief, not entirely understanding Graves's final words but glad that Graves had used only words rather than a pointed pistol. They stayed in New Orleans two days more, and when they left Theo learned that the tavern had been burned to the ground by a fire that started in the middle of the night: a fire that had become explosive when the tavern's alcohol ignited.

Theo watched Broadgirdle now as he glared at the protestors, feeling once again the sense of dread. With effort, Broadgirdle took a deep breath. He continued, ignoring the interruption. "Your representatives in the Western Party have a message, I say. And the message is in the name. We are the last, best hope of the west. Ours is the Western Party. We must go west!"

This was the end of the speech, and there were cheers and applause, but they were less thunderous than Broadgirdle had hoped. Peel was already trembling in anticipation; his future promised a wave of fury rather than a wave of glorious westward expansion. Broadgirdle stalked into the long corridors of the State House, Theo and Peel hurrying in his wake.

By the time they reached the office, Broadgirdle had regained his composure. "Peel, I will remind you that we are meeting tonight at eighteen-hour after the announcement is made."

"Yes, sir."

"When we meet," he added, "I would like to know who leads that group of Indian protesters." He folded his speech in half and handed it to Peel with a significant smile. "A name will be sufficient. I can take it from there."

Theo listened to the exchange, wondering how he could warn the protesters. Another part of him insisted that he needed to pursue his lead so that he could prove what Broadgirdle had done.

With Nettie and Winnie's assistance, Theo had developed a theory that neatly accounted for all of Broadgirdle's machinations—almost all. He had captured the Weatherers, and when Goldenrod came in search of them, he had sent a Sandman to attack her. He had killed Bligh for knowing the location of the missing Eerie, and framing Shadrack for the murder was a neat way of gaining leverage on the most famous cartologer in New Occident.

Theo's newest piece of information had explained why.

Broadgirdle's Nihilismian sympathies largely drove his ambitions for westward expansion. Theo understood that a Nihilismian, even a lapsed Nihilismian, would find significance in the book written by the other Shadrack Elli: it meant that this Shadrack, of New Occident, was destined to create maps of the western lands they would acquire.

What was missing—in more ways than one—were the three Eerie. Without knowing where they were or why Broadgirdle had taken them, the whole edifice could not stand.

He had already decided, on the day of the final speech, that he would find a way to ask about the Eerie, even if it cost him the position. The charade had gone on long enough. Now, with Broadgirdle distracted by the protesters, would be as good a time as any. "Sir," he said timidly.

"Yes, Slade?"

"You may remember the question you asked during our interview. The question about overhearing something. Which you ask of everyone who works in your office?" He looked from Broadgirdle to Peel, the very image of nervous hesitation. The nervousness, at least, was not feigned.

Broadgirdle's eyes sharpened. "Yes, I do. Certainly."

"I am afraid a similar situation has arisen. I have overheard something. And I think you should know about it."

"What is it?"

Theo swallowed. "I overheard two men discussing the plan for westward expansion. They . . . were critical of it. But it seemed unimportant, until I heard them mention the Eerie."

Broadgirdle's face froze. Only his eyes, lit by a kind of slow fire, seemed to register Theo's words. "What, exactly, did they say?"

Theo had practiced this part of the gamble. It had to sound precise and plausible, while still vague enough to cover all the possibilities of the facts he did not understand. "One of them said, 'The three missing Eerie are no secret,' and the other one said, 'Though Broadgirdle would like them to be.' I apologize, sir. That was him addressing you without a title, not me."

Broadgirdle's eyes had a faraway look. "I quite understand. And who were these men, Slade?"

This was the dangerous part. Theo had no wish to bring Broadgirdle's wrath down upon any two men working at the State House, and yet his story depended upon their existence. "I didn't recognize them. They were both older gentlemen. Dressed well but not overly so. One with gray hair and a mustache, the other with brown hair and a close beard." He had given descriptions that could fit half the working population of the State House. He hoped it would be sufficient. "If I see them again I could point them out," Theo offered.

"That would be helpful," Broadgirdle agreed. "Thank you for bringing this to my attention." He glanced at Peel, who had been standing by, looking at turns furious and at turns lost. "Perhaps, Slade, it would be a good idea if you joined us this evening after the election results are in." Peel now looked injured, as if Theo had won a prize intended for him. "We will be discussing our plans for the future, and I believe you may have an important place in them."

Theo bowed his head slightly in appreciation. "Certainly, sir! Thank you."

Broadgirdle turned to Peel. "And now, if you could take a few letters."

"Of course, sir. Happy to." Peel carried his portable wooden desk into the inner office.

That desk has seen every word Broadgirdle has dictated for months, Theo thought. *If only it could talk.* He sat, unsure why the idea of a writing desk that could talk was sticking in his mind. There was some connection, but it was just out of reach. He stared at the surface of his own desk and tried to follow the thought. Then he realized what it was: the writing desk's flat surface reminded him of a map—a memory map that would tell him everything that had transpired in Broadgirdle's office.

Suddenly, Theo pushed back his chair. *But there is a memory map: a map that's been right in front of me and that I've been ignoring like an idiot. The wooden ruler! It isn't a cipher or a message or a reminder. It's a map.*

Without bothering to tidy his desk, Theo snatched up his jacket and made for the door. He had to get the wooden rule from Nettie.

Inspector Roscoe Grey was home, for once. Theo watched him through the window with desperate impatience. Grey had already spent twenty minutes dawdling in the piano room with Nettie, looking like the most relaxed person in the world. *Will he never leave?* Theo thought, fiddling with the mustache in his pocket. Finally, nearing fifteen-hour, he stood, patted Nettie gently on the head, and left, closing the door behind him.

Theo sprang out of his hiding place in the neighbor's rhodo-dendron and tapped urgently on the window.

"Charles, what *is* it?" Nettie asked, leaning out.

"I have no time. It's urgent. I need the ruler. I have to borrow it for a little while."

She frowned. "You've discovered something. Tell me."

"It's only a theory. But I need to try it out."

"What theory?"

"Can I please just have it? I don't have time to argue."

Nettie scowled. "Fine. But the minute you test the theory, you have to tell me what it is." She went to the piano bench and opened it. "Here," she said, handing him the ruler through the window.

"Thanks, Nettie." Theo flashed her a broad grin. "You're the best."

"The minute you test it," she said, eyes narrowed.

THEO BURST INTO the kitchen of 34 East Ending Street.

"Fates above, Theo," Mrs. Clay exclaimed. "What has happened?"

"What do you know about memory maps made of wood?"

She clearly had not expected this question. "Made of wood?"

"Did you ever see any at the Nochtland academy?"

Mrs. Clay blinked. "Yes, I suppose the students worked with wood on occasion. Wood as opposed to paper, you mean."

"Yes, wood—a hard surface. What I want to know is how to wake a wooden map."

Mrs. Clay sat down at the table. "How to wake a wooden map," she echoed. "Let me think." She closed her eyes.

Theo stood by, trying to calm his breathing.

"I'm trying to picture what they would do." She opened her eyes briefly. "You have to understand, I never took part in any of the classes."

"I know," he said impatiently. "Anything you can remember."

She closed her eyes again. "It isn't water or light . . . Why can't I remember? Oh!" she exclaimed, opening her eyes. She gave a smile of triumph. "Smoke."

"Of course!" Theo said. "Smoke." He dashed around the kitchen, collecting a pot, a scrap of brown grocery paper, and a box of matches. He lit the match and held it to the paper until it caught fire. Dropping it into the pot, he held the ruler over it until the smoke had coated every surface. Then he took it away. The ruler looked almost unchanged, but a slender red line had appeared on the unruled side, beside the date. Theo smiled. "I knew it," he said. "This ruler is a memory map."

Mrs. Clay was still perplexed. "A memory map of what?"

"I think it has the memories of the Weatherers who came to Boston. This ruler is going to tell us what happened to them."

—1892, July 1: 16-Hour 11—

There is even rumor of an Age pocketed in the south where all things lost in the world have gone to rest, so that arriving in it the traveler finds himself surrounded by every lost key, lost love, and lost dream ever to have existed. No doubt only the storytellers of the Papal States could believe in the existence of such an Age.

—From Fulgencio Esparragosa's
Complete and Authoritative History of the Papal States

SOPHIA HAD NO notion of time passing. She was not entirely sure of where she was, either. So completely had she submerged herself in the memories of the beaded map, she felt as though she had lived a year in Alvar Cabeza de Cabra's skin. She had seen the parched, harsh world as he saw it, grieved its losses as he grieved them, felt the feeble thread of hope given to him as he had felt it. Somewhere, like a distant echo, she felt these things as Sophia, too: the bitterness of an unknown world that would not yield its answers; the loss of her parents; the pain of knowing what had happened to them; and, with that knowledge, the frail hope of believing they might be alive. Her mind wandered as freely over her own life as it had traveled through the map, grieving and hoping and grieving again, so that when she returned to the room at the inn in the Papal States, she felt that she had been away a lifetime.

She had changed during that lifetime. It was not just the knowledge of what had happened to her parents and the grief of seeing its cause unfold before her eyes. It was something else. Perhaps she had stayed too long with Cabeza de Cabra's memories, or perhaps the thoughts and feelings of Murtea's sheriff were so strong that they had marked her like a brand. Cabeza de Cabra was a man who had lost his faith and sought it. Sophia, emerging from the map, knew that her faith was gone also.

There was no greater meaning to her parents' loss, and there was no guiding hand that would take her to them. What had happened to them was cruel and senseless. Other people had stood by while they suffered. Sophia knew, as entirely and thoroughly as if she had always known it but wished not to: there were no Fates.

No one was leading her anywhere. She was following only herself.

Errol was asleep in his hammock, and Sophia realized she had been brought to awareness by Goldenrod's appearance in the doorway. She was staring at Sophia, her eyes sharp with concern. "What has happened?"

By way of answer, Sophia climbed out of her hammock and held up the beaded map.

"That is an Elodean map," Goldenrod said softly.

Errol stirred and woke, lifting himself from the hammock.

"Yes. They contain one man's memories of a place not far from here." Sophia's own voice sounded strange to her—hoarse and dry. She realized she must have wept at some point without knowing it. "His name is Alvar Cabeza de Cabra, a man from the Papal States who traveled from here to the Eerie Sea in search of his lost faith. He was the sheriff of a town named Murtea. It was the village my parents traveled to when I was little, in search of their friend. This map tells what happened to them."

Errol materialized next to them, his eyes alert. Goldenrod studied Sophia keenly. "Show me," she said.

Sophia spread the map out over the table at the center of the room. "It is one year, which is not marked but must be 1880 and part of 1881. It begins in April. Look at April twentieth at eleven-hour, then December ninth, January eleventh, and March seventeenth—all of them at dawn."

Errol looked confused, but Goldenrod placed her fingers upon the map without a word. She was quiet, her brow furrowed with concentration.

"What is she doing?" Errol whispered to Sophia with frustration.

Having placed the map in Goldenrod's hands, Sophia felt suddenly exhausted, as if all the time she had spent within its boundaries had suddenly caught up to her. "Reading. She will show you how when she is done. I need to rest." She stumbled back to her hammock and crawled into it awkwardly. Before she had lifted her feet up after her, she was asleep.

—July 2: 5-Hour 10—

SOPHIA WOKE, DISORIENTED, to find the room dark and empty. She was unsure of the day or time. Then she remembered the map and all that she had discovered within it, and she felt her body tighten with pain. She got out of the hammock, as if still in a dream, laced up her worn leather boots, and went to find her travel companions.

They were sitting in the candlelit dining room of the inn, speaking quietly to one another at a table while the innkeeper huddled by the fire, wrapped in a woolen shawl as if she were warding off bitter cold. Errol and Goldenrod looked up as one when Sophia entered. She could see at once that something had changed between them.

Sophia reached into her pocket and looked at her watch; it was just after five-hour; she had slept almost until dawn. It felt as though she had been sleeping for days.

Something had happened during the night, and now the falconer and the Eerie had a common purpose. They looked at her with shared knowledge, having come to an agreement. Both pale and serious, their faces had a surprising harmony, even with their contrasting features: Errol's eyes blue and sharp in his angular face, Goldenrod's dark and pensive under her calm brow.

"Did you sleep well?" Goldenrod asked.

Sophia nodded. "Yes, thank you."

"We have read the map." The Eerie's expression turned somber. "We understand what happened to your parents."

Sophia looked at them each in turn, unblinking. "They have almost certainly become Lachrima."

"Yes." Goldenrod said matter-of-factly. She glanced at Errol. "That term is not known here, but I am familiar with it from the Baldlands."

"If we understand correctly," he said, "this man may have followed your parents to the Eerie Sea."

"He did," Sophia replied. "That is where my friends found the map. The man who wrote these memories was already dead. He followed the directions given to him in Ausentinia. And that must mean he followed them—the Lachrima, my parents—all the way there."

"The distance they traveled is a long one," Goldenrod said. "A very long one. You may know that the Wailings—the Lachrima, as you call them—sometimes fade, so that they are less body and more voice."

"Yes, I have heard that," Sophia replied dully.

"This fading happens as they travel. The farther they drift from the Age in which they were made faceless, the less corporeal their presence."

Sophia slumped. "Then it is even worse than I had imagined."

"Perhaps," Goldenrod said. "But perhaps not." She hesitated. "I do not wish to give you false hope."

She turned to Errol, who nodded slightly. "Better to tell her everything, good and bad."

Goldenrod reached out to Sophia. "Come sit beside us," she said. Sophia wearily obliged, sinking onto a wooden stool. Goldenrod pressed her hand, a gesture of encouragement. "There are some among us, among the Elodeans, who are truly marvelous healers in the manner all Eerie are imagined to be. We call them Weatherers. They are seers, visionaries, great interpreters. There are four such among us now, though three are missing. It was these three healers I sought in Boston. You can imagine the need we have for them. They heal every manner of ailment, great and small. And they can heal the Wailings—they can restore their features and their minds."

Sophia looked at her with a stirring of hope. Her mind flew to a distant place: to a dungeon in Nochtland, the capital of the Baldlands, where a veiled woman had spoken to her and issued threats. Blanca, who remembered who she was and found only pain in the memories; Blanca, who was a Lachrima but had recovered her past. *Of course they can be healed,* Sophia realized. *If one man can do it by accident, why should it not be possible on purpose?* "How? How do they heal them?"

Goldenrod shook her head. "I am not a Weatherer. I can only explain what they have related to us, of searching through lifetimes of memory to find the memories of the Wailing before them. But it is possible."

"You have seen them do it?"

"I have. Three times in my life I have seen it done."

"And they are entirely healed?"

"If they are corporeal, yes."

Sophia's hope subsided. "But Lachrima who have traveled

far will fade." She sighed. "Then it makes no difference."

"We do not know. It may or may not have happened to your parents on their long journey. If it has not, then we can seek a Weatherer's aid."

Errol chimed in. "What is your wish, Sophia? Is it your intention to go seek them in this region, near the Eerie Sea?"

Sophia swallowed. She looked away, at the innkeeper, who was staring into the fire as if contemplating a vision. A sound in the room brought the old woman's attention back to the present, and she stood slowly, unbending each limb. With shuffling steps, she left the room. Sophia shivered. "I still wish to see the diary. Those may be my mother's last words. I want to read them now more than ever. But I have decided that I will go to Ausentinia first. I will ask them for a map."

Errol and Goldenrod shared a look.

"But it seems this place, Ausentinia, is gone," Errol objected gently.

Sophia shook her head. "Not gone. Perhaps its borders are shifting. Perhaps the Dark Age holds it captive. But I don't believe it is gone."

Goldenrod regarded her thoughtfully, then gave Errol a significant look. He had been about to speak, but with a knowing look he closed his lips. "Very well," she said.

"We will accompany you east, to this town called Murtea, and help however we can," added Errol.

"I doubt Murtea exists," Sophia told them. "Some months after my parents disappeared, my uncle asked many of his friends—explorers—to visit the Papal States in search of them.

Nothing was ever found. Then, when we received a letter from my father last December, a letter he sent ten years ago that mentioned Ausentinia and the lost signs, my uncle Shadrack sent word to everyone he knew. No one had heard of either.

"I have studied the same maps he studied—in fact, I have them with me here—and they do show Murtea. But the maps are old. They are the same ones he used to help plan my parents' expedition. I think the Dark Age, after surrounding Ausentinia, moved farther outward, taking Murtea with it. Anyone who knew Murtea is gone. And who knows what the place is like now."

There was a strange light in Goldenrod's eyes. "I would not be surprised if you are right," she said softly. "We will go with you nonetheless. If we cannot find Murtea, perhaps we can find Ausentinia. And if not Ausentinia, then we will continue to Granada for the diary." She suddenly became alert. "Someone is riding this way at great speed. Not the Golden Cross. A rider who comes alone. She comes to our aid." She frowned. "But why—"

A rapid shuffling of feet sounded in the doorway. The old innkeeper shouted something at Errol and then rushed away. "Fourwings," Errol said quickly. He took up his bow and quiver and hurried to the doorway. "Come," he called over his shoulder. "We must not remain inside. They will cave in the roof and scavenge. It is what they do."

"But my things—" Sophia started.

"Leave your things, miting, if you value your life." He pulled her through the doorway and into the pale morning.

In the charcoal light of dawn, two winged creatures swooped and whirled overhead. They seemed small, like bats. They cried out, their voices coarse and metallic, like the sound of a knife scraping a grater. Galloping hoofbeats cut into the silence left in their wake, and Sophia saw a pale horse approaching from the east.

"That is the horse and rider," Goldenrod replied to the unasked question. "She means us no harm."

"Stay out in the open," Errol ordered. "It will be safest."

Goldenrod put her arm around Sophia and pulled her close. "Can you talk to them, the fourwings?" Sophia asked. "Like you talk to Seneca?"

"I have already tried," the Eerie said, looking up at them with a vexed expression. "But it is like speaking to a wall. They hear nothing. They say nothing. I've never encountered creatures like these."

They had become alarmingly larger, and their cries erupted again, harsh and bitter. The horse and rider grew closer, too, until Sophia could see the rider's cape billowing and the horse's hooves disturbing the dust.

Suddenly, the fourwings were upon them. One, claws extended, swooped toward the inn. It was covered with gleaming, blue-black feathers. Its beak, slightly curved, shone like a polished scythe. Its great eyes were golden, with no iris at all. The roof crumpled like paper and fell inward beneath the enormous bird's impact, crushing the building where the travelers had just been sitting. Its flapping wings tore at the walls.

"Stay behind me," Errol murmured. "It has not yet seen us.

They will go for the horses first and then us. We must kill both birds in quick succession. Wait for the other one."

The second fourwing called out, whirling down to meet its companion. It had only three wings. Where the fourth would have been was a misshapen lump, dotted with scrawny feathers. The flesh beneath was white. As the second fourwing crashed into the inn, the pale horse drew near, skidding to a halt. The rider dismounted: a woman with a crossbow.

She quickly joined Errol and aimed at the fourwings. "*Ahora,*" she said. "*El roto es mío.*" She loosed the arrow from her crossbow just as Errol loosed his, and the fourwings both recoiled from the impact. They turned toward the four travelers, their golden eyes hard, their cries so loud Sophia covered her ears. The creatures rose up and scrabbled over the broken wall of the inn, advancing toward them.

"*Otra vez,*" Errol said to the woman. Two more arrows struck the birds, and the one with three wings crumpled, an arrow lodged deep in its breast. The other lunged forward, its beak opening with a scream to reveal even white teeth and a long white tongue. The woman shot into its mouth as the beak plunged toward Errol. He drew his sword. Pressing it heavily into the bird's neck, he pinned it to the ground. It flapped and screamed brokenly, and then the wings folded and the golden eyes grew still and glazed.

Sophia found herself clutching Goldenrod's robe. Slowly she released the fabric. Errol's sword was coated with the fourwing's oily black blood. He cleaned it on the dry grass. "Are you all right?" Goldenrod asked.

"Fine," he said. "Thanks to the unexpected aid," he added to the woman with the crossbow.

"You speak English," she said, her own accented but clear. Her green eyes looked them over.

"Yes," he replied. "I am from the Closed Empire. My friends are from New Occident and the Eerie Sea. How is it you speak English? And how did you come to be here at this very moment?"

She tossed her braid over her shoulder and set down her crossbow. Her short frame, compact and strong, belied the fragility of her face and the expression of old grief in her eyes. "I learned English long ago from a dear friend. A man named Bruno. And I came here following the directions given to me on a piece of paper: *When you see seven wings, follow them to the gray pigeon. You will meet the traveler without time.*

"Which of you," she asked, "is the traveler without time?"

35
WHITE STRING, BLUE STRING

—*1892, July 2: 5-Hour 51*—

Since the plague took root, many people in the Papal States have chosen a transient life. In the northern regions, they live in houseboats along the canals. In the drier regions to the south and the mountainous regions, they live in caravans. Ever moving, always on the outskirts, they believe themselves safe from the plague; there is no doubt that they are, at least, more safe from the Orders.

—From Fulgencio Esparragosa's
Complete and Authoritative History of the Papal States

"ROSEMARY," SOPHIA BREATHED.

"Yes," the woman replied. "I am Rosemary. How do you know me?"

The words came out in a torrent. "I know you from a letter that Bruno sent to my parents. My parents—Minna and Bronson Tims. They met you. Do you remember? It was more than ten years ago. And I know of you from a map written by the sheriff of Murtea, Cabeza de Cabra. It tells of you, and what happened to Bruno." Sophia paused. "And my parents."

Rosemary took a step closer. "So you are the traveler without time."

"I have no internal clock," Sophia agreed. "I suppose it could be me. Who described it that way?"

Reaching into her cloak, Rosemary withdrew a scroll tied with white string. "The map given to me in Ausentinia."

Although she had held Ausentinian maps while she was within the sheriff's memories, this was the first time she had seen one as herself. Sophia examined the heavy, gray-tinged paper. Unsteady lines in black ink described a mottled landscape divided by winding paths. She turned it over; the text was inscrutable. "I can't read Castilian," she said.

"I will translate," Rosemary said, taking it back.

"Soundless, we scream in the heart; silent, we wait in the shadows; speechless, we speak of the past. Find us at either end of eleven years.

"Taking the trail of uncertainty, accept the guide who arrives under the full moon. Travel with him into the meadow of friendship, and when the cart breaks, go to the goat's head. Your traveling companion is falsely accused. Speak then, and speak the truth, for both truth and falsehood lead to the steep ravine of loss.

"You will venture alone into the Valley of Vanishing Hope. As you leave the valley, you will encounter the Western Witches and a fork in the path. If the witches go free, you will be led into the Forest of Lingering Sadness, where you will spend many years before you find your way to the Caves of Fear, where Damnation dwells. Your mother's bones will lie forever

undiscovered, bleached by the sun until they crumble into dust.

"If the witches are sentenced, you will journey alone into the Mountains of Solitude, where you will wander for many years. When you see seven wings, follow them to the gray pigeon. You will meet the traveler without time. Give her the map to Ausentinia. She will lead you to your mother's bones, and you will place them on sacred ground so that they may rest in peace."

Rosemary rolled the map carefully and tied the white string around it. "When I saw the two birds, I knew. I took the maps and followed them here."

Sophia felt the thudding of her heart. "There is a map to Ausentinia?" she asked, hardly daring to believe it.

This time, Rosemary produced a scroll tied with blue string. "I have it," she said. "This is the map they gave me so that I would someday give it to you."

It was written in English. She glanced first at the cluster of images with curious names—"The Cave of Blindness" and "Bitter Desert"—before turning to the text on the back. She read it aloud:

"Hidden in plain sight, encircled without a circle, trapped without a trap. Find us at the end of the path you devise, for no others can.

"The hand that blooms must tell you of the old ones. A flock of golden birds will fly east, seeking pursuit, shining in the sun.

"The path divides, leading to the Steep Ridge of Dread or

the Low Dunes of Desire. The Low Dunes lead to Bitter Desert, where you find yourself descending into the Cave of Blindness. From there, you may or may not return.

"Along the Steep Ridge of Dread, the golden birds turn to black. The falconer and the warbler defend you. Do not believe what is said of darkness and shadows. It springs from fear, not truth.

"Beyond the Ridge lies the Labyrinth of Borrowed Remembering. To survive the labyrinth, you must trust your own senses. Emerging from the labyrinth, you have a choice. You defend the illusion or you do not. If the illusion dies, the path leads to Common Pond and, finally, to the Grove of Long Forgotten. Avoid the Grove at all costs. Trust your instincts, as well as your senses. Defend the illusion, taking the Path of the Chimera. Along it you may lose yourself, but you will find Ausentinia.

"When the wind rises, let the old one dwell in your memories, as you have dwelled in the memories of others. Give up the clock you never had. When the wind settles, you will find nothing has been lost."

Sophia reread the paper before her. She looked back up at Rosemary. "How could someone know this? How could this all happen? Has yours come true?"

"It has. Every part of it. There were parts that I did not understand until they were happening, and there were parts that I did not see until they had already passed. But in every case what the map foretold has come true."

"Then we will be pursued by the Golden Cross," Errol said. "'A flock of golden birds.' Not so difficult to predict," he added dryly.

"There is something about these phrases," Sophia said, frowning. "The hand that blooms. The falconer. Errol, these are the words my mother spoke to me in Seville. She said 'the falconer and the hand that blooms will go with you.'"

"What of it?"

"The exact same words as on the map. You are clearly the falconer. And you," she said to Goldenrod, "are the hand that blooms."

Goldenrod spoke for the first time since Rosemary had introduced herself. "Yes, it seems I am."

"What are the old ones?"

The Eerie looked west, her face troubled. "Yes, I understand," she said. "I must tell you of the old ones. But I will tell you while we travel, for there are fifty soldiers of the Golden Cross on the road from Seville, and it does not seem impossible that they are looking for us."

ERROL FOUND THE innkeeper huddled near an almond tree behind the shattered building. After setting her on the path north to her son's farm, he rejoined the others. The room where they had slept, fortunately, was not as damaged as the main room of the inn. Recovering their belongings, they prepared the horses and began riding east.

To Sophia's disgust, Rosemary insisted on taking the eyes of the fourwings. She stored two in her pack and placed two in her caravan, which she had unhitched and left by the road when the fourwings appeared. It surprised Sophia with its colorful beauty: flowers, vines, and birds were painted all over the caravan's walls, and over the door perched a golden swallow, wings spread as if about to take flight.

Rosemary hitched the caravan and they continued east. "This road is well-worn from centuries of travel, though it has not been in great use of late," she said as they rode. "Between here and the perimeter are wells at two leagues and five leagues, but no other inns. There is a shepherd near the fifth league who sells me mutton. Other food we must carry with us."

"And what about the perimeter?" Errol asked. "Won't the guard be there?"

"The guard are not so numerous that they encircle the entire Dark Age. They work in pairs, patrolling lengths of three leagues. I know many of them, and some are not unreasonable."

"I am surprised you think so," Errol said with notable disdain.

Rosemary flashed him a look. "It is a compromise, not a friendship. I have patrolled the perimeter myself for years, waiting for Bruno, and I have many times warned them of approaching fourwings, or the dark storms that drift from within the Age. They have done the same for me. Though our purposes are greatly different, where there is common assistance there can be toleration, or even mutual respect."

"I do not suppose you could draw upon that mutual respect with the fifty riders?"

Rosemary shook her head tersely. "I know none of the Order from Seville." She urged her horse onward and the caravan rolled forward.

Sophia rode with Goldenrod, sitting in front of her this time; she looked at the unbroken morning sky. "Will you tell us of the old ones now?"

"Yes. I said before to Errol and Sophia," she explained for Rosemary's benefit, "that my people, the Elodeans, are interpreters. We can speak to all living beings. Most of them," she qualified. "Even those that are not visible or recognizable as beings."

"Like the plague," Sophia put in.

"Yes, like the wanderers known here through the damage they cause as *lapena*. The old ones are such beings. They are mighty and they are ancient, as our name for them suggests. They have a knowledge of the world that you and I could not begin to fathom. Indeed, most of what they do is difficult to comprehend. Our understanding of them is partial, at best. It is through them—by speaking with them—that I know of things happening at a distance. I asked one for a weirwind when the Golden Cross approached us, and the weirwind appeared. They are powerful—tremendously powerful. Sometimes they do wonderful things with their powers. Sometimes they do terrible things."

"What terrible things?" Sophia asked. "The weirwind?"

"Such as the disturbance known in New Occident as the Great Disruption."

Sophia started. She whirled to look at Goldenrod with astonishment. *"The Great Disruption?"*

"Certainly. It was caused by a conflict among the old ones."

"But what are these 'old ones'?" Errol cut in. "What do they look like? They sound like the pagan gods, and I am fairly certain those do not exist. Are they invisible, or do they take different shapes?"

"They are very much visible," Goldenrod replied. "You see them all the time. Everywhere."

"I do not," Errol declared.

"But you do," Goldenrod insisted. Sophia could hear the smile in her voice. "Perhaps it is more correct to say that you see them, but you do not truly see them. You see them without comprehending what they are. Among the Elodeans, we also call them 'Climes.' In most places, such as New Occident and the Closed Empire, they are known as 'Ages.'"

PART IV
The Rejoinder

—1892, July 2: 6-Hour 30—

Apart from the investigations of explorers, cartologers, and natural philosophers, there is, of course, an entire branch of science devoted to understanding the causes of the Great Disruption. Researchers in this field are so divided in their explanations that their scholarship is marked by bitterness and acrimony. The early belief that a higher power had caused the Disruption as part of some grand plan has been increasingly challenged by those who believe the inhabitants of some future Age are to blame.

—From Shadrack Elli's History of New Occident

FROM HER SEAT upon the horse, in front of Goldenrod, Sophia considered the landscape before her, trying to imagine it as a being: an individual who stretched for miles, containing plains and mountains and caves, who was able to feel the waterways inside itself and the ocean lapping at its edges.

She hesitated, disbelieving. "You mean—this place around us—it is awake?" She could feel Goldenrod breathing.

"Yes," the Eerie said with a smile in her voice. "Awake and aware. It is as sentient as you and I."

Sophia looked at the scrub grass and the yellowed almond trees, the outcroppings of stone, and the pebbly earth, stirred by their passage. "It can . . . hear us?"

"In more ways than you can imagine. Its manner of perceiving and understanding is far more powerful than ours. We do not know how, but it seems the Climes are cognizant of everything that occurs within their sphere."

The sky was an inverted blue bowl overhead. "How big is it—is this one?"

"We are at the edge of a vast Clime that stretches from the coast to include Seville and most of what we see here around us. But farther east, on the road ahead, are two others."

"The Dark Age," Sophia breathed.

"Indeed—the Dark Age. And Ausentinia. I sense its presence, though I cannot hear its voice."

The significance of this worked its way through Sophia's mind. "But you can hear the Dark Age?"

"No," Goldenrod said, troubled. "I cannot. It is unlike any Clime I have ever encountered. It seems . . . absent. But that would be impossible."

Rosemary spoke for the first time. "What you say of these old ones seems very true to me. I have almost suspected this, knowing Ausentinia. The way its paths would appear and reappear, as if the city itself wished to guide us. And the Dark Age, too, though you cannot hear it. For how else would the Ages battle with one another as they have, taking pieces and losing them, fighting for them again?"

"We saw on Cabeza de Cabra's map that the Dark Age had pushed through the hills of Ausentinia, all the way to the stone bridge," Sophia said.

Rosemary gave a sharp nod. "And farther. After the sheriff left, the Dark Age expanded north and east."

"Past Murtea?"

"Well past. One day we woke to find it almost at the village wall. Everyone fled. The next month, I returned with the caravan. Murtea was no more. Before it would take more than three days to ride from Seville to the border of the Dark Age. Now it takes less than two."

"So the Dark Age must be a Clime like any other," Goldenrod mused. "This is what they do when they are unsettled: they shift and grow or contract. It is what happened all at once during the Great Disruption—the War of Climes."

"The War of Climes," Sophia repeated. The words shocked her with the world of meaning they implied. A new map unfurled in her mind: one that was living, breathing, in conflict with itself.

"The Climes themselves have kept its cause hidden, so I cannot tell you what provoked it—one of their many mysteries. But we know that the disagreement grew, became violent, and finally resulted in the alienation and division that we have now. And they have not been still. Of late, especially, there have been hostilities—bitter arguments that change the shape of the world as we know it. Not only here, with the Dark Age."

"The glacier that moved north last year . . ." Sophia began.

"Yes. A southern Clime that rushed northward. Once again, we do not know why."

Sophia fell silent and became lost in thought, her mind

whirling with the consequences of what Goldenrod had explained. Could it be that none of the scholars and scientists in New Occident, none of the cartologers and explorers Shadrack knew—none of them was even close to understanding the Great Disruption, because none of them perceived how the world really was? Sophia felt momentarily dizzy; the learned city of Boston suddenly seemed very tiny and very poor in knowledge. If these Climes existed, then so much of what she had considered inexplicable now made sense. The more she turned it over in her mind, the more undeniably true it appeared.

"So they *are* like the pagan gods," Errol concluded. "They do battle and subject humans to their whims without bothering to consider the consequences."

Goldenrod hesitated. "They are entirely different. But perhaps you could say your pagans understood by some instinct that the old ones existed, and they attempted, imperfectly, to explain them by describing gods with human aspects."

"War is war," Errol said flatly. He held his arm up for Seneca, who landed with a ruffle of feathers. "Only selfish creatures engage in it."

"I do not disagree with you there," Goldenrod said. "You can see why the Eerie hold this knowledge secret. With our capacity to speak to the Climes, perhaps even bend their will through persuasion . . . there are many who would want to use such capacities for terrible ends."

They took cover from the worst of the midday heat in Rose-mary's caravan. Through the white curtains, the sunlight illuminated a room more spacious and more lovely than Sophia had expected. At the front of the wagon, a bed built atop a low wardrobe lay below a window. Two ceiling lamps held the newly scavenged eyes from the fourwings, which were dull and lifeless in the bright sunlight. Shelves and cabinets, many of them painted with gray birds, covered the wall to her right, and these were filled with crockery, jars, and baskets. To the left, a black stove sat short and squat on a large square of painted tiles. Low leather chairs shaped like pincushions had been embroidered in blue and white thread by someone with a patient hand.

It was evident to Sophia that much of the caravan's contents had been made by Rosemary herself. She invited them to sit, taking a loaf of bread and a pot of butter from one of the cabinets painted with gray birds. She poured water from a blue jug.

Sophia thanked her and ate eagerly. She had left the inn without breakfast, and it seemed ages since their meal the previous night.

"You have a comfortable home," Errol said to Rosemary with appreciation.

"It is luxurious compared to how you travel, Errol," Goldenrod remarked, smiling.

"I care little for luxury. But I envy that you are able to carry your home with you," he admitted to Rosemary.

"There is little to envy," Rosemary said matter-of-factly. "I lost an entire farm. What you see are the collected pieces of what survived."

"Forgive me," he apologized. "But you must admit there

is also ingenuity, along with fragments of a lost life. The crossbow—you made it yourself, did you not?"

"I did. I grew tired of fleeing the fourwings every time I heard their detestable cries." She handed him the crossbow and Errol examined it appraisingly. "And you? What of your home?"

Errol handed the crossbow back. "The only shreds of home I carry are the bow and the boots. Everything else you see has been found in the Papal States, from Seneca to the laces."

"You must miss it," Sophia said.

"I do, miting. Oswin, my sister Cat, my mother and father, my grandfather; we are—" He paused. "We were a happy family."

Sophia offered him a smile. "I hope you will be again."

"There is something more you have forgotten," Goldenrod interjected. "Surely you carry your home in your heart and mind."

"That is true," Errol assented. "I carry the green hills, the smell of rain in early spring. Long evenings in winter watching my mother and sister with their sewing. The old ruins where my brother and I would play as children." He sighed.

"We should continue," Rosemary said, rising from her seat. "The next stretch of road is full of abandoned farms, and there are frequent attacks from the fourwings."

AS THEY LEFT the caravan for the midday heat, Errol watched Sophia, chiding himself for mentioning his parents and grandfather. He could see her slipping back into her thoughts, back into the sorrowful memories of the beaded map.

"I will tell you what I miss most about home, miting," Errol said as he helped her up onto the saddle before Goldenrod. "I miss the stories we told each other in the evenings. After a meal, instead of dashing out into blinding sunlight to flee mad clerics, we would tell tales."

Sophia gave a slight smile. "That does sound more agreeable."

"Vastly more agreeable," Errol said, swinging up into his saddle. "Sometimes for laughter, sometimes for tears, sometimes for the lesson contained in the telling. As we ride east toward the Dark Age, I have in mind a story my grandfather would often recount. The story of Edolie and the woodsman. If none of you objects, I will tell it."

"Is it a story about an archer valiantly protecting three women in a dark forest?" Goldenrod asked lightly.

Errol pursed his lips thoughtfully. "That is an even better story. I will tell it to you when we reach Granada. First, Edolie and the woodsman."

As they set off, he gathered his thoughts and finally spoke. "It is a Faierie tale. My grandfather changed it very little over the years, which leads me to believe that it was truer than most. He always began by reminding us of one important thing: Faieries are not all good and not all evil. They are much like us, in that they combine the good and the bad, and they sometimes change before our very eyes, becoming the opposite of what they were. You must judge for yourselves what manner of Faierie this story describes."

And with that, he began.

"There was once a little girl who lived in a small village at the edge of the forest. She was a wayward child, who from the time she was very small came and went as she pleased, venturing into the forest despite its many dangers. Though they tried to keep her close, her parents could not contain her, and at least once with each waning and waxing of the moon the girl disappeared into the forest for hours, driving them to despair until she returned, cheerful and unharmed, recounting in her child's voice the adventures she had had with the Faieries.

"When she grew into adulthood, she began to lose her interest in the forest, and her parents were greatly relieved. There was no more talk of Faieries. Indeed, she no longer remembered them. They began to seem like something she had imagined in those infantile days when she liked to entertain herself with things that were not real. As will happen to young people, she lost her interest in the world of magic and began thinking about love.

"She had heard so many stories about falling in love, a thing both wondrously beautiful and terribly painful, that she watched for it always, the way one watches for a bad cold in winter. But it did not happen. She knew all the people in her village—boys and girls, women and men—and none of them inspired that malady in her. But then, she had known them all her life. Once or twice she felt a pinch of something in her heart—something both beautiful and painful—and wondered if that was it. But no, she decided. That was not love.

"It was customary in this place and time to marry young. When children reached Sophia's age," Errol said, raising his voice slightly, "they could already begin thinking of marriage."

Sophia turned to him in surprise.

Errol smiled. "Not that you should, Sophia. And nor did our heroine, Edolie. In fact, for more than ten years, despite her watchfulness for the arrival of that mysterious ailment, she showed no symptoms of love, nor any interest in marriage, and her parents began to accept that she would never add to their family with a husband and children. Edolie herself began to think less about the malady she had once both dreaded and wished for.

"She realized one morning in early spring, to her great surprise, that the absence of it was a relief. She no longer had to worry about it appearing—about what it would look like or how it would feel. She felt wonderfully unburdened, as if a monumental task that once lay ahead had been suddenly performed, unexpectedly, by someone else. It was no doubt this sense of having cleared her mind and heart that allowed her to see what she had not seen in so many years.

"Walking at the edge of the forest that day, with her mind so newly at ease, Edolie happened to glance into the woods and she saw there, clear as anything, a caped figure retreating. Without a moment's pause, she stepped toward it. 'Hello?' she called. The caped figure turned, and Edolie had a glimpse of a white face before the hood fell forward. It gave a slight whimper before ducking behind a tree. 'Hello? Are you all right?' Edolie asked. The figure limped on, clearly in pain, stopping to rest against one tree and then another. Edolie hurried toward it, all her thoughts focused on catching up. She gained ground quickly, calling out to no avail. Finally, she stopped just beside it. The caped figure stood immobile, its shoulders pitifully hunched. Edolie reached out with her hand. 'Are you hurt? Can I help you?'

"Suddenly the figure turned, and the hood fell away from its face. A Faierie seized Edolie's outstretched hands, and three more Faieries sprang from the trees around her, seizing her by the clothes and hair. Edolie cried out, but she was so surprised that she hardly had strength to resist. The Faierie that had led her into the woods had skin so white one could see the green veins beneath. Her eyes were large and golden, her features pointed—pointed ears, a small sharp nose, and rows of small sharp teeth. The long, translucent wings on her back sharpened to delicate, blackened tips. The hair about her head, fanning and waving as if it moved through water, was golden-white tinged with green. The others were much the same: tall and imposing, beautiful but dreadful, enchanting and yet full of menace. Their sharp-toothed smiles could turn from sweet to wicked in a moment. Edolie was transfixed. Before she knew what had happened, they had wrapped her in their capes, bundling her in darkness that smelled of musty leaves and moss. And then they carried her away, deep into the woods.

"Edolie struggled at first, but the capes seemed to have some magic in them, and the more she struggled, the tighter they wove around her, so she tried to remain still. They traveled for some time, and finally Edolie felt herself drop against the ground. She begged the Faieries to give her air, and after a moment the capes were pulled away. Edolie looked around and found herself in a small clearing surrounded by pines. The four

Faieries were preparing to take their rest on the carpet of pine needles. The one who had led her into the forest took a strand of hair and wrapped it around Edolie's wrists. The golden-white strand, sharp and strong as wire, snapped tightly into place of its own accord. 'Wait,' Edolie protested. 'Why have you taken me? I having nothing that you could want. Please let me go.'

"The Faierie gazed at her with a curious expression. Then she spoke in a whisper that sounded like the rustling of wind in a winter tree. 'You do have something we want. Our king has fallen in love with you, and we are taking you to him.'

"Edolie shook her head. 'You have made a mistake. It is not me he is looking for. I have never met your king.'

"'Have you not?' the Faierie asked. Then, to Edolie's shock, the Faierie took hold of her bound hands and bit her once, hard, on her fingertip.

"Edolie gasped, and the Faierie gave her a cruel smile before turning away and settling down to sleep, her long translucent wings trembling and then growing still. Edolie dared not move; the capes had tightened around her when she had struggled, and she suspected the Faierie's hair would do the same. Her finger ached where the Faierie had bitten her; the tiny punctures made by the sharp teeth were bleeding freely."

Errol paused, taking a moment to settle Seneca on his arm.

"I can see why you are anxious to avoid the company of Faieries," Goldenrod commented.

"Precisely," Errol replied. "They are unpredictable creatures."

"Though as yet I have not bitten any of you. At least that I can recall," Goldenrod said pensively.

"Fortunately, it is Sophia who rides with you, so I will not be bitten first," Errol said solemnly. Sophia laughed. "As the Faieries rested," he continued, "Edolie tried to get her bearings in the forest. It was no use; the sun shone only dimly past the dense tree cover. She could not even tell what time of day it was. The light was gray and violet-tinged, as if it were early morning or early dusk. But as the time passed, the forest seemed to grow darker, and so Edolie surmised that night was falling. The Faieries seemed to be sleeping soundly. Edolie knew this would be her best chance to escape. Rising slowly so as not to cut her wrists, she watched the Faieries for any sign of movement. They slept on. Edolie stepped backward across the pine needles as quietly as she could. Step by step. Still, the Faieries did not wake. Edolie reached the edge of the clearing and went into the woods. She had no idea in which direction her village lay, but it hardly mattered. Taking one silent step and then another, she moved farther from the clearing. It took all her effort to walk slowly when she wanted so desperately to run.

"Then she saw it: a faint flicker of yellow light in the trees ahead. Edolie burst into a run, not caring if the Faieries heard her or if the binding cut her. She ran as fast as she could, restricted as she was, and as she rushed through the trees, the yellow light grew stronger. There it was—she could see it. A cottage, with light in the windows and smoke in the chimney. She sobbed with relief.

"And then she heard a gust of wind and a dim shriek behind

her as the Faieries took to the air. Edolie, with great desperate gasps, ran the last few feet toward the cottage and pounded on the door with her bound hands. She could hear the flutter of the Faieries' wings. She could see them, their white faces and golden-white hair swirling toward her. Their cries were high-pitched whispers, like keening winds rattling in the branches. Edolie watched them with horror, shrinking against the sturdy wooden door of the cottage. And then, at the very edge of the small clearing wherein sat the cottage, they stopped, as if they had arrived at a barrier beyond which they could not pass. At the very same moment, the door opened behind her, and Edolie fell into the room.

"Edolie found herself on a wooden floor that gleamed, honey-colored, in the light of the fire. She looked up to see who had opened the door—who had saved her from the Faieries—and there, standing above her, was a woodsman. He was a stranger. Tall and slim, with dark eyes under heavy brows, he glared forbiddingly. Edolie felt a moment's apprehension. But then, as his eyes locked with hers, the woodsman's face changed. His frown vanished. His dark eyes softened with something like surprise—and then compassion. He had seen the Faierie shackles upon her wrists.

"If you have ever tried it, you know that it is surpassingly difficult to get to your feet when your hands are bound. With some effort, Edolie managed to rise to her knees. The woodsman put out a hand to help her. 'I'm sorry,' he said, in a voice that was low and courteous, 'that I did not open the door sooner. I never have visitors in these woods.' He led her to a chair by the fire.

"'And I am sorry to intrude,' Edolie replied. 'I was being pursued.'

"He nodded, motioning toward her bound hands. 'By the Faieries.'

"'Yes,' said Edolie.

"'Let me get that strand off your wrists,' he said, kneeling before her.

"'I fear it will never come off,' Edolie lamented. 'It is as strong as an iron chain and as sharp as a knife's blade.' And, in fact, poor Edolie's wrists had been cut to bleeding as she ran through the forest and the tight strand of hair sliced into her skin.

"Unexpectedly, the woodsman smiled up at her from where he knelt, holding her hands. Edolie suddenly felt all of the air leave her chest, as if it had been stolen. The woodsman's face— his clear brown eyes, his smile—seemed suddenly so familiar and dear and at the same time so wonderfully rare that she could not imagine life without it. The malady had struck her at last.

"Edolie gazed at him, stunned. 'You will feel a fool,' he said, still smiling, 'when I show you how the Faierie hair is cut.'

"'Will I?' Edolie asked, wonderingly.

"'No blade will cut it. No metal scissor or sharpened glass. How do you think it must be done?'

"Edolie shook her head. 'I don't know.'

"The woodsman bent his face toward her hands, and Edolie stared at him uncomprehendingly. He brought his mouth to her wrist and bit at the thin strand of hair. Instantly, the bond was severed, and the golden-white thread fell to the floor. The woodsman looked up at Edolie, still smiling. 'You see?'

"Despite herself, Edolie smiled back. 'I do.'

"'What you do not see is this. Just as Faierie hair can bind human flesh, so can human hair bind a Faierie. Tie your hair around a Faierie finger, and that Faierie heart is yours forever.' Edolie was astonished. She stared at the strand of golden-white hair on the stone hearth and wondered at the unknown power of ordinary things.

"'Now,' the woodsman said, 'I will clean and bind those cuts, for I can see that they must be painful.'

"And he did clean and bind them, his gentle hands wrapping the bandages around her wrists, while Edolie watched him and told him about the village and how she had strayed into the forest. The woodsman gave her a supper of mushroom stew and dark brown bread. And then he pointed her to an alcove that was tucked away at the top of a ladder: a narrow bed with a railing that overlooked the room. Edolie fell asleep watching the woodsman as he sat by the fire, whittling a stick of wood and humming, just audibly, a tune she could have sworn she knew.

"In the morning, when Edolie awoke, the cabin was quiet and empty. It was an orderly room, with its blue dishes stacked on the shelves and the well-worn broom standing at attention by the cold fireplace. Edolie heard the sound of an ax splitting wood, and she climbed from her perch down into the cabin and peered through the window. There, she saw the woodsman splitting wood just beside his house. The sight of him filled her with a sudden, calm contentment. *He is still here,* Edolie thought to herself. *He is real.*

"Moments later, he entered the cabin, arms laden with firewood. At the sight of her, the woodsman beamed. Edolie felt a murmur in her heart, and she wondered at how the Faieries had been so wise, despite all their petty cruelty, to lead her to this place, in these woods.

"You will imagine how that day passed for Edolie and the woodsman. They spent all morning talking, and then morning gave way to afternoon. The woodsman was wise and funny and just the tiniest bit wistful. Edolie knew she should return to the village, but part of her never wanted to leave. Nor did the woodsman speak of guiding her back to safety. The day grew longer, and finally Edolie felt that she must think of going home, even if she did not want to. 'It will be getting dark soon,' she said regretfully, 'and I should go back.'

"The woodsman looked at her—no longer wistful, but truly sad. 'Do you want to return?'

"Edolie shook her head. 'I don't want to, but I must.'

"'Very well,' the woodsman said, his face heavy with sadness. 'I will lead you back to your village.'

"Edolie did not speak as he made his preparations to leave the cabin. She regretted leaving, but she could not understand the woodsman's grief. After all, she thought to herself, surely she could find her way back to the cabin, or he could find his way to the village. They would see one another again, wouldn't they?

"It was a long journey through the forest. As they walked through the woods in silence, with the pines rustling around them and the still-naked branches of the oaks clattering in reply, Edolie found herself wondering about the Faieries that had taken her captive the night before. She was not sure why it had not occurred to her sooner, but she wondered about the way they had stopped so close to the cabin, when surely they had the power to reach her. And she wondered at how the woodsman traveled through the forest without any concern. How was it that he came to be living there, alone?

"Edolie glanced up at her walking companion and saw, not entirely to her surprise, that his long cape of green wool had taken on the leafy texture of Faierie garments. She could see his strong hands, now and then, lifting aside a branch so that it would not fall upon her, and they were pale in the dappled light. Edolie realized that they were nearing the edge of the forest. She could see, between the tree trunks, the rolling green hills of the field that bordered the forest. 'Stop,' she said.

"The woodsman turned to face her. It was the familiar face she already loved, but altered. There were flecks of gold in his eyes, and those eyes were filled with sadness.

"'How could you?' Edolie asked, aggrieved. She gazed with pain and longing at the face of the Faierie King and understood, at last, how that malady she had heard described could be so terrible and so wondrous at the same time.

"He looked back at her, sharing her distress. 'I did not want to,' he whispered.

"'Why not just speak to me as you are?'

"'I knew you had forgotten me,' he replied, 'and I could not think how to make you remember.' He held out his hand, pale with green veins, and Edolie saw the ring on his forefinger: a strand of hair wound tight, the color of her own. 'We were only children. I would not have held you to the promise, had I been able to forget you, in turn. But I could not.'"

"Edolie gazed with horror at the ring, and she knew that he was right. Those imagined hours in the forest had not been imagined at all. The beloved figure before her, so many years absent, had been in her heart since childhood. And she could see that the Faierie felt as she did, both of them wanting and not wanting that slim bond between them cut. She took his hand. 'What will happen if I cut it?'

"'I cannot say if what exists between us is only the binding power of that strand, or if it is something that stands alone.'

"Quickly, before she could change her mind, Edolie bent toward his hand and cut with her teeth the strand of hair that her childhood self had placed on the finger of the Faierie King. She tossed it to the side and looked up at him, expecting anger or indifference or something worse. Instead, she saw the face of the woodsman who had knelt over her hands by his hearth: smiling, eyes filled with delight at the prospect of surprising her."

Errol rode on, his eyes thoughtful. He glanced up at Seneca, who cast a brief shadow over him.

"That is the end?" Sophia asked.

"That is the end," he replied.

"What does it mean?"

Errol ran his fingers along his chin. "What do you think it means?"

"I think it is about the danger of losing your heart to the forest," Rosemary said promptly. "The danger of being lost so young to a dark force you do not and cannot understand."

"You see it as a warning," Goldenrod reflected. "Perhaps it is. To me, it is about the power of the things we do not remember. Things will happen, and they may vanish from your mind, but they will bind you as tightly as a chain. And this is not always a bad thing."

"I think it is about trusting people," Sophia put in. "And trusting your own heart. Everything Edolie did was dangerous and even foolish, but it ended in happiness."

"Trusting people," Goldenrod echoed. "Perhaps. But is it truly about *people*? Something I have observed about such stories is that they are often about the old ones, even when they do not seem to be. Consider the powerful pull of the forest, the way it drew Edolie without her comprehension. This seems true because it actually happens. The Climes have a way of working through us."

Errol shook his head. "And here I was, thinking it was a simple love story."

"I find it unlikely you thought that," Rosemary said dryly. She pointed ahead. "Your story has carried us far. We are less than an hour from the perimeter."

"I must ask," he said, "what we plan to do when we reach it.

If I understood the sheriff's map correctly, anyone who tries to set foot on the patches of Ausentinia that still remain is made faceless by this wind from the Dark Age."

"It is not the wind," Goldenrod corrected. "It is the moving border."

"However it happens," Errol continued, "you cannot speak to this Clime, the Dark Age, so we cannot negotiate our way forward. And while Sophia's map to Ausentinia may foretell the inevitable, as Rosemary contends, it is not terribly precise. What did it say? 'Dread or Desire'? I somehow doubt we will find signposts at the edge of the Dark Age."

"I have been thinking about it," Sophia said, taking the precious map from her pocket. *"The path divides, leading to the Steep Ridge of Dread or the Low Dunes of Desire. The Low Dunes lead to Bitter Desert, where you find yourself descending into the Cave of Blindness. From there, you may or may not return. Along the Steep Ridge of Dread, the golden birds turn to black. The falconer and the warbler defend you."* She looked at Errol and Rosemary. "Dread or Desire. I think I understand what it is we have to do. We desire to reach Ausentinia, and it would be tempting to find pieces of that Age if we can. But that is the wrong path. Did you notice that in Cabeza de Cabra's map, the Dark Age devoured any portion of Ausentinia where a person stood? But Ausentinia did not do the same."

"I see what you mean," Goldenrod said slowly. "Whatever provokes the Dark Age to shift its border does not so provoke Ausentinia."

"I had the sense reading the map," Sophia said thoughtfully, "that the Dark Age wanted people. But Ausentinia wanted only itself—the land that had been Ausentinian."

"It is well observed, Sophia. I had not seen it this way, but you are right."

"We dread going into the Dark Age. At least I do," Sophia said, rolling up the map. "But that is how we must go. And the golden birds will turn to black. I think that means the Golden Cross will not pursue us into the Dark Age, but the fourwings will be there instead. Errol and Rosemary, you are the falconer and the warbler." She smiled. "You have already defended us once."

"I think it is true that the Golden Cross will not pass into the Dark Age," Rosemary agreed. "They guard the border, and they attempt to kill fourwings that escape it. But they never enter it. If we pass into the Dark Age, they will give us up for lost."

"So they will consider their job done," Errol said. "Very well. Then our path takes us through the Dark Age and not around it."

"And let us hope," Rosemary said, under her breath, "that the worst we encounter are Faieries with sharp teeth and a handsome woodsman."

—1892, June 30: 16-Hour 05—

The United Indies have exported sugar, molasses, rum, and coffee since before the Disruption. New Occident and the Baldlands are its largest markets. To a lesser extent, New Occident has imported the Indies' rice, nutmeg, and cacao. These goods were traditionally sent as raw commodities, but as the Indies grew in wealth and manufacturing sophistication, their exports were increasingly refined.

—From Shadrack Elli's History of New Occident

THE MAP WRITTEN upon the ruler was less a map and more a cluster of memories, inchoate and unclear. Pressing his finger to the wavering red line, Theo felt himself plunged into a dark space heavy with the scent of fear. He was in a dungeon, or a room that felt like a dungeon. The walls were windowless and made of brick. He could not move. He looked down and saw that he was tied hand and foot to a metal chair. Across from him, in identical chairs, sat two others: a young woman and an old man. He could not see them clearly, as dark as it was, but he felt a throb of agonized distress. They were bound just as tightly, and they were slumped, immobile.

The memory ended and another flashed before him, terrible and piercing. It began with a scream. The dungeon was now filled with flame lamps and the smell of burned wood. The girl in the chair thrashed against the ropes that held her. The legs of the chair were blackened. Her skirts were charred at the edges, and flakes of what had been fabric lay strewn around her like black snow. A fire, cunningly devised in a metal tray with a grate, burned near her bare green feet. It had not reached her— yet. A man with long scars at either side of his mouth stood by the tray, inching it toward her with his foot. She pulled back as much as her bonds would allow, trembling with terror. Theo felt that his heart would burst. He could not bear to see her so treated. As he watched, she strained desperately against the rope, and brilliant red blooms sprouted from her palms.

Another memory abruptly intervened. The dungeon was quiet again. The metal tray with its terrible fire had been extinguished, and it lay at the edge of the room, the ashes gray and harmless. There was a broad metal table surrounded by scattered pieces of wood and tools: a hammer, a box of nails, a wooden rule, a saw, and a pencil. Two empty wooden crates, as long and wide as coffins, sat on the floor. The third was on the metal table. The Sandmen had placed the girl within it, and they surrounded her now with loose soil until only her face, white and calm with winter sleep, lay exposed. Theo locked eyes with the old man who sat across from him, tied to the metal chair. His expression said many things at once: *I am sorry. I love you. I am afraid. You can do this.*

He pulled his finger from the map. "Here," he said, passing the rule to Mrs. Clay. "I cannot tell you what it says. You must see it for yourself."

—17-Hour 00—

THE CITY OF Boston stayed up late to learn the news of who would be the next prime minister of New Occident. The polls closed at fifteen-hour, but the results were not announced until seventeen-hour, after the votes were counted. As the city waited and the summer heat stayed high, people roamed the streets, speculating, arguing, and straining the limits of the Boston police force.

MP Broadgirdle and the other two candidates were at the State House, each at the dinners hosted by their respective parties, also waiting. Though the Western Party was widely projected as the winner, the atmosphere of celebration at its dinner was rather forced. Broadgirdle sat at the head of the long dining table and ate energetically, dominating the conversation as the other MPs nervously did their best to impersonate a crowd of jubilant supporters. Peel hovered anxiously in a corner with the rest of the parliament assistants. The servers hurried in and out of the room, carrying trays of steaming fish, pots of fragrant soup, and plates piled high with roasted meat.

Even though they knew they had lost, the mood at the Remember England dinner was more cheerful. Pliny Grimes had given a good speech, and two of the MPs from the Western Party had been brave enough to defect, joining Remember England. This swelled their ranks from five to seven, so the results would not change the shape of parliament, but it was generally felt to be a great success, and the MPs reminded each other—yet again—that they had, at least, the notable accomplishment of having preserved a parliamentary system in New Occident.

At sixteen-hour, the Remember England Party decided to knock on the door of the New States Party dinner at the other end of the corridor, where Gamaliel Shore was attempting to keep spirits high. They were welcomed cordially, and the general anticipation of shared defeat allowed both parties to look upon each other kindly. Raising their warm glasses of sweet wine, they toasted their two parties and the unexpected but fortuitous alliance between them.

Theo was at 34 East Ending Street with Mrs. Clay. Their mood was somber, and not only because of the horrifying memory map. It had offered proof, but Theo knew that proof might not be sufficient for a literal-minded, rule-following police inspector. He wanted a location, which the map did not give. He needed to attend the meeting with Broadgirdle and Peel at the State House to get it.

And so Theo had been forced to confess his ongoing deception to Mrs. Clay. He had meant to persuade her, before heading off, that this meeting would yield the essential final piece of the puzzle.

Instead, Mrs. Clay was persuaded that Theo had been taking an unforgivable risk. She was beside herself. "Oh, Theodore, what would Mr. Elli say?" she kept repeating. She insisted that they tell Inspector Roscoe Grey about Theo's discoveries, so that Grey could investigate Broadgirdle himself. "Let *him* find these poor people," Mrs. Clay urged. "That is what he does for a living. You are putting yourself in real danger."

Theo insisted that he needed more. He wanted to lead the inspector to the brick-walled room. He wanted the inspector to see every scrap of proof he needed. The memory map was not enough.

Finally, having reached no compromise, Theo and Mrs. Clay had a melancholy dinner and waited for the election results. They sat at the kitchen table, each thinking about the people who were missing from East Ending Street and how the evening could have gone differently.

All the clocks in the house struck seventeen-hour, and Mrs. Clay sighed. "They will be announcing it now, then," she said.

Theo pushed his plate aside. "I guess they will."

"Poor Mr. Elli. He worked so hard to overturn the border closure." The housekeeper shook her head.

They sat in silence. Finally, Theo stood up. "Well. I'm off to the meeting."

"Theodore, I beg you one last time. Please stay home. You've done enough already, surely. I cannot force you, but I plead with you to think of the danger. This man is capable of terrible things."

Theo stood, wondering what else he could say to persuade her. Then, in the silence, he heard a sudden pattering of feet on the street beyond the open window. They were decidedly small feet, and they were bare. Theo reached the side door just as the knocking began. He threw the door open to see Winnie, hands resting on his knees, gasping for breath, on the step. "What is it, Winnie?"

Mrs. Clay joined Theo at the door. "Winston, are you hurt?"

Winnie shook his head. "Broadsy won," he gasped. "Announced early. Landslide."

Mrs. Clay sighed. "We were expecting as much. I fear for this Age, I truly do."

Winnie straightened up, still fighting for breath. "Embargo—the Indies declared it."

"What?" Theo exclaimed. "Already?"

"They were waiting in the harbor," Winnie panted, "to declare it. And there's a riot." He took a breath. "At the storehouses. By the harbor. And the ships. Are overrun."

"Fates above," Mrs. Clay gasped. "Over what? Broadgirdle's election?"

Winnie shook his head. "Molasses. Sugar. Rum. Coffee. Before it's all gone."

Theo pulled his jacket off the back of the chair. "I'm going back with you."

"What on earth for?" Mrs. Clay exclaimed. "It will be chaos at the harbor."

"I can report it to Broadgirdle," he said hurriedly. "It's what Slade would do."

"Please don't go, Theodore," she implored. "Both of you should stay here."

"We won't get too close."

Mrs. Clay worried the hair of her disordered bun. "Oh, take care of each other, boys! And may the Fates watch over you."

"Don't worry," Theo suggested, rather unhelpfully.

"Got your mustache?" asked Winnie.

"Got it. Right here." He patted his pocket. "We have to leave by the library window." He gave Mrs. Clay's hand a reassuring squeeze, and they were gone.

—17-Hour 31—

THEY RAN SIDE by side on the cobbled street, Theo's footsteps slow and loud compared to the swift slapping of Winnie's bare soles. Though the streets of the South End were almost empty, the lights were on in many of the houses. People throughout the city were waiting—separately and in the safety of their houses, but nonetheless waiting—for the official announcement of the winner. Winnie reflected as they ran that, as usual, his tweakiness had been well-founded. He'd only caught a glimpse of the mayhem, but he had already seen one ship filled with rum burning in the harbor, the alcohol exploding and sending chunks of splintered wood like fallen leaves into the water.

As they neared the harbor, they began to hear the shouts. The streetlights illumined more and more people who were standing in clusters on the pavement, talking to each other.

Then they turned a corner, and Winnie saw the first sign of trouble. He and Theo were running toward the harbor—but here were people running *away*. And they were not running casually, as he was. They were really running, as if fleeing for their lives.

Theo pulled Winnie to a halt and pushed him to the side of

the street, letting people rush by unimpeded. "What is it?" he called out to one of the men who passed. "What's happened?"

The man didn't answer—he was already gone. Winnie stared at a crumpled shoe that someone had abandoned by the sidewalk. There was a scream from several blocks away. Shouts, more screams, and then a growing din of breaking glass and bursting wood roared toward them.

Winnie and Theo exchanged glances. *"Run!"* someone shouted. *"Run for your lives!"*

Theo stood rooted to the spot, his hand on Winnie's shoulder. Then they both saw it: a dark wave, still a few blocks away, half as tall as the brick buildings on either side of the street. It snuffed out the streetlamps and surged toward them, crushing two men who stood before it. Without a word, Theo and Winnie turned and sprinted.

Theo realized, after only a few paces, that Winnie would not be able to keep up. His short legs, however fast they moved, would not carry him far enough. As he ran, Theo looked over his shoulder and saw the wave moving toward them, carrying debris—broken roofs, carts, and shattered windows—which it hurled against the street and the brick walls and anything else that lay in its path. They would not be able to outrace it. He glanced down at Winnie, short arms pumping. At this rate, the wave and its deadly debris would swallow them whole.

Squinting ahead into the still-illumined street, Theo saw a narrow alley between a bakery and a fish shop, some twenty paces ahead. "We're turning there!" he shouted to Winnie over the churn of the wave and the screams of the people running ahead and beside them.

Winnie gave no sign of having heard. His face was blank with fear. They reached the alley, and Theo pulled Winnie by the torn edge of his shirt. Stumbling over the trash that filled the narrow passage, they dove deeper between the buildings. "The fire ladder!" Theo shouted. "I'll hold you up, then push the ladder down to me."

Theo could just make out the low balcony of a fire ladder ahead. The wave had reached the opening of the alley. It funneled in between the buildings, coursing over the trash as if it were mere dust. Theo lifted Winnie by the waist, almost throwing him at the balcony. For a moment the boy clung to the metal railing, dangling helplessly. Then he scrambled up and threw himself over, onto the rails. Below, the wave had almost reached them.

Theo jumped for the balcony; it was too high. Winnie slammed on the metal ladder with his bare foot, sending it clattering down sharply. Theo jumped again, seizing the ladder, and from there propelled himself up beside Winnie. The wave was already engulfing the base of the ladder, pooling rapidly and rising. "Climb!" Theo cried. "It's going to keep rising— look how high it is on the street."

And, in fact, on the main street beyond the alley, the black glue showed no sign of slackening. Winnie and Theo climbed the metal steps until they reached the roof. Then they stopped, out of breath, and peered down. The wave had engulfed the second-story windows, but it had reached its limit there and could climb no farther. Gasping, Theo walked toward the front of the building to look out onto the street.

All the gas lamps in sight had been extinguished. In the dim light of the moon, he could see the flotsam slowly sinking. Winnie joined him, then lay face up on the roof. His ribs rose and fell. "Whew," he said. He realized now that the tweaky had not been about the election; it had been about this.

Theo took a deep breath and shook his head in disbelief. "It's molasses! Can you smell it?"

"You bet I can smell it," Winnie replied. "Must have been the tank on the Long Wharf."

"You think it burst?"

"They might have tried to make a spigot in it."

Theo threw himself down on the rooftop beside Winnie. "Fitting start for Broadgirdle. A flood of molasses is just about exactly right."

38
LOSING THE MUSTACHE

—*1892, June 30: 18-Hour 11*—

Believe in the world we have lost, not in the world you see, for the present world is mere illusion: a misshapen distortion of the truth. Beyond it, in the evanescence of memory, lies the Age of Verity.

—From the prophet Amitto's Chronicles of the Great Disruption

WHEN THEY HAD rested enough, Winnie and Theo moved on. They discovered a long piece of wood on the far side of the rooftop and used it as a bridge to cross over to the next building. They took the wood with them, bridging the narrow alleyways, until they had reached the end of the block. There, peering over the edge, they saw dry pavement and a great crowd of people moving west as the molasses that was trapped between the buildings seeped outward through the city streets.

The pair scurried down the fire escape and skirted the crowd, running along the edge of the cemetery and toward the State House. The crowds began again on Boston Common: agitated knots of people, some of them weeping and consoling, some of them shouting and pointing. There was no telling how many more had been swallowed by the wave of molasses, and it would be many days before the streets were cleaned and the full damage could be understood.

Winnie and Theo found the State House steps full, but above them the building was quiet and the colonnade dark. "Hey," Theo said to a young man standing by himself, "did we miss the speeches?"

The young man nodded. "Shore and Grimes gave concession speeches. Broadgirdle came out to celebrate his victory."

"Did he say anything about the riot?"

He shook his head. "Nothing. Just more babble about heading west."

Most of the people on the steps were men, and from the look of them, most supported Broadgirdle. There was a good deal of contented chuckling and backslapping. Theo realized that it was only a matter of time before the furious, grieving people who had escaped the molasses flood came to the State House and confronted the smug, victorious supporters of the Western Party. The result would almost certainly be violent.

Winnie, watching Theo's face anxiously, understood what he was thinking. "More rum and fire, isn't it? Rum here, fire there. Won't be pretty when the fire spreads."

"You're very right, Winnie," Theo said, resting a hand on the boy's shoulder.

"I've got a tweaky sense about these things," Winnie said, more mournfully than proudly. He felt that things had gotten tweaky enough, and he was wondering why such excitement could not space itself out a bit, enlivening days that were otherwise boring, rather than occurring all at once and thereby making it difficult to appreciate.

Theo would have asked what he meant by "tweaky," and in fact was about to, but a quick consultation of his watch told him that he was already late. "Winnie," Theo said, shaking his shoulder, "I've got to go meet Broadgirdle and Peel. You shouldn't wait out here, though. This is bound to get ugly. Do me a favor: go back and tell Mrs. Clay that we're all right, would you?" Theo knew that Winnie would never stay overnight at East Ending Street if the invitation seemed an act of kindness. But if he told him to go on an errand, and Mrs. Clay insisted that he stay, then perhaps he would.

Winnie hesitated. "Sure," he said. "Go on now, you're late."

With a brief nod, Theo walked quickly up the steps toward the State House entrance. He did not see Winnie run across the street to where the other scruffy boys were clustered, talking eagerly about all that had happened since midnight. Winnie said something to one of them and pressed a penny into his hand. The boy dashed off across the Common, toward the South End. Winnie hurried back up the State House steps and wedged himself into a tight little corner at the far side of the covered colonnade. From there, he could easily see the main door and the steps while not being seen himself. Winnie crouched down, hugged his knees to his chest, and waited.

As Theo walked along the now empty corridors, he reached into his pocket for his mustache. It was a little the worse for wear, as was his suit. He pressed it onto his upper lip and hoped for the best.

Approaching the offices of MP—now Prime Minister—Broadgirdle, Theo saw that the front room was empty. He could hear Broadgirdle and Peel speaking in Broadgirdle's office. Taking a deep breath, he walked toward it. *This is it,* he thought, nervous but exhilarated.

"Hello?" he called, announcing himself.

"In here, Mr. Slade," Broadgirdle called. "Please join us."

Theo gave Broadgirdle a wide grin. "Congratulations," he said warmly. He realized, as he was about to extend his hand, that he had forgotten his gloves. With an awkward movement, he tucked his hands into his pockets.

Broadgirdle returned Theo's grin in a manner that seemed more menacing than celebratory. "What's wrong, *Mr. Slade*? Forgot your gloves?"

Theo realized then, too late, that he had been played. He had the impulse to turn and flee, his mind flashing through his escape route in an instant, but Peel had already moved behind him to close the door. He looked back at Broadgirdle, wanting to find the right words that would make everything return to how it had been moments earlier, when he was standing in the corridor. But he could think of nothing.

The man Theo knew as Wilkie Graves let out a roar of laughter. "If only you could see your face, Lucky Theo. It is truly priceless. All of the inconvenience has been worth it for that face—so surprised, so utterly deflated." He grinned even more broadly, rising from behind the desk. "Did you truly think I wouldn't recognize you? You've grown a bit, but you're still the same boy: a thief, a liar, and a coward," he said, suddenly reaching out and seizing Theo's arm, "with a hand that looks like it's seen the wrong end of a meat grinder." Theo tried to pull away and failed. Graves, still much stronger and still almost twice his size, had a viselike grip. "I believe this one is my doing, isn't it?" he asked thoughtfully, pointing to the knuckle of Theo's ring finger. "And this one?"

"Let me go," Theo finally said, his voice choked.

"Oh, not a chance, Lucky Theo. Not. A. Chance. For a while it was worth seeing what you were up to, because of your connection to Shadrack Elli. But your speculation on the Eerie has shown that you know nothing. So, lamentably, your little deceptions are not interesting any longer."

"I'll leave the office," Theo agreed.

"Oh, you will, but not just yet," Graves said. He leaned forward and with a quick yank pulled off the mustache. He gave a low laugh. "Really, Lucky Theo. You haven't changed a bit. Still too confident in yourself. Too confident in the good luck that you never really had." His grip tightened painfully and he leaned in close.

Theo felt a wave of disgust as he smelled the familiar scent—smoke and decay, complicated now by a perfumed hair cream. With Graves's face inches from his own, Theo saw that his eyes were slightly bloodshot. His eyebrows were trimmed and plucked into dark bars. And at the edges of his mouth, where the black beard covered so much of his face, Theo saw, to his shock, the thin and hairless stripes made by scars.

He gasped. "You—" he began. "You have the scars. You're a Sandman."

Broadgirdle's brow contracted; his air of jollity vanished. "What do you know about Sandmen?" he asked, biting the words.

"I know, I know what you are," Theo stammered. "I was there when Blanca died. Is that what this is all about? Her crazy plan?"

Graves gave a nasty smile, his composure partially restored. "Actually the plan at the moment is all my own." He eyed Theo coldly, without humor. "As usual, you seem to have all the right instincts and all the wrong facts. My fellows and I survived that woman's persecutions, and we have a far greater purpose now than we did then." He dug his fingers into Theo's arm.

"The closet," Graves called to Peel.

Theo tried to kick his way free, but the two men, despite their different sizes, were easily able to contain him. For a moment, while Peel opened the closet door, Theo was able to squirm out of Graves's grasp. But they were both upon him again instantly, and as they pushed him into the closet, Peel took the opportunity to plant a swift kick with his rather pointy shoe in Theo's stomach. Groaning, he fell back against the closet wall. The door closed, leaving him in total darkness apart from the sliver of light that seeped in at the bottom. The lock clicked. "Lucky Theo," Graves said, his voice once again light, as if he could barely contain his laughter. "Just imagine you're back in the wagon. That should make the time pass quickly." He let out a low chuckle.

Then the light in the office was extinguished, and Theo heard the outer door slam shut.

He reached up and tried the closet door, even though he knew it was locked. He peered through the keyhole. In the faint, silver light that came in through the windows, he could see pieces of the empty office. The writing instruments on the politician's desk gleamed coldly.

Theo sat back and tried to fight the panic welling up inside him. He was sweating, his palms so slick that he could not grip the doorknob. Eyes closed, desperately trying to imagine an escape route, he threw himself against the wall. *He's right*, he thought, the terror pulsing through him like poison. *Graves is right. I'm the same as I was then. I'm just as helpless. I'm just as scared. I will never be any less afraid of him.*

The idea had been planted there, and there was no way to avoid remembering the wagon, just as Graves wanted him to.

ON THAT FIRST day, Graves had set his dog upon him and only pulled the beast back after it had chewed up Theo's hand and forearm. Then, while he groaned in pain, Graves unlocked the wagon. "Get up," he said.

Theo tried to gather himself to run, but the pain was too great, and he couldn't stop cradling his arm. Graves grabbed him by the back of the shirt and hauled him up. "You wanted to get into the wagon," he said with false affability, "and now I'm giving you what you wanted. *Get in.*" He pushed Theo roughly, so that his shins hit the floor. Instinct took over when Graves pushed again, and he jumped up.

He had seen what was in the wagon and he could not believe his eyes. In the brief seconds of light before Graves slammed the door, he gazed at them: four men and one woman, their hands shackled, the shackles attached to chains bolted into the floor. The wagon did, indeed, hold precious cargo, but not of the kind he had imagined. Graves, he realized, was a slaver.

The trip in the wagon was interminable. The people did not speak to him, except for the man next to him who patted him awkwardly on the shoulder when Theo began crying. "Don't worry, my boy. You're much too scrawny. And now your hand is near useless. No one will want to buy you." It did not offer much comfort. But the man was right. Graves had been heading to a slave auction several hours west, and every person in the wagon sold within the day—except for Theo.

Graves did not seem bothered. "Well, you were free to begin with," he said with equanimity. "I guess you can work for me now." He grinned, his metal teeth gleaming.

39
A DARK AGE

—*1892, July 2: 13-Hour 30*—

The circumstances of the first forays into the Dark Age have been lost to time, but soon after the Disruption its nature became known. Any prospect of settlement was quickly abandoned. A Papal expedition of 1433 returned, having lost all but two of its members, and declared that the Age would be prohibited to all inhabitants of the States.

—From Fulgencio Esparragosa's
Complete and Authoritative History of the Papal States

AS THEY RODE the final mile toward the border, Sophia contemplated the changes that had taken place in her since reading Cabeza de Cabra's map. When she thought back on the way she had been in years past, or the last summer, or even the day before, it seemed as though she was contemplating a different person. In all her elaborate fantasies of finding her parents, she had always imagined herself the grateful recipient of some wonderful turn of events. That was gone. In fact, the person capable of feeling that was gone. Her parents would not arrive as a wondrous wish fulfilled by the kindly Fates. Instead, seeking them would be long and arduous. She might not find them. They might truly have vanished as so many others had vanished in the abyss of memories. And should she find the Lachrima that had been her parents, discovering at last those empty faces would be more painful than anything she had ever lived through.

These thoughts did not make her feel helpless, or defeated; on the contrary—they made her feel steady, with a clearer sense of direction. But the realization did make her feel old. She had left the younger Sophia behind in Seville: an innocent girl who believed in the Fates; another phantom to haunt the city's empty streets at dusk.

Was this always part of growing older? Sophia wondered. Perhaps it was: realizing the world was not obliged to give you what you wanted, and, more importantly, deciding what you would do and how you would feel once the realization arrived. Would you sit back and resent the world? Would you make peace with it, and accept the unfairness without rancor? Or would you try to find and take what the world had not provided? Maybe all three, she reflected, at different moments.

She touched the spool in her pocket and ran her thumb along the coiled silver thread. It was strange to think that this token that had meant so much to her, that had seemed to carry the power of the Fates, now seemed lifeless and inert. It was simply a spool of thread. The greatest force it carried was the memories—dear memories—of the last year of her life. There was no other power there.

Sophia could tell that she had grown older because she did not bristle at how Errol treated her. She knew he had related his

Faierie tale for the purpose of distracting her, and she appreciated both the tale and the intention. And when he said, "Well, miting, you are taking us into the dark heart of the Age. You must be sure to stay near Rosemary and myself at all times," she did not feel annoyed at being treated like a child. It gave her a strange sense of wistfulness. She wished she were truly as sturdy and little as Errol imagined her.

"I will," she agreed.

"The caravan will have to stay at the border," Rosemary said with regret. "The spines are too dense." She peered ahead. "I do not see any guards at this portion of the border. It is too bad, for I would have left the caravan in their care."

"The riders are advancing," Goldenrod said, looking over her shoulder.

Sophia, who could not turn around, instead regarded the dark forest. It was unlike any Age, any landscape, that she had ever seen. Though the sheriff's memories had prepared her for a dark Age, they could not fully render the sense of strangeness emanating from the black moss, tinged faintly purple, and the tall black trees, sharp and bright as polished iron.

Rosemary stopped her horse. She dismounted and unhitched the caravan, tying it to a stake which she drove into the ground. As she did so, Goldenrod turned to the west and Sophia saw the cluster of golden birds that the map had foretold riding toward them, glinting here and there as their masks reflected the sun.

"So we enter the Dark Age," Errol said. "Are you certain about this, miting?"

"Almost," Sophia replied nervously.

He gave her a wry smile. "Reassuring." He led his horse forward. "I will go first. Goldenrod and Sophia travel next, then Rosemary with the crossbow."

"Remember that every thorn carries poison in its tip," Rosemary cautioned them. "A single thorn is capable of killing a grown man. I have seen it myself. Do not touch the spines for any reason."

Errol's horse paced the dry ground. The black moss ahead was lush and wet, as if from some hidden moisture. Two tall spines made a black archway that seemed to invite them onward. The sharp thorns on the trunks were as long as Sophia's forearm, and the branches lined with smaller thorns flexed slightly in the breeze.

Errol urged his horse through the archway. Seneca shuddered. For a moment Errol paused, waiting for some rush of wind to sound, but nothing happened. He looked over his shoulder. "It seems you were right, Sophia. So far."

Goldenrod and Rosemary followed, the horses' hoofbeats dulled to silence on the moss. Sophia looked around her, fascinated despite herself. The trees, she could see now, had thin, almost transparent leaves that rustled softly, filling the air with a papery murmur. The branches were unexpectedly beautiful, curving in smooth arcs outward and upward. Vines twined around the spiny trunks, with flowers like purple sponges; they expanded and contracted gently, as if breathing. On one long spine overhead, a long, luminescent worm held itself upright, describing a slow figure-eight in the air.

From the moss below, Sophia heard a faint buzzing, and as she peered downward she saw a trickle of beetles, shiny and black, scurrying in a straight line toward a hole. The patch of soil where they burrowed was dark and rich, far moister than the dry soil of the Papal States that they had left behind.

Sophia frowned, wondering how such a thing could be. The Dark Age lay just beside the Papal States. It received no more rain than did its neighbor, and yet it looked like a landscape that received rain daily. Suddenly Sophia's mind recalled a similar mystery: soil that held heat while the air around it was cold. She caught her breath.

"What is it?" Errol asked sharply, turning in his saddle.

"Nothing. I—I realized something."

He looked at her, waiting.

"I realized something about the Dark Age. Last summer, when we were in the Baldlands, we came across a future Age where the soil was man-made. It could stay warm, even in a cold place. It warmed the water. And it made seeds grow differently, into other kinds of plants. I was thinking . . . Could it be that parts of the Dark Age are man-made? That might be why Goldenrod cannot speak to it."

Goldenrod's body, behind her, stiffened. "Yes," she said. "Of course. If it were man-made, it would not hear me. Or speak."

Errol looked around him, baffled. "That is impossible. How could humans make this?"

"They can," Goldenrod replied. "I have heard that in future Ages, the manipulation and even invention of animate beings is not unheard of. But I had never imagined an entire Age."

Sophia felt her shake her head. "It would be remarkable. But conceivable."

"But the Dark Age is of the remote past, not the future," objected Rosemary.

"How do you know?" Sophia thought of Martin Metl, the botanist, and his soil experiments. She would have to find a way to gather a sample for him. "Perhaps people of the Papal States *assumed* it was from the remote past because it looks like it should be."

"I suppose that is possible." Rosemary shook her head. "Whether made by man or God, it seems to me an abomination."

"I agree," said Errol, and he led his horse onward.

"I think it is rather beautiful," Sophia murmured. Her mind was lit by possibilities. She began to consider what it would mean for a Clime to be both living and artificial: alive and yet not, conscious and yet not. Perhaps the people of this Age had invented ways to adapt, just as the people of the Glacine Age had invented warming soil to counter the extreme cold.

They had progressed some two hundred yards into the forest when Rosemary halted them. "Look behind us," she said. "You will see they stand at the border."

Goldenrod turned her horse carefully in the narrow path, avoiding the leaning branches of the spines. Sophia could see the glint of gold in the distance. One of the men shouted into the forest, his voice hard. "What did he say?" Sophia asked.

"He seems to believe we are witches who live in the Dark Age, and he wishes us a speedy return to our maker." Errol smiled wryly. "Would that we were. But since we are not witches, let me ask a question: We can ride east for some time easily enough, but the path to Ausentinia is gone. Just how are we planning to find it?"

"I had an idea," Sophia said. "The map told me to enter the Labyrinth of Borrowed Remembering."

"Yes," Errol replied. "Very useful advice."

She smiled. "The truth is, I have seen the road east to Murtea and the way to Ausentinia many times. Dozens of times. In Cabeza de Cabra's map."

"And you think you could navigate the route, despite the fact that we are in a different Age?"

"I think so. I have a sense of where we are." Sophia imagined that the Ages were not unlike memory maps, layered one atop the other. She pictured herself in a map of the Dark Age made of metal, seeing through its man-made landscape to the map of clay below it.

"Very well, miting. I will head east, and you will tell me if we should change course."

The afternoon lengthened as they continued at a slow pace, choosing the ways less crowded by spines. The air in the forest was cool, despite the sun overhead, and the quiet rustling of leaves alongside the occasional buzz from the black beetles made the ride deceptively tranquil.

Sophia waited for the fourwings to appear, scanning the patches of sky overhead, but they did not. While she reached for the familiar route in the borrowed memories of Cabeza de Cabra, another part of her mind turned over and over the words from the Ausentinian map. *When you emerge from the labyrinth, you will have a choice. You will defend the illusion or you will not.* She had felt confident that the Labyrinth of Borrowed Remembering meant the sheriff's memories, even if she could not feel confident that she would navigate them perfectly. But she could not fathom what the illusion would be, or how she would defend it. Would it be an illusion of safety? A patch of Ausentinia that would seem safe? Or perhaps the illusion already existed around her: the illusion of a living Clime, which she knew to be false. How would she defend such an illusion?

"Stop," Errol whispered. He halted his horse. He had already drawn his sword.

Sophia raised her head and strained to look past him. A fourwing lay directly in their path. It was curled up at the base of a spine. The nearest thorns dripped a white liquid, and the fourwing's beak was lined with the same milky substance. It raised its head and made a hoarse, halfhearted cry. Then it buried its head in its wing as if to sleep.

Errol waited, but the bird did not move. Slowly, he led them to the right, making a wide circle around the fourwing.

When it lay safely behind them, Sophia turned to look up at Goldenrod. "Was it poisoned?"

"I think it was drunk," Errol replied with a surprised laugh.

"The fourwings nest in the spines," Rosemary put in. "The thorns cannot poison them."

"Then it was drinking from the tree," said the Eerie.

At this, Sophia understood why they had not heard the cries

of the fourwings inside the Dark Age; in their homeland, the creatures were always sated and half intoxicated by the milk of the spines. She marveled again at the possibility that people had created this world. However much its creation was mysterious to her, she could appreciate the symmetry: a forest that protected itself from outsiders, trees that fed the creatures who lived in them, soil that gave water to the moss and trees.

As the sun began to dip toward the horizon, Sophia reckoned that they were reaching the place that had been Murtea. They climbed a hill where the spines were short and sparse. Looking out over the dark landscape ahead of them, Rosemary cried: "There! Do you see it? A yellow patch among the black."

"And another one," Goldenrod pointed.

"Ausentinia still defends itself," Rosemary said proudly. "I feel certain it is there, waiting for us to find it."

"It will be dusk soon," said Errol. "I fear it will be almost impossible to travel safely through the spines in the dark."

"I have brought one of the golden eyes." Rosemary withdrew it from her pack and held it aloft. Slung in a loose net, the orb emitted a penetrating yellow light. "Besides, the forest provides its own illumination, as you will see. I have camped by the perimeter at night and have seen the floor grow bright."

"Nonetheless," Errol replied skeptically, urging his horse onward, "we should move onward while we still have some daylight."

The sky turned a brilliant orange and then faded to violet. The moss around them began to glow softly, as if illuminated from within. "Just as you said, Rosemary," Goldenrod observed. "Perhaps it will not be so difficult to travel at night."

They reached a clearing where the moss underfoot made gentle mounds. A ring of spines around them leaned inward, creating a space like a black chapel of thorns and moss. Errol stopped abruptly. Goldenrod and Rosemary halted behind him. He swung down from his horse and took his bow, which had hung on his shoulder, and a green arrow from his quiver. "You dare follow me here," he said in a hard voice, aiming the arrow.

A figure emerged from the trees. Pale and luminous, it reached its hands out in a gesture of entreaty. *"At the City of Foretelling, you will have a choice."*

"A *spanto*," Rosemary gasped. She crossed herself. "This bodes ill."

Errol's horse, now riderless, backed up, whinnying nervously. Goldenrod reached out and took its reins; she murmured, calming it.

"Do not speak to me of choice," Errol said, his voice strained.
"At the City of Foretelling, you will have a choice."

Errol loosed his arrow, plunging a green stem into the phantom. It crumpled and vanished like a scrap of mist.

"Your arrow felled it." Rosemary's voice was hushed. "I have never seen this done."

"Any green branch will do," Errol said tersely. As he returned to his mount, another figure emerged from the spines: a woman, slight and straight—Minna Tims. The horse suddenly reared; letting out a cry of terror, it turned and fled toward the trees. "No!" Goldenrod cried. "Come back!" Without warning, she seized Sophia and lowered her to the ground. Then she urged her horse toward the trees, diving between the spines.

"Goldenrod! Are you mad?" Errol ran to the edge of the clearing and looked into the trees. With a curse, he pivoted toward Minna's phantom and drew another green arrow from his quiver.

"It advances, Errol," Rosemary warned. She crossed herself again as the pale figure approached.

Suddenly several voices echoed all at once in Sophia's mind. She heard again the phrases Minna's phantom had spoken in Boston: *Missing but not lost, absent but not gone . . .* She heard Errol recounting the tale of Edolie and the woodsman: *The beloved figure before her, so many years absent, had been in her heart since childhood.* She heard Rosemary speaking with pride as she looked out over the hills: *Ausentinia still defends itself*—

"Stop!" she shouted. She raced to put herself between Errol and Minna's phantom. She understood now that it was this illusion—this specter of Minna Tims—that she had to defend.

"What are you doing?" Errol demanded, lowering his bow.

"She's not a phantom." Sophia's heart was pounding. "She's a guide."

"*Trust this companion, though the trust would seem misplaced.*" The voice of Minna's phantom was clear and bright.

"What do you mean, she is a guide?" Errol demanded.

"She is a *spanto*, Sophia," Rosemary said. "A cursed phantom."

"Listen to her words," Sophia urged. "They're like the ones

on the Ausentinian maps. She comes to us from Ausentinia. She is leading us there."

"*Trust this companion, though the trust would seem misplaced,*" Minna repeated.

Errol looked at her. "How would such a thing be possible?"

"I don't know. I don't understand it either, Errol, but I don't think the phantom means us any harm." Sophia took him by the arm, pushing the bow aside. "People say they lead you to oblivion. If the phantoms led here, through the Dark Age to Ausentinia, wouldn't that seem like oblivion? And yet all they are doing is leading us to where the maps we want—the very maps that will guide us to Oswin and my mother—can be found."

Errol regarded her in silence.

"It is too dangerous, Sophia," Rosemary said adamantly.

"She is the illusion that will lead us to Ausentinia." Sophia's voice took on a pleading note. "The map has been right until now."

Errol shook his head. "Very well." He stepped away, returning the green arrow to his quiver, but he drew his sword. "I do not trust this phantom for a moment, but I hope I am right to trust you."

Goldenrod appeared at the edge of the clearing, leading her horse. "Your horse was stung by the thorns," she said sadly to Errol. "I could do nothing for her."

"And yet Sophia would have us believe the phantoms are harmless," Rosemary said.

"I didn't say that," Sophia protested. "I said they could be guides from Ausentinia. Their words sound so much like the maps."

"*Trust this companion, though the trust would seem misplaced,*" Minna repeated. She turned and slipped away among the spines.

"We must follow her."

"Sophia, wait!" Errol called.

"I will not wait," Sophia insisted. "She will be gone in a moment." She plunged into the spines, following the retreating back of the pale specter.

40
MINNA'S PHANTOM

—*1892, July 2: 17-Hour 00*—

Seneca the Younger, a Stoic philosopher from the ancient world, was born in Córdoba in what would become the Papal States. Today he is not popular in the land of his birth, but in the Closed Empire to the north, Seneca is widely taught and admired among scholars.

—From Shadrack Elli's History of the New World

SOPHIA COULD HEAR Errol and Goldenrod call her name. She could hear them fall behind as they tried to follow her twisting route through the spines. But she was fixed on the pale figure before her, and soon their sounds faded.

Minna's phantom moved quickly. Sophia felt a longing in her chest that seemed to steal her breath; at first she thought it was the anxious, fervent wish that she had understood the Ausentinian map correctly. But then she realized it was simply longing to see that pale figure: to never lose sight of it; to follow it wherever it might go, as long as she could continue seeing that beloved face that turned, every few steps, to make sure Sophia was there.

A part of her realized that she was falling under the phantom's spell. This was what had happened to Errol's brother, Oswin, when he pursued the phantom of his horse, heedless of where he was and who else pursued him. But the other part of her, the principal part of her, did not care. This was what she wanted. She wanted to follow Minna. It felt so unquestionably right, but she could not tell if it felt right because she was correct in reasoning that Minna would lead her to Ausentinia or simply because she wanted it to feel right.

Her awareness of the Dark Age around her dimmed, until all she saw was Minna's phantom. The long dress trailed over the moss, sweeping it lightly. When she paused and turned, looking over her shoulder, she smiled in a way that Sophia found achingly familiar. *How could I have forgotten that smile?* Sophia asked herself. She felt in it all the comfort and reassurance that she had missed over the long years of Minna's absence. She began to wait expectantly for Minna to turn her head, to smile once more. Each time it came, Sophia felt a rush of happiness. She quickened her pace over the moss.

The spines had become almost invisible in the darkness. Her path was illuminated only by the moss underfoot and the phantom before her. She lost track of whether they continued to move east—and, as the stepping and pausing, stepping and pausing continued, she lost track of time. Minna had not spoken again after leaving the clearing, but Sophia seemed to hear her nonetheless. It was not words that she spoke, but thoughts and feelings. Minna said that she had not wanted to leave Boston, that she had missed Sophia on every step of the journey, and that it had broken her heart when she realized Sophia would have to wait for her—and wait for her, and wait. But Minna also said something more heartening: *I am here now,* she said to Sophia with every pause, every turn of the head. *Wherever I have been, I am here with you now.*

The dark hills grew more pronounced, and they climbed out of the forest to overlook a valley. She stood before Sophia, hands outstretched. *"You have not yet met fear,"* she said, smiling sweetly, and her eyes filled with tears.

Then she placed her right hand on her heart and lifted her palm, as she had the first time she appeared in Boston. The luminous figure that seemed made of crumpled paper faded slightly and then brightened. *"You have not yet met fear."* Then she was gone.

"Mother!" Sophia exclaimed, rushing forward. She grasped at the air. *"Where are you?"* she cried, her own eyes filling with tears. "Come back!"

She looked around wildly for the pale figure, and as her eyes scanned the middle distance she saw the valley before her. Stopping, dazed, she felt herself emerging from the phantom's spell.

She was at the top of a hill. The forest moss carpeted the ground under her feet and the slope before her. At the hill's base, the black moss met green grass in a vivid boundary. Beyond it the grass grew tall and lush, dotted by wildflowers that turned expectant faces toward the yellow moon. Spruces, cypresses, and pine trees clustered in the valley. Birches and maples lined a dirt path leading to a stone wall, where a gated entrance stood open. The city of Ausentinia shone in the moonlight, its copper roofs gleaming like dozens of white flames.

"Ausentinia," Sophia whispered. With trembling fingers, she pulled the map from her pocket. *"Defend the illusion, taking the Path of the Chimera. Along it, you may lose yourself, but you will find Ausentinia. When the wind rises, let the old one dwell in your memories, as you have dwelled in the memories of others. Give up the clock you never had. When the wind settles, you will find nothing has been lost."*

Sophia looked out at the city she had wanted for so long to find.

Then she turned to where the moss met the green grass of Ausentinia. From the moment Goldenrod described the nature of the old ones, Sophia had suspected what the map would ask of her. Now she knew for certain.

A sudden cry drew her gaze upward. Seneca, swooping toward her, landed abruptly on her pack. Sophia was thrown off balance by the strength of his descent. "Go back, Seneca," she said, over her shoulder. She saw the falcon's dismissive gesture out of the corner of her eye. "Go back," Sophia insisted. "You will have to guide them here. Tell Goldenrod where I have gone."

She let herself plummet downhill, her feet moving quickly over the moss. As she did, Seneca opened his wings and pushed off, taking flight. Sophia felt herself gaining momentum, and she began to brake, wondering suddenly if the weight of her pack would pitch her precipitously into Ausentinia. She threw it off, and her descent slowed.

She stopped at the very edge of the Dark Age, looking out

onto the dirt path that lay only a short step and yet a whole Age away. "I am ready," she said, between gasps.

A gust of powerful wind moved through the birch trees closest to her, unsettling their papery leaves so that they fluttered and came free. The wind struck her face, more sudden and violent than she had expected, and the border of Ausentinia moved through her. She disappeared into the memories of another being: the memories of the place where she stood.

She had no sense of her body. If she had a body, that knowledge was gone.

The world was black and red. All was darkness, except for where the sky was pierced by red flame that turned violently white and then streaked to the earth, filling the air with terrible roars and clouds of dust. When the flames turned white, the landscape was briefly illumined, and there was black, black rock in every direction. A raging impatience simmered in the back of her mind, and she knew that this was not her mind, but Ausentinia's. Impatience and unease—a wish to be everything, to be nothing, to be otherwise. The dark earth, the red flames, the flashes of piercing light, the roaring, and the clouds of dust went on and on. They went on for longer than Sophia thought possible. The restless violence coursed through her, and there seemed no end to it. Flickering somewhere in the endless dark, Sophia in her own self felt a spark of terror: a fear that it would go on forever.

Give up the clock you never had, she reminded herself.

She had to lose track of time, as wholly and irretrievably

as she could, so that she would not spend years wandering aimlessly through the Clime's memories: so that the memories of Ausentinia would not erase her own. She could understand the dread all who had ever become Lachrima must have felt—the great horror of being swallowed whole by an ancient vastness. And she could sense the impulse all who had become Lachrima must have followed—the impulse to cling to oneself fiercely, as if clinging to a rock in a great ocean of time. But this, she knew, was not the way. The way was to give up oneself, to give up one's sense of time—to let go of the rock, to float.

Sophia plunged forward, letting herself plummet through the memories the way she had plunged downhill, the way she had rushed through the beaded map. She moved, and the dark vanished. In a moment, she had passed from a burning world of darkness to a world of water. Waves rose and fell around her. A massive, brilliant moon that seemed close enough to touch hung on the horizon. A steady sense of purpose had replaced the reckless violence: Ausentinia gazed at the moon and felt a stirring of something like contentment. Agitation still lurked below the surface of the waves, but in the air above them was tranquility. Sophia let herself float again, urging herself more quickly through the memories. The waves disappeared. Ice curved away from her in every direction, and the sun hung limply in a pale sky. As she let the time give way, slipping through her fingers rapidly, and then more rapidly, straining her own limits, the ice continued, and only the flickering light of the sun—day and night and day again—assured her that time was indeed passing.

The ice seemed interminable: ice and indifference. A penetrating, immobilizing indifference descended until Sophia could hardly recall anything beyond it. Struggling against a sense of panic, she pushed onward; the endlessness of this unrecognizable world, these incomprehensible memories, threatened at the edges of her consciousness like a terrible promise. There had to be something familiar—somewhere, some time.

Abruptly, as if it had never been gone, the world she knew appeared. She gasped with relief. There were hills and trees, and a bird wheeled down to settle among the rocks. The rocks crumbled and gave way, creating a deep ravine, which filled slowly with rubble. Ausentinia had shed its indifference. Curious, tentative, and searching, it made its way into the world. Sophia recalled trees growing from seed, spreading to cover great expanses, dressing and undressing with the seasons. A path appeared before her, leading three ways, and then, trudging slowly toward her, under a white garment that covered everything but her eyes, came a woman. Sophia paused to watch. The woman drew closer; her eyelashes were caked with dust and she walked wearily, taking the path lined by birches.

Moving onward through Ausentinia's memories, she saw the travelers, at first in small numbers. Then they grew more numerous until they became a blur. Young and old, always alone, they moved along the path. Ausentinia felt a piercing fondness for them. Sophia felt something tugging at her mind: it reached for her, drawing a thread from between her thoughts as if pulling a silver thread from a tapestry. Ausentinia needed to find a route through the Dark Age that had overtaken it, a path out of the darkness, and it tugged at Sophia's memory insistently. The memory came free. The path she had taken through the dark forest unfurled behind her, perfectly recalled in every detail.

Sophia opened her eyes. A light so bright that she felt blinded shone around her. Her body felt strange. Her head was light; her ears throbbed; her throat felt scraped to rawness. When she took a deep breath, her lungs ached. But the air began to restore her.

She lifted her head. Not brilliant light, but complete darkness surrounded her. For a moment she felt a rush of terror: it had happened—she had been transformed into a Lachrima. Her hands flew to her face, and as she felt her familiar features, she realized that the darkness around her was the night sky, deepened by the gathering of clouds above her. The path between the birches to Ausentinia ran true before her.

She had crumpled to the ground, and she raised up slightly, with effort, to look behind her. Leading up the hill through the moss was a dusty path that she knew Ausentinia had made from her memories: a route through the encroaching Age, a safe passage through the darkness.

HALF AN HOUR afterward, Seneca appeared and Errol crested the hill after him to find Sophia curled into herself, lying in the grass by the side of the road. He gave a shout and dropped his horse's reins to rush toward her, Goldenrod and Rosemary hurrying behind him. When he seized her, fearing the worst, Sophia's eyes startled open.

"She's alive," he said, his voice rough with relief.

"I told you she would be," Goldenrod said, though she was nearly as agitated as she dropped to the ground beside them. "Ausentinia promised me that she was well."

"*You will find nothing has been lost,*" Sophia said with a weak smile.

"You are a miracle, Sophia," Rosemary said, clasping her hand. "You have led us to Ausentinia. You have remade the path."

"It was very brave of you," Goldenrod said, pulling her into a sudden embrace, "to lose yourself so completely so that Ausentinia could be found."

41
MAKING THE ARREST

—1892, July 1: 6-Hour 12—

Most in New Occident consider the southern war for New Akan's independence that took place soon after the Disruption sufficient bloodshed, and desire no further conflict with our neighbors. And yet there are those, particularly Nihilismians, who believe that a nation is made in the crucible of war, and they prepare, if not openly plan, for such an eventuality.

—From Shadrack Elli's History of New Occident

INSPECTOR ROSCOE GREY was never home for lunch, and he frequently missed dinner when working on a demanding case. For this reason, the household had a careful morning routine, and it was almost never disrupted. Mrs. Culcutty set the table in the dining room and placed the morning newspaper beside the inspector's plate. The inspector drank coffee and read the paper until Nettie arrived, yawning and with her hair in wrappers, and then they ate breakfast together and discussed the happenings of the previous day and made plans for the day to come.

The morning of July 1, however, did not begin as it was meant to. Roscoe was standing at his mirror, straightening his thin black necktie, when there was a knock on his bedroom door. "Mr. Grey—oh, Mr. Grey, it's Mrs. Culcutty." Her voice was anxious.

With a frown of surprise, he let her in. Mrs. Culcutty was out of breath from having climbed the stairs too quickly. There was a newspaper in her hands.

Inspector Grey had fully expected to read in the morning's paper that the Western Party had won the election and that Gordon Broadgirdle had been named prime minister. So it took him several seconds to comprehend the headlines:

WAR DECLARED

WESTERN PARTY WINS ELECTION: BROADGIRDLE NEW PM

UNITED INDIES DECLARES IMMEDIATE EMBARGO

RIOTS AT THE HARBOR CAUSE TANK EXPLOSION

MOLASSES FLOOD CLAIMS DOZENS OF LIVES

In the early hours of July 1, 1892, a proclamation of secession was issued jointly by the Indian Territories and New Akan. New Occident has made a declaration of war in response.

Shortly after Gordon Broadgirdle, the new prime minister and leader of the elected Western Party, made his victory speech at the Boston

State House and declared his intent to lead New Occident toward immediate expansion westward, the proclamation of secession was delivered by a representative of the two jurisdictions. The proclamation, reproduced in full below the fold, states the intent to form an independent nation. It repudiates many of the prime minister's stated policy objectives, in particular his adherence to the closed-border policy. Prime Minister Broadgirdle was swift in issuing a declaration of war, which was passed by a bare majority in an emergency parliament session. The prime minister plans to speak at the State House this morning to make a call for enlistment.

Gamaliel Shore, the defeated candidate of the New States Party, could not contain his chagrin. "I fear that this secession and this war will be disastrous to New Occident. It all stems from our misguided border policy," Shore argued, "which the New States Party would have overthrown. I am fearful indeed for the future."

An artist's rendition of Broadgirdle at the podium, accompanied by Peel and other members of his party, occupied a box beside the article. Inspector Grey glanced at the other headlines. War? Secession? An embargo? A molasses flood? How had so much happened in a scant six hours? He realized that Mrs. Culcutty was still in front of him, recovering her breath and watching him anxiously. "Thank you, Mrs. Culcutty," he said. "This is grave and urgent news, indeed. I'll come downstairs with you."

"Oh, Mr. Grey, what is the meaning of it all?"

Grey shook his head. "I hardly know. But I do know that Broadgirdle is a determined man, and if he has set us upon this course, it is because he intends to follow it. He is not one to back away from such declarations once they have been made."

As they reached the stairs, Nettie's bedroom door opened and she appeared, swathed in a lavender robe, her head bristling with a colorful assortment of hair wrappers. "Father? What has happened?"

"Come downstairs, Nettie. I will tell you over breakfast."

Nettie was alarmed by her father's unexpected seriousness. "Tell me now, Father."

Grey paused, his hand on the oak newel of the staircase. "New Occident has declared war on the Indian Territories and New Akan."

Nettie gasped. "War?" She followed Mrs. Culcutty and her father hurriedly down toward the dining room, her lilac slippers pattering on the stairs and then the floorboards.

"Yes. The Western Party was elected, which prompted an embargo from the United Indies and a proclamation of secession from the Indian Territories, allied with New Akan." They had reached the dining room. Grey took his seat, and Mrs. Culcutty served him coffee with a trembling hand. "In addition," he went on, scanning the paper, "this seems to have triggered riots at the Boston Harbor and some kind of explosion of a molasses tank. Though how that occurred is beyond my comprehension."

The dining room door opened. Mr. Culcutty wore the same anxious expression as his wife, and he had clearly been waiting for them. Roscoe motioned him inside. "Sit down, Mr. Culcutty, Mrs. Culcutty. Nettie."

"What will happen, Father?"

"I don't know," he said, shaking his head. "We will go to war. Although New Occident has only a small armed force, which means Broadgirdle will need to recruit from the civilian population."

Nettie gazed at her father, wide-eyed. "Will you have to go to war?"

Grey reached out and put his hand over his daughter's. "No, my dear. I almost certainly will not. I am too old, thank the Fates, as is Mr. Culcutty," he said, and the other man nodded. "Unless things change very much, neither one of us will be asked to enlist."

"Unless they change very much?" Nettie echoed. "Does that mean it might happen?"

"Frankly, it is impossible to say, with a prime minister like this one. Broadgirdle is an extremist. He will take extreme measures."

"Oh, I don't like him!" Nettie burst out. "Horrid, horrid man."

At the conclusion of this pronouncement, there was a knock at the front door. Mrs. Culcutty rose and headed for the foyer. The others heard the door open and then the sound of a woman's voice, low and tense. A moment later, the housekeeper returned, accompanied by an older woman wearing an expression of deep distress and a small boy wearing almost nothing at all. Inspector Grey recognized the woman as Mrs. Sissal Clay, Shadrack Elli's housekeeper.

"Mr. Grey," Mrs. Culcutty said, clearly trying to preserve some semblance of normality, "a Mrs. Sissal Clay is here with what she says is an urgent matter. One of your officers accompanied her. He is waiting at the door."

"I'm sorry to interrupt your breakfast, Inspector," Mrs. Clay said apologetically, with a glance at the newspaper on the table. "Especially given the very disturbing news. But I am afraid I am here with a more immediate problem." She paused and suddenly clasped her hands nervously.

"Yes?" prompted Grey.

"It has to do with Prime Minister Broadgirdle and—and Theo. Theodore Constantine Thackary."

"What has happened?"

Mrs. Clay took a deep breath. "You see, Inspector, Theo has taken it upon himself to—well, to investigate the murder of Prime Minister Bligh on his own."

Grey frowned. He sensed an unpleasant difficulty appearing, like a dark cloud on the horizon.

"He has been investigating the murder and has discovered a great deal. But . . ." Mrs. Clay cleared her throat. "But in so doing, he has not been entirely honest with you. In fact, neither of us has been."

Grey's frown deepened.

"Theo believes that Gordon Broadgirdle is responsible for

the murder," she continued, with difficulty. "And he decided to find evidence proving it. He has been working in Broadgirdle's office for more than two weeks now—under a different name—and he has found some suspicious circumstances. But the difficulty is this. Last night, he was with Winston here"— she indicated the boy in rags—"and he went into Broadgirdle's offices for a meeting. Broadgirdle left the State House half an hour later, but Theo never emerged. Winston waited all night for Theo to reappear." She collected herself. "We are concerned for him. We are afraid something may have happened to him in that office."

Grey's frown could deepen no further, but he held his watch in his hand and tapped its cover, a sure sign that his consternation had reached unusual heights. Mrs. Culcutty blinked in astonishment. Mr. Culcutty looked baffled. Nettie was listening intently with a shrewd expression that was very unlike her.

"This is extremely dangerous, what he has done," Inspector Grey finally said. "What is the evidence you spoke of?"

"Theo has a map. It is not an ordinary map, but a map that records recollections. It describes another crime related to the prime minister's murder."

"I see," Grey said skeptically. "And is there any other evidence he has discovered and concealed?"

"I suppose there is," Mrs. Clay said, her face suddenly flushing bright red, "if you consider the gloves and robe found at the murder scene. And the knife."

There was a long pause, during which Mrs. Clay was too

afraid to look up and meet Grey's eye. "What gloves, robe, and knife?" he asked, his voice steely.

She took a deep breath, as if preparing to plunge into an icy pool. She reached into the basket that she was carrying and pulled out a lumpy white bundle. Without asking permission— she was worried that if she spoke, she might not be able to continue—she put the bundle on the table. She unfolded the white sheet. Mr. and Mrs. Culcutty gasped. A pair of gloves and a robe, both bloodstained, along with a short knife, lay on the sheet. "These," Mrs. Clay whispered. She looked down at her shoes.

If she had looked up, she would have seen that Inspector Grey was not so much angry as he was dismayed. He was thinking, not for the first time, that well-intentioned people managed to do very foolish things, not infrequently committing serious crimes in the process. It was one of the circumstances that exasperated him most about his job. Locking up evildoers was easy—even agreeable. But there was no pleasure to be had in pursuing the crimes committed by good people who made very bad mistakes.

"You see, Theo was there," Mrs. Clay exclaimed, reaching out impulsively and putting a hand on the inspector's arm. "He was there, in the room with Mr. Elli and Mr. Countryman, when they found the body. But when the officers arrived he hid, and he took these things with him. He knew Mr. Elli and Mr. Countryman were not guilty, just as he knew these things would incriminate them."

"And these objects have been in your possession?" the inspector asked.

She nodded.

"And you knew that they had been found at the murder scene?"

She nodded again.

Now Grey was angry. He was angry because the investigation had been derailed by these misguided efforts to conceal evidence, and he was angry because now he would have to arrest someone other than Prime Minister Bligh's murderer. He stood. "Sissal Clay," he said evenly. "I am arresting you for the concealment of evidence in connection with the homicide of Prime Minister Bligh."

"Arrest me if you must," Mrs. Clay said, her voice shaking, "as long as I am not deported."

"That may well happen in the sentencing."

Mrs. Clay stared at him for a moment. Then she covered her face with her hands. "Oh, Inspector, please have pity!"

Grey moved to collect the evidence. "I have no choice," he replied, his voice betraying a hint of his anger. "You have withheld evidence and told me so."

"But I came here to tell you that Theo was in danger!" Mrs. Clay protested.

"But in so doing you have admitted to a crime!" Inspector Grey said, exasperated. "The evidence against Broadgirdle is tenuous, at best, but the evidence of your transgressions and Theo's is incontrovertible. Come with me. You have made a fine mess of things."

"What about Theo?" Winnie erupted. "Isn't anyone going to help him?"

Nettie, who to Grey's surprise was considering the grisly murder instruments with something like thoughtful scrutiny, abruptly chimed in. "Oh, yes, Father, we must help him."

Grey shook his head, more irritated by the moment. "I cannot help him, my dear, until I have properly disposed of this evidence and taken in Mrs. Clay."

"He needs help now," insisted Winnie.

"I am sure he is merely pursuing his interfering investigation," Grey said heatedly, "and will reemerge soon enough to make himself a nuisance once more. Come along," he said to Mrs. Clay.

"Father, the arrest can wait! And this boy Theo cannot!"

"Henrietta, I cannot imagine why you care in the first place."

"She cares because she's sweet on Theo," Winnie burst out. "Otherwise known as Charles."

The room grew still. Grey, carefully holding the bundle of evidence, looked sharply at his daughter.

For a moment Nettie stared at Winnie, and vexation flashed across her brow. Then she jumped to her feet with a scream. "Charles!" she cried. "Father, Father—we must help him!" She seized her father by the arm and shook him. "He could be hurt. We have to save him!"

"That's what I'm saying!" Winnie agreed.

"Oh, do please send someone to Broadgirdle's office!" begged Mrs. Clay.

Inspector Grey, standing in his dining room, listening to

the shrieks of his daughter and the appeals of his uninvited guests, felt that few mornings in his life had been as frustrating and inauspicious as this one. Fortunately for Roscoe Grey, he had principles, and when matters grew complicated, he could always rely on them. There was someone standing in front of him who had committed a serious crime. This necessitated action. It was his duty to take her in and deposit the evidence in its proper place. Where his duty was clear, Grey felt no uncertainty. "All right," he said firmly, bringing the room to silence. "That's enough."

"Father—" Nettie began.

"No," he said, holding up his hand. "Do not meddle in what does not concern you, Henrietta. I am taking Mrs. Clay to the station, along with this evidence. And yes, I will send officers to seek out Theodore. As soon as I reach the station, I will do so. He is alleged to have committed a very grave offense, and he is a person of interest in the prime minister's murder. Believe me, I have every intention of finding him."

—*1892, July 1: 7-Hour 15*—

It had to be accepted that if the sole requirement to garner a seat was sufficient funds, some parliament members would have questionable qualifications. Could any restrictions be reasonably set and enforced? Age, sex, soundness of mind? Law has been fairly liberal to date on this point. There are certainly woman MPs, and there are some members who, in their infirmity, have strained to present themselves as functional policymakers. But as yet no child has come forward to test the unstated but tacit age restriction.

—From Shadrack Elli's History of New Occident

AFTER THE FRONT door closed, Nettie stood in the dining room, fists clenched, hair wrappers trembling, fuming with anger. "Me, meddle!" she said furiously. "He said I *meddle!*" Mr. and Mrs. Culcutty knew better than to try to appease her. They watched with concern, hoping the rage would pass or perhaps end in a burst of tears.

Winnie, who perceived in Nettie's anger a possible advantage and even the opportunity to make an unlikely ally, decided to fan the flames and see what would happen. "No one's going to help him, then," he said, crestfallen. "It's just like I thought.

I tried to get him help, and now he'll get no help at all." He sniffled.

Nettie turned to him and glared. For a moment, Winnie feared that he might have miscalculated. "Oh, he'll get help, all right." Winnie was a bit taken aback by her vehemence. "My father is going to deeply, deeply regret this," she said bitterly. "I am going to find Theo myself." She swung around to face the Culcuttys. "You will not even think of stopping me." She swung back around to Winnie. "And you are going to help me."

Winnie blinked. "All right."

Nettie took a deep breath. Then, in a less dragonlike tone, she said, "I just need five minutes to change into something more appropriate. I can't go out in hair wrappers."

He nodded.

Nettie turned on her heel and hurried upstairs. She took out all her hair wrappers, ran a brush quickly through her hair, chose her most sensible gray skirt and a white shirt with six pockets, pulled on gray socks and sturdy brown boots, and, finally, tucked supplies into the pockets of the shirt: string, a magnifying glass, a pencil, folded paper, a pair of gloves, and a handkerchief. Breathless and ready, she ran back downstairs.

Mr. and Mrs. Culcutty had somewhat recovered their wits, and they had decided that a united front would make the greatest impact. As Nettie ran into the dining room, Mr. Culcutty looked stern and Mrs. Culcutty said, "My dear, I don't think it is wise—"

"I'm sorry, but I just don't care what is wise at the moment,"

Nettie said brusquely. "Father was very unwise this morning, and you can tell him when he returns that any unwiseness on my part is a direct result of *his* tremendous, unaccountable, and offensive unwiseness." She turned away from them. "Winston," she said commandingly.

With a barely concealed smile, Winnie nodded.

"We're off."

NETTIE, WITH HER impeccably ironed clothes, and Winnie, with his formidable layer of grime, made an exceedingly odd pair on the State House steps. Winnie hesitated at the entrance. "I can't go in there," he said. "They'll throw me out."

"They have no right to throw you out," Nettie snapped. "You're a citizen of New Occident just like anyone else. And if they so much as look at you funny, I'll give them a piece of my mind."

Winnie, rather enjoying the prospect of such a confrontation, hurriedly followed her into the august building that he had so often seen from the outside and yet never successfully entered.

But no confrontation ensued. No one took any notice of them as they walked through the corridors of the State House. There were too many things happening that morning, and the vigilant clerks, who under normal circumstances would have looked suspiciously at the two mismatched visitors, seemed to accept that secession, war, massive riots, and a molasses flood were bound to bring strange company.

Nettie examined the directory of offices engraved on a metal plate near the grand stairway. "Top floor," she muttered. "Naturally."

Winnie followed Nettie up the stairs, looking with reluctant awe at the ceiling of the rotunda. Normally, Winnie rather disdained the State House, for he had seen the uncharitable and unpleasant side of the people who worked in it, claiming power with apparent ease and yet doing so little with it. He had never told anyone, not even Theo, why he had first gravitated toward the State House.

After his mother's institutionalization, Winnie had been shuttled off to an orphanage, and when he had complained to the warden (by means of incessant shrieks and a desperate left-handed punch) that his mother was not sick and they had no right to lock them both up, the warden had recommended sarcastically that if he wanted to dispute his rights he should take the matter up with his representative in parliament.

Winnie had immediately stopped shrieking, grown thoughtful, and taken the suggestion seriously. It had cost him no small effort to procure the assistance of an older girl who could help him with the letter and send it to the correct address. But he had sent it, and he had waited for a reply, and when he finally received it, the note confused him.

Thank you for your inquiry. MP Riche listens attentively to the comments and questions of all of his constituents. Thank you for your support.

He had hung on to the cream-colored note card, though it was stolen twice, ripped in half once, and finally burned during a terrible showdown with Impy, the orphanage's resident bully. Looking at the ashes, Winnie had decided that it was time to run away and take matters up with MP Riche more personally. He had arrived at the State House a few days later, only to be turned out on his ear before he so much as crossed the threshold.

But to his surprise, he was not the only boy lingering by the steps. Jeff, Barney, Pet (short and furry), and the Eel (who could worm out of anyone's grasp) proved better company than the orphanage crowd. Winnie became one of them, picking up stray errands from the State House when they could be had.

He had expected the occupants to be as dignified and grand as the building, and indeed many of them were. But he learned very soon from his fellows and from his own observations that being grand was not the same thing as being great, and within a week his childish hope of finding justice by writing to MP Riche seemed like the most foolish thing he had ever felt.

But now, as Winnie ascended the grand staircase, he felt some of his old reverence for the place returning. The power of it was real; he could see that in the building itself and in the friction that charged the air around him. What would it be like, he wondered, to use that power as he had once imagined the MPs did? Winnie stopped for a moment, his dirty foot hovering above the burgundy runner of the top step. Was it really so impossible? The people around him were not so great, however much they might be grand. Surely achieving that could not be so difficult.

Winnie smiled. He made a pact with himself, then and there, that he would accomplish it.

"Coming?" Nettie said. "It's this floor."

"Right behind you, Henry."

"Don't call me Henry," Nettie said distractedly as she scanned the name plates beside the office doors.

They walked side by side along the corridor. Though the atmosphere had been hectic on the ground floor, here the halls were hushed and empty. No doubt, Winnie thought to himself, the members of parliament and all their staff were busily meeting with one another and scrambling to find a way to emerge unscathed from the mess Broadgirdle had created.

The door to Broadgirdle's office was open, but the front room with its two desks was empty. Nettie and Winnie looked at one another. "What now?" he asked.

"We look for clues," Nettie determined. "You know that Theo came up here, so we try to find clues of what happened after that. You watch the hallway, and I'll look around."

Winnie took up his post by the door. "Anything?" he asked after a moment.

"Nothing yet," Nettie said, looking through the piles on Peel's desk. She tried the drawers and found them locked, then drifted over to the other desk. The papers there were mostly covered with doodles. "This must be where Theo works," Nettie said in a low voice. "But there's really nothing here." She looked up. "Where do you think those other two doors go?"

"Other offices?"

The first one was locked, but the second opened onto a narrow, carpeted corridor with several closed doors. "Psst," she said.

Winnie abandoned his post, closing the door to the outer office behind them.

"They're all locked," Nettie reported in a whisper. "At least these four. The corridor winds back around that way," she added, pointing.

Winnie suddenly became alert. "Did you hear that?"

"What?"

"Listen."

They stared at one another in silence, and then Winnie heard it again: a series of loud thumps, as if someone was pounding a fist on a door. There were a few seconds of silence, and then, "Graves!" came a muffled shout. "Open the door. I want to negotiate."

"It's Theo!" Winnie cried.

"Theo, it's us—Nettie and Winnie," she called.

There was a moment's silence, and then a quick series of knocks. "Here! I'm here. Inside Broadgirdle's office, in a closet."

"Which is his office?"

"First on the right."

They tried it again, but of course the door was locked. Theo said from inside the room: "You'll have to pick the lock or break it down."

"I don't know how to pick a lock!" Winnie exclaimed, exasperated.

"There's a letter opener in the front office," Nettie ordered. "Run and get it for me."

He scurried out to Peel's desk, took the letter opener, and ran back. Nettie deftly began working away at the lock. Winnie stood inches away, wide-eyed.

"Ah!" Nettie said, her face breaking into a smile. The lock clicked.

Winnie turned the knob and opened the door. "You did it, Henry!" he exclaimed.

"Lots of practice," Nettie said easily. "And don't call me Henry." She closed the door behind them and quickly surveyed the office. It was less luxurious than she had expected. Ample, with a good carpet and a fine leather chair, the office had pin-striped wallpaper and heavy curtains. The desk was spotless. A fine pen, a crystal ink pot, a stack of paper, and a clock were the only items on its surface.

"The closet door is locked, too," Theo said, then added to himself, "obviously."

"I can get it," Nettie said confidently, crouching by the closet door.

She was already working at the lock while Winnie peered out the window. Suddenly, he stiffened. He had heard something. There was no doubt: voices, very nearby. "Nettie!" Winnie said urgently. "Someone's coming."

They heard a door being opened, and the unmistakable boom of Broadgirdle's voice filled the corridor. "The curtains!"

Nettie hissed. She dove behind one of the thick velvet curtains and Winnie scrambled behind the other just as the door opened.

"Peel!" Broadgirdle roared. "Why is my office unlocked?"

"I—I don't know, sir. I haven't opened it this morning."

"You will recall that we left it securely locked last night," Broadgirdle said, his voice smooth.

"I'm very sorry, sir. Perhaps the cleaning staff forgot to lock the door. I will speak to them."

"Do that. Officer, this way, please."

Nettie felt a flood of relief. Her father had come after all. Then, just as suddenly, the sense of relief evaporated.

"With pleasure, Prime Minister," was the oily reply. She recognized at once the voice of Manning Bacon, an officer renowned in the department for his appreciation for beer and his very compatible tendency to misplace evidence.

"This young man has been working under false pretenses in my office, he has spread lies about me to others, and he has stolen papers from my files," Broadgirdle said, his voice hard. "I have no idea what may have been his objective. Blackmail, perhaps. I would not be surprised if he is working for someone else."

"Leave that to me, Prime Minister, leave that to me. We'll soon discover his sinister motives, be assured."

There was a scuffling sound as Broadgirdle opened the door and Theo tussled with Officer Bacon, whose meaty hands were as good as his name.

Theo knew the moment the door was opened that he would

not be able to get past the three men, but he tried. He kicked Bacon's thigh and dove under Broadgirdle's arm. Unfortunately, the much more agile Bertie Peel was standing by the door, and he captured him under one bony arm. Bacon, recovered from the kick, snapped a pair of handcuffs onto Theo's left wrist, then yanked backward and seized his right. Theo winced in pain but uttered no complaint.

As Bacon secured the handcuffs, Theo saw Broadgirdle, calm and complacent, his arms crossed over his chest. *I might be as afraid now as I was then,* Theo told himself. *But that doesn't mean I have to be silent like I was then.*

It took all his strength to look Broadgirdle in the eye. "I know who you are," he said, low and unsteady. "You can lock me away, but you can't lock away the truth. And you were wrong. I'm not the same as I was before, because I'm not alone anymore, with no one to tell. Now I can tell people what you've done. Your plans to murder Bligh. Your years as a slaver. The fact that you're not even from New Occident. That you're a Sandman, and that the Sandmen who work for you tortured three helpless Eerie." His voice had gained strength, and he spoke evenly as he asked, "And once people know, they won't stand for it. Do you think the people of Boston are so spineless that they will fight a war for a scheming slaver from the Baldlands?"

Broadgirdle had watched Theo expressionlessly. Now he gave a hearty laugh. "Perhaps I was wrong, detective, to accuse of him of anything so rational as blackmail. Slaving? Murdering the prime minister? Torturing Eerie? Fates above! Clearly the young man is mad. You may find institutionalization is the right route for a mind so clearly deranged."

Behind the velvet curtain, Winnie stifled a gasp. He pressed his lips together and squeezed his eyes shut and concentrated with all his being on staying silent.

Officer Bacon laughed. "Never you fear, Mr. Prime Minister. I'll find the right place for him."

"And how goes the investigation into Prime Minister Cyril Bligh's terrible murder?" Broadgirdle asked, his voice dripping with concern.

"Very well, Mr. Prime Minister. Very well. Inspector Grey is on the case, and he can be dreadful slow about his investigations, but rumor has it at the station he made a great discovery this morning."

"Really?" Broadgirdle asked, his voice frankly curious.

"Something to do with a map made of wood?" Bacon chuckled. "That Grey is something else. He finds the strangest things, and then snap—suddenly the whole case comes together."

"*You see?*" Theo cut in. "You thought the Eerie were helpless. But they found a way. Even through the fire and the smoke. That map proves what you did. I saw the screaming girl. Grey will see it too, and you're done for."

Bacon looked at him, baffled. "Screaming girl?"

"It's true!" Theo said fiercely. "Ask him."

Broadgirdle regarded him for a moment, mustache twitching. "Another fascinating if rather bizarre invention from this very imaginative young man," he said demurely.

"Inspector Grey is on to you," Theo said, his voice steely. "And he will find out the truth. And he will come after you."

"I think you'd better take him, Officer Bacon," Broadgirdle said.

"Certainly, Mr. Prime Minister." He drew Theo toward the door. "Congratulations once again on your party's success. Enjoy your celebrations."

43
CONFESSING THE CRIME

—1892, July 1: 8-Hour 17—

Dreck is a term borrowed from a future Age. In that Age, it means "rubbish." In New Occident and the Baldlands, where the material is most common, "dreck" is used to designate fragments—like the word itself—that have drifted into our Age from another.

—From Shadrack Elli's History of New Occident

BY THE TIME Inspector Grey finished the paperwork for Sissal Clay, placing her in the custody of the warden for the women's prison, he thought he had already heard as many confessions as he was going to hear that morning. He was wrong. Walking back to his office, he found Officer Bacon, one of the policemen he liked least, waiting at his door with a young man in handcuffs. He recognized Theodore Constantine Thackary.

"He insisted on speaking with you, sir," Officer Bacon said.

"Inspector Grey," someone called behind him. Grey turned to see Officer Kent approaching, accompanied by Bertram Peel. He had a sense of foreboding, as he had experienced earlier that morning, and he knew that something unpleasant was about to transpire.

"What is it, Officer Kent?" Grey asked warily.

"I have here Bertram Peel, from Prime Minister Broadgirdle's office. He wants to make a confession."

Grey raised his eyebrows. "Is that so? What do you wish to confess?" he asked Peel, who stood rigidly, thin fingers clenched into fists at his sides.

Peel stood for a moment longer. His eyes were on the floor, his gaze abstracted. Then he looked up. The inspector was shocked to see tears in his eyes. "I wish to confess to planning and executing the murder of Prime Minister Cyril Bligh."

There was stunned silence in the corridor.

"No!" Theo exclaimed. "He didn't do it. Don't listen to him. It was Broadgirdle who planned it and his guards who did it. He heard me say Inspector Grey had evidence against him. And now he's sending Peel to take the blame."

"I did it," Peel said firmly.

"No, you didn't! He's got something on you. What is it? Don't let him push you around like this, Peel," he said desperately.

"Just as you did not let him push you around?" Peel said quietly.

Theo had no reply.

Grey had watched this exchange without speaking. "Do you truly wish to make this confession, Mr. Peel?"

"I do."

Theo regarded the thin man who had seemed so ridiculous in his zealousness, his exaggerated self-importance, and his loyalty to Broadgirdle. Peel had no pretensions to self-importance now. He was just a man who had lived longer with Broadgirdle's bullying. Theo saw, with surprise, a flicker of something like conviction in Peel's eyes, and he wondered what secret—or what person—Peel was protecting. He tried to reach out to him, but his hands were bound. "I'm sorry, Peel. I am truly sorry. If I had not said what I did in the office . . ."

"I don't know what you mean," he said quietly. "What's done is done, and your words earlier made no difference. One way or another, I would have found myself coming here to confess." He looked at the inspector. "Shall we continue?"

Grey obligingly opened his door and ushered Peel into his office. "Take Thackary to the jail, Officer Bacon," he said. "I can't attend to him at the moment. I will speak with him later today."

THEO DID NOT resist as Officer Bacon led him to the New Jail. His mind was on Peel. He no longer wondered what Peel was protecting; instead, he pondered the steps that would expose Peel's confession as false, so Grey would be forced to turn his investigation to Broadgirdle. He cast about, but no solution presented itself.

As Bacon led him through the cell block, Theo glimpsed its occupants, and his spirits sank. There were men from every walk of life there, to Theo's experienced eye, but they all had one thing in common: stagnation. They had been there some time, and they had no expectation of leaving. Some did not even glance up as Bacon and Theo passed. The few who did look considered him vacantly, without curiosity.

In that moment, all of Theo's speculations about Peel and Broadgirdle vanished. He had to survive his time in the New Jail without acquiring that vacant look, and he turned all of his attention to the problem. "How long do I have to stay here?" he asked Bacon.

"You'll stay until a judge hears your case, which will probably be tomorrow or the day after. Once a case is assembled they're quick, the judges," he said with satisfaction.

"But Shadrack Elli and Miles Countryman have been here for weeks."

"Because the police were assembling the case against them."

"What about my lawyer?"

Bacon laughed. "If you can persuade a lawyer to take your case, congratulations. But I doubt you will find one interested in petty fraud, which at most will earn him a few bills."

Theo considered. "So I have to defend myself in court?"

"I suppose you can try," Bacon shrugged. "It will be an open-and-shut case," he said comfortably. He stopped, ushered Theo into an open cell, and locked the door. "Hands," he said, and Theo put them through the bars. "What did you do to this one?" he chuckled, looking at Theo's right hand as he removed the cuffs. "Turn it inside out?"

"Sure." Theo snapped his fingers into a gun. "It's a trick of mine. I'll show you some time."

"Oh, I doubt I'll be seeing you again," Bacon said complacently. "People tend to get lost here in the New Jail. Look around you," he said, resting his heavy frame against the bars for a moment while he clipped the keys to his belt. "We're in New Occident, where you can buy anything, including time. Why do you think all these men are in here? Because they can't buy a thing. That's how it goes," he said amiably. He ambled off, the keys jangling with each plodding step.

Theo stood for a moment in the center of the cell. He closed his eyes, trying to organize his thoughts—trying to imagine the escape route. He could see none.

"Don't worry, friend," a low voice said nearby. "The officers only ever see one side of this place. They don't know the half of it."

Theo opened his eyes and turned to the adjoining cell, where a man sat loosely on his cot, his hands resting on his knees. He had Theo's complexion, marking him as an outsider from either the Baldlands or the Indian Territories. His expression was easy, and his face was strikingly handsome—half of it was, anyhow. The right side of his face and neck, his right arm and hand, were disfigured by a gruesome burn scar. "What does that mean?" Theo asked dryly. "The New Jail is fun, and the police just don't know it?"

The man got up. He drew a tattered book with no covers from the inside of his shirt and handed it through the bars to Theo. "It has its moments," he said with a gentle smile. "Books are allowed."

Theo took it.

"We pass them around, clockwise. This cell has been empty for a while, so Bullfrog over on the other side of you has been starving for reading material." He lifted his chin to point to the other cell.

Theo turned and saw a squat man with a forlorn expression.

"So if you could read this one quickly and pass it on, I'm sure he'd appreciate it," the scarred man said.

Theo looked at the coverless book in his hands: *Robinson Crusoe*. "I've already read this," he said.

"Perfect," the scarred man replied. "Bullfrog will be happy to have it. It's an adventure story, Bullfrog."

Theo crossed his tiny cell and handed the book to Bullfrog, whose expression brightened slightly. "The last book I read was *King Lear*, and it was very depressing," he said. He immediately propped himself up on his cot and opened the pages.

"How about this one?" the scarred man asked Theo, holding up another coverless volume.

"Lucretius, *The Nature of Things*," Theo read aloud. "Haven't read it."

"Excellent." The man reached through the bars. "I'm called Casanova," he added.

"Theodore Constantine Thackary," Theo said, shaking the scarred hand with his own.

"Ah, the dreck writer. We have one of Thackeray's. I just read it last week," Casanova said thoughtfully.

"No relation," Theo said with a wry grin.

One half of Casanova's face smiled, and Theo realized the

desperation he had felt minutes earlier had faded, and it had been Casanova's intention all along to accomplish it. "You surprise me," Casanova said. "Tell me what you think of Lucretius," he added, sitting back down on his cot. "He rather changed my view of things."

44

AUSENTINIA

—1892, July 2: 19-Hour 52—

Similarly, the people of the Papal States have found use for the Four-wings' feathers. Beautiful as they are, their iridescent black sheen is considered unsightly by most, who prefer to exploit their incredible strength. As flexible as cloth and as strong as metal, the feathers mix with adobe to make walls of remarkable durability.

—From Fulgencio Esparragosa's History of the Dark Age

SOPHIA RODE IN front of Goldenrod, and if the Eerie's arm had not supported her, she would have collapsed. "We are almost there, miting," Errol said, looking up at her with concern. At the top of the hill, she saw an odd, wavering light near the city. The four of them descended, and as they came closer, Sophia realized that what she had thought was one light was many: a collection of flickering candles.

Beyond the gates, their faces lit by the flames they carried, the people of Ausentinia lined the broad cobbled street. Sophia looked around her in astonishment. They smiled at her, their faces glad and curious and expectant. A woman with long white hair stepped forward and bowed to her formally. "You must be the traveler without time," she said. "We have been waiting for you."

The travelers dismounted. Sophia walked forward, leaning on Goldenrod. The Ausentinians made way for them, and Sophia, despite her weariness, gazed in wonder. The cobbled streets were illumined by tall lamps, and she could see the closed map stores behind them, their windows reflecting the candlelight. The white-haired woman led them to a lighted doorway with a wooden sign above it marked THE ASTROLABE. They passed into the great room of a comfortable inn, where the aproned innkeeper gave them a smiling welcome.

"You will rest here," the white-haired woman said, "for I know your journey has been difficult." She bowed. "Until the morning."

The innkeeper led them to their rooms. Sophia drank water from a white pitcher until her stomach hurt. Then she tried to unlace her boots, but it seemed too great an effort. She felt a moment of regret that she would not manage to remove them as she fell forward onto the bed and into sleep.

—July 3: 6-Hour 37—

ERROL FOUND GOLDENROD in the garden of the inn, resting on the soft grass beneath a flowering plum tree. In her sleep, the white scarf that bound her hair had come loose. Her gloves, no doubt pulled off in discomfort at some point in the night, lay crumpled beside her. Her small green feet were bare.

Errol crouched down and studied her face. He could see the shape of the bones beneath her skin. At times she seemed very human. But her hands . . . He turned his gaze to the slender green fingers of her right hand, which lay only a few inches from his own. They seemed like the stems of a young tree. Errol felt that he did not need to understand how she drew strength from the sun and soil; but he did need to understand whether she was human.

Goldenrod stretched out her palm wordlessly. Errol blinked. "You are studying my hand," she said. "You would like to know how the blooms appear there." She placed her hand, palm up, on Errol's knee. "Go ahead. See if you can solve the mystery." Her face was serious, but her voice smiled.

Errol took her hand, cradling it in his own. He stared at the lines of her palm, which were faintly white against the pale green. The fingers were slim and soft compared to his. He placed the thumb of his left hand in the center of her palm and pressed it, then raised his eyes to hers and held her gaze. Slowly, the skin below her cheekbones turned pink.

Errol realized he had been holding his breath. He let the air out, relieved. She was human, after all.

SOPHIA ATE THE apricots and bread that sat on a little table by the balcony, devouring them to the last crumb. Then she peeled off her clothes, piece by piece, and crawled into the copper tub of water that stood in the corner, a bar of soap and a white cloth folded beside it. The water had cooled slightly from steaming to warm. Sophia submerged herself, washing every inch of her skin, then wrapped herself in the vast white cloth. She began to feel her mind finally waking.

When she joined Errol and Goldenrod in the garden, she found them talking quietly, their heads bent toward one another as if even the trees should not hear them. She watched for a moment, wondering at the quiet laugh that spilled from Goldenrod's mouth. It seemed so unlike her. Errol touched her cheek lightly with his thumb, as if to capture the sound.

"Sophia," Goldenrod said, rising to her feet. "How are you feeling?"

"A little better. Still tired," she admitted.

"It will take some time to feel rested," the Eerie said reassuringly, pressing Sophia's hand. She led her to a stone bench beneath the trees. "You shared thoughts with an old one. That requires great endurance."

"Is that what you would call it? Sharing thoughts?"

"I still do not understand it, however many times my Faierie explains it," Errol said, seeming not at all bothered by his lack of comprehension. He smiled at Goldenrod.

Goldenrod smiled back and then turned that smile to Sophia. "Ausentinia read your memories of the route through the Dark Age."

"It is strange to think—now I know how a map feels when it is being read."

"That is how Ausentinia found its way out."

"But I also—saw things. Remembered things."

"The memories of an old one are long and powerful.

You glimpsed pieces of them when Ausentinia shared your thoughts."

"I sensed that. But there is so much else . . ." Sophia shook her head. "Has Ausentinia spoken to you? Do you know more about how it came to be trapped within the Dark Age?"

"Yes, it has," said Goldenrod. "You speculated that the Dark Age was made by human hands. Ausentinia has told me that this is so. The Dark Age is not a Clime, any more than a puppet is a person. But in some ways it behaves like a Clime. And this explains why it has expanded. It was created to sustain natural life—to support the native life within it. Indeed, its only purpose is to support such life; if no creatures remained in it, the Dark Age would fade, like a tree rotted at the root. Once there were many native beings—people, plants, and animals. As it stands now, the entire Age supports only a single native creature."

"The fourwings?"

She shook her head. "The wanderers—the plague. The fourwings were made to sustain them. They are home to it. But, as you know, the people of the Papal States have hunted the fourwings to rarity. Soon after the Disruption, when people first encountered the Dark Age, they attempted to cut down the dangerous spines. The fourwings defended their homes, attacking at the edges and finally flying farther and farther to deter invaders. People of the Papal States destroyed as many fourwings as they could, thereby also destroying the creatures upon which *lapena* survived. And so the plague looked elsewhere—left the Dark Age and wandered to others so that it might survive. Those others, people in the Papal States, are not as strong as the fourwings; they do not bear its presence well."

"So if the fourwings are allowed to live, the plague will return to them?"

"Perhaps. It would take time."

Sophia sat in silence.

"There is another possibility," Goldenrod said.

"The goldenrod," Sophia guessed.

The Eerie nodded. "Any Eerie bloom would do. I happen to have goldenrod." She opened her palm, revealing a small yellow blossom.

"Over the years, the people of the Papal States have spent a fortune on gold," Errol said. "Gold thread. Gold chains. Gold masks. Such a waste."

"It is an old manner of thinking. Shielding oneself from a sickness instead of speaking to it. You cannot blame them for trying," said Goldenrod.

Sophia smiled. "I can imagine the Dark Age filled with goldenrod. It would be very beautiful."

Errol snorted. "The flower would be the only beauty in that wretched place."

"But it would grow differently," Sophia reflected. "If the soil is man-made."

"It well might," agreed Goldenrod. "We will see."

Sophia watched as Goldenrod scattered the yellow petals to the ground beside them. "I want to go with you."

"You need to rest," Errol objected.

"She will rest," Goldenrod told him. "And then we can all go together."

"Every day more people die of the plague," Sophia said. Errol and Goldenrod did not reply. Sophia bit her lip. "You should go soon. What does it look like, Goldenrod?"

"The plague?" She pursed her lips. "Imagine a tiny moth made of light."

Sophia contemplated the existence of such a creature and wondered at the creation of an entire Age to sustain it. As she pictured the small moths, their wings flickering, her eyes closed. She leaned back against the birch and drifted, her breathing easy.

45

RESCUE

—July 3: 12-Hour 21—

I will confess to the reader that I have traveled as far as the border of the Dark Age, and I have gazed into its depths. I find myself wondering, with optimism rather than dread, what the Age would yield if we did not prohibit further exploration.

—From Fulgencio Esparragosa's History of the Dark Age

SOPHIA AWOKE IN her room at the Astrolabe, a pale green blanket tucked around her. Rosemary sat nearby in a wooden chair, looking out through the open doors to the balcony. She held a length of blue fabric in her hands that she fingered absently. Sophia lay quietly for a moment, content and unwilling to move. Rosemary's expression was thoughtful. She drew her hair back with a practiced movement and braided it loosely, then pulled the braid over her shoulder and brushed the tip across her palm, as if writing something onto her skin. Then she took up the blue fabric once more and held it up before her appraisingly. Sophia pushed herself up to sit.

"What is that?" she asked.

"You are awake," Rosemary said, turning to her.

"I must have fallen asleep in the garden."

"Yes. Errol brought you here." She looked down at her lap. "This is my mother's silkshell."

"I've heard about silkshells, but I've never seen one."

Rosemary held it up. "Would you like to?"

"What does it do?" Sophia asked.

"When you feel the silk, you will have a sense of who she was."

Sophia pulled herself to the edge of the bed and took the silk in both hands. The moment she touched it, she felt herself in the presence of a woman—laughing, gentle, easily affectionate. The longer Sophia held the silk, the deeper became her sense of Rosemary's mother. She had been a little too indulgent with her only child, and she felt, with some embarrassment, unrepentant about it. She had struggled all her life with doubts about whom to trust. She had been strong in her faith and flexible in her opinions. She had no fear of death, but she feared, at every moment, pain or hardship for her child.

Sophia handed the silk back, overcome that Rosemary had shared with her something so precious. "It is almost like a memory map," she said. "But without the memories—just powerful emotions."

Rosemary nodded, carefully folding the precious fabric. "It was kind of her to leave it for me at the end."

"And she wore it for you, too," Sophia said. "For many years, it seems." She paused. "I'm sorry we have not found her yet."

Rosemary smiled. "I am sure we will." She stood up. "Are you hungry?"

Sophia realized that she was. "Very much so."

"Alba says you are to ask for whatever you like. She is the elderly woman who brought us to the inn. She is a member of the council of Ausentinia, and she says the city is greatly in your debt." She smiled again. "So what would you like to eat?"

"Anything."

Sophia and Rosemary ate soup and bread and cheese in companionable silence, and when their plates of pudding with honey had been scraped clean, Rosemary suggested they walk the short distance to the border of the Dark Age so they could see what Goldenrod was planting. "That is," she added, "if you feel well enough."

There was no question Sophia would go. It was more tiring than she had imagined to change into her now clean clothes and lace her boots, and she tried to conceal her labored breathing as they walked through the streets of Ausentinia. Everyone they passed smiled, often waving their thanks to the traveler without time.

When they reached the gates, they rested in the shade of the stone wall. "We should go back," Rosemary said. "I do not know why I did not bring the horse."

"It is only a short distance," Sophia insisted, starting along the path that she had taken, only half-aware, the night before. Rosemary followed her reluctantly. "Would you . . ." Sophia hesitated. "Would you tell me what they were like when you met them?" She paused. "Minna and Bronson?"

Rosemary did not answer right away. Her footsteps sounded heavily on the packed earth. "They were very kind," she finally said. "They feared for their lives, and yet they behaved with great compassion. I could see that this was born from their manner of loving. Each other, and, I am sure, you. When I spoke to your mother, I felt reassured." She smiled. "Can you imagine? Though behind bars, she was reassuring *me*. They were—they *are*—wonderful people. They came all this way to rescue a friend. I recognize it does not make it less of a loss to you, but they acted with great selflessness and humanity."

Sophia felt tears spilling onto her cheeks. But she also felt that her feet moved more steadily and with greater energy, and soon they had reached the hill where Ausentinia had extended into the Dark Age, drawing a dirt path through it to the Papal States beyond.

As soon as they crested the hill, Sophia saw what the Eerie had done. In the soil of the Dark Age, the goldenrod had taken lush, explosive root, and great, golden canopies hung over the spines like clouds. Sophia gasped. "So beautiful!" she exclaimed.

"Yes," Rosemary agreed. "Very beautiful. She and Errol are walking the path to the Papal States, and the goldenrod will grow on either side of it." The golden boughs wove through the Dark Age as far as they could see. "A golden specific in a dark Age. The most beautiful remedy for the most brutal plague."

They sat at the top of the hill and watched the blossoms nod and sway in the breeze. When Sophia felt recovered, she rose and looked back at the valley of Ausentinia. Now she could see what had been invisible at night: a path encircling the city, bordered by cypresses and spruce trees. "Rosemary," she said, heading downhill, "let's take the path around the city."

"We should go back so you can rest."

"It will only take a moment," Sophia insisted. The quiet among the trees was profound, disturbed by the occasional conversation of birds in their branches. Sophia felt more energy in the shade, and they walked slowly but steadily. Stopping to lean against the trunk of a maple tree, she admired the world Ausentinia had preserved. Then a glimmer of white caught her eye. She thought at first it was a strange kind of bird, and then she thought it might be an ornament made by some Ausentinian and placed among the trees. "Can you see what that is, Rosemary?"

Rosemary left the path, disappearing from view. Sophia let herself sink down onto the ground, and she rested her head against the maple. Minutes passed. When she opened her eyes, Rosemary had not returned. Sophia checked her watch and found that she had been gone nearly half an hour. With a start, she rose to her feet and walked as fast she could toward the white shape that had caught her eye.

"Rosemary," she called, as she stepped over the pine needles. "Rosemary?" she called again, more urgently.

There was no response, and as she reached the twisted roots of a cypress she saw why. The high, blanched roots made a kind of shelter—a room, a cage—at the tree's base. Rosemary sat beside them. "See, Sophia, where you have led me." Her eyes were swollen from tears. Inside the cypress shelter, as if someone had taken refuge there long ago, was a half-hidden human shape, the fragile white of dried bone. "The cross she wears on a gold chain—I recognize it without doubt."

Sophia knelt down and gazed at the skeletal figure. "You found your mother's resting place," she whispered.

Rosemary nodded. "She came here to escape me—to protect me." Her tears returned, and she covered her face with her hands. "But now I have found her."

—1892, July 5: 8-Hour 00—

One piece of dreck discovered in 1832 created a sensation that cast a long shadow over the politics of New Occident. It was a history written in 1900, and it told of a great war that had divided the nation forty years earlier. For three decades, New Occident waited, to some degree with bated breath. The war did not transpire, of course. It never would. It belonged to a different Age.

—From Shadrack Elli's History of New Occident

"THEO! THEO!" SOMEONE was calling him, but he had difficulty waking from the dream in which he knelt by the prison window, watching the grass outside grow thicker and thicker until it extinguished all the light beyond. The prison cell was dark, and he had trouble waking without the prodding of the sun.

He opened his eyes and saw at once that there were several people standing at the barred door. He sat up. Some part of him, even while he slept, had recognized the voice. "Shadrack?" he asked uncertainly.

"Yes—it's me," came the reply.

"They let you out!" Theo got to his feet. In the dim corridor, he saw Shadrack, Miles, Mrs. Clay, Nettie, and Winnie all clustered at the entrance to his cell. A slow smile crept over his face. "It's good to see you," he said, surprised by how his voice caught. He reached out through the bars to embrace Shadrack.

Miles, his face pressed between the bars, gave him a hug. "Likewise, my boy."

Mrs. Clay, overcome with emotion, was silent as she reached through to pat Theo's arm. Nettie gave him a cool kiss on the cheek. Winnie, not to be deterred, reached through the bars and solemnly hugged Theo around the waist. Theo laughed, tousling the boy's hair and kneeling to return the embrace. "Come to join me, then? There's plenty of room." Winnie gave a little sigh. "Hey, it's not so bad!" Theo said with another laugh. "They sentenced me yesterday—only two months in this confounded place. A bit more than you had to put up with, though," he said with a smile for Shadrack and Miles. "Tell me, how'd you get out?"

"The case against Bertram Peel moved very quickly," Shadrack said. "He gave a full confession, and his knowledge of details from the case that were never disclosed by the police made the proceedings very fast. Fortunately, Mrs. Clay's trial was even faster."

Theo immediately looked to her. "Mrs. Clay?"

"Concealing evidence, my dear." She sniffed. "Nothing serious. Just a little fine, and well worth it."

He shook his head, smiling once more. "What about Broadgirdle?"

"Off scot-free!" Miles burst out with frustration.

"I thought as much," Theo said calmly. He had accepted that Broadgirdle would somehow pin the murder on Peel.

"He claims he knew nothing about it," Miles fumed, "and that Peel acted with the Sandmen of his own initiative—an effort to curry favor. And, curse him, there is no evidence proving otherwise."

"Broadgirdle will remain as prime minister?"

The little group was silent. Shadrack nodded. "I am afraid so."

Theo clasped the bars. "Broadgirdle is a Sandman. He has the scars. I saw them myself. Doesn't that prove he's tied up with this?"

"Nettie and Winnie told us," Shadrack said slowly. "But I'm afraid it doesn't change anything."

Theo noticed that all of them were avoiding his gaze; they looked at the floor, the cell, everywhere but at him. There was something else, he realized, they had not yet told him. "What is it?" Shadrack looked at him anxiously—almost with pity. Theo felt an unexpected tremor of nervousness. "Tell me what it is," he demanded.

"The war in the west that Broadgirdle has begun . . ." Shadrack faltered.

"Yes?"

"New Occident has almost no army to speak of," Shadrack tried again. "Broadgirdle made a call for enlistment, but he has also conscripted . . ." He swallowed. "He has conscripted the prison population of New Occident. It will be announced today—this morning."

Theo stared at him, not comprehending, though the words were clear enough. "Conscripted?" he echoed.

"He's sending the prisoners to fight the war, Theo," Miles said, his voice coldly furious.

Theo was silent. Winnie reached through the bars and took Theo's hand, looking up at him with the most bewildered, forlorn expression Theo had ever seen. He smiled. "Don't worry. You think I'm going to stand there in a uniform while someone throws bullets at me? Not likely. First chance I'll be gone"—he snapped his fingers—"like that."

"Yes, we knew you would say that. But the penalty for desertion is death," Mrs. Clay cried. She buried her face in her handkerchief. Mrs. Clay's outburst was apparently contagious, because Nettie began sniffling and Miles had to turn away and give a series of loud, throat-clearing coughs.

"That's if they can catch me," replied Theo.

"You would not be able to return to New Occident," Shadrack said tightly.

Theo hesitated. Then he glanced down again at Winnie's face, now tear-stained, and grinned. "Well, can't do that, then. But don't worry about me. I'll be fine. This war will be over before we know it."

"I hope it will," Shadrack said. "And I will do everything in my power to ensure it happens."

"You are staying at the ministry?" Theo asked, surprised. "Even with Broadgirdle as prime minister?"

Shadrack looked stricken. "Broadgirdle has . . ." And, again, he swallowed. "He has suggested I stay on in the new government. Something to do with who I was in the Age of Verity. A war map maker."

Theo's eyes narrowed. "He has twisted your arm."

"No, no," Shadrack said too quickly. "It is true that I can do more good in the ministry than in my study at East Ending. And there's the Eerie." He shook his head. "The rule map tells us what happened, but not where. I feel it is my duty to find them."

"What about Sophia?"

"The pirates came to Boston Harbor on June nineteenth and left word that they would depart immediately for Seville, but I have heard nothing else. Miles wishes to sail at once for the Papal States."

"Wouldn't it be better to wait for them?"

"I cannot make up my mind," Shadrack said, passing a hand over his forehead. "I am sick with worry, but I do not see how Miles can reach Seville before Calixta and Burr . . ."

"I think we should wait," Mrs. Clay said quietly.

"And I have decided that I will sail at once," Miles said, having recovered himself sufficiently to deliver this verdict.

"As you see," Shadrack told Theo with a wry smile, "we cannot make up our minds collectively, either."

The sharp trill of a whistle rang through the stone corridor, and the group turned as one to watch the approach of several prison guards. Theo's cell near the end lay farthest from where the head guard stood, whistling once more before beginning his announcement.

"Prisoners of Ward One, come to attention." He paused,

and from behind the fifty barred doors of Ward 1 came a dull scuffling and clanging and a few complaints—a few more rude retorts—before the guard cut in again. "You have been called to serve your nation. By order of Prime Minister Gordon Broadgirdle, you will be taken from this place of incarceration and trained for combat in Camp Monecan. Any prisoner unfit for combat duty will be reassigned by the Minister of War. Prisoners, place your hands through the bars so that they are clearly visible. We will be coming through to lead you from your cells."

The end of the guard's announcement was met with such a din of protest from the prisoners that Theo could hardly hear his friends' good-byes. The inmates shouted and rattled the bars and taunted the guards, who placidly walked from cell to cell, placing handcuffs on the outstretched arms of willing prisoners and, where necessary, wielding their batons to ensure compliance. "Good-bye, Theo," Shadrack said, embracing him through the bars. "We will get you out of this mess."

Theo nodded. "Don't worry about me," he said. "I'll be all right. Find the Weatherers. And find Sophia."

Shadrack nodded and turned away, his face distraught.

Reaching through the bars, Miles wrapped Theo in a bear hug and said in his ear: "It's kind of you to put on a good show for us, Theo. You've got more nerve than any man I know. I admire you, my friend." He pounded Theo roughly on the back and then pulled away, wiping his eyes hastily with his fist.

The guards were making faster progress through the corridor than Theo had expected. They were halfway down, though the noise was only growing greater. "Good-bye, my dear boy," Mrs. Clay said tearfully. As she embraced Theo, her sobs became uncontrollable. "I'm sorry, I'm sorry," she said. "You're being so brave, but I just can't—" She pulled him closer. "Please be careful."

Nettie, who had veered sharply from tears to outrage, hugged him and then shook his hand firmly. "Thank you for coming to see me," Theo said with a crooked smile, "even though I sort of lied to you about who I am."

"I've not forgiven you yet," Nettie replied primly. "You'll have to come back soon and make it up to me."

Theo took her arm. "You're going to stay on the case, aren't you?" he asked in a low voice.

"Of course," she whispered.

"Then you should know something about Broadgirdle. You heard what I said in his office."

"I heard everything. I remember."

"His real name is Wilkie Graves. Might help."

Nettie's eyes narrowed. "You really should have told me earlier," she hissed.

Theo smiled. "Be careful. He's much worse than he looks."

He crouched down to say good-bye to Winnie, but the boy seemed unwilling to come any closer. He stood a few feet away, watching the guards and the raging inmates with evident horror. "Hey, Winnie," Theo called. He reached out for the boy's hand. "Come over here. Say good-bye to me properly."

Winnie reluctantly came closer. "I don't want to say good-bye."

"I know. But hey, look on the bright side. Good thing it's me and not you they're sending off. Wouldn't want to see you out there in the Indian Territories with a pistol!"

Winnie shook his head. He looked at Theo sullenly, and suddenly the tears spilled from his eyes. "I'm so sorry," he said, gulping over the tears. "I should have gotten there sooner. I should have broken in myself. I don't know why I didn't. It was so stupid. Stupid. I'm so sorry, Theo."

Theo felt a painful tug in his throat. Winnie wiped a dirty hand across his eyes with frustration and grief. Theo saw, with sudden illumination, how like him the little boy was—not only because he lived by his wits and took care of himself, but also because having to take care of himself had convinced him that he was older in the world than he really was. He was so certain that the evils around him were his to avert, his to live with if he could not avert them. Winnie could not fathom that those evils would exist, whole and terrible in their consequences, even if he did not.

And to think I was younger than he is now. I could do nothing. I could no more have stopped Graves's slaving than Winnie could stop this war. Theo felt a pulse of heartbreak for the torment it had caused his younger self to take such a burden, then a wave of compassion for the boy he had been, the boy who stood before him now. If only someone could have told him then what he now saw so clearly: *You are blameless. Forgive yourself.*

"Look," Theo insisted, pulling Winnie toward him by the hand. He drew him in so that no one else could hear. "This is not your fault. I would have landed here one way or another. You understand?" Winnie nodded, but did not look up. "Winnie, look at me." Reluctantly, he did. "Even if you only did good things every day, every moment of your life, bad things would still happen."

"The good is not enough," Winnie said sadly.

"It *is* enough. That's what I'm saying. It is enough. The *doing* is what matters." He squeezed Winnie's hand. "Okay?"

Winnie sniffed. "Okay."

"I want you to look after everyone for me. Mrs. Clay is a mess. And Shadrack and Miles are going to argue about what to do until nothing gets done. You're going to have to give them the advice I would if I were here. Talk some sense to them. Can you do that?" Winnie looked back at the ground. Then he gave a short nod. "Right, then." Theo hugged the boy and released him. "Get out of here." He gave him a wink. "Stay out of trouble."

The guards, nearing the dark end of the corridor, had finally caught sight of the visitors. "You can't be here," one of them snapped. "There were to be no visitors after eight-hour."

"We are just leaving," Shadrack said. Putting his arm around the inconsolable Mrs. Clay, he began walking down the corridor, followed by the others.

Theo watched them go. They made a sad little procession, weaving their way through the shouting, jibing prisoners, all the way to the entrance of Ward 1. Theo sighed. He felt a spasm of sadness as Winnie turned in the doorway to wave. Theo swallowed hard and put his hands through the bars. "Theodore Constantine Thackary?" the guard barked.

"Yes."

"You are hereby conscripted to the Armed Forces of New Occident. Your sentence of two months' imprisonment will be considered served when your unit's deployment has ended or, if this be sooner than two months, when your term of incarceration has ended." He turned to the guard beside him. "Manacles." The cuffs closed on Theo's wrists, and the guards made ready to open the cell doors.

EPILOGUE:
THE OFFERED SAIL

—1892, July 15: 12-Hour 00—

SEVILLE: Calle Abades, Libreria del Sabio. The bookstore named for Alfonso "The Wise" specializes in detailed maps of the Papal States. You will not find many useful travel maps for other Ages, but you will find guide maps aplenty for local journeys and pilgrimages.

—From Neville Chipping's Map Vendors in Every (Known) Age

SEVILLE HAD CHANGED. The first few days after the plague had passed, no one could believe it. They considered that the brief respite was only that: a pause in the dreadful progress. But after a week, people began to hope that perhaps, after so many decades, the contagion had finally turned and fled. The hope became relief, which became elation.

From one week to the next, Seville transformed from a shuttered and desolate city to a buoyant, living one; from a clump of dry soil to a tendril of green growth. Doors were unbolted, merchants opened their stores, horses clattered through the streets, children once more played together, and the houses of worship rang with the sound of music.

Most people did not know what had caused the plague to end. But Sophia, as she rode alongside Goldenrod and Errol, with Seneca gliding high above them, knew for certain, and she felt a rush of unexpected happiness thinking of the part she had played. She had to remind herself that she had taken a great risk and expended all her strength in doing so. It was too easy, now, as she rode with her friends, to forget the long journey through the Dark Age and the terror of communing with a Clime.

The time spent in Ausentinia had allowed for recovery. Sophia recovered, albeit slowly, and Ausentinia recovered gradually from its long isolation, and the Papal States recovered yet more gradually from the enduring effects of the plague. When the first traveler to Ausentinia arrived, following the path through the Dark Age and seeking a map for what he had lost, the city celebrated.

During her days in Ausentinia, Sophia spoke frequently to Alba about her journey, and she told her of Minna's phantom. "What I don't understand is where the apparition came from. I was afraid of it at first, but then I became certain that it somehow came from here—from Ausentinia. But how could such a thing be?"

Alba thought for a moment. "You are right that she came from Ausentinia. Let me ask you this: if you had arrived here seeking something you had lost, what would that thing be?"

"My mother and father," Sophia answered without hesitation.

"And if Errol had arrived seeking something he had lost, what would it be?"

Sophia paused. "His brother."

Alba nodded. "You would have sought maps to find these people. The maps guiding you to them, in truth, already exist. They have always existed. They are waiting here for you as they have always waited. But while Ausentinia lay trapped in the Dark Age, no one could approach the city. The guiding impulse that writes the maps of Ausentinia had to reach you, somehow—somehow find and guide you."

Sophia reflected in silence.

"You might say," Alba added, "that the apparition is the map brought to life—the physical presence of the guide that will, someday, lead you to your mother and father."

"So they're not dead?" Sophia whispered.

"They are absent," Alba replied gently. "Not departed."

"Then does that mean—does it mean that bringing me to Ausentinia was part of my finding them?"

Alba smiled. "Yes. You will not see the figure any longer, for you will have the map now to guide you. The map that will lead you to Minna and Bronson. I have been waiting for the right moment." She paused, reaching into the folds of her cloak. "Here it is." She gave Sophia a scroll of paper tied with white string. "And here is the map you will one day pass along to another," she added, handing her a small leather purse fastened with blue string. "Your map will let you know when the moment is right."

Sophia took the scroll and the purse. She looked at the scroll but did not touch the white string. Her hand was trembling.

"I know it has been a long wait, Sophia," Alba said quietly. "I will let you read the map in peace."

SOPHIA PATTED THE purse and the map where they sat in the pocket of her skirt. The purse, curiously, held not a scroll of any kind but a bundle of red stones that Goldenrod said were garnets. The map was similarly mystifying. Most of what was written upon it she did not understand. But the beginning was familiar, and it gave her a clear path to follow:

Missing but not lost, absent but not gone, unseen but not unheard. Find us while we still draw breath.

Leave my last words in the Castle of Verity; they will reach you by another route. When you return to the City of Privation, the man who keeps time by two clocks and follows a third will wait for you. Take the offered sail, and do not regret those you leave behind, for the falconer and the hand that blooms will go with you. Though the route may be long, they will lead you to the ones who weather time. A pair of pistols and a sword will prove fair company.

For now, she was simply happy to know that the path before her lay alongside Goldenrod and Errol. She had no wish to part from them. Errol had received his own map, one as inscrutable as Sophia's, though he believed implicitly that his brother lay at the end of it.

But not all routes led in the same direction. Rosemary, having found what she had sought for so long, took her mother's bones to hallowed ground. She had ridden with them as far as Seville and there said her farewells.

As they neared the port, Sophia's heart soared. The sight of so many ships, their tall masts cluttering the harbor, filled her with excitement. Soon, very soon, she would be home.

"I say we find something to eat before we seek our vessel," Errol said, dismounting. "My Faierie here might subsist on sun and air and water, but you and I need something heartier, Sophia." He rested his hand on Goldenrod's gloved arm and gave her a brief smile.

"What about bread with raisins in it?" Sophia asked, allowing Errol to help her down from the saddle. "Remember the street where you found me? There's someone there I want to thank."

"Very well. Bread with raisins it is." He paused. "Can I be of service?" he asked, rather stiffly.

Sophia turned to look at the man who stood nearby, looking keenly at the trio. He was tall, with skin bronzed almost to brown, and his broad grin flashed a row of even, white teeth.

"It is I who wish to be of service."

"Richard," Goldenrod said comfortably. She gave a warm smile as she extended her gloved hand. "It is very good to see you. I had word that you had arrived, and I understood at long last my very unusual Atlantic voyage."

"You are impossible to surprise," the tall man said, bowing slightly. He spoke English with a broad accent that pulled his mouth into a smile. "But I am very glad to see *you*, too, safe and sound. And you," he said, turning to Sophia, "must be Sophia Tims."

Sophia nodded, surprised. "Yes. How did you know?"

"Very pleased to make your acquaintance," he said, shaking her hand. "My name is Captain Richard Wren. I was given your description. I have been anchored in the port of Seville for some time, waiting for your arrival." As if by habit, he reached into his pocket and pulled out a watch, examining it through an amber-tinted monocle. "Fifteen days and seven hours, to be exact." He flashed his brilliant smile and returned the watch to his pocket.

Sophia noticed, with sudden awareness, that he had two pocket-watch chains. "Captain Wren?" she asked, her pulse quickening. The name was familiar: Cabeza de Cabra had recorded it in his map, in his memory of watching Minna and Bronson as they prepared to cross the bridge into Ausentinia. "Who gave you my description?"

"My associate in Boston, who, I believe," he said with a hint of vexation, "instructed you to meet me here at the port of Seville."

His reply recalled her to what seemed a remote past. "*Remorse?*"

"The very same. It seems there have been some unexpected mishaps and detours, but at least you are here now."

Sophia was astonished. "I—How—" She shook her head. "I am confused."

Wren gave a hearty laugh. "All will be explained, I promise. Perhaps this will help—I have here the document you have been seeking." Captain Wren handed Sophia a packet of folded papers. "It is a copy I made of a diary in Granada, and I brought it with me for our meeting to demonstrate my good intentions. And, as you shall see, it is in small part about me." He said this abashedly, as if he had taken a great liberty by appearing in the pages of the diary.

Sophia took the packet of papers and stared at the cover sheet. It read:

Personal Diary of Wilhelmina Tims.
From the original found at the Granada Depository.
Copied on June 25, 1892, by Richard Wren.

Sophia's eyes opened wide. She looked up at the captain. "The diary! She wrote about you?"

Captain Wren nodded. "Your mother and father sailed with me in 1881. Not long after, they sent a message asking for my help. For several reasons, I could not come to their aid. I am arriving now, many years later, hoping I am not too late to be of some assistance."

Sophia stared at the pages in silence, hardly believing she finally held her mother's words in her hands. "Thank you," she said, looking up at Captain Wren. "Thank you."

The captain bowed, beaming with satisfaction. "You are very welcome." Turning to Errol, he gave another small bow. "And I have not yet had the pleasure of meeting . . . ?"

"Errol Forsyth, of York," Errol said, shaking hands with the captain. He had at first watched the man with suspicion; this had gradually faded, giving way to a cautious curiosity. "I am pleased to know someone who offered aid to Sophia's parents, Captain Wren."

"Please call me Richard. I am very glad to make your acquaintance. And if I could," he said, gesturing toward the harbor, "I would recommend that we negotiate for passage with one of these ships. We are heading west to find the author of that document, are we not?" He smiled at Sophia.

Sophia nodded, overcome.

Wren grinned. "Excellent. I wish the vessel your parents knew, the *Roost*, was here with me, but for reasons I will explain I had to find other means of travel. But we will find suitable arrangements." He led them toward the harbor, holding one large, weathered hand over his eyes to shield them.

The sun, as it always did in Seville, shone down so brightly that Sophia had difficulty making out all the various flags and sails that fluttered in the harbor. But as the sun hid behind a tall mast, Sophia suddenly spotted one particular flag that made her heart stop. Her eyes followed down the mast to the ship, searching eagerly for the ship's name. There it was: the *Swan*. A broad smile broke out across

Sophia's face. "A pair of pistols and a sword," she said aloud. "Fair company, indeed."

The hope flared up in her, quick and sudden, that Theo had found his way aboard. She could not wait to see him. "I think I know who will take us west," she said, making her way to the dock.

ACKNOWLEDGMENTS

A heartfelt thanks to all the readers, booksellers, librarians, and fellow writers—young and old—who received *The Glass Sentence* with such warmth and enthusiasm. Your readership is inspiring, and it encouraged me to take some risks in this world of the Great Disruption.

To the readers who grappled with early versions of *The Golden Specific*—Pablo, Alejandra, Paul, Tom, Moneeka, and Sean—your comments were invaluable to the shaping of this book. Thank you for your willingness to read those very unpolished drafts, in some cases multiple times!

I feel extremely lucky that the Mapmakers books have a home with Viking and the Penguin Young Readers Group; thank you to Ken Wright and so many others who have supported these rather unusual creations in countless ways. The experience of working with Jessica Shoffel, Tara Shanahan, and the rest of the marketing team has changed my view of how books reach readers—entirely for the better. I am grateful to them and to Jim Hoover, Eileen Savage, Janet Pascal, Tricia Callahan, Abigail Powers, Krista Ahlberg, and the outstanding sales force at PYRG for transforming the stages that follow solitary writing. They used to be daunting, and now, thanks to you, they seem exciting and fun.

I am grateful to Dave A. Stevenson for bringing Shadrack to life once again through such wonderful maps and to Stephanie Hans for capturing so perfectly a sense of mystery, adventure, and foreboding in her artwork.

Laura Bonner has somehow persuaded readers in places all around the globe to take the Mapmakers books in hand, and I am so thankful (and amazed) to know that this intentionally global story will be read globally.

I am deeply grateful to Sharyn November for caring about this world and these characters as if they were just as vital, just as real, as the ones around us. Sharyn, your passion for these people brings out the best in them. (And maybe sometimes the worst. No one will ever loathe Broadgirdle like you do!)

As ever, I feel lucky beyond words to benefit from the infallible reading sense of Dorian Karchmar. Thank you for your insights and sensibilities, which I have come to rely upon so greatly. I trust your judgment more than my own!

I am grateful to my mother for affirming in her every statement the value and importance of writing, to my father for all of the spirited ideas (even the ones I didn't take), and to my brother for the sharp-eyed readings and rereadings—despite the fact that this is "*fahn*-tasy."

As he flipped through the first galleys of this book, tearing out my sticky notes, Rowan offered exuberant exclamations that I think were complimentary. Thank you, Rowan, for somehow putting it all in perspective.

Lastly, I wish to thank Alton, to whom this book is dedicated. Thank you for reading section by section, chapter by chapter, over and over and over. Thank you for making the best efforts of my imagination—Theo's humor, Errol's gallantry, and Goldenrod's wisdom—pale in comparison.

TURN THE PAGE FOR A SAMPLE
OF THE THRILLING CONCLUSION
TO SOPHIA'S JOURNEY IN

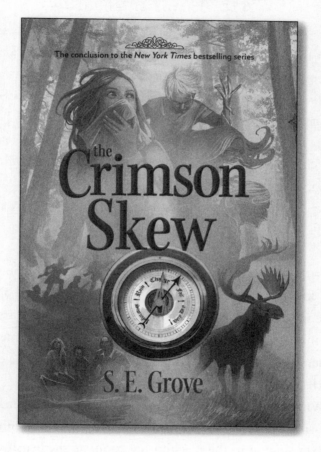

The conclusion to the *New York Times* bestselling series

the
Crimson
Skew

S. E. Grove

1

HISPANIOLA

—*1892, August 2: 7-Hour 20*—

Though the United Indies makes a legal distinction between merchants and pirates, safeguarding the privileges of the one while prosecuting (on occasion) the crimes of the other, in practice they are almost indistinguishable. Both hold property in the Indies— sometimes lavish property. Both exert considerable influence on the Indies' government. Both enjoy access to the seas and trade with foreign Ages. Indeed, it is, for the outsider, difficult to see where merchants end and pirates begin.

—From *Shadrack Elli's* History of the New World

SOPHIA AWOKE TO the sound of a woman singing. The voice was low and languid and sweet, as if the singer had all the time in the world; it sang of mermaids and silvery stars and moonbeams shining on the sea. It took Sophia a moment to remember where she was: Calixta and Burton Morris's estate on Hispaniola.

With a sigh of contentment, Sophia stretched against the soft sheets. She lay in bed with her eyes closed, listening to Calixta singing in the neighboring room as she brushed her hair and dressed. Suddenly the song was interrupted by a shout of dismay and a thump, as if from a booted foot striking a trunk. *"Where are my tortoiseshell combs?"* Calixta wailed.

Sophia opened her eyes and smiled. Splinters of light were pushing their way into the dark room. As the protests next door became fervent curses, she got out of bed and opened the tall wooden shutters, revealing a small balcony. The sunlight of Hispaniola was blinding. Sophia shielded her eyes until they adjusted, and then she caught her breath with delight at the sight before her: the grounds of the estate and, beyond the grounds, the shining ocean. Marble steps led down to a long lawn bordered by bougainvillea, jasmine, and birds-of-paradise. A straight path paved in white stone cut through the lawn to the beach. The *Swan*, anchored at the private dock, bobbed serenely on the sparkling waters.

"Sophia!" Calixta called. Sophia reluctantly made her way back into the bedroom, where Calixta stood holding what appeared to be a billowing curtain in a shocking shade of fuchsia. "Look what I found," she declared triumphantly. "This will fit you perfectly!"

"What is it?" Sophia asked dubiously.

"Only the finest silk New Orleans has to offer," Calixta exclaimed. "Try it on."

"Now?"

"It's midmorning, you lazy thing! We have plans to make and people to see, and I insist you be well dressed for it."

"Very well," Sophia replied agreeably. *Of course Calixta already has plans made,* she said to herself, *and of course she already has outfits chosen for everyone as part of those plans.* Sophia had found on the voyage from Seville, across the Atlantic, that it was almost always better to let the pirate captain have her way.

She slipped out of her nightgown and let Calixta help her into the silk dress, which was indeed beautiful. Sophia examined herself skeptically in the tall standing mirror beside the bed. "I look like a little girl impersonating the famous pirate Calixta Morris. And I can barely breathe." She reached for the shoulder strap. "I'm taking it off."

Calixta laughed. "No, you're not! We'll do your hair properly and get you stockings and shoes. A little powder and orange-flower water. That's all." She gave Sophia a quick kiss on the cheek. "And you're not a little girl anymore, sweetheart." She turned to the doorway. "Yes, Millie?"

A maid wearing a black-and-white uniform stood in the doorway. "Will you want breakfast here or downstairs, Captain Morris?"

"Have the others woken?"

"They are all downstairs, Captain, except for your brother."

"Still snoring soundly, no doubt," Calixta muttered. "We'll join the others downstairs, Millie—thank you."

Millie left the room with a brief nod.

"Let me just get my things," Sophia said, moving to gather her satchel.

Calixta stopped her, taking her hand. "You're safe here, Sophia," she said. "Our home is yours, and you have nothing to fear. We won't have to bolt at a moment's notice. You can leave your things in your bedroom."

Sophia pressed Calixta's hand. "I know. Thank you. Let me find my watch."

S. E. GROVE

Damask curtains, gilded mirrors, and delicate furniture upholstered in cream and blue: Calixta's hand lay behind the effortless luxury. Sophia's pack, satchel, books, and clothes—gray and worn from two Atlantic crossings and a perilous journey through the Papal States—made a dirty pile that seemed to have no place in the sumptuous room. "Got it!" She tucked the watch into a hidden pocket of the fuchsia dress.

"Down we go, then," Calixta said. Not to be outdone by the fuchsia, she was wearing a lemon-colored silk with gold trim. She trailed a hand along the polished banister as they descended the wide marble steps to the main floor.

Their travel companions were in the comfortable breakfast room. Sitting side by side on a white couch beside the windows, Errol Forsyth, a falconer from the Closed Empire, and Goldenrod, an Eerie from the edges of the Prehistoric Snows, looked out at the ocean with rather dazed expressions. Sophia thought to herself, not without amusement, that they seemed just as out of place in the gilded mansion as she felt in the fuchsia dress. Goldenrod sat stiffly, her pale-green hands folded in her lap, her long hair wild and windblown. She looked like a tuft of grass on a plate of porcelain. Errol, his clothes even more worn than Sophia's, rubbed the scruff of his chin, pondering the view. Seneca, Errol's falcon, blinked unhappily from his perch on the archer's shoulder.

At least Richard Wren, the Australian sea captain, seemed at ease. He stood in a wide stance before the windows, happily munching a piece of toast as he took in the view.

"I trust you all slept well?" Calixta asked, gliding toward the table, where fruit and pastries, butter and jam, coffee and sugar awaited.

"I can't remember the last time I slept so well," Wren exclaimed, saluting her appreciatively with his toast. "The most soothing sound of the waves, the softest pillows, the most comfortable bed. Calixta, I am afraid that once this search concludes, you will find me at your doorstep, an uninvited but eager guest."

"You are most welcome," Calixta replied, pleased.

"Thank you for your hospitality," Goldenrod said, rising from the couch. "It is wonderful to be at last on land and in safe circumstances. You and your brother have given us the safest of safe havens."

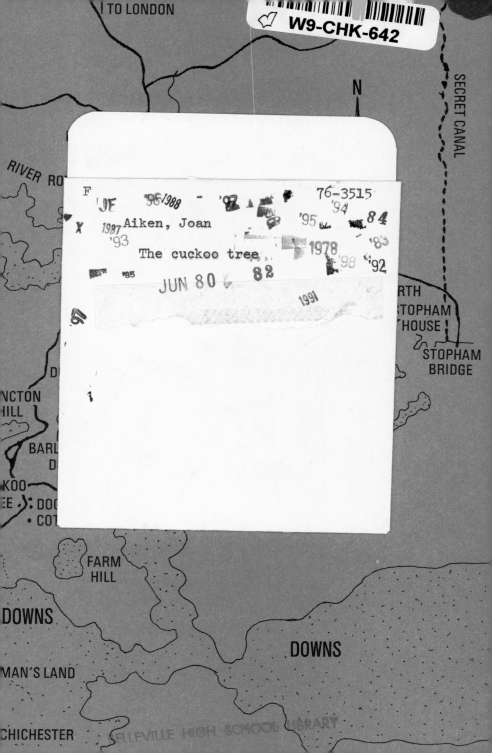

The
Cuckoo
Tree

The Cuckoo Tree

Joan Aiken

Illustrated by Susan Obrant

Doubleday & Company, Inc.
Garden City, New York

F
Aiken
76-3515

ISBN: 0-385-03071-1 TRADE
0-385-04715-0 PREBOUND
Library of Congress Catalog Card Number 76–157569
Copyright © 1971 by Joan Aiken
All Rights Reserved
Printed in the United States of America

9 8 7 6 5 4 3

The other passenger appeared to have been dozing. It was dark inside the chaise and little could be seen of him, save that he was a tall man, muffled in numerous capes and rugs. Except for an eye slit, left so that he could see out, his head was entirely wrapped in bandages, over which he wore an enormous fur hat. He spoke weakly, but with an air of authority.

"It's our driver," returned the girl in a low voice. "I suspicioned he was a bit bosky at the start, and now I reckon he's just about half-seas over. Trouble was, none o' the drivers would leave for London at five o'clock in the evening."

"I cannot imagine why not! They might ask what fee they liked, since we are traveling on government business, with dispatches for the Admiralty. Did you not tell them they should be handsomely rewarded?"

"Didn't make a mite o' difference. None of them'd stir—said as how we might meet with Gentlemen on the road." The girl glanced doubtfully at the black trees on either side.

"Gentlemen!" her companion exclaimed weakly but testily. "Pish! What moonshine!"

The driver had evidently caught some part of their conversation, for he suddenly burst into raucous song:

"Captain Hughes and young Miss Twite
Went for a drive—hic!—one shiny night
If they don't end in the Cuckoo Tree
Pickle my brains in eau-de-vie!"

"Attend to your business, my man!" snapped the bandaged passenger, for the horses were now dashing faster and faster down a long, winding hill, and the carriage was beginning to sway alarmingly.

But the driver only replied, "Tooral-eye-ooral, fiddle-eye-ay!" and cracked his whip in a very carefree manner.

"Put your arm through the strap, Cap'n!" young Miss Twite exclaimed anxiously, and since, blinkered as he was by his bandages, her companion was unable to find the arm hold, she scrambled across the rocking vehicle and slid the heavy leather loop over his elbow.

"Ah! Thanks, my child!"

She had secured him only just in time. Next instant the coach gave a particularly violent lurch and over-turned completely. Young Miss Twite still had hold of the strap; she clung to it tenaciously as she and her companion were flung backward against the padded seat, and then down on to the door of the carriage, which had come to rest lying on its side.

"Cap'n! Cap'n Hughes! Are you all right?"

No answer. Anxiously, Miss Twite felt his chest and discovered that he still breathed.

"Fry that coachman!" she exclaimed, attempting to disentangle herself from her companion.

"Who are you? What's happened?" he muttered con-fusedly.

"It's Dido, Cap'n—Dido Twite. We've had a turnup, but don't fret; I'll see to everything. *Mussy* knows how," she added to herself, "seeing I don't even know

[13]

how I'm a-going to get *out* of here—and the driver's about as much use as a herring in a hockey match. Maybe he's dead. Anyways, thank goodness the Cap'n isn't."

By stretching up to her full height (which was not great) she was just able to reach the arm strap dangling from the upper door; she pulled herself up by this, digging her toes into the indentations in the upholstery. Luckily one of the windows had fallen open, and she was able to edge her way through and climb on to the hedge bank. Searching about, she found the coachman, dead or unconscious, in a patch of long grass and thistles; he had apparently been thrown off his box at the first jolt. One of the horses stood with hanging head, very lame; the other was plunging about nervously; it had kicked its way clear of the shafts but was still held by its traces.

"Easy now, mate," the girl said, approaching it warily. "You and me has got to get better acquainted. Here, have a slab o' Sussex pudden; it's a bit squashed, but the landlady at the Dolphin said it would do for supper and breakfast too; you're welcome to the soggy stuff if it'll settle your spirits. It's better inside you than in my pocket, anyways."

The large, damp, sweet lump of suet pudding did prove soothing to the horse, and Dido was presently able to unhitch it, and lead it around to the side of the overturned coach.

"Cap'n!" she called. "Can you hear me, Cap'n Hughes? I can't get you out by myself, and I can't

[14]

right the coach, so I'm a-going for help. All rug? Shan't be long—I hope," she added to herself.

No reply came from inside; it seemed likely that the unfortunate captain had fainted again. Dido led the horse alongside the hedge bank, which was about three feet high, and from the top, managed to scramble on to the animal. Unused to being ridden, it started affrightedly, threw up its head, and set off at a canter; clinging like a monkey to its mane, Dido was jounced in a most uncomfortable manner from side to side of its broad back. By now her eyes were accustomed to the darkness and she was able to make out that they were in a narrow muddy lane with wooded hills sloping away on either side; no lights or houses were to be seen anywhere.

"Of all the God-forsaken spots to get tippled up in! *Don't* pull so, what's-your-name, Dobbin, my arms is weaker than seaweed already with all that scrabbling about in the coach."

Fairly soon the horse slowed to a steady trot better suited to its solid build; this was even more bone-shaking for Dido but she did not feel in such imminent danger of being tossed off and having to continue her quest on foot.

"How much o' this nook-shotten wilderness is there?" she wondered. "It seems to go on forever—not a house, nor an inn, nor a bakery shop anywheres! Downright wasteful it is, if you ask me."

After about ten minutes' riding she came to a crossroads—or to be more accurate, a spot where four or five tracks met.

"Now where?" Dido wondered, dragging on the traces to bring her steed to a halt. "Choose the wrong path and I reckon I'll be wandering for hours—and never find my way back to the carriage, which is worse; and if I don't get back with help pretty nippily, poor Cap'n Hughes is liable to *die,* I shouldn't wonder, with all this hugger-mugger on top o' that head wound he's got."

She bit her lip in anxiety and indecision, but at this moment a dark shape emerged in complete silence from the trees over to her left, stepped up beside her, and whispered,

"Tarrydiddle?"

"*I'll* say it's tarrydiddle," Dido replied. "Likewise hocus-pocus and how-de-do! Who the blazes are you, hoppiting about in the woods like a poltergeist?"

At this reply, evidently not what the newcomer expected, he put his fingers to his mouth and let out a soft whistle; in an instant seven more figures darted out from the trees; somebody took hold of the horse's bridle. Dido felt cold metal pressing against her leg, and saw a gleam of light move up and down something that looked extremely like the barrel of a blunderbuss. She also smelt, rather surprisingly, a strong, sweet scent, roses and cloves, mixed with ambergris and orange blossom.

"Who are you?" somebody hissed in her ear.

"Who'm I? I'm Dido Twite," she replied with spirit. "Our coach tippled over along there, acos the coachman was drunk as a wheelbarrow, and there's a hurt man inside, and I'm a-going for help. So I'll take it kind if you gentlemen will step back along with me and turn the coach topsides, and tell me where there's a house or a barn or *summat* where I can take poor Cap'n Hughes for the night."

As she spoke, the word *gentlemen* reminded her of the landlady's warning: "You'll not find a driver at this time o' day, love, they're all too scared o' the Gentlemen. All except Bosky Dick that is, and I wouldn't call him reliable."

" 'Tis a child," somebody whispered. "Do ee reckon that be a true tale?"

"The nag be Ben Noakes's gray from the Dolphin, sure enough. I did hear tell as how Bosky Dick was hired to drive a party to Lunnon town."

"Who else be in the coach, maidy?"

"Cap'n Hughes, I tell you, and he's hurt bad."

"What like of a cap'n is he?" someone asked suspiciously. "Be he one o' they Preventive Men, Bush officers?"

"What's they? No, he's a navy cap'n, and he was wounded at sea, in a battle—oh, *please* come and help me with him!"

"Us can't do that, my duck. Us has to goo t'other way to meet some friends, see? That's one reason, and another is, we dassn't, do we might meet some niffy chaps as we don't fancy."

"Well, then, can you tell me where I *can* get some help?" said Dido impatiently.

"Arr! Ee wants to goo upalong to the Manor House.

Owd Lady Tegleaze'll help ee surelye. She'll send some o' the chaps from the estate, sartin sure."

"Which way to the Manor House, then?"

One of the men holding the bridle turned Noakes's gray and led it into the track on Dido's left.

"Up yonder, my liddle maid. Through the big gates and on up the dene till ee see the lights. They'll help ee, up at the Manor. But don't ee goo speaking arter now, about who ee've seen here, eh? 'Twouldn't be wise, see?"

"How can I?" said Dido tartly. "I *haven't* seen you. Who are you anyways?"

She heard soft chuckles in the darkness. "Wouldn't ee like to know? Well, then, listen: we're Yan, Tan, Tethera, Methera, Pip—"

"Sethera, Wineberry," the other voices took it up, "Wagtail, Tarrydiddle, and Den! Now ee knows all that's good for ee."

"And a mighty big help you've been *I'm* sure," Dido muttered—rather ungratefully, since they had, at least, set her on the right way—as her horse cantered up the loamy ride, under an avenue of tall trees whose branches creaked mournfully in the wind overhead.

Just before she left them she heard one phrase not meant for her ears:

"Quick yourselves a bit, then, lads, or us'll be late at the Cuckoo Tree!"

This reminded her of the coachman's rhyme,

> "If they don't end in the Cuckoo Tree
> Pickle my brains in eau-de-vie!"

She wondered vaguely what it meant, but almost at once anxiety about Captain Hughes drove out all other considerations. Luckily she soon came to a pair of massive stone pillars, evidently the gates the man calling himself Yan had alluded to; when she passed between them the path took a sharp bend to the left around a hummock of ground, and beyond this she could distinguish a cluster of lights not far ahead. Five minutes more, and Noakes's gray drew up in front of what was plainly a very large mansion, set in a fold of the hillside, with a dark mass of trees behind it and a broad sweep of grass in front. Little else was visible in the dark rainy night. Considering that the time could not yet be much after eight o'clock, Dido was somewhat surprised not to see more windows lit—there seemed to be but half a dozen, and these with wide spaces between them, as if the inhabitants of this great place were so unsociably inclined that they preferred to keep as separate from one another as possible.

There was a portico with white marble pillars, and some iron staples, roughly driven into these, were evidently meant for tethering horses.

Dido slid off the gray's back with relief. "Though dear knows how I'll ever get back on," she thought, seeing no mounting block. Ignoring a slight palpitation of the heart at the grandeur of this place—the double doors, under the portico, were so huge that a medium-sized whale could easily have passed between them, given enough water to swim in—she tugged briskly at a brass bellpull.

The house had seemed so silent, as if all its inmates were elsewhere or asleep, that she was a little startled when the doors flew open at once; they had been pulled back, she discovered, by a pair of liveried footmen in powdered wigs, and directly in front of her a butler stood bowing.

"Can you help me—" Dido began. He interrupted her with raised hand.

"This way, my lady. Please to follow me."

"Poor old fellow," Dido thought, following. "I suppose in a place as grand as this he ain't allowed to give orders for help on his own, but has to ask the lord or duke or whoever lives here."

They crossed a wide hall, decorated with a great many pairs of deer's antlers, ascended several flights of marble stairs—very slowly; the butler was a very aged man—and proceeded along several wide passageways until, it seemed to Dido, they must have reached the very end of the house.

"Coo, it's a big place, ennit?" she remarked. "Must take a deal o' sweeping. I'm right sorry for the housemaid."

The aged butler, in the act of knocking at a door, turned and surveyed her with some surprise. The sight of her clothes, which he had not observed in the darkness of the portico, appeared to surprise him still more.

"I'd take it kind if you'd ask someone to keep an eye on my nag while I'm up here," Dido added. "If I'd a known we'd have to come sich a perishing way I'd a tied him up a mite tighter."

"But—did your ladyship not come in a carriage?"

"That's just what I'd a told you if you'd waited—" Dido was beginning impatiently, when an equally impatient voice inside the door shouted,

"How the deuce many times do I have to say, come in?"

Flustered, the butler threw open the door, bowed, stood aside, and announced, as Dido entered,

"The Lady Rowena Palindrome!"

"There! I might a known there was some mux-up," Dido said. "Bless your socks, I ain't Lady Rowena Thingummy."

"Never mind, I daresay you'll do just as well," said the room's occupant. "Come in and sit down. Can you play tiddlywinks? Gusset, there's a draft; don't stand there, go out and shut the door behind you."

"I beg your pardon, Sir Tobit. But if the young lady isn't who she said she was—"

"I didn't say I is, I said I isn't!" Dido put in. "My stars! I was told I'd get *help* here, not a lot of argufication—"

"I had better inform her ladyship," the butler muttered worriedly. "She won't be best pleased, I'm afraid. What name *did* you say, missie?"

"I didn't say *any* name, but it's Dido Twite."

"Dido Twite. Dwido Tite. Twido Dite. Twito Died. Dwighto Tied," the butler repeated, and left the room, closing the door.

"Oh, bother! Now Grandmother will come along and there'll be a lot of fuss. Why did you have to say you weren't Rowena Palindrome? What does it matter who you are? Sit down, anyway, and amuse me till the old girl comes—it'll take her a while to get up."

"I haven't *got* a while," said Dido crossly. "There's a chap out there, dying, maybe, in an overset carriage, and the driver's knocked silly—not that he was much at the start—and I'd be obliged if you'd kindly send out those two coves as has nothing better to do than open and shut doors to fetch the poor souls here and see arter 'em a bit."

"An overset carriage? How do you know?"

"How do I know? Acos I was in it—that's how."

"You were in a carriage that overturned? Aren't you lucky!"

"Rummy notion o' luck you has," Dido said, studying her companion with curiosity. And certainly he was an unusual figure—a boy of twelve or thirteen, tall and thin, with a pale face and a mop of black hair. More singular still, he was dressed in clothes at least two hundred years out of date—the sort of clothes worn by gentry in Charles the First's day: a frilled shirt with long lace cuffs, a long-skirted embroidered waistcoat, a sword, velvet breeches, and buckled shoes. His hair was tied back with a velvet ribbon. A huge furry white dog lay at his feet; it had a pointed nose, like a bear, and the tongue lolling from its jaws was blue.

Her host, for his part, studied Dido with almost equal astonishment; he saw a sun-tanned girl, her brown hair cut untidily short; she wore long, wide trousers

[22]

of dark-blue duffel, a white shirt with a sailor collar, and a tight-fitting pea jacket with brass buttons.

"Why do you wear such peculiar clothes?" he said.

"These? They're a midshipman's rig; mighty comfortable too. I jist got back from sea, that's why. Going up to London with dispatches for the Fust Lord o' the Admiralty, and our numbskull of a driver has to overturn us afore we've gone twenty miles, and poor Cap'n Hughes wounded in the Chinese wars and weak as a snail—"

"You've been at *sea*—you, a girl?" Sir Tobit stared at her round-eyed. "Why?"

"That'd be a long tale. That'd be several long tales. What about those hurt men?"

"Oh, we can do nothing for them till my grandmother has given permission," he said carelessly. "So you may as well sit down and tell me your stories till she comes. Are you hungry? Would you like something to eat?"

He pushed toward her a tray carved from some silvery foreign wood. On it were several plates, wooden likewise, containing a few wrinkled apples, some nuts, and a large lump of cheese.

"We never eat anything but fruit and cheese; my grandmother thinks it best. Cowslip wine?"

The cowslip wine, pale yellow in color, was served in an earthenware pitcher. Sir Tobit poured some into a wooden mug.

"Thankee." Dido rejected the nuts—which were wizened, strange-looking little things—but helped herself to

[23]

an apple and a lump of cheese. There had been no time for supper at the Port of Chichester, so she was glad of them. The dog snarled a little as she moved, and Sir Tobit, cuffing him lightly, said,

"Quiet, Lion!"

Glancing around the room as she ate, Dido was struck by the oddity of the contents. In a mansion this size she would have expected richness and grandeur; gold doorknobs, maybe, and crystal chandeliers, such as her friend Simon once told her were to be seen at the duke's castle in Battersea. But here everything looked dusty and worn, and seemed to be made of the plainest materials—wooden chests, straw matting, loosely woven curtains in queer, bright colors, looking as if they had been sewn by people living in grass huts on some distant foreign isle. The lights were the commonest kind of tallow candles and not too plentiful. There were strangely shaped, strangely colored clay pots, and numerous little statues and images in wood and pottery. And books were piled everywhere, higgledy-piggledy—on the chests, the floor, the chairs, and on a curious little round table which looked as if it had been carved with a toothpick from the trunk of a tree. It was rather a nasty little table, Dido thought, looking at it more closely—the top and bottom were solid disks of wood, connected by a crisscross wooden network; at every join a little wooden face grinned maliciously with white-painted teeth and eyes. The room was a large one and the farther end was almost in darkness, but Dido had an uneasy feeling that somebody was there in the shadows watching—occasionally the corner of her eye caught a movement. Perhaps it was another dog?

"Tell about the carriage accident," Sir Tobit demanded. "What happened? Were you waylaid? Was there a fight?"

"No, no, it was just an accident—nothing out o' the common."

"But how did it come about?"

"Land sakes, hain't you never seen a carriage turn topsy-turvy? The driver was a bit tossicated, that's all; I reckon he runned one o' the wheels against the bank. So over we went. And Cap'n Hughes was stuck inside. I managed to scramble out."

"Where did it happen?" Sir Tobit was asking, when the door was opened by Gusset the butler and a lady swept into the room.

Although Lady Tegleaze was plainly very old, her age was not her most striking feature. What most impressed Dido about her was a feeling of *queerness*—as if her very bright eyes were set most of the time on things that nobody else could see, as if she were listening to sounds or voices that nobody else could catch. Like her grandson, she was tall and thin, she limped slightly and walked with a stick, she wore what must surely be a wig of flowing gray curls, and had carelessly flung around her a lavender-colored satin overdress, trimmed with point lace. It was faded and slightly torn. As she came in, Dido heard a door close softly in the shadows at the far end of the room.

"Not so close!" Lady Tegleaze exclaimed, limping

swiftly toward Dido and tapping her with the stick. "Not so close to Sir Tobit—remove yourself, pray!"

The dog Lion growled softly to himself.

Rather taken aback, Dido scrambled to her feet and stepped back, ducking her head in a mixture between a bow and a curtsy. What in tarnation does the old girl think I'm a-going to do—*bite* him? she wondered, but the very oddness of Lady Tegleaze commanded respect.

"Now then," she continued, fixing Dido with those curiously bright, curiously distant eyes, "what is all this about? Who is this young person? Why is she here and where is Lady Rowena Palindrome?"

"Please, your ladyship, the young lady is Miss Twido Dite; and Frill just gave me this; he said a messenger brought it not ten minutes since." The butler handed Lady Tegleaze a note.

"Humph," she said, unfolding and reading it: "From the duchess—too late—too far—too rainy for the horses—cried off. Pish! When I was a gel horses were horses and could stand a bit of rain."

"They always cry off," Sir Tobit languidly observed. "No one wishes to come here. Why should they? You won't let *me* go to *them.*"

"So who are you?" The old lady's gaze returned to Dido. Absently she took a handful of nuts from the dish and munched them.

"She had an accident to her carriage," Sir Tobit explained. "On the London road. There are two hurt men and she wants our help to fetch them. One of them's a sea captain, carrying dispatches."

[26]

"A sea captain? You have come off a ship?"

"Yes, ma'am."

"From what country? What ship?"

"A navy ship, ma'am, the *Thrush;* she was a-coming home from the China wars and stepped from her course to chase a Hanoverian schooner, and picked me up off'n the isle of Nantucket."

"*China! Nantucket!*" Lady Tegleaze could not have been more horrified if Dido had said Devil's Island. "And you come here—from such places—reeking of typhus, yellow fever, and every kind of infection! Pray stand over by the door!"

"I don't wish to stand anywhere, ma'am, if you'll only send someone to help right our coach and tend to those hurt chaps," Dido said rather aggrievedly, removing herself to the desired location.

"Gusset, have two of the men go back with this young person. But the injured people certainly cannot come *here;* that is quite out of the question. Suppose Sir Tobit caught some noxious illness from them, and it so near to his coming of age!"

"Where should they be taken then, marm?" Gusset inquired doubtfully.

"Someone on the estate can take them in!"

"There bain't many *left* on the estate now, your ladyship."

"There are some tenants in Dogkennel Cottages still, are there not? Old Mr. Firkin—Mrs. Lubbage? Very well—take them there."

Gusset looked even more doubtful, and Dido was not

too happy at the sound of Dogkennel Cottages. Still, it's only for a night, she thought; tomorrow I can stop the mail coach or summat. "Maybe your ladyship could tell me where I can get hold of a doctor?" she asked politely.

"A doctor?" Lady Tegleaze seemed vaguely surprised.

"Dr. Subito is here, playing tiddlywinks with Mr. Wilfred," the butler reminded her. "I could ask him to step along to the cottages."

"Why, yes, I suppose he *could* do so, if the child absolutely demands it; though I would not wish *him* to pick up any infection. But come, child, come along; every minute you are here increases the risk to my grandson."

Lady Tegleaze limped to the door.

"There, I said how it would be," muttered Sir Tobit sulkily. "Just when I had the chance to hear some new tales, instead of having to make up my own."

But Dido was eager to be off. "Thanks for the wine and cheese," she called back, and followed Lady Tegleaze.

At the top of the stairs, Lady Tegleaze came to a halt.

"Where is Tante Sannie?" she asked Gusset.

The butler paused a moment before answering. Then he said, in a peculiarly expressionless voice,

"She was in Mas'r Tobit's room. I reckon she be in your ladyship's room now. Would you wish for me to search?"

"No—no. I will go myself. Follow me, child."

Oh crumpet it, Dido thought; now what?

[28]

However she followed along another series of passages. Lady Tegleaze halted outside a door.

"Wait here," she commanded Dido. She opened the door and called, "Sannie?"

Through this door Dido could see another large dimly lit chamber filled with a clutter of foreign-looking furniture, draperies, and scattered clothing. A faint, sickly waft of aromatic smoke drifted out. This is a rum house and no mistake, Dido thought.

Next moment the skin on the back of her neck prickled as something small and dark scuttled from the shadows inside the room out through the door. It was too small for a person, surely? Could it be a large dog? Or an enormous spider?

Then she saw that it was in fact a tiny, bent old woman, wrapped in a kind of embroidered blanket, black and white, which covered her entirely except for two very bright eyes which peered up at Dido from under her head swathings.

"Sannie," said Lady Tegleaze. "You see this girl?"

"I see her, princessie-ma'am!"

"Look at her hand for me, Sannie!"

Dido was disconcerted when a minute, skinny brown claw shot out of the black-and-white draperies and grabbed her hand, turning it over so that the palm came uppermost. The old woman bent over it, mumbling to herself.

"This girl strong girl—much temper, much willful. Can be angry to push over a house. Can kindly love too. I see her holding gold crown in this hand—she picking it up from ground, she putting it on someone head. I see great pink fish too—"

"Is this in the past or the future?" interrupted Lady Tegleaze.

"Past, future, princessie-ma'am—all one."

"Well, has she any sickness? Is she infectious? Will she harm my grandson?"

Tante Sannie bent over the hand once more.

"For mussy's *sake,*" thought Dido, "what a potheration! All over five minutes' chat with a boy that I'll likely never see again."

"Not sick—no. Strong girl. But something strange here —tree, tree growing. Can't see clear—tree growing, spreading branches over hand. Voices talking in tree— two voices, t'ree voices? Can't see who, tree too thick, too dark. Can't see, can't see, princessie-ma'am!"

The old woman flung down Dido's hand angrily, as if it burnt her, and hobbled away, muttering to herself in a foreign language that sounded like the resentful snarling of cats before they attack one another.

Lady Tegleaze gazed after her rather blankly and stood a moment as if undecided. Then, saying to Dido, "That will do—you may go," she limped into her chamber and shut the door.

Ho, I may, may I? Dido thought crossly. There's gentry for you; full of notions and fancies one minute; then drops you like a bit of orange peel in the midst o' nowhere and leaves you to chart your own course for home.

She darted back the way they had come. Born and

bred in the alleys of Battersea, she had no difficulty in retracing her steps through the maze of passages; she found the marble stairs and ran down them.

Gusset was waiting at the foot.

"Frill and Pelmett have set out already, Missie Dwight," he told Dido. "I reckoned you'd rather they started. Be you able to find your way back to the carriage or shall I step along wi' you?"

"Thanks, mister—that's mighty kind of you. But I guess I can manage," Dido said gruffly, touched by the frail old man's thoughtfulness.

"Might I ask summat, Missie Twide?"

"O' course—what is it?"

"I heeard you say as how you were *told* you'd get help here. Might I ax *who* told you?"

"Why—" Dido began. Then she recollected the caution that had been administered by Yan, Tan, Tethera, and the others.

"It was a chap I met along the road, mister. I don't know who he was. He couldn't stop—was a-going the other way, and all in a pucker acos he was going to meet someone."

"You don't know where he was a-going, missie?"

"Why yes, matter o' fact, I do." Dido wondered why the butler was so inquisitive. "I heeard him say he was a-going to a tree—the Cuckoo Tree."

The old man paled slightly. Dido, glancing about the large, bare hall, did not notice this.

"Excuse me," she said civilly, "but would there be a chair somewheres in this here barracks, Mister Gusset?"

"A chair, missie? I'll see if I can find one for you." Puzzled, worried, but anxious to oblige, he hobbled off, murmuring to himself.

"She couldn't have heard wrong, could she? The Cuckoo Tree, she said plain enough. Butter my wig, I wish I weren't so pumple-footed."

In a little while—evidently chairs were not too plentiful on the ground floor of Tegleaze Manor—he came slowly back, carrying a rush-bottomed ladderback with a burst seat.

"Here you be, then, missie; was you wishful to sit down?"

"Thankee, mister; no, it's to get back on my nag," Dido explained. She carried the chair out to the portico, planted it down beside Noakes's gray, and climbed aboard.

"Giddap, Dobbin; you musta had a good rest by now, let's get back quick, eh? Good night, Mister Gusset, and thanks for all you done."

"Good night, Missie Dite." Gusset untied the traces and watched her trot off into the rainy dark. For a few minutes after that he stood indecisively, scratching his white whiskers; then he picked up a sack from a heap lying out in the portico, muffled it about his head and shoulders, closed the great doors behind him, and set off in his turn down the pitch-black avenue.

2

By the time that Dido arrived back at the overturned carriage a dank and dripping moon was groping out from behind the rain clouds and giving a little light; she saw that the two footmen, Frill and Pelmett, had fastened a rope to the driver's box and were trying to pull the carriage up on to its wheels again.

"That's a cack-handed way o' going on," Dido muttered as, after some unavailing struggles, they stopped and blew their noses.

"What would *you* suggest, then?" Pelmett inquired sourly.

"Why, pass the rope over a tree branch, o' course!"

This was such obvious sense that the two men received it in silence; Frill, without more ado, climbed up on to the bank and tossed the free end of the rope over a stout beech bough that extended some fifteen feet above the road. With the extra purchase thus obtained, it was not difficult to right the chaise. Its only damage proved to be a snapped shaft.

"Will it go?" asked Dido.

"Reckon so. The gray nag looks a bit swymy, though. Best unharness him and put-to the bay again."

While they were doing this Dido climbed into the carriage and found that the unfortunate Captain Hughes was still unconscious.

"Hey, Mister Frill!" she called softly. "Could you help me set the poor chap back on the seat?"

As he assisted her to do so the moon came out fully and Dido was astonished to discover that the upholstery of the chaise had been violently slashed and ripped; the horsehair stuffing lay tossed in thick mounds and masses all over seats and floor.

"How in mussy's name did that come about?" she exclaimed, brushing a handful of horsehair from the Captain's cravat.

"Cushions split in the upset, o' course," Frill said rather scornfully.

Dido thought this improbable, but she made no further comment. Discovering with relief that Captain Hughes was still breathing, she spread rugs over him and then, while the two footmen searched for Bosky Dick, she went around to the luggage compartment of the chaise, opened the lid, and found, as she had expected, that their two portmanteaux and the Captain's dispatch box were gaping open, and the contents strewn about. She pressed her lips together and nodded to herself.

"Hey, miss! Where did you say the driver was a-lying?" Frill asked. "He don't seem to be noways hereabouts."

"He was in a patch of thistle just there by the road."

Dido walked up the track, now chalk white in the moonlight, to where the two men were standing. But the crushed thistle patch was empty; the driver lay there no longer.

"Musta come to hisself and wandered off," Pelmett said.

"Ah, that'll be it, I'll lay," Frill agreed, nodding wisely. "Bosky Dick allus had a larmentable hard head. Reckon he be halfway back to Chichester by now."

"Well, if you think he'll be all right," Dido said doubtfully, "there's no sense hanging about for him. He warn't no shakes as a driver, anyhows, and I want to get the poor Cap'n bedded and tended as quick as possible. Let's be off."

Pelmett went to the bay's head and they started at a cautious pace, Dido walking beside the carriage, Frill leading the lame gray horse. Captain Hughes stirred and moaned a little.

"Can you go a bit faster, Mister Pelmett?" Dido urged anxiously.

"Just so long's the wheels don't come off," Pelmett agreed, and increased the pace. They had by now reached the spot where Dido met her mysterious guides.

"How far is it to this Dogkennel Cottages?"

"Dogkennel. Cottages? Jigger it, is that where we've got to take him?" Pelmett was plainly startled and not too happy at this news.

"That's what the old lady said. She said someone called Mr. Firkin or—or Mrs.—some name like Libbege —'ud look arter him."

"Mrs. Lubbage." Pelmett pronounced the name with distaste. "Well, I dessay she would if she'd a mind to; she'm a wise woman. But *I* ain't so unaccountable keen to have dealings wi' the old besom. Frill, you can do the talking."

"Not I," Frill said uneasily. "Let the lass talk for herself."

Both men quickened their pace, as if anxious to get the meeting with Mrs. Lubbage over as soon as possible. The white track, now winding between gentle grassy slopes, led into a long shallow valley at the far end of which, under a hill round and bare as a bald head, Dido could see a little row of cottages with one or two outbuildings and a couple of haystacks.

"Them's Dogkennels," Pelmett said with relief.

As they drew near, Dido saw that the cottages were flint built and looked very poverty-stricken. Some of the windows were broken; a few cabbage stalks grew in the derelict garden patches. A dim glimmer of light showed in one window; the rest of the cottages, some three or four in all, were dark.

"I'm skeered," Frill said shivering. "This is an unket place—fair gives me the twets. Can't we stop here?"

"We'd best carry the chap in," Pelmett said. "Old

Mis' is sure to ax if we did. Sides, there's the doctor's cob; while he's about she 'on't do anything twort."

A stout gray cob was tethered by the door of the cottage with the light in its window. Pelmett looked about him, picked up a rock, and as if reluctant even to touch the door, used the rock to hammer on it.

The door shot open. Plainly they were expected.

"My daffy-down-dilly!" exclaimed the man who opened to them. "What in the world kept you so long, my dear souls? Have you brought my patient? How is the sad sufferer? Let us fetch him in, *molto, molto allegro!*"

Pelmett and Frill lifted the unconscious man out of the carriage.

"Where'll we set him, gaffer?" Pelmett asked, plainly reluctant to set foot inside the cottage.

"In here, where elsewise?"

But Dido had stepped inside the open door.

"This don't smell right to set a sick man in—it smells downright horrible," she said bluntly. The little room she had entered was slightly below ground level, dimly lit by a rush dip, and it had indeed an evil smell—a damp, warm, sickly, fusty, rotten smell, of old filthy rags, and food gone bad, and burning rubbish, and a queer faint choking sweetness over all. "Ask me," Dido went on, "the air in this place is enough to *make* a body ill."

"Oh, it is, is it? And who asked your opinion, Miss Prussy?" inquired a voice at her elbow. She turned around sharply.

[37]

Beside her, studying her with hostility, stood an enormously fat woman, who wore a grubby print dress, and a grubby print apron, and trodden-down slippers. She had her arms folded across the front of the apron. Her face, with tiers of double chins, and small twinkling eyes set in folds of fat, and curly gray hair atop, should have been friendly and jolly, but although the mouth pretended to smile, the unwinking stare of the sharp little eyes made Dido feel very uncomfortable.

"N-no offense, missus," she said politely, "b-but the Cap'n there, being a sailor, is used to lots o' fresh air, and he can't abide being cooped up anywhere stuffy. Reckon he'd be better in a barn or hayloft, if you has one? 'Sides, if this is your kitchen, you won't want a sick person cluttering about in it."

He can't stay here, that's for sure, she thought, her eyes, now used to the dimness, taking in the horrible squalor of the little kitchen, the piles of soiled rags and rotting vegetables, greasy puddles on the uneven brick floor, and peeling, blackened walls.

"Eh! High-up, flarsky, and hoity-toity we are," Mrs. Lubbage said sourly. "Still, there's empty housen a-plenty; if my kitchen's not good enough for you you can take yourself next door. *I* ain't pitickler where you sleeps, it's all one to *me*. Her ladyship sends a message for me to have an eye to the poor sick gentleman; that's all *I* knows."

"Perchance it would be better to take the patient next door," Dr. Subito agreed with ill-concealed relief.

[38]

"Can you carry the poor languisher there, my good fellows?"

Not at all reluctant, Pelmett and Frill carried Captain Hughes to another of the empty cottages. The first they tried had been used for keeping chickens in, and was not much better than Mrs. Lubbage's kitchen. But the next was empty and clean enough; it even had a rickety old bedstead which Pelmett stacked with hay while Frill fetched sticks and kindled a fire in the little hearth. By the light of this, and some tapers which the men had brought with them, Dr. Subito was able to examine the Captain.

"A leg is broken, alas, which I will set," he announced, and proceeded to do so, swiftly and deftly. "Otherwise he suffers only from fever and inflammation of his head wound, that is all. The wound received at sea, I understand? Since how long? Two months? And he is recovering *con brio*, up to now?"

"Chirpy as a cricket," Dido said. "The surgeon on board his ship—that's the *Thrush*—told him how when he got to London the doctors there'd likely say he could have his bandages off. It's a plaguy shame this had to happen now. How long'll he be poorly again, mister doctor?"

"He should not be moved for two weeks—three, if this fever does not slip down very quickly. I will come back tomorrow—*subito*—meantime you will find that the large lady—Mrs. Lubbage—is a famous nurse."

"She don't look it—I'd as lief not trouble her," Dido said, wrinkling her nose at the thought of that kitchen.

[39]

"*Senti,* young lady, she has the gift of healing, she knows about herbs and charms, *molto, molto,*" Dr. Subito said earnestly. He was a small, spare man, with a sallow complexion and an anxious expression; his large black mustaches were his most lively and vigorous feature. When he spoke about Mrs. Lubbage he glanced somewhat nervously behind him and made an odd, jerky sign with two fingers. "If it were not for the intervention of Mrs. Lubbage, many, many of my patients would not have recovered!" Under his breath he muttered, "And many, many of them would not have fallen ill, *presto alla tedesca!*"

"Fire's going nice and sprackish now, sir," said Pelmett. "And I've put the lame nag in the shippen with a bit o' feed, and reckon us'd better ride the other one back to the Manor, or ol' Mis'll be turble tiffy and bumblesome, axing where we've got to."

Plainly he was dying to get away.

"I will accompany you, my good fellows, *allegro vivace,*" the doctor said quickly. "Give the patient this draught, young lady, when he awakens, and another dose at morningtide. He should have light feedings— milk, eggs, white wine. No meat. I will return *domani* —tomorrow. *Addio!* To the re-see!"

"Hey! Where am I to find eggs and wine and so forth in this back end?" Dido called after him, but he did not hear, or did not choose to.

Dido suddenly found herself left alone with the sick man; the sound of hoofs died away outside and after that, strain her ears how she might, there was nothing to be heard at all, save a distant sighing of trees.

"This is a fubsy kind o' set-out," she said to herself. "Still, no use bawling over botched butter—have to make the best of it. I'd as soon not tangle overmuch wi' that old witch next door though. Only thing is, how are we going to get summat to eat? Oh, well, maybe old Lady Tegleaze'll send some soup and jelly—or cheese and apples—no use fretting ahead. Queer old cuss *she* is, too—all those rooms in that great workus of a place, and she has to send us to a ken that ain't much bigger than a chicken coop."

She made sure the Captain was sleeping peacefully, packed the hay tight under him, and straightened the capes and carriage rugs over him. Next she brought in their valises, which would serve as tables or chairs, made up the fire, piled more hay in a corner for her own bed, and bolted the front and back doors of the cottage, which consisted of two ground-floor rooms with a loft above.

Lastly Dido pulled a packet from the front of her midshipman's shirt and carefully inspected it. It was addressed to the First Lord of the Admiralty and was covered in large red unbroken seals.

"All hunky-dory," she muttered to herself in satisfaction. "Likely enough it was *you* as whoever rummaged over the carriage was a-looking for—seeing as how nothing else was stole. But they didn't find you, and so long as we're in this neck o' the woods, or till I can lay

[41]

hands on some trustable chap to take you to London, you stays right inside my shimmy shirt."

She replaced the packet, blew out the tapers, and curled up in her sweet-smelling nest.

About half an hour later she heard somebody cautiously try first the front, then the back door.

"Hilloo?" Dido called out. "Is that the baker's boy? One white, one brown, two pints o' dairy fresh *with* the top on, half o' rashers, and a dozen best pullets', *if* you please."

Dead silence greeted this request, and though Dido listened alertly for some time after, there was no further disturbance. Presently, satisfied, she fell asleep.

Early next morning, well before daybreak, Dido was wakened by the crowing of roosters near at hand. Beyond the roosters, plaintive in the dark, she could hear sheep bleating—high and low, near and far—it sounded as if the hills were covered with an immense flock of sheep, full of unappeased longing for breakfast.

"And I could do with a peck myself," thought Dido, rolling off her flattened pile of hay. "Croopus, don't they half have it noisy in the country! Still, I reckon' it's time for the Cap to take another dram o' physic. Hey, Cap'n Hughes!" she said softly. "How are you a-feeling today?"

His forehead was cool and his eyes, when they opened, recognized her.

"It's the young passenger—Miss Twite," he murmured. "I will escort her to London when I carry the

Dispatch—Osbaldeston will continue in command until the end of my sick furlough. Ah, thank you, my dear—"

Obediently he swallowed down the draught which Dido had prepared for him and fell asleep at once. Satisfied that he was doing well, Dido blew up the embers of the fire and fed it with dry sticks. Now, how could she go out leaving the sick man secure from intrusion? There were bolts on both doors, and a lock on the front one, but no key.

"Nothing bigger than a cat could get in at the windows, so that's no worry," she decided. "Wonder if I could get out through the loft?"

Entry to this was through a trap door in the ceiling. She piled the cases one on another and from the top one was just able to spring up, grab the edge of the opening, and pull herself through like a squirrel.

Plainly the loft had been used in the past for housing pigeons. A number of miscellaneous oddments had also been stored up here at one time or another and then forgotten; probing about cautiously in the half dark Dido found some pewter dishes, half a dozen clay pipes (broken), a stringless lute, a box of mildewy books, an iron candlestick, a three-legged stool, some earthenware crocks, and a hip bath.

"Some o' these'll come in useful," she decided. "Now, what's out back?"

A couple of tiles had been removed from the roof to make an entrance for the pigeons. Putting her face to the hole, Dido looked out and in the growing dawn light saw that a neglected, weed-grown farmyard lay behind the row of cottages. With great care she removed another tile, enlarging the hole enough to stick her head through, and looked sideways. A big rain-water barrel could be seen to her right, just below the edge of the roof.

"Guess if I could get on to that I could climb down from it," Dido thought, measuring its height with her eye. She began taking more tiles from the hole, slipping each carefully off its pair of wooden pegs and laying it on the floor, until there was a gap large enough to climb through. Once a tile escaped her and slid down, landing with a crash on the cobbles below, but nobody appeared to have heard. When the hole was big enough she squeezed through and went down the roof on fingers and toes until she was above the big wooden cask. Prodding it first, to make sure the top would take her weight, she scrambled on to it. A broken wooden handbarrow leaned against the wall below.

"That'll do for climbing back," she thought with satisfaction, and jumped nimbly to the ground. Hardly had she done so when she heard footsteps; an old man carrying two buckets on a yoke across his shoulders walked around the corner of the cottages and across the yard away from Dido. He had not seen her but his dog, following a few yards behind, did, and gave one sharp formal wuff. The old man turned himself around —he could not turn just his head because of the yoke.

"What be fidgeting ee, Toby?" he said.

The dog barked again.

[44]

"Why, dag me, 'tis a boy. No it bean't, it be a liddle maid. Where be you from so early, darter?"

"Are you Mr. Firkin?" Dido asked. "Lady Tegleaze said you'd help me."

"Owd Tom Firkin I be, and this yer's my dog Toby."

"What kind of a dog's that? I've never seen one like him before."

Toby was a grayish sandy color, as big as a sheep, and so extremely shaggy that it was hard to tell which way he was facing.

"Old-fashioned ship dog ee be," Mr. Firkin said.

"Old-fashioned! He looks like something out o' the ark."

"Ah, he be a wunnerful clever dog wi' the ship; we ne'er loses one at lambing time."

While he was speaking Mr. Firkin continued on his way and Dido followed into a cowshed where a brindled cow stood waiting to be milked. Mr. Firkin hung his yoke over a wooden partition, took off the buckets, and sat down to milk on a three-legged wooden stool like the one in the loft, leaning his head against the cow's side. He wore a battered hard felt hat, painted gray, with a pheasant's feather in it, and a sort of jerkin and apron made of sacking over velveteen breeches and leather boots. He had a long bushy white beard, which at the moment was inconveniencing him very much; it stuck out and got in the way of the milk flow and if he pushed it to one side with his elbow it dangled into the pail.

"You want a bit o' string for that, mister," said Dido.

[45]

She had one in her pocket, with which she tied the beard, doubled up in a neat bunch.

"Nay! That's nim," he said admiringly. "I can tell ee must be a trig liddle maid. Why don't ee feed my chickens while I tend to owd Clover here, then us'll git our breakfasses."

He showed her where the hens were shut up at night "for fear o' foxy owd Mus' Reynolds" and gave her a round tin pan with a wooden handle.

"Chickens' grub be in the posnet yonder."

Outside the cottage at the far end of the row from Mrs. Lubbage's, Dido saw a kind of caldron on legs, which proved to be full of potato peelings. Under Mr. Firkin's directions, she mixed these with a measure of corn. Then she opened the fowl-house door, letting loose a knee-deep flood of brown, white, and speckled poultry into the yard, and fed them by flinging out handfuls of the mixture until they were all busily pecking and the pan was empty. Meanwhile Mr. Firkin had finished milking and carried the two full pails back to his cottage.

Dido followed and found him there carefully wringing his beard into one of the pails.

"Now then, what's all this nabble about ol' Lady Tegleaze?" he said, putting a pan of water to boil over the fire. While he cut slices off a loaf and a side of bacon and laid them in a skillet, Dido told him about the accident: how Captain Hughes, wounded in the Chinese wars, had been coming home on sick leave, when his ship the *Thrush* had become involved in another battle, against the French this time, and had captured a French frigate.

"And we was taking a Dispatch to London about it all when this roust-up had to happen."

Mr. Firkin was deeply interested in her tale.

"Yon sick Cap'n's lying with a busted leg in the empty cottage? Eh, I'll take him a posset; that'll furbish him up."

He poured milk into another pan (not from the pail into which he had wrung his beard, Dido was relieved to notice), warmed it, added sugar, eggs, and a golden fluid from a leather bottle.

"What's yon, mister?"

"Dandelion wine, darter."

The posset was yellow and frothy and smelt wonderful—like a whole field of dandelions. Dido ran back along the yard, clambered by means of the wheelbarrow on to the cask and so to the roof, through the pigeon hole, down through the loft entrance, and was able to unbolt the cottage's front door just as Mr. Firkin arrived.

Captain Hughes was stirring again, more wakeful this time, and very glad of the posset.

"Puts me in mind of the Chinese lily soup we used to get in Poohoo province," he said. It soon made him drowsy, and he slept again.

"D'you think he looks all right, mister, or d'you reckon he's feverish?" Dido asked Mr. Firkin.

"Nay, I'm bline, darter, I can't see him! Mis' Lubbage'll be the one to tell ee how he'm faring."

"*Blind? You* are?" Dido was astonished. The old man's eyes were so bright, and he was so deft in everything he did, that it seemed as if he could see better than most.

"Blinded forty year agone, struck by lightning sitting under a snottygog tree on Barlton Down. Turble fierce thunderstorms we had when I were a lad."

"How ever did you know I was a girl?" Dido asked, thinking back.

"Why, my dog Toby told me, surelye! There bain't much as my dog Toby can't tell me." The shaggy Toby wagged his tail knowledgeably and thrust his head under his master's arm.

Dido was somewhat dashed to realize that she would still have to apply to Mrs. Lubbage for sick nursing.

"Anyhows, you don't want to rouse her yet awhile or she'll be sidy," Mr. Firkin said. "She be a late lier, owd Mis' Lubbage. Come ee back and eat a rasher o' my bacon, cardenly."

Since she would be next door and within earshot of the Captain, Dido accepted.

Mr. Firkin's bacon was delicious, and so was his homemade bread-and-butter, and so was his tea "that thunderin' strong ye could trot a mouldywarp on it." After breakfast Dido washed up for him, peeled potatoes for his dinner, and swept out his kitchen, which was the same size as that of Mrs. Lubbage but exquisitely neat. Then she chopped some firewood because Mr. Firkin told her that was the one job he was sure to make a boffle of. His woodshed contained a

[48]

large untidy pile of dry boughs and a small neat pile of kindling already chopped to the right size. Dido wondered who had done it.

"Mr. Firkin," she said, "if I wanted to get a letter taken to London, who'd I best ask? Is there a regular mail coach as goes by this way?"

"Once every two days Jem Hoadley takes mail so far as Petworth."

"Is he reliable? What happens to it there?"

"Nay, he's a bit shravey, Jem is; times folks's letters has gone no-one-wheres. And if the mail does get to Petworth, I dunnasay what comes to it there."

Dido resolved not to trust Captain Hughes's Dispatch to the shravey Jem until she had tried him out.

"D'you think Mrs. Lubbage'll be stirring by now? Maybe I'd best go and see her or she'll be offended?"

"Ah, she'm a taffety one," he agreed. "There's some as dassn't go anigh her, 'case she puts a mischief on 'em. Some reckons she's a wise 'ooman, others say she's downright a witch."

"What do you reckon, mister?"

"I ain't afeered o' the owd skaddle, however skrow she be. But then I wears mouldywarpses' toeses; she can't mischief *me*." He pulled out and showed Dido two moles' claws on a leather bootlace around his neck. "Powerful good agin the toothache they be and against the powers o' dark too. Tell ee what, darter, I'll give ee a pair; then ee 'on't come to no harm."

He picked another pair of feet from a wooden box full of very strong-smelling tobacco and threaded them on a string; Dido slung them around her neck and tucked them out of sight along with Captain Hughes's Dispatch.

Mr. Firkin and Toby then set off up the smooth steep grassy slope of the hill behind Dogkennel Cottages—which he had told her was called Barlton Down—to look after the sheep; Dido walked along to Mrs. Lubbage's cottage. Outside the door she paused with her hand upraised to knock. She could hear voices inside—or rather, one voice, very angry. It was Mrs. Lubbage.

"Show your face down here again between sunup and moonup and I'll give ee such a dose of hazel oil, ye 'on't be able to set down for a week. Hear what I say? Maybe that'll teach ee!"

There was a thud and a stifled cry.

"Now be off outa my sight," said Mrs. Lubbage's voice. There was no reply.

Dido knocked loudly on the door.

A long silence followed. Then Mrs. Lubbage—much closer to—said, "Who's that?"

"It's me, from next door," Dido called. "Come to ask you to take a look at the hurt man."

After another long wait the door opened a crack and Mrs. Lubbage's large red face peered suspiciously around it. The smell from her kitchen also came out through the crack; it seemed to have thickened and strengthened during the night.

"Oh, it's you, is it?" Mrs. Lubbage said, and opened

the door completely. Dido looked past her, but nobody else was there.

"Spose I better come along, and hob him up," the wise woman said in a surly tone. "I'll jest fetch my things."

She retired to rummage in a chest in her back room; no one else was there. But of course they might have gone out the back door. And there was a loft entrance similar to that in Dido's cottage; perhaps the other person was up there.

Dido felt sorry for anyone who lived with Mrs. Lubbage.

"Right, then, here I be," said the wise woman, emerging with a cloth bag. She glanced at Dido out of the corners of her sharp little eyes, and said, "Did ee hear me a-thumping my owd Tibbie jest now?"

"Maybe, missus," Dido said cautiously. "Why did you do that, then?"

"He be a turble owd thief, my Tib; he sucked up a pan o' milk while my back was turned, so I was a-larruping of him. He be my magico; helps me cast spells."

Dido made no reply to this, but opened the door to let Mrs. Lubbage into the Captain's sickroom. Mr. Firkin had run his fingers sensitively through a tray of oddments in his tool shed and found a pair of keys, one of which fitted the lock of her front door. She saw the sharp little eyes take note of the lock and the key.

It became plain at once that Mrs. Lubbage knew

quite a bit about nursing. She carefully removed the bandages, inspected the healing wound on the Captain's head, and dusted it with some powder from a small jar.

"What's that, missus?"

"Powdered sungreen, it be; wunnerful good for a healing cut. Now I'll put a handful o' cobwebs atop"— she did so—"and you leave them lay, and in tuthree days he'll be sprackish enough and through this liddle toss o' fever. If he gets fretful, soak these in water"— she passed Dido a handful of dried berries like raisins— "give him the water to drink, that'll ease him till he sweats."

"What are they?"

"Mortal quizzitive you be," Mrs. Lubbage said sourly. "Where *I* was reared, children kept their eyes open and their mouthses shut. Dried pethwine they be—if *that* learns you."

It did not, and Dido resolved to throw the berries away and give Captain Hughes nothing but the doctor's medicine. Mrs. Lubbage then inspected the broken leg, which she said was mending well and not inflamed.

"I'm obliged to you, missus," Dido said politely. "Can I dig your garden or do aught useful for you?"

"You can muck out my chicken house if ye've a mind to."

Dido was not enthusiastic about this task but at least it would be pleasanter than cleaning out Mrs. Lubbage's horrible kitchen. First making sure that the Captain was once more peacefully asleep and had a drink within easy reach if he were to wake, she locked him in. Whoever had searched their baggage might return for another look; besides, Dido did not trust the sly-eyed Mrs. Lubbage, good nurse or no.

Mr. Firkin's chickens had been plump, well-feathered, and lively; Mrs. Lubbage's were scrawny, mopey, and molting. You'd think a wise woman'd be able to take better care of her poultry, Dido thought, carrying baskets of shed feathers and dirty straw from the chicken coop to a pile of rubbish at the bottom of Mrs. Lubbage's muddy garden. While doing so, she observed a pony and trap trot briskly along the road and come to a halt in front of Dogkennel Cottages. Old Gusset, the butler, descended with a white-covered basket.

"Aha, there's the soup and jelly!" Dido stuck her pitchfork into a straw stack and started toward the butler, but before she reached him, Mrs. Lubbage opened her door and beckoned Gusset inside. He went after several doubtful and uneasy glances about him. The door closed. Dido, still a fair way off, then noticed another figure slip out from under the seat of the trap, look sharply around, and hurry off around the corner of the cottages.

The day was a misty, murky one; what Mr. Firkin called driply weather; but even through the damp rainy grayness this second caller, though bundled up like a chrysalis in draperies, had a familiar appearance.

"It's the funny old gal that Lady Tegleaze called Tante Sannie," Dido thought. "Why's she stealing a ride with the butler?"

In a moment Gusset appeared, looking glad to have completed his errand. He caught sight of Dido. Coming up, she noticed that he held a little carved wooden pistol, about the size of a radish, threaded on a leather thong. He pocketed it, saying in an embarrassed way, "'Tis a luck-charm," and pulled out a note, folded like a cocked hat, "I was to bring you this, Missie Twito Dide. And I've left some things for the sick gen'lman with Mrs. Lubbage. Good day to ee, missie."

He climbed back into the pony trap and drove off without apparently noticing that he had had a passenger on the ride down who was now missing.

Dido, not wishing to read her note where she could be seen from the windows, retired behind the hen house.

"Come up to the South Door after dark," she read, "follow the track, turn right at the top, across the tilting-yard, up the steps, along the terrace, through the lavender court, and I'll be waiting inside the door."

No signature—unless the smudge at the bottom was a T. And the writing was very untidy.

"Oh, that's naffy!" Dido thought. "Sposing I go all that way and nobody's there? Well, I'll wait and see what the weather's like, and how the Cap'n's fettling. Now, what about these here delicacies?"

She started back toward the cottages but before she reached them Mrs. Lubbage came out, wrapped in a man's coat and with a sack over her head. The shawled figure of Tante Sannie darted from behind a barn and joined her. The two talked together, then Mrs. Lubbage locked her door, and they set off side by side along the road away from Tegleaze Manor.

"Proper pair of old witches they be," thought Dido. "Right good company for each other. I'm not weeping millstones that old Madam Lubbage is out o' the road for a bit. But it's a cuss about the locked door."

Through the window the basket of provisions could be seen, very tantalizingly, on her kitchen table.

"What's the odds she'd never hand it over unless I ask for it? Oh well, let's have a wash and see what can be done."

The hen house being as clean as she could make it, Dido drew a pail of water from the rain butt, heated it over Mr. Firkin's fire, and had an enjoyable splash.

Then she re-entered her own cottage and climbed up into the loft.

As she had noticed before, the partition between one loft and the next was formed only of wattles. It was easy enough to push a way through this thin barrier.

But what was her surprise, when she started doing so, to hear, evidently from the loft over the empty cottage, a voice singing softly to itself in a strange little chant:

"Dwah, dwah, dwahdy dwahdy dwee
I can't see you but you can see me—
Canarack, stanarack, out of the blue
You can see me but I can't see you—"

Mystified, Dido parted two wattles and laid her eye against the partition.

Someone was sitting cross-legged in the shadows—someone about Dido's size, dark-haired, wearing ragged trousers and a shirt. That was all Dido had a chance to see, for she had made a slight noise pulling the withies apart; the singer turned a startled face toward her, sprang up, made a dart for a hole in the roof, and vanished through it. Dido heard a scrambling outside on the tiles and then a thud; evidently she was not the only one to use the water butt as an escape route.

"Drabbit it!" Dido exclaimed. "There's altogether too many mysteries around here. Now, what'd I best do—keep an eye on the Cap or go arter this here hop o' my thumb?"

Curiosity won. "The Cap'll come to no harm in ten minutes," she decided, scrambled out her own hole, and slid down the roof. As she did so she observed a small distant figure cross the field and take the chalk track that ran from Dogkennel Cottages between Barlton Down and the next big grassy hill. Almost at once the figure was out of sight in the mist, but Dido, hurrying to the chalk track, found a trail of new footprints in the white oozy mud.

"My stars," she thought, hearing no sound ahead, "whoever it is can't half cover the ground."

Luckily Dido herself was no mean runner; even so she began to wonder if she would ever catch up. The chalk road climbed steeply. High hedges on either side cut off the view. At the topmost point between the two hills, where the track started to descend, the footprints suddenly came to a stop. Dido, questing about, noticed a trail of scuffled leaves under some big beech trees to her left. She followed this clue, and came out from the trees into a wide, hammock-shaped grassy place; beyond it rose the big dome of Barlton Down. Far ahead Dido could see her quarry, running along a grass path that led around the side of the hill.

"Plague take the critter," Dido muttered, picking her way at top speed through damp knee-high tussocks of coarse downland grass. "At this rate we'll be halfway to London before I get any closer. Another five minutes and I give up!"

However once she reached the grass path, which was flat and smooth as a shelf, the pursuit was easier. On her right, the grassy slope ran steeply down into mist; a few big, dark-green bushy trees dotted the uphill slope to her left.

"All we want's a few candles and there'd be enough Christmas trees here for every soul in the country. Croopus, this is a funny sort o' place. There's so *much* of it; naught but trees and grass, and no people, and all tipped up like the side of a roof."

She was fairly out of breath, but the trail of foot-prints in the short, dewy grass of the path was easy to follow. As she ran soundlessly along the smooth turf she heard the voice again singing its queer little rune:

"Canarack, stanarack, out of the blue
    You can see me but I can't see you—"

"What does the silly perisher mean?" wondered Dido. "Dunno whether he can see me, but I sure as Sunday can't see *him.*"

The voice was close at hand, up the hill to her left; she stood still and then began cautiously climbing the steep slope through mist, which here was suddenly much thicker. After a moment or two the voice seemed to be straight ahead. Dido stood still again.

"There you are at last as well," the voice said in a conversational tone. "I couldn't come before; Auntie Daisy was beating me."

Silence for a moment. Dido moved another step or two. Where *was* the voice coming from?

"Why did she beat me? For coming out of the loft to get a bit of bread. It didn't matter as well—beating's not the worst."

Dido stopped once more. She had thought the voice was speaking to her; now she realized it was not. Who else was there, then? Who was answering? Where in the mist were they?

"I don't mind anything so long as I can talk to you as well."

As well? Dido thought. As well as what?

She took another step.

"*Dear* Aswell," said the voice. "I do love you."

Aswell?

Another silent step. Dido felt something tickle her nose: a gossamer-spangled sprig of yew. Peering ahead into the mist she saw that she was close to a small tree which stuck out at right angles from the steep hillside.

"canarack, Stanarack,
out of the blue
you can see me
but i can't see you"

It was a curious little stunted yew, not much more than twelve feet high; the foliage began about four feet above the ground, thick, bushy, and flattened as if the top had been chopped off, so that the tree resembled a finger with a round cake balanced on its tip. The cake was composed of close-set branches and twigs covered with dark-green yew needles and luminous red yew berries; while the finger—the trunk—was so twisted and knobbed and grooved that Dido could see it would be very easy to climb: just like walking upstairs. And the voice now came from directly above her.

"What have *you* been doing, Aswell?"

"This is getting too spooky," Dido thought. "I'm a-going up to find who's atop there."

Ducking, she edged under the branches and looked up the trunk, which was about as thick as a gatepost. The trunk turned sideways just above Dido's head, and three or four branches came out from it, like the spokes of a bent wheel. There was a gap in the greenery just big enough to climb through. Dido could see a pair of feet in very patched, broken boots, resting on one branch.

Still very silently, she set foot on the lowest knob, caught hold of two spoke branches, and with one rapid movement pulled and thrust herself up the sloping trunk, so that her head suddenly shot out through the central hole.

"*Oh!*" said the voice.

Dido found herself face to face—almost nose to nose —with the boy who had been in the loft.

[60]

"Blimey, he's thin!" was Dido's first thought. Then she looked around. They were sitting—it was impossible not to sit at once—in a kind of soup bowl of green yew needles—the foliage was so thickly massed that it held them like a cushion, with their feet in the middle, resting on the central spokes.

The boy would have bolted again, but Dido was in his way—he could not escape. Besides—

"*Please* don't skedaddle!" Dido said. "Croopus, I can do with a bit o' company in this wilderness! I'm lonesome! What d'you think I've bin a-chasing you for?"

The boy took a deep breath. It was plain that Dido's sudden appearance had frightened him badly—she could almost see his heart thumping under the thin torn shirt. He looked nice, though. He was amazingly dirty —smeared with grime, wet from the drizzle, wrapped in a filthy matted old sheepskin jacket. His dark hair was cut raggedly short and festooned with cobwebs, as if he spent most of his time in the loft. But he looked far, very far, from stupid.

"Who are you?" he brought out presently.

"I'm Dido Twite. I'm stopping in one o' those Dog-kennel Cottages with a hurt chap—Mrs. Lubbage is tending him."

"Please," said the boy earnestly, "*please* don't tell Mrs. Lubbage that you saw me!"

"*Course* I won't." Dido was affronted. "I ain't a blobtongue. What'd happen—would she beat you?"

"I don't mind being beaten. She does worse things than that."

[61]

He looked as if he would rather not discuss it. Dido asked instead,

"Is she your auntie Daisy?"

"Not really. All my family are dead. I used to live with another old woman in Suffolk—I think she was Auntie Daisy's cousin. She wasn't any kin of mine. Then she died—that was last year—and Auntie Daisy fetched me here. She said no one must ever find out I was living with her. I don't much like it here. It was better in Suffolk. Sometimes the rector used to teach me."

"Why mustn't anyone find out?"

"I don't know. Maybe she's not allowed to have children because she's a witch."

"Is she *really* a witch?" Dido asked.

"*She* thinks she is."

"Are you scared of her?"

The boy pondered, his gray eyes fixed on distance. "I'm more scared of the other one," he said at length.

"Which?"

"Her friend. Tante Sannie." He looked a little impatient—as if, Dido suddenly thought, he expected her to know all this already. She glanced around her at the bushy little dark-green tree, which could have held about two more people as well as themselves, but did not, and asked,

"Who were you a-talking to when I climbed up?"

He looked still more surprised. "I was talking to Aswell, of course."

"Who's Aswell?"

"My friend. Can't you hear him? He's talking now."

"No I can't," Dido said crossly. Was the boy touched in the upper works?

"No you can't," the boy agreed, after listening again. "Aswell says I'm the only one who can hear him."

"Where is he?" Dido asked rather disbelievingly.

The boy frowned, getting his thought into words. "In a way he seems to be here. Sometimes when we first start talking I can feel him—feel him put his hands between mine. But it's hard for him to do that—it only lasts a minute. *Really* he's thousands of miles away."

"Where—in the *sky?*"

"I suppose so. He'll come when I call. Not always but sometimes. And more often here in the Cuckoo Tree than back in the loft."

Dido was suddenly enlightened.

"You fetches him by singing that funny rhyme— canarack, stanarack?"

"Of course." He seemed as if he found Dido dreadfully slow-witted, and she felt a little forlorn.

"What's your name?" she asked.

"Cris."

"Well, Cris, why don't you run away from Auntie Daisy? Croopus, I would, if I had to live in the loft all the time."

"They'd find me," Cris said. "Even if Auntie Daisy couldn't, Tante Sannie would be sure to find me, wherever I went. And I couldn't bear that. She can do things." He shivered. "Besides, Aswell says it's better

[63]

if I stay. Aswell knows much more than I do. And I can help the old man—Mr. Firkin."

"Does he know you're there?"

"He doesn't *let* himself know—I expect he guesses Auntie Daisy would be angry," Cris said, thinking again. Dido suddenly realized that he was not at all *used* to having a conversation—it took him a minute to translate her questions into his thoughts and back again. "But I think he does know. He leaves food for me. And Toby knows, of course."

Dido nodded. "Don't you see *no* one else?"

Cris looked puzzled. "Who could I see? I'm supposed to stay in the loft while it's light. But Auntie Daisy's too fat to come up, so most days I come here."

"It's nice." Dido leaned back against a spicy, springy cushion of yew. "Reckon you could just about *live* in this tree. Can you eat the berries?"

"The red squashy part you can—but it's not very nice, it's sickly. The green seed in the middle is poisonous."

"Do cuckoos build their nests here?" asked ignorant Dido.

"Cuckoos don't build. They lay their eggs in other birds' nests."

"Then why's it called the Cuckoo Tree?"

Cris listened a minute.

"Aswell says it's always been called that—since Charles the First's time. Because it's such a funny shape."

At this moment the sun, which had been battling with the mist for the last ten minutes, suddenly burst through. The clouds lifted in a great spongy, steamy mass, melting skyward into the blue.

"Saints save us!" exclaimed Dido.

She had not realized how high up they were. Below the Cuckoo Tree the wooded hill shot steeply down for six hundred feet, and at its foot flat country began which stretched away—field after field, wood after wood—into the far blue distance. There were villages, churches, a town with a tall steeple, a pair of lakes not far off, reflecting the color of the sky. On either hand the downs rolled away, one behind the other, like green grassy waves. And the beech trees in the woods down below blazed red and gold in their autumn plumage.

"Where's London?"

"You can't see that from here—it's over fifty miles."

"Not that town there?" Dido was disappointed.

"No, that's Petworth."

The name reminded Dido of Captain Hughes and his Dispatch.

"I'd best be getting back," she said regretfully. "What about you?"

"I daren't come back now the mist's lifted. I'll have to wait till it's dark."

"Don't you get hungry?"

"Used to it. Maybe I'll find some blackberries or nuts left."

Dido felt in her pockets and discovered a couple of eggs which she had picked up in Auntie Daisy's hen house. One of the eggs had broken.

"Ugh!" She pulled out her fingers slimy and dripping. "Lucky the other one ain't bust. Sposing it's not addled, that is. You could build a little fire and roast it."

"Thanks." Cris took the egg. His thin, serious face broke into a smile which made Dido wonder if he had ever smiled before.

"My stars!" She suddenly remembered. "The doc's sposed to be coming at noon to look at my Cap'n. I'd best scarper. Tooralooral, Cris. See you in the loft, maybe."

Cris turned rather pale. "You'll be careful? If Auntie Daisy heard you up there—"

"Mum as a mouse in a mad cat's ear," Dido promised, and climbed nimbly backward down the trunk. It was like going down the companionway of a ship.

At the foot she noticed an odd thing: a corkscrew, which somebody had screwed several turns into the reddish, flaky bark. A small piece of green ribbon was tied to the handle.

"Daffy idea to leave a corkscrew in a tree trunk!" Dido thought. "No bottles hereabouts? Wonder why Cris has it there?"

It was not until she had started the steady jog trot back to Dogkennel Cottages that she remembered Yan, Tan, Tethera, and the rest. They too had been planning to come to the Cuckoo Tree. Could the corkscrew belong to them, rather than to Cris? And did Cris know about them?

She reached the top of the hill and started running down the slope toward the little row of cottages. Away

[66]

to her left she could see Mr. Firkin, with his dog Toby, sitting in the middle of a huge flock of sheep.

"Ask me," said Dido to herself, "Mr. Firkin and Toby are about the only two around here that ain't muxed up in some kind of havey-cavey business. Blight it, there comes old Sawbones Subito on his nag; I'd best hustle."

3

The doctor's verdict on his patient was favorable.

"Another two weeks," he declared, "and we shall have him *con moto, allegro assai!* It is a strong constitution, fortunately—*fortissimo!* Continue with the treatment along the lines I have laid down. The *signora* Lubbage—she has seen him?"

"Yes," said Dido, "she put these here cobwebs on him. She ain't home just now."

"Ah, that is good—I mean, that is good she has seen him. *Eccolo,* I will return on Friday," said Dr. Subito, and made off at top speed, casting wary glances along the road in either direction.

Captain Hughes was wakeful, after the doctor's inspection, and somewhat fretful.

"I could eat a sturgeon, bones and all," he announced, and Dido glanced around the bare little room.

"We're clean out of prog, Cap," she said. "Wait a couple o' minutes and I'll see what I can fetch in."

Mr. Firkin still sat out in the hillside with his sheep, a couple of miles away, but the basket from Tegleaze Manor was close at hand, temptingly in view through Mrs. Lubbage's kitchen window.

"I spose she did lock the door?" Dido said to herself.

She walked along to the witch's cottage carrying Captain Hughes's clasp knife, with which she thought it would be easy enough to force the door. She tried it to make certain: yes, locked. Just as she was about to insert the knife blade between door and doorpost she experienced a curious prickling sensation in her hands; at the same time a small buzzing voice—where? inside her head perhaps—said, faintly but audibly,

"This is a hoodoo lock. Beware. Do not touch it."

"Eh?" Dido looked sharply behind her. Nobody was there. "Have I got a screw loose?" she wondered, and approached the knife blade to the crack once more.

Again she heard the voice, distant but distinct, impossible to locate, like the drone of a loud mosquito:

"This is a hoodoo lock. Beware. Do not touch it."

"Rabbit me!" Dido, thoroughly discomposed and uneasy, stepped back, eying the door as if it might fly open and thump her. "This is a right mirksy set-out! Talking doors—I spose when I goes to lay hands on the basket of grub it'll get up and walk away! Well, the old crone may have hoodoo'd her front door, but I'll lay she didn't think to set one o' her spooky booby traps in the attic—blow me if I don't fetch the vittles out that way just to serve her right for her nasty suspicious nature."

Somewhat to the surprise of the Captain she returned to his room, piled up their luggage, and climbed into the loft. Then she made her way along through the series of lofts until she reached that of Mrs. Lubbage, whose trap door was open. Jamming a broomstick across the hole, Dido tied a length of cord to it, and slid down.

Mrs. Lubbage's kitchen smelt even worse with the door shut; the smell was like a solid, threatening presence in the room.

Just our luck if it's turned the grub sour, Dido thought, moving carefully and warily across the greasy bricks toward the table on which stood the hamper of provisions. A label on the handle reinforced her courage: it said in large clear print:

FOR THE SICK GENTLEMAN
AT DOGKENNEL COTTAGES

Bet we wouldn't a-seen a crumb of it if I hadn't come to fetch it, Dido thought, grasping the handle. Next moment, with a startled gasp, she almost dropped the whole supply on the bricks for, sitting on the table close by and revealed when she picked the basket up, was the largest rat she had ever seen, brindled, with a tail that must have been fully two feet long. It did not scurry away, as an ordinary rat would have done, but turned its head slowly and gave her a steady look; Dido felt a cold sensation between her shoulder-blades.

However she returned the look boldly.

"*You*'ll know me again, Frederick, that's for sure," she said to it. "And I just hope you've kept your long whiskery nose out o' the Cap'n's cheese. Now, how'm I going to get yon basket up the rope?"

She solved this problem by attaching the basket to the end of the rope and pulling it up after her; watched, meanwhile, by the rat, "as if," thought Dido, "he was learning how so he could do it himself next time."

The rat was not the only creature that seemed to be watching her; she noticed, in a corner of Mrs. Lubbage's kitchen, a small carved wooden table exactly like the one she had seen at Tegleaze Manor, with little black faces and white-painted eyes that seemed to follow her.

"If I never go back into that boggarty place again it'll be soon enough," she thought, scrambling back into her own loft; "blest if I know how Cris can stand *living* there. No wonder he seems a bit out o' the common.

"Anyways, we got the grub."

She lowered it down into Captain Hughes's sick-room, jumped down herself, and unpacked the hamper with exclamations of satisfaction.

"Bread—butter—cold roast chicken—flask o' soup—cheese—red currant jelly—grapes—oranges—and a bottle o' wine. Couldn't a done you better if you'd been Admiral o' the Fleet," she told the Captain, and proceeded to heat up some of the soup for him and toast some of the bread.

"I've poured in a dram o' wine as well, so it's right stingo stuff," she said, giving him a bowlful. She herself ate an orange and a leg of chicken to hearten her for the scene which she felt certain must follow Mrs. Lubbage's return and discovery that the basket was missing.

Sure enough, at about sunset there was a tremendous thump on the door.

"Hush! You'll wake the Cap'n!" Dido hissed, opening it.

Outside stood Mrs. Lubbage, brawny arms akimbo, little black eyes snapping with rage.

"Evening, missus," Dido greeted her politely, slipping out and closing the door. "Guess you was wanting to ask about the basket o' prog Lady Tegleaze sent down for us. Cap'n Hughes was fair clemmed wi' hunger, and you hadn't left word when you'd be back, so I jist nipped along and helped myself—hope that was all hunky-dory."

The witch stared at her for a moment, started to say something, and then changed her mind.

"How did you get in?" she asked at length, in a surly tone.

Dido could not mention the loft, because of Cris, so she opened her eyes wide and innocently replied,

"Why, how d'you think? Down the chimbley?"

Mrs. Lubbage seemed annoyed but baffled by this answer and was about to ask another question; luckily at that moment a distant bleating, which had been drawing closer, became so loud that no further conversation was possible; Mr. Firkin had arrived home with his flock. Mrs. Lubbage stumped off angrily to her own cottage; Dido ran to help Mr. Firkin and Toby persuade the sheep to file through a gap between two hurdles and so into the pasture at the rear of the farmyard.

As they passed through the gap, Mr. Firkin touched each sheep with his white crook, and Dido could hear him counting,

"Yan, Tan, Tethera, Methera, Pip—"

Each time he came to *Den* he moved his hand down the crook, which had notches in it.

"Mr. Firkin," said Dido, when the sheep were all safe in the field, and she was scrubbing potatoes in the old man's kitchen, and setting them to bake among the glowing logs in his fireplace.

"Yes, darter?"

"What was that you were saying when you counted the sheep?"

"I was a-counting of them, darter."

"Yes, but what were those words—Yan, Tan, Tethera—"

"That be ship-counting lingo. Lingo for counting ship," Mr. Firkin explained kindly.

"Oh, cranberries! We're a-going round like a merry-go-round! Well, suppose I was to meet some chaps as called 'emselves Yan, Tan, and so forth; I'm not saying I *did,* but suppose I was to—"

Mr. Firkin's old brown face took on a cautious expression.

"Nay, I'd say let well alone, darter. Mebbe 'tis all talk but I've heard tell as how there be folk called Wineberry Men as 'tis best not to meddle with."

"Smugglers, maybe?"

"Hush! Nay, more like kind o' civil service gentry," Mr. Firkin said hastily. "Best not to talk about 'em, darter. Wallses do have earses."

Deciding that the Wineberry Men almost certainly were smugglers, Dido returned to Captain Hughes and found him wakeful and fidgety.

"What about our Dispatch?" he demanded. "Do you have it safe, child?"

"Yes, yes, Cap'n. All rug. Right here." Dido tapped her chest, which crackled reassuringly.

"We must get it to London somehow," the Captain fretted. "What day is it today?"

"Fust o' November, Cap. All Saints' Day."

"And the coronation next week! It is desperately important that the Dispatch should reach the First Lord before then."

"Doc says you mustn't be moved afore two weeks," Dido pointed out.

"Then we must find a reliable messenger."

Dido bit her thumb. "I knows that," she said gloomily. "But trying to find a reliable cove in these parts is about as likely as picking up a pink pearl in Piccadilly. Everyone's up to the neck in summat. There's a carrier called Jem; today's his day to call, seemingly; but Mr. Firkin says he's shravey. Best not give him the Dispatch. What I thought I might do, Cap, if you're agreeable, is send a note by Jem to a cove I knows in London asking him to step down and help us."

"Is your friend reliable?" the Captain asked, pressing a hand to his aching head.

"Sure as a gun, he is!"

Since Captain Hughes, who was beginning to feel weak and feverish again, could think of no better plan, he agreed to this.

Dido sat down to the unaccustomed task of writing a letter. Borrowing the Captain's traveling inkhorn and quill, using a bit of paper the cheese had been wrapped in, she wrote:

"Dere Simon. I doo hop yore stil alive. I am all rug— wuz piked up by wailing ship an hadd Grate Times abord her. Brung home in Man o' War like Roilty. Wil tel more wen I see yoo. I do hop yore stil alive. Iff yoo can pleez cum hear wear I am stuk at preznt or send relleye relible cove. I badly need sum wun. I doo hop yore stil alive. Lots ov luv. Dido."

She folded it and addressed it: "Simon as used to livv in Rose Alley, Care of Doc Furniss, The art Skool, Chellsey, London."

She had scarcely finished this when voices were heard outside, there came a knock on the door, and Mr. Firkin ushered in a lank, greasy-haired individual in a moleskin cap and gaiters.

"This yer's Jem Mugridge, as'll take your letter to Perroth, darter."

One glance at him was enough to make Dido thankful she had not planned to entrust Captain Hughes's Dispatch to the shravey Jem; he looked about as reliable as a stoat.

"That'll be five-and-a-tanner," he said, receiving the letter, his little pink-rimmed eyes meanwhile darting into every corner of the room.

Dido was fairly sure that a letter to London should not cost so much, but Captain Hughes counted five shillings and sixpence out of a purse which he brought from under his pillow, Jem's eyes following every movement and every coin.

"I thankee sir and missie. That'll be in Pet'orth by breakfast time."

"So I should hope, if Petworth is but five miles distant," the Captain remarked testily.

When Jem had departed on his flea-bitten mare, Dido asked the Captain if he would have any objection to her stepping up the road to Tegleaze Manor.

"There's a cove there as asked to see me, and it seems only civil to go, seeing they sent us the basket o' prog. Mebbe I'll find someone as we can trust there; you never can tell."

Captain Hughes agreed to this; but since he seemed rather low-spirited at the prospect of being left alone, Mr. Firkin was easily persuaded to come and keep him company. Mr. Firkin's brother, it turned out, had been a seafaring man and a great singer; the two men were soon absorbed in discussing sea shanties and comparing tunes. Leaving them to it, Dido slipped off.

As she left the cottage some animal scuttled away, quick and quiet, along the wall. It might have been a rabbit or a large rat.

"I'll be glad when we can shift out o' this hurrah's nest," she thought with a shiver. "You gets the notion someone's everlastingly a-peering over your shoulder."

However, nothing else seemed to be stirring in the cold, moonshiny night. She walked up the beech avenue toward the Manor, turned right at the top as instructed, and found herself on the edge of an enormous sunk lawn.

"Guess this must be the tilting-yard," Dido thought. "The sides is tilted, anyhows; it's like a dripping pan." She scrambled down the steep grassy slope and walked across turf that was silver with icy dew. Black yew trees, once clipped to resemble giant pineapples, but, from neglect, grown into many strange shapes, were placed about the lawn in pairs, like sentries. Dido slipped from one pair of shadows to the next and ran softly up a flight of steps toward the house. She passed along a terrace above the lawn, through a wicket gate, through a small walled garden, and so came to a side door, half hidden under a great vine. While she was wondering whether to knock, the door opened.

"Hallo! I saw you come up the steps. Make haste—after me. Isn't this capital!" breathed Sir Tobit. Dido felt her hand taken; she was pulled into the dark; the door shut quietly behind her. She allowed herself to be led up a narrow flight of stairs, along a passage, and so presently found herself in the room where she had been before. It was just as dusty and untidy as it had been on the previous evening.

"Now we can talk," said Sir Tobit, throwing himself comfortably in a chair. "Grandmother is in bed with one of her headaches, so she won't trouble us."

"Talk, what about?"

"You can tell me your adventures. I've read all my books. So the only way I can amuse myself now is to make up stories—and that's very boring because I know what the end is going to be. Well, go on—begin!"

Dido was not eager. However she felt some sympathy for Sir Tobit's solitude and boredom, so she obliged with a brief account of how she had been shipwrecked, picked up by a whaler and carried to Nantucket, and brought home by his majesty's sloop *Thrush*.

"And I must let someone in London know that Cap'n Hughes is stuck here with a broken gam," she finished. "I've sent a letter to a pal o' mine, but I don't trust that carrier Jem above half; is there any reliable cove you can suggest?"

"There aren't many men left on the estate," Tobit said. "We're so poor, everyone has left, except Frill and Pelmett, and I wouldn't trust *them*."

"Poor? In a place this size?" Dido was surprised.

"You see, Grandmother has a great fondness for betting on the horses. When she was a girl she loved riding; then she was thrown and broke her leg. So now as she can't ride, she bets instead; since I've been living

here I believe she has gambled away, oh, hundreds of
thousands of pounds. Yesterday she gave FitzPickwick
her last diamond ring to sell. That's why I have to wear
these clothes; we can't afford to buy new ones. But
luckily there are lots of old ones about the house."

"How long *have* you lived here, then?"

"Oh, ever since I was a baby. I was born in the
West Indies, on Tiburon Island; we have—used to have
—estates there. Papa and Mamma lived there, but they
were killed in a hurricane, so Tante Sannie brought
me here. I don't remember that. Sannie didn't know
what it would be like here; she's homesick, but there
isn't enough money to send her back." He spoke in-
differently, but Dido felt that, since he was lonely himself, he ought to have more sympathy for the old
woman's plight, stuck here in this great dusty cold
house, so far from her own warm island.

"I'd better be getting back." She prowled restlessly
about the untidy, shadowy room. "Is that you?"

A picture on the wall showed three children, dressed
in clothes such as Tobit wore. The boy in the middle,
holding hands of the other two, who stood slightly behind him, might have been Tobit at a younger age.

"No, that's three ancestors—two brothers and a sister
who lived in Charles the First's time. They were triplets—all the same age."

"It'd be grand to be a triplet—you'd never be lonely
then," Dido said, studying them with some envy. "What
happened to them?"

"They quarreled," Tobit said coolly. "One fought on

the king's side, one on Cromwell's, and the third one went overseas and vanished. The other two lost all their money in the Civil War, so ever since then triplets have been thought unlucky in our family."

"Have there been many more?"

"No, none; but we've had bad luck just the same. . . . Come along; I'll show you Cousin Wilfred's dolls' house."

He pulled the reluctant Dido—croopus, dolls' houses at his age! she thought—out of the room, along passages and downstairs into the main hall—empty tonight; and through an open door into a small room at one side of it.

"Come on—old Wilfred isn't here, he's playing tiddly-winks with Sawbones Subito. Look—isn't it queer!"

Cousin Wilfred's room was as shabby as Tobit's, but in a different way. The furniture here was old, and had once been handsome, but was now falling to bits: the wood was worm-eaten, the satin upholstery faded and torn. Only the dolls' house looked well-cared-for. It was a faithful copy of Tegleaze Manor, beautifully made, furnished to the last detail with curtains, carpets, plates on the tables, pictures on the walls, even a carriage in the stables. There were no dolls, but tiny suits of clothes like Tobit's hung in the closets.

"He made it all himself, from old prints of the house as it used to be," Tobit said, carelessly throwing open the front.

"Even the pictures?"

These were oval miniatures, carefully framed, no bigger than postage stamps.

"No, those are real. Some ancestor collected them.

[80]

Some of them were quite valuable, but Grandmother sold those—all except one, which isn't here. She'd like to sell *that*, but it belongs to me—or will when I come of age."

"When's that?"

"Next week—on my fourteenth birthday."

"Where's the picture now?"

"At the lawyers'—they don't trust her. Come on." Tobit was restless—nothing seemed to interest him for long. He moved to the window. Dido took a last look at the nursery with its three white-spread beds, box of tiny toys, hoop leaning against the wall, and dappled rocking-horse which might just have stopped swaying, as if three children had rushed out of the room, slammed the door, and gone their different ways.

"Hey!" whispered Tobit. "Look!"

He beckoned Dido to the window. They were looking out on the moonlit tilting-yard. Two figures paced across it and vanished into the shade of a pair of yew trees.

"It's old FitzPickwick—wonder what *he's* doing here at this time of night. And who that is he's talking to. Tell you what—let's go out and stalk 'em, that'd be famous fun. Wait, have I got my peashooter on me?"

Tobit rummaged in his black velvet pockets.

"I druther have a word with your butler—is he any-wheres about?" Dido said, impatient at the prospect of such a childish sport.

"*Gusset?* Why? Anyhow, you can't, it's his evening off; he goes to see his son. Ah, two shooters and lots of peas. Here, have one." He thrust a slender pipe into her hand and poured into the pocket of her duffel jacket what felt like about a pound of heavy little dry objects.

"Ain't we a bit old for sich goings-on?"

"What else is there to do in this moldering barracks—except make up stories? I'm a dead shot," he boasted. "With a sling I can hit a hare at a hundred yards. Only there aren't any hares. Oh, *do* come along."

"What's that?" Dido asked, as they passed a large chart on the wall.

"Family tree—all the way back to the Saxons." He pulled her along yet another dark passage.

"Who's old FitzPickwick?"

"Our bailiff—he's a toffee-nosed sort of fellow. It's my belief he's feathered his nest handsomely out of Tegleaze Manor," Tobit said, sounding all of a sudden surprisingly shrewd. "He sells Grandmother's jewelry for her, and places her bets."

"Doesn't give her very good advice, if she always loses."

"Hush!"

They had come out into a brick-paved stable-yard, like that of the dolls' house. A gate and a flagged path brought them back to the terrace overlooking the tilting-yard.

"When Jamie Three had *his* coronation," Tobit muttered discontentedly, leading Dido down the steps and along in the shadow of the high yew hedge that bordered the lawn, "Granny and Grandpa had a pageant here, with champagne and roast peacock for all the tenants. But now there are hardly any tenants, and no

[82]

cash—not even enough for me to go up to London to *see* the coronation."

"Would your gran let you?" Dido asked. "I thought she was so set agin your going out in case you catch summat nasty?"

"Oh, she won't care what happens to me once I come of age—and my birthday's before the coronation—I'm fourteen on Monday, the coronation's on Wednesday, I daresay you didn't know, just home from sea? Old Jamie Three died, and now it's going to be his son. He's always been called Prince Davie but he's going to be Richard the Fourth. And there's going to be fireworks on Ludgate Hill, and oxes roasted in Stuart Square, and processions, and all sorts of high jinks—don't I just wish I was going."

Mention of the coronation reminded Dido of her own worries. "If Gusset isn't here I guess *I'll* be going, back to Dogkennel," she said. "Please to thank your gran for the prog."

"The what?"

"The grub—the basket o' vittles."

"Oh, *she* won't have sent anything—far too mean. No, if some food came, I daresay Gusset sent it. Hush—there they are!"

He dragged Dido into an alcove in the yew hedge, where they lurked in the shadow.

Low voices gradually became audible as the two men paced across the immense lawn.

"Oh, *I* won't expose your little g-games—don't think it, my dear f-fellow. It's n-nothing to *me,* believe me,

[83]

if you've pocketed a rent roll as long as the M-Mississippi River. Money is of s-small interest to me."

The speaker's voice had a curiously deep, grating quality, broken by his occasional stammer.

"What is, then?"

"That's old Colonel FitzP," whispered Tobit in Dido's ear. "But I'm blest if I know who the other one is."

"The name! The place! You d-don't understand what it means—when one has s-spent all one's life in a lumber camp as n-nobody—Miles Tuggles—pah! To change that I'd commit any c- any crime. As to your peccadilloes—what's the old lady to me? Or the b-brat either? I give you my word, my research into your d-dealings was solely to effect an introduction so that we could meet on equal t-terms—"

"I wonder?" Colonel FitzPickwick's soft mutter was overheard only by the two eavesdroppers.

"But harkee now," the first man went on. "I hold you in a cleft stick. I know so much, I promise you I could c-cook your goose with six words, dropped in the right quarter. S-so it is in your interest to help me. I n-need a pretext for remaining in the neighborhood—"

The two men moved away. The word "puppets" was all that Dido could catch of the next remark.

"Puppets!" muttered Tobit discontentedly. "Old Fitz-Pickwick's mad about puppets; they're his hobby. He's always boring on about them."

"—be a first-rate cover," FitzPickwick was saying, when the two men next strolled in the direction of the watchers.

"That will do. Now tell me the rest—you have n-no choice. This Godwit you mention—"

They turned and paced away again.

"Let's go after them!" breathed Tobit, and tweaked Dido's hand; the two listeners slipped from their hiding place and crossed to the shadow of a pair of yews.

"—rollers," they heard Colonel FitzPickwick say. "They are fixed already. And the diamond will pay for half. But the rest of the money—" The two men passed behind a tree and their words were lost. "—still to come," the Colonel was saying when they reappeared. "If Lady Tegleaze—" another pair of trees cut off his words—"certain His Highness Prince George would lend a favorable ear to your claim."

"Rot it, so I should hope! But as to these rollers—"

the stammering man was beginning, when Dido heard a soft hiss beside her, a phtt! and Colonel FitzPickwick raised a hand to his cheek.

"Strange! I could have sworn I felt a hailstone. Yet there's not a cloud in the sky."

"Oh, famous!" Tobit breathed in Dido's ear. "I got him fair and square."

" 'Twas a m-mosquito, I daresay. Rollers, now: rollers are all very fine. But where's your motive power?"

"A mosquito? You forget you are in England in November, my dear sir. If the weather's breaking I must be off. My mare's a thoroughbred—she has an aversion to hail."

"You shoot now!" whispered Tobit. "Go on—I dare you!"

"I druther listen," Dido muttered crossly. "Hush! I've a notion—"

"Motive power yet remains to be found. Godwit thinks a system of levers. Now, if humans were as easily moved as my mannikins—Devil take it! That was certainly a hailstone. It hit me on the ear."

Tobit was suffocating with suppressed laughter.

"Got the old windbag again. Him and his mannikins!"

Colonel FitzPickwick turned and walked off decisively, his companion following with reluctance, turning back for many glances at the house.

The shadows of the two men followed them like long black-velvet trains.

"Now we ain't sure what it was all about," Dido complained when they were out of earshot.

"Oh, pho, what does it matter? Just old Pickwick's usual hocus-pocus about puppets."

"But it seemed to be about your grandmother and this place."

"What do I care about this place? As soon as I'm of age I shall run off to sea and turn pirate. Yo, ho, ho, and the jolly black flag," said Sir Tobit, and aimed a broadside of peas into the yew tree. "Come on, we'll spy on old Wilfred and the sawbones." He tugged Dido at a run along the yew hedge, up the steps, and around the end of the house. They looked through a window into a small room where, by the light of one dim candle, two men were crouched over a tiddlywinks board. Dido recognized the doctor; the other was a little tiny gray-haired old fellow like a water rat in a velvet robe and nightcap.

"Pity the window's shut," Tobit muttered. "I'd like to give old Wilfred a fright, in return for all the games of tiddlywinks he's bored me with. D'you dare me to break the window?"

"O' course not! What a mutton-headed notion."

Dido, becoming more and more impatient, was about to take her leave, when a sudden fierce whisper from behind startled them both.

"Bad, bad boy! What you doing, what you about?"

Like a black, angry dragonfly the tiny figure of Tante Sannie darted from a patch of shadow, hissing reproaches at Tobit.

"You not allowed out after darkfall, you know that!

Spose a memory bird hear you, spose the Night Lady catch you in her claws?"

"Oh, stuff. Don't talk such nonsense, Sannie," Tobit said, but he glanced behind him uneasily, then put a couple of peas in his mouth. "Anyway, I'll be of age next week and can do as I please!"

"Also, who is *this?*" Sannie peered up at Dido. Over the black-and-white draperies muffling the lower part of the old woman's face, her tiny eyes glittered like the points of nails. "Hah! I know you! You little bad sickness girl, Sir Tobit not allowed to play with you. Lady Tegleaze be very angry when she hear."

"We weren't playing," Sir Tobit said sulkily. "I was showing her the grounds by moonlight."

"Don't you false-talk me, boy! What this?" Sannie twitched the peashooter from his hand. "Ho! You be of age next week, be you? You got no more sense than baby picknie. Out after darkfall, shooting Joobie nuts! Spose hit somebody in him eye, sent to prison? Then you never come of age, you know that!"

"Oh, fiddle. Nobody gets sent to prison for shooting with a peashooter. I shall shoot as many as I like." Rebelliously he snatched back the tube and blew a pea at the window. It bounced off the glass with an audible ping, but the two men inside, absorbed in their game, never even lifted their heads.

"Oh, so brave little feller!" Sannie's tone became silky as syrup. "So brave to shoot Joobie nuts. But don't you dare swallow nut!"

"I'll do that too, if I want!" He swallowed the two

nuts he was sucking, eying the old woman with defiance. But almost at once a curious change came over his face. He glanced behind him again, twice, and gave a violent shiver.

"Is cold, my little thingling? Is hearing some noise in bushes, memory bird, maybe?"

Tobit shivered again, glancing about with dread.

"Come along then, come in quick before the Night Lady fly over. Come along, little thingling. Old Sannie make you cup of thistle tea."

She took his hand and led him off; Tobit followed meekly.

"Croopus!" muttered Dido, when they were out of sight.

She was so startled by the change in Tobit that she remained where she was for several minutes, pondering. "It was those peas—Joobie nuts, or whatever she called them. What the blazes can they be?"

She pulled a handful of the heavy little dry things from her duffel pocket and eyed them suspiciously. In the moonlight they looked gray, wrinkled, harmless enough; about the size of nasturtium seeds; they felt faintly gritty, as if they had been dusted with salt. Warily Dido tried one with the tip of her tongue. It did taste salty. She spat, and glanced behind her, suddenly overcome with an almost irresistible urge to duck: it seemed as if she could hear the whizz of giant wings overhead. Out of the corner of her eye she thought she saw a huge shadow flit over the moonlit grass. But when she turned and looked there was nothing.

"Shiver my timbers!" She stared again at the peas in her hand; was about to throw them on the ground; but in the end, tipped them back into her pocket and ran fast and quietly away from the house. Suddenly the night seemed full of noises: a cold, liquid call, some bird maybe; a soft drumming tick; a rattle—or was it a chuckle?—coming from the yew hedge. Dido darted across the tilting-lawn, where the pairs of yew trees seemed to be shifting just a little, changing their positions after she passed them; she did not look back but had the notion that they were moving together behind her, perhaps coming after her, as in the game Grandmother's Footsteps.

"Rabbit me if I ever taste another o' them perishing Joobie nuts," Dido muttered. "No wonder Tobit and his granny both seem a bit totty-headed, if they keep a-chawing o' the nasty little things."

Ahead of her now lay the beech avenue, with its bands of moonlight and shade. She felt some reluctance to go down it, but shook herself angrily and ran on at top speed. Then, coming toward her, she saw a black figure. It seemed to vary in size—wavered—grew tall—shrank again.

Dido gulped.

"This here's nothing but a load o' foolishness," she told herself, and went on firmly. The figure seemed now to have no head and three legs. But of course when she came closer she saw that it was merely old Gusset, hobbling back from his evening off, wearing a sack over his head, helping himself along with a stick.

[90]

"Hey there, Mister Gusset!" Dido greeted him warmly when they were within speaking distance. "I'm tickled I didn't miss you—wanted to say thanks again for the basket o' vittles—Tobit said as how likely you'd sent 'em your own self."

"Oh, no trouble, missie." The butler seemed embarrassed. "Glad to do it for the poor sick gennleman— I heeard tell as how he's a naval captain? And you've been a-visiting Mas'r Tobit, have you, missie? That's good, that is—he can do with a bit o' young company."

"That he can," Dido agreed. "Ask me, he has his head in the clouds most o' the time, he's got some right cork-brained notions. And that old witch as sees arter him—Sannie or whatever she calls herself—it's a plaguy shame she couldn't be shipped back to Thingummy Island, her and her Joobie nuts."

Gusset glanced around him warily. "You're right there, missie," he said, sinking his voice.

"What are those Joobie nuts, anyways?"

"Summat she brought with her from Tiburon, Missie Twido. She grows 'em from seed, up where the old asparagus bed used to be. She allus has a plenty of 'em. Don't you go a-swallowing they hampery things, missie— they'll give you the hot chills, don't they give you wuss."

"What happens when Tobit comes of age next week?"

"Why, nothing much, missie. I reckon things'll goo on pretty much as usual."

"He doesn't come into any cash, so's he could go off to school?"

"No, missie. Only the heirloom."

"What's the heirloom?" Gusset had spoken as if everyone would know of it.

"It be a liddle painting, Missie Dwite. Only small, smaller than the palm of your liddle hand, but it be painted on ivory, and I've heeard tell as it be worth thousands and thousands—enough to put everything to rights round here."

"Fancy! What's it of?" Dido asked curiously.

"'Tis a picture o' the Tower of Babel, missie. 'Tis painted by a famous painter, I've heeard tell. Anybody can see it—they keeps it at Perrorth, at the lawyers', a-set in a glass case in the wall."

Mention of Petworth recalled Dido to her own problems.

"Mister Gusset, I've got to get a message to London, urgent. How can I send it? I gave a letter to that Jem, but he don't look reliable to me."

"Jem Mugridge, missie? No, he ain't noways reliable."

"Well, then, what'd I best do? The message has to get to London before the—before the end o' next week."

"Best to goo yourself, missie."

"But I didn't oughta leave Cap'n Hughes while he's sick."

Gusset pushed back the sack in order to scratch his white head. He reflected.

"Well, missie," he said at length. "There's some chaps I know as gooes up and down to London regular. Trading chaps they be. Some mightn't say as how they was reliable, but I speak as I find, and I've allus found 'em trustable."

"D'you reckon they'd help me, mister?"

"I'd hatta ask," Gusset said cautiously. "I couldn't promise, see?"

"When will you see them?"

Gusset seemed unwilling to commit himself, but said he'd see them by Friday, maybe, and would try to let Dido know on that day.

"Now I'd best be getting in, missie. 'Tis turble late."

"Good night, then, Mister Gusset, and thanks."

The old man hobbled off, and Dido ran on down the avenue toward Dogkennel Cottages. Her talk with Gusset had cheered her and the queer visions and sounds that had troubled her before seemed to have died away; she whistled as she ran, and jumped over patches of shadow in the chalk cartway. But just this side of the cottages she came to an abrupt stop. Something—*surely* it was a dragon?—lay on the weedy grass in front of the little row of houses. Its eyes glittered. When it saw Dido it stretched slightly, and spread out its wings.

Dido bit her thumb, hard. Then she stooped, picked up a sizable chunk of flint from the track, and hurled it at the monster, which broke into about seven different sections. Three of them were sheep, which trotted nervously away. Two or three more were chickens, flapping and flustered. One, which might have been a rat, scurried into the shadow of Mrs. Lubbage's cottage.

Mrs. Lubbage herself was sitting by her door on a

broken-backed chair, gazing, apparently, into a pail of water.

"Evening, missus," Dido said civilly as she passed. The wise woman lifted her head and gave Dido a long, expressionless stare. But she said nothing.

"Utchy old besom," Dido thought, taking her key from under a stone, where Mr. Firkin had left it. "Anyone can tell as manners weren't thought much of where *you* was reared!"

Rather more clumsily than usual, she fitted the key into the lock.

And all the time, as she turned it, opened the door, and let herself in, she could feel Mrs. Lubbage's malevolent stare boring into her shoulder blades.

4

"Consarn it!" exclaimed Dido, as the bucket of chicken food slipped out of her hand, falling heavily on her toe.

"What's to do, darter?" mildly inquired old Mr. Firkin, coming out of the cowshed with his two pails of milk.

"I dunno why it is—my fingers is all thumbs today. I spilt a bowl o' hot water on the Cap'n's bed, and I dropped our breakfast eggs in the fire, and hit my thumb with a hammer when I was a-fixing the leaky window, and caught the other one in the rat trap you lent me, and broke my tortoise-shell comb that a friend in Ameriky gave me, and now I've bin and dropped the hens' grub all over my feet—not that the hens care."

Dido was standing in a sea of chickens, who were vigorously pecking her toes and ankles.

"My hands feel greasy all the time," she grumbled. "I wash and wash, and it don't right 'em."

"Sounds to me like Mrs. Lubbage overlooked ye,"
Mr. Firkin said gravely. "Have ye got on the mouldywarpses' clawses?"

Dido clapped a hand to her neck and remembered
that she had taken off Mr. Firkin's protective charm
when she went to bed.

"My stars! Do you really think—"

But she remembered the wise woman's long, angry
stare as she sat before her door in the moonlight.

"I'll fetch those claws right away," Dido declared,
and did so, before sitting down to breakfast with Mr.
Firkin. And whether it was because the claws gave her
more confidence, or really had power against bad wishes,
her run of ill luck seemed to have ended for the time;
she gave the Captain his breakfast, made up his bed, and
had the satisfaction of hearing him say that he felt
somewhat better and thought his leg was mending.

"I fancy that by tomorrow or the next day I could
walk with a crutch, if one could be procured," he said.

Mr. Firkin, when asked, said he could fettle one up,
but it would take him two-three days. Or there was a
chap in Petworth, Godwit by name, who generally had
one or two crutches and such gear in his shop.

"The lame gray coach horse is a-mending, too," Dido
said. "Reckon if the doc agrees it's all rug for Cap'n
Hughes to walk a bit, I could ride in to Petworth,
tomorrow maybe, and see what this Godwit has in
stock." Godwit, she thought; I heard that name somewheres just lately; where was it now?

Dr. Subito did not come that day, however, and meanwhile the Captain, really not as strong as he made out, was glad enough to lie and doze, wake for a short time, eat or drink a little of the invalid fare provided by Gusset, and sleep again.

During the afternoon, when the invalid was in a sound slumber and seemed likely to remain so for some time, Dido, first carefully locking him in, slipped away to the Cuckoo Tree, taking a roundabout route in case anybody was watching. Mr. Firkin was off with his flock at a distance, Mrs. Lubbage nowhere to be seen. There had been no sight or sound, either, of Cris all day, though Dido had once or twice stuck her head through the loft opening and listened intently. She could not help feeling a bit anxious about Cris. Mrs. Lubbage had seemed so very angry about the basket of food—and Cris was the nearest scapegoat at hand, unless you counted the brindled rat.

But when she at length reached the Cuckoo Tree, on its steep slope of grassy hillside, Dido thought at first there was nobody in it.

"Cris? Are you there?" she called softly.

No sound came from the dark, thickly massed foliage above.

"Might as well climb up, though," Dido thought, noticing that the corkscrew with its bit of ribbon had been removed from the trunk. "Looks like someone's been here."

Up she went, quick as a squirrel—and found Cris, lying in a bushy hammock of yew needles.

"Hey, didn't you hear me—" Dido began, and then

saw that Cris was fast asleep, curled up, knees to chin, one cheek pillowed on a fold of dirty sheepswool jacket, which he had thrown around him, and clutched like a comforter. His cheeks were streaked with tears and one had a mark on it, half bruise, half cut.

"Blame it," Dido thought angrily, "that old scrow has been a-larruping of him, and it's my fault, partly; I ought to a waited till she came home, 'stead o' taking the basket. But the Cap'n was *that* hungry—how's a body to act?"

Troubled, uncertain what to do for the best, she sat and watched the sleeping Cris. Time passed, and the pale November sun moved toward a furry shoulder of hill behind which it would soon dip. "Hadn't I best wake him?" Dido wondered. "It'll be right parky soon—and the Cap'll be stirring presently. But Cris does sleep *so* sound."

Presently, though, the sleep began to be broken by little whimpers and twitches; letting go of his sheepswool jacket, Cris started to suck his thumb; a tear trickled from the corner of his closed eye; then the eyes opened, and he was awake, and terrified.

"Easy there; easy!" Dido arrested his first frantic scramble for the trunk. "It's only me—Dido, remember? We was talking here afore. I brought you some vittles. Mr. Gusset fetched some down from the Manor, and I reckoned as how you might be glad of a bite. Here—it's only bread and cheese, but it's good."

She went on talking calmly while she pulled out the packet of food and handed Cris a large slice of brown bread and hunk of cheese. "You get that inside you, you'll feel better. There's apples, too, for afters; I didn't like to carry a bottle o' drink in case old Madam Lubbage was a-looking out her back window."

Cris took one or two cautious bites and then bolted the food down ravenously, eating all the cheese first, and the bread next; his trembling quieted and presently he gave a deep sigh.

"Did the old girl beat you much?" Dido asked quietly.

Cris nodded. "She was in a rage last night when I got home. She asked me where I'd been and I wouldn't say, so she beat me. Being beaten's nothing. But she said she was going to listen to my dreams all night and then she'd know where I'd gone. I don't know what I'd do if she found this place."

"Croopus," muttered Dido. "D'you reckon she could listen to your dreams?"

"I don't know," Cris said. "I stayed awake. I stood up all night and pricked my arm with a bramble thorn so I wouldn't fall asleep. That was why I was so tired today. Auntie Daisy went off at noon to physick someone's sick cow, so as soon as she left I came here."

Between sentences Cris was taking bites from the second apple; he finished by chewing and swallowing the core. Then he sighed again.

Dido gulped and said gruffly, "Cris, it was my fault the old girl beat ye, acos I nicked a basket o' groceries outa her nasty dirty kitchen and that riled her. So I feel right bad about it and this is to say I'm sorry. Well, go on, take it: it's for you!"

Cris stared wonderingly at the little object that Dido held out in the palm of her hand. It was a tiny whale, carved from ivory.

"I brought it back from Ameriky," Dido explained. "The sailors make 'em on the whaleboats when they've nowt else to do."

Timidly Cris took it and turned it over and over. "It's pretty."

"You could wear it round your neck on a string— there's a loop on the tail, see? Maybe it'd keep off back luck—like Mr. Firkin's mouldywarpses' claws."

Cris made no answer.

Dido, rather hurt, was beginning to wonder if he didn't think much of her gift—which she had really hated to part with—when he suddenly said,

"It *is* lucky. Aswell says so. It will help me find— something I never knew—that I had lost."

He spoke in a dreamy, listening way, as if he merely passed on the words of someone else, and then lay back, relaxed and peaceful in his thickset hammock, smiling at the twilit sky. "Thank you for coming, Aswell! I was afraid you wouldn't today, I was so tired."

Dido shivered. All at once the place felt unchancy to her.

"Guess I'd best be going," she mumbled.

"Isn't the sky beautiful up there," Cris went on without heeding her. "Look, there's the first star. When I lie here I seem to be looking *down* into the sky, not up— it's like a huge well, don't you think? I feel as if I could jump right into it."

"Cris!" Dido exclaimed. "You hadn't oughta talk that way! It's not sensible."

"What is sensible, then?"

Cris turned his filthy, bruised face inquiringly toward Dido, who found herself at a loss.

"Oh, I dunno! Ask me, this is a right spooky part o' the world—*nothing's* sensible round here. Well, don't get downhearted, Cris, anyhows—if the old baggage wallops you any more, holler out, and I'll come and give you a hand—the two of us oughta be a match for her."

With a sad smile, like the wind ripple over a field of long grass, Cris said,

"All right. I'll remember."

Dido slithered down the trunk. "Powerful scent o' honeysuckle or summat round hereabouts," she thought. "Didn't know you got honeysuckle at this time o' year, but there's no telling what you'll get in these cockeyed parts. The mischief is, there's too many wrong 'uns and not enough right 'uns. And what right 'uns there is, is blind, like Mr. Firkin, or in poor twig, like my Cap, or too old to be very spry, like Mr. Gusset. And the *young* 'uns is next door to addle-pated, Tobit a-playing with them unnatural peas, and Cris a-talking to somebody in the sky. There's hardly an ounce of sense betwixt the pair of 'em. Pity they couldn't meet, they'd deal together like porridge and cream."

Thinking about them, as she trotted over the hill, she was struck by the similarity between the situations of Tobit and Cris: both of them forced to live so lonesome and mopish, their lives made a burden to them by queer-natured old crones. "And that spooky Tante Sannie is friends with Mrs. Lubbage—wonder if she knows about Cris? If I hadn't enough to worry about, getting Cap'n Hughes's Dispatch to London," Dido thought, "there's an awful lot wants setting to rights round here."

Mrs. Lubbage had returned from her cow doctoring, and was picking herbs from a tangled, nettle-grown patch under her kitchen window.

"Oh. So you're back, are you?" she said, giving Dido a hard stare with her little sharp eyes. "Well? Do ye want me to have a look at the sick chap or not? 'Tis all one to me."

Dido conquered an impulse to refuse. Best be polite, she thought.

"Yes, please, missus."

"I'll get my things, then."

While Mrs. Lubbage was dressing the Captain's wound, Dido noticed the brindled rat slip through the open door and along the angle of the wall and floor. Without pausing a second, Dido grabbed a heavy beech root from the firewood heap and slung it hard at the rat, which squealed indignantly and scurried out, limping.

"What was that?" exclaimed the Captain, startled.

"Jist an old rat, Cap; if he shows his snout in here again I'll pepper his whiskers," Dido said cheerfully. Mrs. Lubbage darted a black look at her but said nothing.

When she had finished her doctoring—it took less time today, for the wound was better—she said to Dido, "You step outside with me, missie!"

"Back directly!" Dido told the Captain.

Outside it was quite dark. A ray of lantern light from the doorway illuminated Mrs. Lubbage's broad face. Dido did not care for its expression.

"Now, harkee, gal," said the wise woman. "And pay heed, for I don't reckon to say things over. You crossed my path twice already, you went spanneling into my kitchen 'thoughten leave, and you hurted my old Tibbie-rat."

"*Your* rat, missus? How was I to know?"

"Don't aggle at me, gal! I'm warning ee, if I have any more mizmaze from ee, I'll make things right skaddle for ee, *and* for that chap in there. 'Twouldn't take but a pinch o' naughty-man's-plaything to set his wound into a mortification. And as for you—you puny little windshaken emmet—I could make you wish you'd never been borned."

Dido was silent. Mrs. Lubbage evidently took her silence for defiance; she went on,

"And I hear you bin upalong to Tegleaze, where you've no right nor business, making a sossabout, upsiding Mas'r Tobit. You leave that boy be! Do he land hisself in trouble before he come of age, then he won't noways inherit his grandpa's luck-piece."

Mrs. Lubbage might have said more, but she was interrupted at this moment by Gusset, in the trap, who came to a halt by them.

"Evening, Missis Lubbage," he greeted the wise woman politely. "Evening, Missie Twido Dight. I brought ye some more stuff for the sick navy gennleman."

With a surly jerk of her head, Mrs. Lubbage retired to her own house.

Dido would have taken the heavy basket from Gusset, but he insisted on carrying it in. As he did so, Dido's quick eye caught sight of Sannie, as on the previous occasion, slipping from the back of the trap and darting off to visit her friend.

"Don't I just wish I was that flea-bitten rat for five minutes to hear what the old crows is a-talking about in there," Dido thought. "I bet it's nothing good."

Gusset, it turned out, was dying to have a word with Captain Hughes.

"I did hear, Cap'n, sir," he quavered politely, "as how your ship was the *Thrush?*"

"You heard right," answered the Captain who, propped against rolled-up sheeps' fleeces, was drinking barley soup.

"I've a nevvy on that vessel," explained Gusset. "Able seaman Noah Gusset. Did ee e'er come across the boy, Cap'n, sir? Do 'e still be live and kicking?"

"Why, certainly! He is a fine fellow—will probably end up as Master Gunner. I have often spoken to him," the Captain said cordially. Old Gusset's face lit up at this news. "My brother Ed'ard'll be in a rare proud scarrifunge when I tell him!" he said, and could not do too much for the Captain; he bustled about, toasting bits of bread and warming up a mixture of wine and spices which he said would make the Captain "sleep like a juggy."

Dido, seeing that she was not needed for a few moments, said quietly to Gusset, "I'm jist going aloft a minute, mister, to see arter summat; shan't be long," and nipped up into the roof. Using the utmost caution she crept along to the loft over Mrs. Lubbage's kitchen. The moon had risen by now and slivers of light, finding their way through cracks between the tiles, showed that Cris was not there; most likely, Dido guessed, having had his hunger stayed with bread and cheese, he had gone back to sleep, and would not return all night in case Mrs. Lubbage should listen to his dreams.

"Blest if I'd want her a-listening to mine. Though I dessay it's all rubbish," Dido thought.

Mrs. Lubbage's trap door was closed, but Dido lay with her ear pressed against the crack, through which came a faint gleam of candlelight.

"Tell me about it again," she heard Mrs. Lubbage say.

"I done tell you many, many time!"

"Aye, but I had dunnamany things go caterwise on me today. The cow died, and my Tib-rat got hurted, and yon flarksy little madam nabbling at me—I could do wi' hearing summat brightsome."

"Is all green and warm," Sannie said. "Green and warm from east to west, from north to south. Orange trees, mango trees, love apples, sweet grass and honey flowers, all a-blowing and a-blooming. The sea she do sing by day and by night, white sea a-breaking on the black rocks. Old Fire Mountain, he up above, a-muttering in he sleep but never waking. And in that island, isn't no rudeness, isn't no mocking of old people; old

people paid proper respect, is loved, is given the callum drink and bonita bread, quilt stuffed with happiness feathers, wherever they do fancy to warm they bones."

"That's the place for me," Mrs. Lubbage said. "Round hereaways they treats you like dirt, even if they *is* scairt of you. Treats you like dirt and owes you money. If they gets to owe you too much, then they takes and drowns you in Black Pond."

"Never mind—never mind! Old Sir Tobit's luck-piece going to bring us luck, going to change all that. In three weeks—maybe two weeks—us'll be on a great white ship, a-sailing, sailing—"

"Over the white waves and the black waves—"

"A-wrapped in silk satin and treated like two queens—"

Plainly this was a conversation the two friends had held many times before.

"Until we comes to Tiburon Island—"

"Till we steps ashore and they cries, 'Is Tante Sannie come a-home! Is dear old Tante Sannie!'"

"And her friend what's come to live with her!"

"And they give us the callum drink and bonita bread and wrap us in quilt stuffed with happiness feathers!"

"All on account of Sir Tobit's ivory luck-piece."

What the dickens is all *that* about? Dido wondered. She stuck her eye to the crack. Down below she could see the top of Mrs. Lubbage's table, on which were a bottle, a saucer, and two teacups, which were removed, emptied, and refilled at regular intervals. Sometimes she could see the rat's pointed, whiskery snout drinking wine from the saucer.

But do they reckon to *steal* Tobit's luck-piece? Dido wondered.

She crawled back silently to her own loft and dropped down. Gusset had heated up a quantity of water in the hens' breakfast pan and was slowly but expertly shaving Captain Hughes, who appeared to be greatly enjoying this attention and was meanwhile relating all he could remember about the life and exploits of Able Seaman Noah Gusset.

Dido put away the provisions and squatted down by the fire on the three-legged stool.

"Mister Gusset," she inquired presently. "This little ivory painting you was a-telling me about, is that what they call Sir Tobit's luck-piece?"

"Why, yes, missie, acos the first Sir Tobit brought it back from furrin parts a couple o' hundred years agone, in oughteen sixty-summat. He reckoned it'd bring him luck, see?"

"Did it?"

"No, miss, it didn't. Some say as 'twas because it was stole—but I dunno if that be a true tale."

"What'll happen when this Sir Tobit gets it?"

"I reckon 'twill be passed over to his gran to take care of, like the rest o' the property."

Dido would have liked to ask if Gusset thought the old lady would get Colonel FitzPickwick to sell the heirloom and use the money for bets, but this did not seem a very polite question.

"And that happens next week?"

"Yes, missie. Unless Sir Tobit should die or go to prison first wards."

"Go to *prison*? Why in the name o' judgment should he get sent to clink?"

"Oh, no reason, Missie Twido; only it says in the will that if the heir be thrown in jail afore coming of age, then he loses the right to the heirloom."

"I see. Who gets it then? Lady Tegleaze?"

"No, missie. The next heir 'ud get it if there was one. But, being as there ain't, I believe it do go to some museum."

"No wonder Lady Tegleaze is in such a twit to see Tobit don't get in bad company."

Captain Hughes had been silent for the last few minutes and was now found to be asleep, so Gusset took his leave. Dido had wondered if he bore any message from Tobit, but none was forthcoming, so it seemed probable that the heir was still subdued by the effects of Sannie's scolding, or the Joobie nuts.

Two days passed quietly. Captain Hughes continued to mend, though slowly; Dido took care not to offend Mrs. Lubbage, and did various odd jobs for her and Mr. Firkin; Cris was not seen, but gifts of food that Dido left for him in the loft were taken. Mrs. Lubbage did not leave her cottage and so Dido, who would have liked to go to the Cuckoo Tree, did not think it safe to risk leading the witch to Cris's retreat.

On Friday Dr. Subito returned for another of his brief, nervous visits, and pronounced Captain Hughes well enough for a little gentle exercise on crutches if they could be obtained.

"Don't you reckon I'm well enough to hire a coach and go on up to London, doctor?"

"*Non tanto*—never, never! It is not to be thought of! The jolting—the swaying—*piu mozzo*—*doppio movimento* —*furioso*—it would inflame the head injury—bring on a syncope—a cataclysm—if not death itself! No—no, slowly we return to health, *poco a poco.*"

"Don't set yourself in a pelter, now, Cap," soothed Dido. "I'll be off to Petworth this very arternoon and get you a pair o' crutches."

But she herself was decidedly restless and uneasy; four days had passed and there had been no word from her friend Simon. Was he no longer living in London, or had her letter gone astray?

Addio! To the re-see," said the little doctor. "I return next week. In the meantime—*legato, non, non troppo!*"

He placed his finger to his lips, bowed, and departed at speed.

Not long after his departure, Gusset arrived with more provisions. After chatting a little to the Captain he glanced around cautiously and drew Dido away to the middle of Mr. Firkin's paddock, where they might be seen but could not be overheard.

"About that message you wanted sent, missie."

"Yes?" said Dido eagerly.

"Those chaps as I spoke of is willing to meet you and

talk it over. They be a darksy lot, see, they 'on't carry for every which-who, they're pitickler."

"That's all rug," said Dido. "The Cap's pitickler too; this is a very pitickler message."

"Ah!" said Gusset. He looked around again, advanced his mouth closer to Dido's ear, and murmured, "Do ee have the letter right, tight, and safe, missie?"

"That I do!" replied Dido, curbing an impulse to feel for the Dispatch inside her jacket.

"That's good," said Gusset. "Acos I did hear as how yon coach upset of yourn were fixed by somebody as wanted to lay hands on that there bit o' scribing. I dunno if 'tis true, but that's what I did hear."

Dido nodded. She was not surprised, having come to the same conclusion.

"Have you any notion who mighta done it, Mister Gusset?"

He came so close that his white whiskers tickled her ear dreadfully.

"That I dassn't say! But be that letter anywise connected wi' guvment business?"

Dido nodded, warily.

"I reckoned so!" said Gusset triumphantly. "I could tell as Cap'n Hughes must be a jonnick guvment man. Well, missie, round Tegleaze there be a pesky lot o' them Georgians."

"Hanoverians? The ones as wants to get rid o' the king?"

"That's the ticket! 'Twas one o' they fixed the accident."

"But how about these chaps o' yours? *They're* all hunky-dory?"

Mr. Gusset was affronted. He drew himself up. "My boy Yan's a true-blue king's man," he declared proudly. "Why, didn't he carry Gentleman's Gargle and twisty-corks every month for Jamie Three his own self—aye, and Oil o' Primroses for Her Majesty, bless her sweet face?"

"Your boy Yan? Why then—"

"Eh, massypanme! What have I bin and said?" Mr. Gusset was dreadfully upset. "Now, Missie Twido, don't ee let on as how I told ee that, don't ee, please! My boy Yan'd be turble taffety if he knew."

"Why, Mr. Gusset, I wouldn't dream of such a thing arter you been so kind to us and brought us all these vittles."

"Promise, do ee? Well, then, I was to tell ee, when ee be in Perrorth 'sarternoon, to go to a pub called The Fighting Cocks—at the end o' Middle Street, it be—don't ee go into the pub, now, but go ee round up a little twitten lane to the back, where they holds the cock-fights. Go ee there roundabout four o'clock. And there prensly a chap'll come up to ee and say, 'Larmentable scuddy weather we be having.'"

"And what do I say?" Dido inquired briskly.

"Don't ee say nowt, but goo along o' him, missie, and he'll talk over about taking yon message. And ee won't let on as I by-named my boy Yan?"

"No, no, Mr. Gusset, o' course I won't."

After Dido had reassured the old man several times he took his leave, still very shocked at his lapse.

Dido ran back to the cottage with a lighter heart. "Things is looking up, Cap, I reckon. As far as I can puzzle it out, old Mr. Gusset's friendly with a set o' they moonshine men, what the folks round here calls Gentlemen. And this lot is a mighty high-up crew, seemingly; used to carrying stuff to the king hisself."

"Never?" exclaimed Captain Hughes, much shocked. "His Majesty buying smuggled goods?"

"Well," said Dido, "I did hear tell as how the corkscrew tax was perishing stiff; I dessay old Jamie Three had better things to spend his dibs on. Corkscrews! O' course! What a muttonhead I am!"

"I beg your pardon, my child?"

"Nothing, nothing, Cap!" said Dido hastily. "Anyways, if they really takes run stuff to the palace, and all the nobs, they're the boys for us, ain't they? You want your Dispatch taken to the Fust Lord o' the Admiralty—like as not he's on their list for Organ-Grinders' Oil, or his lady for Parsley Face-powder."

Captain Hughes was obliged to admit the truth of this.

"Well, child—see what you think of them. Do not decide rashly. If you have the least doubt as to their trustworthiness, take no further steps. So much is at stake! Confound it—I wish my head did not still ache so—I wish I were not so wretchedly weak."

"Now don't you fret, Cap! If I can, I'll get one o' the chaps to come back here and have a word with you."

"Do. Do, child."

"I'm to meet 'em in Petworth at four this afternoon. Come to think," said Dido, rubbing her brow, "how did old Gusset know so quick that I was a-going to Petworth?"

Captain Hughes supposed the doctor must have mentioned it. "Does he not spend most of his time at Tegleaze Manor?"

"He does, that's so," agreed Dido thoughtfully. "Jist the same, I wish news didn't travel quite so fast in this back end."

When she had given the Captain his dinner she went out to the shippen and untethered the gray coach horse.

"Come on, Dapple, you lucky old prancer; you're a-going to have a change of air."

Since she had been giving him his feed all week and fomenting his lame leg with potato poultices under Mr. Firkin's directions, the gray had become very friendly. He allowed Dido to put on his bridle and to strap a sheepskin for a saddle around his barrel-shaped middle; she climbed on him from the water butt; and they were off. It was no use waving to Mr. Firkin, sitting with his flock on the hillside, but Toby wagged his tail amicably as they passed, and so Dido waved to *him*; her spirits rose as she left the quiet little valley.

"Pity the weather's so misty and murky; but anyways, it's grand to be out on the gad."

5

Mr. Firkin had told Dido the way to Petworth. It lay first down an exceedingly steep descent, on which Dapple slipped and snorted and complained. Above, on the misty hillside, dim glimpses of great beech trees in their flaming autumn colors reminded Dido of red-hot embers hidden under a layer of ash.

The road then twisted through a small hamlet of thatched houses: Duncton, Mr. Firkin had said this was called.

Growing accustomed, by the time they had left Duncton behind them, to Dapple's jerky trot, Dido rode thoughtfully, pondering about Tegleaze Manor and its inhabitants, and the conversation they had overheard between Colonel FitzPickwick and the other man, Miles Tuggles. What was all *that* about? Tobit had not seemed in the least interested, but Tobit was a totty-headed boy;

wouldn't know an egg from an Austrian. Nonetheless it seemed to Dido that the talk concerned Tobit quite closely; so far as *she* could make out, Colonel Fitz-Pickwick had been doing something he shouldn't, stealing money from old Lady Tegleaze, like as not—maybe that was why she never had any luck with her bets, maybe they never got placed at all—and the other fellow had got to know about this somehow and was threatening FitzPickwick with exposure unless he assisted in some further plot, something connected with Tobit and Lady Tegleaze and the Manor itself—otherwise, what had he meant by "the place—to get all this I'd commit any crime?"

Havey-cavey goings-on, without any doubt whatsoever.

Goodness knows what all the talk of rollers and motive power was about; but at that point the two men had been a little farther away; perhaps Dido had misheard them.

Well, she thought, if Yan, Tan, Tethera, and their mates will take the Cap'n's Dispatch to London so *that's* off my mind, I reckon I oughta do something about old gravel-voice Miles Tuggles. Dear knows what, though. Tell the Bow Street officers? That'd mean going to Bow Street; can't do it till the Cap's better. Warn Tobit? No use, he'd only start on about pirates or peashooters. Warn Lady Tegleaze? She'd never heed *me*. Maybe the lawyers in Petworth, the ones as looks after the heirloom, maybe they'd have some sense? Might be worth talking to them. Anyways, I'd like to see old Sir Tobit's luck-piece.

It had taken her the best part of an hour to reach Petworth; as she rode up the long straight track that led into the little walled, red-roofed town, she wondered at the lack of people; all the houses seemed shut and empty. But when she reached the sloping central market place this fact was explained: a fair was in full swing there.

It was mostly a farming fair: stalls around the sides of the square and overflowing into the streets nearby offered every kind of produce—eggs, butter, cheeses, apples, red and gold, bunches of late roses and purple daisies, farming tools and equipment; there were pens of cattle and sheep, crates of poultry; girls with pails offered their services as dairymaids, Dido saw shepherds with smocks and crooks and carters with whips. But as well as these there were various entertainments and peep shows, a band playing country dances, and a central merry-go-round, which had horses gorgeously painted in red, gold, and white.

"Better-looking than you, poor old Dapple," Dido told her steed. "Guess we'd better find somewhere to leave you out of all this mollocking."

Following Gusset's directions she located The Fighting Cocks Inn at the end of Middle Street, and asked permission to tie up Dapple in its stable-yard. Then she returned to the central square on foot, for at one side of it she had seen a shop window containing scythes, fowling pieces, wooden hayrakes, stools, ladles, and copper cooking pots. Sure enough, when she approached it more closely, she found a small painted sign over the door which read: Godwit & Son, Ironmongers & Conspirators.

"Humph," said Dido, considering this. "Well, I reckon the two things does go together, so it's kind of handy having 'em under the same roof; I spose they can fettle you up a riot, weapons, trimmings, and all, at wholesale rates."

She walked in, and demanded of a thin, wizened little man in rimless spectacles if he had any crutches in stock. He did have a pair, slightly too long for Captain Hughes (whose measurements Dido had taken before setting out); he promised to shorten them, put leather padding on the arm rests, and have them ready for her in an hour's time.

"I daresay you can amuse yourself at the fair meanwhile," he said with a meager smile.

Dido, who had decided that he was a soapy-faced fellow, replied that she had plenty of errands to occupy herself, and asked if he could direct her to an apothecary's, and also to the lawyers who had charge of the Tegleaze heirloom? At which Mr. Godwit (for it was he) raised his thin gray eyebrows and darted a very sharp glance at her indeed through the rimless glasses, but told her, still smiling gently, that she would find Wm. Pelmett, Chymist & Chirurgeon, on one side of his shop, downhill, and Messrs. Pickwick, FitzPickwick, and Wily, Solicitors and Attorneys-at-Law, on the other side, uphill.

Dido did not care for the sound of this. Still, I guess

as it's to be expected they'd all be cousins or kindred in a small place like Petworth, she reflected.

She went downhill first, and bought some ointment which the doctor had recommended for the Captain's wound, and a roll of bandage, since, even in Mrs. Lubbage's exceedingly dusty house, the supply of spider-web was running low. Wm. Pelmett, Chymist, bore a strong and unprepossessing resemblance to Pelmett the footman.

Next Dido turned uphill toward the lawyers' office, but before she reached the doorway she was startled to observe, set in a glass-fronted case in the wall of the building, what must surely be the Tegleaze luck-piece itself.

"But that could never have hung in a dolls' house," she thought. "It's far too big." Then she realized that the whole front of the case was in fact a powerful magnifying glass; the oval picture painted on a piece of ivory mounted in the case, though appearing to be about the size of a man's face, was really not much bigger than a gull's egg.

"It's a right naffy bit o' work, I will allow," Dido thought, studying it with interest. "I still don't see how it could be worth such a *deal* of dibs, but whoever done it put plenty of elbow grease into the job, I can see that, special considering how tiny it is. Musta been at it for hours."

The picture showed a very high tower, encircled by a spiral ramp. Hundreds of little people were rushing up and down the ramp, were occupied in building the tower, climbing ladders, at work with trowels and buckets of mortar; others were setting bricks, wheeling barrows, or consulting plans; but many others were just arguing, or even fighting, presumably about how the tower should be built; and in any case the tower had been struck by lightning and was falling down, so a great many people were trying to escape from it and trampling over each other in the process; some devils, down below, were finding the whole affair very funny indeed, and some angels, up above, seemed sad about it. The picture was painted in very bright, beautiful colors, reds and greens, browns and yellows; it seemed even gayer than the merry-go-round horses. The faces of all the little people were done with wonderful skill, no two the same, each with something strange, unexpected, yet lifelike about it; the painter's name, P. Bruegel, was neatly written in one corner.

"Fancy just leaving it there, where anybody might bust the glass and walk off with it," Dido murmured wonderingly.

"Oh, there's no risk of *that*. For one thing, the glass is specially strong: you'd need a diamond to cut it; for another, everybody round here thinks it's unlucky; no one would buy it from the thief."

Dido looked around in surprise at this unexpected reply; for a moment she thought that it was Cris standing behind her; then she recognized Tobit in what he plainly considered to be disguise; he had abandoned his black velvet and ruffles; instead he wore a frieze coat

P. Brüeghel

and pantaloons. The lower half of his face was concealed by a red muffler.

"Tobit! What the plague are you doing here?"

Dido was not best pleased to see him; his presence would make it difficult to go into the office of the family lawyers and say she suspected a plot against the family; they would probably think it was just some of Tobit's romancing.

"Anyway, how in the world did you get leave of your gran?"

"Oh, I took French leave," said Tobit boastfully. "Pelmett told me Petworth fair was on, and I didn't see why, as I'm not going to the coronation, I shouldn't at least come to *this;* so I put a lot of minced-up Joobie nuts in Grandmother's gruel, and she's gone to bed with one of her headaches; and now I'm going to have a fine time, I can tell you."

"Did Sannie know?"

"She kicked up a bit of a dust, but I didn't pay any heed. After all, I'm nearly of age."

"How did you get here?"

"Came with Frill in the trap; he's doing some errands for Colonel FitzPickwick. Come on—let's go and look at the shows." He grabbed her hand.

Dido went with some reluctance; she glanced back toward the offices of Pickwick, FitzPickwick, and Wily; but at this moment the heavy black outer door opened and two very elderly gentlemen came out, followed by one somewhat younger; the first two were so extremely old and frail that they could get along only by leaning against one another; they looked like ancient hairless mice; while the younger one, presumably Mr. Wily, had such an extremely villainous, untrustworthy countenance that Dido at once decided there would be no sense in going for advice and entrusting her suspicions to *him.* "All in whatever it is, hand and glove together, like as not," she thought.

Tobit did not wish to go on the roundabout; he said it would most likely make him sick; but he spent a good deal of money at the shooting gallery and the houp-la stall; it did not seem to occur to him to treat Dido, who had no cash for such amusements, but he liked her to watch him.

"This time I really will get it over—you'll see—I am a prime shot, once my eye is in! Oh, confound it! All the stands are just too big for the hoops, if you ask *me.* That wasn't my fault. Can I have another six shots for ninepence?"

"How did you come by all the mint sauce?" Dido asked, noticing his pockets heavy with coins.

"Frill lent me some; said he'd just been paid. He's a good-natured fellow. Now—this time I'll *certainly* get it over—you just watch, you'll see."

But he did not. Presently he became bored with the houp-la and moved on to a skittle stall.

Dido, tiring of his unjustified optimism, wandered along to the next booth, which was a kind of Punch-and-Judy show, apparently. A crowd was collecting in front of it. Weird and melancholy music was being played on a hoboy, somewhere behind the booth, by an

[123]

unseen performer; to Dido there was something tanta-lizingly familiar about this music, but she could not name it.

"Walk up, walk up, ladies and gentlemen: watch M-Miles M-Mystery's amazingly M-Mysterious Manni-kins; what m-makes them move about? See the g-grandest show of its kind in the world—the *only* show of its kind in the world! And it's all f-free—free, gratis, not a penny to pay. Watch the M-Mystery of the Miller's Daughter; the M-Macbeth Murder case; the Strange Tale of the Loch N-Ness Monster; see the dragon s-swallow St. George!"

Since the show was free, Dido stood on the outskirts of the group and waited. After a while the red-and-yellow curtain was pulled up, letting out a cloud of tobacco smoke, and revealing the little stage, lit by a baleful greenish light. There were some bits of painted wooden scenery and a backcloth representing a millhouse with a large water wheel.

"The Mystery of the Miller's Daughter! Ladies and gentlemen, you will now be the first spectators of this amazingly blood-curdling drama, the only one of its k-kind!"

The hoboy played a melancholy and off-key version of the "Miller of Dee."

"L-ladies and gentlemen, if any of you should have the m-misfortune to suffer from weak nerves, p-palpita-tions, sympathetic vibrations, digestive disorders, heart-burn, high t-tension, low spirits, vapors, or m-melancholy, you will be p-pleased to hear that soothing refreshments are on s-sale, at the extremely reasonable price of six-pence a packet."

Sure enough, a boy was going around with a tray containing little paper twists. Dido had not sixpence to spare, nor did she suffer from any of the ailments mentioned, but she looked with curiosity to see what the refreshments could be that would cure so many different troubles: so far as she could make out, each packet contained a small quantity of Joobie nuts.

The Mystery of the Miller's Daughter was heralded by an extra-loud flourish of hoboy music; then two puppets came hopping on to the stage: Rosie, the Miller's Daughter, and her sweetheart.

"Why," Dido thought scornfully, "they ain't but glove puppets; I can see what makes 'em move."

She had to admit, though, that they were unusually large, lifelike glove puppets, with something eye-catchingly strange and wild about their appearance. "I know what it is: the bloke as made them had been studying that picture, Grandpa Tegleaze's luck-piece."

The play was very comical at first: all about the efforts of Rosie and her sweetheart to escape the vigilance of her stern father, the Miller; they hid in all sorts of ingenious places—behind the mill wheel, up the apple tree, in the copper—while the Miller, completely bamboozled, rushed about the stage hunting for them, puffing and panting with fury.

But Dido soon became more interested in watching the audience than the play. The people in front nearly split their sides at the funny scenes; they staggered about and bumped into each other, bawling advice to the Miller which he always followed just too late. In their enthusiasm most of them had swallowed down all their Joobie nuts, and the boy with the tray, going around again, did a brisk sale; the sixpenny packets, Dido noticed, had been replaced by slightly larger ones which cost a shilling. Having swallowed a few more, the audience became almost hysterical with excitement, shouting, clapping, and screaming, as if they had before them the finest actors in the world. It seemed as if they saw more than was actually taking place on the stage and Dido, remembering what she had seen after merely tasting a Joobie nut, was not surprised.

She glanced at the church clock, set high on a tower, just visible over the red roofs: ten minutes to four. Time to go and meet Mr. Gusset's boy Yan.

Tobit, luckily, was absorbed in front of a stall where the game was to swing an iron ring hanging on a long cord so as to hook it over a peg on a panel at the back. It looked easy enough, but was evidently not so, judging by his lack of success. The prizes were goldfish, swimming in little semi-transparent bags made of pigs' bladder filled with water and tied up with twine. Wonder if Cap'n Hughes would like a goldfish to keep him company, Dido thought. But then I dessay it'd hate the coach trip up to London presently. Anyway, Tobit's happy enough and he won't notice if I skice off; hope Frill takes him home afore he notices the puppet show and starts stuffing down Joobie nuts.

She made her way back to The Fighting Cocks Inn,

and, following Gusset's instructions, turned under a low archway at the side, around a corner, and up a steep and narrow cobbled alley. This brought her into a little courtyard, where twenty or thirty men were standing in a circle, apparently waiting for a cockfight to begin. Two, in the middle, were taking their birds out of baskets, looking them over, strapping them into their fighting gear, and talking to them encouragingly, while the crowd laid bets and shouted advice. Dido had seen cockfights in London and did not like them, but this one made a good excuse for loitering in the court, so she stood at the back of the crowd and pretended to be examining her purchases.

In a minute she heard a familiar voice.

"Arternoon, maidy! Larmentable thick weather, 'tis!"

"Right fretful," Dido agreed politely.

The speaker was a well-set-up young fellow in a shepherd's smock; he had curly dark hair, cut rather short, a brown weathered complexion, and very bright observant brown eyes; he gave Dido a friendly grin and jerked his head, indicating that she should follow him in an inconspicuous manner. Everyone's attention was fixed on the cockfight, now starting, so they slipped away. He did not lead her back into the street; they went up a flight of steps from the alley into a big, bare, barnlike upper chamber, where there were two or three long trestle tables and a quantity of benches and stools.

"'Tis the inn banquet hall," Yan explained. "My uncle Jarge, he owns the inn. There'll be grand junketings here, come Coronation Day."

He sat down on a stool and Dido perched on another; she noticed that he smelt powerfully of clove pinks and orange blossom.

"It be the perfume," he explained apologetically, noticing her sniff. "Do what us may, *some* of it leaks out. And the mischief is that they Bush officers are training special hounds, now, to goo arter it; like truffle hounds they be."

"Couldn't you disguise it with onions or summat? Or strew pepper, to go up their noses?"

"Pepper costs terrible dear, lovie; but 'tisn't a bad notion. I can see my old gaffer's right—a nim, trustable little maid you be. So now, how can us Wineberry Men help ee?"

One look at Yan Wineberry in daylight had assured Dido that here was the right person to help her; she explained that she needed a letter taken to the First Lord of the Admiralty.

"Oh, no trouble about *that,* my duck. Us takes grog to old Lord Forecastle regular. Next trip Sunday night. He'll get it Tuesday maybe, Wednesday for sartin."

"Not before?"

"Us travels slow, you see, love; for one thing it 'on't do to joggle the grog, the old Crozier of Winchester created turble one time when the sediment got shook up in his pipe o' port wine; then there's deliveries along the way—us has a private way, slow and sure, what the Bush officers don't know about."

"Oh well, guess the Cap'll be agreeable, so it's

[128]

Wednesday for sure. Could you come and see my old Cap? Just so he'll feel easy about it?"

"I'll need to wait till arter dark, then, lovie. I'll come Saturday night—Dogkennel Cottages, ben't it? Owd Mis' Lubbage, therealong, be a terrible untrustworthy woman, no friend o' mine. Dunked in Black Pond she'd a bin, long agone, done she hadn't bin so thick wi' the Preventives and the Hanoverians."

"What are the Hanoverians doing mixed up with the Preventives?" Dido asked, puzzled. "I thought as how the Preventives were government revenue officers? And the Hanoverians are *agin* the government, surely? My pa used to be one; he was in a plot to blow up Battersea Castle; but he got found out and run off and no one's seen him since."

"Oh, it be simple enough," Yan said. "Nobody likes the Preventives—always clapping gurt dratted taxes on grog and twistycorks that honest folk has taken trouble to fetch over from France; and nobody likes the Hanoverians either, allus a-trying to blow up poor old King Jamie, and now his son, that's a-going to be Dick Four. So as nobody liked *either* lot, they just nature-ally set up together."

"I see. Now, how about the letter—will I give it you tomorrow night?"

"That'll be best," he agreed. "Now—if you wants to get in touch with me afore then—do ee know the Cuckoo Tree?"

"Yes I do."

[129]

"Well, if you wants me, just ee stick a twistycork in the Cuckoo Tree trunk and come back there the next noon or midnight arter—someone'll meet ee. Right?"

"Right."

"Us'd best leave by onesomes—I'll goo first and when you hear me whistle, you follow."

He gave her ear a friendly tweak and slipped down the narrow steps, quieter than a shadow. Dido waited until she heard his soft all-clear whistle from the street, then silently followed him.

Even more silently, when she had gone, a tiny figure unfolded itself from under one of the trestle tables and stole away in a different direction: Tante Sannie, aged, bent, frail as a bunch of cobwebs, quick as a spider.

Dido went back to Godwit & Son, Ironmongers & Conspirators. Mr. Godwit had the crutches ready, neatly tied up with cord so that she could sling them on her back. She paid, and was leaving his shop when she heard a disturbance from the upper end of the square, where Miles Mystery had his Mysterious Mannikins. People were shouting, "Stop thief!" and a portion of the crowd had broken away and was racing up a small cobbled lane that led in the direction of the church.

"What's it about?" Dido asked a fat man.

"Some lad nicked a couple o' goldfish off of the goldfish stall. Got caught red-handed—or rather, wet-pocketed," the man said, with a loud laugh at his own wit. "They're arter him now—they'll catch him soon enough." Too fat to run himself, he filled his lungs with air and shouted, "Stop thief! Catch the pesky ragamuffin. Stop thief!"

By now all the upper portion of the square had emptied; Mr. Mystery's theatre was empty and unattended. Dido took the opportunity for a quick examination of the puppets, which had been left, lolling and lifeless, on the stage. "They ain't bad," she thought critically, "but they're no better than what Pa used to make, when I was little."

She turned back in the direction of Middle Street; the ground hereabouts was white with the little twists of paper in which Joobie nuts had been wrapped. Suddenly her eye was caught by something familiar in the look of one of them: she picked it up and read her own handwriting: "Dere Simon. I doo hop yore . . . I am all rug . . . an hadd Grate Times." The paper had been torn into four; scuffling with her foot she found another piece. So much for the shravey Jem! No wonder her letter had not been answered. It had traveled no farther than Petworth Square. But how had it come to be wrapped around a packet of Joobie nuts?

"I jist hope Yan, Tan, and co are a bit more trustable," she thought, greatly cast down by this discovery.

She walked on feeling thoroughly uneasy, she could not think why. After all there was no reason to suppose that the boy who had stolen the goldfish—

But as she reached the top of New Street the hue and cry, which had swung in a circle around past the church and back toward the center of the town, came surging in her direction.

Ahead of the crowd, but only just, she was horrified to see Tobit, gasping and wild-eyed. Half a dozen yards from Dido he tripped and fell, as a tall man sprang forward and tackled him.

"Got the little varmint!" shouted the crowd.

Tobit was on his feet again, fighting frenziedly.

"I didn't take it, I tell you I didn't!"

"Ah, how did it come to be in your pocket, then? Why did you run off?"

> "Little Tommy Tittlemouse
> Went to the skittle-show
> Lined his breeches
> With other men's fishes!"

somebody sang derisively.

"Someone must have slipped it in my pocket."

"A likely tale! Tell that to the magistrate!"

A constabulary officer, conspicuous with his truncheon and top hat, was making his way through the crowd.

"What happened?" he asked.

"Why, it was l-like this, officer," said the man who had caught Tobit. Dido studied him curiously. He was very tall, very thin, with a long, flat face, not ill-looking but very yellow in complexion; his hair was dusty dark and his eyes, big, yellowish-gray, and slanting, were strangely like those of a goat. Dido noticed that his hands, though they retained a vicelike grip on Tobit, shook all the time; it seemed that he could not control their shaking. "I r-run the m-mannikin show in the square—Mr. M-Mystery, you know. I was just coming to

[132]

the end of my M-Miller's Daughter play when, l-looking out at the crowd through a slit in the curtain, I s-saw this boy steal a couple of g-goldfish from the next stall and slip them into his p-pocket."

"That's a lie!" shouted Tobit. "I never did any such thing! Why, if I wanted, I could easily buy a goldfish— I've plenty of cash."

He brought out a handful as proof—it was wet, and bits of pig's bladder were mixed up with it.

"Stole the money too, like as not," somebody commented.

"Did anybody else witness this?" the constable asked.

"Yes, I did!" Somebody was shouldering his way to the front of the crowd; Dido was shocked to recognize Frill the footman. "With my own eyes I saw him," Frill went on sorrowfully. "Oh, Mas'r Tobit, how could ee do such a thing, boy, bringing down your poor old grandma's white hairs?"

"I never did, I tell you! Someone must have planted it on me."

"He's right!" said Dido, angrily coming forward. "It's all a plot against him, so he'll be sent to prison and won't come into his luck-piece. You know that," she said accusingly to Frill. "I bet your tale's naught but a pack o' lies." He gazed at her as if he had never laid eyes on her before.

"Oh, and did you see the occurrence, miss?" said the officer.

"Well, no, I didn't, but—"

"Just a-wanting to keep your playmate out o' trouble,

eh? Well, my advice to you, maidy, is, don't poke your liddle nose into matters as don't consarn you, or you'll be in trouble too. Come along you," he said sharply, grabbing Tobit's arm. "We'll see if a night in the stone jug'll cool you down and make you more biddable—then tomorrow you'll go afore the beak."

The crowd followed as he hurried Tobit away. Frill and Mr. Mystery strode alongside.

Dido started after, but a hand on her arm checked her.

"You'll never do no good that way, lovie," said a warning voice. "Best not get imbrangled."

She looked up into the eyes of Yan Wineberry.

"But it was all a put-up job—" she began indignantly.

"Whisht! O' course it was. That Amos Frill is as crooked as one o' my twistycorks. But no sense in making a potheration now, or what'll come of it? You'll be run in too, for nabbling at a constable in pursoot o' his dooty."

"What'll I do then?"

"Best tell old Lady Tegleaze first. The magistrate's a friend o' hers—old Sir Fritz FitzPickwick. Reckon she'll be able to put matters right wi' him."

"D'you reckon so?" Dido said doubtfully. "What if that don't work?"

"If that don't work us Wineberry Men'll see what we can do."

Somewhat comforted by this assurance, Dido fetched out her nag, mounted him from the steps in front of The Fighting Cocks Inn, and made for home as fast as possible. But Dapple had no great turn of speed, and as she passed through Duncton in the misty twilight she was overtaken by a trap bowling rapidly along. It was driven by Frill, who passed her without a sign of recognition; the trap's other passenger, bundled up like a sackful of shadows, was not visible to Dido.

"Blame it!" she thought. "Now he'll get home first and tell his tale."

She delivered the crutches to Captain Hughes, who was delighted with them, gave him a hasty summary of the afternoon's events, including the satisfactory interview with Yan Wineberry, and explained that she must hurry on to Tegleaze Manor.

"That you must," agreed the Captain. "Not a doubt but the boy's been framed, by the sound of it; makes one's blood boil. Why, when I think how I'd feel if my own boy, Owen, got into such a fix—I've a good mind to come along with you and talk to this Lady Tegleaze."

However his indignation and the effort of attempting to leave his bed made his head swim so badly that Dido was alarmed and begged him not to overexert himself.

She prepared him a hasty meal, explained her intentions to Mr. Firkin, who promised to keep the Captain company and, observing that Mrs. Lubbage's house was in darkness, remounted the dismayed Dapple and continued on her way.

As she neared Tegleaze Manor she saw one faint glimmer of light in an upstairs window, and when she pounded on the door, Gusset presently appeared with a candle.

"Oh, Missie Dwighto Tide!" he exclaimed dolefully. "There be desprit tidings of Mas'r Tobit—caught a poaching goldyfishes and clapped in clink!"

"I know, I was there! But it's all a pack o' lies, you know, Mister Gusset—he didn't do it." As she said this, though, a sudden doubt assailed her. Tobit was such an unaccountable, impulsive boy—supposing he had done it? But no, why should he? "I've come to tell Lady Tegleaze the truth," she went on stoutly.

"Oh, that's good, that's good, Missie Dide—I'll take ee to her directly," Gusset quavered, and escorted her upstairs so slowly and shakily that he scattered great drops of candle grease on every step.

In Lady Tegleaze's dim, dusty bedroom, Dido found a conclave assembled. Frill was there, looking thoroughly hypocritical; the corners of his mouth were turned down as far as they would go, and his hair had been parted in the middle with a wet comb. Dr. Subito was there with a finger on the pulse of Lady Tegleaze, who lay on a couch looking pale and haggard; Sannie, wielding a large ostrich-feather fan; old Cousin Wilfred in his dressing gown, holding a bottle of smelling salts and looking somewhat bewildered; Pelmett stood with an untouched plateful of nut cutlets; and another member of the group, greatly to Dido's astonishment, was Mrs. Lubbage, whose solemn expression did not disguise a gleam of excitement and malice in her twinkling little eyes. Tobit's big white dog Lion had crept in and was lying in the middle of the room with his head on his paws, flattened out, like a thick white fur rug; every now and then he let out a mournful whimper.

"Who is *that?*" demanded Lady Tegleaze as Dido entered; then, recognizing her, added fretfully, "Why, it's that quarantine child who forced her way in once before. I daresay she began all the trouble, putting ideas in the boy's head. Tell her to be off, Subito; she is not wanted, specially at such a time as this."

"But my lady," pleaded Gusset, "she be come about Mas'r Tobit; says as how it be all a pack of lies that he took the fish."

"Nonsense, man! Frill himself saw the incident. A devoted family servant would hardly lie, would he? Oh! to think I should have to suffer such a blow. My own grandson convicted of poaching, three days before his coming of age. Such a vulgar crime, too. It is crushing— entirely crushing."

"But ma'am—I am sure that it is all a plot."

Dido wished that some of these people would go away, so that she could talk to Lady Tegleaze in private.

"Who would plot against me—and why, pray?"

"Colonel FitzPickwick—" began Dido, but at that moment the Colonel himself entered the room. Seen in daylight his hair and mustaches were so white that Dido wondered if he dipped them in bleach; they formed a decided contrast to the whites of his liver-brown eyes which were a blood-veined mud color; his teeth, when he showed them, looked as if inside somewhere they must be labeled "Best Staffordshire porcelain."

"Dear lady—who speaks of me?" he said, coming forward.

"What news?" Lady Tegleaze demanded. "What news of my grandson?"

"He will appear before the magistrates at ten tomorrow; my cousin Fritz presiding; let us hope that as it is a first offense, Fritz will be lenient; ten years in Lewes Gaol, perhaps, rather than a life sentence in Botany Bay."

"Oh, what difference does it make to me where he gets sent?" Lady Tegleaze said pettishly. "Or for how long? The main thing is that we lose the heirloom. When I think of the trouble I have wasted in rearing that child—and all for this! Stupid, ungovernable boy! Well, I wash my hands of him—I wish now I had kept the other instead."

"Other?" twittered the mouselike Cousin Wilfred, evidently much startled. "What other, Catherine?"

"Why, surely you remember that there were twins? Or rather, triplets, but one died at birth. Sannie brought the other two from Tiburon when their parents died. But *I* said that it wasn't to be expected that I should have the trouble of looking after *two* grandchildren; one would be quite enough work; so I kept only the boy."

"And I said, princessie-ma'am, two-baby twins bring always bad, bad luck in family, almost as bad as three-baby; better get rid of one, better keep boy, just."

[138]

"Good gracious! Mean to say you just *disposed* of one?" mumbled Cousin Wilfred, really shocked.

And Dido thought, "Well! I allus did say she was a queer old trout but, ask me, that's downright heartless! Fancy tossing out your own grandbaby like summat you'd give a rag-and-bone man."

"Oh well, Sannie said she'd find a home for it somewhere, in an orphanage or something; you'll just have to find it again now, Sannie, and double-quick too, now Tobit's no use to me."

"That's not easy," said Tante Sannie, wrinkling her leathery, monkeylike forehead under its sparse silvery hairs. "Not easy, that! Who know, who know where that baby be now? Far, far away, daresay; cost a much, much money to find her. Hundred, t'ousand pound."

"Well, the money'll have to be found somehow," snapped Lady Tegleaze. "FitzPickwick, you'll have to arrange it. Sell one of the chimneys—or the portico, that's made of marble, isn't it?"

Dido, meanwhile, had been struck by a blinding flash of inspiration. Without pausing to listen to anything else she turned hastily toward the door, noticing two faces only on her way: Gusset's, full of reproach at her supposed desertion; and that of Colonel Fitz-Pickwick who looked as if he had received an utterly staggering blow; his jaw had dropped in disbelief, his large porcelain teeth stuck up like Dapple's, and he was directing a look of pure fury at Tante Sannie, who took no notice whatsoever.

6

Back at Dogkennel Cottages, Dido briskly approached that of Mrs. Lubbage. It was unlit, as before, and the door was locked. When she tried it, the little voice buzzed in her ear:

"Beware! This is a hoodoo lock."

"Oh, be blowed to that," thought Dido impatiently. "If old Sannie and Mrs. Lubbage are hoping to squeeze a thousand quid out o' Lady Tegleaze before they'll produce Tobit's sister, they're liable to be pretty riled with me anyways, sposing I spile their game; busting the old crone's witchlock can't make matters much worse, I reckon."

She found a lump of rock and gave the ramshackle door a vigorous thump; it burst inward.

From up above an alarmed voice cried, "Who's that?"

"Cris? It's me—Dido!"

She walked into the kitchen—which smelt even worse than on her last visit—and looked up. Framed in the black square of the loft opening was a pale, scared face.

"I thought it must be people coming to duck Auntie Daisy," breathed Cris. "She said once that some day they will do. But, Dido, you won't half catch it when she finds you here! And so shall I! Breaking down the door, too—didn't her hoodoo lock work on you?"

"Yes, a bit," said Dido, crossly rubbing her hands. "My fingers tingles as if I'd been pulling stinging nettles. But I don't believe in such stuff! Anyways, come down, Cris; I wants to talk to you."

"Where's Auntie Daisy?"

"Up at Tegleaze Manor."

Encouraged by this, Cris jumped lightly down.

"Why did you let on you was a boy?" Dido snapped out.

"I—I—Auntie Daisy said I must, always. For *goodness'* sake don't tell her you found out," Cris gasped, looking frightened almost to death.

"That'll be all right—don't you worry. What's your real name, then?"

"It is Cris—Cristin. She said if anyone got to know, she'd put a freezing spell on me, so I was shivering cold to the end of my days. She can too—she did to old Mrs. Ruffle at Open Winkins."

"Rubbidge. Mrs. Ruffle probably had the ague. Now, listen, Cris—I've lots o' things to tell you. But there's no

[141]

time to lose, so you come along o' me, and I'll explain as we go—agreeable?"

"Go where?"

"I'd as soon not say till we're farther along," Dido said cautiously.

"Supposing Auntie Daisy comes back?"

"I don't reckon she will jist yet."

"I can't go without asking Aswell!"

"Oh, croopus," Dido thought. But she felt some sympathy for Cris—plainly the unusualness and suddenness of her arrival had thrown the girl into such a state of fright and indecision that she was almost paralyzed. She stood trembling, huddling the ragged sheepskin jacket around her thin shoulders, her huge dark eyes fixed hauntedly on Dido.

"All right, go on, ask Aswell then," Dido said patiently. "But I think we'd best get outside, hadn't we? Shouldn't think Aswell'd fancy coming into a murky den like this."

They went out into the little weedy front yard, dark now, and misty; Cris sang or chanted her curious rhyme:

"Dwah, dwah, dwuddy dwuddy dwee—
I can't see you but you can see me—"

Dido perched on the yard wall. Cris stood with her eyes shut and hands stretched out. There was a long pause, of expectation and strain; then Cris gave a short sigh.

"It's all right. Aswell says I ought to go."

"Well, so I should hope!" Dido muttered to herself, but aloud she merely remarked, "Come along, then— can you trot? That's the dandy—" catching hold of Cris's hand. She had stabled Dapple, who had certainly done his part for the day, before coming to find Cris.

The two girls ran along the chalk track at a steady pace, and Dido said,

"Right, listening, are you? Now, Cris, do you know what twins are?"

"Brothers and sisters the same age?" Cris said doubtfully.

"That's it. Now, how'd you feel, Cris, sposing I was to say you had a twin brother nobody'd ever told you about?"

There was a long silence. Then Cris's voice came hesitantly out of the dark.

"Could you say that again?"

Dido said it again.

"Dido?"

"Yes, Cris?"

"Do—do you mean that I really *have* got a brother?"

"Yes, Cris. His name's Tobit. He's in pokey at the moment, but we'll get him out someways."

"Pokey?"

"Jail. Prison."

"Why?"

"Someone fadged up a tale against him o' summat he hadn't done."

"I've got a brother called Tobit." Cris was trying

[143]

over the words to see how they sounded. "I have a brother. Do you know—everything seems *warm* all of a sudden. As if the air was warm and I could swim in it like a fish. I've got a brother," she said again.

"Hey, hold on!" Dido became a bit anxious. "He's jist an ordinary boy—not an angel!" Leastways he's not all *that* ordinary, she thought; but anyway I reckon Cris would take to him if he had three legs and a sword on his snout.

"Now, there's lots more to tell you, Cris, so pay attention; that ain't all by a long chalk."

"What else?" But Cris sounded vague as if, in spite of Dido's caution, her attention was not fully engaged.

"It's like this. As well as Brother Tobit, you've got some grand relations up at Tegleaze Manor. Old Lady Tegleaze is your granny. And there's Cousin Wilfred. They're a-going to be right pleased to see you," she added thoughtfully, "acos now Tobit's been in jug he's lost his right to the luck-piece. At least I spose he has; jail's jail, even if it's on a skrimped-up charge."

"Lady Tegleaze is my grandmother?" Cris murmured dazedly.

"That's right. Mind, don't go running off wi' the notion that life up at Tegleaze Manor is going to be everlasting sherry cobbler and larks on toast—it ain't so. Lady T has gambled away all her dibs on the races. But at least it'll be a whole heap better than life with Mother Lubbage. You won't have to lurk up in the loft and live on spud scrapings. And old Auntie Daisy'll hatta treat you civil from now on."

[144]

"Sannie's there," Cris said, half to herself. "I'm scared of Sannie."

Dido frowned. She too had thought about this.

"Well, we just got to find a way to put a damper on that old spider monkey. And, whatever you do, Cris, *don't* you go eating of those Joobie nuts; you lay off 'em."

"Will I have to stay up at the Manor always, now?" Cris was sounding more and more doubtful.

"Now, Cris! Dido began scoldingly. In her heart, though, she was uncertain enough. Would Cris be happier up at the Manor with all those funny old things? But *surely* it was better than life at Dogkennel Cottages?

There was another pause, then Cris sighed again.

"Aswell says I belong there."

Thanks a million, Aswell, Dido commented inwardly. You're a real pal.

Five minutes' more trotting and they reached the Manor. Dido walked in without knocking. No one was about; she guessed that everybody was still assembled upstairs.

"Come along; this way. Crumpet, Cris, don't gawp so—you'll hatta get used to the place."

She led Cris over the marble paving, up the stairs, and then turned in the direction of Tobit's room. "Here, this won't take but a moment and I reckon it'll help—"

Rummaging in Tobit's untidy apartment she found several of his black velvet suits.

"Put one o' these on, it looks to be just your size.

Lawks, gal, you're nought but skin and bone, it surely is time we got you outa that old devil's clutches. Now, where does the boy wash?"

Investigating, Dido found a dressing closet and washstand with pewter basin and ewer. She soaped a cloth and briskly scrubbed the inattentive face of Cris, who had found the picture of the three children and was standing riveted in front of it.

"That's *Aswell!*"

"You said you'd never seen Aswell," said Dido, buttoning cuffs.

"No, but that's how I imagine him."

"It's *you*. Here, look at yourself—" Dido wheeled her to face the looking glass over the mantel. Cris gazed in astonishment.

"Is that me? I never saw myself before."

"Croopus, Cris, you ain't half got a lot to learn," Dido muttered, hard at work with a molting silver hairbrush. "Right! We're ready, come along."

She led Cris through the maze of passages to Lady Tegleaze's room.

The conclave was still assembled, but now something mysterious was going on. Sannie and Mrs. Lubbage, evidently at the request of Lady Tegleaze, were doing a bit of conjuring. Another pewter washbasin had been filled with what looked like ink. Sannie had lit a lot of incense sticks which, stuck about in egg cups and toilet jars, were filling the room with white choking smoke. Frill, Pelmett, Gusset, the doctor, Cousin Wilfred, and the Colonel were standing in a ring looking nervous and ill at ease; Lady Tegleaze still reclined on her couch; Mrs. Lubbage was gazing into the basin of ink while Sannie chanted foreign words in a shrill unearthly tone.

"Ah, now I begins to see clear," Mrs. Lubbage was saying, as Dido poked her head around the door. "Yes, I can see a face. Yes, it be the face of your granddaughter Cristin, my lady. . . ."

"Where is she?" Lady Tegleaze asked eagerly.

"Wait a minute—wait a minute—the driply mist be a-thickening again. Ah, now 'tis clearing. Cristin be a turble long way from here, my lady—over hill and dale, over bush and briar, over sand and swamp and sea. Far, far away, she be; 'twill cost a power o' money to fetch her home."

"Now, *that's* a funny thing," Dido said, stepping in briskly and dragging the nervous Cris behind her. "I'd a notion she was no farther away than right here, and it'd cost nothing at all to fetch her!"

Three things then happened simultaneously: Lady Tegleaze shrieked, Colonel FitzPickwick let out a fearful oath, and Mrs. Lubbage, startled almost out of her wits, upset the basin of ink, which poured in a black flood all over the carpet.

"My granddaughter!" Ignoring the fact that her lavender satin was trailing in the ink and that her wig was awry, Lady Tegleaze rose, swept forward, and enveloped Cris in a bony embrace from which the latter, looking somewhat taken aback, freed herself as soon as she could.

[147]

"Knavery! Arrant deception! Dear lady, do but think! What possibility can there be that this come-by-chance brat could be your grandchild? It is a piece of bare-faced imposture!" Colonel FitzPickwick had recovered and strode forward, casting looks of rage at Sannie and Mrs. Lubbage.

"Imposture?" snapped Lady Tegleaze. "Nonsense! Look at the child's face. Besides—look at the dog."

The dog Lion, who would go to no one but Tobit, was standing on his hind legs, with a paw on each of Cris's shoulders, crying with joy, and licking her face with a large blue tongue. She put her arms around his white furry neck and hugged him back.

"Pity I washed her face," Dido thought regretfully. "It would a been prime to have it come plain when the dog licked it. Never mind, she's *in,* that's the main thing."

For it was plain that by Lady Tegleaze, by Cousin Wilfred, and by Gusset, Cris had been unhesitatingly accepted. The two witches, biting their lips with cha-grin, were quarreling in furious undertones. Frill, Pel-mett and the Colonel, pale and angry, were on the point of quitting the room when Lady Tegleaze said to Cris,

"Now, tell me, what do you want, dear child? What do you need? Food, clothes—er, toys?"

"Nothing, thank you, my lady," Cris said politely, "only—"

"Call me Grandmother!" snapped the old lady. "Only? Well, what?"

"Only to see my brother Tobit."

"Oh, *that* is quite out of the question. He has done for himself. I've washed my hands of *him.*"

"But, Lady Tegleaze," said Dido, "I'm sure as ninepence he didn't steal those fish. They was palmed off on him. Arter all, who in the name o' thunder would be so totty-headed as to stick a pair o' goldfish in his britches pocket?"

"Whether he stole them or not, it is all one. If he had not disobeyed me and gone to Petworth, he would not have exposed himself to such a risk. I have no more interest in him. If he is sent to Botany Bay it is no concern of mine."

"But, Grandmother—" Cris began.

"No more, miss!"

Botheration, thought Dido. What an old tarmigan. This alters the look o' matters.

She had expected that, in gratitude for the production of Cris, Lady Tegleaze would be prepared to exert herself on Tobit's behalf, but plainly that was not going to happen.

Murmuring, "Well, enjoy yourself, Cris, see you Turpentine Sunday," Dido slipped away, following the Colonel who, without noticing her, had walked rapidly to the back stairs, down them, and out along the path to the tilting-yard.

The pale moon was beginning to struggle out, throwing long spindly shadows on the mist. Dido saw another shadow, with its owner, move out from one of the yew trees.

[150]

"Well?" Dido recognized the grating tone of Miles Mystery. "How did it g-go? Will the boy get a stiff sentence? How did the old lady take the n-news?"

"Oh, as expected. But—"

"But what?" Mystery said sharply.

"Our plans are overset. Another grandchild has turned up."

"Devil take it! What are you telling me? How can there be another grandchild?"

"It seems there was a twin sister of Tobit, mislaid or farmed out in infancy. Those two old hags, Sannie and Mrs. Lubbage, have been playing deuce-ace with us—they knew of this other child all along, and planned to demand a handsome sum from Lady Tegleaze as the price for producing her when Tobit was knocked out of the game."

"Wait till I lay my hands on the d-double-dealing old witches! They'll reckon that money hard-earned!"

"But they never got the money!"

"S-so? Why not?"

"That strange child—the one who is lodging at Dog-kennel with the navy captain—she suddenly sprang the plot and produced the missing grandchild."

"How in Lucifer's name did she know about it?"

"Lord knows. We shall have to do something about her. She may know too much for comfort."

"Not only her. We shall have to get rid of the other grandchild."

"How?"

"If she was lost once—she m-must be lost again."

[151]

Dido's blood ran cold at the calm way in which Miles Mystery uttered these words. Plainly the Colonel also felt a qualm for he said,

"No violence, Tuggles. You know I draw the line at violence. It's too dangerous."

"Oh, call me Tegleaze! It is my name, after all. Hark, what was that?"

Dido held her breath. Had they seen her, crouching by the hedge? But then she saw Mrs. Lubbage and Aunt Sannie, still bickering angrily, come down the steps and start to cross the lawn. They had not noticed the two men, and appeared somewhat confused when Colonel FitzPickwick accosted them.

"A f-fine trick you played us, you miserable pair of old scarecrows!" Mr. Mystery exclaimed angrily. "You needn't think I'll stir myself to send you to Tiburon Island *now*. Pretending to help us with Tobit and the old lady—and all the time you had another grandchild hidden up your sleeves!"

"Is not pretending!" Sannie said fiercely. "*Is* helping! Number two grandchild—pooh! T'ousand pound in pocket, why not, then get rid, easy as Tobit."

"Only you didn't get the thousand pounds," Mr. Mystery pointed out unkindly. "And *I'm* not weeping millstones—you deceitful pair of old crows! Well, you can whistle for your great white ship to Tiburon after that—you'll not get it from me, even when I come in to the estate."

"Just you bide a minute, you fine Mr. Mystery!" hissed Sannie, scuttling after him like a scorpion as he turned away. "You cast us off now, you fine fellow, you be sad and sorry, afore long soon, when the ground gape black under you foot, when the water snatch you in she claws, when the luck-piece hang over you head and you can't reach!"

"Best keep the old beldames in a good humor," Colonel FitzPickwick urged in a low tone.

Mystery jerked his head reluctantly. The two men and the two old women were slowly moving away, their unnaturally long shadows trailing behind them on the mist like black wings.

"Drat!" said Dido. "I wish I could a heard a bit more."

She ran softly across the lawn, but the two couples had separated, and the men were mounting horses in the stable-yard.

Slowly and thoughtfully, Dido made her way home. As she neared Dogkennel Cottages she recalled Mrs. Lubbage's make-believe dragon, and quailed a little at the thought of what might be in store for her tonight. But whatever it is, I'll just throw a rock at it, she decided.

Tonight there was no dragon, nor was Mrs. Lubbage herself to be seen. Suspicious of the silence and darkness, remembering Mrs. Lubbage's broken lock, Dido approached her own cottage and looked for the key under the stone. But the key was not there. A glimmer of candlelight showed in the window and the door was open. Surely it was late for Mr. Firkin still to be sitting with the Captain.

Dido pushed the door back and went in.

Mr. Firkin was not there. Instead, Mrs. Lubbage and Tante Sannie were sitting in silence, one on either side of the Captain's bed. He did not stir as Dido entered; he appeared to be sleeping.

A dreadful apprehension filled her; she darted forward to the bed and leaned over it.

"Cap'n! Cap'n Hughes! Are you all right?"

He neither moved nor stirred. The sharp eyes of Tante Sannie and Mrs. Lubbage moved up and fixed on Dido like pins in a map.

"Cap'n Hughes! Please say summat!" She shook him a little, but he did not answer. He breathed, but only just; his mouth was a little open, his face deadly pale, what could be seen of it under the bandages.

"If you've killed him, you old—" burst out Dido, choking with grief and terror, "if you've hurted him— Oh, what have you *done* to him? What'll happen to him?"

"Wait and see, Miss Prussy! Wait and see!" Mrs. Lubbage gave Dido a look of malignant satisfaction. "And maybe this'll teach ye a lesson not to be so quick to meddle in other folks' concerns! Come, Sannie; us'll leave, eh, now the fine young lady's come a-home. *She* can look arter him."

Dido hardly noticed when they left. She was frantically rubbing the Captain's cold hands. She filled a stone bottle with hot ginger ale and put it to his feet; she mixed a mustard plaster and laid it on his stomach; she fetched in a bundle of chicken feathers and set light to them, filling the room with foul-smelling fumes; she tickled his feet and held a warm flatiron to them, and sprinkled snuff under his nose. None of these remedies had the least effect; the Captain continued to lie still as a log, hardly alive, yet not quite dead.

In despair, Dido went and roused Mr. Firkin who came quickly when she had made him understand the gravity of the case. He felt the Captain all over with careful, wise old hands.

"Arr; she've overlooked him, surelye. Deary me, darter, that *is* misfortunate, just when he was a-coming along so nimbly."

"Is he dying?" asked Dido, gulping.

"Nay, I wouldn't say that, darter, not here-an-nows. But die he may, don't she take the spell off'n him again. He can't eat, see, not while he be thisaway; he be like to starve."

"What'll I do?" Dido muttered, half to herself.

"Ee'll have to eat humble pie, darter; I dunno how ee harmed owd Mis' Lubbage, but ee'll have to undo it, and ask her to take off the overlooking."

"She never would. And *I* never would," said Dido flatly. "It didn't even *advantage* her any to hurt the Cap'n; she just did it out o' pure malicefulness. I'll cure him somehow. Or I'll *make* her take the spell off. Anyways, I don't believe in spells!" She was half crying.

"Well, darter, us'll try this and us'll try that. A drop o' Blue Ruin wi' red pepper in it works wonders for my old ewes, time they suffers from the sheepshrink; I'll see how that gooes down."

It did go down; and the Captain blinked, as if it had given him a lively minute's dream; but it did not rouse him.

"Anyhows, that shows we can feed him," said Dido, recovering, and rather ashamed of her loss of control. "Why, when I was in a swound on board the whaler they fed me for nigh on ten months with whale oil and molasses. I'll get some molasses in Petworth tomorrow."

"Music," muttered Mr. Firkin. "Music be a powerful strong tonic agin sorcery and spells. I dunno why but so 'tis. I'll sing the Cap'n a shanty or two."

"Just afore you gets going," said Dido, visited by a sudden idea, "Mr. Firkin, does you have sich a thing as a corkscrew?"

Mr. Firkin, who had opened his mouth to sing, paused in midbreath.

"A twistycork, darter? Surelye. Look ee in the chest in my tool shed, ee'll find one there." He filled his lungs again.

Dido found the corkscrew, whispered to the Rio-bound Mr. Firkin that she would be back in twenty minutes or so, and set off at a fast run for the Cuckoo Tree.

The next day dawned gloomy and lowering. Dido awoke very dejected. Captain Hughes still lay in the same stupor; his condition had not changed despite all Mr. Firkin's songs; and she could not help blaming

[156]

herself bitterly. Supposing he *never* recovered? And what other forms might Mrs. Lubbage's ill will take? Suppose the witches made Cris's life miserable at Tegleaze Manor? Suppose they prevented the Dispatch from reaching London?

Trying to shake off these thoughts, she gave Dapple an extra handful of feed.

"Eat up, old mate, us has to go into Petworth and get some spermaceti and treacle."

Just before she left, Gusset arrived with more provisions and a bottle of blackberry wine.

"Old Lady Tegleaze be rare and spry," he told Dido. "Reckon she thinks a granddaughter be a better bargain than a grandson."

"How's Cris settling?"

"A mite peaky and homesick; it do all seem turble big and grand to her, poor young maidy. How be the Cap'n?"

When Dido told Gusset what had happened he shook his head in an anxious and gloomy manner, and promised to send Dr. Subito as soon as possible.

"Though I doubt he'll not be able to do anything, missie; old Mis' Lubbage's spells be desprit powerful when she's roused. 'Tis better to keep on the right side of her, or she can do deadly harm. I know, who better." A shadow passed over his aged face.

"I've got to get him away from here," Dido said, biting her lip with anxiety. "You don't think Frill or Pelmett'd help—I could borrow the trap and take him to an inn—he can't be wuss off than he is here."

"Pelmett's gone, missie."

"Gone? When?"

"Said he had an offer of a sitiwation wi' better pay and took his bundle and went off last night."

"Sounds a bit havey-cavey? What about Frill?"

"I doubt he be going to follow. We shan't miss 'em, they warn't much use."

Gusset took his leave, casting a wary eye in the direction of Mrs. Lubbage's house, and promising he would ask about the trap. But, he said, he thought it very unlikely that Lady Tegleaze would be willing to lend it.

Dido left the Captain in the care of Mr. Firkin, who usually spent Saturday cleaning his cottage. Dido promised to do this when she returned, and also to buy him some provisions.

When she reached Petworth, she could not help noticing that it seemed to be in an extreme state of turmoil and uproar. People were rushing hither and thither, up and down the streets, in what seemed a purposeless way, like ants when their nest has been disturbed.

Dido stopped a man and asked him in which street the Magistrates' Court was to be found. He gave her a blank stare and replied,

"What's the use o' that, pray? It's gone. No use locking the stable door arter the horse has skedaddled," and strode away.

When she inquired of another he replied, "They sat early. The Court's closed now."

[158]

"Why? They was due to sit at ten; 'tis only quarter to, now."

But the man had not waited; he was roaming up the street, peering into every cranny as if he expected to find an emerald brooch there.

Dido noticed a remarkable number of constables about, too, whose behavior was of the same wandering kind; they stopped, they started, poked with their staffs in flower beds and window boxes, rummaged in the baskets of goods exhibited for sale outside shops.

Out of patience at last, Dido went to the apothecary's, bought a pound of spermaceti and a gallon of treacle, and asked Mr. Pelmett what the mischief was the matter with everybody, and why had the Magistrates' Court sat early?

"Constabulary was needed elsewhere," Mr. Pelmett said curtly. He looked, Dido thought, put out about something; had a face as long as a rolling pin.

"What for?"

"Every man jack of them's out looking for the Tegleaze heirloom."

"W-what?" gasped Dido. "You mean—"

"It's been stolen."

"But I thought the glass case was burglar proof."

"It was cut by a diamond. Expert cracksmen have been at work."

"My stars," muttered Dido. "Here's a fine flummeration. I spose that perishing Mystery decided he better get his paws on it right away, without waiting for any

[159]

more hocus-pocus over grandchildren. I'd dearly like to know who that Mystery *is*—a-calling of himself Tegleaze and a-reckoning to polish off heirs right, left, and rat's ramble—it's plain he's close connected with the family someway."

There was no sign, today, of Mystery's puppet theatre; the whole of the fair had been expeditiously tidied away.

Dido could get no information from anybody about what had happened at the Court session, and she did not dare linger in Petworth asking questions for fear the doctor should arrive before she returned. She urged Dapple back at what he considered a most unreasonable speed for an animal with a gallon can of molasses banging about on his withers.

In fact the doctor did not arrive until half past eleven and Dido was becoming wildly impatient before his cob drew up at the gate. Furthermore, he seemed very reluctant either to come in or, when he did enter, and saw the Captain's condition, to advise anything at all helpful.

In answer to all Dido's questions as to whether the patient needed new medicines, or new treatment, or new diet, he merely reiterated,

"*Tranquillamente—lusingando—amabile—poco a poco!* Only the utmost care will save him."

"But can't you advise anything, Doc?"

"*Non troppo*—I think not," replied the doctor, casting a hunted glance in the direction of Mrs. Lubbage's quarters.

[160]

"Don't you reckon it'd be a good thing to shift him from here?"

"*Largamente*—yes; yes I *do* think so." Dr. Subito made this answer in an undertone, finger on lips, and the moment after, took his leave, going off so fast that he forgot to pocket the five-shilling fee Dido had laid ready for him on the table. Oh well, he had hardly earned it, she decided.

It wanted but twenty minutes to noon by the Captain's chronometer. Dido flew to Mr. Firkin's cottage, swept, mopped, and set all to rights; laid out his groceries on the dresser where he could feel them over; and then, telling him she would be back as soon as possible, ran off in the direction of the Cuckoo Tree. No time to take a roundabout way; she hoped that she was not observed.

Behind the little tree, stretching away around the far side of the Down, was a thickish yew wood; as Dido approached the Cuckoo Tree from one side, a figure slipped quietly through the wood on the other, and they met by the Cuckoo Tree trunk, from which Dido's corkscrew still protruded.

"Well, love; what be the trouble?" said Yan Wineberry.

"Old Ma Lubbage has overlooked my Cap'n," Dido gulped out. "He's struck speechless; so there ain't much sense in your coming to see him tonight. And I dunno what to *do* about him."

"Humph," said Yan. "Things is tolerable troublesome all round then, for *I* found out that the magistrates had a private session this morning and sentenced that young Tobit to ten years' transportation. Which is as much as to say a lifer."

"But that's wicked!" Dido was horrified. "How could they—with no one there to speak up for him?"

"Well, they did." Yan was somber. "But," he added more cheerfully, "that's no skin off'n our nosen, for we're a-going to break into Petworth Jail 'sevening, for to fetch out Pip, my number five, who got hisself buckled up by mistake, and we'll fetch out young Mas'r Tobit at the same time."

"Oh, Yan, that's prime!" Dido hugged him. "Can I come too? So Tobit knows it's friends?"

"But what about your Cap'n?"

"Yan, is there any lodgings in Petworth where I could get him fixed up? I jist can't abear leaving him alongside that old fiend any longer."

"Well, reckon Uncle Jarge might have him," Yan said, scratching his head. "That is, if he's not a Scotchman; Uncle Jarge can't abide them."

"No, he ain't a Scotchman; he told me he comes from Pennygaff in Wales, and got a boy there called Owen. Is that your uncle Jarge as owns The Fighting Cocks pub?"

"That's right, lovie. My aunt Sary, she'm a wonderful comfortable woman; I dessay she'd take tolerable good care of the Cap'n if he be that sick; she'm a famous nurse."

"How could we get him there?"

Yan seemed to have unlimited relatives.

"My cousin 'Tholomew, over to Benges, guess he'd lend his haycart. Put the Cap'n on a bit of hay, he won't feel the jounces so bad."

Dido could hardly speak, the idea of getting the Captain away from Dogkennel Cottages was such a relief. She picked a sprig of yew and carefully stripped off all the tiny dark-green leaves. When she had her voice under control she said,

"What time should I have the Cap ready to shift? When are you breaking into the—"

"Hush! Who's that?"

They had been speaking very softly, but now he dropped his voice to a breath and laid a finger on her lips. Above them a voice began to sing:

> "Dwah, dwah, dwuddy, dwuddy, dwee
> I can't see you but you can see me—"

"*Cris!*" exclaimed Dido. "What in the Blue Blazes are you doing up there?"

A silence followed, then a timid voice said,

"Dido? Is that you?"

"Well, o' course it's me, gal! But why the plague are you here, 'stead of up at the Manor, eating your dinner with a silver spoon? I call that downright ungrateful!"

There was another long pause, then Cris slid down the trunk. Her face was pale, and there were traces of tears on it; she had the old sheepskin jacket huddled over her velvets.

"Aswell won't come to me at the Manor," she said miserably.

"Oh, botheration," Dido muttered.

"Who be this, then?" Yan asked in an undertone. He had been even more startled than Dido by Cris's sudden appearance.

"Tobit's twin sister," Dido explained in the same tone. "Old Ma Lubbage had her hidden away all these years in her attic, ready for a bit o' blackmailing tick-tacks when Tobit got put away."

"Have you been up yonder tree afore, ducky?" Yan asked Cris.

"Many times. More than I can count," she told him.

"Then that explains a power o' puzzlement. Some o' my Wineberry Men would have it that there was a liddle Pharisee lived up the tree," said Yan, grinning.

"But, listen, Cris," said Dido, who was anxious to get back to the Captain. "You can't run off from Tegleaze Manor, you gotta give it a fair trial. Why, gal, you're in clover there, in the lap of thingummy—all found, four square meals a day—"

"It's lonesome!"

"Oh, crumpet it—"

"It would be different if my brother was there."

"Well, we're a-going to rescue him from quod this very arternoon. Though what us'll do with him then—"

"*Are* you?" Cris's face lit up. "I'll come too!"

Disconcerted, Dido and Yan stared at one another.

At this moment another voice broke in.

"Well!" it said gloatingly. "So I found ye out at last, did I? This is where ee went skrimshanking off to outa my loft, was it? The old Cuckoo Tree, eh?"

Mrs. Lubbage stood before them, arms akimbo, her face red with hurry and triumph.

Cris turned white as her ruffles, Dido drew a sharp breath.

"Make a slap-up liddle nestie for to play hide-and-seek in, did it? Well, I'll soon tell Amos Frill abouten it, time he'll bring his scoring axe and chop it down!"

"No!" cried Cris, and laid her hand protectively on the trunk.

"Ah! But I say yes, my young madam. And ee'd best come back to Tegleaze with me now; Sannie an' me'll put ee to bed with a shovel, I can tell ee!"

"Hold your tongue, you sidy old witch, or by the pize I'll give ee summat that'll misagree with ee," interrupted Yan angrily. "Let's have none o' that moonshine about cutting down the Cuckoo Tree. You know well, if ye was to lay a finger on it, there'd be no roof over your head by nightfall."

Mrs. Lubbage seemed to swell like a slug with rage; she darted an evil look at Yan.

"Moonshine is it, Yan Gusset? I know a thing or two about moonshine too! If ee have the roof off my head, I'll give ee neighbor's fare."

"There's nought ye could do wuss than ye done already," Yan said bitterly. "You poisoned my mum, putting nightshade in her morgan-tea, I know full well."

"Prove it! Ye can't!" Mrs. Lubbage grinned spitefully.

"I can too." The smile vanished from her face. "I've a witness. That wouldn't bring my mum back, though. But you'd best mind your ways, you old canker-moll. Go

[165]

back to your crony. Tell her the Tegleaze luck-piece is stole, you can mumble your jaws over that together."

Mrs. Lubbage's jaw did indeed drop at this piece of news. Without another word she turned and waddled away as fast as she could over the steep hillside.

"That'll give 'em summat to worrit about," Yan said with satisfaction.

"Who stole it, Yan, d'you reckon?" Dido asked.

"Ah, that's a black mystery, that is."

"I'll lay it *was* old Mystery. Croopus, time's a-wasting —I must get back to the poor old Cap. Cris, are you going to come along o' me, then?"

Cris nodded; she was still pale and speechless from the scene with Mrs. Lubbage.

"I'll send my cousin 'Tholomew round with the hay-cart, come cock-shut time then," Yan said with his friendly nod, and slipped away into the yew wood.

Dido and Cris returned to Dogkennel Cottages—not without some terror on the part of Cris in case they should meet Mrs. Lubbage. But Mrs. Lubbage was no-where to be seen—doubtless she had hurried off to take counsel with Tante Sannie.

"I hope she'll stay away till we've gone," said Cris trembling.

Dido considered her thoughtfully. "What are we a-going to do with Cris," she wondered. "If she won't go back to the Manor, and wants to be with Tobit—and if we rescue Tobit—*he*'ll have to stay hid somewhere till we can find a witness as'll say his arrest was a put-up job—where can we stow the pair of 'em? Oh well—no sense getting into a sussel about it yet."

She fed the unconscious Captain some treacle and spermaceti, gave herself and Cris something more substantial, and then packed up their things in readiness for departure. What food remained she took around to Mr. Firkin and told him they were leaving.

"Nay, that be ernful news, darter," he said sadly. "Mind, I ain't saying you're wrong—I dessay the Cap'n'll do better if he bain't anigh that old grummut—but ee've been brightsome company and I'll grieve to part from ee."

Dido grieved too. She had grown fond of the kind old man.

"Spose old Mother Lubbage gets swarly with you when we've flitted?"

"She 'ont harm me, darter; I ain't afeered of her, see?"

Just the same Dido felt a pang when, after Cousin 'Tholomew had turned up with his wagon and they had loaded the Captain and their boxes on to the layers of hay inside, they drove off leaving Mr. Firkin with Toby beside him, standing at his cottage door, listening, listening, and waving as long as he could hear the sound of the wheels. He looked so old and so frail to be left there alone.

"You oughta have him to live up at the Manor, Cris," she said, swallowing, "when we've got Tobit out of jug and—and things is all settled."

Cris looked as if she thought it unlikely that such a time would ever come.

Cousin 'Tholomew was a red-faced, silent, curly-headed giant who drove them to Petworth at a slow walk, with Dapple harnessed alongside his own cart horse, and refused to accept any payment.

"Nay, 'tweren't no manner o' trouble. I had to come anyhows, to get a new Canterbury hoe," he said gruffly, and made his escape as soon as he had left them at the inn.

Uncle Jarge and his boy Ted received them kindly at The Fighting Cocks, and Captain Hughes was carried upstairs to a little white-walled room at the very top of the house, "where," said Miss Sarah Gusset, "he won't be disturbed by the street noises or the cockfighting."

Dido only wished he *would* be disturbed; he lay so pale and silent. But plump, smiling Miss Sarah seemed a kind and resourceful nurse; she had a bed so stuffed with hot bricks that it was like a Roman bathhouse, a whole tub full of aromatic vinegar, and a great quantity of hickory pepper, to make him sneeze. So he lay warm and sneezing, and at least by this they knew he was still alive.

"Now," said Miss Sarah, when the Captain was settled, "I had a message for you from that scamp, my nevvy Yan. I'd best not miscall him, though, had I? George gets all his corkscrews and Blue Ruin and Dutch Stingo and Calais Cordial from Yan—mum's the word! He surely is a member, that lad! Anyway, you're to meet him under the arch at six sharp, so you'd best have a bit of supper first, by the kitchen fire."

Miss Gusset's kitchen fire blazed in a huge open hearth by which hung hams and dried fish and bunches of herbs. Dido and Cris sat on stools in the hearth itself and were given earthenware pipkins of the best soup they had ever tasted and bread fresh out of the big oven, while Miss Sarah bustled about getting supper for the customers, and Uncle Jarge looked after the bar, occasionally putting his head through a little hatch to tell them the latest gossip.

"Harwood's pig be loose again! Foxhounds to meet here, Saturday's a fortnight. That Mr. Mystery, as he calls hisself, is still in the town, lodging with Hoadleys at the Angel; going to give another show. Asked could he lodge here and give his show in our yard, but I said we were full up."

Croopus, Dido thought, that was a near squeak!

"We'd best get you out o' them velvets, Cris, they're too noticeable. I've a notion old Mystery means no good by you; anyways you're too like Tobit by half; anyone might pounce on you thinking you was him. You'd best wear my spare midshipman's rig."

The midshipman's gear included a canvas smock, like enough to a shepherd's smock so that Cris would pass unnoticed in the street; and besides this, Miss Sarah rummaged out a sheepskin cap from a collection of odds and ends left behind by visitors to the inn. This covered up her dark hair.

At a minute before six they slipped out the back door and found Yan already waiting under the arch, with a couple of other men, muffled up like carters in sacking. They carried long brushes, a ladder, and bags of soot.

"Naught better than to look like a chimbley-sweep

when you're fixing to break into a jail," whispered Yan cheerfully. "It's a good reason for having the ladder with you, likewise for blacking your face; and if things comes to a roughhouse, a handful o' soot's wonderful boffling does it hit the other chap in the face."

He nodded approval of the girls' dark-blue rig, gave Dido a large sheet of very sticky paper to carry, and led off up the alley in the direction of the jail.

When they were halfway along, a man slipped silently past them, going in the opposite direction. It was too dark to see his face, but Dido gave two or three sharp sniffs after he had passed by.

"What's amiss, my duck?" whispered Yan, who was amazingly quick to notice anything that happened near him.

"The smell o' that chap's tobacco," Dido whispered back. "I knowed someone afore who smoked that kind—Vosper's Nautical Cut." She stopped to unstick the paper which had caught against itself—it was spread with treacle, Yan explained. He remarked that with a sniffer like hers, Dido was wasted outside the scent trade, and then they had arrived at the jail, a small brick building that stood beside a windmill on the outskirts of the town. It did not appear as if the jail were put to very frequent use; grass grew over the doorstep. There were bars on the ground-floor windows, but not on the upper ones. A watchman was seated on the mounting block outside the jail, drinking something from a leather bottle. Yan stole up behind him and gave him a brisk, deft thump with a sock full of soot; he toppled silently off the block and the contents of his bottle spilled on to the grass.

"Organ-grinder's oil," said Yan, sniffing; "wonder where he got it? Why, 'tis Sam Pelmett, I thought he was in service up to Tegleaze."

"He left there this morning," Dido said.

"We'd best put his head in a bag and tie him up middling tight."

This done, Yan took the treacled paper from Dido, ran up the ladder as nimbly as if chimney-sweeping were really his profession, smoothed the paper against a windowpane, and then tapped it with his soot-filled sock. The pane broke, but stuck to the paper, which he passed down to his mates. He then put an arm through the window, found the catch, opened it, and disappeared inside.

Five minutes of somewhat uneasy silence went by. At last one figure, two figures, suddenly and softly appeared around the corner of the building.

"It's us!" whispered Yan. "Came out the back door—dang me, it wasn't even locked."

"But where's Tobit?" Dido asked anxiously, for Yan's companion was a grown man.

"That be the mischief of it, ducky—he ain't there."

"Are you *sure?*" Dido made a movement toward the jail, but Yan grabbed her arm.

"Sure as Sunday—we went over the whole place, there's not another soul inside. But Pip here, who was in the next cell, says that not half an hour agone he heard some chaps come along, mouching and mum-chance, have a word wi' the watchman, open up the boy's cell, and take him off wi' them. What d'you make o' that?"

"Oh my stars!" said Dido. "I reckon that there Mystery's gone and kidnapped him!"

7

Tobit had been horribly bored in jail. He was shut into a little upstairs room that looked out on to a pigsty with three pigs in it. Beyond that lay a grass-grown yard in which there was a well. The well appeared to be disused: it was covered by a millstone with moss on it; the wellhead was weatherworn, the handle and chain rusty. A pile of old farm implements lay in a corner of the yard, half grown over with brambles. On the other side of the yard was a windmill with some doves on its roof.

Tobit had plenty of time to study all these details.

For a while he tried to amuse himself by firing Joobie nuts through his peashooter at the pigs, but their hides were so thick that they didn't notice; it was very poor sport and he presently gave up. For a while, too, he tried to cheer himself by hoping that his grandmother would send to have him released, or that some witness would come forward to say that he had been wrongfully arrested, but time passed, and his hopes sank lower and lower. Night fell. When he had been sitting in the dark for a couple of hours somebody opened his door and thrust in a rush dip, a loaf of brown bread, and a mug of weak beer; he had no more visitors that evening. It took him a long time to go to sleep; he made up dozens of different stories about how he was rescued by highwaymen, by Hanoverians, by outlaws; how he managed to escape by tearing his sheets into strips and climbing out of the window. But nobody rescued him, there were no sheets, it was a long drop to the ground, and then there were the pigs underneath; Tobit had a great dislike of pigs.

He thought of swallowing a Joobie nut. When he was little, Sannie had given him Joobie nuts to suck for toothache and there had been a fearful fascination about the things they made him see—trolls, giant bats, griffins. Then Sannie had forbidden Joobie nuts, which of course added to the excitement of sucking them. But now Sannie was not here to provoke, and he didn't fancy the kind of visions that Joobie nuts might produce in the little dark prison room. He counted sheep instead and at last fell asleep.

Next morning, not particularly early, the door opened and he was surprised to see Pelmett, who brought a loaf of brown bread and a cup of watery milk. Tobit's heart leapt up.

"Has Grandmother sent to have me let out?"

Pelmett dumped the cup and loaf on the floor, then stood regarding Tobit with folded arms and a scornful smile.

"Old Lady T? Not middling likely! You've cooked your goose with *her,* my boy—she've cut you off. There'll be no more airs and graces, Mas'r Tobit now! Yes, Sir Tobit, no, Sir Tobit, what can I fetch for you, Sir Tobit—ugh, you spoilt young twort! You'll be pulled afore the Beak this morning, and you'll be given a lifer in Botany Bay, and serve you right. All for a couple of fourpenny shubunkins!" He laughed in a sneering manner as if he knew more than he was prepared to say, picked up the empty beer mug, spat into it, and retired, slamming the door.

Presently two constables appeared and hustled Tobit into a downstairs room.

Three gentlemen were already seated there, behind a table. He recognized the Tegleaze family lawyers, and hope rose in him again. But the two old gentlemen, Pickwick and FitzPickwick, stared vacantly about as if they had not noticed him come in, while young Mr. Wily flipped through a bunch of papers, stood up, and proceeded to read aloud in a rapid gabble:

"Accused was seen to steal two shubunkin fish, worth fourpence-three-farthings, property of Miss Betsy Smith; fish were subsequently discovered in accused's pocket."

"Shocking, shocking," mumbled the two old gentlemen. One of them asked, "Where is Miss Smith now?"

"She has left town."

"Names of witnesses?" croaked the other old gentleman. They seemed half asleep, and as if they were unable to distinguish objects more than two or three feet away.

"Mrs. Aker, Mrs. Baker, Mr. Caker, Miss Daker, Mrs. Eaker, Mr. Faker—all ratepayers; a Mr. Twite, and a Mr. Mystery, who happened to be passing through the town, and Amos Frill, footman at Tegleaze Manor."

"Ah yes, mumble mumble; very respectable, Tegleaze Manor. Mumble mumble," said one of the two old men.

"And the culprit's name?"

As the younger lawyer read out Tobit's name, both constables fell into such a fit of coughing that it seemed almost impossible the old gentlemen should have heard it, but this did not seem to make any difference.

"Guilt clearly proved then," said one. "I think we are all agreed on that? Mumble mumble."

"Indeed yes, mumble," said the other. "And the sentence? Are we agreed on that?"

"Ten years in Botany Bay, I think we decided before coming in?"

Here it was young Mr. Wily's turn to cough in a reproving way.

"Did you hear, young man?" said old Mr. FitzPickwick, blinking in Tobit's direction. "You are sentenced to ten years' transportation, and we hope you are duly grateful for the leniency of your sentence."

Tobit's mouth was so dry with astonishment and dismay that he was incapable of making any reply, but nobody noticed; young Wily snapped out,

[177]

"Constables, remove him!" and he was hustled back to his cell.

"You'll be taken off on Tuesday, when a gang goes down to the convict ships at Pompey," one of the constables told him. "Ah, and am I thankful I'm not in *your* shoes!"

They dumped down his dinner—more brown bread and a bowl of weak pea soup. After that, nothing happened for a number of hours and Tobit was left to his own miserable reflections. He tried to tell himself stories about how he escaped on the way to Portsmouth; how he was rescued by smugglers, by French privateers, by pirates from the convict ship—but none of the stories rang particularly true, and even if they had, they left a lot of time ahead of him which would have to be spent in a very disagreeable manner.

By five o'clock that evening it is probable that he was the most unhappy boy in Petworth.

He was sunk in a sort of melancholy daze when he became aware of low voices having a conversation just outside his door, and the sound of coins chinking. Then the door was softly opened. Tobit, who had been staring gloomily out at the pigs, turned his head, but before he could see who had come in a neckerchief was whipped over his eyes and a noose was drawn tight over his hands. Something pricked him between the shoulder blades.

"D'you feel that?" inquired a voice in his ear. "If you want it to go another six inches in, just holler! It'd go in as easy as a knitting needle into a ball o' yarn."

[178]

Tobit prudently remained silent and was half pulled, half pushed very rapidly and, as far as he could make out, by at least two men, downstairs, out into the frosty night, a short distance over cobbles, a shorter distance over grass, and into a building that seemed large, to judge by the echoes, and had a strong, not unpleasant odor of bran, sacking, and grain. He could hear a regular creaking, and the mutter of distant voices. A door slammed behind him and a bolt rattled. The cloth was removed from his face and he discovered that he was in a large, round, dimly lit room; sacks, some full, some empty, were piled against the walls; in the center was an arrangement of ropes and pulleys leading up through a hole in the high ceiling. The floor was thick with dust or flour. He realized that he must be in the windmill; the creak was the regular noise of the great sails as they went around.

A small oil lamp burned on a trestle table about ten feet from where he stood; beyond the table sat a man whose face could not at the moment be seen because he was leaning forward, looking down intently at a small object that lay between him and the light.

Presently the man raised his eyes from their gloating scrutiny and peered past the lamp. Tobit recognized the puppet master.

He spoke harshly and abruptly.

"Where's your sister, b-boy?" he demanded.

Tobit remained silent, thinking the question could not have been addressed to him.

But the man repeated impatiently.

"You have a tongue—use it, or b-by the powers, I'll d-drag it out of you. Where's your sister? Where will she have hidden herself?"

"I—I haven't got a sister!" gulped Tobit.

Here another man, who had been standing in the shadows, moved forward. So low were Tobit's spirits that he was not particularly surprised to recognize Colonel FitzPickwick. The Colonel remonstrated.

"What difference does it make where the girl is, Tegleaze—since you have the heirloom?"

These words made Tobit start forward, but he was dragged sharply back by the cord around his wrists; Pelmett and another man still stood behind him.

"I tell you, I'll have no contenders for the title!" said the man addressed as Tegleaze. "When the Hanoverians come to power I want my claim clear. The boy is to be transported—very well, *he's* out of the running. But where's the g-girl? Where has she run off t-to?" he snarled at Tobit.

"I don't know what you are talking about!"

"He never met his sister," interposed FitzPickwick again. "He did not even know she existed. But doubtless we can soon track her down. She was friendly with the pair who have just decamped from Dogkennel Cottages —she may be with them. They'll not have gone far."

"She m-must be found."

"What will you do then?" the Colonel asked uneasily.

"Ship her overseas t-too, perhaps—back to Tiburon. Or m-marry her, maybe! How can I tell till I find her?"

"I don't understand you, Tegleaze!" the Colonel ex-

[180]

claimed. "You are so changeable. First you were going to wait till the boy came of age so that his grandmother would get her hands on the heirloom; I could have persuaded her to part with it as with all her other geegaws, for gambling money."

"Are you so sure?" interjected the other man. "The old lady is afraid of the luck-piece—Sannie told me so. She may be too willful and scatterbrained to scruple over gambling away family jewels and money, but the heirloom is something different. She believes, Sannie told me, that it has some uncanny power—that when it is in her hands it will bring her *luck*."

"But *you* do not believe such superstitious nonsense?"

"N-no." Tegleaze seemed to hesitate. "But perhaps I do not altogether t-trust you, FitzPickwick! You might, after all, if you *had* succeeded in getting it from her, have kept the luck-piece for yourself! After all, those two old hags of yours were playing a fine double g-game. If it had not been for their suddenly producing this precious girl, I could have made my claim as heir, once Tobit was out of the count. B-but that won't be so s-simple now—even if we get rid of the g-girl people might ask awkward questions; you can d-dispatch *one* rival heir without arousing suspicion, but if there are *two*, you have to be more c-careful! Until King George is on the throne and our c-cause has triumphed I'll stay in the b-background—now I have the luck-piece I c-can afford to wait. Our f-friends will see I have my rights after we have dealt with the Wren's N-Nest."

"Well—very well. Shall I deliver the luck-piece to the

[181]

Margrave of Bad Fallingoff? He will give all the jewels in his crown to see it safe!"

"Thank-ee, FitzPickwick," the other man said dryly. "I'll take care of that little m-matter myself!"

"What about Godwit—what about payment for moving the Wren's Nest?"

"Have no fear—you can trust *me!* Tell him to set his wits to work on the matter—he will receive f-funds within the w-week."

The seated man picked up the little object that lay before him; it was slung on a thin black cord, which he proceeded to tie in a knot. His hands, while doing this, shook so violently that two or three times he nearly dropped it; it swung crazily from side to side and Tobit could not get a clear view of it, though he could guess what it was.

"I wonder you care to part with it—since it is the family treasure?" Colonel FitzPickwick said inquisitively.

"The *family?* The family that does not even know of my existence? Pah! I should like to c-crush it to dust!" the other man said with such violent anger in his voice that the Colonel took an instinctive step forward. "S-set your mind at rest, however—I shall n-not do so! After all, this little t-trifle is going to pay for our t-triumph—it will set your humble servant back in his rightful place as well as K-King George. But, C-Colonel, I detain you —you have other engagements, I am s-sure. Pray don't let me inc-inconvenience you."

The Colonel seemed reluctant to leave.

"What about the boy—you'll not harm him?"

"Pelmett and Twite shall take him back to jail—ready for export. I see you were right. He c-can tell us nothing useful. G-good night, my dear sir."

He stood up and stepped to escort Colonel FitzPickwick from the place, carelessly slinging the black cord around his neck as he did so. But the cord, insecurely tied, came unknotted, and the pendant slipped off it and fell without a sound on to the dusty floor. They exchanged a few last words at the door, then the Colonel went out and mounted a horse, which could then be heard trotting away.

"Now," Tegleaze said briskly returning. "Give Fitz-Pickwick a few minutes to get clear, then dispose of the b-boy."

"Back to the lock-up, eh?" Pelmett said with a meaning wink.

Tegleaze did not reply; Tobit felt a sudden oddness in the atmosphere.

"Who are you?" he blurted out.

"Found your t-tongue, eh?" Mr. Mystery gave Tobit a long, strange, chill stare. "Well, it won't do you much good now. And it won't do you much good to know who I am. But I'll tell you—I'm your cousin—your cousin Miles Tegleaze. Our great-great-great-grandfathers were brothers, back in Cromwell's day. Yours fought on the king's side and prospered; mine went overseas to the Americas and f-fell on hard times. So did his son and his son's son. But n-now it is *my* turn to crow."

He swung away as if the sight of Tobit fidgeted him, and studied some plans that lay on the table. "Right," he said presently without looking around, "t-take him out."

Pelmett and the man called Twite grabbed Tobit's arms again and urged him toward the door. But he tripped over an iron bolt that fastened a trap entrance in the floor and, unable to keep his balance with his arms behind him, fell flat on his face.

Just before he hit the floor he saw something to his left in the thick, floury dust: a small, round, brightly colored object—the Tegleaze luck-piece. By pushing himself sideways, as if struggling to get up, Tobit was just able to gulp it into his mouth—along with a lot of dust—before the two men dragged him upright again.

Once outside the mill they did not, as he had expected, take him back toward the jail. Instead, Twite held him, while Pelmett moved a few feet away.

"Dark as the inside of a cow," Tobit heard him mutter. "Where is the plaguy thing—Ah—" There came a strange grinding creak as if heavy metal or stone had been slowly opened or dragged to one side. With an indescribable pang of terror Tobit remembered the disused well in the windmill yard.

"Too bad about this, young feller-me-lad," muttered the man called Twite. "But orders is orders—that Mystery knows enough about me to have me strung up by the heels from Temple Bar. I'll undo your hands though —you can swim if you've a mind to."

Tobit felt the noose gently slipped from his wrists— next minute he was pushed violently forward—trod on nothing—and fell, gasping with shock and fright. The luck-piece flew out of his mouth as he fell. Something struck his arm and he made an instinctive clutch at it, first with one hand, then with the other. It was the well rope, which burnt and scraped his palms as he shot helplessly downward. Another loud grinding creak overhead told him that the well's lid had been shut above him; at the same moment his fall was checked; he came to rest on something cold and sharp that cut and bruised his knees and shins: the bucket. Tobit and the bucket together dropped a few more feet; then, apparently, the rope caught, or had come to the end of its length.

Dangling in the dark, Tobit reached out with one hand; he could feel the circular brick wall of the well all around him, nothing above or below. He found a Joobie nut in his pocket and dropped it, but could hear no splash; either the well was dry, or the water was too far down for the sound to be audible. Up above, he could see a tiny circle of night sky, about the size of a button, with a single star in it. This must be the round hole in the middle of the millstone.

"I am hanging on a bucket in a well," thought Tobit very slowly and carefully. "I don't know how deep it is, but it may be *very* deep. I daren't shout for help because the nearest person is probably that man who says he is my cousin, and he wants me to die, I suppose so he can be sure of getting Tegleaze Manor. I have lost the luck-piece, which is at the bottom of the well. The only other people who know where I am are Pelmett and that man who undid the rope. Everybody else will think

I have escaped from the jail. Grandmother has cut me off. No one will care what has happened to me."

With a tremendous effort he managed to wriggle up so that he was half kneeling on the bucket. It was difficult because the bucket swung about and tipped, and when he had changed his position the metal rim hurt his legs, but at least some of the weight was off his arms. He wondered if the rope would break.

After a while he tried to make up a story about how he was rescued from the well, but no possible story seemed to meet the case.

He began to feel painful cramps in his arms and legs, but there was no way that he could move to ease them; he could find no comfort, either for mind or body.

He had thought himself to be miserable in jail, but in comparison with his present situation the jail seemed quite a cozy, homelike place. He wondered if he could be dreaming—having a nightmare—but it was all so unlikely that he was sure it must be real. The dreams from Joobie nuts were nothing like as frightening as this.

Joobie nuts. He felt them rattling in his pocket like heavy little peas. He could chew a couple and give himself a different kind of dream—but then he would go to sleep and fall off the bucket and that would be the end of him.

Presently, for no better reason than to distract his mind from the hopelessness of his plight, he began puzzling over the talk between Tegleaze and Colonel FitzPickwick.

"Where's your sister?" Tegleaze had asked. And Fitz-Pickwick had said, "He didn't know she existed."

What could they have meant? Surely they were not talking about him?

"I haven't got a sister," Tobit repeated obstinately. After another very long pause he added,

"Have I?"

Dido, Cris, and the three Wineberry Men stood in dismay, at a loss, out by the jail, until Pip said in an urgent whisper.

"Butter my wig, boys, let's scarper! Us doesn't want to be picked up by the constables spannelling around outside the lock-up."

"He's right," said Yan. "You two liddle maids'd best get back to The Fighting Cocks, smartish. If there's kidnappers abroad 'tis time for honest folk to be under cover."

"But what'll us do about Tobit?" said Dido worriedly. "I don't trust that Mystery—he'd pinch the birdseed from a blind canary. What'd he want to kidnap Tobit from jail for?"

No one could answer this.

"I'll nip round to the Angel, where he was staying, and have a word with the landlord," said Yan. "He be my great-aunt Gertrude's godson. He'll tell me if old Mystery's stirred out lately and where he's been. You two lads, Tan and Pip, quick yourselves out o' town and get to work on tomorrow's load, I'll see you presently.

And if I pick up any news at the Angel I'll leave word with Aunt Sary."

They separated, going in three different directions. Dido and Cris started down the alley, back toward The Fighting Cocks. But Cris went slower and slower, presently stopped altogether.

"What ails you, gal?" Dido said in an impatient whisper. "Bustle on, can't you?"

"I—I feel as if Aswell were trying to say something," Cris whispered back. "But I can't quite hear—can't make out what it is. Wait—wait just a minute!"

She stood still, then turned slowly back the way they had come, like a water diviner questing for the pull of the rod.

"Oh, rummage it," Dido muttered. "This is a fine time for Aswell to feel like a chat."

Very unwillingly she followed Cris, who was now proceeding at a steady pace back along the alleyway. At the top she went left, passing the jail again, and entered a grass-grown yard at the side of a windmill. Someone was inside the mill: there was a faint rim of light around the door. Dido looked inquiringly at Cris, who shook her head.

"Hush! I can almost hear it now!" she breathed. "Why are you so faint, Aswell?"

Their eyes were used to the dark; they could see the round stone in the middle of the yard, and the wellhead. Cris moved slowly toward this, listening all the time. Dido took two or three steps after her, glancing warily around.

[188]

"*Cris!* Yan said we oughta get under cover!" she whispered urgently.

"Hush!" Cris, heedless of Dido's warning, seemed to be listening through every pore of her skin. She murmured, "I can't make it out—Aswell seems to be in trouble—"

There followed a pause which seemed nerve-rackingly long to Dido, then Cris added with the beginnings of doubt in her voice,

"*Is* it Aswell?"

At that moment something struck Dido on her wrist. She rubbed the place and whispered, "*Do* come on, gal, we dassn't stay scambling about here so near the lock-up—"

"Could Aswell be down *there?*"

Like a bird dog, Cris was pointing to the well—not with her hand, but with her whole attention.

"In the *well?* Look, Cris, it just ain't sensible to stay here—"

Two more pellets struck Dido's hand; purely by chance she caught one of them and rolled it unthinkingly between her fingers. Something about the feel and shape of it attracted her notice; she sniffed it, peered at it, tested it with the tip of her tongue. It was a Joobie nut.

"Hey! Where did that come from?"

She knelt down to look at the millstone covering the well; as she did so, a fourth nut hit her on the cheek. It had come, there was no doubt at all, through the round hole in the well lid.

[189]

"What the dickens is going on round here?" she whispered to Cris. "Surely to goodness Aswell ain't shooting Joobie nuts at us from down the well?"

Even while she said the words her mind had leapt ahead and found the explanation.

"Tobit!"

She squatted down by the stone and leaned so that her face was over the hole. A nut struck her cheek. "Hey, Tobit!" she called softly. "Are you down there, boy?"

She could feel the well's hollowness carry her voice downward.

"Yes!" An urgent whisper came echoing back. "I'm halfway down here, hanging on a bucket. Can you pull me up? Some men threw me down here. Is that Dido? Are you on your own?"

"Rabbit me, *now* what are we going to do?" Dido muttered. "We don't dare waste time hunting for Yan—how does this pesky well open up?"

She felt all over the millstone; tugged upward; it was immovable.

"They musta shifted the stone somehow to get him *in*—"

All this time Cris had been standing silent, apparently dumbstruck; now she murmured in bewilderment,

"It's *not* Aswell!"

"O' course it's not Aswell, you noddy!" whispered Dido, hauling unavailingly at the millstone. "It's your brother. It's Tobit. Give us a hand, do!"

"No, but Aswell *is* saying something now—listen! Aswell says—wait, I'm getting it—Aswell says sideways. Push the stone sideways."

"What, like this?" More than doubtful, Dido gave the stone a shove, and nearly tumbled headlong in herself as it swung around, evidently on a pivot, to reveal a black crescent-shaped hole. The loud grinding rumble it made terrified the girls; Cris ran on tiptoe around to the far side of the stone; she and Dido eased it farther around, inch by inch; even so it seemed to make a hideous row in the quiet night. It would not go all the way; feeling around, Dido discovered that the rope had somehow jammed underneath it, which was why, evidently, the bucket had stuck halfway down and broken Tobit's fall.

"Anyways, I reckon there's room for him to clamber through," she whispered to Cris. "We can't wind up the bucket, though—we'll just have to haul him up. Brace yourself, Cris! It's lucky Tobit's skinny like you."

Heaving and straining, trying to stifle their gasps, they dragged Tobit on the bucket nearer and nearer to the top. When he was only a few feet down, Dido, changing places with Cris to get a closer purchase on the rope, fell or stumbled against the millstone and contrived to loosen it so that with a loud rasping thud it shot back the final foot; the freed rope would have run back down the well but Dido flung herself on it and reached down a hand to grab Tobit. She caught his hair and he let out a yell.

"*Quiet!* Grip on my hand, boy! Cris, you hold my feet."

[191]

Somehow, all struggling together on the brink, they managed to haul him out, losing a good deal of skin in the process.

There was a noise from inside the mill. Rapid steps came toward the door and they heard the sound of bolts being drawn.

"Quick!" gasped Tobit. "*He's* in there!"

No one asked who. Without a word they flew around to the back of the mill and dropped behind a stack of old farm implements grown over with brambles.

They heard the door open and a voice shout, "Pelmett? Where the devil are you?"

Somebody ran out. There was another shout, then silence.

"They've seen the well's open," Dido guessed. "Now what'll they do? Go off into the town, most like—they'd not expect anyone to be hiding around here."

Cris, Dido, and Tobit huddled in a heap, among the nettles and the rusty harrow blades.

"Keep your breathing down, you two—try *not* to breathe, can't you!" Dido whispered.

There was no more sound from the other side of the mill.

After five minutes had gone by, Dido said,

"Guess it'd be all right to mizzle off? We'd best climb over this wall behind us and circle round. Agreeable? Tobit, give Cris a hoist over the wall, can you?"

With the utmost caution they climbed, by means of the junk heap, on to the wall, which was not very high. There was much more of a drop down on the far side, into a field; Dido realized that this was in fact the town wall.

Without speaking, Dido grabbed Cris's hand, gestured her to take that of Tobit, and led off at a silent trot, under the wall, until they came to a small copse. Striking a footpath, they turned along it, through a gate, across another field, all the time skirting around the edge of Petworth which they could see as a few twinkling lights in the distance. At last their path met another which led back toward the town; they followed this warily, ready to duck into the hedge if they heard anybody approaching. But they met no one, and the path presently brought them out beside a big house at the bottom of the High Street.

"Right," muttered Dido. "You two bide here—duck down behind them bushes if you hear anybody coming—and I'll scout on ahead and make sure all's clear. Don't either of you dare to say a word!"

8

Luckily there was no cockfight that evening, and the yard at the rear of The Fighting Cocks Inn was empty and dark. Before going in, Dido glanced through the kitchen window and saw Miss Sarah Gusset knitting socks by the fire; nobody else was in the room. Dido slipped softly in the back door.

"There you are, then, dearie," Miss Sarah remarked placidly, finishing off her sock and adding it to a large heap of others. "Where's t'other little lass? And did you find the one you went to look for?" She spoke as if rescuing people from jail were a perfectly normal occupation.

"Yes, ma'am, we did," Dido said quietly. "They're a-waiting outside—I was wondering where we'd best put 'em—it wouldn't do for anyone to lay eyes on 'em."

"No indeed, dearie. They'd best go in our Gentlemen's cellar, the one the Wineberry lads uses in winter-time; they'll be cozy as two mice in a nest there. Just you fetch them in, poor little scrumplings—I daresay you can all do with a bowl of my soup."

Reassured by this calm welcome, Dido went off to fetch her companions. Halfway down the High Street an alley led in from the left. Just as Dido reached its entrance, a man came hurrying out of it; unable to check herself in time, she ran straight into him.

"Croopus, I'm sorry, mister—" she began, and then, getting a sudden glimpse of his face by the glimmer of a street lantern, "Why, it's *Pa!*"

The man's mouth fell open in utter dismay. "Great fish swallow us, it can't be Dido?" he muttered, gave her a hunted look, and made off at top speed up the hill.

Dido stared after him for a moment, biting her knuckle. But the first need was to get Tobit and Cris under cover; she went on down the hill. When she reached the point at which she had left them they were not to be seen. She gave a soft whistle.

"All clear, it's me—Dido!"

After a pause, long enough for her to grow anxious, Tobit and Cris crept out from behind two bay trees in tubs that ornamented the closed front of a greengrocer's shop.

"That man came by," Tobit whispered nervously. "I think he was hunting for me."

"Humph," Dido muttered to herself. "Here's a fine start. How's my pa got muxed up in this?" But aloud she was encouraging: "There was a chap, but he's gone —went off up the hill. Come on now—look sharp!"

Silently as three fish in a river they ran up the High Street and around to the back of The Fighting Cocks. Miss Sarah was waiting at the back door to let them in.

"That's the dandy," she said comfortably. "Come you down into the cellar now, while there's no folk about."

An iron spike with a side of bacon hanging from it stuck out of the bricks on one side of the big kitchen fireplace. Miss Sarah gave this a sharp tug; a large section of bricks opened outward like a door, revealing a narrow flight of stone steps.

"Take this rush dip, sweetheart, and go you down," Miss Sarah told Dido. "I put the soup on the hob and I've a pair of beds a-warming—I daresay the liddle 'uns'll be middling weary." She spoke as if Tobit and Cris were about six years old and gave them a kindly smile. "Then, when you've settled 'em, dearie, you come up and tap twice to be let out—I know you'll be wanting to have a look at your Cap'n. He's no different, but seems comfortable. Oh, just take the socks as you're a-going down, lovey, will you—I try to keep those Wineberry chaps socked up regular, their poor feet do get so wet."

The brick door closed behind them.

After descending about twenty winding steps they found themselves in a dry, brick-paved, brick-vaulted cellar which was so large that Dido guessed it must extend under the house next door as well as the inn kitchen. At the far end were about forty massive casks, labeled Sack, Rhenish, Canaries, Oporto, etc.; there were also bales of tobacco, crates of corkscrews and clay pipes, and half a dozen fourteen-quart kegs of brandy. Ten hammocks were slung from the ceiling, neatly made up with patchwork quilts; from two of them the handles of copper warming pans protruded. Ten seats, made from sawn-off sections of tree trunk, were ranged in front of a small but hot fire which burned in a kind of hollow pillar, open at one side, in the middle of the room; evidently its chimney ran up into that of the kitchen fireplace in the room above. A pot of soup stood on the hob.

"Jeeminy, this is snug," Dido said with approval. "It's a sight better than jail, *or* Mother Lubbage's parlor, hey, Cris?" Cris gazed around wonderingly; so did Tobit. Then Dido recollected something.

"Oh, Cris, this here's your brother Tobit; Tobit, meet your sis; reckon you ain't hardly had a chance to look at each other yet."

There followed a silence while they did so and Dido added with friendly impatience, "Well—go on! Don't you want to *say* summat to one another?"

It seemed they did not. They stared and stared. Tobit twisted a lock of his hair around his finger; Cris sucked a finger and rubbed it against the collar of her sheepskin jacket. At last Dido said, "Well, if you don't feel like talking, best eat," and ladled soup into earthenware bowls. Tobit gulped his down ravenously; Cris almost forgot to eat, watching every movement he made. Still neither of them spoke.

"Rumple me," Dido thought. "If I'd only just met my brother for the first time I'd have a sight more to say, I reckon. What a rum pair they are!" She stacked the soup bowls, put a couple of logs on the fire, and added aloud,

"Sweet dreams, then, mates. Us'll talk about plans in the morning. Now, don't you go a-making any ruckus, or chattering all night. Those is your hammocks a-warming. I'd best go and look after my Cap'n now."

She left, feeling that the silence behind her was closing and thickening, and becoming colored, like water into which a brilliant dye is slowly being poured; she had the fancy that if she turned and tried to go down the stairs again she would find it almost impossible to push her way.

When she had tapped twice and been let out by Miss Sarah, she went up to the attic and hung anxiously over Captain Hughes. His condition was unchanged, but he certainly seemed peaceful enough, and appeared to have been tidied up a good deal.

"I took off all those nasty old cobwebs," Miss Sarah explained, "and wrapped him up from head to toe in brandy leaves; that's why he smells so medical."

"What's brandy leaves, missus?"

"Lily leaves soaked in brandy; my old mother always used to say they'd cure any trouble but a broken heart. Now don't you fret about him, dearie, we'll get him better one way or another. My stars! He's a fine-looking fellow, isn't he—handsome as a herring. Yan sent a message to say he'd be round in the banquet hall at screech o' dawn for a confabulation. He went to the Angel but could get no news, he said to tell you. So you'd best get a bit o' sleep yourself. I had to put you in the loft, as all our guest rooms are full, but you'll sleep as soft as a silkworm there, for that's where the owlers keep their packs."

"What's owlers, ma'am?" Dido asked, as Miss Sarah opened a small trap door over the attic stairs, which led to the roof.

"Wool smugglers, dearie."

And indeed Dido discovered that all the space between the joists was packed with wool to a depth of several feet, so that it was like sleeping on a marvelously thick, springy mattress the size of a whole room. She burrowed herself a nest and lay in luxury. She could hear genuine owls calling, among the chimney pots outside; the owl hoots changed imperceptibly into the chattering of starlings, and she found that splinters of light were making their way between the tiles and that Miss Sarah had stuck her head through the trap door and was calling softly,

"Morning time, love! There's a bowl o' porridge keeping hot for you in the kitchen!"

While Dido gulped down her porridge, Miss Sarah, busy frying twenty eggs for the inn guests, said,

"I'll see to the Cap'n presently, don't you fret your head about him. And I reckon the liddle 'uns down below can sleep a bit longer yet; I've not heard chirp nor cheep from them. You can take down their breakfastses when you come back from seeing my nevvy Yan."

So Dido slipped out to the banquet hall and found Yan Wineberry already there, carving a whistle from an elder twig. His brown face looked less cheerful than usual and he greeted Dido soberly.

"I've not been able to find out anything about the boy, my duck. That Tegleaze be missing too—" he was beginning, when Dido, first glancing cautiously about the big empty room, whispered,

"Hush! It's all rug, we got him!"

"Nay! You never!"

As Dido described the mysterious way in which Cris had discovered, without being told, that Tobit was down the well, he looked more and more astonished.

"Well! That beats cockfighting!" he said at length. "I'd allus heard as twins was a bit uncanny and could understand each other wi'out talking but I never heard naught to equal that! And fancy you two liddle things being able to shove that gurt stone back and wrastle him out—he'd a bin drowned for sure by now, if you hadn't. That well be a hundred foot deep, easy. Who put him down there?"

"He just said some men. He and Cris was both a bit dumbstruck when I got 'em back here last night. But I reckon as how it was old Mystery."

Yan nodded. "Cousin Will said he'd not been back to the Angel all night, nor that mate of his, the fellow who plays the hoboy. They must still be out, searching

[200]

for the boy—guessed he'd climbed outa the well when they saw the top shoved back, I daresay."

"What can we do with Tobit and Cris?" Dido said. "They can't stop in your aunt Sary's cellar forever."

"I've been thinking about that, duck. I reckon it'd be best if they came up to London with us, on our run."

"Croopus," said Dido, somewhat taken aback. But then she began to see that this was a sensible suggestion. "It'd keep them out o' trouble here for sure; and no one'd be looking for them in London. But what about on the way—how can you keep them hid?"

"We're all hid together, duckie—'tis a secret way we go, see?"

"And what happens when you get there?"

"Well," Yan said, "they could stop with my auntie Grissie in Wardrobe Court, where we always puts up; she'd keep an eye on 'em. And I was thinking—we always takes a load o' corkscrews and two-three tubs of Hollands to Sir Percy Tipstaff—he's the Lord Chief Justice, you know—I could tell him as how there'd been a frame-up on young Tobit. Sir Percy knows I'm a trustable chap—I reckon he'd pay heed to me."

"Oh, Yan!" Dido hugged him warmly. "That's a prime plan. It's no use talking to old Lady Tegleaze or any of the nobs down here—the ones as hasn't a screw loose is all in it together, thick as gutter mud."

"And I'll take your letter to Lord Forecastle too."

"I wish I could come along," Dido said wistfully.

"You're kindly welcome, my duck."

"No, I'd best stay with poor old Cap'n Hughes. And

[201]

if I'm seen about the town, Mr. Mystery and Sannie
and the rest of 'em'll likely think that Tobit and Cris
are still stowed here too, and that'll put 'em off the
scent."

Yan agreed with this.

"But you take care of *your*self, lovey," he cautioned
her. "Don't you go getting chucked down a well."

"I'm fly!" said Dido. "No one's liable to sneak up on
me 'thout my hearing 'em. Now, where should Tobit
and Cris come—where do you start your run?"

"We meets at the Cuckoo Tree. The ten-shilling men
pick up the stuff at Appledram Camber and fetch it so
far—then five of us takes it on to London."

"Cris and Tobit better not go back to the Cuckoo Tree
now old goody Lubbage knows that's where Cris used
to go."

"No," Yan agreed. "I reckon they'd best get the carrier's cart to Pulborough—my uncle Ned's the driver,
he'll take 'em hid inside a pair o' cider barrels or summat—get off at the White Hart pub by Stopham Bridge,
and one of us Wineberry chaps'll meet 'em there. And
you give them Cap'n Hughes's letter and I'll see it's
delivered."

This sounded like a watertight plan, but still Dido
hesitated.

"Which day d'you reckon to get to London?"

"Tuesday—if we don't have too many deliveries along
the way."

"Suppose there was trouble here—spose summat went

wrong and I wanted to get in touch with you afore you got to London?"

"There's three pubs along the way where I'll ask for a message: the Rose at Run Common, the Ring o' Bells at Ripley, and the Rising Sun in Wandsworth."

"The Rose, the Ring, and the Rising Sun—that's easy to remember. And you'll take mortal good care o' the Cap'n's Dispatch, won't you—I've a notion it's someway connected wi' the coronation, and that's why the Cap was so desperate anxious to get it there the day before."

"Don't you worrit—I'll keep it locked up, along o' the Lord Mayor's dallop of tea and the Lady Mayoress's pipkin of pink lemon perfume," he promised.

"And if so be as you're chatting with old Lord Fore-castle," Dido said, "could you ask him to send a decent doctor down here? That Subito's too scared of Mother Lubbage to be any more use than a pastry pickaxe."

Yan said he would see to it.

That seemed to take care of everything. "I'll be getting back then," Dido said, and slipped into the alley, looking vigilantly all around her. After a cautious interval, Yan followed her.

Dido carried bowls of porridge down to Cris and Tobit. They were awake, and seemed quite content with each other's company, but still could not, or need not, talk together. They had gone back to their old occupation of staring at one another's faces.

Dido, finding their silence rather fidgeting, asked Tobit how he had come to be in the well, and he told her the whole tale.

"So it *was* old Mystery—and he's your cousin from furrin parts. No wonder he likes to come a-sneaking around Tegleaze after cockshut, measuring the flower-beds and sizing up the pigsties," Dido said thoughtfully. "But what a murksy set-out to push you down the well. Anyway I bet he's in a proper taking now—a-looking for you right, left, and rat's ramble. And you say the luck-piece fell down the well too?"

"I should think it must have. And so far as I care, it can stay there—Grandmother was only waiting for me to come of age so she could get hold of it and sell it for gambling money, my cousin wants it to sell to the Margrave of Bad Somewhere to pay for a Hanoverian plot—and it's never done *me* any good."

Dido was inclined to agree.

"Anyhow it can bide there for the time—nobody but us knows it's there, reckon it's safe enough." She chuckled. "I'll lay old Mystery's tearing out his hair in handfuls wondering where it's got to—he probably reckoned *you* made off with it."

"Well, so I did," said Tobit proudly.

Dido had observed a change in him since his adventure. It was hard to put into words, but he seemed more sensible, less given to play-acting and senseless dares.

She explained the plan in regard to Uncle Ned and the carrier's cart and the trip to London. Tobit's eyes certainly brightened at the thought of perhaps being able to see the coronation after all, but he was not so

wildly excited as Dido had thought he would be; while Cris seemed very little interested in the prospect.

"The cart don't pass here till dusk, so you'll have to stay down here for the day. You'd better play cat's cradle or summat—you can't just sit *staring* all day."

Neither Tobit nor Cris knew how to play cat's cradle; Dido pulled a length of string out of her pocket and instructed them, looping it over Tobit's hands, crossing it, and showing Cris how to take hold of the crisscrosses, pull them under and out, and so make a new framework. In no time they had got the hang of it and were completely absorbed.

Dido dumped a log on the fire and went upstairs, feeling rather lonely.

I wish I *was* a-going up to London with them and the Wineberry Men, and not staying here in this spooky little town, she thought enviously. And don't I just hope the Fust Lord of the Admiralty sends back some decent doctor as can put the poor old Cap'n to rights.

It was another driply foggy day; twilight came early, long before the arrival of Uncle Ned. During the afternoon Dido helped Uncle Jarge and his son Ted pack Tobit and Cris into sacks, with handfuls of wool and all the smugglers' socks Miss Sarah had knitted to stuff out the crannies so that they looked like a load of grain or seed. Then Uncle Ted arrived in his ancient covered wagon drawn by a spavined gray mare who went along so slowly that her driver never bothered to stop her, but simply loaded and unloaded as she wandered along. The canvas cover was pulled aside, the two sacks were placed on the cart. Dido did not dare call good-bye, as two or three other people were hoisting goods on at the same time, so she gave each sack a friendly pat under pretext of settling them in place, and jumped down on to the cobbles again.

"Eh, dear," she thought. "I do hope Cap'n Hughes's Dispatch will really be all right."

She had given it to Tobit, with strict instructions to hand it over to Yan Wineberry as soon as they were alone together.

"Jub on, mare," said Uncle Ned, the mare plodded slowly on up the hill, and Dido went off to Wm. Pelmett, Chymist, to get some more treacle, since Captain Hughes had finished the first gallon. The apothecary's shop was open for an hour on Sunday evenings, for the sale of treacle and cough jujubes, because so many people made themselves hoarse singing hymns in church.

"I can see you've a sweet tooth, missie," said Mr. Pelmett, handing her the treacle with a gluey smile.

Dido gave him a scowl in return.

As she was carrying the heavy jar up the High Street she caught a glimpse, in the distance, of a lanky, familiar figure, just turning left in the direction of the church.

"I'll not lose him twice!" Dido vowed. Thrusting the jar of treacle into the arms of a startled small boy she told him to carry it to The Fighting Cocks Inn and ask Miss Sarah for a spoonful.

"Say I said you was to have one!" And she made off at top speed in pursuit of the retreating figure. As he had not seen her and did not realize she was after him, she was able to dodge swiftly around the block and so meet him face to face in front of the church.

"Hello, Pa dear!" she greeted him affably. "Ain't you a-going to speak to me? Your own little Dido? How's Ma? And Penny-lope?"

Mr. Twite—for it was undoubtedly Dido's father— would have turned and run once again, but his daughter had him firmly by the jacket buttons.

"Now, Pa! Don't you try and scarper! Jigger it, some dads would be *pleased* to see their child as had been twice round the world and given up for drownded. Come and sit down on a tombstone and tell us the family news."

"Why, there's none that I know of, my chickadee. Indeed, for the last year or so I have been a happy man, free from family afflictions." But seeing there was no help for it, he allowed her to lead him to a dry tombstone behind a hollybush in the churchyard, where they could talk unobserved. "Your dear lamented mother was lost to us when Battersea Castle blew up—so was your aunt Tinty and your cousins—your sister eloped with a very ineligible young fellow who traveled in button-hooks—and *I* am under the painful necessity of supplying hoboy music for a strolling puppet troupe, since the Bow Street runners conceived a wholly unjustified suspicion that I was in some way connected with the Battersea Castle explosion."

"Swelp me," said Dido. "The whole family's gone, then?" She was not particularly cast down, since her mother had never been at all fond of her. "But what about Simon? And our house in Rose Alley?"

"Sold, sold, alas—or so I understand, not having been able to inquire personally—to pay some few trifling debts. So I have not even a home to offer you. As to Simon— the young boy who used to lodge with us?—I really cannot say." Mr. Twite sighed. He pulled a hoboy from the front of his waistcoat and played a few melancholy notes on it, then, becoming enthusiastic, launched out into a spirited jig.

"Ah," said Dido, "I suspicioned it was you playing, soon as I heard the hoboy tuning up for old Mystery's Mannikin show. So you're Mystery's mate, are you? How long've you been with him, Pa?"

"Why, but a few weeks, child. I was introduced to him by a most respectable gentleman, a Colonel Fitz-Pickwick. I understand Mr. Mystery has only recently come from one of our delightful colonies."

"And is already up to his whiskers in a plot to pinch Tegleaze Manor and put Bonnie Prince Georgie on the throne, helped by those old witches and that dicey pair o' footmen; Pa, Pa," said Dido sorrowfully, "why *will* you let yourself get imbrangled with such a jammy-fingered set o' coves? It's sure to lead to trouble."

"Not if we succeed, my dove; it'll be all garnets and gravy then, and Sir Desmond Twite, conductor at Sadlers Wells, and a house in Cheyne Walk."

"But you won't succeed, Pa."

"Oh? And why not, my sprite?" Mr. Twite gave her a sharp look.

Dido was tempted to tell him that the Tegleaze luck-piece, which was to have paid for the conspiracy, had been dropped in a well, but she resisted the urge. She said,

"Stealing may be respectable in your circles, Pa, but attempted murder ain't going to be so easy to laugh off."

"Humph," muttered Mr. Twite. "I wondered, when I came back and found the well stone had been pushed aside, if your little meddling hands had been at work. I had the devil of a job to get it back. So the boy *did* escape, did he?"

"Some trustable chaps as I know of are on their way to London this minute to lay an information about the whole affair before the Lord Chief Justice," Dido went on, impressively. "So if I was you, Pa, I'd mizzle while the mizzling's good."

"Oh, ho!" said Mr. Twite gaily, not a bit impressed. "But suppose I told *you*, my dear little chickadee, that some trustworthy chaps *I* know are perfectly informed about *your* trustworthy chaps and plan to get their information off them and destroy it before they reach London. Hey, dee, marathon me, what a set of simple souls those Jacobites be!" he hummed.

Dido gaped at him, utterly taken aback by this news.

"Yes, yes," Mr. Twite went on agreeably, "our friend Mystery—ah, there's a clever spark for you—got an equally clever old lady called Mrs. Lubbage to find out through some timid-hearted relative of one of those gallant Wineberry Men all about their so-called secret route to London. Unknown to the Preventive Men, maybe, but not to us; a concealed canal, I understand, all the way from the Arun River to the Thames, along which the barge of contraband plies its worthy way. With *one* extra crew member on board, ho ho, snug between the lavender water and the Lapsang Souchong and the spirits of licorice! So this famous Dispatch will vanish before it ever reaches London; and by Thursday, you know, it won't matter if *twenty* Lord Chief Justices know about the affair, it will be too late; too late, too late, too late, to retaliate," he sang joyously.

> "Sir Christopher Wren
> Let fall his goosefeather pen
> But, he said, whatever else falls
> It won't be St. Paul's.

Ah me, ah me, even the best of us are sometimes faulty in our judgments, are we not?"

"Sir Christopher Wren?" said Dido slowly. "The Wren's Nest?"

Mr. Twite suddenly stopped short in his caroling.

"You didn't know that, then, my duckling? Well, as it's too late now to prevent it, I'll strike a bargain with you. I will unfold to you the whole Wren's Nest project —ah, and what a startlingly sublime and sweepingly satisfactory scheme it is—in return for one small piece of information which doubtless you have at your clever little fingertips. What has become of that volatile pair, the youthful Tegleaze heir and his bewitching twin, like as one pin to another pin? Oh where and oh where can they be, with their noses turned up and their toes turned out, afloat on the bonnie blue sea? Or words to that effect," he added, suddenly darting another sharp look at his daughter.

But Dido was hardly heeding him.

"I couldn't say where they are, Pa, I'm sure," she truthfully replied.

"Oh, well, in that case, no cash, no crumpet."

"That's right," Dido said inattentively. "I must go, Pa, my Cap'll be wanting a dose of treacle."

"Indeed, indeed, the gallant Dispatch bearer. Poor fellow, what a misfortune that his coach should overturn, and he on his way to town with tidings of such urgent import."

"So long, Pa." As impatient to leave him as she had been to question him, Dido gave her father a hasty nod and almost ran in the direction of The Fighting Cocks. Had she looked back she would have seen him staring thoughtfully after her. But she did not look back.

9

Dido was panting and breathless when she arrived back at The Fighting Cocks Inn.

"Gracious, dearie, what's amiss?" inquired Miss Sarah, placidly stirring a caldron of soup with a spoon in one hand while she rotated five sizzling chickens on a spit with the other.

"Miss Sarah, I've got to get arter those Wineberry chaps at once! There's a spy among 'em that's going to pinch the Cap's Dispatch!"

"Eh, dear, there's a fanteague. Who could that be, I wonder?" Miss Sarah, still unruffled, basted her chickens, took a china mug down off the mantelshelf, and counted out five gold guineas from it. "Well, that Dapple horse is still there eating his head off in our stable, they've never sent for him from the Dolphin, so you'd best take him. Here's a bit o' cash—it never comes amiss."

"The Cap'n—" Dido began.

"Bless your heart, don't you worrit about him, dearie, I'll see to him as careful as if he was my Hannibal that was struck by lightning in a rowboat full of corkscrews, fifteen year last Michaelmas. Terrible fierce thunderstorms we had in those parts when I was a girl. Ah, it's a hard profession being a Gentleman."

Dido ran up to have a last look at the Captain, who seemed to be having pleasant dreams, lapped in his brandied lily leaves.

"Wrap up warm against the sea fret now," warned Miss Sarah when she came down. "Do you know where to go?"

"To the White Hart Inn?"

"That's it, but don't you cross the river. There's an old narrow bridge they call Stopham Bridge; *you* stop on this side, and follow the river upstream. Then you'll come to where the secret canal begins—"

"How be as it's so secret, ma'am?"

"Well, you see, dearie, it's a long way from any highroad, running through the farmers' fields. O' course the farmers knows about it, but they don't reckon to mention it, not when they finds a keg of Bergamo Water or two-three corkscrews in the hay barn now and again. And the canal's all grown over with maybushes, right the whole way up, so you'd hardly notice it was there. Ah, dear, in May month it surely is a pretty way to go to London, a-gliding along under the maybushes and a-listening to the nightingales sing—many's the time I've done it with my Hannibal in bygone days. Well, when you find the canal, 'tis easy enough; all you've to do is follow along till you come up with the barge, the *Gentlemen's Relish* she's called; she doesn't go faster than mule pace, it shouldn't take you that long to catch up with her. If you meet anybody, just you say Yan, Tan, Tethera, Methera, and they'll know you're on Gentlemen's business and not hinder you."

"I'm obliged to you, ma'am. And I'll pay back the dibs as soon as I can—or work it off helping you in the kitchen."

"Ah, pshaw, child, run along with you."

Dapple was not pleased to be harnessed and ridden off along the Pulborough road on a foggy November night, but he had been well fed and rested in the stable of The Fighting Cocks; he went briskly and biddably enough, through the little village of Fittleworth, up a long hill, and then down a winding road through evergreen woods. Now Dido began to smell water; they were coming into a valley. Ahead of her the road curled around and she could just make out a narrow stone bridge spanning the misty river; on the far side glowed the lighted windows of the White Hart pub.

"Keep on this side, Miss Sarah said. Us wants a gate, Dapple." Dido reined him in, and walked him along, searching for a way into the water meadows; with her head turned to the left she never heard quick soft footsteps; never heard a rope whistle through the air; the first thing she knew was that a noose dropped over her, tightening sharply and jerking her from Dapple's back. That was the last thing she knew, too; she fell, helplessly, her head thudded against the road's stony surface, and the dark fog seemed to rush in through her eyes, nose, and ears.

The party on board the *Gentlemen's Relish* were carefree enough. She was a forty-foot barge, with a galley bigger than the bar parlor of The Fighting Cocks, and below that, a series of roomy holds, packed now with corkscrews, orris root, eau de cologne, eau de vie, eau de nil, and spirits of licorice; in fact she smelt like a mixture between a scent factory and a distillery as she glided along, drawn by Moke and Choke, a pair of mules who picked their careful way up the towpath, heads lowered to avoid the overhanging red-berried, rusty-leaved branches of the hawthorn trees.

"Well, yes, *'tis* a bit okkerd, the hogo," Yan agreed when Tobit remarked on the smell. "That's why we likes to come canal-way because it's fine and far from the turnpike. In springtime, o' course, no one'd be like to notice, because o' the scent o' the may-blow, but at this time o' year it *is* a bit remarkable."

There were five Wineberry Men on the boat, looking after cargo and navigation: Yan, Tan, Tethera, and Methera (who were brothers) and Pip, recently rescued from jail. The other five, Yan explained, did the ten-shilling run from the sea to the Cuckoo Tree.

"But o' course we all shares the profits; 'tis a grand steady line o' trade."

"Don't you have adventures?" said Tobit, disappointed.

"Not if we can help it, my duck," said Yan, grinning. "That's why we keeps the paddlequacks, see?" Tobit and Cris had wondered why there were so many ducks on board: half a dozen different families, all with broods of lanky pin-feathered ducklings. "There be naught to equal a paddlequack for a night watchman; rouse up if a stranger comes within a hundred yards, they will."

"What do you do then?" Tobit asked, all agog.

"Why, we rummage off, right smart; up the bank and away."

"And just leave the boat and cargo?" Tobit thought this very poor-spirited. "I'd stay and fight!"

"Nay, that'd be right ardle-headed," remonstrated Tethera, a bony redhead, who spoke little but seemed extremely devoted to, and popular with the ducks; whenever he sat down, as many as could find room came and perched on him. "What's the *ship*, what's the *cargo?* Uncle Samson, in Appledram Camber, he'd allus fettle us up another barge; and we can allus get us another cargo; but it ain't so easy to get another *us.*"

A slow smile broke over the face of Cris. She, like Tethera, played little part in the long, lazy conversations, but she enjoyed listening, and the ducks had taken to her at once, too; she had a brood of parti-colored ducklings now, scrabbling for the warm place under her chin. Bunches of red-leaved thorn twigs and swags of golden bracken were fastened thickly all over the decks and cabin of the *Gentlemen's Relish,* to help her merge into the background as she floated along; Cris and the ducks had burrowed themselves a kind of nest in the bracken, and there they were all snuggled together in the mild November sun.

Pip and Tethera jumped ashore and mounted Moke and Choke (whose real names were Mercy and Charity) to encourage them to amble along a little faster; Tan and Methera went below to re-stow some of the corkscrew cargo, which had worked loose and was clanking. Yan sat in the stern steering, when it was needful, playing on his devil's box, or harmonium, in between times, and softly singing old songs—"The Milkmaid of Wisborough Green," "Sweet Sally of Smock Alley," and a very aged ditty that seemed to consist principally of the words,

> "Eh! how they do bound about
> . At Roundabout."

"How about a game of cat's cradle?" Tobit said to Cris.

She nodded, and pulled a length of string from her pocket. They had hardly spoken since leaving Dido; after coming aboard the previous evening, they, with the rest of the crew, had been busy for a couple of hours, fastening down the cargo, then Yan had shown them a pair of sweet-scented little cabins between the orris root and the eau de cologne, where they had slept in bracken-lined bunks, until called on deck for a breakfast of brown bread, scrambled duck eggs, and licorice tea.

After they had been playing for a while, Tobit said, "D'you know what? It's our birthday!"

"So it is!"

"We're of age!"

They both thought this very funny. Cris, leaning back and looking up at the gleams of sunshine coming through as they moved along under red hawthorn leaves, said,

"I didn't even know what coming of age meant, this time last week."

Presently Tobit said,

"Do you remember me at all?"

She shook her head.

"Or the place where we were born?"

"No."

"I didn't think I did, but since I've seen you I'm beginning to. I can remember a pair of big iron gates, and two rows of trees with moss on them. There was a fountain."

"Why," said Cris slowly, "so there was. And a big white house with balconies—wasn't there a sandy track under the trees? They used to put us there in our wicker cradles—"

"That's right!" said Tobit excitedly. "And once—there was a snake in the sand—"

"And our father came and killed it!"

"He was a big man with a black beard."

"He used to sing—he used to sing a song about the

[219]

moon and a mockingbird," said Cris, frowning with effort as she dragged the memory from some nearly closed cupboard in her mind. Then she added rather slowly, "Can you remember our mother?"

Tobit thought for a minute.

"A yellow dress?"

"Yes! And a necklace of big orange beads. I used to bite them when my gums were sore."

"Father used to hold us both at the same time, one in each arm."

"Oh," said Cris—she was crying a bit, "what happened to them? Why aren't they here?"

"There was a storm—a very bad storm."

"So there was. First it was hot—and a lot of crabs came—"

"And the wind blew like a scream that went on and on."

"All the trees fell down."

"The house fell down too."

"I don't want to remember any more." Cris rubbed her eyes. "It's too miserable."

"They got killed in the storm," Tobit said soberly. "I can remember someone saying. They were out in the carriage. We were in the cellar with Tante Sannie so we were all right."

"Horrible old Tante Sannie. Why didn't I remember that?"

"She wasn't horrible then. It was only in England that she turned horrible."

"We used to have a parrot that sat on a perch."

[220]

"That's right—so we did! Mother used to give it bits of orange peel."

"Father named it when someone gave it to us—he called it—he called it—"

"Polygot!" said Tobit triumphantly. They beamed at one another. Then, remembering something Tethera had said half an hour before, he added, "I tell you what, Cris, it's miserable that Father and Mother were killed in the storm, but aren't we lucky to have found us!"

Dido was unconscious a long time. When she began to take notice again, she found that she was lying on a damp stone floor listening to voices which apparently were discussing her future.

"Polish off the little canker, I say. Drop her in the river," suggested one voice, which Dido recognized, with little enthusiasm, as that of Mrs. Lubbage.

"Is much best," agreed Tante Sannie's voice. "Isn't no more trouble from her then."

"Here, hold hard!" protested a man—Dido's father. "The individual you allude to in this utilitarian way is my own chick—the youngest living sprig on the tree of Twite. Consider a father's feelings, I beg!"

"Does she know about the Wren's Nest?" That was Colonel FitzPickwick.

"She says not. She appears ignorant of the matter."

"So, once that meddlesome Captain's Dispatch is destroyed, she can't give a warning?"

"No."

"Oh well, in that case, all we need do is leave her trussed up here for two days—that will serve our turn. Wind an extra length of cord about her wrists and secure her to the pillar."

Dido was dragged a few feet across gritty ground; her wrists were jerked out in front of her and made fast to a post. Nevertheless she went on resolutely keeping her eyes shut.

At this moment she heard footsteps.

"Who's that?" said Colonel FitzPickwick sharply. "Oh, it's you, Godwit. What kept you, man? Have you the levers—the machinery? Are you ready to start?"

"No I haven't, and I'm not, and I'm not coming," replied a thin, dry voice—Dido instantly recalled the wrinkled little ironmonger and conspirator in his rimless glasses.

"*What's* that? Not *coming*? What the deuce has got into you? Explain yourself, man!"

"I supplied rollers as per specification. I installed them by night, encountering difficulties which would make—which would make a *camel* weep," said Godwit. "Have I been paid? I have not—bar a mere pittance. Now you ask me to do this other job which is a difficult job and a highly risky job. Very well, I say. Where's the money for the rollers? Where's the money for the next job? Any more work I undertake on behalf of you and your colleagues is strictly cash in advance."

Colonel FitzPickwick let out an oath.

"I tell you, Godwit, the money's as good as in the bank. Tegleaze has gone to sell the miniature to the

[222]

Margrave of Bad Fallingoff. He will be back anytime this next seven days."

"That wasn't what *I* heard," said Godwit. *"I* heard as how he'd scarpered from the Angel leaving his luggage and without paying his score, and it was thought he'd pocketed the Tegleaze luck-piece and gone back to the Americas. That's the talk in the town."

"Rubbish, man!" Colonel FitzPickwick spoke with forced confidence. "Twite here will say that's a pack of moonshine, won't you, Twite. You'll pay the score at the Angel, won't you, Twite?"

"Not pesky likely!" replied Mr. Twite. "What, when that unfeeling Mystery required me to sleep in the stable along with those heathen mannikins—*me,* an artist on the hoboy as has played before all the margraves and pagraves of Europe in my palmier days? No, if Mystery has really snudged off, I'm clearing off too; unless you're wishful to pay the month's wages he owed me, Colonel?"

"Don't be ridiculous, man; of course you will be paid in full when our cause triumphs."

"If I had an ounce of flour for every time I'd heard *that,*" muttered Twite, "I'd be able to make a birthday cake the size of the Houses of Parliament. No, friends and colleagues, this is where Twite says good night. I like plots as is carried on businesslike and money down; none o' this havey-cavey cabbing around on credit. You a-going back to Petworth, Mr. Godwit? I'll ask the favor of a lift in your conveyance."

There was a long silence after the two men had left.

The Colonel began cursing in an undertone. "Flay, spike, and hamstring that Mystery. I wonder if he *has* made off with the luck-piece. If so, what'll we do? By the great Coolin, it's enough to make a man become a —a fishmonger; to have the whole project so near coming off, and then to be at a stand for want of a bit of motive power!"

"Me and Sannie could do your little job for you, Colonel," said Mrs. Lubbage softly. "Us doesn't need all that gurt old machinery and levers. All us needs is *folk*, hey, Sannie?"

Sannie didn't answer in words, but she gave a little chuckle that made Dido's hair prickle.

"*Could* you now?" said the Colonel thoughtfully. "Could you really?"

"Ah, we could! We could make a right avick as'd finish off King Dick for ye once and for all. And the only pay we'd want'd be a passage to Tiburon—"

"On a great white ship a-sailing, sailing—"

"Over the white waves and the black waves—"

"With us a-wrapped in silk satin—"

"Well, well, I daresay that could be arranged without undue trouble," the Colonel said hastily.

"It better had," Mrs. Lubbage muttered. "Or who's to say our fine Colonel won't end up in the same mizmaze as old piecrust-promises Mystery?"

"What's that, you old hag?" the Colonel said sharply. "What do you know about Mystery?"

"Why, nothing, Colonel, nothing! He be in Bad Fallingoff, you said so your own self!"

"Humph!" the Colonel grunted, sounding only half satisfied. "Well, wherever he is, *we* had best start for London without delay. There is no time to be lost. I left my carriage at the White Hart yonder. I'll tell them to set-to new horses, and will expect you in ten minutes."

"Us'll have to go back to Petworth, Colonel-mister," said Sannie. "For to get Mystery's mannikin box."

"What d'you want that for? How do you know he has not taken it with him?"

"He not take it, no, no," Sannie said chuckling. "He not need mannikins where he be now, in Bad Fallingoff. Those mannikins a-waiting in Angel stable, a-lying so still. Those mannikins like to play new game, old Sannie teach to play new game."

Lying on the wet stone floor Dido was cold already, but Sannie's tone made her feel even colder.

"Right; back to Petworth and pick up the puppets. What about the girl; should she not be gagged?"

"No need; old Sannie put her to sleep directly."

Oh no you don't, missus, Dido thought.

"Ten minutes, then." The Colonel left.

"Open eyes, dearie! Old Sannie knows you not be asleep."

Despite her intention not to, Dido opened her eyes.

She was in a curious little octagon room, quite bare and empty. It had small windows in each of its eight walls, and an iron pillar in the middle, to which she was tied. Beyond the open door she could see weeping willows, and the river flowing. But in front of her stood

Mrs. Lubbage and Tante Sannie with their four eyes fixed on her like four glittering metal skewers.

"Now, miss!" The face of Mrs. Lubbage was red and shiny and gleeful. She looked as if she had been given a splendid birthday present. "Where's Cris and Tobit? You'd best tell us or you'll be turble sorry, I can promise ee."

"*That* I won't!" said Dido stoutly. But her heart sank at the expression on their faces.

"You like spiders?" Sannie asked softly. "You like spiders come and climb on you?"

Spiders happened to be things that Dido particularly disliked. But she shrugged, in what she hoped was an indifferent manner.

Crouched in front of Dido, wrapped in her black-and-white blanket, old Sannie looked like the Queen of the Spiders herself. She reached out a tiny, bony, furry arm, flicking her fingers sideways in front of Dido's face, and Dido felt something tickle her cheek; a thread of spiderweb had caught and attached itself crossways. With her hands tied, she could not rub it away; she moved her head, trying to dislodge it.

"Now another!" whispered Sannie, and moved her hand upward; a thread crossed Dido's eye and stuck to her eyelash.

"Now one for the other eye," chuckled Mrs. Lubbage, and drew her hand across Dido's face so that five tendrils of sticky thread, one from each finger it seemed, clutched and clung simultaneously.

"Stop it, you old witches!" Dido shouted angrily.

"Weren't it for you," crooned Mrs. Lubbage, drawing another handful of spiderwebs along Dido's cheek and around the back of her neck, "weren't it for you, Miss Fine-Airs, we'd be sailing to Tiburon on a white ship this minute. You don't like spiders, eh?"

"I don't mind 'em, I tell you."

"Oh, so you don't mind 'em, dearie? Well—before your eyes is all matted over with black webs—jest you have a look by the wall there, eh?"

By the wall there seemed to be a heaving mass of things about the size of bantams' eggs, each with a pair of tiny red eyes, all looking at Dido.

"Take your nasty little cold claw off'n the back of my neck, will you, missus Sannie?" Dido said politely, quelling a horrible heave of her heart. "Yan, Tan, Tethera," she said to herself, "Methera, Pip, Sethera, Wineberry, Wagtail, Tarrydiddle, and Den! It's all a load of hocus-pocus. There's nothing by the wall but a pile o' dead leaves."

She looked at the wall again. Were they dead leaves —or were they hairy, wicked-looking spiders, beginning to scurry silently in her direction?

She stared and stared—so hard that she did not notice the shadow in the doorway, nor hear the patter of paws on the stone floor, until Mrs. Lubbage suddenly let out a wild screech of terror, which was echoed an instant later by Sannie. The two old women sprang away from Dido and bolted for the door, jibbering and wailing— struggled in the entrance a moment, each trying to get

out first—then Sannie slipped ahead, Mrs. Lubbage followed her, and they were gone.

"Well!" Dido muttered, trying to get her breath—and the spiders *were* only dead leaves—"That was sudden, but I won't say it warn't a welcome riddance. Whatever put the old besoms in sich a fright, though?"

Whatever it was had gone around to the back of her; she could hear a sniffing and snuffling close behind, and feel warmth on her hands, tied to the metal post. With some difficulty she worked her head sideways against the pillar, so as to peer out of the corner of her eye, and saw quite a large tiger, all black and yellow stripes, with a head the size of a cider barrel, and eyes that blazed like marigolds.

"Oops!" said Dido.

"Yan," Tobit asked, as the crew of the *Gentlemen's Relish* sat in the galley eating supper (brown bread and fried ducks' eggs) "why ever did the ducks kick up such a row last night? They were quacking away for over an hour? What was the trouble?"

"Well, I don't rightly know," said Yan. "I was in a rare puzzle myself about it. When I heard them kick up all the ruckus I thought there must be Bush officers a-tracking us, but Pip and I had a good sharp look-around, up the cut and down the cut, and there wasn't a soul for miles. Then it seemed as if the paddlequacks was a-fussing about summat *on* the boat, so we had a look-see all around the cargo, in case anyone had got down there that shouldn't."

"Yes," Cris said softly. "I thought it was something down in the hold that was upsetting them. I had Lady Webb and her children with me in my bunk, and they all acted the way chickens do when there's a rat in the nesting box, stealing the eggs."

"Oh well," Yan said, "maybe it was a rat. Rats never yet took to eating orris root and eau de cologne and corkscrews, not as *I* heard of. A rat aboard won't do us much harm."

10

Dido was still gazing over her shoulder at the tiger, and the tiger was still sniffing thoughtfully at the back of her neck, when a huge gray shadow obscured the door and four windows of the octagon room, as if a battleship had berthed outside.

Dido heard a kind of scuffling slither, a gentle voice said, "Stand, if you please, Rachel," and a gentleman entered the room.

"Dear me," he said. "Sunflower, come here."

The tiger—Sunflower was its name, apparently—padded around, rubbed its head against the gentleman very lovingly, and sat down beside him. Dido studied him with interest. He really *was* a gentleman, she decided—as opposed to a Gentleman. He wore black small-clothes, white silk stockings, black shoes with silver buckles, a black velvet jacket, and a snowy white stock, beautifully tied. His hair, what little there was of it, was also snowy, like very clean thistledown. His face looked as if he sat indoors a good deal, reading, but the eyes behind gold-rimmed pince-nez were a very clear bright blue. On one hand he wore a silver ring with a large pink stone in it.

"Dear me," he said again. "That waygoing fellow gave me to understand that there were picnickers, and he was quite right, evidently. When *will* the public learn that this is private property? Not that I mind in principle, you understand—they do little real damage beyond leaving orange peel and bits of marrowbone pie on the ground—but it is frightening for the animals to have strangers about. But people will do it—they come up the river in boats—"

Shaking his head he crossed to Dido, absently surveyed the rope that tied her to the pillar, drew from his pocket first an inkhorn, then a snuffbox, finally a small silver penknife with which he cut the cord—

"Eat their lunch in my gazebo, play ring-o'-roses in my park, and then go on without saying so much as good afternoon or thank you," he continued sadly.

"I'm sorry, sir," said Dido. "I didn't come here a-purpose. I was fetched."

She rubbed her wrists to get the stiffness out of them; then her face. There were no cobwebs on it. "My name's Dido Twite," she added.

"Lord Sope," said the gentleman.

"Soop?"

"You spell it s-o-p-e and pronounce it soup—confusing, I agree. What can I do for you, Miss Twite?"

"I suppose there ain't a dapple-gray horse outside?" she said hopefully.

He looked out, and drew his head in again to say, "Not a *horse,* not at present. You have lost a horse?"

"I was supposed to be taking an urgent message, you see, to some chaps a-going up to London. But I was stopped and tied up in here, and I spose that mardy lot have gone off with my Dapple. D'you reckon I could hire a nag at the White Hart, sir? Mister? Lord?"

"You need a horse? I could accommodate you with one I imagine—I am almost certain I have a horse."

Dido stood up, and nearly fell down again from weakness. It suddenly seemed a terribly long time since her last bowl of soup at The Fighting Cocks. Yesterday? The day before?

"You are a little enfeebled," said Lord Sope. "Allow me." He took her arm and piloted her from the gazebo, the tiger padding behind them. Just outside stood an elephant, with a kind of opera box on its back, from which dangled a rope ladder made of red silk cord.

"After you, Miss Twite."

Rather shakily, Dido climbed the rope ladder and sat on one of the red velvet chairs. Lord Sope followed and took his place beside her.

"Home, if you please, Rachel," he said. The elephant started, at a deceptively smooth stroll which carried them rapidly across an open grassy park to a handsome gray stone mansion. On the way Dido observed a couple

of giraffes, a small group of zebra, and a lynx rolling about on its back and playing with some dead leaves, watched in a vaguely puzzled manner by a flock of sheep.

"Doesn't some of 'em chase the others?" asked Dido.

"I teach them not to, of course," Lord Sope replied.

The elephant reached the house by climbing on to a terrace.

"Just wait outside here a short time if you please, Rachel," Lord Sope instructed it, and politely assisted Dido down the ladder.

Passing through a pair of french windows into a library, he took down a speaking tube from a hook on the wall, said into it, "Lunch, if you please, Diggens," and replaced it.

"Pray sit down," he said to Dido, "and excuse me one moment."

Left alone in the library, Dido gazed rather blankly at the leather and gilt volumes, and the numerous paintings of wild animals that covered the walls. She felt tired, and hungry, and sad. Too much had been happening; she was suddenly shaken by a small, dry sob.

"I wisht Pa hadn't gone off like that and left me," she thought.

Lord Sope returned, followed almost immediately by a footman in a beautifully powdered wig, who arranged dishes on two small tables beside Dido and his master, and then withdrew.

"Frumenty," said Lord Sope. "And I think this note

[234]

must be for you: the waygoing character who told me about the picnickers left it."

The note, simply addressed to DIDO, said, "Dear Daughter, maybe you were right. Things is somewhat Sticky, so I am going to Cut and Run. If I was you, I would do Similar. But I reckon you will be Alright; you always was a Clever Chick. See you some Turpentine Sunday. Your loving Pa."

Frumenty seemed to be a kind of porridge made with wine and spice; after two spoonfuls Dido felt wonderfully better. It was followed by apple pie, with cheese, and a jam-lined omelet, which was very good but difficult to eat politely.

"Now—you say you require to go to London quite fast?" said Lord Sope, removing his jammy stock, throwing it into the fire, and receiving a clean one from the footman who had come back to clear away the dishes.

"Yes. It's to do with the coronation. An urgent message may have gone astray," Dido explained, licking a blob of jam off her elbow.

"In that case, without a doubt, the best thing I can do is to put Rachel at your disposal. She is quicker than any horse, and very reliable. Also, she is well acquainted with the route, for I nearly always take her when I go up to my club."

"Croopus; I mean—that's ever so kind of you, mister —lord. Will she go for me, d'you reckon?"

"She is particularly partial to being ridden by a young female."

"I need to call at three pubs on the way—the Rose, the Ring o' Bells and the Rising Sun."

"There will be no difficulty about that. Rachel is quite accustomed to wait for me outside places of refreshment. In fact she will stop automatically at such places."

"Well, I *am* obliged to you, sir—lord," said Dido. "If you really means it, I'd best be on my way directly. Oh—please can you tell me what day it is?"

"It is Monday, Miss Twite. You do not wish to wait for the two old ladies whom I observed making off at some speed as I approached the gazebo?"

"No, thank you, lord. They wasn't really friends." She put Mr. Twite's note in her pocket and went out on to the terrace, where the wigged footman was just descending the red cord ladder after placing a hamper in the box seat on top.

"I thought you might be glad of a few provisions on the way," Lord Sope explained. "I usually reckon that it takes nine or ten hours to reach London—with the usual pauses for refreshment, of course. Now, Rachel, you are to stop at the Rose, the Ring of Bells, and the Rising Sun—and anywhere else the young lady requires, naturally. Is that perfectly clear? Capital. Allow me, Miss Twite."

He helped her up the ladder.

"I'm *ever* so obliged," Dido said again. "I'll bring her back directly after the coronation."

"Such a lot of extravagant fuss and display," sighed

[236]

Lord Sope. "Still, kings have to be crowned, I understand. On your way, Rachel."

He raised his hand in farewell, Dido settled herself in the red velvet seat, and Rachel rolled off smoothly across the park.

It was plain that when Lord Sope and Rachel went to London, they followed a direct, cross-country route; Rachel ambled through fields and woods, over streams and rivers, by copses and commons, but seldom went near a road. Presently it began to rain; Dido discovered that various capes and covers were provided against this contingency, waterproof on the outside, lined with camel fur. She wrapped herself up snugly and, lulled by Rachel's smooth-flowing motion, went to sleep.

An hour or so later she woke because Rachel had stopped. Night, she found, had fallen; they were halted outside a small, cheerful-looking public house situated by a canal lock; its sign, illuminated by a lantern, showed a red rose.

"Crumble me—thanks, Rachel," muttered Dido, yawning and scrambling to her feet. "I'd never awoken if you hadn't stopped. Just hang on a minute, will you, while I pop in and inquire."

The landlady of the Rose was black-eyed, pink-cheeked, and smiling.

"Well I never!" she exclaimed, looking past Dido. "If that isn't Lord Sope's elephant. Aren't you a lucky young lady! Going up for the coronation, then, are you? Is Lord Sope going too? I *am* surprised!"

"No, ma'am. He says he can't abide fuss," said Dido, drinking the glass of milk she had ordered.

"I daresay his elephant'll be glad of her usual bite," said the landlady and went to fetch this, which turned out to be a bagful of buttered buns.

"Ma'am," said Dido as Rachel munched, "could you tell me, please, if a barge called the *Gentlemen's Relish* has been past yet?"

"Why yes, dearie, they went by early this morning, afore sunup. They'll be a long way up the cut by now."

Dido thanked her, and tried to pay for the buns, but the landlady refused, saying that Lord Sope was an old friend. The refreshment appeared to have been very welcome to Rachel; the minute her passenger was aboard again she started off as if competing in the Calcutta Derby.

Since there was nothing to be seen in the dark wet night, Dido went back to sleep.

Next morning, at gray of dawn, they came to the Ring of Bells, and again Rachel stopped of her own accord. Dido had hoped that, swinging along at Rachel's more rapid pace, they might have caught up with the barge by now but the landlord, whom she found dousing his head under a pump in the yard at the back, reported that the *Gentlemen's Relish* had passed by early the previous evening.

By now Rachel was beginning to grumble and mutter as she rolled along, and to look back at her rider in a reproachful and significant way, which Dido took to be an intimation that it was time for rest and breakfast; so they halted in a hazel copse near Esher. Rachel, after more buns, provided by the Ring of Bells, had a standing nap, with her huge ears folded tidily over her eyes, while Dido sampled Lord Sope's hamper. It proved to contain egg salad in a silver bucket, currant wine, cheese straws, and a marmalade pie. There was also a pot of frumenty, and instructions for heating it up in a chafing dish to be found under the red velvet seat, but Dido was impatient to press on, ate it cold, and gave the marmalade pie to Rachel as compensation for having to start again after an hour's nap.

By now they were no great distance from London and houses were more frequent: large, handsome mansions, most of them; many were gaily decorated with flags and wreaths and colored bunting in honor of the next day's event.

Dido had expected to cause some surprise by riding through the suburbs on an elephant, the more so as Rachel, cheered by her nap and breakfast, was now trumpeting cheerfully to herself as she proceeded; but in fact no one seemed to find their appearance at all remarkable, either because this was Lord Sope's regular route, or because people took it for granted that Rachel was to form part of the coronation procession.

"Gee up, Jumbo, you'll be late for the crowning!" shouted a cheerful group of boys coming out from morning school in Merton village; they showered Rachel and her passenger with peppermint drops and Michaelmas daisies, which Rachel rapidly sorted, swallowing the former and tossing back the latter with a dexterity that filled the boys with admiration.

"How far to the Rising Sun in Wandsworth?" Dido called, leaning over the side of her box.

"Matter o' five mile, duck; she'll do it before you can make these into a daisy chain," they called back, bombarding her with the rejected daisies.

Wandsworth was a small, ancient village, not unlike Dido's native Battersea, situated about a mile south of the river Thames, and perhaps eight or nine miles up that winding river from London Bridge. The Rising Sun was evidently not one of the inns where Lord Sope was accustomed to stop for refreshment. There had been a good many of these along the way and Rachel was beginning to grumble again at being expected to pass them by without her usual fifteen-minute pause outside each. So both companions were pleased to arrive at their third point of inquiry, which proved to be a tiny, gabled public house in Allfarthing Lane, on the banks of the river Wandle.

"Has the *Gentlemen's Relish* been by yet?" Dido asked the landlord.

He was a thin, sandy-haired, sharp-faced character; he gave her a very searching scrutiny before replying:

"No, missie. She ain't. And what's more she's powerful late—I've been expecting her these three-four hours."

Dido's heart sank. What could have happened to delay the barge? Had she better start back along the banks of the Wandle? She was not quite sure where this river was joined by the Gentlemen's secret canal, but if she followed the towpath she must be sure to find the junction somewhere. But then she would be farther away from London when they met, and would have to bring the Dispatch all the way back again—it was difficult to know what to do for the best. In the end she decided to remain by the Ring of Bells for two hours and then, if the *Gentlemen's Relish* had not yet arrived, start back.

On the west bank of the Wandle just at this point there was a pleasant little park, so they crossed the river —Rachel preferred to swim, ignoring a perfectly good bridge—Dido, dismounting, sat under a tree and Rachel sank down alongside like a neat and silent avalanche.

They waited. There was no difficulty in telling the hour hereabouts. Three churches, just across the Wandle, struck all the quarters, and if they did not agree absolutely to the minute, at least there was a general certainty that time was passing. One o'clock, half past, quarter to two, quarter past. And still the *Gentlemen's Relish* did not appear.

"Rachel," said Dido at three o'clock, "I reckon we'd better go back along the towpath."

Rachel, who had been asleep, lifted her ears away from her eyes with a movement like a shrug, and began gloomily clambering to her feet.

But just at that moment, far away along the winding Wandle, something came into view that might have been a traveling hedge, or a sliding grove, or a piece of moving moorland.

"Hang on a minute, Rachel. What's that?"

The landlord of the Rising Sun had come out of his bar parlor and was standing on the opposite river bank gazing upstream. He nodded to Dido.

"That's the old *Relish,*" he called. "Dear knows why she's so late."

Dido ran across the bridge and Rachel waded through the river.

"Don't they worry about Preventives?" Dido asked. "Coming along in daylight, so bold?"

"Not in these parts, bless you—we're all good King's men round here. Nary a Bush officer'd dare show his face."

At last the garlanded barge slid alongside. Yan and Tan, who had been riding the tow mules, tied them to a lamppost.

"Well, Yan?" called the landlord, "Brought my drop of licorice water, have ye? What makes ee so late?"

"Hollo there, Bob. We had a bit o' trouble in the night wi' our paddlequacks." Then Yan saw Dido and the elephant. "Hey!" he said. "What's amiss? I didn't think to see you here, dearie."

"Oh, Yan! Am I pleased to see *you!*" Dido was about to jump on board, but she thought better of it, and beckoned him to come around the corner into Allfarthing Street.

"Listen!" she whispered urgently, "You've got a spy on board! Where's the Dispatch?"

"A *spy?* Nay, dearie, that just can't be! All us chaps has worked together since we was lads at school."

[243]

"Just the same, there is one." Dido repeated what Mr. Twite had said. "Is the Dispatch safe?"

"Surelye! I've got it packed in among the orris root."

"What was that about trouble in the night?"

"Our paddlequacks all swam away. We had the devil's own job a-pacifying and a-fetching them back—running up and down the banks, they was, roosting in trees, quacking and clacking and carrying-on—took us hours to catch 'em all, and when we'd caught 'em there was nothing for it but to shut the lot of 'em in young Cris's cabin—they takes kindly to *her*."

"What upset them?"

"'Twas a black mystery—we never did find out. There was no stranger around. And the cargo was trig enough —not a corkscrew out o' place. In the end we reckoned as it might a bin an outsize rat as scared the ducklings."

"A *rat*?" Dido stared at Yan, her eyes big as saucers. "Here—come back on board, *quick!* Show us where you've got the Dispatch."

She grabbed his hand and fairly raced him back to the barge. They picked their way hastily across the bushy deck while Tethera, Methera, and Pip, who were unloading kegs of licorice spirit for the Rising Sun, gazed at them in astonishment.

"Where's Cris and Tobit?" Dido panted, as they dropped down the hatch into the galley.

"Playing cat's cradle, I. reckon. They spends most o' the day doing that, and hashing over old times," Yan said tolerantly. He led Dido through the spacious galley with its central stove, kitchen table, and benches. Here, before continuing, he took a lantern from a hook, lit it, and gave it to Dido to carry. They crossed a series of communicating cabins filled with bales and crates which smelt strongly of lavender and licorice, then came to a passageway leading between closed doors. Yan tapped on one of these and threw it open.

Inside, an extremely cozy scene was revealed. Cris and Tobit were sitting on the floor playing cat's cradle. Dido noticed at once that they had made great strides in this game since she had given them their basic instruction—when? Two days ago? Tobit held between his outspread fingers an immensely complicated network of string like the mesh of colored ribbons around a maypole. Cris was carefully studying it from all angles.

Perched all around the cabin, and on Cris's head and shoulders, were thirty or forty ducks and ducklings, also, it seemed, attentively watching the game.

However, when the door opened everybody looked around.

"Why, it's Dido!" said Cris with mild surprise.

"All right, everyone in here, are you?" Yan asked.

"Yes, why?" Tobit said. "Look, Cris, take those two with your hands and *those* two with your teeth—" he pointed with his nose.

"Ducks all right? No more upsets? We're a-going down below to make sure the Dispatch is safe."

"We'll come too," said Tobit jumping up, but carefully so as not to disturb any ducks, or his network, which he carried along with him.

[245]

Yan led the way down two more ladders and into a dark, narrow region, even more strongly scented, where they had to scramble over and between large prickly sacks of corkscrews and tacky bales of licorice.

"Now—" Yan paused in front of a shut door and pulled out a bunch of keys—"I keeps the Dispatch in the lock-up—no one goes in here but me." He carefully inserted the largest key, turned it, and flung open the door.

Dido, just behind him, held the lantern high.

There was a sudden scuffle and scurry. Something jumped off the wide shelf which ran around three sides of this hold, and dashed across the shadowy floor. But Tobit, acting with most unexpected dispatch and address, bounded forward past Yan, his hands held low and wide with the net stretched tight between them, and caught the thing on the floor, instantly twisting and gripping his net to prevent its escape.

"*Dang* it, what's that?" exclaimed Yan. "Here, Dido, bring the light closer!"

The creature in Tobit's net screamed. It was a horrible sound—a scream of rage and defiance, not fear at all. It was like a human scream but higher and shriller. The creature struggled, causing the net to swing furiously.

"Halloo, what's amiss—what the devil's going on below there?" cried startled voices from the deck. Tan and Methera came clattering down.

"Mercy sakes, what *have* you got hold of?" Tan gasped. Dido held the lantern close and Tobit's prisoner was

[246]

revealed as an immense brindled rat, its eyes flashing, its whiskers bristling, its long yellow fangs bare in fury.

"Don't you let it bite you, boy," Yan warned. "I'll lay every one o' those grinders is as full o' poison as a deadly adder's tooth."

As they stared at the beast Cris said rather shakily, "That's Auntie Daisy's rat."

"Are ye certain, gal?"

"Yes, I reckon she's right," Dido said. "It's brindled just the same."

Yan began to curse.

"What a gurt muttonheaded fool I am. Why didn't I think? Where the dickens did the brute get in?"

"Never mind that, where's the Dispatch?"

"'Twas on the coaming yonder," said Yan with a groan. "In an oilskin packet—"

"Here's a bit of it on the floor," Cris said, springing forward. "The rat must have knocked it off—"

She picked it up gingerly. The red string and seal fell to the floor with a shower of leaf-sized bits of paper. Half the document had been gnawed away.

"Let's go up where it's light and have a look at what's left," Dido said. "Maybe we can make out what it's about. Mind how you hold that monster, Tobit—don't let him get away."

"Wait till I fetch my qualiver, I'll blow him to forty bits," vowed Yan. The rat squealed angrily.

They went on deck. "All that cat's cradle come in handy, anyhows," muttered Tan to Tethera. "Which was more than I'd a prognotified yesterday."

Tobit was having great difficulty in keeping a grip on the struggling rat which darted its head this way and that, trying to squeeze through the meshes of the net. Nobody could take it from him because it snapped so savagely.

Just as Yan came back with his hand gun the rat finally succeeded in thrusting its body through a gap and bounded on to the deck, screeching with triumph. Yan fired but missed. The rat scurried over the side and could be seen swimming across the river, a dark V of water spreading away behind its pointed head.

"*Plague* on it—" Yan hurriedly reloaded. But as he did so, Tobit sprang over the side and went after the rat.

"Tobit! Come back, boy! You'll never catch it!"

"Oh, Tobit!" wailed Cris. "Do be careful."

But he did not answer. Hunter and quarry both disappeared into the dusk on the far side of the Wandle.

"Well, here's a right hugger-mugger!" said Yan furiously.

Dido had spread the rest of the chewed Dispatch on the cabin roof and was poring over it, by the light of the lantern and the last rays of the setting sun.

"To my Lord Forecastle Master of the
lace horse and Westminster Foxhou
First Lord of the Admiralty.
Sir: Whilst interrogating prisoner
captured French frigate *Madame de Ma*
I was lucky enough to discover detail
laid and diabolical plot to assassina
well-beloved Prince of Wales on the oc

his Coronation. The details are as
Cathedral of St. Paul's has already be
mined & its foundations rest merely
at a given signal or impetus these rol
set in motion and the whole Sacred Edif
slide with uncontrollable speed in
River Thames. Proof of this can
visiting the Crypt. I there
it right to communicate the fright
tidings without delay. I remain
    Your lordship's
    Charles Tran
    Rear-Admi

Dido read through this very carefully three times.

"Holy Peggotty!" she said then. "What time's the coronation tomorrow?"

"Ten in the morning."

"Us has got to hustle," Dido said.

"Why, what's it about?" Yan peered over her shoulder at the damaged Dispatch. But he said, "You've got more book-learning than I have, reckon, ducky; blest if I can make trotter nor tail of it. What's it say?"

"Why," said Dido, "near as I can reckon, some admiral is writing to this here Lord Forecastle about a plot to push St. Paul's Cathedral into the Thames, with the whole coronation a-going on inside it. That's what they means when they keeps talking about the Wren's Nest! Oh, the villains! Here, I'm off—where does Lord Forecastle live, Yan?"

"House in the Strand. How'll you get there?"

"Lord Sope lent me his elephant."

"I was wondering where that came from," Tethera said.

"Shall I come with ee, duck?" said Yan. "Old Lord Forecastle is a tiddy bit slow and given to argufication. But he knows me, reckon I could help get the notion into his noodle as there's need to hurry."

"That'd be prime, Yan. How about the ship?"

"The others can bring her on the reg'lar way, and we'll all meet at Aunt Grissie's in Wardrobe Court."

"But Tobit!" said Cris, half crying.

"Look, gal, us simply can't wait to hunt for him now," Dido said. "But he's got sense. He can ask his way to Wardrobe Court—you told him where that is?" Yan nodded. "He'll be all right, I reckon. Besides, wouldn't Aswell give you a warning if he was in any kind o' trouble?"

"Aswell?" Cris looked vaguely puzzled.

Dido stared at her, equally astonished. Had she already forgotten about Aswell? But there was really not an instant to waste. Yan slipped what was left of the Dispatch into another oilskin case, he and Dido jumped ashore, and ran to where the elephant was patiently waiting.

11

Steering Rachel through the streets of London to Lord Forecastle's residence proved considerably more difficult than letting her find her own way from Stopham Park to Wandsworth. In fact it proved impossible. Rachel had her own theories about the right route into London and whether they threatened, pleaded, thumped, or tried to lead her, she pursued her own course, quite regardless of their wishes.

"Oh well, let her take her own way," said Dido at length. "She seems to have a powerful strong notion o' where she wants to go."

She took them across Wandsworth Bridge and along the King's Road, Chelsea.

"Why," exclaimed Dido, "that's Doc Furneaux's Academy of Art! Hang on just a moment, Rachel, my ducky, I used to have a pal as learnt painting there. I'll just nip in and ax if anyone knows where he is. I've been trying to get in touch with him—he'd be a right useful cove in a fussation like this—chap called Simon."

And she slid down the rope ladder like a powder monkey, muttering to herself.

"Oh I *does* hope he's still alive."

But Dr. Furneaux's Academy of Arts presented a very blank and silent aspect: in the wide forecourt, usually choc-a-block with students eating impromptu meals and doing their laundry in the fountain, no one was to be seen but an aged Chelsea pensioner, who was slowly and thoughtfully trying to remove a Dutch cheese from the hole in the middle of a statue where someone had rammed it.

"Where's all the folk?" Dido asked. The old man turned bleary eyes on her.

"What folk?"

"The students!" Dido said impatiently. "And the teachers! And Doc Furneaux! Where are they?"

"Gone for to put up the decorations in the cathedral. And in Threadneedle Street and Paternoster Row and Cheapside. Fancy wasting a good bit o' cheese like that," said the old man in disgust, giving it another vain poke.

Dido scurried back to the elephant.

"No good . . . You can roll on, Rachel." So Rachel continued, looking neither to right nor left, along the King's Road, across Sloane Square, through Belgravia, across Green Park, and presently drew up outside what was presumably Lord Sope's club in St. James's. It was called Toffy's and, judging by the white steps, polished brass, window boxes, and the uniformed porter, was very grand indeed.

"What'll us do now?" Dido said. "Leave Rachel here and call a cab?"

But Yan, all excited, exclaimed, "There! There he is!"

"Who?"

"Lord Forecastle. He just got out of that phaeton and went into the club."

"Oh, well, that's prime," Dido said. "We'll go in too."

But this was easier said than done.

The uniformed porter, who was about seven feet tall, said coldly,

"Lord Sope's elephant always gets taken around to the back."

"Well, you do that, will you?" Dido said. "Us has an urgent errand with Lord Forecastle. Just ax him to step back and speak to us for a minute, can you?"

"I *beg* your pardon," the porter said in frozen tones. "I fear that will be quite out of the question."

"Why?" demanded Dido.

"Gentlemen when availing themselves of the facilities of this establishment may not be disturbed for *any* reason whato*ever* by *any*body. It is the first club rule. Why, when the Battle of Trafalgar was won, they had to wait for two days till Mr. Pitt came out before they could tell him."

"What did he say? I'll bet he was right vlothered that everyone else had known for two days before him."

"History does not relate," the porter said snubbingly.

[253]

Then his tone changed to one of outrage and he exclaimed,

"*Where* do you think you are going?"

"In, to look for Lord Forecastle, if you won't."

"Persons of the female sex are not on *any* account *ever* allowed into these premises."

"Yan, *you* better go," Dido said crossly.

Yan looked daunted.

"When d'you reckon his lordship's liable to come out?" he asked the porter.

"I cannot possibly undertake to say."

"Oh, drabbit!" said Dido. She retired to the street, filled her lungs to their maximum capacity with air, and bawled,

"LORD FORECASTLE!"

Yan, approving of this tactic, joined her, filled *his* lungs, and shouted even louder,

"LORD FORECASTLE!"

Rachel, entering into the spirit of the enterprise, joyfully trumpeted. Windows were opened in clubs all up and down St. James's. About a hundred white-wigged heads and scandalized old faces poked out. "Like cheese mites," Dido said.

The elderly gentleman who all this time had been slowly climbing the red-velvet-carpeted stairs of Toffy's club, slowly retraced his steps.

"What is all the commotion about, Prothero?" he demanded. "Pray cause it to cease."

"Begging your humble pardon, your lordship, but

there is a—a person, and a—a *young* person that are desirous to have words with your lordship."

"Indeed? Where are they?" inquired Lord Forecastle icily.

"In the street, your lordship."

"I can hardly converse with them in the street, can I?"

"The young person is of the female sex, your lordship."

This might have been insoluble, but luckily Lord Forecastle, peering through the entrance, observed,

"Dear me, there is old Plantagenet Sope's elephant. I'd no notion he was coming up for the crowning. Planty! Planty! D'you care to come and take a dish of tay with me?"

"Lord Forecastle!" said Yan, springing on him like an active thrush on a very ancient snail, before he could discover his mistake and retreat inside the club again. "You knows me—Yan Wineberry, as delivers your corkscrews and organ-grinder's oil."

"Good gracious, my good fellow—" Lord Forecastle was scandalized, "St. James's Street is *not* the place to allude to such commodities."

"Well, I ain't a-going to," Yan said reasonably. "We bring you half a Dispatch from Rear-Admiral Charles Tran."

"Charles Tran? I have no acquaintance of that designation. And in any case, this is not a suitable place to bring me a dispatch, or half a dispatch. I am off duty, I am in mufti! Take it to the office—take it to the

Admiralty. I will look at it on Friday. Or, no, on Friday I shoot partridge at Ravenscourt Park—Monday. Monday will be better. Charles Tran? Some imposter, I daresay; never heard of the fellow."

"Look, Lord Fo'c'stle, this is *urgent*," said Dido. "We borrowed Lord Sope's elephant special to come and find you. Are you a-going to the coronation tomorrow?"

"Of course I am, child. What has that to say to anything?"

"Well then you won't be in the Admiralty on Monday, I can tell you that. You'll be squished in sixteen feet o' Thames mud under twenty thousand ton dead-weight o' fancy stonework."

"My dear young person, are you raving? Shall I be obliged to call the Watch?"

"See here," said Dido, and spread out the gnawed Dispatch under his eyes.

"Tut! What is this rigmarole?" he said peevishly. "French frigate Madame de Ma? There is no such vessel. Cathedral has been mined? Unthinkable rubbish. Why, the fellow who wrote this must have been drunk —half the sentences are incomplete. Either drunk or mad! Tush—take it away—I dare swear the whole thing is an arrant fraud."

"It ain't!" said Dido indignantly. "Captain Hughes o' the *Thrush* asked us to bring it to you."

"Ha!" said Lord Forecastle triumphantly. "*I* know Hughes—sensible, reliable, gentlemanly sort of officer —excellent disciplinarian—know *he'd* never act in such an irregular manner. Why not bring it himself, pray?"

"He's ill—he was wounded at sea, and in a carriage accident, and overlooked by a witch."

"Fiddledeedee! Be off with you, miss—pray don't try such Billingsgate stories on me. A witch—Owen Hughes —there's a likely fairy tale. Why, my great friend Rear-Admiral Charles Transome, under whom he serves, thinks the world of Hughes."

"Transome!" exclaimed Dido. "Don't you see this letter *is* from Transome, you clutter-headed old—"

"Steady, steady, ducks!" cautioned Yan. "No use setting his whiskers on fire!"

Lord Forecastle was indeed in a dangerously empurpled condition.

"Wineberry!" he sputtered. "I've always found you a businesslike fellow in our dealings. What you are doing with this disgracefully impudent young person who appears to be mentally deranged as well, I cannot imagine, but I wish you will take her away!"

"But, sir, what she says is quite true. 'Tis they bothering Hanoverians, at it again—digging away under St. Paul's like mouldywarps, they be."

Lord Forecastle cooled down a little. He read the Dispatch again.

"Well," he said at length, "if this really is from Charlie Transome—though why he cannot sign himself properly I quite fail to comprehend—"

"The Dispatch was gnawed by a rat—"

"A rat? Oh, good gad, man, how can you expect me to believe such a farrago of preposterous balderdash?"

"Because it's the truth!" exclaimed Dido, with such

indignant and passionate conviction that a number of people in the street turned to look at her.

A spare, shrewd-looking gray-headed gentleman who happened to be driving past in a curricle reined in his horses.

"Evening, Fo'c'stle!" he called. "Is Planty Sope in town, then? I see his beast there."

"No, he is not," said Lord Forecastle peevishly. "So far as I can make out this precious pair appear to have purloined his elephant in order to come and tell me a ramshackle tale of rats and witches and a plot to dig up St. Paul's—I wish you will call up your constables, Sir Percy, and have them consigned to the Tower—"

"Sir Percy!" exclaimed Yan joyfully, while the gray-headed gentleman, seeing Yan at the same moment, remarked,

"Nay, that's young Wineberry, who brings me my Hollands every month, regular as the Bank of England. I can't believe he'd be mixed up in anything havey-cavey."

"Sir Percy, do but take a look at yon message!" Yan begged. "It bean't a ramshackle tale, indeed it bean't. It got chawed by a rat aboard the *Gentleman's Relish*, but you can see it's from Rear-Admiral Transome and it's mortal important—"

With obvious relief, Lord Forecastle passed over the Dispatch to the gentleman in the curricle, who read it attentively.

"That's Sir Percy Tipstaff," Yan muttered in Dido's ear. "He'll pay a bit more heed, I'll lay—"

"Humph," grunted Sir Percy. "This certainly bears *some* appearance of a genuine warning. I feel it had best be looked into. I'll put matters in train, shall I, Fo'c'stle, and spare you the trouble?"

"Do, Tipstaff—do—if you really think it is not a hoax. And now, if you'll pardon me, I am sadly late for an appointment to play backgammon with the Bishop of Bayswater—" Plainly much relieved at being able to wash his hands of the business, Lord Forecastle gave a final disapproving glare at Dido and Yan, turned, and stumped up the steps of Toffy's club.

"You two had best come in my carriage," said the Lord Chief Justice. "Then you can tell me the details as we ride."

"What about the elephant?"

"Prothero!" called Sir Percy.

"Yes, sir? What can I do for you, Sir Percy?"

"Put away this elephant; see she is fed and rubbed down."

"Begging your pardon, sir, can't undertake to stable her without Lord Sope himself personally consigns her to our stable."

"Oh, tush—" Sir Percy was beginning, when Yan interposed.

"Excuse me, sir, but best not waste time in arguing; I daresay my auntie Grissie will oblige if they ain't willing here."

So Rachel was allowed to follow behind Sir Percy's curricle, and this was perhaps just as well, for it was plain that she had every intention of doing so anyway.

Yan and Dido sprang into the vehicle, Sir Percy touched up his horses, and the procession whirled away toward Piccadilly.

"Now," said the Lord Chief Justice, skillfully guiding his team through the crowds, which became denser and denser as they approached the City of London, "you know more about this murky business than is mentioned in the Dispatch, hey? How do the miscreants propose to topple over St. Paul's?"

"Well, sir," Dido told him. "One night I heard two coves, as I know to be mixed up in this, a-talking together and one of 'em said, 'The rollers is mounted already. All we want now is motive power.'"

"Rollers? Good gracious. Do you mean to suggest that the whole cathedral is already mounted on castors like —like a sofa?"

"Yes, sir. We reckons so."

"How very shocking. Well, proceed! What about the motive power—have you ascertained how they propose to give it the final push?"

"They ran into a bit o' trouble when it came to that, sir," said Dido, and explained about the defection of Mr. Godwit. "Someone run off with a valuable bit o' property that they was going to sell to pay for the levers and stuff, you see."

"So our worries are at an end? They cannot start the cathedral rolling?"

"I ain't so sure about that, sir," said Dido. "There's these two old witches—"

"*Witches?* Come, come, child. Do not try my credulity

too far. Rollers are one thing, witches are quite another. Let us leave magic and spookery out of the business, pray!"

"But they *can* do queer things, sir! They put poor Cap'n Hughes in a sleep and no one can't rouse him—"

"A drug or a blow on the head would do as much—"

"They can make folk see things as isn't there—"

"Bah!"

"Well, anyways, Colonel FitzPickwick believes they can fix it."

"FitzPickwick, eh? I always suspected he had Hanoverian leanings," Sir Percy said thoughtfully. "But this talk of sorcery and such jiggery-pokery, you know, is the outside of enough."

By now the curricle, with Rachel in anxious pursuit, had rolled briskly along the Strand, along Fleet Street, up Ludgate Hill, and had turned left below the towering bulk of St. Paul's Cathedral. They drew up outside the Old Bailey.

"The Yeoman of the Guard and just about the whole of the London constabulary are quartered here in readiness for tomorrow," Sir Percy explained. "And Lord Raven, the Home Secretary, is certain to be here, so we can put the whole matter before him and decide on a proper course of action."

This sounded promising. But when Lord Raven presently appeared, in a small gloomy office to which Sir Percy had led them, Dido's heart sank.

The Home Secretary was a tall, gaunt, draggled-looking character with rusty black hair and a rusty black beard and such very thick drooping black eyebrows that it seemed unlikely that he could see much unless he looked sidelong.

He listened to Sir Percy's outline of the plot to dispose of King Richard the Fourth, along with the Archbishop of Canterbury, all the nobility and gentry of the land, as well as members of parliament, clergy, choir, St. Paul's Cathedral itself, and a congregation of several thousand, in a discouraging silence.

"So you see," concluded Sir Percy, "whether or not these dastardly plotters have, since our young friends left them, actually discovered a means of shifting the edifice or not, it is urgently necessary to survey the foundations before tomorrow's ceremony, so as to remove any risk of such an attempt."

The Home Secretary ran one hand through his beard, looked at it, ran the other hand through, looked at it, and after a thoughtful pause replied,

"Can't be done."

"What is that you say, man?" exclaimed Sir Percy. "How do you mean, can't be done?"

"Cathedral's not my province. Can't set foot in it without permission of the Dean. Certainly can't arrest anyone in it."

"But, good heavens, man, there's a double cordon of your constabulary officers all around the place this minute. I noticed them as we came up Ludgate Hill."

"That's to keep people out," replied Lord Raven. "Cathedral's already filling up fast—tomorrow's congregation will all be there by invitation. About the only

[263]

ones left to come now are members of parliament and peers."

"The congregation's there already?"

"A cathedral's not like a teapot—you can't fill it and empty it in five minutes," Lord Raven said sourly. "Every person who'll be there tomorrow has to have a pass—every pass has to be countersigned by ten different constabulary officers—takes hours to get 'em all in and out again."

"Well, we must obtain passes so that we can go and look at the crypt—I presume that is where the male-factors will have placed their rollers," said Sir Percy impatiently. "And surely conspirators could be arrested in the crypt?"

Lord Raven ran one hand through his beard, ran the other hand through, and replied, "Can't get passes."

"Why not, in the name of St. Pancras?" demanded the Lord Chief Justice, in a high state of exasperation.

"Passes have to be issued by the Dean."

"Very well, then let us go to the Dean, for goodness' sake."

"Can't. The Dean is passing the night with His Majesty, in meditation and serious talk."

"Oh." Sir Percy considered, and then said, "Just the same, in a case of such danger and urgency—Where are they having this talk?"

"In St. Paul's library."

"In the *cathedral?* You mean His Majesty is there *already?*"

"That is so. He arrived just after lunch, and will not leave until after tomorrow's ceremony."

"But, in that case—good gracious, don't you see that the danger is critical *now*? Why, if everybody is inside it already—except the peers and M.P.s and who cares about them—if the plotters have by now found some means of moving the building, there's not a thing to stop them doing so *at any time*—supposing they knew His Majesty is in there. Good heavens, man, the whole thing is perched at the top of Ludgate Hill like a boot on a roller-skate, just waiting for someone to give it a shove. We *must* get inside, I tell you!"

"Can't, without a pass," replied the Home Secretary immovably.

Dido plucked Yan's hand and drew him from the room.

"Come on," she whispered outside. "That pair will be at it for hours, to and fro. I wouldn't give a buttered biscuit for Sir Percy's chances of getting into St. Paul's. Dismal old croaker, that Lord Raven, ain't he?"

Yan could only agree.

"What'll us do? Got any notion, duck?"

"Let's go up to your aunt Grissie's," Dido suggested. "If she lives in Wardrobe Court, that's right handy for St. Paul's, and maybe the others'll have got there by now; they might have some good ideas."

They walked up the short but steep hill—Rachel following—and admired the great west front of the cathedral, which had been garlanded all over, presumably by the

[265]

students of Dr. Furneaux's Academy, with purple daisies and bunches of red autumn berries. The roadway down toward the City of Westminster had been kept clear by Yeomen, but in all the houses, and everywhere that people were allowed to stand, the crowds were massing thicker and thicker. People were all in their holiday best. There was an atmosphere everywhere of jubilation and expectancy.

Yan turned right, off Ludgate Hill, into a tiny cobbled street, and right again, under an arch. Rachel, unable to squeeze through, trumpeted mournfully.

"Just you wait there a minute, Rachel my duck, and we'll bring you something nice," Dido reassured her.

Wardrobe Court was a tiny enclosure, in which two plane trees were dropping their pale yellow leaves on to soft green grass. Around the sides of the court were peaceful little old houses which looked as if they had grown there, like the trees. Up above, the sky, for once, was clear; its luminous green, with one or two stars prickling out, gave promise that the next day would be fine.

They knocked at Number Four. Aunt Grissie, a small cheerful old lady exactly like a nut, hugged Yan and said, "There! I made sure I'd see you directly. I've been a-watching the old *Relish* a-tying up at Mermaid Wharf from my kitchen window. But how is it you're ahead of her, Yan, boy?"

"We had a bit o' business to do, Auntie, so we left the ship at Wandsworth. This here's Dido Twite, and we've left an elephant outside, if so be as you've any buns."

Aunt Grissie made no difficulty about producing buns —"I always lays in plenty of provisions when the Wineberry lads are due," she explained to Dido, giving her a trayful. While Aunt Grissie and Yan were exchanging family news in the neat little kitchen Dido wandered back through the parlor—with its painted glass ornaments, pictures made from butterflies' wings, red chenille tablecloth, and wax fruit under glass domes. Outside the window a larger dome, that of St. Paul's, faced the house over the roofs of Wardrobe Court.

"If St. Paul's does go a-skating down into the river," Dido thought, carrying the buns to Rachel, "it'll take Aunt Grissie's house with it. *And* topple in right on top of the old *Gentlemen's Relish*."

Rachel, appeased by buns, was content to wait in the street. As Dido returned to the house the rest of the *Gentlemen's Relish* crew trooped into the court, hungry, highly scented, and cheerful.

"Well, did you fix things with his lordship?" asked Tethera.

Cris ran to Dido and caught her by the hand.

"Oh Dido—I'm so worried about Tobit!"

"He's not back yet? Oh well, I daresay he'll be along by and by," Dido soothed her.

"But *I keep getting messages from him!*"

Dido's skin prickled.

"Like when he was in the well?"

"Yes! No, not quite like that—it doesn't seem so much that he's in danger—but he's stuck somewhere and can't get out, and he wants to tell me something and I can't understand it."

"Like it was with Aswell sometimes?"

"Aswell?"

Blimey, thought Dido, has she clean forgotten? "You remember Aswell, that you used to talk to in the Cuckoo Tree?"

"Oh," said Cris slowly, "yes—I *think* I do—but I was just a child then. That was a long time ago. Was it someone I used to believe was up in the sky? I've almost forgotten."

"Oh well, no matter. D'you reckon if we went upstairs, or somewhere quiet, you might hear better?"

Cris thought this might help. As the tiny house was now crammed with Wineberry Men shaving, washing their socks, eating bacon and eggs, and discussing Lord Raven's behavior, Dido and Cris went out through Wardrobe Court, gave Rachel a passing pat, and strolled on into St. Paul's churchyard.

"This is better—but let's keep going." Cris tugged Dido along toward the cathedral. Since the double line of constables prevented the crowd from entering and kept urging people to move on, Dido and Cris continued going east—anti-clockwise—until they were around on the north side of St. Paul's. Here the crowd was thicker still. Every now and then somebody who had a pass showed it and was allowed to go in.

[268]

"Can't *we* go in?" Cris said impatiently. "I'm almost sure Tobit's voice is coming from inside there."

"That's funny," Dido thought. "Well, I suppose if Tobit had come straight, he *could* have got here while we was argufying with old Fo'c'stle, but why? And how did he fetch up inside? And how can we?"

Her last question was answered at once.

"Buy a pass, dearie?" muttered a voice in her ear. "Only two guineas to *you,* for I've took a fancy to you. You've a lucky face."

She turned to find a little man like a blackbeetle at her elbow. "Passes for the North Door and Lord Mayor's Vestry—you'll never be sorry you took the chance," he urged her. "Only two guineas—in an hour's time you won't be able to get 'em for twenty!"

"Does I look as if I had two guineas?" Dido began tartly, and then remembered that as a matter of fact she *had;* thanks to Miss Sarah Gusset she had five. She glanced about and realized that in fact a brisk trade in illegal passes was going on. Pity old Raven couldn't come up here and buy a few, she thought.

"Please, *please* let's go in," besought Cris, who had seen Dido's hand move toward her pocket.

"Oh, very well!" Dido brought out four of the five guinea pieces, and received in exchange two large pieces of pasteboard all covered with lions, unicorns, balls, crosses, and croziers, that said, "Admit bearer to North Transept. (Signed) Thos. Talisman, Dean." They looked very official.

[269]

The salesman, having taken their money, vanished into the crowd like a lemming. Cris and Dido showed their passes, were allowed through the double line of constables, and climbed the steps to the North Door. "Wonder if I oughta let Yan know?" Dido thought. "But we needn't stay long, and this does seem a chance. We mightn't get in so easy another time."

12

Although born and bred in London, Dido had never before set foot inside St. Paul's Cathedral. When they had passed through the entrance vestibule and came out into the north transept, she was amazed at the size of the place. It was like being in some clearing among giant trees. Underfoot were black and white marble squares, an enormous checkerboard stretching away in every direction. Massive pillars led the eye upward to a roof that was a series of lofty white domes, encircled by dark-brown rings. Although there were so many people already in the cathedral, they seemed tiny in its hugeness.

The students from Dr. Furneaux's Art Academy were still running to and fro, busily at work on the decorations. Up and down the pillars, on the choir stalls, statues, monuments—wherever stone, wood, marble, or ironwork provided a hold, they were fastening great festoons of autumn leaves, brown, gold, and rust colored. And among the leaves hung oranges and lemons in profusion, so that the principal color everywhere was gold—it seemed like a forest of gilded trees, seen in the half dark, with the infrequent rays of light picking out pale gold, bright gold, rich gold, dark gold. The tiny flickering tapers carried by the students to give light for their labors enhanced this effect—the dusk among the majestic pillars, under the soaring arches, seemed powdered with a dazzling shimmer.

"Why all the oranges and lemons?" Dido asked a boy who carried a basket of these fruits and was pinning them with skewers among bunches of oak and beech boughs over the tomb of an old gentleman who was lying uncomfortably balanced on a pile of cannons.

"The new king is very fond of marmalade."

"My stars!" murmured Dido. "He'll be able to make enough outa what's here to last him the rest of his days." Then she asked the boy,

"Hey, are you from Doc Furneaux's place?"

"That's right."

"D'you know a cove called Simon—Simon as used to live in Rose Alley?"

He shook his head. "Can't say as I do. The only Simon I know is the Duke of Battersea. He's the gaffer in charge of all this set-out—Master of the King's Garlandries, he is."

"Oh, no, it wouldn't be him," Dido said, greatly disappointed. Cris plucked her arm.

"Can we go up, do you suppose? The voice seems to be coming from up there."

She pointed toward the white vault overhead.

"*Can* we go up?" Dido asked the boy.

"Sure—if you can get through the crowd. Door to the stairs over there on the south side." He pointed across the nave.

They edged their way through, Cris tugging Dido's hand, and found the door; beyond it, the crowd thinned somewhat, and they were able to make their way up the stairs. These were wide, shallow wooden steps, winding upward in what seemed an endless spiral; Dido lost count after a hundred and fifty.

"What the blazes would Tobit be doing up here?" she panted. "If all the doings is down below?" But Cris kept on doggedly.

At last, however, she turned off through a little doorway into a stone passage so narrow that if two people had met in it, one would have had to go back. After following this, up steps and down, mostly feeling their way in the dark, though it was lit by an occasional lantern, they emerged in a great circular gallery that must have lain under the central dome, for it looked down directly into the middle of the cathedral; the students below, scurrying hither and thither with their festoons of leaves, looked like ants carrying tiny shreds of grass.

"Ah: now it's *loud*," murmured Cris. "Where can he be?" She started walking around the gallery. Echoes

[273]

came strangely to them in this place; Dido felt as if she, too, could hear Tobit, urging them to hurry.

On the opposite side of the gallery another little passage led off; Cris followed it, past some doors, and presently paused outside one that seemed made for dwarfs. She tried it: it appeared to be locked. But a voice from inside whispered,

"Cris? Is that you?"

"Yes!"

A key rattled and the door opened; Cris and Dido slipped through into a tiny stone room that looked out on to a leaded roof. Tobit was there. He and Cris looked at one another in that queer way they had; as if, Dido thought, nobody else existed.

"What a time you took to get here!" he said.

"I came as fast as I could."

"Listen, we must do something fast! Old Sannie and FitzPickwick and Mother Lubbage are down below—"

"How did *you* get here, Tobit?"

"I followed the rat," he said impatiently. "I kept peppering it with Joobie nuts from my peashooter, and it ate one or two and got slow and sleepy—*I'm* not ever going to touch those things again, I can tell you—it went wandering along a lot of dirty streets and across a bridge —I couldn't catch it but I could keep it in sight. Over the bridge—Blackfriars, it was called—the rat crawled into an empty house. There were cellar stairs, and the rat went down, and I went down, and there was a passage, and I went along it, and it came out under here."

"In the crypt?"

"No, under that. There's a huge open space, big as—big as Tegleaze park, with all these rollers."

"What are they made of?"

"I dunno—iron—some kind of metal—all wrapped around with sheepswool. They're big—higher than me—and there's hundreds of them. The whole place is sitting on top of them. The rat went staggering out into this place and then it fell over and went to sleep. I was having a look around when I heard Sannie and Fitz-Pickwick and old Lubbage, so I hid behind a roller to listen."

"Not Mr. Mystery?"

"No, he wasn't there."

"What are they fixing to do?"

"It's something to do with old Mystery's puppet show. They've got the theatre down there, and baskets full of puppets, and they're planning to bring it up by and by—they've got leaves tied all over, so it looks like the rest of the decorations. And they've got trays and trays of Joobie nuts and two boys to take them round—"

"Oh, rabbit it," said Dido. "I reckon I know what they're a-going to do. Did they see you?"

"No, while they were dressing the puppets I found a ladder up to the crypt behind one of the rollers, so I thought I'd try to get out and find you. But you can't get out of the cathedral once you're in—the line of constables won't let you past."

"Couldn't you get back along the passage?"

"I thought of that, but when I went back FitzPickwick and the others were just coming up into the crypt—I only just got away without being seen. And I could feel you weren't far off, Cris, so I hoped you'd come."

"And how d'you reckon *we're* going to get out if you couldn't?" inquired Dido acidly.

Tobit's face fell. "I don't know. Can't you think of something?"

"We'd best find the Dean," she said more kindly. "He's somewhere about, a-chatting to the king and helping him with his cogitations."

"And he'll get in some of the constables to deal with FitzPickwick?"

"I ain't so sure about that," Dido said. "I reckon we has to go as if we was a-walking on eggs. We *are* on eggs. Start a ruckus wi' the Hanoverians, and we may set the whole place a-rolling. I can feel it rock right now."

It was true, there was a strange uncertain vibration in the cathedral, more plainly to be felt in its upper rooms and galleries. The whole building swayed gently, like the branches of a tree, like an anchored ship in a slight swell.

"Hushaby, Kingy," muttered Dido. "Let's hope it don't blow a gale in the night, or we may all get a surprise, FitzPickwick as well."

She led the way from Tobit's hiding place back toward the great circular gallery. Looking down over the rail they could see that the cathedral had filled up considerably even in the short time they had been talking.

Some girl students from the Chelsea Art Academy had

threaded goodness knows how many oranges and lemons alternately on to a long rope and were busy hanging this enormous necklace in swags all around from the balustrade of the gallery.

"Can you tell me," Dido asked one of them, "where his Reverence and King Dick are having their chat?"

The girl put her finger on her lips. "Hush! Nobody's supposed to know the king's here yet."

"But he is here, ain't he?"

"Oh yes; Doctor Furneaux just took them in a basket of oranges and a bottle of marmalade wine because the Dean sent a message to say they were getting rather dry. They're in the north gallery. But of course they mustn't be disturbed."

"O' course not," said Dido, and led the way past a sign that said "To the North Gallery."

After more stairs, more passages, they came to a closed door with a sign: "No Entry Except by Special Permission of the Dean." Dido considered knocking, and decided against it. She walked boldly in. Tobit and Cris followed with less confidence, Cris holding on to Tobit's hand.

They found themselves in a long room furnished with a refectory table, chairs, and gorgeously colored Persian rugs; on the walls were maps of London and pictures of Old St. Paul's before the Great Fire; a small fire burned briskly in a marble fireplace; nearby stood an open clavichord with some music on it; in front of the fire, on a low table inlaid with silver, two men were building card houses. In the corner of the room opposite the door hung a set of coronation robes, glimmering in the firelight; for a moment, as Dido entered, she fancied this was a ghost.

Cris shut the door softly behind her. At the same moment the card house, which had reached seven stories, fell down.

"May the foul fiend fly away wi' the cartes!" exclaimed the younger of the two men. "What ails ma hand this e'en, that I canna build higher than seven?"

He started building again.

"It must be the wind, your Majesty; I notice the smoke from the fire keeps eddying out in a most unusual manner."

"But 'tis a braw, still nicht, man! Nae breeze at a'!"

"It ain't the breeze, your Royalship," said Dido, walking forward. "It's on account of a mess o' Hanoverians down in the cellar who've stuck the church up on rollers. That's why it keeps rocking back and forth."

The king's hand paused for a second in the act of delicately depositing a card; then he laid it carefully in place. Next moment there was another puff of smoke from the fire and the new card house fell down.

"You see," said Dido.

"There wad appear tae be a possibeelity that the lassie is speaking the truth," said the king. "What is your opeenion, Reverence?"

The Dean had jumped to his feet, very scandalized at such an unauthorized intrusion.

"Who in the world gave you leave—" he began.

"Whisht, man! Let's hear what they have tae say. Explain yersel', lass!"

Dido and Tobit told their tale, keeping it as short as possible. When Dido mentioned Captain Hughes, as being the original bearer of the Dispatch, the king exclaimed,

"That's no' Captain Owen Hughes, o' the sloop *Thrush?* Why, I ken his son weel, and a canny braw laddie he is, and ettling to carry my train the morn's morn."

"Captain Hughes's son? In London?" Dido was delighted. "Why, then he can come back with me to Sussex—I reckon that'll be more likely to rouse the old Cap than anything. We can't wake him, you see," and she went on to explain why, and what she suspected the Hanoverians were planning.

"Aweel, aweel," said the king, "ilka path has its puddle. My puir auld dad had trouble wi' the Hanoverians aft eneugh, it wisna tae be expectit that I'd gang free o' them. Whit had we best do, Reverence?"

The fire smoked again, and the room gave a perceptible lurch. It was plain that, as the cathedral filled up and more people were moving around downstairs, the whole structure was becoming more tippy and unstable.

"Your Majesty must leave the building at once—without losing a minute!" announced the Dean.

"Na, na, man, I'll not do sid a thing while a' the folk doon yonder are in danger."

"Well then we must get *them* out—" the Dean began.

[280]

Then he stopped short and exclaimed, "Botheration!" in tones of the deepest dismay.

"What fashes ye, sir?"

"Nobody is to be allowed out before tomorrow's ceremony unless they have a special pass signed by the Home Secretary."

"Weel, send someone for him, man!"

"They couldn't get out."

"Losh," said the king thoughtfully, after a pause. "Here's a powsowdie. Whit'll we do the noo?"

"*You* could leave, your Reverence, surely—and fix things with Lord Raven?" suggested Tobit with some diffidence.

"Leave his Majesty in such peril? Never!" declared the Dean.

"Seems to me," said Dido, "no disrespect to your Royalty and your Reverence, that there's a lot of obstinate, clung-headed thinking going on round here."

"*Really*—" the Dean began, but King Richard said,

"Nay, I like a plain-spoken lass. Let her have her crack."

"Well then. Us doesn't want any scrimmage, right? Acos that would start the place a-rocking. So no sense sending for a lot o' big flat-footed constables. The *main* thing is to get the place pegged down someway, so we needs to send a message about that."

"But how—"

"Fust of all, though," pursued Dido, "is there any food in the place?"

"Food? Not a crumb," said the Dean. "Except for the choirboys' buttons, of course."

"What's those?"

The Dean explained that in the fourteenth century, when choirboys were likely to faint from hunger, an act had been passed requiring the regular supply of small macaroons to the cathedral by city bakers. Choirboys were better fed nowadays, but the act had never been repealed, and over the centuries a large supply of these cakes had accumulated; they were kept in a special lead-lined room, safe from fire and mice.

"They'll do," said Dido. "Have 'em taken round and handed out free to everyone downstairs. Folk who've had a bite already ain't so likely to nibble on Joobie nuts."

The Dean departed to arrange for this, murmuring that it was all sadly irregular and how he would account for the disbursement to the Church Commissioners, heaven only knew.

"Now," Dido went on. "Us needs a lot o' rope."

"Lord Forecastle wad be the proper pairson to apply to, I jalouse."

"He *is* such a picksome old cuss, though," objected Dido. "Could *you* write him a note, mister king? He'd pay heed to you, likely."

"Aye, lassie; I'll stress the oorgency o' the matter. Two thousand ells o' best cable," the king said, scribbling. "But who'll deleever the message?"

"We know five active, sensible chaps not a stone's throw from here. All we need *is* a stone," said Dido, and glanced about. On a glass-fronted shelf were some

[282]

carved pieces of masonry—relics of Old St. Paul's before the fire. "That's the dandy." She selected one. "Now for a bit o' leather."

At this juncture the Dean returned, having arranged for free distribution of choirboys' buttons. When applied to for leather he seemed puzzled, but thought the librarian would undoubtedly have a supply, for bookbinding; at a nod from Dido, Tobit went with him to choose a suitable strip.

"Odds fishikins," said the king, laughing, "ye should ha' been a general, lassie—whit name do ye go by?"

"I'm Dido Twite, your Royalship."

"Dido Twite? Nay, I've heard *yon* name before—and on the lips of an auld friend. Dido Twite. Well, weel! He'll be blythe and canty to hear ye are weel."

"A friend of your *Majesty*—who in the world—?" Dido began, but now Tobit and the Dean reappeared with a leather strip and some thongs, from which Tobit constructed a sling with considerable dispatch and skill. While he did so the Dean, on the king's instruction, signed five cathedral passes for Yan, Tan, Tethera, Methera, and Pip. ("I know yon names too," said His Majesty, "they used tae supply claret wine to my dad") and Dido wrote a letter:

"Dere Yan, Were stuk in Sint Palls. Things is disey. Can yoo tell Home Seck to see Sint Palls is tide down tite as quik as poss. Then slope allong here fast for Them Hanno Veerins is agwine to Brake loose enny minnit. luv Dido.

"P.S. His Majesty sez this is troo."

"You sign it too, sir, then he can show it to Lord Raven and Sir Percy."

So the king signed Dido's letter, which was then, with the note about rope to Lord Forecastle, and the five passes, and a note from the Dean to Lord Raven asking that no more people be allowed into the cathedral, all placed together in an outer covering addressed to Mrs. Grissie Gusset, 4 Wardrobe Court, One ginny reward to him as Delivers this, and Dido's last guinea was enclosed, since neither the king nor the Dean had any money on them. The whole package was securely tied to the lump of stone.

"The foot of Saint Erconwald! The only piece of his tomb left!" lamented the Dean.

"Wheesht, man! Ye'll get it back."

"Now, where's the best place to send it from?" Dido asked Tobit.

"Higher up."

So the whole party left the north gallery.

"Your Majesty had best remain out of sight," remonstrated the Dean; but the king said, havers, this was the daftest ploy he'd been engaged in since he was a sackless callant, and naething would gar him miss any o' the whim-whams.

They had to pass around the circular gallery in order to reach the southwest tower, which Tobit reckoned would be the best spot for his purpose.

Looking down over the balustrade into the nave, Dido let out a groan.

[284]

"Confizzle it! They're a-setting up that blessed theatre. Us'd best make haste."

"In my north aisle!" said the Dean, outraged. "Wait till I go and—"

"No, your Reverence! We *dassn't* start a row! Feel how the place sways."

The motion was even more noticeable now, and sometimes, when there was a sudden shift in the crowd below, the cathedral bells could be heard faintly jangling in the north tower.

"The rollers are uneven sizes," Tobit said. "I heard FitzPickwick complaining that Godwit had cast them in small batches and they were all different."

"The skrimping skellums," muttered King Richard.

They hastened on to the south tower, climbed up a steep, narrow spiral stair, past the works of the cathedral clock with its three massive bells, Great Tom, Great Paul, and Great Fred, on, up, to a high outer gallery from which half London could be seen, smoky and twinkling in the clear frosty twilight.

"By my certie," said the king, "yon's a braw parochine! Where do you aim, laddie?"

"Down yonder." Tobit showed him the tiny oblong of Wardrobe Court, easily to be recognized by its two plane trees. He inserted the stone foot of Saint Erconwald, with message attached, into his sling, took careful aim, and let fly. The projectile whirled away, soaring over the churchyard, over the rooftops, dropped, and was lost to view.

"Send it lands on the planestanes, and disna smash some citizen's losen-glass!" said the king anxiously.

They waited, peering, straining their eyes. One minute went by—two—five—seven.

"If there's no one about in Wardrobe Court," Dido muttered.

"If it lodged in a tree—fell in a window box—" Cris worried.

But then suddenly a figure appeared on the roof of a house that must, surely, be on the south side of Wardrobe Court. The light was too dim and he was too far off to be recognized, but he carried a long pole attached to the end of which was, without any shadow of doubt, Aunt Grissie's red chenille tablecloth. He waved the pole once, twice, three times, and the watchers on the tower let out a unanimous gasp of joy and relief.

"Though dear knows we're nae oot o' the wanchancie business yet," remarked the king, as they retraced their steps down the spiral stair. "Let's see what yon skytes are abune the noo."

When they returned to the gallery and looked down they could see that a change had taken place in the random shifting and drifting motion of the great crowd assembled below. The crowd's attention was now focused on the puppet theatre which a figure in black fur, wearing a mask, had almost finished erecting in the north transept. Dido stared fixedly at this character. From his height she guessed him to be Colonel Fitz-Pickwick—or was it Mystery come back? She could not be certain.

[286]

There was an upheaval going on in the crowd. People were pressing and massing in front of the theatre. With another fourteen long hours before the coronation ceremonies would begin, any promise of distraction was welcome as water in the desert.

Evidently this commotion did not suit the puppeteer's purpose, for he could be seen to send out a sharp message; presumably that no performance was to be expected for a long time yet; a disappointed ripple passed through the crowd, which eddied back.

"Forbye, they're growing fretful and capernoited," muttered the king, knitting his brows. "Where be your laddies wi' the cakes, Dean?"

"There they go." The Dean pointed downward to where a dozen choirboys in white surplices could be seen threading their way among the crowd, each carrying a big silver tray heaped high with macaroons. These were handed out liberally, and eagerly received; for the moment the puppet theatre was forgotten. Plainly this development did not meet with the puppet master's approval; he consulted with two shorter assistants, also masked—were they Sannie and Mrs. Lubbage?

"What'll they do?" Dido wondered. "They're as stuck as we are; they dassn't start a performance too soon."

At this moment, however, King Richard solved the puppeteers' problem, while adding greatly to that of his own supporters. Observing the giant necklace of citrus fruit that hung in swags around the balustrade, he reached down with his penknife to remove an orange and, by mischance, cut right through the cord; the entire necklace of fruit went cascading down on to the crowd in the nave, who naturally looked up to see what had caused this rain of oranges and lemons.

A great gasping murmur went up!

"The King! Granny, look, 'tis His Highness! Ma! look up there, it's His Majesty's own self!"

"Sir!" exclaimed Dido. "Duck! Don't let the Hanoverians see you!"

Too late! Plainly the puppet master and his two assistants had discovered the king's presence. Full of excitement and purpose, they were bustling about their theatre. And some smaller assistants were now making their way up and down the nave carrying trays full of what were presumably Joobie nuts.

"Oh, croopus," Dido said. "Sir, you'll have to talk to the people. Now the Hanoverians know you're here I reckon it don't make much odds."

"I am e'en o' the same mind," agreed the king and, leaning over the balustrade, he called, in a voice that, though not particularly loud, was remarkably clear and carrying:

"Friends! Will ye leesten tae me a meenit? This is yer ain appointit king, Davie Jamie Charlie Neddie Geordie Harry Dick Tudor-Stuart, wishfu' tae hae a crack wi' ye. I came tae spend the nicht here, in seerious meditation afore being crownit tomorrow, and blythe I am tae see sae mony o' ye keeping me company. But, friends, I maun warn ye. There's *un*friends amang us too."

"For *mussy's* sake, sir, don't mention the rollers!"

Dido whispered urgently in his ear. "It'd start a panic—they'd all helter-skelter for the doors. It'd be murder!"

King Richard nodded reassuringly, while continuing to address the crowd.

"These unfriends, wha I willna scruple tae ca' by their richtfu' name, which is Hanoverians, are aboot tae gang aroond, offering ye nuts. *Dinna eat yon nuts!* They are a kind of poison, they will mak' ye sick, and in your sickness ye will see ghosties and hobgoblins and deil kens what! Drop the nuts on the floor, wamp them under foot!"

"No, no! Not on my tiles!" the Dean was heard to protest in agony.

"But, friends, if ye are hungry—and it's a lang watch till the morn—my gude friend, his Reverence the Dean here has kindly sent oot some almond cakies—those ye can eat a' ye've a mind to."

The crowd down below could be seen responding to this advice by dropping handfuls of Joobie nuts on the black-and-white tiles and scrunching them underfoot as instructed; the puppeteers were plainly angered and taken aback by this development; King Richard nodded with satisfaction.

"Now: anither thing, friends. Bear wi' me patiently and I'll not trouble ye much farther. These ill-deedy Hanoverians have also set up yon puppet theatre in the cathedral. They plan to distract yer minds with gal-dragonries and marvels! Weel, 'tis a free country—thank the Lord—I'll not forbeed ye tae look. But dinna tak it unco seeriously. (But dinna mistreat the Hanoverians

[289]

either—we want nae rampauging in the cathedral.) Those that love me best, and loved my old dad, Jamie Three, will maybe not look at a'. For my part, I like plays and puppetries fine, but I jalouse they arena whit I'd wish tae watch the nicht afore I'm crownit. This nicht I aim tae spend in seerious thocht and hymn singing. And I'm aboot tae commence noo. Any friends wha care tae join in are kindly welcome!"

Without more ado, King Richard lifted his voice—a resonant baritone—in a tuneful rendering of Metrical Psalm 23.

There was a moment's pause, then a gale of sound followed him. The entire congregation had joined in.

"Saints save us!" breathed Dido. "Don't I just hope the noise ain't enough to upset the rollers."

The Dean, terribly agitated, glanced around him at his beloved building, waiting for the landslide to start. But the sound of the singing, though tremendous, was steady and ordered. The cathedral vibrated like a chimney in a storm, but it kept its position.

"Good boy, good boy!" murmured the Dean. "Ah, he'll make a decent king, if we're all spared. Only, does he know enough hymns to keep them going all night?"

The Dean bustled off to find a hymnbook. Dido, seeing that for the moment King Richard had the situation under control, turned back and climbed the spiral stair to the outer stone gallery below the dome, and looked down to see what was happening in the streets.

What she saw filled her with amazement and thankfulness.

On the north side of the cathedral the crowd had scattered to a considerable extent and the reason for this was that Yan, mounted on an elephant, presumably Rachel, was riding in and out, unrolling as he went what seemed an endless reel of rope. Each time he came close to the cathedral he tossed a loop of this rope to another of the Wineberry Men—Dido could not see which—who stood waiting to receive and make it fast; then the elephant dashed away to the outer perimeter of the open space around the cathedral, where another Wineberry Man stood ready to receive another loop of rope and tether it to whatever was at hand.

"Pegging it down just like a tent, bless 'em," muttered Dido, and rubbed the back of her hand across her eyes. "I might a known they'd do the job decent and seamanly. They surely never got the stuff from old Lord Fo'c'stle, though; I can't believe he'd come through with it so quick."

Yan, having secured St. Paul's at about forty different points on the north side, took a turn of rope completely around the cathedral and disappeared lickety-spit northward in the direction of Newgate, presumably to pass the rope round the block formed by Paternoster Row and Ivy Lane.

"Just so long as the rope holds," said Tobit anxiously. He had followed Dido on to the stone gallery. "I bet the cathedral's pretty heavy, once it starts to slide."

Cris ran out and caught Tobit's hand.

"Come quick! Things aren't so good inside."

They dashed at top speed down the shallow spiral stairs and back to the inner gallery.

When they looked down they saw that the puppet master had started his play. It was not, from where they stood, possible to see the puppets themselves, but, judging from the behavior of the audience, what they were doing was very sinister; remembering the Miller's Daughter, Dido knew how wild and strange they could be, even when acting something comical. The people standing near were gaspingly attentive; every now and then, at some bit of action, a portion of the crowd would jump nervously back.

"Blame it," Dido said. "It won't do to have much o' *that.*"

As if to underline her words, there was an uneasy surge of the crowd at some startling occurrence, and the cathedral rocked on its unstable foundations.

Meanwhile the king, steadily singing, beating time as he sang, was still carrying a good half of the congregation with him, at the same time keeping a wary eye on the activities of the Hanoverians.

"Some o' the daft fules ate the nuts in spite o' the warning," he told Dido between two verses. "That's why they're sae nairvous and rintheroutacious."

It seemed that events on the puppet stage were approaching a climax. The light from the theatre shone blue and evil.

"I wonder what Sannie and co. plan to do if they start the church a-sliding?" said Dido.

"Oh, I heard that," Tobit told her. "They reckon it'll

slide south, that's why they put the theatre near the north door—as soon as it starts to move, they slip out the back way."

"Not so easily now, they can't." Dido grinned, thinking of Yan's network of rope. "I'm a-going down," she went on, "I want to see these here mannikins."

Cris and Tobit followed her. The stairs were beginning to fill up, as early-comers were crowded out of the nave and transepts; it was hard to squeeze their way down, but people were kind about letting them through; everybody was singing, even on the stairs, and there was a general atmosphere of cheerfulness and good will.

Out in the nave it was different.

About three quarters of the huge crowd now assembled in the body of the cathedral were singing. Those who could see the king were taking their time and tune from him, and the rest were following *them* (with some exceptions: Dido distinctly heard one old lady singing "O where and O where is my little dog gone," looking around her with a melancholy expression, which was certainly justified if she had brought her little dog into the cathedral). But the crowd, several hundred strong, directly in front of the puppet theatre were not singing; they were following the action on the stage with strained attention.

Wriggling, gliding, edging their way, Dido, Tobit, and Cris moved in the direction of the theatre. People in the crowd here were by no means so friendly and helpful as those on the stairs; they met with glares and mutters of "Keep back there! Give over shoving!" One man gave Cris a clout as she slid under his elbow; three more linked arms and tried to stop them getting through.

As, in spite of this opposition, they neared the stage, they began to hear the music: a sad, hypnotic wailing drone. It was the same tune that Mr. Twite had played on his hoboy, but it was now being rendered, Dido saw, by Tante Sannie and Mrs. Lubbage, wearing black fur clothes and black masks, playing on black combs wrapped in black tissue paper.

At last, by standing on tiptoe and craning sideways, they were able to get a view of the puppets.

The play was evidently about a war between goblins and humans. The humans were losing the war. And the goblins—little dark creatures, their faces wizened with malice, their eyes blazing with green light—were winning. They had poisoned blades to their swords and daggers; they sang a magic song which killed its hearers. Louder and louder wailed the sad, spooky music.

"Oh, Alfred, I feel rotten queer," said the woman beside Dido, absently swallowing a couple of Joobie nuts she held. "I believe I'm going to faint." She swayed, but there was hardly room to fall over. "You *can't* faint here, Lil, hold up, do!" said the man with her anxiously. However at this moment another woman did faint, crumpling on to the black-and-white tiles.

"We have won!" screamed the goblin king on the stage, triumphantly waving his poisoned sword. "Not one of our enemies is left alive!"

He turned toward the audience, his eyes blazing green,

[294]

his army of dark, wicked little soldiers massing behind him—more and more of them came piling on to the stage. "And *now*," hissed the king, "now, my friends, we are coming to get *you!*"

The whole army of goblins poured off the stage.

There were screams, shouts of fright and disgust, gasps, moans. Both Dido's feet were stamped on heavily, as the crowd surged backward. Three more women fainted.

The situation in the nave was now as if one piece of a jigsaw were trying to shove its way through the rest of the completed puzzle; there was no room to move at all, and yet a whole huge section of the crowd was frantically pushing and struggling to get away from the puppet theatre.

Cris pounced forward and grabbed one of the puppets from the floor.

"Look!" she cried to the woman called Lil. "It's only a doll! It won't hurt you!"

But the woman, screaming and hysterical, was in no state to listen to sense.

"It's alive, it wriggled! I saw it!" she wailed. "It's got a poisoned dagger!" And she fought like a crazy creature to get away from it. Kicked and knocked by frantic feet, the puppets skidded about on the smooth tiles, and wherever they were seen they spread terror and pandemonium.

"They aren't alive!" shouted Dido at the top of her lungs. "Stand still! They can't hurt you!"

But at that moment she distinctly saw one of the little

creatures move toward her foot, jerking itself along the ground. Quelling a horrible swoop of her heart, she picked it up, and realized that it was propelled by a simple mechanism of a twig, a notched cotton reel, and a stretched, twisted piece of catgut. *"Look!* It's only a toy!"

She might as well have said so to Niagara.

"STAND STILL!" shouted the king. "Keep your heads! Stand still!"

But the crowd, five hundred strong, heaved sideways, once, twice, three times.

"Hold them!" shouted the king to the people farther away from the puppet theatre, who, unaffected by the panic, were still keeping their position and singing away. "Link your hands round and hold them!"

The cathedral began to rock.

"Guess this is what an earthquake's like," Dido said to Cris. They had been washed up against a pillar, as if by a flood; Dido grabbed an arm of Tobit, an arm of Cris, and braced herself against the stone. "Hark at the bells! Don't they half ring!"

The chandeliers with their tapers were swinging wildly; shadows leapt about; oranges and lemons rained down from the high vaulted roof. The puppet theatre toppled and fell, crushing a good many puppets underneath it. Dido peered through the mass of people, trying to discover where the puppet master and his two assistants had got to. She could not see them in the general muddle. It was like a battle; it *was* a battle.

The cathedral rocked a fourth time.

"Do you think it's starting to slide?" Cris said. She was rather pale. She let go of Dido's hand and clung to Tobit.

"Dunno. With all the ruckus, it's hard to say *what's* happening."

But at that moment the cathedral did something definite. With a tremendous noise, louder than any sound hitherto produced by the crowd, with a kind of thunderous, rumbling scrunch, St. Paul's lurched sideways—shuddered in every stone—and sank about six feet into the ground, canted over at an angle of fifteen degrees.

And stood still.

"Some of the rollers must have buckled and given way," said Tobit.

"That's so—on account of Yan's anchoring it so tight," agreed Dido. "With all that rocking about, and the ropes holding fast, the rollers jist couldn't take the strain. Oh well—guess the old place is safe enough now—though it's going to be a right puzzle for his Reverence to jack it up level again. Why, look—there *is* Yan!"

At the moment of the cathedral's final subsidence, the north doors had swung open. There was a movement of the crowd to try and get out, but due to the angle at which St. Paul's was tilted, down at the southwest corner, the north entrance was now above ground level. Moreover Rachel the elephant was standing outside, blocking the way. The five Wineberry Men leapt in, off her back.

"The puppets!" called Dido. "Pick 'em up! Put 'em away!"

She, Cris, and Tobit, began tossing all the puppets they could see into a wicker hamper, evidently the container in which they had been brought. The Wineberry Men helped. Seeing this, the crowd began to settle down.

"Friends!" shouted the king from above. "It wad mateerially asseest matters if ye'd a' sit doon on the ground. The cathedral is quite safe—just a wee bit canted o'er. Ye hae nae groonds for appreheension!"

People were only too pleased to comply—with three exceptions. As the whole congregation sank limply to the floor, three desperate figures were seen trying to make their way to the south entrance: Sannie, Mrs. Lubbage, and the puppet master, who had been foiled in their attempt to get out at the north door.

"Get them, lads!" shouted Yan.

The three separated, Sannie and Mrs. Lubbage fleeing toward the crypt, while the puppet master darted through the door to the spiral stair.

Dido, Tobit, and Yan followed him.

"I'm afeered he means mischief to the king," Dido panted. "We mustn't let him get to the gallery!"

Yan nodded, pounding ahead. But there was really no risk, as they saw when they reached the narrow gallery entrance; it was jammed with people and the fugitive had evidently abandoned his plan and, in desperation, continued onward and upward with Yan close at his heels.

"Stop, you fool!" Yan shouted after him. "You can't escape that way!"

The puppet master evidently thought otherwise. Pausing an instant to discard his black fur cloak and hood, which were hampering him, he rushed along a narrow passage that led off the stairs. Now they could recognize the fair hair and mustache of Colonel FitzPickwick.

"He can't escape that way," said a voice behind Dido. She looked around and saw the Dean. "It leads only to the roof."

But FitzPickwick had unbolted the door and sprang out into darkness, followed, an instant later, by Yan. Light from inside showed a lead-lined valley between two roof ridges.

"Yan! Take care!" called Dido anxiously.

She started after him, but the Dean grabbed her arm.

"Don't go, child! It's too dangerous in the dark: That's the nave roof—it ends in a sheer drop over the west front."

Nonetheless, Dido would have gone—but at that moment they heard a wild shout of rage, or defiance, or despair. A moment later Yan came back to them, looking pale and appalled.

"He jumped . . . clean off the end of the roof."

"Heaven forgive him," said the Dean.

Downstairs, they found that a general calming-down and tidying-up process had taken place. Another issue of choirboys' buttons had been dealt round and most people, exhausted by all the excitement, had gone to sleep, lying as comfortably as they could on the sloping cathedral floor. The king, having delivered a calming speech, had retired to the north gallery. Here the Wineberry Men were summoned to be thanked for the speed and skill with which they had secured the cathedral.

"You saved it from destruction," the Dean kept repeating, with tears in his eyes. "I'll never forget it, never!"

"Losh, lads, ye did wonders," agreed the king.

"How did you get the rope so quick?" Dido wanted to know.

"Got it from the Old Bailey. They've allus got plenty there—for tying up prisoners. Sir Percy fixed for us to have it—he and Lord Raven were still arguing when we took along his Reverence's note. We could see the cathedral a-swaying about from there, so I reckoned there wasn't time to go along and argue the toss wi' Lord Fo'c'stle."

"I'll no' say but that ye were richt," agreed the king. "Weel, lads, if ye wish for pensionable, kenspeckit poseetions in the government, Davie Jamie Charlie Neddie Geordie Harry Dick Tudor-Stuart's the man tae see ye'll get them."

Yan and the rest thanked him politely, but said on the whole they would prefer to continue plying their trade as Gentlemen.

"'Tis what we're used to, you see, sir."

"Aweel, I'll no' quarrel with ye; 'tis a gey frack profession, fit for gallant lads like yersel's. Whene'er ye veesit Westminster I'll be blythe tae buy claret from ye as my dad did afore me. And I hereby gie ye leave to write Appointit tae His Majesty on the brattach o' your boat."

Much impressed by this royal favor, the Wineberry Men withdrew, pulling their forelocks.

"Would Your Grace wish to see the two prisoners?" the Dean inquired.

"I canna say I do, but I doubt I had better," said the king reluctantly.

Tante Sannie and Mrs. Lubbage were led in; they had been taken in the crypt without difficulty, for the subterranean passage was blocked when the southwest corner of the cathedral sank into the ground.

The two witches were a sorry spectacle. Sannie seemed to have shrunk; she had always been small, now she was tiny, hardly bigger than a five-year-old. She whimpered out miserably, on seeing the king,

"Oh, dear King-sir! Is will be kind to poor old Sannie? Old Sannie never meant harm! Only to go back where the sea she do sing, and isn't no cold nor rudeness, but love apples and sweet grass, and old people is loved and given quilt stuffed with happiness feathers—"

"What does she mean?" asked the king.

"She wants to go back to Tiburon," Dido said.

"And the other one?"

But no one, ever again, would be able to tell what Mrs. Lubbage wanted—if she wanted anything. She had half a dozen Joobie nuts, with which she played, smiling like a baby, trickling them from one hand to the other without speaking; she never said another word.

"Take them away," said the king. For the first time he sounded tired. "Take them away and let them be looked after somewhere. . . ."

"Shall you let them go back to Tiburon, sir?" Dido asked when they had gone.

"Och, weel, they'd be out of mischief there."

But old Sannie died in the night; whether from age, or lost hope, no one could say.

"Whit aboot ye three?" the king said to Dido, Cris, and Tobit. "Gin ye hadna brought yon message in the faurst place, we'd nane of us be here noo. I'd be blythe for ye tae carry my train the morn, alang wi' young Owen Hughes—would ye like to?"

Dido glanced at the others; they nodded.

"Thanks, Mister King; we'd be right pleased. If I can get back to Sussex directly arter, that is; I shan't feel easy till I see how my old Cap's a-getting on. And I promised Lord Sope I'd return his elephant."

So that was how Dido Twite, along with Tobit and Cristin Tegleaze, came to carry the train of King Richard IV at his coronation. And the Master of the King's Garlandries, arriving at the last minute for the ceremony, because he and his helpers had been working all night replacing the scattered decorations on the cathedral, looked down from the Whispering Gallery and exclaimed,

"Good heavens! That's Dido!"

13

Dido, Tobit, and Cris started for Sussex the very instant the ceremony, which was held at six in the morning, had finished. They had been invited to stay for the junketings, but declined. Dido was anxious to get back to her Captain; Tobit and Cris, armed with an injunction, signed by the Lord Chief Justice, against anybody trying to stop them taking possession of Tegleaze Manor, in particular one Miles Tuggles, alias Tegleaze, alias Mystery, were anxious to see what was happening at home; and Rachel, too, was dreadfully homesick; right through the crowning she had stood just outside, in St. Paul's churchyard, trumpeting mournfully.

Just before they left, Dido received a message to say that the Duke of Battersea would like to see her, as soon as he had fixed up some toppling garlands.

"Duke o' Battersea? Who's he?" she said, puzzled.

"Well, look, tell him I'm right sorry but I can't wait now. Ax him to write to me."

Rachel swung through the outskirts of London at a rattling pace. Along with Dido, Tobit, and Cris, traveled Captain Hughes's son Owen; he seemed a pleasant enough boy, though rather silent and anxious at the moment. This was hardly surprising, since the Captain's family had not heard from him for several years, had thought him dead in the Chinese wars, and now the news of his mysterious illness was hardly encouraging.

"Don't you fret, though, I reckon the king's doctor will be able to set him to rights," Dido kept saying consolingly. "He seemed a right sensible cove."

The king's doctor, who had an allergy to elephants, was to follow them in his own curricle with a supply of medicines, directly the coronation banquet was over.

Rachel took them over heath and common, through woods, fields and copses, straight as a bird to Stopham House, where she trumpeted outside the library window until Lord Sope came out and patted her cheek.

"Well, well, well, Rachel; that will do! I am delighted to see you back, but do not deafen me, pray! How do you do, Miss Twite," he said to Dido. "Were you able to deliver your message? That's good, that's good. . . . I see you have friends with you. Would you all care for a little refreshment?"

"That's ever so kind of your lordship, but I reckon we'd best get on. Oh, here's a note from Lord Forecastle, inviting you to take a dish of tay with him next time you're in town. He sent a messenger posting after us with it on a Derby 'chaser.'"

Dido had been planning to hire a carriage at the White Hart for the last bit of the journey, but Lord Sope hospitably put his phaeton at their disposal, so they drove in it on to Petworth, where they received a great welcome from the Gusset family at The Fighting Cocks.

"There, I *am* pleased to see you, dearies!" exclaimed Aunt Sarah, embracing them all impartially. "You'll never guess what's happened, *never!*"

"What?" Dido asked anxiously. "Is the Cap'n all right?"

"At twelve o'clock midnight last night," said Miss Sarah impressively, "just as I was a-taking a last look at the Cap'n, poor dear soul, sleeping up in the attic, so innocent and quiet as a babby, what does he do?"

"What *does* he do?"

"Sits up! Looks about him calm as a Christian and, if you'll believe me, says, 'Ma'am, who are *you?* Where the deuce am I? What's become of my Dispatch? And where's Dido Twite?' He's sitting in an armchair in the little parlor—a bit weak, but a-mending fast—drinking a mugful of huckle-my-buff—at this very minute. He *will* be pleased to know you're back, dearie."

"He'll be even more pleased than that," said Dido. "This here's his son Owen, that he hasn't seen for dunnamany years."

"Oh, dearie! He'll be right dumbfounded with joy."

"Owen," Dido suggested, "why don't *you* go in and

[306]

see your pa fust—he won't want too many of us a-crash-ing in on him if he's weak yet."

Owen nodded, and went through the door indicated by Mrs. Gusset. They heard him say,

"Father?" and Captain Hughes exclaim,

"That's never *Owen?*"

Then there was a long silence.

"Eh, bless him! That'll do him more good than doc-tor's medicine," said Aunt Sarah, wiping her eyes. "Now, how about the rest of you? Would you like a bowl of my soup, eh?"

They were glad of soup, having had nothing since a scanty breakfast before the ceremony, and while they ate they told Aunt Sarah, Uncle Jarge, and his boy Ted the whole tale of the events leading up to the coronation, and discussed the astonishing fact that, at the exact time when Mrs. Lubbage and Tante Sannie realized their plan had failed, Captain Hughes had recovered the use of his senses.

"There's something mighty odd about it all," Miss Sarah said over and over. "But I'm right glad he's on the mend, for I've not laid eyes on a better-looking man since my Hannibal was struck by lightning in the row-boat full of corkscrews. And that's a nice-looking boy, too; do you reckon *he'd* fancy a bowl of my soup?"

"Guess he would," Dido said. "While you're giving it to him, ma'am, I'll take Tobit and Cris on to Tegleaze, before it gets dark, and then come back to have a talk with the Cap. Oh, there's a letter for him from Lord

Fo'c'stle giving him six months' leave so's he can go home to Wales."

"I've always fancied a holiday in Wales," Miss Sarah said thoughtfully, tucking Lord Forecastle's letter in her apron pocket.

Dido, Tobit, and Cris returned to the phaeton and continued on their way. Some three quarters of an hour after their departure, the doctor's curricle arrived. The doctor had brought with him a passenger who inquired for Miss Dido Twite and, on hearing that she had gone to Tegleaze Manor, decided to follow her, after a brief pause for refreshments.

Dido, Cris, and Tobit drove through the village of Duncton, and up steep Duncton hill, where they dismounted and walked beside the horse. Dido was rather silent, but Tobit and Cris kept up a nonstop flow of talk.

"We'll keep a lot of sheep—Mr. Firkin will be the chief shepherd—and we'll breed horses again—Granny will like that, she knows a lot about horses when she's off the Joobie nuts—we'll mend all the things that are falling to bits—have Dogkennel Cottages repaired and find new tenants—set Tegleaze Manor to rights—"

"What'll you use for cash?" Dido asked.

"Well, there's bound to be *some,* now old FitzPickwick isn't taking it all for his Hanoverian plots—"

"What about the luck-piece?"

"Oh, well, it won't run away. We'll give it to that museum in London. Neither of us wants it. But there's other things to do first—that can wait."

[308]

(It waited for a year, and when they finally sent down a diver to rescue the Breughel miniature, which was dangling from a nail in the brickwork of the well, they also found the bones of Miles Tegleaze, alias Miles Mystery, lying at the bottom, where he had fallen when he rushed from the mill that dark November night.)

"And we'll do something about those magistrates in Petworth, so people can't be transported on false evidence," Tobit said.

"And we'll look after poor old women, so they don't get a grudge against everybody and take to witchcraft," said Cris.

They passed Dogkennel Cottages. Mr. Firkin was up on the side of the down with his sheep and dog Toby.

"I'll go and see him tomorrow," Cris said.

They reached Tegleaze Manor. While Dido was tethering Lord Sope's horse to the marble pillar, Tobit and Cris walked through the great door hand in hand. The big white dog Lion flew down the stairs like a bolt from a catapult, barking and whining with joy. When he saw that there were *two* of them, he was quite astounded, and did not know which face to lick first. Old Gusset, wandering about the hall with a feather duster, also nearly fainted from astonishment.

"Mas'r Tobit, sir! Miss Crissie! Bean't you transported to van Dieman's Land? Nor murdered? Nor taken up by the Bow Street runners? Nor magicked by Mother Lubbage?"

"None of those things," Tobit said. "And Tante

Sannie's never coming back, nor Colonel FitzPickwick, and we're never going to allow another Joobie nut on the place, and things'll all be different from now on. Where's Granny?"

"Why, she's been a bit brighter than usual, Mas'r Tobit. She be in Mr. Wilfred's bedroom, a-playing tiddlywinks with him."

"We'll go up and surprise her. Want to come, Dido?"

But Dido said she thought she would be getting back.

"Thanks for the ride, then. Maybe we'll come over to Petworth tomorrow to see you."

Hand in hand, without looking back, they ran up the stairs.

Old Gusset, gazing after them, shook his head.

"Well, I declare! Who'd a beleft it? So all's right, is it, Missie Twido Dite?"

"Yes," said Dido slowly. "All's right, Mister Gusset. The king's been crowned, and Cap'n Hughes is better, and if that Mystery turns up again, he'll get his comeuppance. And your boy Yan got a special thanks from the king, and permission to put By Royal Thingummy on the *Gentlemen's Relish*. And they're coming back by the cut, and he said to tell you he'd see you at the Cuckoo Tree the day arter tomorrow."

"Ah, that be champion," the old man said happily. "I knew nothing'd harm my boy Yan, acos I bought him that liddle wooden charm piece from owd Mother Lubbage—but thanked by His Majesty! Think o' that!"

He looked up the stairs again, thoughtfully rubbing his whiskers with the feather duster.

"All the same," he muttered, "those two young 'uns ought to offered you a glass o' cowslip wine. Uncivil, that was. Or would ee like a biscuit, now, missie?"

"That's ever so kind of you, Mister Gusset, but I really does want to be getting back."

Just the same, before doing so, Dido went into Cousin Wilfred's little study to have a look at the Tegleaze family tree. Triplets, back in Charles the First's time: Tobias, Christopher, and Miles Aswell Tegleaze.

"Mister Gusset?"

"Yes, Missie Dwite?"

"Do you know the name of the other triplet? Tobit and Cris's brother who died at birth?"

"No, missie. I never did hear. Likely he was never christened."

"Maybe not."

Dido unhitched the phaeton, and drove off. All of a sudden she felt lonely—almost choked with loneliness. Tobit's got Cris, she thought, and Cap'n Hughes has his boy Owen, but who've I got?

Such thoughts were not sensible, she knew. A warm welcome awaited her back at The Fighting Cocks. She could probably go to Wales with Captain Hughes and Owen, if she wanted, the king had invited her to stay at Westminster, and Mr. Firkin would certainly be pleased if she went back to Dogkennel Cottages. But all the hospitality in the world is not the same as having someone of your own.

As she neared Dogkennel Cottages she saw that the sheep were down in the pasture, which meant that Mr.

Firkin was home. So she stopped in to tell him about Captain Hughes's recovery and the collapse of Mrs. Lubbage. While she was telling her tale, a curricle dashed by, going toward Tegleaze.

"Eh, fancy old Mis' Lubbage being brung so low!" Mr. Firkin exclaimed wonderingly. "The poor owd mawther! Like a babby, is she? Tell 'em to send her back here, darter, and I'll keep an eye on her, surelye; she 'on't come to no harm herealong when folks knows she'm afflicted."

Dido promised she would do this.

"Mr. Firkin," she said suddenly. "I've a fancy to walk along to the Cuckoo Tree. Can I leave the carriage here for twenty minutes?"

"O' course, darter! And time ee comes back, I'll have a cup o' tea a-mashed for ee."

Dido walked across the pasture, up the chalk track, through the beech grove, across the saddle of rough down grass, along the path under the hanging yew trees. And she finally came to the little crooked, aged Cuckoo Tree, leaning out sideways from the slope of the hill, as it had leaned for many, many hundreds of years, and would lean for many hundreds of years more.

"I wonder if a cuckoo ever really did build a nest in it?" she thought. "No, Cris said cuckoos don't build nests. Cuckoos don't *have* nests. All they have is other birds' nests."

She climbed up into the tree and looked down at the wide, spreading stretch of country below, beginning now to be hazy with the blue of evening. She remem-

bered how she had first come to the tree and heard Cris, apparently talking to nobody.

"It was right queer about Aswell, Cris just forgot him, once she met Tobit. I wonder if *he's* lonely too."

Half seriously, half not, she put out both hands and shut her eyes. She remembered Cris saying, "When we first start talking I can feel him put his hands in mine."

"Aswell?" said Dido. "Is you there, poor old Aswell? Can you hear me?"

She waited.

And waited. But nothing happened, and presently she opened her eyes again.

And, meanwhile, through the beech grove, across the saddle of down, along the yew-hung path, her friend Simon, Sixth Duke of Battersea, came searching for her, following the directions Mr. Firkin had given him.

JOAN AIKEN, daughter of American writer Conrad Aiken, was born in Rye, Sussex, England. She has engaged in a variety of professions, including features editor for a magazine and copywriter for a large London advertising agency. Now she devotes her time to writing.

In 1969, Miss Aiken received the *Manchester Guardian* award for children's fiction.

Her hobbies are painting and gardening at her home, an ex-pub in Petworth, Sussex, England, where she lives with her two children.

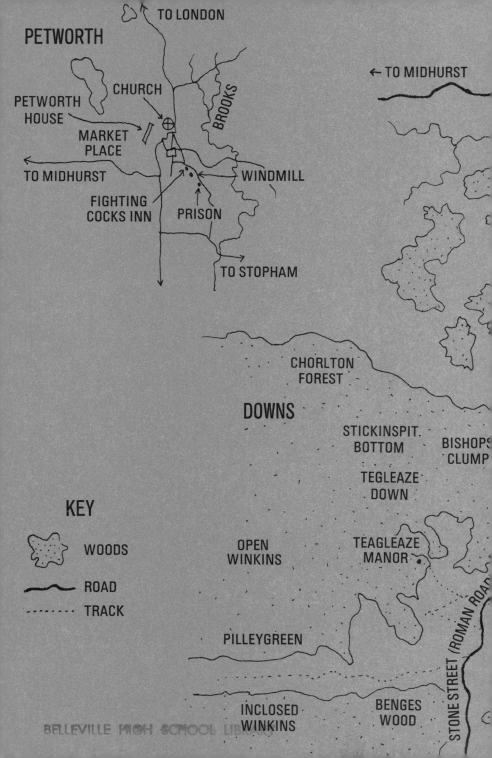